ISA

To Jack,

Embrace your inner strength and rise.

G. G. McNeil

25.8.20

ALSO BY L.L. MCNEIL

WORLD OF LINARIA

NOVELS

Moroda

Palom

Amarah

Isa

NOVELLAS

Rise of a Sky Pirate

KOUZLO SAGA

NOVELS

Crimson Eyes

Crimson Bone

Crimson Fang

Crimson Soul

NOVELLAS

Pandemonium Rift

ISA

WORLD OF LINARIA BOOK 4

L.L. MCNEIL

THREE DRAGON
PUBLISHING

First published in Great Britain in 2020.

Printed and bound in Great Britain by Clays Ltd, Elcograf S.p.A.

Three Dragon Publishing
www.llmcneil.com

Cover by Holly Jameson
www.hollyjameson.co.uk

For Pipkin, who supplies me with all the tea I can drink, all the biscuits I can dunk, and all the hugs when everything becomes too much.

ACKNOWLEDGMENTS

This book would not exist without Olivia.

Your keen eyes, constant banter, and encouragement helped me reach the end - and ensure it was the best book it could be. Not to mention your ruthlessness with my overzealous commas, your confusion when entirely the wrong character appeared in one chapter, and your ability to keep me motivated when I struggled. I cannot thank you enough for your unending patience, support, advice, and encouragement. Thank you.

To anyone who purchases my book, I am eternally grateful. It would mean the world and more if you would be kind enough to review *Isa*.

SUMMARY OF AMARAH

Princess Isa, half-sister to King Sapora, has turned traitor. The divide between their ideals has widened since Sapora came to power, and along with the bullying tactics of Tacio, have driven a wedge between them, pushing Isa away. In Taban Yul, the capital city of Val Sharis, Isa leads the rebel uprising attempt to rescue their leader, Palom's former lover, Lathri. The attempt fails, resulting in Kylos being captured and subsequently tortured by Tacio, while Isa feigns innocence to keep herself safe.

Amarah travels with an old sky pirate ally, Traego, and his crew on a treasure hunt for a huge bounty. Although Traego is sketchy on the details, Amarah needs the gold to get herself a new airship—having lost both *Khanna* and an eye to the Arillian, Jato. Kohl, Jato's father and another ally of Amarah's, travels with her.

While flying through a low mountain range, they come across Morgen, who is posted in Povmar, a remote town in the distant reaches of Corhaven—where he is hiding from Sapora's wrath. Amarah invites him to join her, which he declines.

It transpires that the "treasure" is of Varkain origin—an

ancient, living weapon known as an Ark—of which four were created, but lost to Linaria millennia ago. Amarah and Kohl are terrified of the Ark, but Traego is driven by gold, and steals a sword from Veynothi's tomb as proof to his buyer—King Sapora.

Meanwhile, in the far north of Val Sharis, Palom and his dragon companion *Leillu* guard a large convoy of Ittallan heading to the capital from rampaging dragons and opportunistic thieves—unaware they are part of a rebel faction who stand against Sapora. Odi, the son of an Archigo, is the influential leader of this group. Palom is accompanied by a young Ittallan, Karvou, who he reluctantly takes under his wing.

Having seen his old ally, Morgen rethinks his life. Having committed treason by aiding Isa, he fled the Corhaven capital for fear of Sapora tracking him down. He decides to abandon the Imperial Guard and travel to Amarah's old tutor, Topeko, in the mage city of Berel. The Samolen magic can be manipulated in countless forms, and he hopes to figure out how to resurrect those lost to Linaria—perhaps bringing Moroda back.

While travelling to Traego's base in Estoria, a collection of tropical islands to the south-east of Linaria, Amarah and Traego are set upon by sky pirates. A battle ensues in the sky, during which Traego is the victor after using Samolen magic-fuelled weapons. Veynothi's sword falls overboard in the chaos. Amarah leaps into the ocean to claim it before it is lost, and ends up fleeing from an enormous sea monster that seems drawn to the Varkain blade.

During Palom's journey south, the Ittallan encounter Jato and her Arillians hunting down dragons—narrowly escaping their attacks. They observe an adult dragon burning a tiny hamlet to the ground, and Palom fears their wrath, for it seems to know no bounds.

With Sapora more distant than ever, and feeling trapped during the preparations for Summercourt, one of the largest events in Taban Yul during which all the country's leaders come together to create a new council, Isa takes advantage of a window of opportunity and frees Kylos. She is caught red-handed by Tacio, but Sapora appears at the last minute to pardon her.

Amarah meets the rest of Traego's crew when they return to his base. The sky pirates of Estoria are carefree but lead violent lives—going as far as trapping Arillians in their "drowning pits" to claim gold for their capture. Traego sends one of his pilots, Antar, to Taban Yul to negotiate Veynothi's bounty reward with Sapora.

Disheartened by seeing his people slaughtered for gold, Kohl grows distant, and walks along a remote beach. He comes across Fogu, a former general in the Arillian army, and one of his oldest friends. They are overjoyed at seeing one another, especially after surviving the horrors of Aciel's campaign. They decide to leave Estoria and return home—though Kohl wishes to visit Berel first. He believes the Arks and the *Valta Forinja* are evil, and driving the dragons' rage. The original *Valta Forinja* are all held in Berel University, and would therefore be a clear target. Instead of running and hiding, he wants to warn the scholars of Berel and offer them what help he can, before returning to his people on the floating islands.

Antar arrives in Taban Yul and claims his Captain, Traego, has knowledge of Veynothi's location. Sapora is skeptical and wants proof, but he gives the sky pirate gold to encourage him. Recognising Traego as a famous sky pirate, Isa chases Antar down and asks him to deliver a message to Amarah for her: come here and help. She hopes the sky pirate's skill will free Lathri and finally get her away from the nest of vipers.

During Summercourt, many Archigo and leaders arrive from across Val Sharis and Sereth—including Vasil and his full retinue. Sapora speaks with his father's Valendrin—a blood mage—and discusses breaking the Arks' seals with only himself, Tacio, and Isa present.

Realising Sapora is close to releasing the Arks, Isa races away—warning Solvi, now part of the Ittallan uprising—only to be arrested by Tacio for conspiracy and treason.

Dragons attack the mage city of Berel and burn parts of the university. Although Morgen has been studying the life magic of *Ra* and the peaceful teachings of the Samolen, he cannot stand by and not help others. Ignoring the orders of the Kalos—teachers—Morgen grabs his forbidden *Valta Forinja* and defends himself and the city—injuring a dragon and driving it away. Instead of praise, Morgen is severely reprimanded for breaking their laws. His *Valta Forinja* is taken—locked in the university, and some of his memories are wiped by Topeko prior to his judgement from the Arch-Kalos.

In Estoria, the sea monster attacks again—Kohl spots it before anyone else and warns the sky pirates. A battle ensues on the shores of the beach. Amarah uses her *Valta Forinja*, but is crippled by a panic attack from the weapon's dark influence. Traego kicks it away, relieving her. They manage to drive off the monster, and Traego loans Amarah the gold to get herself a new airship.

Palom, *Leillu*, Odi, Karvou, and their convoy arrive in Taban Yul. One of their number, an old woman named Yfaila, immediately leaves the Ittallan and is escorted into the city by some Cerastes who have been awaiting her arrival. She has sold them information in return for her safety and plenty of gold—the location of an Ark. Angered at Yfaila's betrayal, Palom enters Taban Yul and sees how much it has changed. Varkain are everywhere, Sapora's

Sevastos flies overhead, and parts of the city are still damaged. He is reunited with his niece, Solvi, and sees Isa's arrest. Solvi says Isa has a plan and they are to await help from Amarah.

Having said his goodbyes to Amarah, Kohl heads to his rendezvous with Fogu, but is captured mid-air by another sky pirate troupe. Fogu sees Kohl's capture, and frees him from the drowning pits, obliterating part of Estoria in doing so, and the two flee the country.

Amarah navigates the enormous Arillian storm surrounding Taban Yul—created by Jato and her Arillians—and arrives in Taban Yul with some sky pirates on Traego's ship, as her new one is still being refurbished, and time is of the essence according to Isa's desperate plea. She has brought Veynothi's sword as proof for Sapora's bounty.. She is met at the hangar by Kylos, who brings them to a tavern where the sky pirates are reunited with Palom and the rebels. They hatch a plan to free Isa, Lathri, and their followers.

Sapora meets Amarah and the sky pirates to determine Veynothi's location. Although she lies, the Valendrin takes blood from her. Able to discern the truth with his magic, he obtains the true location of the Ark. Sapora arrests Amarah and the others immediately, and armed with the correct information, flies off on his Sevastos with the Valendrin to resurrect her. He fills an airship with almost all the prisoners of his dungeon to be sacrificed in a blood ritual to resurrect the Ark.

Amarah leads the jailbreak, rescuing Isa and Lathri. They also discover Yfaila locked up—Tacio going back on his promise to keep her safe and pay her for the information. Unwilling to leave her to rot, they free her. Amarah and Isa fight their way out, both women getting injured. Isa fights Tacio one on one and is overcome by blood lust.

Amarah pleads with Isa to leave him and escape, but it falls on deaf ears. Amarah is losing too much blood to wait, and clambers up to the top of the tower where *Otella* is waiting to fly them to safety.

Eventually, Isa follows, and the group take to the air—although Amarah is on the brink of death.

They meet with Palom and the other rebels outside the city walls, who all clamber aboard and fly away. Traego is waiting a short distance away on Amarah's new airship, *RaKhanna*, as back up, and the ships flee Taban Yul.

In the far reaches of Corhaven, Sapora discovers Veynothi's tomb and resurrects the Ark. But she detests him immediately for being a mongrel king.

Amarah falls from the ship's wheel, succumbing to her wounds. Lathri heals her, although the effort of saving Amarah's life is too much after weeks of torture in the dungeons, and she passes away.

Isa is now free from her brothers, but on the run with a rag-tag group of Ittallan rebels and sky pirates.

1

In the wetlands of eastern Val Sharis, crisp, cold mornings usually belied rain to follow. Lingering mist often meant a frost that refused to lift, which would turn the muddy waters into cold sludge. Today's dawn was still. Calm. Even the ocean waves seemed to lap gently against the shore. As if all of Linaria held its breath, waiting to see what secrets the new day would reveal.

But a sunrise hotter than it should have been was fair warning that the day would not be in Princess Isa's favour. There would be heat not just from the sun, but from the frayed tempers of people she'd betrayed, and the dark rage of sorrow of those who'd lost loved ones. Whose deaths she'd caused.

Isa pushed her sleeves up over her elbows as the heat from the southern sun prickled her skin. Her clothes were torn and bloody from her fight with Tacio the night before, but she ignored them. Clothes could be washed or discarded.

And her brother's blood was the least of her worries.

She'd never been so far from the capital before. Certainly not unescorted. Not only did she have an unknown vastness ahead of her, but now, her hidden secrets had been revealed to all—her true intentions stripped bare. She stood on the edge of Val Sharis as if awaiting judgement from both her past and future.

The island nation of Estoria, both a tropical paradise for the rich and a seedy underbelly for sky pirates away from any nation's jurisdiction, was just out of sight on the horizon, a smudge somewhere below the rising sun. Yet, it seemed so close that she could reach out and touch it. There, she'd be safe.

Hidden from Tacio and Sapora after her escape.

She hadn't realised how hot the dawn would be, and at any other time, she might have enjoyed sunning herself on a quiet rooftop, perhaps taken a mug of cold, sweet tea with her. She'd never once thought she'd be mourning with her fellow Ittallan, grieving at the funeral of the woman who had wanted both her brothers dead.

She wondered what more would change that day.

Isa swallowed thickly, her throat raw and dry. It was as if her entire life's worth of trials and tribulations had spilled over, leaving her an emotional wreck.

She was a wanted fugitive.

A betrayer to the king.

A traitor to her brother.

She'd known it was coming. Of course she had. She wasn't an idiot.

Begging a sky pirate for help to orchestrate a jailbreak was never going to be easy, nor forgivable. She'd known there would be deaths. "Collateral damage," Sapora had always called it. But it was one thing when nameless, faceless people fell in the pursuit of greater power. It was another when you knew them personally. When their deaths weighed heavy on your conscience.

Isa stood in the waterlogged mud that marked the edge

of the Val Sharis wetlands, a plethora of sky pirates and Ittallan rebels behind her, and Estoria lay waiting across the ocean.

She knew there was no coming back from this. Sapora had given her chance after chance, defended her against Tacio time and time again, and yet she had turned into a rat.

Tacio probably expected her to hide like a rat, too. Disappear like frightened vermin, never to be seen again. But she wouldn't disappear. She hadn't run away simply to escape his torment—her skin was thicker than that. She'd escaped as a prisoner, and she had every intention of returning as a queen.

The *true* Queen of Val Sharis. Even if it had to be taken in blood.

Isa balled her hands into fists to mask her trembling.

To her right, Palom coughed awkwardly. 'My princess…?'

She looked away, keeping her eyes on the sea ahead. Its gentle waves seemed to calm her, and she took several seconds to gather herself. This moment wasn't about her. Wasn't about what she'd lost, nor the upcoming mountains she had to climb.

It was about Lathri. The woman who had given her life for Isa's cause.

Everyone who stood with Isa also stood with Lathri. The Ittallan healer had been the one who'd brought the rebels together, had given her people hope in the face of the snakes moving into their homes. Provided sanctuary in a suddenly dangerous and terrifying city, where saying the wrong thing could get you killed.

Without Lathri, Isa wouldn't be where she was. She'd never have had the guts to stand up to Sapora, or fight Tacio to gain her freedom. If being on the run could be considered freedom.

She heard Palom take a tentative step towards her, the

ground squelching under his heavy boot. With a sudden whoosh of heat, his travelling companion, *Leillu*, scampered along the soft mud and halted by her feet. The innocence of the gesture startled Isa, and she looked away from the waves and into the young dragon's eyes.

Leillu chirped, wings beating frantically, and Isa knelt, trailing the back of her fingers along *Leillu's* lengthening horns, much to the little dragon's delight.

Despite the fact Isa was not in the mood to talk, she *was* curious about her fellow Ittallan's companion. Dragons were wild creatures. Untameable. The oldest ones were revered as gods. How had Palom managed to hatch and raise such a creature?

'*Leillu* is wanting friends with you, Princess.' His voice was flat.

Isa drew in a breath and pushed her face into a mask of impassivity. 'Yes, it appears so.'

'I am learning about *Leillu* every day,' Palom continued, his broad frame obscuring the bright sunlight and throwing Isa and *Leillu* into shadow. Hailing from a remote village deep in the Rio Neva forest, Palom's mastery of the common tongue was limited at best.

But Isa had dealt with his sort of people before and ignored his stilted speech and missing vocabulary. She had to be accepting of any and all Ittallan if she was to be their queen. Many Goldstones were judgemental, and she was keen to distance herself from that sort of thinking.

When she didn't reply, Palom said, 'It is good you are with us. *Leillu* does not like strangers.'

Isa smirked at Palom's attempt to hide his own concern for her through his dragon, even through his grief. She appreciated it, though. After being locked up in the palace, she was glad of company that wasn't a condescending Varkain. 'Well, it's good that *Leillu* wishes to be friendly with me. How will the young dragon fare in Estoria? It's quite busy there, from what I've heard.' Isa turned fully to Palom now.

Her life had changed so dramatically since Aciel's war. Now, she'd left her city, her people, to her bloodthirsty brothers. What kind of princess was she to allow that? Would everything collapse into ruin?

She wondered what kind of ruler she would be if she *did* manage to overthrow Sapora and take the throne. That was in the future, though. She needed to be a leader of this rebellion, first. She'd wished desperately for power and independence, and now she had exactly that, she hadn't expected to feel so afraid.

'*Leillu* will be okay I think. If I am there with her.'

Isa raised an eyebrow. 'Her?'

'Or him.' Palom shrugged. 'In old tongue we use only one word for person.'

She knew the old languages as well as Palom did, she'd been well-schooled after all. But teasing him was bringing the beginnings of a smile to her face, something she didn't think possible on that day of mourning, so she continued. 'Person? *Leillu* is a dragon.'

'*Leillu* is people.'

She laughed aloud at that and stroked the young dragon again. *Leillu's* blue scales were beginning to fade in colour, even in the short time that had passed since their escape from Taban Yul. The dragon's eyes weren't as bright as they'd seemed the previous night, and one appeared milky. 'Best keep *Leillu* close, just in case.'

Moored on the wetlands behind them, Captain Traego's enormous airship, *Otella*, underwent repairs. His crew scampered up and down the masts and ladders like ants, pulling at ropes and carrying wood, calling to one another over the brisk wind, and leaving the Ittallan to their mourning. The ship had been damaged by Tacio during their escape, with part of the hull suffering the most. A gaping hole yawned wide, and his crew attempted to patch it up as quickly as they could.

Beside it sat Amarah's un-named warship, equally glorious in the dawn sun, and without so much as a single scratch. On *Otella's* other side, Amarah herself strolled across the deck of her new airship, *RaKhanna*.

Smaller than the two warships, and less formidable, *RaKhanna* was a ship that leaned more towards speed than power. Amarah inspected every inch of it with a critical eye, hands on her hips as she progressed. Isa smiled as she watched the sky pirate. She hadn't known the woman for very long, and she'd changed drastically since she'd last seen her. For a start, Amarah had lost her right eye and now wore an eyepatch with a dragon insignia stitched into the fabric. Secondly, her original airship, *Khanna*, was gone. Thirdly, her comrade, an Arillian by the name of Kohl, no longer travelled with her.

Isa had many questions for the sky pirate, particularly surrounding what had occurred since she and the Arillian had left Taban Yul in search of a way to free Moroda. Clearly they'd failed, as Moroda was still sealed in crystal on the outskirts of Taban Yul. Although curious, her questions could wait.

Amarah hadn't asked *her* a thousand questions either, which Isa had been half-expecting and had braced for. Isa was therefore happy to extend the same courtesy to the sky pirate.

Three ships wasn't much of a fleet, considering she was used to managing the Imperial ships of Taban Yul, but it was better than nothing. Her own pair of tiny class five airships were safely tucked away on board *Otella*. Her fleet technically consisted of five ships—though hers had no firepower.

Isa was sure that with Amarah, Traego, and the rest of their sky pirates on her side, she'd be able to get more ships under her belt. She needed every advantage she could get.

With Jato's Arillians, Sapora's Sevastos, random dragon attacks, and now potentially an Ark on the loose, Val Sharis was a definite no-fly zone. And it would take more than a show of strength to win her crown, at any rate. She needed to strategise and get the people of her country behind her, or at least against her brothers. Val Sharis was in a state of unrest, and she planned to leverage that.

Isa's lip twitched as she remembered her battle with Tacio and she looked down at the blood on her sleeves. She'd been able to release part of her rage, against him. He'd not soon forget her claws.

Palom strode forward, wading into the saltwater, *Leillu* clutching his shoulder, until he was waist-deep. He said nothing, returning to his usual stoic quietness at their lapse in conversation.

Isa was no healer, nor had she any training from the mage cities of Ranski, but she could feel the grief and sorrow radiating from the man. It encompassed him like smoke.

Palom and his niece, Solvi, had wrapped Lathri's body in linen and whatever fabrics could be spared, and given her a burial at sea. It wasn't uncommon in the more remote villages of Val Sharis, but she knew Palom wanted his former lover buried with dignity in the shining capital city of Taban Yul. Preferably in a sun-drenched room within the mausoleum, where her spirit could easily find lasting peace.

But that couldn't happen.

'Look, Palom. I...With everything so chaotic during the flight here, I never had the chance to speak to you about Lathri. I want you to know—'

'Is not your fault.' Palom cut her off. He turned his head

slightly, only enough to look her in the eye. 'Is nothing to be said about it. Yes?'

Isa wanted to argue, wanted to offer her heartfelt condolences, her apologies, and promise that Lathri would be avenged. Wanted him to hear how genuine her words were and force him to listen to them. But when she saw the red-tinge in Palom's eyes, his steely gaze, and the barely-hidden wrath of the tiger behind it, she decided to hold her tongue. Instead, she stepped back—giving Palom and his dragon their space.

Behind her, scattered along the wetlands, were the beginnings of her army. Mostly, they were Ittallan who Lathri had gathered together. Those who believed in her as their queen. Many were fighters—Aetos, Kylos, Solvi, even Chyro, a young captain of the guard. Formerly, of the guard.

Isa trusted those Ittallan with her life.

They stood against Sapora. His Sevastos,and the Arks. She had no idea if they would be enough.

'Princess Isa.'

She whirled around at the sound of her name, eyes scanning the crowd for who had called her.

A man strode over, his boots leaving deep prints in the mud. He was tall, his jacket open and blowing in the wind, a long, curved sword at his hip. 'Glad my crew and ships could be o' service ta ya.' He tapped his hat when he reached her and offered a wide smile.

Isa evaluated him for a brief moment. 'I appreciate the assistance...Captain Traego?' It was an educated guess. She knew who *Otella* belonged to, and the sky pirate Traego's reputation was well-known throughout Val Sharis, even if she'd never met the man before.

At her words, Traego's grin broadened, revealing gold teeth at the back of his mouth. 'Unfortunately, *Otella* was a little damaged while *assistin'* ya. We're able ta patch her up, but she won't be able ta be repaired properly until we get back ta base.'

She knew what he was fishing for. 'You'll be paid for the damages, don't worry.'

Traego grunted in response. 'I'd hope so. Things are gonna get more'n a little sketchy from now on, ya know.'

Fear coiled in her stomach. What was to stop one of the pirates in Estoria from handing her right back into Tacio and Sapora's waiting claws? She had some eighty or so armed Ittallan gathered. Her followers. The others were from Traego's crew of sky pirates. Fewer than ten of them, but still a force to be reckoned with. Could *any* of them be trusted?

Pirates worked for gold. That's what drove them. When she became queen, she'd have more than enough coin to satiate their appetites. They'd stood with her and freed her. If she promised them further riches, they'd be in her pocket, and she'd have another fleet at her disposal. 'I'm sure I can count on you, Traego. Even if things...get rough?'

Traego considered her, then nodded. 'For the moment.'

Isa was under no illusions. Allying with the sky pirates was only temporary. 'Good. I'll need your famous silver tongue once we reach Estoria.'

'Putting me back ta work already? Ain't even recovered from this rescue mission!' Traego laughed and jabbed a thumb towards *Otella*, as if to illustrate his point.

Isa ignored him. 'My followers aren't enough, even as strong as they are. I need ships. A fleet. I need you to help convince the other sky pirates of Estoria to join my cause, lend me their ships and crews. I can't fight for my throne without an army, not facing the arsenal Sapora has at his disposal. And you won't get much gold until I'm queen.'

Traego laughed again, a deep belly laugh that shook his entire body.

Isa fought to keep a scowl from her face, and waited until he stopped.

'What's all this?' Amarah asked, approaching the two, several loops of rope held over one shoulder, her scythe clasped loosely in her other hand. 'I miss a joke or something?'

'Amarah! How are you feeling?' Isa asked. She saw Amarah's corpse in her mind's eye, suddenly, prone and bleeding out on the deck of *Otella*. She bit her thumbnail and forced the memory away.

The other woman shrugged and shifted her weight. 'I'm alive.' Her gaze flicked to the sea, where Palom and *Leillu* stood. Overhead, gulls cried as they worried the fish in the shallows, but Palom remained motionless. Amarah returned her attention to Isa a moment later. 'What's so funny, then?'

'Your princess wants the captains on Estoria to give her their ships,' Traego answered.

'*And* crew,' Isa added. 'Empty ships aren't any good. I need competent people in the air, too.'

The black fabric of Amarah's eyepatch flapped a little in the wind. 'You...uh...you sure that's what you wanna do? Best thing would be to lay low after a job like this, to be honest. You don't wanna go back to them snakes so soon after breaking outta their prison? Be suicide.'

Isa tilted her head. 'We're going to Estoria, anyway. I need to take my throne. That's why all these Ittallan are here, following me. There are plenty of resources on the Estorian islands that I could use—the airships and crews being a major one.'

Amarah and Traego traded glances.

'What's the problem?'

'Convincing sky pirates ta do *anything* is harder than pullin' a dragon's tooth. I dunno how much luck you'll have,' Traego said.

'You're both helping me, aren't you?' Isa countered.

'I had a personal reason to help you. Most pirates don't give a shit about anything other than how much gold they can grab,' Amarah said.

'And I'll have gold to give them. Or have you forgotten I'm royalty?' Isa folded her arms. She didn't need this uphill battle to be any harder.

Traego scratched his eyebrow. 'With all respect, Princess. Ya ain't got nothin' ta give 'em now, have ya? What's their incentive? Hope you beat the snakes and make good on ya promise? Most o' us never do jobs for royalty for a reason. Heck, even Goldstones on the islands have trouble getting us ta do stuff unless they pay in full in advance. These are troublin' times. Everyone'll be on edge. They're more likely ta throw ya back ta Sapora than do anythin' else.'

'What would you suggest instead?'

Traego looked back at Amarah. 'I dunno. I'm just sayin' it's probably gonna be harder than ya think. Ya might technically be a princess, but as far as Estoria is concerned, ya just another outcast. People ain't gonna jump at ya every command, so ya might wanna get used to the change.' He gave her a somewhat apologetic grin, then headed back towards *Otella*, barking orders at Antar and the others as he went.

Amarah lingered, watching Traego go. Antar argued with his captain and the two had a brief standoff.

'What do you think?' Isa asked.

'Anything's possible if you're willing to work for it,' Amarah said, almost aggressively. 'Traeg's got a point. Ain't gonna be plain sailing with the Estorian crowd, let me tell you! But, we'll see if we can't persuade a few of 'em.'

Isa chewed the inside of her lip and glanced at Amarah's scythe, weighing up her options. It wasn't the same dragon ore-infused weapon of destruction that Palom had made—

the *Valta Forinja* that had given them the edge over Aciel, his Arillians, and the army of thralls he'd commanded. Isa wondered where it was.

That was exactly the sort of advantage she wanted.

She knew she was foolish to keep trusting Amarah, but she'd never have been able to escape the palace if not for the woman's aid. Amarah had literally given her life during the jailbreak, only just brought back from the brink by Lathri's healing magic. Regardless of what Traego warned, or claimed sky pirates were like, Isa was convinced that Amarah, at least, would be on her side. Gold, or no gold.

'Incoming!' Antar barked from atop *Otella's* deck, his strong voice carrying across the shoreline.

Isa immediately turned towards the sea, where a small class five airship hurtled towards them at breakneck speed. Her breath caught. It couldn't possibly be one of her brothers' spies, could it? She'd only fled the palace the night before, and they'd not been trailed. The *Thief Shrouds* had made sure of that.

'Looks like one o' Captain Ipot's, if I'm seein' that sigil right,' Traego said, only a handful of steps from *Otella*. He rested one hand on his sword as he stared at the approaching ship.

Evidently Captain Ipot wasn't a friend, if Traego was so ready to defend himself.

Kylos and Solvi made their way over to Isa and stood beside her, almost as though they were an honour-guard. Isa appreciated the gesture, but it didn't make her feel any safer. If that airship had weaponry and decided to fire, they'd all be sitting ducks.

'Might want to keep yeh distance,' Kylos whispered. The fierce woman could hold her own in a scrap, but she was also recovering from weeks of Tacio's torture. Isa didn't consider her fighting fit.

'It's just another sky pirate. Shouldn't be a problem, right? They're allies?' Isa's words held more confidence than her voice.

'We do not know which of them we can trust, Princess,' Solvi said. At eighteen, loyal to a fault, the young woman had a strong, athletic build, and was one of the bravest people Isa had ever met. She shouldn't be surprised, considering Palom was her uncle.

The sky pirate navigated his ship towards them, pulling his sails out wide to slow his approach and briefly blotting out the sun. The ship didn't seem to be anything special. The wooden hull hadn't even been painted, and remained a mottled mix of natural browns and greys. The sails had been dyed dark, forest green, and showed a silver chalice insignia in the centre. Isa recognised it as one of the various sky pirate sigils, but she couldn't identify anything more than that.

'Cap'n Traeg!' the pirate yelled down from on deck. He turned the wheel violently, forcing the ship to brake in mid-air, and almost spin 180 degrees with the force of the manoeuvre. As the ship shifted, Isa noticed the back half of it was blackened—by fire? 'Dragons above, what you doin' out here in the mud, Traeg? No. Never mind, I don't care. Glad I found you! You gotta get back to Estoria! There's been trouble, and it's all your doing!'

Traego kept his hand on the hilt of his sword and made no move to get closer to the landing ship or greet the other pirate. The rest of his crew remained at their posts, dotted about *Otella*, and all watched with a wolf's wariness.

Traego said calmly, 'What trouble, Reg?'

'Arillians! Blasted the drowning pits to pieces and took most of the hillside with it. Killed dozens of us, and Goldies, too! Cap'n Ipot's in a bad way. We lost half our ships, Traeg! *And* two pilots!'

Isa's heart thudded in her chest. She looked back at the horizon and stared. The distant smudge of land was Estoria —or was the darkness actually smoke from the Arillian attack?

As far as she was aware, there weren't any Arillians this far south, aside from Jato's crowd—and they certainly weren't in Estoria when their target was the capital city.

She tried to swallow and realised she had a lump in her throat. Returning her attention to the sky pirates, she noticed Amarah biting her lip.

It was the only nervous giveaway in her otherwise relaxed stance.

Why was *she* nervous?

Wait. Arillians. It couldn't be Kohl...could it ?

'He doesn't seem to know yeh here, Princess,' Kylos whispered. 'He can't be after yeh.'

Isa nodded, trying to keep the gesture small. She didn't want to draw attention to herself if Reg was more interested in screaming at Traego.

Traego shifted his weight and shrugged, giving no outward indication of any emotion save mild amusement. 'Some captains have been bringin' in Arillians for the bounty. Yours, too. A bit o' wayward lightning damage is ta be expected with their sort. How's that my fault? I ain't even *been* in Estoria the past few days.'

Reg shook his head, frantic, as he cut the ship's engine and scrambled over the side. In his haste, he tripped in the wet mud and smeared the dirty, grey stuff down his front. He ignored both the state of himself and the watching Ittallan, and made straight for Traego, marching every step. 'No! It ain't a few desperate prisoners being difficult. It was a fucking massacre. One of 'em came down from the sky like Rhea herself and cut us all to ribbons. And it's all *your damned fault*!'

Isa noticed as he came closer that his muddied clothes were stained with blood and ash, and his face was twisted in rage. Thin slashes lined his arms and legs, streaks of red on his dirty skin.

'Oh, really?' Traego lifted his shoulders, again refusing to give in to Reg's allegation. His finger twitched on the hilt of his sword, as though he'd been about to unsheath it, but held himself back at the last second. 'I don't see how it's any o' my concern. All my crew are here with me. We're actually in the middle of a job right now, Reg, so if ya wouldn't mind—'

Reg looked up at *Otella*, took in the faces on board, and scowled. '*Her*!' He jabbed an accusatory finger in Amarah's direction. '*You're* responsible for this, Captain Traego, because it was the Arillian what came to Estoria wiv *her*!'

2

Flying to Corhaven, Sapora had been full of nervous excitement and apprehension. Returning to Taban Yul was the exact opposite. He felt like the god he had freed. Nothing in Linaria could touch him.

His Sevastos flew ahead of the airship, clearing the way of rogue dragons or Arillians, and even those on the ground scattered before its wings. The creature despised him, he knew, but forces greater than itself bound its actions to Sapora's words, so the king paid the thread of malice little mind.

He was used to people resenting him.

Sapora travelled in his father's luxurious airship, *The Jade Crown*, with a small complement of Cerastes headed up by his personal guard Roke, and of course his newest weapon: Veynothi.

She'd been robed in red silks secured with leather bindings, the most she had permitted, and the rest of her remained as wild and ferocious as any Varkain of the Old Guard. Her cold eyes surveyed those on board and the world below with faint disdain, and Sapora wondered how much Linaria had changed since she'd last drawn breath.

It *had* been several thousand years.

Although he flew in a royal airship with a Sevastos as an escort, he wondered where the Imperial Guard were. There had been numerous checkpoints set up in the mountains on the approach to Povmar, and every single one had been empty. What was to stop any number of thieves from looting Veynothi's tomb? Or helping themselves to ancient Varkain treasures?

He'd need to request Roke make some investigations. As king, technically he was responsible for the Imperial Guard. If they were slacking, or there were problems among their ranks, he needed to do something about it.

He glanced at the dark vein that stood out on the back of his left hand—a new appearance following Veynothi's resurrection—and wondered at its meaning.

Approaching footsteps and a panicked heartbeat broke Sapora from his thoughts. He pulled his sleeves down to cover his marked skin and counted the seconds in his mind before the inevitable knock on the door to the king's quarters.

'My liege, forgive the disturbance. I have an urgent message from the palace, may I enter?'

'You may.' Sapora remained in the plush chair at the back of his quarters, gazing out the window as the world sailed by. His Sevastos was resplendent in the sunshine, an escort that even he never grew tired of seeing.

A large cruiser, *The Jade Crown* travelled slowly, providing a gentle journey to all those it ferried around. Despite his eagerness to return to the palace, Sapora could take his time to admire the workmanship of the vessel. It was nothing at all like the shabby airship *Khanna* he'd been forced to travel upon for weeks.

The Jade Crown enjoyed gold and mahogany, silks and fabrics, and even tapestries hung in the king's quarters. His bed had been stuffed with goose down, and the chandelier which hung from the ceiling glittered gently in the sunlight, made from the same crystals as the chandelier in the grand ballroom back in the palace.

It was the perfect ship to make a statement in.

Sapora looked up at the young Varkain soldier who entered. He stood almost a head shorter than himself, and wore silvered jewels in both ears. Perhaps he looked up to Tacio. The peacock.

'An Ittallan messenger approached the ship moments ago. She'd flown from Taban Yul.'

Sapora narrowed his eyes. They were still at least a day's travel from the capital. What could be so urgent that it couldn't wait until he arrived?

The young guard swallowed, eyes darting to the window, where the Sevastos's wings were in full view.

'Well? What's the message?'

'There's...something happened at the palace, my liege.'

Sapora stood up. Now the messenger had his full attention.

'Some of the prisoners escaped...'

'Isa?' Sapora asked, thoughts only on his sister.

'She was among them, yes. The sky pirate Amarah, too. And Lathri. Along with the remaining survivors of the rebel attack. They've...they've all escaped.'

Sapora licked one of his fangs in an attempt to steady his breathing. 'Tacio...?'

'Is alive and well—'

'I *know* he's alive and well! Where *was* he?'

The young man took an involuntary step back. 'The messenger left before that could be ascertained, my liege. But...he is believed to have been overpowered by those aiding the escape.'

'And *who* aided them...?' Sapora could hardly keep the snarl from his voice.

'We don't know, but they appeared to be sky pirates. Assumed from Estoria? Their ships were unmarked, and were last seen fleeing to the south-east. Unfortunately, the Cerastes lost them near the border.'

'You're dismissed.'

At the king's command, the young Varkain practically ran from his quarters. Sapora returned to the window. He didn't want anyone to see his expression and realise how high his emotions ran. The veins pulsed with his heartbeat, seeming to darken before his eyes. He exhaled slowly and looked back out the window.

After his greatest success, he couldn't even rely on Tacio to manage the palace for a handful of days. Everyone had been locked up. The palace had been quiet. He literally did not have to lift a finger!

Sapora suppressed a snarl of frustration. He'd wanted to question Isa personally. Without his brother's presence.

Now, he wouldn't even have that chance.

Tacio believed her to be a traitor, and wouldn't be persuaded otherwise. Sapora struggled with that. There had been no reason for Isa to betray him, and yet he couldn't ignore the facts.

She'd aided Lathri and her rebels. Orchestrated two escape attempts—one of which while she herself was held prisoner.

Perhaps he had been too soft on her, unwilling to see her for what she had been all along. Just another Ittallan traitor who despised a snake in power. He dreaded to think how much truth was in that.

'I sense *such* turmoil within you, *King* Sapora.'

Veynothi's icy voice sent shivers down his spine, particularly because he hadn't heard or sensed her approach. He recovered as quickly as he could. 'You presume much of me, Ark. And you didn't request entry.'

'I didn't need to,' she replied. 'Your door was open.'

Sapora glanced at the doorway and scowled. Evidently in his haste to get away, the young guard had left his door wide open.

He didn't enjoy the fact that Veynothi had invited herself in, nor that she utterly terrified him, much as he hoped to mask it with indifference or annoyance. 'You are most impolite, then.'

She grinned, fangs on display. She undoubtedly enjoyed tormenting people. 'Where are the others?'

He didn't have to ask her to clarify. Her mind had been on the other Arks from the moment she'd stepped out of her tomb. 'Malashash is close to the border.' He walked past her to close the door, pulling the handle up to lock it. He didn't want anyone else sauntering in unexpectedly. 'I've yet to confirm the locations of Brahm and Karekis.'

Veynothi frowned, her eyes darkening. 'That's *Prince* Karekis. I do not like working alone. Malashash and Brahm are guards. Prince Karekis and I are fighters.'

'You should be grateful I woke you up at all. There is much to do and little time to do it.'

'Many setbacks for the king.' She pouted. Childish.

Sapora ran a hand through his hair. He hadn't been sure what to expect from the Arks, but petulance and defiance hadn't crossed his mind. 'My sister is missing. Finding her and bringing her back to the palace is my first priority.'

Veynothi's pout grew. 'You said the Arks were your first priority.'

'They have been waiting a few thousand years already. Waiting a bit longer will make no difference. Sometimes priorities shift, Veynothi.' He fought to keep from sneering.

She flicked out her tongue. Long, and black, the fork

tasted the air for several seconds. 'What are you afraid of, my king?'

'I'm afraid of nothing,' Sapora replied, too quickly.

Her pout shifted into a chilling smile. 'Are you afraid of us? Of *me*? Is that why you're waiting to release the others? Want to see if you can *control* me, first?' She stepped towards him and the air around her surged with magic. It tightened, making every breath difficult.

Sapora watched as she raised her left arm, and one of the six swords attached to her back flung out into her open hand. She grasped the blade and pointed it at him, the tip a hair's breadth from his throat.

'I could kill you right here, right now, young mongrel king. Drain you of every drop of blood and gift it to the Valendrin. Present it in a golden bowl decorated with the jades from your crown. Pluck out your eyes and let them float in it, so his face is the last thing you ever see. And then I would free my brothers. Who would stop me?' She pressed the sword against his skin.

Sapora glared at her, but held his ground, unflinching. 'Then my hold on the Sevastos would break, and you would once again be sealed in stone. Lost and forgotten forever more. You cannot threaten or bribe me, Veynothi. Do as I say, and I'll make your servitude more bearable.'

He allowed himself a flicker of a smile at her disgust at the word *servitude*. She had to know her place, otherwise he had no hope of controlling her or the other Arks.

She huffed and put her sword back, though her predatory gaze lingered on him.

'You will hunt down Princess Isa and bring her back—alive and unharmed. Once you've completed this task, I will look to release your brothers.'

Veynothi sneered and the air crackled with her power. 'I am an *Ark*, Sapora! I ravage towns, destroy armies, crush any who stand in my path! You want me to...to...be your *sniffer dog* to track one worthless woman? Another mongrel, no doubt?'

Sapora's smile grew. 'I am *ordering* you to find her.'

She glowered at him. 'I am *not* a Cerastes to be commanded! I am the *greatest* of the Varkain!'

His ears popped as magic rushed from her, sending the papers on his desk fluttering away, the chandelier clinking as it moved. 'Then you'll have no trouble finding her for me. When we reach Taban Yul, I will give you a ship, Cerastes, anything you need for your task. Understand?'

Veynothi's pupils constricted to slits and she sent another wave of energy around the room. The blast made Sapora stagger, but she wrenched the door from its hinges and stormed out of the cabin.

He had *something*, at least. Some hold, no matter how small, over the Ark. She hadn't been seen in generations, yet the memory of her destruction would sound loud and clear in the hearts of every Ittallan who saw her. If nothing else, she would put a stop to any lingering rebel activity in Taban Yul. It would become a golden city for the Varkain and those few Ittallan who swore him true allegiance.

Having an Ark under his control showed the world who he was, *what* he was.

Sapora inspected the broken door and pulled at a few of the splinters which jutted out from the wood. A shame. The door had been beautifully carved with patterns from Sereth, and Veynothi had smashed it to pieces in her tantrum. He shuddered to think how much it would cost to repair.

Veynothi only obeyed him out of fear of being returned to stone.

Unchecked, the Ark could storm Linaria and kill everyone she found unworthy.

Would Aciel be able to stand up to her?

He hoped not.

He was *banking* on the fact that he couldn't, that Veynothi and the other Arks would be immune to his compulsion. If the Valendrin was accurate in his knowledge, it might be the only way Linaria would truly be free of the Arillian's poison.

Sapora closed his eyes and thought things through. He knew he walked a fine line. But every step, every risk, was calculated. He could not afford to lose and refused to let himself or his people suffer through his mistakes.

As the sun reached its zenith, he spied the tips of the palace towers in the far distance as they approached the city of Taban Yul. Gold and gemstones reflected the light in a dazzling display of colour and rainbows.

The Sevastos roared overhead as it swooped forwards, wings sending waves of wind over *The Jade Crown* and rattling the ship. At least he had the dragon. Without the Sevastos, he'd lose his already tenuous grip on the Ark, and everything would collapse into chaos.

At least there was no way that bond could be broken.

~

SAPORA STROLLED through the palace halls towards his council chamber, having paused for only a few minutes to get changed into something that didn't stink of blood. The robe he'd selected had long sleeves, but they didn't quite cover his hands. So he'd opted for moleskin gloves to hide the dark veins. When it came to the Varkain, the less attention he drew to perceived weaknesses, the better.

The Cerastes and Valendrin had gone ahead to the council chamber, and only Roke stayed by his side.

The bright tapestries adorning the walls mocked him as he walked past. His own tapestry wasn't there, of course.

Sapora had had it moved to his suite to cover the door to his room of mirrors lest anyone stumbled in and discovered it. It meant the last tapestry he walked past was always the previous royal in power—his father, the warrior-king, Vasil. The double-headed tapestry leered at him. Either as a man or a snake, Vasil's dismissive disappointment became a tangible cloud through which Sapora had to navigate to reach the council chamber.

He stared at his father's likeness and compared it to his own *naja* form. There could be no doubt that Sapora was royalty. He'd done everything that had been asked of him, and more. Completed his errantry, learned what he could of Linaria and the forces moving across it. Beaten his trials and slain a member of the Old Guard in front of an audience—including Vasil and Tacio.

Yet he was still mocked or begrudgingly served.

The hairs on the back of his neck stood up, and Sapora whirled around in time to see Veynothi saunter around the corner, surrounded by an elite group of Cerastes in full armour and holding spears, their tips pointed at the ceiling.

'Ready for your grand introduction?' Sapora asked as she approached.

Veynothi blinked slowly. 'I am *always* ready to hunt. Must you put me on show?'

'It is expected. The council will wonder where I've been the past few days, and if I mention your name without proof, it would reflect poorly.'

She smirked. 'Even your servants have little faith in you.'

Sapora bit his tongue and waved her through, disgusted with himself at how on edge she put him. The Arks were the ultimate weapons of the Varkain. The stuff of legend—or nightmares, depending on whose side you were on.

He'd been foolish to assume they would bow to him and kiss his feet as the Ittallan servants did.

Once the doors to the council chambers closed behind Veynothi and her guards, Sapora turned back to the tapestry of Vasil. He wondered what his father would have done. And whether anything he did was good enough for the warrior-king's approval.

The tapestry remained silent, though Vasil's eyes seemed to be watching him.

'Are you ready, my liege?' Roke asked after several long moments.

With a final glance at the image, Sapora led the way down the hall and into the waiting chamber.

~

THE STUNNED SILENCE that greeted Sapora lengthened as he strode alongside the table and took his seat at the throne at its head, Roke only a few steps behind him.

Tacio sat to his right, Koraki to his left. The Valendrin sat beside his brother, paper-thin skin barely clutching to the bones underneath. A handful of other council members were present, but most chairs remained empty, and he felt Isa's missing presence more strongly than he cared to admit.

While Tacio and the Valendrin gave him a polite nod, the rest stared at Veynothi—who stood motionless at the end of the table, hands clasped behind her back, eyes closed.

Sapora could hardly believe the state of Tacio. His normally immaculate brother had bruises and welts on his skin, his face marred by knife and claw. He'd put coloured powder on his face to mask them, but it was clear he'd recently been on the receiving end of a brutal encounter.

Isa.

'I thank you for convening on such short notice,' Sapora began, ignoring the standard pleasantries and jumping right into business. 'There are several issues I wish to discuss, however I would first like to introduce you to Veynothi.' He held out a gloved hand in her direction, but she remained immovable. Even with his keen senses, Sapora couldn't detect so much as a breath from her.

Unperturbed, he continued, 'As you are no doubt aware, Veynothi is unlike any Varkain alive, even among the Old Guard. She is an Ark, one of only four from the time of our war, and will stamp down on the Arillians and protect the Varkain—and Ittallan—from outside threats.'

Sapora hadn't been sure what to expect. A round of applause would be too uncouth, yet the gathered council remained as deathly quiet as when he'd walked in.

Irritation grew.

'Veynothi. Do you have anything to say to the ruling council of Sereth and Val Sharis?'

With deliberate slowness, Veynothi opened her eyes. Her gold irises seemed to light the room, and she took a step back to lower her head in a short bow. As her head dropped, the six blades attached to her back shimmered, and she filled the room with a sudden pulse of energy.

Sapora braced himself for it—at least he knew what to expect having experienced it in her tomb when he'd first woken her. She only took a little energy from them, but Sapora immediately wanted to sit down and catch his breath.

Her magic snapped them out of their reverie, and the council bowed back to her, before breaking out in excited chatter. Some directed questions at her, others at Sapora or Tacio.

Sapora permitted them their excitement for almost two minutes before holding a hand up to cease the talk. 'Veynothi has been tasked with tracking down Princess Isa and bringing her back to the palace. In my absence, I have learned she was kidnapped by a group of sky pirates led by an old associate of mine: Amarah. Veynothi, I have no doubt, will complete this task with the efficiency for which the Arks are known.'

He heard Tacio's breathing quicken. Stating to the council that his sister had been captured, instead of escaped, saved face. Openly admitting she'd turned traitor and betrayed them would not go down well for Isa when she was brought back.

Veynothi, for her part, remained emotionless.

The council murmured to themselves, making various noises of assent.

Sapora smiled inwardly. Despite everything that she'd done, he was still protecting Isa. Perhaps he *was* soft. He added, 'Koraki. Please have new writs drawn up for the arrest of the sky pirate Amarah.'

The head steward wrote frantically. 'Yes, my liege. The bounty?'

'Two thousand crowns.'

Koraki almost dropped the quill. 'My liege?'

'Five thousand crowns alive,' Sapora corrected. He held Koraki's gaze, and the steward hurried to note everything down.

Tacio jumped in, eager to appear useful, 'Captain Doro, as the new Fleet Master, would you kindly provide Veynothi with a suitable vessel for her trip?'

The Ittallan—one of the few who'd made it onto Sapora's council through Summercourt—stood up immediately. His large belly pressed against the table and he dabbed his sweating brow with a pocket kerchief. 'Of course my lord Tacio. We have been steadily building since...since...the winter. I'm sure we have several suitable for the great Ark, Veynothi.' He turned awkwardly to look at her, as if seeking approval.

'If you have any requirements, please speak to one of my aides. Koraki, or one of his stewards, will provide you with anything you need. That will be all,' Sapora said to Veynothi. He enjoyed being able to dismiss her in front of the council. It was about the only way he could assert any of his power in front of the Ark.

He sensed her disdain, but she stepped back and allowed herself to be escorted out of the chamber without another word. Captain Doro hurried after her, along with a pair of Cerastes. Not that an Ark needed any protecting.

Perhaps she was pleased enough to get going that she would overlook Sapora's display of dominance this time.

With the Ark gone, the chamber visibly relaxed, and normal business resumed.

Koraki noted down things that were said, and by whom, what was to be done, and by whom, and anything he'd read between the lines that Sapora needed to learn or be made aware of.

Chief on everyone's list was the sickness in the city, which had worsened with the Arillian presence growing on their doorstep.

'Have any cracks appeared? Anything that might show the crystal weakening or changing?' Sapora asked. He hated how much seemed to have changed in the few days he'd been away.

'No, my liege. Nothing. Yet the power within pulses. Aciel is not dead, I fear.' The Varkain beside the Valendrin spoke quietly, and inclined his head in a far more reserved display of obedience. He wore the dark blue-black scaled armour of the Cerastes, and Sapora recalled Tacio putting him forward to assist on the council. Tethkari, if Sapora recalled correctly. Recently promoted to captain.

'Keep your soldiers as far away from the crystal as is safe for them. We can't afford to lose good fighters. After freeing

Veynothi, my next step is to bolster Taban Yul's defences by releasing Malashash.'

Captain Tethkari raised his eyebrows. 'My liege, if such a feat could be achieved, that would be most gratefully received.'

'I am taking matters into my own claws. I'll not abandon you.'

Captain Tethkari dropped his shoulders and relaxed, visibly happier.

'Aside from Veynothi, I want all ships grounded until we know Jato's intentions. We have enough provisions to last several months, do we not? Let's stop any accidents before they have a chance to happen. From my understanding, she's not launched any direct attacks on the city?'

'That's right,' Tacio fiddled with one of his rings. 'We've fired warning shots when she's flown too close to the city walls from our ballista, but otherwise she's just set up a perimeter of storms around Taban Yul.'

Sapora laced his fingers together and rested his elbows on the table. 'One threat at a time. Let Jato wear herself out by throwing up her storm wall. If we need to get urgent supplies into the city, my Sevastos is more than a match for her little birds. I believe she is trying to get to Aciel, but as for what she might be able to do, I cannot say. Maintain your watches, let me know the moment any of her movements change.'

The council nodded as bells rang out in the city to mark midday.

Sapora had wanted to discuss more, but decided it was enough for now. It wasn't every day an Ark walked among them. He waved a hand to dismiss the council.

Tacio pushed his chair back to stand, but Sapora raised a finger. 'Not you, brother. I need to speak with you once they've gone.'

Tacio's face shifted from relief into frustration, resentment, and finally grudging acceptance.

Sapora glanced at Roke, then nodded. Despite his personal guard's questioning look, Roke did as he was bid, and left the room with the others.

Once the doors were closed and they could no longer hear the council's excited chatter, Sapora dropped his amiable act and lashed out at Tacio. 'How in *Rhea's name* did you let Isa escape? You were overpowered by *Amarah*? And a handful of her friends?'

Tacio's fangs lengthened in response to the challenge. 'You left the palace unguarded! How was I to know they were after Isa? All attempts had been on Lathri!'

'The princess was our key priority. I was gone a few days, Tacio! A few days, and you let everything fall apart!'

Tacio snarled, pupils contracting. 'She would have escaped even with you there.'

'No. She wouldn't. Because *I'd* have been watching her cell myself. You're too distracted playing torture games with the other prisoners and prowling the city at night. I should have you ripped apart and sent back to Sereth in pieces.'

'If only you knew what she did to me!' Tacio's nose flared and he stood up, kicking the chair away in his anger. 'I've been telling you for weeks there was something *wrong* with her!'

'Perhaps she always has been one of us, until *you* pushed her away,' Sapora retaliated. 'I've never had a problem with her. Perhaps if you'd bothered to visit Taban Yul once in a while during your youth, you would have realised that for yourself! It's a shame you're so spoiled down there.'

Tacio snorted. 'Don't accuse me of never visiting. I travelled here with Vasil once or twice! Besides, there is no reason for me to come to this damned palace. I have everything I need in Sereth! It's comfortable, I'm surrounded by my own kind. None of that back talking or disgust you get up here with the Ittallan. Even now, it still goes on. You're an idiot if you don't think so.'

Sapora snarled, thinking of Vasil's tapestry, Veynothi's callous words, and even the way the Ittallan on his council looked at him. 'Of course I hear it, brother. But now I have Veynothi. She'll put a stop to everything before the year is up. Just you wait.'

3

The howling winds carried Jato's unbridled rage.

Her anger was palpable—Kohl felt it in every breath he took.

He and Fogu had made a point of avoiding the centre of Val Sharis, and had kept to the ridge of mountains running along the spine of the land as they flew south. The mountains divided Val Sharis and Sereth, yet even this far away from the capital city of Taban Yul, Jato's power and strength was evident in the winds that swirled relentlessly against the Feor Mountains.

After Fogu's attack on the Estorian sky pirates, and Kohl's subsequent rescue, the last thing they wanted was to bump into any Linarians. But it wasn't because of guilt. After seeing what the pirates had done to his people—drowning them for gold—Kohl felt little remorse.

He wanted to keep them out of his sight lest he couldn't contain his fury.

Every Arillian death weighed heavy on his shoulders. His responsibility, because he'd failed to defeat Aciel. The vigilante had led his people—no, forced them—into a war they had no right to partake in. The pirates were doing what they did naturally. Working for gold. It just happened to be against Arillians, this time.

They'd needed to keep checking over their shoulder frequently in case they were followed during their flight. Fogu had ensured he'd crippled or outright destroyed all the airships he could see within two leagues of the drowning pits, however some pirates may have given chase.

It would take the pirates weeks, if not months, to recover.

Kohl wished they wouldn't ever recover.

Since reuniting with Fogu, Kohl had felt a glimmer of his old self resurface. His true personality—before losing Jato, before his exile. He remembered that he was a leader, that he had power. It had been well and truly squashed after losing his daughter twice over to Aciel. He'd been alone, save Jato, and she was a lost cause. Amarah had seen to that.

Fogu had provided him with friendship, genuine compassion, and even humour.

Kohl felt for the first time in close to fifty years that he had a purpose. That Fogu believed in him. That it was not too late to take a stand and change what he'd always believed to be unchangeable.

His eyes were open. Linaria was on the brink of destruction. Dragons burned indiscriminately now people wielded *Valta Forinja* and the Arks were being reawakened. Nowhere felt safe any longer, and he had to warn the scholars of Berel before yet another country was destroyed.

In his naivety, he'd allowed the sky pirates to get the better of him. Amarah and Traego had had the decency to warn him, and he'd been foolish enough to ignore their words, succumbing to Captain Ipot's trap.

Even Fogu had used a *Shroud* in Estoria to hide who—what—he was. It was common sense.

Kohl had grown too lax, wallowing in his own misery.

Fogu had thought nothing of it when he'd blasted the

pits open to save him. He'd slaughtered the Estorians keeping guard—and anyone else unlucky enough to be within range.

Kohl had been ready to accept his death, dishonourable and terrifying as it was.

He'd given up hope. Jato was lost. Aciel had been defeated by someone other than himself—someone who wasn't even an Arillian. And even when he'd returned to Oren, his people had given him little more than a cool welcome.

Many believed in Aciel more than himself as leader—even though Aciel's conquest had been terrible, and ended with Arillians dead or worse—at least Aciel had *done* something.

Kohl had not reacted. He'd wanted peace for his people, and ignored that fact that sometimes you had to fight for it. Fighting only meant a worse outcome for all involved.

'My lord, do you wish to rest?' Fogu called from somewhere above and to his left.

A fine rain had fallen, bringing an extra layer of misery to an already dreary, overcast afternoon. It was the type of deluge that always seemed to end up in your eyes, and taking a break from it wasn't a bad idea. Kohl hovered and looked around for anything suitable. There wasn't much they could use for shelter in the sparse mountain landscape, but they had been flying for most of the morning, and his back ached in a way it hadn't a few decades before. If they flew much higher, the rain would turn to sleet, and eventually snow. The violent gusts blasting in from the west—more of his daughter's anger—made flying particularly uncomfortable. 'Soon as there's any shelter, we can take a break.'

'What about that cave there?' Fogu dropped into Kohl's field of view and pointed at a large outcropping a short distance ahead. Snow covered the grey rock, and the mottled colours almost masked the cave's entrance. It was as good a place as any, out in the middle of nowhere. 'Should keep the worst of the wind off our backs? Until the skies clear?'

'Good spot. Let's go.' Kohl held his hat with one hand, using it to keep the worst of the rain out of his eyes, and followed Fogu down to the ground.

When his boots crunched into the compact snow, slippery in the rain, Kohl took several steadying breaths. It really had been too long since he'd flown properly. It had taken the best part of a week to recover from the drowning pits, and when he slept, he had nightmares of freezing, salty water rushing in around him, trapping him in darkness until he woke himself up, clawing at his own throat in a futile attempt to breathe.

'My lord?'

Kohl realised he'd been standing motionless for too long. 'I feel I need a sit down.' He chuckled at the thought. To fly was to rest, for an Arillian. To sit down? Wasn't that simply inviting death? He'd been down on the Linarian mainlands for too long.

He ignored Fogu's concerned glance, and walked past him into the cave, stooping to enter through its mouth. His hat brushed past stalactites, and he held it tight to his head as he made his way along the short tunnel and out of the frigid rain. Bits of the cave roof broke away at its entrance, sending down a shower of pebbles and dust that clattered to the frozen ground.

Fogu joined him a few moments later, and set to pulling out loose sticks and the firewood he carried in his pack. He spent a brief moment arranging them into a pile in the centre of the cave floor, making minor adjustments as he added handfuls of kindling. Once satisfied, Fogu flicked his wrist—sending a small bolt of lightning at the dry material. It incinerated on impact, and a fire spurted into life with a happy crackle.

Kohl removed his hat and sat it by his feet, enjoying the meagre warmth from the flames. Fat drops of water dripped from slowly melting ice, echoing all around them, and making the cave feel much larger than it was. The two broken fingers on his left hand ached terribly. He'd bound them with grasses and used a stick as a splint, but he doubted they'd ever be straight again. Yet it was a price he was more than happy to pay, considering he'd left Estoria with his life. 'Thank you, Fogu. You've saved me.'

'Nonsense. I owe it to you after everything...'

Kohl rested an arm on the Arillian's shoulder. 'You weren't yourself, then. Everyone knows that. I know that. You're more loyal a friend than I've any right to have.'

Fogu dropped his eyes to the ground. 'My lord.'

'I can't run anymore. Linaria is on the brink of collapse. Even you must have realised that, hidden away in Estoria? It's time to act. The dragons are key. If they house the original *Valta Forinja*, the Samolen will become a target of the dragons' fury. If the only good I can do is warning the scholars of Berel before the dragons bring ruin, I would be happy.'

Fogu grunted. It could have been assent or disgust.

'Sapora, as much as he seems to want to raise the Varkain from the shadows, is playing with forces too great to be controlled by one person. Aciel started things with the dragons, and now look where it's led. Jato is trying to finish his work and Sapora is messing with dragon gods. The Samolen prophecies may be truer than we think.'

'From dragon-flame...?' Fogu looked up.

'Indeed.' He needed to get across the Sea of Nami sooner rather than later. The University of Berel surely would contain scholars wise enough to listen to reason. Who would be able to act. Influence the powers of Corhaven and Val Sharis, before the world burned. Topeko had been welcoming, and Kohl hoped there would be others like him. Having an associate on the mainland had its benefits.

They sat in silence a long while, both staring into the fire while they contemplated their own thoughts.

Fogu occasionally stoked the flames to keep up their source of light and warmth. It reminded Kohl of the fire-pit back on Oren. The stories shared there, his friends and followers gathered. He wondered whether the Ice Golems could truly take on the Sevastos and the Arks, if they were attacked by those god-like powers. Whether they could bring an end to the fighting, as Moroda had tried to do.

It seemed like a lifetime ago, yet he vividly remembered the battle in the sky above Taban Yul. The air had been thick with lightning from Aciel and his Arillians, and cannon-fire from the Imperial Fleet had filled the sky with dense smoke. And everywhere, the blood-curdling screams of violence and death.

He'd sought Aciel across the maze of the battlefield. Hoped to take him out by himself, as he should have done when Aciel first came to power.

Aciel had been weakened then. He'd barely recovered from Sapora and Amarah's attack on the warship, and was making his move against Taban Yul out of desperation. Kohl's lip twitched. He *should* have been able to crush Aciel like an insect. A chill ran down his palm at the thought. Frost-touch.

Jato had been lost, but he'd hoped—a tiny flicker of hope—that perhaps by sparing Aciel, she would come back to him. Would love him again.

But he'd been too slow, and Moroda had been the one forced to make the ultimate sacrifice.

Because he'd been too afraid and too stupid to see the truth for what it was.

It had taken Amarah fighting Jato for him to realise his daughter was lost. Truly lost. He hoped their paths never crossed again, for fear they'd try to kill one another.

'Do you know how far it is to the nearest town?' Kohl asked, pushing the dark thoughts out of his mind. He wanted to get back to the present and stay there.

Fogu shifted in his seat, his wings brushing against the cave wall and floor. 'We're not far from the Sea of Nami. There's a small town on the coast. I believe the Ittallan call it Gur Bano.'

'A coastal town will have a harbour. Ships that travel across the sea.'

'Most likely, yes.'

'I hope they have airships. I would rather cross by air than by water.'

'Why don't we fly?'

'And potentially reveal ourselves again? I'll take no such risks, Fogu.'

The General frowned, deep lines crossing his face. 'My lord. We can outfly anything these Linarians have built. Especially in such a remote area.'

'I'm sure. But I would prefer we travelled by their ships. It'll draw less attention. We need to be more wary than ever. King Sapora's bounty will be in effect all over Linaria, not just in the pirate-infested islands of Estoria.'

'I thought speed was of the essence? Even if they have a fast airship out in the middle of nowhere, it'll take twice as long to cross the sea as it would take us. Your scholars may already be in danger—there are dragons everywhere. Besides, if anyone realises what we are, we've both strength enough to put them down.' Lightning crackled around his knuckles as he spoke.

Kohl couldn't ignore the logic in Fogu's argument. But after what had happened to his people in Estoria—what had happened to *him*—he didn't want to take any more chances, nor did he wish to add to the death toll he was responsible for. Slower was ultimately safer.

Rain continued to pummel the mountainside outside and the wind howled.

Kohl ran a hand through his hair. It had thinned over the years, and he forced it back with his fingers into some semblance of tidiness. He was tired of it all. Of everything—the hate and greed of the world. And the overwhelming guilt.

'I honestly don't see how it is any of our concern.' Fogu turned away, his mouth a thin line.

It was no wonder Arillians lived so high, believing Linaria's troubles beneath them. It was the lie they told themselves to justify their own exile.

'You would sit there and do nothing? Knowing these people are going to burn to death? I cannot. I've sat and done nothing for too long. Those people still died. I was just as responsible as the ones who killed them.'

Fogu didn't answer.

Eryn and Anahrik's deaths weighed on his mind. He'd refused to challenge his daughter and left them to die. Even Moroda wouldn't have perished if he'd done something about Aciel when he'd had the chance. The young Goldstone would never have been pushed to desperation, otherwise.

Kohl was so lost in his thoughts that he nearly missed the low rumble outside.

He rose to his feet quickly, breath held.

Another rumble.

'Thunder...? Is it Jato?' Fogu shuffled forward, wings half-open and ready to fly.

Kohl raised a finger to his lips and took a step towards the cave entrance, carefully placing his feet so he made no noise, and peered out into the rain, listening intently.

It wasn't the rumble of distant thunder—Arillian or otherwise. This was the deep breathing of a massive creature. He'd tracked those noises for too long to misinterpret it.

Kohl turned his head slightly. 'It's a dragon.'

Fogu masked his intake of breath well, then slipped into his battle stance. He raised both hands, but refrained from summoning any lightning—the crackle could mask the dragon's attack.

Kohl turned his attention back outside, pleased that Fogu was an experienced fighter, and didn't need to be told exactly what to do in such a situation. He took another step forward, so close to the entrance that the rain splashed onto his face.

The rumble shifted into a deep snarl that made his blood run cold.

Kohl leapt from the cave, Fogu on his heels. The two Arillians spread their wings and wheeled away in opposite directions as flames consumed the cave mouth. The edge of his cloak sizzled as fire caught the edge, but was doused almost immediately by the pouring rain.

'*Archon*! We are not your enemy!' Kohl straightened out, but kept himself out of range of the dragon's breath. He hovered, waiting for understanding or at least acknowledgement. But the dragon simply swooped overhead, lashing its spiked tail towards him, and he had to dart out of the way.

Plainly the dragon wasn't in the mood to listen.

It moved too quickly for Kohl to get a good look at it, but by its size, it had to be an old dragon, its rusted bronze scales dull in the overcast sky.

'I'm not sure speaking to it is the best idea,' Fogu called from some distance to Kohl's right. 'Assault or flee, my lord?'

'We're not attacking it!' Kohl yelled back, keeping his eyes locked on the massive beast as it swerved to avoid colliding with the side of the mountain.

It was a dragon elder, for certain. It had to be close to sixty feet long, with a wingspan so vast it brought the mountain into shadow. Its scales were a mix of brown and bronze, with golden spines that rippled with every breath, and talons like spears.

Kohl had seen the senseless rage of young drakes on the hunt, driven by instinct and emotion. But an elder dragon had more intelligence than that. They could speak. Reason. They were above their baser instincts.

Besides, attacking the dragon—even in self-defense—would add fuel to a fire that already burned too hot. He *had* to quell the dragon's fury—it was the only way to guarantee all three of them would get out of the encounter uninjured. The dragon's life was just as sacred as their own.

'Foul storm-bringers!'

Kohl flinched as the dragon bellowed. The heat from its breath vaporised the rain and turned the surrounding air into hot steam.

'Blight on my mountain!' It contorted, massive wings beating waves of superheated air towards them. Thick smoke coiled around its flared nostrils, and when it spoke, it revealed fangs longer than Kohl's arm. An apex predator, its attention squarely on them. 'You have slain your last dragon, storm-bringers. My kin have fallen, their blood stains the ground. Runs deeper than any river. Any sea! Their deaths cannot be undone! You steal from us our sacred power, you flush out our young, slaughter them as soon as they are seen. Your treachery will be your undoing!'

It sucked in a breath, and on the exhale, spurted a column of fire.

Kohl pivoted away, avoiding the plume. He wanted to speak with the dragon, to show that he and Fogu weren't a threat. But it saw them as the enemy and had decided to attack first. 'Please, *Archon*! We have slain none of your kin!'

The dragon roared in response, sweeping overhead like a murderous shadow, its intense heat knocking them off balance. It swiped at them with outstretched talons. 'I'll *not* hear you speak!'

Its growl almost deafened Kohl, and he struggled to move in the hot turbulence of the dragon's passage.

'It's of no use! You can't reason with the beast!' Fogu called.

Kohl couldn't see his companion, the rain, steam, and smoke were too thick. But Fogu was right. This elder dragon had no intention of speaking with them. It wanted vengeance.

'I will burn you to ash. Crush your bodies until your bones shatter. I will leave your flesh to rot on this mountain, a feast for vultures!'

Again the dragon swooped overhead, and again, Kohl narrowly avoided being incinerated. Yet, he refused to fight back. If he did, he'd simply make true the dragon's argument. However, by abstaining, he was leaving himself and Fogu vulnerable to the dragon's relentless attacks.

'I forbid you from life. Your kind bring nothing but destruction!'

'Jato is the one who is killing dragons! Not us!' Fogu cried out.

Kohl flinched. He hadn't wanted the dragon's attention to turn on his daughter.

The General's words made the elder dragon pause in its attack. 'I know that name. The storm-bringer who travels in a pack like a wolf. Who seeks to undo our glorious Sevastos's sacrifice.'

Kohl took the reprieve to catch his breath. He flew higher and joined Fogu a short distance above the dragon—just out of range of its flames.

'It matters not. You will all perish. You have forgotten your place and purpose, and thus shall be wiped from this world.' With a snarl, the dragon launched itself higher, teeth snapping at the two Arillians.

'Peace, *Archon*! We are not attacking you! Let us by!' Kohl tried again, narrowly avoiding its burning mouth.

The dragon ignored him. It slashed with its forelimbs—one talon slicing into the edge of his cloak and tearing it practically in two. The wash of heat as the dragon careened past was nearly as hot as the fire itself—its scales like burning coals. Kohl summoned his own frost power to shield himself from the worst of the intense heat, before spiralling away just in time to avoid the dragon's next dive.

'My lord, we must flee!'

'If we flee, it'll just chase us down.'

'Split up, then! It cannot follow both of us!'

'I'm not putting you in danger!' Kohl spread his wings to slow his descent and regain control of his movement. He was too weak to get away, and he didn't want to run. He was sick of running. '*Archon*! I warn you, we are *not* your enemy! Stand down or you will suffer!'

The dragon replied with a roar that seemed to shake the very mountains.

'You're wasting your time, my lord!' Fogu snapped. 'Let me end this. You know I can do it quickly.'

Kohl shook his head, his gaze locked on the dragon. 'Absolutely not, Fogu. No more dragons will be killed!'

'Then what are we to do? Let it burn us alive? After

everything we've been through, I'd rather live, thank you.' Venom laced Fogu's words.

Kohl couldn't blame him. But he needed to do something quickly, else his inaction here would have the same consequences as it had in every other aspect of his life. People getting hurt. Or worse.

He took a deep breath. This wasn't going to be easy, but the dragon had refused to speak, and given him no alternative. 'Stay back, Fogu.'

The dragon beat its massive wings, swooping round with another bellow, and coming level with the two Arillians. It glared at them with eyes of molten gold. It let out a hiss of steam, readying itself to breathe fire again.

Lightning crackled from Kohl's palms as he prepared to meet it. His body cooled, numbed, as Frost-touch flowed over his skin, steeling himself from damage, and powering his body with the ancient magic of his ancestors. He drew more and more, his hands flickering with ice-blue light as he concentrated. He whispered, 'Forgive me, *Archon*.'

As the dragon's jaw opened, Kohl acted. He threw his hands forwards, blasting the dragon with a gale of freezing wind. Shards of ice formed on its scales, singing and immediately turning to steam.

Kohl threw out more and more power. It cancelled out the dragon's fire faster than the creature could breathe it, and larger chunks of ice appeared over the dragon—its forelimbs, flanks, wings. The dragon snarled, bit down on the ice, shattering several pieces, but Kohl was relentless, and did not give the creature the chance to destroy it.

In less than a minute, the dragon's entire front half was encased in ice.

It wobbled in the air, suddenly too heavy to remain aloft.

'Fogu. Help it to the ground,' Kohl said through

clenched teeth. He continued to attack the beast. Ice crept up every scale, slowly, but surely covering its body.

As it fell, Fogu swooped in, his own wind whipping up and slowing the dragon's descent. Bits of ice fell off, cracked or melted from the creature's internal heat or constant thrashing. But Kohl's Frost-touch was too much for the creature. With every attack, every attempt to burn away the ice, the dragon weakened.

By the time it reached solid ground, it had given up. The hateful glare it gave them was nothing short of murderous. 'You say you are not my enemy, storm-bringer, yet you imprison me. I know you are the Lord of the Arillians. My forefathers knew your Frost-touch. Knew how it could wipe all fire from Linaria and reduce the dragons to dust. I should sunder you where you stand.'

Kohl landed heavily, and sank to one knee. He didn't feel the snow, the Frost-touch was too powerful, but his whole body was numb. Fogu came over and rested a hand on his shoulder. He, too, breathed heavily from the ordeal.

The dragon let out a snarl of impatience.

'You gave me no choice, *Archon*. I'm not here to kill you. I want to help you,' Kohl replied, getting shakily to his feet.

'You are a *storm-bringer*. You cannot help me.'

Kohl allowed himself to catch his breath. It was the most amount of energy he could remember exerting in a long while, and every limb felt suddenly weak—as if he were newborn.

Fogu dropped his voice. 'What is your plan, my lord?'

Kohl patted his comrade and turned his attention squarely to the dragon once he had his breath back. He didn't want to appear any weaker than he was. 'I am *more* than any other Arillian. You know of my Frost-touch, you know I am a Lord of Arillians. Does that not merit a conversation, at least?'

'It merits your death.' The dragon attempted to move. Cracks appeared, running the length of the ice, but it did not break. It snarled again, but was too weak to do anything other than grumble. 'And why should it warrant conversation? Linarians stole our power. We burn Linarians in recompense. And it is past time the storm-bringers were brought to justice.'

'Aciel is gone,' Fogu said, interjecting. 'There's no need to burn Arillians.'

Laughter rattled around the dragon's chest. 'Aciel disrupted the power of Linaria. Murdered and stole from us. One Sevastos gave its life to correct the mistake, yet things are worse than before. Our powers taken and manipulated for war. Jato continues to slay us. There can be no forgiveness.'

Kohl thought carefully. Their powers manipulated for war? His reasoning for the dragons' fury had been correct all along. Had this dragon confirmed his suspicion? 'The *Valta Forinja*?'

'This is the name you use for those stolen weapons,' the dragon spat, 'you ripped away the power of a Sevastos and used it beyond the agreed price. This is *not* how we bargain. I swear that you will *all* burn for your transgressions.'

4

Isa stayed with her own followers while the sky pirates argued amongst themselves about what was to be done with the accusations. Reg claimed Traego owed his captain for the damages caused by Kohl because the Arillian had come to Estoria with Traego and Amarah in the first place.

Amarah had taken Reg's accusations with little more than a snort, but even Isa could tell that she was on edge. Arillians didn't have the greatest reputation—understandably so. She knew there was a bounty on them but hadn't realised so many had fled to Estoria. She'd just assumed they'd go back to their own lands, lick their wounds, and keep away from the rest of Linaria for the next few generations.

Jato was an outlier. A powerful one, yes, but not unbeatable. The fact they had all fled once Aciel was entombed made that perfectly clear.

If Kohl had been in Estoria—which was more than likely given he'd been travelling with Amarah—she wondered if he truly *had* been responsible for the devastation that Reg claimed. After delivering his message—along with several choice words to insult Amarah, Traego, and his crew—he'd headed back to Estoria to let Ipot know his message had been delivered, and the warning had been given if Traego didn't cover the costs.

Isa remembered Kohl as an unwilling fighter. Someone who participated in events because he couldn't flee from them. She didn't remember him to have much of a temper—nothing like Palom—nor could she imagine him attacking innocents.

'Kohl betrayed us. Killed Anahrik. Eryn,' Palom said, as if reading her thoughts. He had his arms folded tight to his chest as he watched Amarah, Traego, and the other pirates aboard *Otella*. The massive warship still required additional repairs, but Traego seemed keen to get back in the air as quickly as possible. He was arguing the point with Antar so loudly their words carried down to the beach.

Palom said, 'I would not put anything past Kohl. He is desperate. Without leadership. Without daughter. Many people do terrible things when desperate.' His voice shifted into a low growl at the end of his sentence, and Isa wondered if he was referring to himself. Some terrible act *he'd* committed through desperation.

Kylos approached cautiously from behind. 'Princess Isa?'

She turned. 'What's the matter, Kylos?'

'We want teh know yeh plan. How we can help. We're tending the sick and injured for now, but everyone's worried Sapora and the Varkain will be on our trail before we know it. There's a lotta restless Ittallan here.'

Isa shared their concerns. 'We're heading east, all the way to Estoria.'

'So, more than just enlisting pirates, we're going teh sleep in their bed?'

Isa sighed. 'Our resources are low. Sapora has no claim to Estoria. We'll lie low there until everyone is fighting fit. I plan to enlist more pirates, get ourselves a fleet which will enable us to travel unhindered.'

'You are not going to attack Taban Yul?' Palom asked.

'Not straight away. Our numbers are too low. We'll need to bolster our followers and fighters. I won't lead us into a massacre.'

Isa could tell from Kylos's firm expression that she didn't think much of her plan. Kylos and her brother, Aetos, had followed Lathri—the healer was to be the leader of this entire operation. Isa was a figurehead, only rallying people when needed.

She hadn't expected to actually *lead* the resistance herself. And it showed.

Isa thought back to the palace escape. Amarah had fought beside her the whole way to the ship. Solvi, too, had fought. Judd and Antar may have only been in it for the gold, but they'd been with her.

Although they'd made an excellent team, she didn't want to rush back into that until they were ready.

'My father is a warrior king. I'm not proud of my Varkain heritage, but I cannot change it. I shall be a warrior queen, if I must. I know all eight Archigo of Val Sharis. That's more than can be said for any of the Varkain, or anyone on the present council—aside from perhaps Koraki. That'll be to our advantage. I'll work with Odi to get letters written to start persuading them. As for us? We'll leave just as soon as *Otella* is airborne again. Get everyone ready to move.'

Kylos bowed her head, then headed back into the throng of Ittallan, barking orders and putting out campfires.

'I am with you, Princess,' Palom said. *Leillu*, clutched to the huge Ittallan's shoulder, chirped in assent.

Isa smiled. 'Good. We'll need everyone in the battles to come.'

RaKhanna WAS A RATHER BEAUTIFUL AIRSHIP, Isa had to admit. With the cobalt sea glistening below and a warm sun on her back, Isa could forget the circumstances that led her here. Going against her brothers—her only family—and throwing her lot in with a bunch of thieves and despondent Ittallan. All on the word of one healer who said she'd make a better ruler than Sapora.

In her head, she believed it.

But her heart hated everything about the coup, the escape, and the ongoing rebellion.

Palom travelled alongside her on *RaKhanna*, with *Leillu*, Solvi, Odi, and several other Ittallan.

Kylos didn't trust the sky pirates now the job was over, and opted to fly with Traego and his crew on the warship, *Otella*, to keep an eye on them.

Isa had asked Chyro to fly on Amarah's other warship, piloted by Antar. That way, she had people she could trust on all three ships. She'd also noticed Antar and Traego trading verbal blows, and wanted a close eye kept on him in case he tried anything. As Solvi had reminded her—sky pirates couldn't be trusted.

Aetos flew himself, the black eagle keeping high above the airships, eyes on everything below.

Her heart thudded in her chest. This wasn't just conversations and arguments anymore. It was *real*. Whatever decisions she made now, would stick.

She kept on deck, peering over the side as Amarah flew them towards Estoria. She'd always loved people-watching, had spent hours every day doing it, hidden across the rooftops of Taban Yul, and had soon noticed a young lad who stuck to Palom's side like a shadow. Karvou, his name was. The son of a blacksmith from the distant town of Tum

Metsa in the Val Sharis north, where the Everwinter ruled. He was too young to have come into his *meraki* yet, but he watched Palom like a hawk, shadowing him often, and asking dozens of questions when Palom was in a mood to talk.

It didn't take long before Estoria's glorious coastline to come into view. Pristine white beaches almost glistening against the jewelled waves. A tropical paradise for anyone with enough money to travel to the islands. Despite the brisk wind on the deck of *RaKhanna*, the sun burned into Isa's skin, and it didn't take long for it to redden.

She was relying on Traego to keep them safe when they reached Estoria. To give them a place to stay while they worked out their next moves. While many of the Ittallan had expressed their concern, it made sense to Isa. Although she was putting herself deeper into the sky pirate's debt, she reasoned that he wasn't likely to carve them up while he could get more gold out of you later. Therefore an alliance with Traego made sense for the time being.

It was only temporary.

All of it was only temporary.

Just as soon as she was on the throne, everything would be all right again.

She ignored the fact that she skipped over the part where she'd have to confront Sapora, kick him away from his new life—one that was his by rights—and push him back into the tunnels of Sereth. She wouldn't kill him.

She wouldn't.

Thick black smoke rose slowly from the north-eastern side of the main island. Isa narrowed her eyes to get a better look. 'Palom, do you see that?'

'I smelled it from few leagues away. That pirate messenger was speaking truth.'

'This is going to make our new base somewhat more

dangerous,' Odi said. The old Ittallan made his way towards them from below deck, his thick robes dragging behind him. 'Princess Isa, we should turn around. Tum Metsa would be safe, and just as far away from the capital as Estoria if distance is what you wish for?'

Isa kept her gaze on the approaching islands. 'Tum Metsa is under my brother's rule. It's leagues away from anywhere, and tiny. Estoria is more central, with more resources. We won't stay there any longer than we need to. A few weeks at most.'

Odi said, 'I will of course obey your orders, but I really must insist. Hiding among pirates on the rampage isn't going to be as easy as you think. They will look at you and see nothing but gold.'

Isa scowled. He was the second person to accuse her of being too naive. 'We'll be fine. You managed to join a rebellion in the capital, right under Sapora's nose. I'm sure you can all handle a few weeks on a tropical beach.'

'Looks like a right mess,' Amarah said from the wheel.

Isa made her way up the deck and looked out again. Small fires dotted the clifftops, trees had been blasted apart, their bark split and peeling, and even the lush green foliage had been blackened. 'The sooner we speak to the other captains, the better.'

'You sure about that? Even after what me and Traeg said?'

'I have no choice, Amarah. If I don't have a fleet, I've just resigned myself and all these Ittallan to the life of a refugee. Taken them out of their homes, away from friends and family, and dumped them on an island in the middle of nowhere.'

'Don't say it like that. Estoria's quite nice, you know.'

Isa appreciated the woman's humour. But she knew she had to act quickly. The pirates would be fired up over the

Arillian attacks. Now might actually be the best time to get them signed up to her cause. Traego's words bothered her, though. What *did* she have to offer them as an incentive?

All she *could* offer was a promise. She wasn't sure it would be enough.

If she were Sapora, he'd threaten and intimidate them until he got what he wanted.

She resolved to be different.

Traego was well-respected, wasn't he? Would he vouch for her? It might be enough to sway the others, if he did.

Her faltering confidence disappeared the moment Amarah brought them in to land. A small crowd of pirates had gathered in a clearing below, most of whom held swords, spears, bows, and other weapons. Their chatter descended into aggressive jeering when they spotted the ships, though they were thankfully more interested in *Otella* than *RaKhanna* or Amarah's other warship.

The crowd set upon *Otella* the moment it landed. Above the shouting, people called for Traego or members of his crew. Isa struggled to keep her nerves from overwhelming her. Any of them could be one of Tacio's spies, looking to attack and kill her on the spot. Or worse, drag her back to the palace.

It took only a minute for Isa to realise they were more annoyed about the destruction caused by Arillians, and angrily demanding information on when Traego would be paying them their damages. Their outrage set the others on edge, and Palom kept closer to her side than ever.

Thankfully, the mob were so focussed on *Otella*, that Amarah was able to sneak everyone off her ship without being hassled. Isa and the others hurried after her as she led them through the jungle trees and away from the baying crowd.

'This lot love getting themselves riled up over nothing,'

Amarah said with a sly grin. She glanced over her shoulder to ensure they kept up, and no doubt to check they weren't being followed. 'If one person has a complaint, suddenly all of Estoria has, too. Egging each other on like a pack of crows. It's funny, really.'

'No honour here. I am not surprised,' Palom grunted.

Amarah rolled her eye. 'We'll head to Traeg's base. It's up here, just past Falice. He has a big lodge and there's half a field pretty much for your lot to set up camp.'

That name rang a bell. 'I'm sure I had a pair of boots made in Falice,' Isa said.

'Wouldn't surprise me. Great seamsters in that part of town.'

Isa halted underneath a palm tree, enjoying the shade from its broad leaves. Odi led two dozen Ittallan off *RaKhanna*, marshalling them through the trees and after Amarah's lead. They carried bundles of equipment, clothes, food, tools, and weapons. A miniature army on the march.

Pride swelled in her chest at the sight of so many determined faces ready to lend her their strength. To stand with her against her enemies, and help her triumph. Old and young, hunters and fodder both. Everyone had stood together for Lathri—and for her.

The majority had sweat-slicked hair, their clothes damp and clinging to their skin, but none complained. They took their cues from Odi and the others, most nodded to her as they passed, some even saluted—if they didn't have their arms full. Excited chatter broke out among the Ittallan, most of whom seemed happy enough to be on solid ground again. A few even laughed.

Isa inclined her head and watched as the procession moved quickly through the trees. She tried to peer over to *Otella*, to see if the rest of her followers were able to get away from the mob of pirates, but her view was masked by the trees and *RaKhanna's* hull.

Aetos circled above. She had to put her faith in him—he'd be able to lead the others and help them catch up.

Isa had lingered long enough. She wheeled around and hurried along the heavily-trodden path, making her way past the others until she had caught up with Amarah and Palom at the head of the line. Estoria's jungle foliage was thick and unforgiving. Grasping vines and thorns protruded from the sandy ground, and Isa carefully watched every step lest something sharp and piercing went straight through her foot.

The trees thinned, and sand gave way to paved streets as Amarah led them out of the jungle and into the Falice district. Tall wooden houses rose on either side of the main parade, many with heavily thatched roofs, and although there were already plenty of Estorians out and going about their daily business, few gave them more than a cursory glance.

Sudden boatloads of arrivals—many of whom were rich and eccentric—was obviously a common enough occurrence it didn't warrant much attention.

Isa's skin prickled, and it wasn't just the heat.

These weren't her fellow Ittallan here. They were complete strangers, with little knowledge of who she was. A mix of pirates and Goldstones, travellers from as far as Corhaven and Ranski. Holiday-goers, and those who had decided to move to Estoria to enjoy a better climate.

A completely different world.

'Keep moving, Princess Isa. The sooner we are off the streets, the better.'

Isa glanced up to see Solvi sat on the outstretched branch of a nearby tree, legs dangling over the side as if she was perfectly at home. Solvi said, 'I do not trust Traego's pirates, so we should stay close to Amarah.'

'Oi! You! Amarah!' another pirate shouted from halfway down the street.

Isa stared over the crowd of Ittallan in time to see Amarah wave her scythe at the man who had called to her, and continue on as if no-one had spoken.

'Looks like the welcome here isn't very warm,' Solvi muttered.

Isa fought to keep from frowning. Once everyone was safely at Traego's base, she could relax. They were vulnerable while they moved. 'Stay with the others, Solvi, in case we're attacked.'

The young woman leapt from the treetops and landed neatly several feet away. She darted ahead, slipping along the street and down another one to catch up with Amarah.

Isa followed, but in her peripheral vision, saw more and more pirates slinking onto the street behind them with weapons unsheathed. They appeared like rats, from alleyways and rooftops, as though drawn like moths to a flame.

They were after Amarah, that much was clear. But Isa still found their presence unnerving, like being trailed by carrion vultures.

She rounded a corner to find her followers at a dead stop, all talk silenced.

Isa wasn't particularly tall, so she bounced on her tiptoes to see over the heads of the crowd, and try to figure out the issue.

There, not twenty paces ahead of them, in front of a long, wooden cabin, three sky pirate captains and their crews blocked the path. They were focussed on Amarah, for the most part, who shouted obscenities at them, and threatened what would happen if they weren't out of her way in five seconds flat. But even the pirates, for all their bluster and drawn swords, were beginning to see they were outnumbered at least three to one by the Ittallan. Even with the pirates that had followed boosting their numbers, they were still outmatched.

'What's the hold up?' Isa asked, barging her way through the crowd and trying to assert some sort of authority. She couldn't have pirates ruining the entire situation before she'd even got off the ground.

'This ain't none of your concern,' one pirate glanced down at her, 'Goldie. Official clan business. Keep you and your Ittallan moving.'

Isa narrowed her eyes. 'Who are you?'

The pirate turned to face her. He was tall, heavily muscled, with broad shoulders, and looked as if he could probably wrestle even Palom to the ground. 'Like I said, Goldie, it ain't nothing to do with you.'

'I'll knock her flat, Basir,' the man beside him spoke. He was short and stocky, with a thick neck and tattoos snacking down both arms. He tapped the end of his cudgel into his palm and stepped closer to Isa.

She stayed put. Non-threatening, but unwilling to budge, or show fear in the face of their aggression. She'd come too far to fall at the first hurdle, especially in front of her followers. She needed to prove to them she could be as capable as Lathri had promised. 'Hmmm, captain, are you? I came to talk to you, as it happens. You and the other sky pirate captains. I've a proposition for you.'

Basir let out a hearty laugh. 'Goldstone business can wait. We got a debt to sort out here, and if Traego don't show up to pay, we're cutting it out of your one-eyed snake-in-the-grass friend.' He levelled his sword at Amarah, but she didn't flinch.

'I don't have the luxury of time, captain,' Isa said. She widened her stance slightly, trying to turn their attention away from Amarah and onto her. 'Traego will be along soon enough. As I said, I've come to talk to *all* the sky pirate captains of Estoria. And it's not some low-class jewel theft or a heist that'll give you a little bit of gold. What I plan to do is going to change the face of Linaria as we know it.'

The pirates let out a laugh. 'Goldie, you been in the sun too long! Get down to the beach and take a dip. That'll sort you right out.'

'Basir. You *might* wanna stop calling the Princess of Val Sharis, "Goldie",' Amarah said.

He stopped laughing so abruptly, he almost choked.

Isa pressed her advantage. 'As I said, Traego will be along shortly enough. You're gathered here, so you've saved me a job in tracking you down. Where can we talk? In *private*.'

Basir struggled to catch his breath and glanced at his comrades, obviously floored to discover he was speaking with royalty.

Chatter broke out among the pirates, many looking at one another, uncertain.

'Cap'n! We got Traeg an' 'is crew!'

More chatter from behind, and movement as the original mob of pirates caught up with the crowd. The new pirates shoved forward, parting through the Ittallan with little concern, pushing Traego ahead. His arms had been bound behind his back, along with everyone on his ship—including Kylos, who looked none-too-pleased about it. She snarled her fury at the burly crew members, but they held her firm.

'Basir, what's with all the rough treatment? What I ever do ta ya?' Traego asked, calm despite the fact he and his crew were surrounded. 'This ain't really necessary, is it?'

At once, Basir spun away from Isa and focused his attention on the new arrivals. 'Actually, Traeg, I reckon I'm being too soft after what *your* Arillian did to my ships and crew!'

'*My* Arillian?' Traego raised his shoulders as much as the rope allowed. 'I don't see no Arillian here. Do you?'

'It destroyed everything and flew off. *You* tell me where it is. And if you can't, then you're paying for everything I lost!' Spittle flew from his lips as he berated Traego.

Isa—and several others—took a step back to avoid being splattered. She needed to stop this before things escalated more than they had already.

Slipping a short blade out of her sleeve, she crouched, then leapt high—sailing over the gathered pirates to land exactly behind Traego. She slashed down in one, quick movement, severing the ropes that bound his hands. Before anyone could react, she gestured broadly to the Ittallan gathered. 'Captain Basir. I said I was going to change the face of Linaria. Do you really want to ignore me, and your chance at becoming the richest pirate in the world? I thought your hospitality was better than that. I've come a long way to speak with you.'

Many of the Ittallan laughed.

Amarah twirled her scythe.

Traego grinned and shook out his hands, now free from their bindings.. 'There we go! Much more civil! Why don't we have a drink o' that gold rum I keep in my lodge. We ain't animals are we, Basir? Uh, no offence, Princess.'

'All right, all right, you win, *your highness*. My boys can have a drink, and we can have a *talk*. Traeg—you best be bringing gold—rum *and* coin,' Basir said, rubbing his nose and smearing dirt across his face in the same movement.

Isa took a breath, savouring her first minor victory. She followed Basir and Traego as they led the unorthodox pack of pirates back to the main street through Falice.

This was it. Here, Isa was going to build her fleet.

5

Morgen woke with a scream. His chest rose and fell painfully, and he tried to slow his hyperventilation with mixed results. He balled his hands, realising he sat in sweat-soaked sheets that were rapidly cooling. They were only damp silk sheets. Not slick snake skin coiling around his body.

He wasn't under attack by the Varkain. Not yet.

Despite his certainty that he was safe in Topeko's house in the middle of Berel, he couldn't shake the feeling that somewhere, somehow, Sapora was drawing near.

Morgen had been sure to remove all mirrors from his room the moment he moved in, and had even "accidentally" broken or misplaced other mirrors from the scholar's residence. The idea that Sapora could be watching his every move from any mirror absolutely terrified him. He was sure that wasn't exactly how the Varkain blood magic worked, that Sapora needed a shard of the mirror first, but Morgen didn't want to take any chances.

Mistakes hurt. Cost lives. Why risk it?

He lay shivering for a long while after his breathing had calmed and his heart no longer felt as if it would burst from his chest. Dawn had yet to arrive, and although he enjoyed the peace before birdsong erupted, he couldn't relax.

Morgen wished he had a sword to hand. Somehow, holding a weapon made him feel less vulnerable. But every sword, every object that could be used as a weapon, had been taken from him. The walls of his room seemed more a prison than ever before. A hole he was trapped in. He worried he'd die in it.

He wet his lips as he sat up in bed, trying to force away memories of his vivid nightmare. Whenever he closed his eyes, he could see snakeskin glistening in the moonlight. Could feel fangs against his skin, piercing his flesh and leaking venom into his body.

Morgen shivered, then threw off his bedsheets. He needed a cold shower, and to throw himself back into his studies. At least they required so much focus and dedication that he had no capacity to think about anything else.

And there was another problem; Arch-Kalos Dhabra. If ever there was a man who came close to terrifying him as much as Sapora, it was the Arch-Kalos. Topeko couldn't be sure when he'd be back, so Morgen had spent days walking on eggshells, waiting for judgement to appear without warning.

The faintest whisper of a flute drifted through the air. It brought with it a cool freshness that chased away the remnants of sleep from Morgen's limbs. Even after so long living among the Samolen, Morgen found the magic of the Kaloset incredible. It was amazing to think that no matter how hard the labour of the day before, their magic would rejuvenate you completely. It meant that sickness never lasted long, nor did fatigue, rage, or hatred. At first, he hadn't been keen on the idea of being kept docile, like some obedient puppy. Then, he'd realised it took the edge off the most aggressive emotions. He could seethe in quiet, passive fury for the rest of his life, if he wanted. But he was far less likely to end up in a brawl over a disagreement or perceived slight.

If anything, he could name more than a few towns in Corhaven that could do with that kind of calming influence.

He only wished it could chase away his nightmares as easily as the aches of manual work.

And his lingering fears.

With a final shiver, he forced himself to his feet and hurried to get ready. Cold water on the face chased away much of his worries, and set him up for his upcoming day. A morning habit, one that Morgen put much stock in, and by the time he'd dressed in light-weight cotton robes, he'd completely forgotten about Varkain stalking him.

Topeko had left out a spiced lentil wrap and a mug of cold tea for him. Morgen swallowed over half the wrap in a single bite, downed the tea, and raced out the door while chewing the rest of his breakfast. For all the Samolen magic, cities weren't rebuilt in a day.

Although up before dawn, Morgen was far from the first to arrive in Berel Old Town. Thankfully, the pathways bridging the old and new towns hadn't been badly damaged by the dragon attack—most of the Kalos's magical shields had protected them—but there were significant chunks of the university that had been scorched or broken apart by the beasts' massive claws.

As the university was the most important place in Berel, their rebuilding efforts had been focussed on clearing debris, reinforcing the archways, and restoring the university to its former glory. Kalosai and visitors still attended the university every day, therefore getting it back to normal as quickly as possible was of the utmost importance.

He'd lost count of how many times he'd crossed the main bridge to the Old Town. And yet every time he crossed the lake, a shiver crept up his spine and gooseflesh pimpled his arms. Rhea's breath. The source of all Samolen magic, inherited from the dragons themselves. Topeko's words filled his mind. The scholar's teachings and his books on theory had been all-consuming while he'd been in Berel.

Ahead, the cheek jewels of Samolen already up and working glowed in the pre-dawn gloom.

Blue. Green. Yellow. Red.

He quickened his pace. After his public admonishment, Morgen knew he needed to prove himself to the other Samolen. Already he was an outsider—from Corhaven, without a drop of magical blood in his veins. Yet, Topeko vouched for him. So had Andel, though the student's opinion carried less weight.

Morgen desperately tried not to throw it away, not now he had a second chance.

And not now Arch-Kalos Dhabra's seemingly all-seeing-eyes were turned towards him.

He shivered again when he passed through the two pillars beside the courtyard entrance to the university, stone dragons carved into them, wings half-folded, tails twisting down to the ground. Other robed Samolen moved around in pairs or threes, already set to the day's work.

'Kalosai Morgen, good morning.' One of the Kalos stood to greet him. A tall man in purple robes, the Kalos was one Morgen had seen several times. He had skill in managing teams of Samolen to get the best out of them when it came to the rebuilding effort. Thankfully, he wasn't one of the many Kalos who seemed to despise Morgen.

'Good morning Kalos.' Morgen lowered his head in a short but respectful bow.

The Kalos pointed to the edge of the circular courtyard, where a large pile of wooden crates and hemp sacks lay heavy against a large fountain. 'You're to assist Kalosai Mahlu by transporting these supplies into the university. More will be arriving through the day, so the quicker you get them moving, the sooner you can rest.'

Morgen masked his grimace. 'What supplies?'

'Oh, nothing special. Food, clothing and the like.'

Heavy supplies, then. One sack of potatoes might not be particularly heavy, but fifty of them carried back and forth over the hard, sandy earth and the cold flagstone university floor would quickly become back-breaking work. He hoped Kalosai Mahlu, whoever that was, wasn't too slow. He wasn't a stranger to this sort of menial task, and knew many people would try to shirk their duties given half a chance.

While the Samolen seemed to have a better work ethic than the general recruits in the Imperial Guard, Morgen knew this sort of work wasn't fun for anyone.

'Have you seen Kalos Topeko?' Morgen asked, already rolling up his sleeves.

'I haven't, but I know he's teaching today.'

Morgen walked away. He missed Andel and hoped the Kalosai was getting on okay, wherever he was. He hadn't realised how lonely he was without the younger Kalosai's positivity and light humour. As much as he loved his own company, Topeko's home felt empty without the Kalosai.

To his left, the five enormous Sevastos stones loomed like silent, ever-watchful guardians. A circle of them commanded the courtyard's centre, showcasing the knowledge and power of the university, and by extension, Berel. Almost eight feet tall, they dwarfed anyone who stood by them, and Morgen glanced at the nearest one. He didn't know which stone Palom had taken a shard from to build his *Valta Forinja*, and it amazed him that something so powerful could come from such a tiny piece.

He wondered what the Sevastoses who'd given their stones to the Samolen would think of him after *he'd* attacked a dragon. Would they, too, despise him?

Probably.

Morgen rubbed his eyes and approached the pile of supplies. The names of various Kalosai had been scrawled in black ink on the top of the crate, and he took several seconds to decipher the wiry handwriting. Reading had never been his strong suit, but he'd improved massively since studying under Topeko. Yet he struggled to work out where he was supposed to take it.

'It's going to the Kalosai chambers!' A high-pitched voice called cheerily from across the courtyard.

'Kalosai chambers?' Morgen looked towards the sound of the voice and saw a tall, blonde woman in deep red robes that were well scuffed at the hem and sleeves. She didn't have a cheek jewel.

'Yes. Where the Kalosai sleep?' she said, as if it were the most obvious thing in the world.

Morgen swallowed. He hadn't realised he and Andel were special by staying in Topeko's home. Of course there were more Kalosai than could stay with all their individual Kalos. It made sense there would be quarters set aside for the students of the university. It had simply never crossed his mind.

She made her way over to him and peered down at the scrawl as if to double-check. 'Yep, same as the ones I moved earlier. Ready?'

'Um, sure.' He hadn't expected someone to take the lead with such gusto, certainly not so early in the morning. 'I'm Morgen. I mean, Kalosai Morgen.'

'Pleased to meet you! I'm Mahlu.' She grinned at him, her light blue eyes twinkling in the dawn light, then grabbed one side of the crate with both hands.

He mirrored her action, and the pair of them heaved the massive box off the ground. 'This loaded with steel boots? Dragons above, it's heavy!'

Mahlu laughed. 'I haven't actually checked inside. Could well be!'

The two of them shimmied across to the open side door of the university building, and Morgen was suddenly pleased that the heat of the desert sun wasn't fully upon them yet. He followed Mahlu's lead and they made their way down the corridors of the lower university, through wide entranceways and into a vast room warmed by a large fire. A plush red and gold carpet ran across the length of the room, though it was fraying at the edges from years of wear. Cushioned sofas and wooden armchairs littered the room, along with several wide desks, rows of bookshelves, and stacks of papers. There was a chill in the room that the fire attempted to remove, which was strange considering the university was in the middle of a desert.

A handful of Kalosai lounged around, many half-asleep, thumbing through books and papers, their blue cheek jewels glowing faintly in the firelight. One or two glanced up at their arrival, but most paid them no mind.

Being ignored was better than being glared at.

'Where is it going?' Morgen looked around for the other crates Mahlu said she had moved earlier.

Mahlu gestured with her chin to a space in front of the largest sofa. 'We'll start stacking them over there. The others must've already been taken through.'

Together, they dropped the crate by the sofa, earning them an annoyed grunt from the Kalosai sat reading, and straightened up. Morgen dusted his hands, irritated that dirt had smeared across his palm from whatever grime the crate had picked up while travelling. No doubt it had been imported from somewhere in Corhaven.

He wiped his hands on his robes and wondered where Mahlu was from. From her accent and humour, he guessed she was from Corhaven too, but beyond that, he couldn't tell. He'd never been good at figuring out where people came from. It was part of the reason he'd joined the Imperial Guard—he could be told what to do and when, and he didn't need to give it much more thought than that.

She kept their pace up, almost jogging back and forth between the Kalosai quarters and the courtyard, and hauling the heavy crates with more gusto than anyone had any right to so early in the morning.

They dropped the fifth crate down, sending dust floating up. Morgen wiped his forehead. A whole day of this to look forward to. Great.

'Cheer up, Morgen!' Mahlu said, affectionately punching his arm. 'No need to be so glum!'

'I didn't leave the Imperial Guard to do more manual labour here,' he replied before he could think. 'Um, that is... I want to get back to training. Magic training, I mean.'

'I know what you mean,' Mahlu said. She headed back out into the corridor, Morgen following. 'You're not really what I expected.'

Morgen frowned. 'Expected?'

'Kalos Ettas told me you'd be helping out today. And, well, after everything...I was expecting something else...'

She turned away suddenly, and Morgen noticed a thin scar on her left cheek, just under her eye. Was it from a cheek jewel? Or the removal of one? 'Yeah, I noticed everyone seems to think they know me just because of what they've been told.' He couldn't keep the bitterness from his voice. 'Anyway, I haven't done anything wrong. Least, not until the Arch-Kalos passes judgement.'

Mahlu stopped mid-step and sucked in a sharp breath.

'Mahlu?' Morgen looked back at her.

She faced away from him, then pulled out a sheet of parchment from her pocket and made a show of smoothing it down. She cleared her throat. 'There's eighteen more crates, and fifty-four sacks. We need to get a move on.' Her cheery demeanour had vanished.

Morgen watched as she all but marched past, wondering what had caused her sudden change. He tried not to think about it for too long, and followed her out to continue with their task.

He didn't press the matter, but on the next crate, she couldn't stay silent anymore.

'Sometimes I wonder if this is my eternal punishment,' Mahlu muttered.

'Punishment? What for?'

She headed back across the room and Morgen followed. 'Oh, you know. Just the usual. The wrong blood.'

Morgen was confused. He frowned, but she was heading off at such a pace that he had to jog to keep up. But her behaviour made him wonder. 'You mean the Arch-Kalos?'

Mahlu didn't reply. They entered the courtyard and made their way to the next crate. She grabbed her side again, and Morgen mirrored the action.

Once they'd managed to heave it into the building, she glanced up, eyes darting left and right as if expecting someone to leap out at them. 'You've met him?'

Morgen didn't think he'd ever forget, even if Topeko wiped his mind again. But her fearful gaze had replaced her cheeriness so completely that Morgen was almost afraid. 'What did he do to you?' He wanted to know what she'd been through, firstly. Secondly, he wanted to know what manner of judgement awaited *him* when Arch-Kalos Dhabra returned.

They both remained in place, and gently lowered the crate to the cool flagstone floor. She said, 'I only came to Berel three days ago. I've been studying in Tarika, to the south.'

Morgen had almost forgotten there were other universities in Ranski. Berel was simply the largest and most famous. He pondered how it might be different, and whether moving there might be safer—considering the Arch-Kalos was due to return to Berel any day now.

Mahlu shook her head. 'I don't...I shouldn't...'

'What is it, Mahlu? What happened?' Dragons above, he wished he had his *Valta Forinja* when Dhabra had turned up. Actually, it had been locked up somewhere in the university, hadn't it? Perhaps he could have a quick scout while he was here...

Mahlu took a breath then lifted her side of the crate again. 'It's nothing. Come on. We have a lot of work to get through.'

Morgen didn't like her dismissing what she'd been through, but said nothing. He'd have to ask another time, perhaps after she'd known him for more than five minutes. If there was anything he could do to help—even if it was simply sharing in the misery—then he would.

He sighed. She reminded him of Eryn—unafraid to speak her mind and cheery with the right people. But he'd not been able to save Eryn. Perhaps he could redeem himself by helping Mahlu.

~

MORGEN WAS QUITE certain his back had broken at some point during the day, yet Ettas and the other Kalos had expected him to continue moving sacks and crates through the scorching heat without rest.

It had been quite some time since his work had been this physical, and by evening, his hands were covered in blisters and his sleeves had been torn to shreds. While his Samolen robes covered his arms and shoulders from the worst of the sun's heat, his hands had been rubbed raw by the heavy rope and linens of the loads he carried.

'Alright Kalosai Morgen, that'll do for today,' Ettas said at length.

Before the words were out of his mouth, Morgen collapsed against the wall surrounding the courtyard, and rolled his head back. Sweat poured from his brow and trickled down the side of his face and neck, and he was so exhausted that he didn't notice Mahlu approach with a pitcher of water.

'Here, you look desperate!' she said, offering him the pitcher.

Morgen grunted his appreciation—too tired to speak—and drank the cold water in enormous gulps. He struggled for breath between swallowing, and poured what was left over his head and the back of his neck.

The water ran brown with sweat and grime, but he didn't care. He'd tried to count the hours, but soon lost track as everything blurred into one. Mahlu had regained her cheerfulness quickly enough after their mention of the Arch-Kalos, but they'd been too busy to have much time to chat.

Morgen hoped never to rebuild a town again, after seeing the devastation of Niversai, but here, he was an integral part of restoring Berel. He felt guilty for what had happened, and needed to restore the Kalos's confidence in himself.

Truthfully, Morgen couldn't care less about the damaged buildings. He was simply sick of more massacres caused by dragons, and wondered whether there was actually anywhere in Linaria he could go to in order to escape it all.

It was part of the reason he'd returned to Berel in the first place—to get away from the war spreading across Linaria, instigated by Sapora and the Arillians in equal measure. Ranski was a country of peace, a neutral zone where fighting was banned by law. It had seemed the perfect place to hide away and learn, and yet Berel, capital of Ranski, had succumbed to the dragon's maddening rage.

Topeko had been shocked at the attack, but not surprised. The older man had muttered to himself about balance of power, about prophecies, and how they were all doomed. Morgen was done with it all.

Mahlu sat down beside him and sighed heavily.

He offered her the rest of his water, which she gratefully drank. After a long swig, she said, 'Sometimes I feel like Linaria's gone mad.'

'Tell me about it.'

'Look at us,' Mahlu said, staring at the empty pitcher. 'We're both a long way from home, caught up in something we never thought we'd be part of.'

'How'd you know I'm far from home?'

Mahlu smiled at him. 'You're from Karoun, right? Or Kebbe? You've got the accent.'

He couldn't argue against that. 'What about you?'

'Iryl. I miss the sea.'

Morgen had never been there, but he knew it was a very pretty town. With the Itila Mountains as a backdrop, Iryl sat on the banks of the Seli River, the Sea of Nami surrounding the land to the east and south. Rich green grass, and no dragons, it was a beautiful town coveted by many Goldstones.

Far above his station.

'If *Ra* is life,' Morgen said, producing a flame from his

fingertips, 'and *He* is death,' he balled his hand into a fist and the fire flickered out, 'then...surely then, the dragons are the root of it all. Life. Death. *Ra*. *He*. All of it. It's them.'

Mahlu ignored his voiced thoughts on dragons.

Morgen licked his chapped lips. 'I thought this place was sacred. Why were we attacked?'

Mahlu shrugged. 'Berel is sacred to the Samolen. Maybe not to the dragons. There's nothing really here for them to hunt, and they don't bother us. But with Linaria as it is... Maybe they just saw Berel and decided we'd get burned next.'

'Doesn't seem fair,' Morgen said, aware he was slipping into a sulk.

'Dragons are the dominant predators. That's why they're revered as gods, all magic aside. If they want something, they take it. Not a lot you can do about that.'

'I suppose.' Morgen thought about his *Valta Forinja*. It had to be in the university, locked away somewhere. He understood the Samolen relationship with their magic, but he'd rather be permitted to defend himself than be able to move flames across a room. 'We've got these giant Sevastos stones. Can't we do something with them? Use their power?' He stared up at them. Unmoving sentinels.

'You mean like Aciel did?' Mahlu asked.

Morgen scratched his chin—it itched terribly where he'd shaved off his beard. 'Not to that extent. Just enough to make them stop. Do we have to take cover and not fight back?'

'We *can't* fight back. We can control the damage and protect ourselves, but that's it. Killing dragons will only make it worse. If Aciel hadn't done that in the first place, we wouldn't have this problem now. HisArillians did more damage than the dragons ever have.'

'And the Sevastos. If Sapora didn't have one, we probably

wouldn't have this problem now, either.'

'Probably not. I don't think a Sevastos would serve us like a dog or horse,' Mahlu said, staring at the empty pitcher. 'I don't think there's any record of it ever happening. How Sapora's managed it is anyone's guess. I don't think he realises what that's doing to the rest of Linaria, though. Not while he's tucked up safe and sound in that golden palace.'

Morgen snorted and shook his head, wondering how many mirror gateways Sapora had access to throughout Linaria. 'Oh, he's smart enough to know. Don't think he cares, though.' He didn't know why he was speaking so candidly to her. He blamed it on being exhausted. The evening's music couldn't come soon enough.

Mahlu pursed her lips. 'He can't hold onto that dragon forever. Maybe he only has it for a certain amount of time?'

Morgen shrugged. His guess would be as good as anyone else's. 'I reckon if there were no dragons, we'd have no problems. That prophecy? Dragon-flame undone? That wouldn't matter any more if there *were* no dragons to burn us all.'

Mahlu looked at Morgen for a long moment. She held his gaze until Morgen became uncomfortable and turned away. 'You've worked so hard, Morgen. You're more than what everyone here claims you to be. Maybe tomorrow you should take a rest day? Cleanse yourself of these dark thoughts. I'll ask Kalos Ettas for you, shall I?'

Morgen held in his huff of indignation. Evidently, Mahlu thought he was a savage for spending a couple of years in the Imperial Guard. Before Aciel's war, he'd never so much as stabbed anyone, much less killed them. The Arillians he had attacked weren't necessarily dead, either. In the chaos of battle, he had no idea of knowing who he'd injured and who he'd killed.

Various Samolen looked at him strangely from time to time, almost as if they pitied him, so Morgen had thrown himself into his lectures and their work with as much enthusiasm as he could manage in the hopes he'd learn a new way out of his situation.

Perhaps even to bring Moroda back.

Perhaps.

Before, he'd been convinced coming to Berel had been the right move.

Now, after the dragon attack and their constant peace talk, Morgen wasn't so sure.

He'd avoided Sapora, at least. That had been part of the main reason why he'd fled to Ranski—he was away from the Varkain King and could not be held accountable for anything he had, or hadn't done. Not to mention there was less chance of his name being mentioned as associated with the Imperial attack on Taban Yul.

Morgen was under no illusions—Sapora would likely execute him the moment he realised he'd been betrayed. And he had no interest in remaining anywhere the snake could get him for that to happen.

Even Topeko hadn't known—he'd left Niversai about a week before he'd received Princess Isa's letter begging help. Where was she now, he wondered. Was she safe in the palace, living inside the viper's pit? Had she also fled, like him?

Isa had been a formidable force of cunning and strength. Yet even she had buckled under the Varkain's oppressive rule.

He daren't risk sending another letter to the palace. He didn't know any kind of code to put in the message were it to be intercepted by one of the Varkain there, or worse, Sapora himself. He had to wait in silence and hope she was okay.

He knew he didn't owe her anything, and in fact by helping Isa, he'd put his own life at risk. He wondered if she even realised that.

'Kalosai Morgen?' Ettas barked his name.

Morgen struggled to his feet, his knees as weak as a fawn's. 'Yes, sir?' He took a moment to rub his eyes, and only then realised that there was someone else beside Ettas. 'Kalos Topeko!'

'A job well done, Kalosai,' Topeko said with a wide smile.

Just seeing Topeko's grin warmed Morgen and lessened his body's aches. 'Thank you! Kalosai Mahlu helped me a lot.'

Topeko tilted his head slightly, eyes darting over to where she remained against the wall. Mahlu waved happily, then turned her attention back to the pitcher, fiddling with the cork.

Kalos Topeko said, 'I thought you might want to know that one of my Kalosai is finishing his training tonight. If you aren't too tired, you might wish to accompany us to the ceremony? You'd be more than welcome.'

Mahlu looked up sharply, her eyes wide. She opened her mouth to say something, but Morgen didn't understand. He turned back to Topeko. 'Ceremony, sir...?'

'They will no longer be a Kalosai. It is the ceremony where they will ask Rhea to turn her breath into a jewel of their very own as they take the first steps into their speciality.'

It was the first step to becoming part of Samolen society again. The ritual was one he'd been deeply curious about, but had never been allowed to witness. Mahlu subtly shook her head, but Morgen didn't understand her reluctance. Yes, he was tired, but he was sure he'd be able to stay awake to watch something so ingrained in Samolen culture. It would be a leap towards true forgiveness for his transgressions.

'Thank you for the honoured invitation, Kalos Topeko. I'd love to come.'

6

Darkness permeated the former wine cellar. The sconces Sapora had lit had long since burned out, leaving only the faintest whiff of smoke in the vast stone basement under his suite of rooms. Mirrors lined every wall, his eyes and ears into distant parts of Linaria, both above and underground.

Cold seeped into him like poison, but he remained fixed in his position, unwilling to move. Perhaps it was just as well. He was unwilling to budge on most matters, and despite his discomfort, he remained exactly where he was, and would, until he'd spoken with Vasil.

He didn't know *why* he was reporting to his father. It wasn't like he was still on errantry, nor living with him. He was a King, and Vasil no more than a distant advisor, who'd spent the minimum amount of time in Val Sharis for Summercourt before scuttling back to the tunnels of Sereth.

And yet there was something about Vasil's authority that Sapora couldn't shake. Some desperate, child-like need to impress him, to have Vasil agree that he'd done well. That he was proud.

Sapora snorted. *Proud*? Since when did *he* crave that sort of acceptance?

He was a Varkain. Royalty. He did as he wished, regardless of what others thought.

Linarians despised and feared him by default. Well. He'd give them something to despise and fear.

He sat in the dark, his breathing and heart slowed, waiting to speak with Vasil.

Somewhere above him, just outside his chambers, Roke stood guard. Sapora wasn't sure exactly when, or how, but Roke had moved from being a simple member of his guard to being the King's personal bodyguard. Roke followed only his orders, not those of any Cerastes. Not even Tacio's commands.

Roke was a grizzled old Varkain, of too low a caste to ever be inducted into the Cerastes, yet Sapora had seen the man's potential and brought him along to Taban Yul. As far as Sapora was concerned, blood was of little consequence. He was far more interested in what someone could do, their own strengths, than some arbitrary measure of worth as dictated by a Valendrin.

He, himself looked no different to Tacio, and yet he'd been competing with his half-brother all his life.

Sapora had assumed when he wore the Jade Crown, things would have become more equal, if not skewed in his own favour. But a lifetime of being looked down upon was never going to disappear overnight. Perhaps that was why he went to greater and greater lengths to prove himself to his doubters. Took more risks. Pushed more boundaries.

If he could just *prove* that he wasn't the failure everyone believed him to be...

'Ah, Sapora, is that you waiting?' Vasil's low voice slithered from the mirror.

Sapora exhaled, awakening from his stasis. 'Vasil. I trust your travel went well?'

'After the business of Summercourt, I am happy to be back in Sereth,' Vasil replied. 'How is the Valendrin?'

Sapora nodded, curt. He wasn't sure how to break the news of Veynothi's return to his father. He didn't want to brag and boast, as Tacio would. Nor did he wish to downplay the gravitas of what he had achieved. It was a delicate balance.

He ran his tongue over a fang as he considered. 'The Valendrin has proved himself to be of great use. Thanks to his input, I have achieved something long since deemed impossible.'

Vasil raised an eyebrow, but his pale face showed little emotion.

Sapora's heart thumped, but his father gave him nothing else. 'I am pleased to announce the Ark Veynothi has been restored. She is—' he cut himself off. Vasil didn't know about Isa yet, and he wanted to keep it that way. It was no secret that Vasil cared least of all for his daughter, and he didn't want to give him any more reason to dislike her. 'Veynothi is carrying out my orders. I am working on the seals for the other three as we speak.'

Sapora stared at Vasil, waiting for any hint of reaction.

His father bowed his head. 'That is most incredible, Sapora. But, may I ask, is it wise? After what they did...Why have you gone to such lengths to restore one? I hadn't thought it possible. Does the Sevastos trouble you?'

There it was. Always a critique, regardless of what he did. At least it had come alongside one of Vasil's rare compliments. Sapora chose his words carefully. 'I am aware you are safe in your tunnels, but I am responsible for Val Sharis. I'll not have Arillians ruining my country, nor threatening my people.'

'Your people are here, in Sereth,' Vasil countered. 'The Ittallan do a decent enough job of ruling themselves. You only need to visit to ensure their tributes are being paid on time. And if you were in trouble, why ask for a Valendrin? A blood mage won't be of much use. Why not one of the Old Guard?'

Sapora let out a low hiss. So much for praise. 'I am *not* in trouble. I am bringing the Arks back to ensure none of us are ever in trouble again.' He knew he was raising his voice but struggled to keep hold of himself. Only his father, Tacio, and Isa ever seemed able to get him to raise his voice.

He hated himself for it.

'My King?' Roke's uncertain voice drifted down from the top of the stairs. 'I apologise for disturbing you, but the report you requested is here. You said to let you know the instant it did.'

Sapora tried to mask his conflicting emotions. If Vasil hadn't been so late, this clash of priorities wouldn't have happened. Then again, Roke's news was a welcome distraction from his father's condescending gaze. 'Thank you, Roke. Wait for me in the antechamber.'

Roke's footsteps died away as he retreated from the stairwell.

'More trouble?' Vasil asked.

Sapora exhaled slowly. If he knew Vasil's game, then he wouldn't let it get to him. 'Not at all, father. Just business to attend to. We'll speak later.' He didn't give Vasil the satisfaction of a proper farewell and turned the mirror to face the stone wall.

After all his accomplishments, it wasn't enough. At this rate, Sapora didn't know if anything he did would *ever* be enough.

He closed his eyes for a moment, trying to re-centre himself. Veynothi was out and on the hunt. He should have been the epitome of relaxation. Instead, he skulked about as if waiting for something to jump out and attack him at any minute.

This was the exact opposite of what he'd hoped for.

He tried to push the negative thoughts out of his mind as he ascended the stairway. At least he could still depend on Roke. All he needed were two dozen more like him, and he'd have things under control.

Slipping out of the doorway hidden behind the tapestry of himself, Sapora tried to regain his composure. Vasil always had the ability to put him on the back foot. He'd be off-kilter for days.

His antechamber was warm after being in the old wine cellar, and he relished it.

Roke stood at attention by the door to his chambers, spear resting against the wall, but within easy reach if needed. He didn't presume to approach the king, nor address him. Roke knew Sapora would speak to him when he was good and ready.

'Come in,' Sapora said, unlocking the door to his personal chambers. The fireplace lay empty, plush chairs gathered before it but rarely used. Beside the fireplace, there was a shelf of wine and rum in bottles of various sizes. Those hadn't been used either. In fact, most sported a thick layer of dust. Sapora ignored it all and made his way over to the window. It looked down on the Lower Quarter of Taban Yul—which had yet to be repaired after the attack on the palace, although various workers had been assigned to the district, getting materials and resources through Jato's storm had proved difficult, and work was slow going.

The shadow of the Sevastos moved over the city like a thundercloud.

That, if nothing else, gave Sapora peace of mind.

Seeing the Sevastos reminded him of the report and its importance. 'Go ahead, Roke. I'm listening.'

The Varkain moved his spear across the door lest anyone tried to barge in. Raising his chin, Roke brandished a thick bundle of rather sodden papers, 'King Sapora. These are the reports from the Imperial Guard in Povmar.'

'It took a while.'

'I'm sorry, my liege. I had to put quite a bit of force on them. Seems their captain abandoned his post and hasn't been seen for weeks. They're behind on their reporting.'

Sapora took the papers from Roke and glanced over them. A few airships had passed through, mostly carrying hardened merchants and necessary supplies. *The Bellflower. Zartanius. Otella.*

He frowned. *Otella*. Why was *Otella* familiar? 'Who was the captain posted there?' Sapora asked, unable to discern the information quickly enough. 'Any chance they were taken by a griffin?'

'A newly promoted one, far as I can tell,' Roke said. 'Comes from the town of Kebbe, somewhere in the north of Corhaven, but was shipped over from Niversai. Morgen's the name.'

Sapora had spent years masking his emotions from others, lest they saw any sign of weakness and attacked him. Even though he trusted Roke implicitly, his instinct to hide his true reaction was stronger than any bond he shared with the other Varkain.

Morgen. It appeared he had fled the capital and taken up a patrol in Povmar. What would cause him to travel to the middle of nowhere so suddenly? Especially when he'd had work to do for him! Morgen couldn't possibly know about Veynothi, could he? Perhaps he did. Perhaps that was why he abandoned his post. 'Any idea where Captain Morgen might've gone?'

'No, sir. Trail's cold. No tickets in his name by ship or sea, and there aren't many ways out of Povmar as I understand.'

Sapora narrowed his eyes. People vanished all the time. That was the way of the world. Especially considering the griffins in that part of Corhaven. But for a Captain of the Imperial Guard to disappear? Especially when Sapora was so interested in him...

It seemed rather convenient. Which made it suspicious.

'Do you want me to send some Varkain to Povmar, my liege?'

'I need everyone here. It's too dangerous to fly with Jato and her Arillians around, anyway.' Sapora glared out the window at the distant lightning. She was becoming more of a nuisance every day. Hopefully Veynothi would be back with Isa before too long, but he knew he couldn't rely on the Ark fixing all his problems.

He needed Malashash. And the other two.

Why was he always clutching at ever-shortening straws?

'Of course, my liege, but if this is important, time may be of the essence. Povmar is remote, is it not? It shouldn't be too difficult to question people and figure out the direction of travel. I'd be happy to go myself—'

'I'd rather you were here. But, I need the job done properly. I leave the hunt to you.' Sapora folded his arms. He needed to increase pressure in many different ways. If Isa was in the palace, it would be the perfect mission for her. She excelled at tracking, eavesdropping, and figuring out people's motives. Plus, it would get her out of the palace and away from Tacio for a while—something they'd all benefit from.

But he couldn't.

He only had himself to rely on.

'I'll see that it's done at once,' Roke said. He grabbed his spear, then paused and half-turned back to Sapora. 'If...If I may, my liege. The Valendrin has been rather insistent on speaking with you since we returned to the palace. Shall I have him moved elsewhere? Away from your chambers so he is less of a bother?'

'No. It's fine. I simply needed to deal with some personal matters that I'd rather he wasn't privy to. No doubt he'll find me and say whatever's on his mind before too long. You're dismissed.'

Roke hesitated a moment longer, as if weighing up some internal idea. Then, he nodded brusquely and exited Sapora's chamber.

Sapora glanced down at his gloved hands. The Valendrin was key to releasing the other Arks...but Sapora didn't want to consider what that might do to the rest of his body. He now had invisible threads linking him to two gods; the Sevastos and Veynothi. Would he be able to manage three more?

Barely two minutes passed before footsteps approached. By their distinct pattern, Sapora knew at once that it was Tacio. Had he come to grovel and seek forgiveness? Or had he come to gloat about some other minor achievement?

Sapora had no patience for his brother at the best of times. But, much like Isa, he needed him. So he had to indulge his younger brother's visits. 'Come in, Tacio. It's obvious that you're desperate to tell me something.'

Tacio's laughter preceded his arrival. He sauntered into the room, every bit the prince Sapora remembered. His damaged skin had been well covered, his hair freshly oiled, and he wore twice the amount of gaudy jewellery to draw attention away from his face. He limped slightly—Tacio put less pressure on his left leg than normal, and his steps were shorter—but Tacio played a good act.

'Are you feeling better now you've had time to recover?' Sapora asked lightly.

Tacio ignored the barb and made his way to the bar beside the fireplace, where he took a minute to select a bottle of wine. He pulled out a goblet and filled it. 'Such good stock here, but you never taste it. Utterly wasted on you.'

'It's for appearances' sake more than anything else,' Sapora said. Frankly, he didn't like how alcohol dulled his senses. 'Go on, then. What is it you want? My time is valuable.'

Tacio drained half the goblet and smacked his lips noisily. '*Very* good stock. I should have Koraki order another crate.'

'You *do* realise we have a small army of Arillians on our doorstep? It's unlikely we'll have ships deliver anything until *she's* dealt with.'

Tacio waved a hand dismissively and topped up the goblet. 'Just have that dragon of yours deal with it. I don't understand the hold up.'

Sapora's thread to the dragon seemed to vibrate angrily. Because it detested him. 'What did you come here for?' Sapora snapped.

'I wanted to know when you planned to return,' Tacio said, unusually direct.

'Return? What do you mean?'

'To Sereth. You've done Summercourt, you have a new council in place, people to run things for you. Your dragon patrols the skies, your Ark does your bidding. Remind me why we're still up here with these sun-dwellers? Don't you miss home?'

Sapora bristled. 'You *do* remember I was born here, right? I only came to Sereth at sixteen.'

'So? Sereth is your home, wherever you were born. You're a *naja*. Like me. Like Vasil. Our place is in Sereth.

Why stay up here any longer than you have to? It's not even like Isa is here.'

Sapora suppressed a hiss at his callous words and the way he dismissed their sister. 'There is work to be done.'

'Like what?'

Sapora pointed out the window. 'Like Jato. Like Aciel.'

'Since when have Varkain ever cared for Arillians? The birds'll get bored and fly away soon enough. If they want to attack the city, let them. The Sevastos will keep them at bay or chase them off, and the Ittallan can look after themselves. We don't need to be here and endure it.'

Sapora huffed. Tacio made several good points, and his opinions mirrored Vasil's. In truth, if Sapora was any other Varkain, he probably would have returned to Sereth long ago. The idea *was* appealing. The council would run things. The Sevastos would ward off all major threats. And the Arks would be his go-between, ensuring no-one ever challenged him again.

Yet, he couldn't ignore the rot growing in the heart of Taban Yul. Aciel's influence spread like a disease, and the pressure applied by Jato made him more than a little edgy. What kind of ruler would he be if he fled to the tunnels and left the city ripe for a siege? Besides, if he was the one to personally bring the brewing war to a stop, the whole world would see him as their saviour. He'd be untouchable.

Whatever happened, he needed to stand by his decisions.

'This is my kingdom, too,' Sapora said at length.

Tacio snorted, exasperated. 'Why don't we just go back to Sereth? Rule there? Why d'you need to come all the way out here and try to squash the Ittallan? Now you've brought back an Ark, there'll be war between us again. You know that, right? You're going to undo everything Vasil worked for to end all that constant fighting. You and I need to get back to Sereth before it kicks off. What happens when they storm the palace?'

Sapora decided to not rise to his brother's bait. He'd already had this conversation once before with Isa. Why was everyone blind to what he was trying to do? Did they believe so little in him?

He was trying to *prevent* an uprising, not instigate one.

'What I'm doing is my business, brother.' Sapora needed Tacio to remember his own shortcomings before trying to give him orders. He wasn't one of his damned Cerastes, grovelling at his feet.

'You don't need the Arks. You have me, you know. If you'd stop trying to side with the Ittallan and meddle in their affairs, perhaps you'd see that!'

Sapora folded his arms. 'Anyway, Tacio, I'd like to know exactly how *you* plan to make up for your failure in letting Princess Isa and the others escape. Maybe I ought to ask Vasil to send someone from the Old Guard to keep an eye on you.'

Tacio snarled audibly. 'How *dare* you! I don't need a babysitter!'

Sapora laughed. 'Don't you? You're here to manage the Cerastes in the city, advise in council meetings, and obey me. I've seen precious little of that.'

Tacio rolled his eyes and put his empty goblet down. 'Brother, you don't make it easy. Especially when you've ignored every bit of advice I *have* given you since you won the jade crown. About Isa. About the Ittallan. Now about this war you're on the brink of unleashing.'

'Isa is no traitor! If you hadn't messed up, I'd have been able to question her!'

'She attacked me!' Tacio said, pulling down his jacket collar to show Sapora the healing scars on his neck. 'Damned feral cat!'

Sapora scowled. It didn't mean anything. 'Force anyone into a corner and they'll lash out. If you'd only left her alone—'

'She'd probably have slit our throats while we slept!' Tacio interrupted.

He didn't believe it. Tacio had locked her up. She'd been vulnerable. Afraid. Amarah and her sky pirates had influenced her, badly. She'd lashed out at Tacio when she'd left.

That was the narrative he told himself. It was what he believed.

'I don't know why you hate her,' Sapora said.

Tacio snorted in response, shaking his head and eyeing a different bottle of wine. He unstoppered it and poured a drizzle into his goblet before bringing it to his nose for a deep inhale.

Sapora refused to let it go. 'I'll not have another word said of Isa.'

'You're so blinded by your soft-heart for the Ittallan—'

'Fine. *You* lost her. *You* can bring her back. Perhaps you'll make less of a mess of things outside the palace than within it. But I can't see how you'd succeed over Veynothi.'

Tacio stood silent for a moment, stunned. 'You...*excuse* me? I don't go out unless I choose to.'

Sapora strode across the room, plucked Tacio's goblet from his hand, and threw it into the empty fireplace where it shattered, splattering deep red across the ashes. 'Roke is off doing missions for me. Are you saying Roke is a better Varkain than you?'

'That old cretin? Hardly,' Tacio spat. 'I cannot believe you're *dismissing* me!'

'I'm *using* you, Tacio. You wanted to be helpful, here's your chance. Prove me wrong about needing the Arks.'

Something shifted in Tacio. His eyes narrowed and his whole body stiffened, as if he'd reached the end of some internal debate. Instead of raging, he spoke coldly, 'Just you wait and see.'

Sapora ignored the instinctive concern. 'Go then. But I want her *alive*. Do *not* kill her, do you understand? If she has so much as a *scratch*, I'll throw you into the pits back home with every fighting thrall we have.'

7

Just as Isa had feared, several of the sky pirates wanted to bind her and deliver her straight to the snake king the moment they realised who she was. They wanted their riches *now*. Although Sapora had not formally listed a bounty for her, they were certain he'd pay handsomely for the return of his royal prisoner.

She'd had to overcome their need for instant gratification by explaining that standing *with* her would be far more beneficial than standing with Sapora—especially considering she had a small army of armed Ittallan already with her.

Most of the pirates were born and bred Estorians—bold, fearless, and able to tell when they were being deceived. Getting them to see things long-term was about as easy as convincing a Varkain that her official title was not the "kitten princess." Thankfully, the captains were a little more far-sighted than their crews, but it was a tense and tricky night of conversation to negotiate.

Amarah had been right about Traego—he seemed to be the only one there who could think more than one step ahead, to consider more than simply the next job, or where things might lead to. And the fact that they were already allies helped, of course.

The two Captains Ipot and Basir wanted vengeance and payment from Traego for allowing an Arillian to travel with his crew—who had later churned up a chunk of Estoria and caused them significant losses. Traego's masterful silver tongue always steered the conversation back to Isa's needs, and the sheer rarity of royalty in Estoria was enough to keep the pirates' attentions off him and on the Ittallan's cause for the time being.

Isa had discovered that there were countless thief troupes, not to mention those who worked alone or in pairs. Each looked out for themselves above anything else, and she had at least thirty to convince. These were, apparently, the most influential of the sky pirates in Estoria, and didn't speak for the others who were based elsewhere in Linaria.

Of course, most sky pirates worth their salt set up base in Estoria, where there was no fear of the Imperial Guard, but Isa had an uphill battle. Most of the troupe leaders were arrogant, overconfident, and refused to listen. Captain Hanzel, an old woman who was the bitterest of them all, was particularly tricky to convince. She and her First Mate, Rimir, whose glass eye rolled about every time he moved his head, had put up a show of aggressive arguing all night that left Isa frazzled.

Isa had offered herself and her followers' time rebuilding their lost cabins as a show of faith to the pirate captains. Ipot had lost the most in the Arillian attack, and therefore argued for the most work. Isa would happily offer their labour to help rebuild what had been damaged, and restore what they could. It satiated Ipot enough to listen to her proposals, though he still threw Traego filthy looks from time to time.

At least the Ittallan would stay busy while she worked out the details of her next steps, and offering the pirates work would certainly endear them to her cause.

And it showed that she didn't expect things for free. She would help as much as her followers.

Thankfully, when talk grew too heated, Traego and Amarah could knock sense into the pirates—Amarah literally with an old captain called Idas, who had to be in his sixties and smoked a cigar the entire evening—but by the end of it, Isa thought maybe a third of those present would consider her proposal.

The fact of the matter was asking a ship captain to risk their vessel, crew, and livelihood, on the hope that one day Isa would be queen and reward them for their service, was not easy. After all, she was the same queen who would command the Imperial Guard—historically the greatest enemy of sky pirates and their endeavours.

Isa understood from their standpoint that it was asking a lot, especially when the skies of Val Sharis were now more treacherous than ever with dragons and Arillians, and Isa could do nothing to prevent that.

Amarah had taken the angle of adventure and bravery—didn't they want to prove they were better in the sky than a handful of birds and some fire-breathing lizards? Her challenge had turned the table for a lot of them, who were now more open to the idea of flying through Val Sharis than before.

The main questions on everyone's lips were: why would she return to Val Sharis so soon after being rescued? What did she plan to do next? And of course, when would they be paid for their efforts to ferry her and her followers around?

By dawn, most of the sky pirates had returned to their own bases, leaving Isa alone with Traego, Amarah, Antar, and Palom. Even Solvi, desperate to stay a part of the discussions, had been taken to bed shortly before dawn. Kylos had wanted to stay, but Palom assured her he would keep watch over the princess, letting her rest while she could.

Outside, her followers had set up camp in the clear land beside Traego's lodge. It would be a bustle of activity once everyone was up and awake, but for now, most of the tents lay quiet.

Isa rubbed her eyes and tried to stifle a yawn.

'I'd say that went well, Isa,' Traego said, folding his arms and leaning back on his wooden chair.

'Well?'

'We tend not ta discuss major movements with each other,' he explained. 'Gettin' 'em all here an' on the same page was great. No killin's either. A good night! Ipot'll definitely grab me today, though. That's gonna be fun.' His tone suggested that it would not, in fact, be any fun at all.

'Time's are changing. Maybe it's better we stick together for a bit. Good to have someone strong to rally behind for once,' Amarah said.

Isa was running out of energy. 'Thank you for your confidence. It won't be easy going up against Sapora. Things seemed…less complicated when I was back at the palace.'

'Of course. You are princess,' Palom said. He sat beside Traego, *Leillu* curled up on his lap. The dragon was getting so big that her lower half and tail snaked along the floor. *Leillu* let out a small puff of smoke with every snore, oblivious to the conversation.

Isa didn't fully trust any of the pirates—how could she, when her own brother had locked her up? 'I need the support of the Ittallan more than the support of the pirates.'

'The Ittallan are behind you,' Palom said. He gestured through the small window of Traego's base to the numerous tents outside.

'They aren't enough. I need to go to the towns of Val Sharis, rally up the people, get them on my side. I can't talk to Sapora. Not after what I've done. Having him step down isn't going to be possible, and I could never defeat him in single combat.' Weariness pressed down on Isa's shoulders. 'I need Val Sharis, the whole country, united behind me. And even then it might not be enough. Odi has begun to write letters that I will take to the Archigo to plead my case and bolster our numbers.'

'Sapora's Sevastos is pretty powerful...And now the Arks...' Amarah muttered.

'I know.' Isa rubbed the back of her neck and shut her eyes. 'I know...I know.'

'Maybe ya should just give up on all that. Hide out here with us. Become a pirate!' Traego laughed.

She couldn't believe he'd joke about something like that. Not after all the work they'd just done talking to the other captains. Four of the most influential of them; Ipot, Basir, Hanzel, and Idas, had each agreed to loan her the use of one ship—class four or five—once they had prepared them. In three days' time, she and her followers would be able to move. 'I can't. I owe the Ittallan more than that. They've all risked a lot just to get me here. I need to do something for them. Fight on their behalf. They're afraid of Sapora. They need someone to stand up to him and the other Varkain.'

'Maybe do what Palom does. Find your own *Leillu*?' Traego suggested with another laugh.

'*Leillu* is mine!' Palom said, putting a protective arm over the dragon's snout.

Isa shook her head. 'I don't want to get into a battle of who has the biggest teeth! That's just what Sapora's doing, anyway.'

'Ya can't match Sapora, you said it yourself. Say you get

these ships. Crews to fill 'em. How do ya plan on beating him if ya ain't playing his own game?' Traego asked.

Isa turned to Palom. 'You made weapons before, didn't you? The *Valta Forinja*? Could you make me one? To fight against Sapora? If I could...If I could get him alone...'

'Ya just said ya *can't* fight him one-on-one,' Traego said.

Isa stood up and paced the table. 'I know. But. But if I had an edge... Something he didn't know, something he couldn't fight. I could weaken him enough. *Make* him flee.'

Amarah said, 'I'll fight him for ya. I ain't got no problems killing him. Anyone can see that you have a problem, though.'

Isa swallowed. 'It's my fight, Amarah.'

'Why are we talking about killing our brothers? Just make him leave. If you are stronger in battle, then retreat is better than death, no?' Palom asked.

Amarah snorted. 'Sapora's too proud for that. It'll be death or nothing with his type.'

'Let's not get too hasty. Ya just escaped from Tacio and the dungeons, and ya wanna go back an' fight Sapora straight away? Probably not the smartest move, Isa,' Traego said, whacking a hand flat on the table. 'Ya got a few pirates on ya side that'll ferry ya about. Help ya get ya new followers. But don't forget there's more than one way ta skin a cat.'

Isa faced him and raised an expectant eyebrow.

'Ya want the people on ya side, right? Best way ta get that is ta do something for 'em. For free. Why don't ya stop the dragons burnin' their homes? Or stop Jato stormin' up the place? Take full credit for it. Isa, saviour of Val Sharis! The Ittallan will see ya as their hero, not Sapora. Ya win 'em over without risking yourself in a fight against the snake.'

Isa frowned, considering. He had a point. She didn't *have* to tackle Sapora head on. She could work alone, on her own campaign, and weaken Sapora without ever confronting him directly. Not until she was good and ready. That would be better. She wasn't sure she could *actually* face him after her betrayal.

'Ya gone quiet. Somethin' I said?' Traego asked, grinning.

'It's a good point,' Isa conceded. 'Best sleep on it. As much as I appreciate the other pirates' offers, I would prefer to fly in *Otella*. Can you have the ship ready on the same deadline as the others? Three days? The sooner I get back to Val Sharis and talking with the Archigo, the sooner this'll be over.'

Traego shrugged. 'Fare is two crowns a day if ya want a cabin. I'll do it for a crown a day if ya happy to sleep on deck like the rest o' us.'

'What? You'd *charge* me?'

'Isa, I gotta make a livin'! While ya an' Sapora are off stirring up trouble, I got no income! That bit o' gold he gave me for Veynothi's sword ain't covering much. Come on then queenie, ya gonna pay up?'

'This is future queen, you are talking to!' Palom said so loudly that *Leillu* jerked awake.

'I know exactly who I'm talking ta, that's why I know what ta charge!'.

Isa scowled. She'd owe the sky pirates for the rest of her life with rates like those.

'You can fly on *RaKhanna* if ya want, but I got my own business to see to, first,' Amarah said, coming to her rescue. 'Jato is number one on my list now you're safe.'

Isa huffed, exasperated. She had to expect as such. These were sky pirates, they weren't her loyal soldiers or members of her guard. They would continue to live their own lives.

'Do not be so hasty, princess,' Palom said. 'You have few

days here safe, at least. Wait and rest. There is no rush to act. Then you will know what to do first.'

The Ittallan had a point, she knew. Rushing into things had put her in more trouble than she'd bargained for—with Mateli, with Lathri, and now with Sapora and Tacio. 'Okay, I'll rest for the next couple of nights and plan my route through Val Sharis. Do I have to pay for *that*?'

Traego laughed. 'Royal guests get a great rate. I'll add it to ya tab for when ya're queen.'

'You should be honoured royalty even wishes to *be* your guest,' Palom grumbled.

Isa smirked at the sky pirate. It would be the best she'd get, no doubt. 'I appreciate your *kind* offer, Captain Traego.' Stifling another yawn, Isa stretched her arms high above her head, joints popping.

She needed to get outside. The room was hot and stuffy, and she'd spent too long in their company for her liking. Outside space—peace and quiet. It was probably the only chance she'd get for a long while. 'If we're done? You should all get some rest.'

The others mumbled their assent and she stood up. Her lower half had gone completely numb, even in the cushioned wooden chair, and her first few steps were wobbly. By the fifth step, she'd regained most of the feeling in her legs and feet, and hurried out into the sunshine before anyone could come with her.

This time yesterday, she was on a beach saying her goodbyes to Lathri. The day before? She was locked in her room, a prisoner of Tacio. Who knew what tomorrow would bring.

In a flash of light, she transformed, tapping into her *meraki*. The last time she'd shifted had been too long to recall.

She didn't hesitate. Four powerful legs propelled her

forward faster than she ever could be on two, and she shot off into the jungle.

She dived between trees, the jungle leaflitter now a springboard for her every step. The sun dazzled her for a moment, and she raced up the nearest tree, leaping from branch to branch, getting higher and higher, until she reached the flat palm leaves at the very top.

Inhaling deeply, the salty air filled her lungs and she revelled in the feeling of being alone with the most stunning view she'd ever seen. As a princess, Isa knew she was recognisable by most, even in Estoria. But in her true form? Far less so. She was just another wildcat out hunting.

Isa leapt from one tree top to another, making her way past the three airships she'd arrived with—Traego's crew still working on *Otella's* damaged hull—and down towards where the land gave way to sea. Her fatigue shrank away to nothing as she prowled the jungle rooftops and watched the Estorians going about their morning routines, completely unaware that the Princess of Val Sharis was in their midst.

High above, a black eagle circled, and Isa recognised the shrill cry of Aetos. So much for him resting. With Aetos, Kylos, Odi, and other Ittallan here, it felt like some of Val Sharis had travelled with her to this distant place. The thought brought her comfort as she continued to the edge of the trees, and looked out onto the sandy beach as it spread along the breadth of the island.

For a moment, she thought of Traego's laughable suggestion. Remaining here, hidden away in this jewel of a place, *did* appeal. Estoria had everything she needed—food, drink, shelter, familiar people. If you ignored the constant threat of violence with sky pirates in such close proximity.

But that would be cowardly.

She owed the Ittallan more than that. And they hadn't all

risked their lives to rescue her so she could live a life of luxury on a sandy beach until her last days.

She was their princess. She would be their queen. Despite her terrible upbringing, there *were* Ittallan who saw her as more than one of Vasil's bastard children. Lathri had made that clear.

She'd spent too long in isolation, so afraid of rejection that she saw it wherever she went. The constant negative inference meant she constantly doubted herself, her qualities, her true power.

Taking down Jato *would* be a good first step to dispelling that. Dispersing some of the smaller dragons, too, would be feasible. It meant the pirates would put their ships under greater risk, however, and they would need more convincing to do that.

Who else could she call on for a favour? Morgen had gone quiet since her request for aid, but he had certainly answered it. Sapora hadn't guessed her part in the attack, but since then, her messages to the man had gone unanswered, with two letters being returned.

Topeko, the scholar, had spent time with him. Perhaps it would be worth visiting Berel, or at least sending him a message, to see whether he knew where Morgen was.

Surely turning up in the peaceful nation in strength would not win any votes to her cause. A letter would be the better route. If Morgen had comrades in the Imperial Guard who would be persuaded to join her...That would certainly bolster her numbers, particularly with those who knew how to fight and were disciplined. All those from Corhaven and other Ittallan who had been pushed out of the Imperial Guard and replaced by Varkain would surely dislike Sapora enough to stand with her.

Isa strode along the clifftop, the white beaches sprawled out in front of her. Behind, thick smoke rose slowly in the non-existent breeze. She hadn't yet seen the devastation caused by the Arillian attack for herself, but would need to later that day, when her followers were helping the pirates rebuild.

She found a shady spot under a line of palm trees and sat down in the soft, warm sand. She shifted out of her true form, and rested her head against the trunk of the nearest tree. Atop the cliff, she could see for leagues. Isa counted eighteen small fishing boats coming into shore, most with nets full of silver-blue fish wriggling in their traps, scales glistening in the sun. Her stomach growled, but she ignored it.

Staying hungry kept her sharp.

She certainly needed her wits about her if she was to survive Estoria and its power—and gold—hungry pirates.

Slowly, while she watched the calm waters of the Central Ocean, Isa began to piece her plans together. Her next steps, counter moves, and defences should things take a turn for the worst. Trade routes used often by merchant ships would be the quickest way across the mainland. Amarah and Traego would know those, as well as which ones were patrolled by the Imperial Guard. It made sense to work with people used to smuggling to travel undetected across Val Sharis.

Considering Jato's presence, she assumed much of the Imperial Guard were thin on the ground, pulled back to defend the capital. With their attention elsewhere, she'd be able to move her burgeoning fleet in safety. She hoped.

As far as she was concerned, she'd suffered her greatest defeats already. She refused to lose any more battles—or people—because of her haste or mistakes. Lathri's death would forever eat at her conscience, even more so when she looked at Palom, and saw the hurt and sorrow in his eyes.

Amarah had done more than rescue her, she'd given her

another chance at power. Another chance to make right the wrongs she'd allowed to happen.

Perhaps once, she and Sapora would have been able to rule. But a childish fantasy of getting your own back against those who did you harm was one thing, and actually killing them was something else.

She should have realised the night of the ball that she and Sapoa were not the same. They did not share the commonalities she'd thought they had. He was ambitious and selfish. He would do whatever it took to get the results he wanted.

She would *not* mindlessly kill.

They may have shared Varkain blood and a warrior father, but she was no snake.

And she never would be.

The thought saddened her—she'd been trying all her life to be accepted by her family. Her father and brother both had abandoned her. Now she had to stand on her own two legs and show the world what a true queen was capable of.

'Funny, you found my spot.'

Isa was on her feet in a heartbeat, knives in her hands, ready. 'Oh. Amarah. I didn't hear you.'

'I'd be a shit thief if you did. I like watching the water from here.'

Isa could understand that, but she didn't want to leave. After everything that had happened, all the emotions and talking, the fear and panic of fleeing, she was simply exhausted. She watched as Amarah, quite comfortable in her presence, sat down against the tree beside hers, and let out a long sigh.

After waiting for a few seconds and realising they weren't going to be joined by Traego or any other sky pirates, Isa returned to her spot. It was comfortable and cool, and the height of the cliffs enabled them to enjoy the mild sea breeze. 'You have a beautiful home.'

'It ain't home. But yeah, it's nice enough.'

Curiosity gnawed at the princess. 'How did you end up here?'

'Same as all the others.'

When Amarah didn't elaborate, Isa prompted, 'Which is...?'

'Washed up with the tide.'

The two women enjoyed a companionable silence, with naught but the waves and distant chatter from the beach drifting up. Isa struggled a little. She hadn't known Amarah very long, yet she had risked her own life to instigate the jailbreak, when she could so very easily have laughed at Antar's message and continued on as if nothing had happened.

She'd lost her eye and her ship, yet marched ever onwards, as though those things were barely stumbling blocks in her path instead of life-altering obstacles.

Isa wasn't sure how *she'd* cope if she lost an eye. The thought of it made her feel sick with anxiety. Perhaps Amarah was good at masking it? Isa couldn't hear the heartbeats of people like Sapora could—for all her sharpened senses, they weren't as sharp as a Varkain's—but she could see nervous ticks, or people sweating. Amarah hardly seemed bothered by anything.

'You're tough, you know,' Isa murmured.

'What? Where'd that come from?'

Isa raised her shoulders, her gaze still on the horizon. 'You ran away from home as a child. Lived on the streets. You could have ended up in a dungeon. As a Varkain's thrall. But it never happened. That life...painful and hard as it must have been...I suppose it toughened you up?'

Amarah let out a snort of laughter. 'Running away from home didn't make me tough.'

Isa looked at her. 'No?'

'I was tough *because* I ran away from home. I've always been tough. That's what helped me get through those shit times. Not the other way around. I came through it even better than before. Learned lots. If I weren't tough, I'd have ended up dead or worse. Don't get it wrong.'

Isa smiled. She needed to give Amarah credit for the decisions she'd made, not assume that those experiences had turned her into something she wasn't. 'That makes sense.'

'Course it does. Same as you. You're stronger than them snakes are. That's why you got all these Ittallan following you. Why you did what you did. If you were stupid and naive like they say, you'd still be locked in your room, doing what you been told like a good girl.'

Isa didn't know. She knew what she *wanted* to do, but she was afraid. Afraid of messing up and doing the wrong thing. Being berated or attacked because of it. It was no longer just her. There were dozens of people whose lives were in her hands. If she messed up, they'd *all* suffer for it. 'Don't you ever get scared of messing up?'

Amarah took a minute to think about it. 'Sometimes. But...everything's calculated, right? I ain't gonna rush into something that'll *definitely* kill me.'

Isa stared at the woman's eye patch but didn't interrupt.

Amarah followed her gaze and cackled. 'Most of the time. But if you don't do something, you aren't allowed to complain when things don't go your way. You know how things are right now. If you're happy with it, stay there. If you ain't, then do something.'

'Easier said than done.'

'Yep. That's why you gotta pick your moment. Bide your

time. Then go for it when you can. Hesitate, and you might as well give up on ever changing.'

Isa shrugged again. Amarah made it sound so easy. Perhaps it was, when you looked at the world in terms of black and white.

'...sometimes you go your whole life waiting for that chance.' Amarah had dropped her voice, and Isa had to lean forward to hear. 'Sometimes it never comes. So you jump into the darkness, no idea if you're gonna hit a wall or if you'll break through. But I'd rather get hurt and know I tried than give in and suffer.'

Isa wondered what she meant—what event in her life made her think like that. What fate had she narrowly escaped, if she'd been so desperate to change her life's course?

'Anyway. I don't wanna get sentimental. Life's easier that way.'

'I know. Ruling is hard enough without emotions.'

'Hah. You don't wanna sound like Sapora, do you?' Amarah grinned.

'Never!' Isa and Sapora had much in common, that was true enough. But they'd grown into very distinct people, even without their different *meraki*.

Her whole life had revolved around her brother—growing up with him, then comparing herself to him once she came of age. When he'd left, it had revolved around waiting for him to visit the palace and keep the Goldstones and council off her. Waiting for him to be king. And now it had all happened, it still revolved around him giving up the throne to her.

Her eyes prickled with the threat of tears, and Isa bit her bottom lip.

She could have stayed. Been a good princess and did as she was told by Tacio, Sapora, and whoever else. She wouldn't have been happy, but it was *safe.* If they were happy, it was easier for everyone else.

Amarah's words rolled around in her mind. What she was doing now was dangerous. She was stumbling ahead in the dark, unknown. She had no idea of the risks and dangers she'd face until it was too late.

But, even if she failed, at least she had tried.

8

Kohl and Fogu flew further west, putting as much distance between themselves and the mountain as they could. It wouldn't be long before the dragon freed itself from its icy tomb, and Kohl had no wish to be anywhere near when that happened. As their current behaviour showed, dragons were vengeful creatures that held grudges over a lifetime.

Fogu agreed, and pushed the pace as much as he could without one of them getting exhausted.

It was ironic, however, that the *Valta Forinja* Palom created to defeat Aciel were directly responsible for the wrath of the dragons now. There was always a consequence to power.

A shame that so many were now suffering because of ignorance, and those in Berel would be sitting ducks with more of those cursed weapons locked away. He needed to do what he could to warn them before they burned.

At least Palom had made the weapons in good faith. Although they'd been created to fight against his kin, the blacksmith hadn't forged the *Valta Forinja* out of personal greed.

That had to count for something.

It wasn't long before the expanse of the Sea of Nami came into view, a blue-grey streak under the overcast day. Far below them, directly on the shore, a large town grew like fungus—white cobblestone streets trailing along crevices and flats as if they sprouted from the land itself. They stretched out in all directions from the town's centre, as though trying to reach distant lands. A large port spread out over the water's surface, with several large ships docked, their enormous sails rippling in the wind. To the side, a square hanger rose high—no doubt where the townspeople kept their airships.

'That would be Gur Bano, my lord,' Fogu announced, hovering. 'Shall we keep going, across the sea? That'll put plenty of distance between ourselves and that dragon.'

'Yes, but we shall travel by airship, as I said before.' Kohl didn't want to take any chances with the dragon, but surely the airship would be as much a disguise for them as a method of transport. He hoped the town still had ships flying. If there weren't any more transport vessels until the following day, they'd have to fly themselves unless they spent the night. That was a risk he didn't want to take, so waiting until the morrow was out of the question.

Fogu stiffened, but said nothing, plainly unhappy with the decision to mingle with Linarians. Still, he followed Kohl's lead obediently, scoping out their surroundings with ruthless efficiency. At least Kohl knew he could rely on the general in case he spotted any threats.

Their main priority was to land nearby without being spotted, and enter the town while covering their wings. To most people in Corhaven—who rarely knew any better—they could pass as Ittallan. But in Val Sharis, they'd have a harder time convincing the locals they were Ittallan, too.

They needed to spend as little time in the town as possible without arousing suspicion.

Kohl glanced down to his hand. His broken fingers pained him less than before, and he wondered if it was too late for someone to take a look at them. If they healed crookedly, it wouldn't be the worst thing—although he worried it might affect his control over the Frost-touch.

He tried to clench his fists as they descended into some woodland, using a nearby bluff for cover. These would be the first people he'd seen since being attacked by sky pirates. He knew the Ittallan here had nothing to do with the people of Estoria, but he was nervous about being among people who were not his kind.

If Fogu was to be believed, everyone who wasn't an Arillian was their enemy.

Kohl knew it wasn't that black and white, but tensions were high across Linaria, and there was nothing to be lost by remaining cautious.

'I think we've bought ourselves enough breathing room from that dragon,' Kohl said, dusting himself off. 'My cloak?'

Fogu fumbled around in his pack for a moment and silently withdrew Kohl's travelling cloak. It was muddy and covered in sand from his time in Estoria, and part of it had ripped at the bottom—no doubt from his mistreatment at the hands of the sky pirates. But, mercifully, it was dry.

Kohl carefully adjusted it, ensuring his wings were fully hidden from view, and let it drape down to the ground.

The noises of Gur Bano drifted up through the trees. Dockworkers talking, wood and metal thrown around. Crashes and banging. The smell of pipe smoke and fish. And above all, the salt-rich scent of the sea.

Kohl's lips went dry. It was similar to Estoria, just without the intense heat and stagnant sweat. He tried to remind himself that he'd travelled through various towns in Corhaven without being discovered—including the capital city. It would be easy to fool the people from a small town on the edge of Val Sharis.

Fogu made his way through the trees once Kohl had readied himself, leading the pair of them down a path he'd evidently discovered. His own cloak was equally as long as Kohl's, and he stooped somewhat, further reducing his appearance from Arillian to a weary traveller of unknown origin.

At least Kohl wasn't on his own anymore, even if Fogu didn't agree with all his decisions.

They formulated their story as they walked, should they be questioned by any nosy Ittallan, or even the Imperial Guard. Deciding to pass as Samolen—for they had incredible variance in their appearance and tongues—seemed the safest course of action. Although they didn't have anything even faintly resembling a Samolen cheek jewel, there were plenty of those from Ranski who didn't go on to study the magical arts. It was the best option they had, and would also explain why they were travelling to Berel.

Of course, if there were any of King Sapora's Varkain in town, their cover would be blown. They might be able to fool Ittallan as to their true nature, but a Varkain's senses were too sharp for such a farce.

Kohl reasoned that the town was some way from Taban Yul, and Sapora would have no reason to send his Varkain here.

Fogu argued it was a foolish risk to take, especially after what had happened in Estoria.

'We are not Aciel. And we are not Jato. If we always distance ourselves from Linarians, they'll never regain their trust in us,' Kohl said when they were less than half a league from the town gates. They'd left the cover of the trees and were making their way across farmers' fields.

'We're still hiding our true nature. Why not avoid the town altogether and simply fly over it? My lord, I don't wish to be rude, nor press the point if you are absolutely certain, but it seems a pointless risk to take. Simply because you want to...you want to...*mingle*?'

'News travels quickly. We've been in Estoria ever since the siege of Taban Yul. Who knows what's really been happening in Linaria since.' Kohl noted the four Imperial Guard Posts outside Gur Bano were each manned only by a single Ittallan. Definitely not the tight security Fogu had been concerned about.

Fogu dismissed him with a scoff. 'Gossip, that's all these towns are good for.'

'You'd rather believe the papers? King Sapora will be in charge of those, you know. Anything you read in there will be biased towards the Varkain.'

Fogu snorted. 'We're above these petty matters.'

'We'll be back in Oren soon enough, my friend.' Kohl clasped a hand on Fogu's shoulder, sure to avoid his wings, and the two walked side by side down the dirt path towards the farmland that surrounded Gur Bano.

They made their way in between two fields, cabbages in one, radishes in the other. The plants were still young, and they weren't much more than greenery above the soil, but both Arillians took care where they stepped to not inadvertently damage any of the vegetables. It was an oft frequented walkway, as evidenced by the grass and weeds that lingered on the edge of the fields had been worn away, creating a rudimentary path of hard mud.

Summer insects buzzed, flitting from one flower to the next, heedless to the Arillians passing through their small world.

A few farmhands worked the fields, but most were interested in their own jobs, and ignored them. Three hands worked to put up a scarecrow near the centre of the cabbage field, the sounds of their strained grunts carrying easily across the flat land.

'If only our lands were this fertile,' Fogu said, unable to keep the bitterness from his voice. 'What I'd give to grow these foods for our people.'

'It's the price we must pay for the Great War,' Kohl replied to Fogu's lament, watching the workers all the while.

'I know. Yet, I often think we don't deserve those barren rocks..'

Kohl didn't reply. He'd happily live on bread and water for the rest of his life, if it meant he and his people would be safe from invaders or being drawn into another war. It was a shame that many of his people disagreed.

'WE'VE close family in Berel. It's urgent we get there as quickly as possible,' Fogu said, with a passable Samolen accent that mostly disguised his upbringing and rank.

The gatekeeper had no interest in them, reeling off his questions and marking down their answers with apathy. 'Your intended time of stay in Gur Bano?'

'As soon as the next airship leaves, we'll be gone. I don't suppose you've the day's schedule?'

'And what about your return?' He rubbed his nose with the back of one hand, ignoring Fogu's question and moving down to the next question on his checklist.

'We'll be travelling via a new route.' Fogu masked his irritation well, but Kohl could tell the Arillian was on edge. His shoulders tensed, and he squared his jaw, peering down his nose at the gatekeeper who hadn't even bothered to stand at their approach.

Neither of them mentioned the dragon they'd encountered only a few leagues away.

With a final yawn, the gatekeeper waved them through and settled back on the bench—no doubt to resume the nap he'd been in the middle of when they'd arrived.

'I say, that's not the best security I've ever seen,' Fogu muttered once they were out of earshot. 'No wonder the snakes rose up and conquered them all. What laziness!'

'Nothing much happens out here, I suppose,' Kohl replied. They walked down the main street of the town, buildings rising on either side of the road. From afar, the cobblestones had appeared white. Now they walked upon them, it was clear they were a dirty grey. Most of the buildings were only one or two storeys high, nothing like the vast townhouses of Taban Yul, or the crooked buildings all piled on top of one another in Niversai. The smell of the sea was stronger than ever, and in between every building, it glinted like a blue streak on the horizon. The sun attempted to breach the thick clouds overhead, and every so often it sent down a warm ray that lit the dreary seaside town.

Most of the buildings had been bleached grey-white from decades in the sun, and were made of hefty chunks of stone that were no doubt chosen for their ability to survive the extreme weather on the seafront. Although the sea appeared calm at the moment, Kohl was certain that it turned into a frothing, violent rage during winter storms.

On Oren, aside from the amount of light every day, all the seasons appeared much the same. That was part and parcel of the Everwinter so far north.

The Ittallan here were mostly fishing folk, from their dress, behaviour, and smell. Many carried long rods or baskets over their shoulders, and chatted easily with one another. Peals of laughter drifted along the streets. Their carefree attitude almost made Kohl less nervous, but he couldn't rid himself of the feeling he was walking right into the enemies' camp. That he'd be a sitting target as soon as they—inevitably—saw through his disguise and realised they could earn a hefty amount of gold from Sapora's bounty on Arillians.

Fogu didn't appear to share Kohl's concerns. He was committed, now, and led them steadily towards the docks, where they hoped to figure out the airships' schedules and barter passage across the sea to Ranski.

The sky above was clear, aside from clouds and birds, and very unlike Taban Yul or Niversai, whose skies were always thick with airships. Kohl followed Fogu along the steadily narrowing streets as they dropped down towards the sea.

Several Ittallan glanced over to them—they were a pair of strange, tall, cloaked travellers, after all—but they quickly darted down a side street or turned a corner before any conversations could be struck up.

Most of the talk Kohl heard as they moved through the town was related to that morning's catch, the limited trade to the northern towns and cities, and whether the dragon threat would reach them tucked away on the coast.

Berthed along the pier, Kohl counted six large sailing ships, and over a dozen smaller vessels. They all looked kitted out for fishing or crabbing, and certainly weren't long-haul ships that would transport anyone across the sea.

The airship hangar lay further south, half the size of the docks. Upon spotting it, and noting how small it was, he suddenly worried it wasn't large enough to house more than two or three good-sized airships. Travelling from a relatively small town certainly had its disadvantages.

Kohl cast his gaze back towards the Feor Mountains. They were too distant to see with much clarity, but no dragon-shaped shadow made its way towards them.

'...I tell ya. We'd be better off with *anyone* else than those bloody snakes. Always trying to take what ain't theirs.' An angry voice cursed from across the half-full docks. A large group of Ittallan congregated around a full net of fish and a small boat that had been tipped on its side. Most of them smoked long, slender pipes as they loitered. While the younger members of their groups scurried around, stacking crates and weighing crabs.

It didn't take long before Kohl spotted the cause of their ire.

Two Varkain in dark blue armour lingered on the far side of the docks, speaking with one another in hushed tones. Every so often, one gestured to the catch. Kohl narrowed his eyes. He'd never seen Varkain in that sort of armour before. It certainly wasn't the red and gold livery of the Imperial Guard. Both looked like they knew how to fight, and had sheathed longswords at their backs.

'We should keep away,' Fogu whispered, keen to keep everyone's attention off them. 'There, the entrance to the hangar. There must be a Fleet Master or equivalent with whom we can speak.'

Kohl nodded, half-listening. The two Varkain looked to be of their warrior caste, and their presence put him on edge. He allowed Fogu to steer them to the far side of the docks, away from the Varkain and angered fishers, towards several tall guardhouses, their officers thumbing through paperwork or staring idly out over the water and the docked boats. It seemed the guard at the town gates wasn't the only one who suffered from apathy.

Kohl looked away quickly when one of the Varkain glanced in his direction, hoping he'd not been recognised as an Arillian.

He and Fogu walked quickly, and Kohl forced himself to look ahead. He was certain the Varkain would know they were Arillians, but there were no shouts to halt, no threats launched in their direction.

It wasn't until they were out of earshot that Kohl released the breath he held. He whispered, 'Why are there Varkain here?'

'Does it matter? We must keep away from them. It'll be harder to escape their claws than it was to get away from those pirates in Estoria!' Fogu adjusted his cloak, drawing it up higher around his neck. 'Thank the Ice Golems they are more interested in the catch of the day than in us.'

Kohl had to agree, but he couldn't shake his curiosity for their presence. Was it a coincidence? Or had they been sent specifically by Sapora for some other purpose? There was no way the king could know their location. Up until a few days ago, he'd been hidden away in Estoria.

It *had* to be a coincidence.

But it meant that the Linarian mainland had become more dangerous than ever for his people.

Sky pirates ruled in Estoria. It was only expected that crime levels would be high. But in other, more respectable locales? If the Varkain influence had truly gained a foothold, then Arillians wouldn't be safe anywhere aside from the floating islands they'd been banished to so many generations prior.

They needed to make their trip to Ranski as brief as possible and get back to Oren. He was already putting himself and Fogu at risk by travelling there, but he couldn't stand the thought of fleeing without acting. That had been the behaviour that had put him into trouble in the first place.

Fogu's desire to return made sense. But Kohl refused to abandon Linaria, not if there was something he could do to help it avoid a fate that ended in dragonfire. Right now, it was imparting knowledge.

A tingle of Frost-touch ran through his fingers, and he clenched them. What were the Varkain up to? Surely they had no business in such a remote town that cared only about fish and crabs?

'Looks like I can make an enquiry about the airships in there,' Fogu said, grabbing Kohl by the elbow and pulling him away. 'My lord. Stare at a snake too long, and it'll stare back at you.'

Kohl knew the saying, knew Fogu was right, but he couldn't help but let his curiosity grow. 'Go ahead and ask, I'll keep watch.'

Fogu gave him a long look, glanced around to ensure there weren't any Ittallan or Varkain near, then entered the building.

Kohl settled against the wall of the guardhouse, his back against the stone, where he was able to watch the two armoured Varkain move.

'Where's the shipment report?' One of the Varkain stormed over to the group of Ittallan fishermen near the crates. 'We're meant to receive weekly reports of what's been sent. There's nothing for the past five weeks.'

'I dunno if you noticed, snake, but the skies ain't exactly safe. Half our ships get attacked by dragons the moment we leave town. The rest are blasted to bits by that Arillian outside the capital.' The Ittallan who answered him was tall and burly, with shoulders and arms grown by years of hauling barrels and rope. He looked like a mountain against the lean, wiry Varkain, and refused to be intimidated. 'We do what we can. If they ain't getting there, it's *King Snake* who's the reason why.'

The Varkain's lip curled, and he made for the sword at his back. 'You'll show King Sapora more respect than that! *You're* responsible for getting the shipment to Taban Yul. And *you're* responsible for the fines if it goes missing. The capital is under siege, you ought to be doing your part to keep the people fed.'

The gathered Ittallan grumbled loudly, some even stamped their feet. 'How's it my fault if your king can't keep the airways clear for us?'

'Why's he so interested in our fish anyway?'

'Why don't he leave us alone like Vasil did?'

'Tripling the order leaves us hardly anything! Not to mention higher taxes!'

'*Our* king is no babysitter,' the Varkain said, raising his voice above the chatter and bringing it to a halt. 'I ought to *double* your fine for your treasonous tongue. We've travelled out first thing to get here early, and this is the welcome we receive?'

All the snickering stopped immediately. Even Kohl, several feet away, felt the venom in the Varkain's tone. Taban Yul under siege? Had Jato caused so much trouble? It would explain why were the Varkain so interested in receiving a shipment of seafood—any resources would be desperately needed to help the people survive.

Kohl noticed the second Varkain had stalked away from the others, more interested in peering among crates and fishing equipment than in the conversation his colleague was having. He kept his sword sheathed, but moved purposefully along the dock as if searching for something.

'Where's the Archigo here?' The first Varkain asked, drawing himself up to his full height.

Many of the Ittallan shrank away. 'Gur Bano don't have one.'

'No? Then who's in charge of all this?' He gestured vaguely to the ships bobbing in the shallows.

'Archigo Gralla covers Tannon Sona,' the bolder Ittallan shuffled another step back, 'she comes here every few weeks to check on things. But last we saw her was before Summercourt.'

The Varkain shifted his weight and flexed his claws. 'We need to get our shipments to the capital. If we don't—'

Rustling behind him caught Kohl's attention, and he glanced back to the office to see Fogu emerging grim-faced. 'What's the verdict?'

'There's an airship leaving in the morning for Ranski. Nothing before. I even tried to *bribe* them.' Fogu almost spat the word. 'I don't know how we're going to stay in town all day and night without encountering those Varkain.'

'They aren't interested in us,' Kohl said. The second Varkain had returned to his partner, but didn't appear particularly interested in the conversation. He kept sighing and glancing around, as if he'd rather be anywhere but there. 'We may be safe.'

'*May*? Is that truly a risk you wish to take? What if they decide to question everyone in town, resident or traveller? What then, my lord? It's too dangerous. We ought to be halfway across the sea by now!'

Kohl frowned, as the Ittallan and Varkain continued their argument.

'I've learned Taban Yul is under siege. Not only is there a sickness within the city, but enemies are at the gates.'

'Jato?'

'Most likely. The sickness, though? I wonder...'

Kohl couldn't shake the feeling that Arillians were the ones causing Linaria's strife. The Great War had ended generations ago, yet his people remained banished to the distant north. Today, Jato remained a threat, and even Aciel—though sealed in crystal—remained alive.

Perhaps it *would* be easier to fly, especially now there were Varkain in Gur Bano that would pose a threat. He still didn't like the fact they were there, putting him on the back foot. This was supposed to be a straightforward trip to the mage city of Berel, doing his bit to aid in Linaria's strife, before returning home.

Now, it seemed, the world had bigger plans than even he could fathom.

9

At some point after dawn, just as the birds began to sing, Amarah woke to an incessant hammering on her door.

Other than on her airship, there was only one place she knew she'd be able to snatch at least a few hours of uninterrupted sleep, and that was in Traego's base. She had the only key to her room, and the windows were so high and narrow, barely more than slits, that there was no chance of anyone being able to break in.

She was infuriated that someone had decided to wake her up before she was good and ready. 'What d'ya want?' Amarah pushed the sheets off and shoved her bare feet into her waiting boots. She grabbed the long dagger she kept under her bed, and stretched.

'Amarah, you have to see this *right now*!' It was Carav, and she could hardly get the words out over her panicked breathing.

Pulling her clothes on, Amarah marched to the door, slid the bolts open, and unlocked it with her key. Before she had a chance to fully pull the door open, Carav barged in and thrust a sheet of paper in her face.

'Wait, wait.' Amarah stepped back and adjusted her eye patch. 'I can't read, you know—'

'Look at the *picture*!' Carav pulled the door shut behind her. 'You see?'

Amarah blinked and held the paper out at arm's length while her groggy vision came into focus. It was a rudimentary sketch of a woman with short, messy hair, and an eyepatch. The clothes and boots seemed oddly familiar. 'That's...that's me?'

Carav nodded, her head moving so fast Amarah thought it might separate from her neck. 'The reward, Amarah! Look at the *reward*! He'll give *three thousand* crowns for you. *Alive*!'

Amarah didn't need to ask who *he* was. There was only one person in Linaria who would care about her—and what she'd done—enough to put a life-changing bounty like *that* on her head.

Even proof of Veynothi's tomb hadn't been that high.

Amarah shrugged and folded the paper over and over into a small square. She'd been expecting a bounty for escaping the palace. She'd been a prisoner of the king. 'He's wanted to kill me for ages. It's nothing new.'

'Maybe, but he hasn't told the whole world how much he'd pay to actually do it until now! You freed his sister! And the others! He blames *you* for that!' Carav was close to hysterical now.

'I freed myself! He locked me up, too. Shoulda killed me when he had the chance if he wanted to do it that badly. Dragons above, *breathe*, Carav! You'll pass out!'

The other woman swallowed, her multiple necklaces jingling as she took the paper back from Amarah and opened it up again, hands trembling as she read it. She moved her finger along each line of text as she read aloud, 'He's calling you a traitor to Linaria. Wants you brought in on charges of treason for kidnapping the princess! Your ships are to be shot down on sight—'

'My ships?'

Carav nodded, not lifting her eyes from the writ. 'Both of them. *Khanna* and the warship—which he also says is royal property and stolen from his palace. Anyone seen working with you is to be killed—not arrested! *Killed*! No bargaining, no leverage. He's *serious*, Amarah. You ever have a damned snake hunt you? It's ***not*** fun!'

Amarah hadn't realised Sapora would mark her down for kidnapping. She'd only expected a bounty for escaping the dungeon. Nothing more. She shrugged away the gnawing worry. 'Well, *Khanna* don't exist no more anyway. And if he don't know about *RaKhanna*, there's no problem, is there? I could fly right under his nose and he'd have no clue it was me.' Amarah rolled her eye and took the paper from Carav. She glanced down at it, but the writing was an incomprehensible mess of black squiggles that writhed around on the page. In one swift movement, she tore the sheet in half. 'There. That's better, ain't it?'

'You don't get it! These arrived in the island's shipment this morning. At dawn! By lunchtime, half the pirates in Estoria will be hunting you down for this!'

'Half the pirates in Estoria wanna work with me.'

Carav's eyes darted from left to right. 'Even *Traego* said he'd be interested!'

That made Amarah pause. Her oldest ally and closest friend? The man who'd called on her services for the Ark hunt? Whose crew she was now technically part of?

Carav looked at her with such sincerity that Amarah held her tongue. The usual rebuttal fell short as the gravity of Sapora's ludicrous bounty slowly settled in. Three thousand crowns?

He'd basically signed her death warrant.

Forget Estoria, anyone in Linaria who spotted a one-eyed woman would be looking to take their chances for a slice of that bounty.

'Surely not.' Her words were barely above a murmur, and she looked down at the ripped paper where it had settled on the floor. Nothing mattered above coin.

'Amarah, you're always talking about living a free life. Doing what you want. Maybe...maybe you should get away?'

'I'm *not* being pushed out of here. I won't let them!' Her voice came out as a bark in her sudden emotion. 'You tell Traego and anyone else that wants to have a go, they're welcome to try me. "Any treasure for whoever can get it," I know the rules of Estoria. But I ain't no treasure, and I ain't sitting around waiting to be plucked by someone who fancies some gold. The bounty is high because I'll *kill* anyone who fucking tries me!'

Carav shrank away from Amarah's outburst, but Amarah saw a flicker of a smile mixed in with the younger woman's concern.

'You deliver that message for me, right? And if I leave Estoria, it's 'cause I *want* to, not 'cause anyone made me. Got it?'

'Got it.' Carav leaned forward to pick up the ripped papers.

'That stays here. Tear up any of those posters you happen to find. Don't need anyone thinking they can get lucky.'

'Done.' But Carav didn't leave. 'Amarah...you think...you think you might need a hand on *RaKhanna*? 'Cause I could help, you know. Traeg's always got Antar or Oris or the others to help.'

Amarah bit her lip. Running away was how she'd always survived. But she'd be going back on her promise. She *had* said she'd help Isa. Offer her ships to aid the princess in her vendetta against Sapora, and help her retake her crown. She prided herself on keeping promises and repaying debts.

But that was before the bounty.

Wasn't it always everyone for themselves? Wasn't that how she'd survived so long?

It wasn't as if Isa *needed* her anymore. Not now she had four more ships from the other sky pirate captains at her disposal. Plus, she had all her followers. All those Ittallan were better than her. Far more useful.

And if Traego himself was interested in the bounty, none of his crew could be trusted. Unless she did something...

Maybe this was a sign from Rhea to get out of Estoria and make good on the promises she'd made—finding a Sevastos to free Moroda; hunting Jato down and getting her revenge. Maybe this was the opportunity she'd been waiting for.

Amarah didn't like how conflicted she felt, but she didn't have time to think it through. 'Maybe I might do that, then. Get your stuff. Meet me at *RaKhanna* if you want in.'

Carav nodded again, her wolfish smile making her seem far older than she was, before she darted out of the room, slamming the door shut behind her.

Amarah exhaled slowly and waited until she couldn't hear Carav's disappearing footsteps anymore. Most days, she was pleased with her choice to become a sky pirate. Her network of allies had come in useful on more than one occasion. Not just for herself, but for other friends of hers.

She smirked at the thought of having *friends*.

But today, she cursed Sapora, and she cursed those same sky pirates for loving gold more than loyalty.

She doubted Isa's stirring speeches and negotiations would keep them from seeing what three thousand crowns could buy. Probably their own island with private security to keep said mountains of treasure safe.

Thieving bastards.

Would they really trust a snake to pay an insane bounty like that over staying loyal to one of their own?

The icy chill in the pit of her stomach told her they would. Most would be daring enough to give it a try, at least. Look at how Cyd had died after the Ark, and that bounty had only been five hundred crowns.

So much for laying low in Estoria with Isa and enjoying some peace and quiet. It would be straight back to old times. Her against the world, as it always had been. Unless she could grab some allies to keep Traego off her back.

Her throat tightened suddenly.

This was a feeling she'd not had in a long while.

She squeezed her eye shut. 'I won't cry. I won't!'

Footsteps raced along outside, kicking up sand and snapping twigs as they hurried around. Such movement wasn't in itself unusual, but after Carav's warning, Amarah's paranoia told her that every pair of footsteps was another pirate coming to claim what gold they could get from her.

She *wouldn't* be bartered with or bargained for.

Carav hadn't had to warn her—she was part of Traego's troupe. Going against the captain's orders was tantamount to treason. And what about the rest of his crew? Antar was Traego's second-in-command, although they'd not been seeing eye-to-eye recently. He was a competent pilot, too, having flown her own warship. Amarah couldn't fly two ships at once—perhaps he could be bargained with if he got a warship out of the deal? Even flying her colours, a free ship, no-strings-attached, was nothing to sneeze at.

It might be enough to get him to leave Traego and side with her.

Judd, that soft touch, was a decent pilot, too. But she doubted he'd have the backbone to stand against Traego. Likewise, Malot was in Traego's pocket. Or bed. Probably both. She couldn't rely on her, either, even if they were from the same country.

Ernold and Farlan were both indebted to Traego, serving him until their contract expired.

Other than Antar, it only left the runts of Traego's crew. Carav and Oris.

And Isa? The princess trusted her. Owed her. She had dozens of Ittallan at her side, who quite literally would follow her to the ends of Linaria. But they were already entwining themselves in the sky pirates' pockets—if not Traego directly, then the other captains now that they had an accord.

Amarah had to get away with whoever she could before the noose closed on her.

Isa was the final piece in the mix. She'd promised the princess she'd help, and fleeing Estoria meant breaking her word. Turning tail and running before helping with Isa's campaign didn't sit well with Amarah, even if she was leaving to keep herself safe.

If Isa came with her, though...She wouldn't owe the princess anything for fleeing Estoria.

And if Traego was going to come after her for that bounty, she'd need back up. Especially considering Traego had *dragon's breath* and unlimited Samolen magic thanks to Malot.

Palom, though? Solvi?

She didn't know which allies she could talk to, or ask to join her. There were too many variables, and time was short. It wouldn't be long before the pirates would all be awake and looking for her. Carav's assessment that the pirates would be after her by lunchtime might be a little too generous.

Best thing was to get out now.

She needed to speak to Antar and Isa, as quickly as

possible. Even if she just spoke to Antar, they didn't need to leave at the same time. Getting Traego's main pilot on her side would weaken Traego's crew. She'd have more chance of getting away, and staying away with him on her side. They could set up a rendezvous point later on—she just needed to tell him when and where, and he could leave of his own accord. It would arouse less suspicion that way, too.

More than keeping her warship and gaining a competent pilot as an ally, she'd weaken Traego and his ability to chase. That said nothing of her *Thief's Ink*, the magical substance tattooed on her wrist that enabled Traego to track her down anywhere, but she'd cross that bridge when she came to it. Traego could be dealt with. All the other pirates would be too much.

Birds called out to one another outside and their cries wafted through the thin window. She chewed on the inside of her lip and ignored them, straining to hear approaching footsteps or voices—anything that might signal people coming closer to her cabin. Amarah packed the rest of her clothes in her satchel, shoving things in haphazardly, and grabbed whatever food she could. Dried fruit, crackers, a tin of peaches she was saving for a treat later. Once her room had been emptied of anything valuable, she ran her hands through her hair, and ensured she had a healthy collection of knives concealed about herself.

Satisfied, she grabbed her scythe, gave it a preemptive smack on the floor, then unlocked the door and stepped out into the blazing morning sunshine.

The few people who were gathered nearby were residents of the row of cabins—mostly used as holiday homes charged at extortionate prices—sat in the morning sun, sipping their coffees. She paid them no mind. There were plenty of rich Linarians who owned cabins out here, or travelled to stay in one owned by someone else. Just because

Estoria was where most thieves and pirates had their bases, didn't mean *everyone* was part of a troupe.

With all the turmoil in Linaria at the moment, Estoria had more visitors than ever. No doubt people were trying to hide away in paradise while the world sorted itself out. Amarah gave them a cursory glance and saw no-one of interest. Scratching her nose absently, she half-walked, half-marched down the pathway through the trees to Traego's main base.

She had to walk through Isa's makeshift camp to reach his lodge, and dozens of white and brown tents had been erected across the clearing. Even at this early hour, there was plenty of activity. Cookpots bubbled away, clothes hung out on several lines, and there was the tell-tale clink of a hammer on metal.

It wasn't a holiday for them.

'Amarah? What brings yeh here so early?' A woman stepped out from behind one of the larger tents, keeping herself out of sight while she was on watch. She was armed, but kept her sword in its sheath. It took Amarah a moment to recognise her—Isa's second-in-command, Kylos.

Amarah paused and glanced around. No pirates that she could see. 'Where's Isa?'

'Princess Isa is out at the moment. What's the matter?' Kylos asked, eyes alert and suspicious.

Solvi and Chyro exited the tent and stood by Kylos. The younger Ittallan stepped forward and embraced Amarah in a warm hug. 'Good morning, Amarah! Are you well? This place is *incredible*! The food, I've never seen the like! Estoria is—'

'Solvi. Don't yeh have work assigned this morning?' Kylos snapped, her eyes never leaving Amarah.

Solvi released Amarah and looked away, sheepish. 'Yes, Kylos. I was just saying—'

'Best yeh get on with it then. And yeh Chyro. Off with yeh both.'

There was no arguing with Kylos's authority, and the two Ittallan murmured their goodbyes and headed off into the thick Estorian jungle, looking back frequently.

Kylos rested her hands on her hips. 'Now. What's this about that's got yeh so worked up, Amarah? Any trouble we ought teh know about?'

Amarah considered coming clean about Sapora's bounty, but she didn't know if she could trust Kylos. The Ittallan was a decent fighter, for sure, but she didn't know her well enough to make a judgement. She was leaving Estoria to save her own skin. It would be like one of Isa's party defecting.

She doubted Kylos would approve. 'It's all good,' Amarah grunted. 'Tell Isa to come see me when she gets back. I'll be on *RaKhanna*. But not for long.'

Kylos narrowed her eyes slightly, then seemed to release any tension she'd been holding. 'I'll pass on the message for yeh.'

At least Kylos hadn't read the news yet. All the better.

She skirted around the edge of Traego's lodge and hurried through the trees towards where her airships lay. Amarah glanced around, looking for any signs of people trailing her. She hoped for a friendly face, but she knew at best she'd encounter no-one. Her heart thumped painfully as she made her way along. Every breath of wind could be an eager pirate following her, every snapped twig a precursor to an attack.

She tried to stay cautious and not let her paranoia get the best of her, but it was difficult.

In the distance, the sea crashed against the beaches and cliffs of the island's edge, and Amarah tasted salt on her lips.

Another home she'd been forced to run away from because of other people's twisted ideals of value.

Who knew how long it'd be before she'd be allowed to return? Perhaps she never would.

When she saw *RaKhanna* nestled among the trees, she breathed a sigh of relief. If the shoe was on the other foot, and *she* was after a sky pirate, their ship would be her first target. Thankfully no-one had thought to sabotage *RaKhanna* yet.

She'd be able to get away.

After giving *RaKhanna* a quick once over, Amarah headed over to her warship, and grinned when she noticed Antar sewing up one of the torn side sails. A spot of luck. She clapped her hands once to announce herself, and he looked down with a jump.

'She ready to fly?' Amarah asked.

'Yeah, just wanted to sort out the ripped edge. Annoyed me the whole flight back, kept shaking the whole ship.'

'Get loaded up with food and weapons, as much as you can take.'

Thankfully Antar was on his feet in an instant, all smiles gone. 'Where you going?'

He hadn't heard the bounty either, it seemed. '*We* are going away for a little trip. Got some scores to settle. Promises to keep. And some good old fashioned revenge. Might be we give Isa a bit of a head-start too, if I can find her. Unless you'd rather stay working for Traeg, flying *Otella* when he lets you.'

Antar frowned. 'Amarah...What you suggesting...?'

'Look, d'you wanna fly that warship full time or not? I'm kind of in a hurry, so—'

'Yeah, I want it.'

That was all it took. 'Good. Get the ship loaded. Meet me at...' She frowned, suddenly wondering where it would be safe to rendezvous. It couldn't be too far, couldn't be too obvious. 'Esta Cona. The small town. You know it?'

'That's in the wetlands? Near where we stopped before?'

'Yup. There's an inlet, maybe five leagues north of the town. Don't tell no-one where you're going. I'll be there by dark.'

Antar debated with himself for several seconds before pocketing his sewing needle and thread. 'Anything else I need to bring?'

Amarah had already started back up the path. She *had* to find Isa. At least then she'd have done everything she could.

She yelled over her shoulder, 'Dress warm.'

~

'Isa where in Rhea's name are you…' Amarah muttered to herself. She didn't have the time to waste looking for the princess, yet she couldn't leave without at least speaking with her.

Amarah had searched for the best part of an hour, and with the sun high in the sky and more people out than ever, she knew her time had all but run out.

She looked skywards, but couldn't see the black eagle that meant Aetos watched. Then, realisation hit her. The island was a jungle paradise, with trees stretching throughout the land until the sea, where it bloomed into sandy beaches or rocky cliffs.

Isa could shift into a wildcat. She'd give ten crowns that the princess was up a tree somewhere.

No wonder she'd not been able to find her.

'You look lost.'

Amarah whirled around at the voice, scythe raised, when she realised it was Palom.

He'd made a small clearing for himself among the thick

jungle foliage, axe in hand, splitting logs of wood in front of him. 'I thought you knew this place. This is home for you?'

'I know it well enough. I'm looking for Isa. Have you seen her?'

Palom lined up the axe, took a swing, and split another log. 'Princess Isa? No, I have not seen her today. Why?'

For all his faults, Palom was a formidable fighter. In his tiger form, there was little that could stand against him. An ally she'd lost and found—she didn't want to lose him again if she didn't have to. 'Kinda need to talk to her. Now. Where's *Leillu*? Can your dragon fly? Can she find her?'

Palom shrugged but didn't answer until he'd split the next log. '*Leillu* is not dog. *Leillu* is *Leillu*. She can fly, yes but I am not sure about asking to find Princess Isa.'

Amarah's shoulders slumped. 'Well, tell Isa to come to *RaKhanna* as soon as you see her, okay?'

'I can ask Princess Isa for you, but I am not ordering her about.'

Thwack.

Another log split.

Amarah scowled. 'You can stay and split logs all day if you want. I'm heading off. Away from Estoria. Coming?'

Thwack.

'I said to Traego I would split these logs for him. Apparently the artisans of Sereth use Estorian wood for their wares. He is paying me six florins for this pile.' He gestured to a veritable mountain of logs beside him. Although he was strong, that amount of work would take him hours to get through.

Karvou, the young Ittallan Palom seemed to have adopted, appeared from the trees with another armful of logs. He grinned broadly at Amarah. 'Good morning! Want ta give me a hand with these?'

Scratch that. It would take Palom all day if the wood pile kept growing.

Palom said, 'Karvou. Go see Traego when you are finished. See if he has more work.'

The young Ittallan dropped his bundle with the rest and returned to the jungle, no doubt to fetch more.

Damn. She'd have liked to have Palom with her again, especially after everything that had happened with Lathri. Guilt twinged, tightening her stomach. 'You sure you don't wanna come? You don't have to chop logs all day with me!'

'I do not mind. Is good work.'

Thwack.

'That young lad can come, too. I don't mind, long as he keeps outta my way.'

Thwack.

'Karvou works with me here.'

Stupid, stubborn tiger. She didn't want to openly talk about the bounty, not when anyone could be listening. She shifted her weight from foot to foot. 'If you change your mind, you got less than an hour.' She'd tried. Amarah turned around and almost tripped over *Leillu* with her next step. 'Dragons above!' She stumbled, tried to correct her step, and ended up in a heap on the sandy ground. '*Leillu*!'

Palom set down the axe and walked over. 'This is not *Leillu*.'

'What...? But it...' Amarah muttered, rubbing her eye. 'It's skin!' She was back on her feet in an instant.

'Yes, *Leillu* has been very slow recently. Sleeping much. She has shed skin. See?' Palom beamed like a proud father.

Amarah swallowed hard as a sudden shadow blotted out the sun trickling through the thick canopy above, and *Leillu* fluttered down, her broad wings shaking the leaves and vines on the trees and foliage below. Amarah took a few steps back to make room for her—*Leillu* seemed a third bigger than she had been just last night.

Previously, she'd been the size of a boarhound. Now, she would rival a small horse, and that didn't even include her growing wingspan. Her horns seemed thicker, too, with a slight curve that matched the dragon's neck. *Leillu's* scales had shifted from sea-blue to bright cobalt, more vivid than before, and speckled with flecks of pale green and silver that shimmered when the sun caught them.

At any other time, Amarah would have been curious to discover more, but she knew the other pirates would be looking for her soon—if they weren't already—and she needed to get in the air where it was safe. 'Like I said, I'm off. I don't know if I'll be coming back here, to tell the truth. You know where *RaKhanna* is if you want to come with me. Might be fighting Arillians...'

She saw Palom's eye twitch, and she raced away without another word. Perhaps she'd get him to come with her by playing on his dislike of Arillians. She knew he hadn't forgiven Kohl for what he'd done to cause Anahrik and Eryn's deaths, and any sort of revenge was something he'd probably be interested in taking up.

At least, she hoped.

Deciding to save herself, Amarah raced back through the trees to her airships. Antar was nowhere to be seen, but she'd expected that. He'd be along when he could—that wouldn't slow her down. Carav wanted to come as well, so she'd give her a few more minutes if she wasn't already hiding on board.

Amarah clambered up the steps carved into *RaKhanna's* side and heaved herself onto the deck with a small grunt. 'Oh! Isa! You got my message then!' Amarah was shocked to see the princess already on deck, standing by the railing, peering over the edge.

At her voice, the princess turned around. She opened her mouth to say something in response, froze for an instant, then let out a scream.

It was all the warning Amarah had before a small sack smelling strongly of fish wrapped around her head and tightened at her throat.

10

As morning dragged on, Palom continued to split wood for Traego, hoping to do more than asked and earn a handsome profit on the sky pirate's initial offer.

'You see, *Leillu*? You keep word. You do hard day's work. This is how it should be.' He looked over at the young dragon as he dusted off his hands.

The dragon chirped and flapped her wings, but Palom had no idea if the creature really understood what he said, or if she just enjoyed the sound of his voice.

'And best part of hard work? You know what this is?' Palom asked, reaching into his pocket and pulling out a florin. He waved it in front of *Leillu*. 'You get to enjoy nice drink. Dark ale is good. It lines the belly and keeps core strong.' To show what he meant, Palom thwacked his stomach with his hand.

Leillu snapped her teeth together and let out a small flame.

'Exactly.'

He'd sent Karvou away to report to Traego, in case the

sky pirate had any other work for him that day. While he had the opportunity to earn himself a little gold, it seemed foolish not to take it.

Solvi and Chyro were hard workers, if a little distracted, and he couldn't ignore how the young captain—former captain—looked at his niece when the sun caught her. And although Karvou was barely more than a boy, he was eager to help and never seemed to tire.

Princess Isa had struck up an accord with four of the sky pirate captains, and her plans would be set in motion within the next few days.

Although his heart was heavy at the loss of Lathri, the world seemed to be straightening itself out.

Only Amarah's sudden nervousness troubled him. But the woman was a crook and a criminal, and she had no doubt got herself into a new heap of trouble. He would have gone with her, truth be told, if he was not already committed to his work. Once he was finished, he'd see if Amarah was still here, and help out if he could. Her desire to leave immediately was probably a ploy to get him to go with her right then and there, and he wasn't going to fall for it.

'Ah, there you are, Palom! Traego told me I'd find you out here.' It was Odi, the son of the Gal Etra Archigo, and perhaps the most senior ranking Ittallan out of the whole camp, save Princess Isa herself. Odi had been the defacto leader of the convoy of Ittallan who travelled to the capital city. Palom respected the older Ittallan—who had to be in his late fifties—especially for the sound advice he imparted.

Odi said, 'Back at work so soon?'

'I am just helping out Traego,' Palom replied. He lowered his head in respectful greeting as Odi shuffled across the clearing. His long, grey and purple robe dragged on the ground behind him and had picked up all manner of dust and debris, including a thorned vine that had snagged in the fabric.

'I must say, I'm not much of a fan of this intense heat. I can hardly remember the last time we even *saw* the ground back home!'

'Gal Etra is on edge of Arillian Everwinter,' Palom commented, explaining the weather difference. He picked up the axe and inspected the blade to ensure it hadn't warped after the morning's slog. 'Are you okay?'

'I've been looking for Princess Isa. We were to have a discussion this morning after everyone had rested about contacting the other Archigo. But she didn't arrive for the meeting.'

Palom frowned. Why was everyone suddenly looking for the princess? 'She may have gone for long walk. Is big jungle here. Easy to lose time.'

Odi shrugged. 'We've seldom little time to lose. So much for building our resistance against Sapora here. With our leader...unavailable, what are we supposed to do? We're meant to fly in less than three days.'

'Princess Isa will have her reasons for being away, I am sure. She will be back soon. We must carry on her work. Have other messages written to send to Ittallan all across Val Sharis.'

'Oh? And what might these messages say?'

'Sapora will not save you from dragons or Jato's Arillians. Princess Isa will protect you. Come to Estoria.' It felt incredibly simple when he spelled it out like that, but somehow, Odi didn't seem to cheer up.

Odi sighed. 'When I learned that...Lathri was gathering everyone in Taban Yul, it was a covert resistance. A few Ittallan who didn't like the way things were going. Wanted to get away from Varkain who'd taken over their homes or businesses, away from the fear. Now, it's a full-fledged rebellion. If Sapora doesn't step down, we'll be at war. So many people have been hurt. So many deaths.'

Palom rubbed the back of his neck wearily. 'This *is* war. People die. You know this.'

'And if it's all for naught?'

'Why would it be? You are here. The Ittallan are here. More will join.' He looked over at *Leillu*, who scraped her claws up and down a tree like a cat. 'I am here, too. Whatever is needed, we will stand behind Princess Isa. She is our queen. If that is here. If that is in Val Sharis. Wherever she commands.'

Odi smiled then. 'Well, it's a start. I'll work on getting the letters written ready for Princess Isa to approve and seal. We'll start with some of the smaller towns and villages, the ones where people can move more freely. Esta Cona, Gur Bano, places like that. Where the Arichigo are already friendly.'

'Is good idea. What can I do?'

Odi let out a long, slow breath. 'There'll be plenty of fighting to come. I can feel it. We'll need your forge and a supply of weapons and armour. Your very best.'

'If Traego can give me place to work, is no problem. I can help arm us.'

'What about the *Valta Forinja*? Can you remake those?'

'No.' Palom wasn't going to entertain that idea. Not after what he'd been through. And even if he wanted to, he no longer had the shard of Sevastos stone—he'd used up his meagre supply when he made them before. He'd need to travel to Berel and somehow obtain more—an impossibility, now the scholars knew what he'd done with the shard.

'If it's resources you need, don't forget, we have access to ships. As long as these pirate captains keep their word, of course—'

'No more *Valta Forinja*. I'm not making these. No special weapons.'

Odi pursed his lips for a moment. 'What about the ones you already made? Did you sell them? If we can bring them back, we'd have a huge advantage and—'

'Stop, Odi. I told you, I do not have my sword anymore—'

'But you made *others*, didn't you? Could we not call upon them? Surely you can see how much it would help Princess Isa's cause. Why, the Varkain might even take one look at them and throw down their arms, and save the need for any fighting at all.'

'*Or* they will launch the Arks at us and it will be like old war all over again! This should not be battle of who has bigger teeth. Everything will be destroyed this way. Sapora already has Veynothi, do not forget.'

'But the *Valta Forinja* might match her power!'

Palom snarled. 'I have said *no*, Odi! You may be son of Archigo, but do not test me with this.'

Odi stepped back, his eyes wide in the face of Palom's fury.

Ignoring him, Palom said, 'I need steel to make weapons. I will speak with Traego about supplies. With steel and wood, I can forge again.'

'Yes, Palom, of course. When I get back to the lodge, I'll speak with Captain Traego about getting you set up.' Odi bowed his head, then turned on his heel, walking back into the trees with more speed than Palom had seen him ever muster before.

He sighed, his heart heavy. Lathri had known the *Valta Forinja* were *emonos*. Perhaps he did too, deep in his heart of hearts. But he'd been absorbed by its curse and pushed everyone away.

It was too late for him. He didn't deserve redemption.

If he'd been with Lathri, perhaps she'd never have been arrested and tortured by the snakes. She'd certainly not have died saving Amarah.

He couldn't be angry with Amarah, though. Nor Isa. He'd gladly give his life for his princess, as would any of her other followers. And Amarah had clearly changed—she'd thrown away her *Valta Forinja* after learning what it was doing to her.

Anahrik's daggers were buried with him in the mausoleum in Taban Yul. And Morgen? Well, there was no reason why Morgen wouldn't still have his sword, but he was half a world away and had no part in Isa's cause. It would be cruel to drag him back into the conflict.

The only other *Valta Forinja* in existence were the originals in Berel University, and the scholars would never in their right mind allow Odi—or anyone, for that matter—to take them and use them in war.

The time of the *Valta Forinja* was over. They needed to stop relying on gods and monsters and fight for themselves, before they destroyed Linaria in their desperation.

'That seemed harsh,' Solvi said, 'poor Odi.'

Palom glanced overhead to see his niece sitting on a tree branch, legs dangling. 'He was pushing.'

'I know that.' She leapt from her perch and landed on the ground beside him, ignoring all the wood shavings and dust. 'But you could have been nicer about it.'

Palom shook his head. He adored Solvi, but very often she said something naive that reminded him of just how young she was. It wasn't fair that she'd been dragged into this war, not when she could be safe at home. 'Solvi, when are you going back home?'

'When...the war is over, I think?'

'You should not have left Sol.'

'I wanted to help Princess Isa...and Lathri.'

'I know, and you did. I was surprised to see you in Taban Yul. More surprised to hear you had been friends with Lathri and her people.'

Solvi giggled as *Leillu* flew around her, knocking her back with the strength in her wings as she darted up and down, side to side.

Quite what he was going to do with the dragon, Palom didn't know. Would *Leillu* one day decide she felt the rage of the other dragons in Linaria and attack them? Would she decide to return to others of her kind? Steal away in the night without so much as a look back?

'She's like a duck,' Solvi said, racing in circles in the small patch of green beside the stack of neatly split logs, arms trailing as *Leillu* chased her.

'*Leillu* is dragon.'

'Yes, but...Ducklings follow their mothers when they hatch, don't they? Wherever she goes, they go. It's the same with *Leillu*?'

He hadn't considered that before. Hadn't given it much thought at all.

Palom had been in an extremely low place, and *Leillu* had helped pull him out of it with her utter innocence and dependability on him. 'Maybe there is likeness. They both come from eggs.'

Solvi sat cross-legged, her bare legs caked in tree sap and mud, but she didn't seem to notice. *Leillu* came to sit by her. She stroked the top of the dragon's head with the back of her hands, and *Leillu* chirped.

Overhead, two warships floated past, the leaves above swaying in the wake of their passing. Palom wondered whether the sky pirates had tightened their security after the Arillian attack. Surely none of them wanted a repeat of it.

He was just grateful that he, Solvi, Princess Isa, and the

others hadn't been caught up in it. If they'd reached Estoria a day or two earlier, they could well have been blown apart, too.

He growled low as he thought of Kohl's betrayal. Amarah hadn't said anything, but it was clear he'd been with her for a time, and had been in Estoria during the attacks. If he'd turned traitor a second time, then he deserved to rot.

An answering growl echoed through the trees.

Palom and Solvi jumped to their feet, and even *Leillu* hissed.

'Solvi...' Palom said, keeping his eyes on the surrounding jungle. He definitely hadn't imagined that snarl. Whatever it was, it sounded enormous.

'Palom! Solvi!' Karvou burst into the clearing, his face pale. 'There's...there's something...I don't know—'

'Arillians again?' Solvi asked.

Karvou skidded to a halt, almost toppling over the stacks of wood. 'No it's...I've never seen anything like it! Some sort of monster!'

'Monster?' Solvi repeated. 'Calm down. Are you sure it's just not some animal you've not seen before?'

Chyro appeared from the clearing's other side, a sack held over his shoulder. Bars of bent and twisted metal protruded from the opening. 'Traego wants these straightening out, Palom. Said he'd give half a crown if—' He stopped mid-sentence, taking in Karvou's terrified expression. 'What's happened?'

Solvi hugged Karvou, trying to calm him down, but the young lad trembled, tears trickling down his cheeks. 'He says there's something in the jungle. Some monster.'

'Monster? Should we check it out?' Chyro dropped the sack and hurried over to the other Ittallan, immediately focussing his attention on the potential threat.

'Karvou, maybe you should return to lodge for rest of day. Jungles are not safe for young Ittallan without *meraki*,' Palom said, trying to figure out the best way to keep him safe and calm.

Karvou sniffed and wiped his nose. He couldn't be more than a year away from coming into his *meraki*, but he'd also grown up in a tiny, remote village at the end of the world. Anything normal to the rest of Linaria would probably terrify him.

Palom sighed, trying to remind himself why he'd agreed to look after the young lad, and wondering if he could find Jek among Isa's followers and have the trader keep watch.

'Maybe...will you come with me, Palom?' Karvou asked, his bottom lip trembling.

'Of course.'

Before they could take a single step, Solvi cried out, 'Hey, *Leillu*, wait!' She raced off.

Palom glanced up in time to see a flash of blue as *Leillu* disappeared into the thick foliage, Solvi just a few steps behind.

'Solvi!'

Nothing.

'Solvi?'

He stepped away from Karvou and Chyro, and leaned forward to listen.

'SOLVI!'

Birds leapt into the air at his roar, but his niece did not call to him or return.

The low growl rumbled again, making Palom's decision for him. 'Karvou. Chryo. With me!'

Chyro grabbed Karvou without hesitation, and they raced through the trees.

Palom followed the fading sound of Solvi's footsteps churning up the litter of the jungle floor, heedless to grasping vines or stones and rocks in his way. Adrenaline coursed through him, powering on every step through the deeping trees, towards the growling as it grew louder.

11

Without Roke trailing his every move, Tacio sauntering in with an insult or jibe, and with Isa missing, Sapora felt alone and empty for the first time since his errantry. The palace had begun to get busy again, with Goldstones visiting, viewing the galleries, dining in the ballrooms, and Koraki arranging palace tours. It was practically back to normal—nobility visited, bringing gold that would bolster the royal treasury, despite the fact that a significant part of Taban Yul still needed repairs following the battle between Imperial ships and his Sevastos. Considering airships leaving or arriving into the city had been drastically reduced due to Jato's storm, the Goldstones didn't seem to notice. Many had their own private stashes of supplies, and enough gold to pay the most desperate couriers to risk life and limb to bring in treats from beyond the city. Even though Sapora utterly despised the raven, Koraki was the head steward, and had been in that role most of his adult life. He did most of the work revolving around the palace and council, and it was his job to ensure the royal coffers remained healthy.

It meant Sapora had one less thing to worry about.

At least with Tacio out of his way, he could think clearly and act without being second-guessed every minute of the day.

It was amusing how much time Sapora had spent cooped up in the palace, mocked and detested by those who surrounded him. Either fawning Goldstones who acted subservient out of fear, or Tacio's Cerastes who considered him a temporary inconvenience, not worthy of the throne.

Idly, he scratched the back of his hand, the vein pulsing dark and angry against his grey skin. The Valendrin hadn't told him what to expect when he'd released Veynothi, but Sapora wanted to have a talk with him *before* he resurrected Malashash. If his arm was going to fall off should he release a second Ark, he might reconsider his approach.

Then again, the Arks hadn't been seen in generations. It was possible that even though the Valendrin knew the ritual, he didn't know about the after-effects of releasing Veynothi. The blood mage wasn't all-knowing.

Thankfully, Sapora didn't *feel* any different. His senses hadn't been dulled, and physically he was just as capable as before. Admittedly, he slept little and ate less, but he could survive for months on limited sustenance. That in itself wasn't out of the ordinary.

It was the mark on his skin that worried him. It had to mean *something*, and it was definitely linked to Veynothi—having appeared only after she'd awoken.

He made his way down a winding flight of stairs, descending one of the palace's many towers. As he followed the familiar paths, he remembered his childhood—racing up and down the steep stairs with his sister, trying to see who was fastest.

Where *was* Isa?

Had she willingly run away?

Had she been tricked into leaving by Amarah and the

other sky pirates? There had to be some simple, reasonable explanation for her behaviour. They were in this together—surely she wouldn't have thrown it all away?

Would she?

Whatever Tacio accused, Sapora and Isa had had a plan, a goal. Things hadn't run smoothly—none of them could have predicted Aciel's siege, the Arillian attack, and now the dragons' wrath. But he was doing everything he could to mitigate those threats. Surely she could understand that? He'd even told her when she'd pressed him for an explanation.

It was why he needed to turn his attention to Malashash. One Ark free was an incredible accomplishment, but he needed to do more. And that would be tricky with Aciel's will poisoning his city, and Jato's storm siege outside limiting travel in and out.

The Sevastos detested him, but Sapora didn't care. The dragon was bound by its own magic, and Sapora was simply the one who'd used that thread.

If Malashash was much the same as Veynothi, he'd have his work cut out keeping both Arks in line. He had the Sevastos to help, but they were still tenuous holds on some of Linaria's greatest powers. If his veins were anything to go by, the strain of balancing everything was already starting to take its toll on his body.

Sapora straightened his jacket and ensured any blemishes on his skin were fully covered.

There was no need to add the topics the palace staff gossiped about.

He had business to attend to.

The Valendrin had taken up residence in one of the guest suites on the third floor of the palace. He'd originally wanted to be closer to the ground—under it, actually—but Sapora couldn't be bothered to waste time traipsing up and down dozens of stairs every time he wanted to speak with the blood mage.

He knew the Valendrin—like most of the Varkain working for him—wanted to be back in the tunnels of Sereth. Even *he* did, in some strange way. However, with the way things were in the world, they were needed above ground until all the immediate threats had been dealt with.

Sapora had never taken much interest in blood magic, had always thought it an archaic relic of the Varkain that had endured over generations—like keeping thralls and the fighting pits. Now, he could see its true use. If only the Valendrin would speak to him with the respect he showed Vasil.

Pairs of guards stood along the corridors and at most of the doors where the public were not permitted. Mostly these were at hallways leading to the airship hangar, the dungeons, any of the council's personal quarters, as well as the council chamber itself. Sapora had wanted to close the palace library to the public, too, but apparently that would tarnish his image, so he'd had to permit more roaming than he was entirely comfortable with.

It meant dealing with them every time he moved through the palace, and he curled his lip as today was no different.

Several Goldstones lowered their heads as Sapora passed, many offering their condolences on Princess Isa's kidnap and their certainty that he would put it to rights. A few even congratulated him on Veynothi's release—though it surprised him that the news had travelled *so* quickly. He'd only notified the council the previous day.

The scent of their oils and perfumes reminded him of Tacio, and he hid his grimace as best he could behind the high collar of his jacket. Without Roke keeping them back with a stern gaze, many bowed and tried to hurry forward to grasp his hand, or even present him with gifts. 'Yes, yes. Much appreciated. I have urgent business to which I must attend. Please, excuse me.' Sapora sidestepped the small gathered crowd, ignoring their proffered gifts, and continued down the hall as quickly as he could without running.

He was so focussed on getting away from the gathered visitors that he almost missed the Valendrin.

The blood mage stood alone halfway down the hallway —the Goldstones giving him a wide berth, even with his hood up. He peered through the massive floor to ceiling windows, seeming to admire the view of Taban Yul below. Without pulling his attention from the window, he said, 'Nothing speaks the truth like our blood.'

At first, Sapora thought he'd misheard. He quickly crossed the space between them and peered down at the city, expecting to see violence of some sort.

The section below was part of the Lower Quarter. Street beggars tended to congregate on the roads leading to the palace—the unguarded ones—pleading for alms from Goldstones and visitors. Ramshackle markets sprung up on a daily basis, vendors selling souvenirs from the palace or artefacts purported to be from various past members of Ittallan or Varkain royalty. Most of it was counterfeit, and the Imperial Guard were always kept busy shooing them off and issuing fines, but the opportunists could earn so much money within a couple of hours that most risked the fines—or even the sharp side of a spear.

Although the hallway Sapora stood on had to be four storeys high, he could clearly see the antics of the Lower Quarter below. People bustled across the cobblestones, calling to one another or gesturing wildly to be seen over the hubbub.

Sapora wasn't sure why the Valendrin had spoken, and

was about to ask for clarification, when the crowd below parted.

Two Cerastes in gleaming black-blue armour marched down the road approaching the palace, grasping a large sack between them. From the way they struggled, the bundle held some weight. Ittallan and Varkain both moved aside for the elite caste, whispering and pointing once the Cerastes had passed.

'You know what they carry?' Sapora asked, though he kept his gaze on the street below.

'Indeed,' the Valendrin replied, 'you and your people speak of a poison in the city. Who better to study it than one such as I? You did not come to me with this problem, so I thought I would make a request and see what I could do to assess the situation for myself.'

Sapora fought to keep his temper with the interfering blood mage. There was no poison in the city. It was simply the fable they'd spread to keep the citizens from panicking at the knowledge of Aciel still being alive. Apparently, the Valendrin hadn't received the message, and had decided to meddle.

'I'd appreciate you *not* taking these matters into your own hands. I have the issue under control. I need your assistance with the Arks. Nothing more.'

'Do you have it under control? I heard from Captain Tethkari this morning that another twelve dead were discovered on the floor of a tavern, and over thirty more had been locked up at a healer's station for fear they'd end up much the same way.' The Valendrin's tone held the same condescension Tacio and the Cerastes used.

Sapora *had* missed the report, but the numbers didn't surprise him. It was much the same every day, and only affected the city's poorer sections, which didn't affect anything in the palace. It was also why he was working so hard to find the next Ark and put a stop to this madness.

The Valendrin took advantage of Sapora's silence. 'Considering the panic rippling through the dregs of the city with Arillians looming overhead, I thought it might be pertinent to see if I could provide some...enlightenment to this... sickness. I know you care more for your Goldstones than those who live in Taban Yul's underbelly. But *they* are the ones who are dying. What if it spreads to your richer citizens, hmm? Who knows how this alleged poison works.'

It was clear that the blood mage didn't believe a word of what was spouted about a sickness in the city, and Sapora couldn't blame him for that. One didn't become Vasil's personal mage without a great deal of intellect. He only wished the Valendrin had a little more shrewdness. 'Yes. I see you meant well. But as I have said before, you are best suited for the Ark hunt. *That* is what you will focus on.'

The blood mage turned to him and lowered his hood, revealing the thin, pale flesh clinging to his skull. In a withering voice, he said, 'I have been alive almost four hundred years. Longer than most Arillians. You are the first...Varkain to make such significant changes.'

Sapora ignored the Valendrin's hesitation. 'You speak as if change is a bad thing.'

'Is it?'

'I fail to see how sitting in the dark, never moving forward, while Linaria despises us is of any value.' Sapora glared at the creature before him. A shell of a Varkain, twisted beyond all reckoning. The blood mage had no lips, no hair, and skin so thin it looked like it might evaporate. Every inch of him had been drained to boost his own power. Dark veins snaked up his face and hands—no longer grey, just a translucent, sickly skin that barely clung to his bones.

Sapora's fingers twitched and he thought of the veins on his own hands.

'Ah. Well you are young, and wish to make a name for yourself. It is the same of Prince Tacio. In time, you will see that the Varkain way of life is what is best: leaving Linaria to its fate while we endure.'

Sapora wasn't sure he liked the Valendrin's tone. 'You dislike the sun?'

'Yes. We are not Ittallan, who need to parade outside and adorn themselves in all this garish materialistic vanity.' He opened his arms, gesturing not just to the palace but the entire city. 'We are more civilised than all this braying and bellowing at one another.'

Sapora could understand the sentiment. It was something he'd heard from his father and brother one time or another, not to mention it was the general feeling of many Varkain in Sereth.

But, as was clear from those who had made the trip to Taban Yul, enlisted in the Imperial Guard, or taken up work elsewhere in Val Sharis, it was not a sentiment shared by all. Why silence their needs when other Varkain wished to hide in their tunnels until the end of time?

He certainly didn't.

It was something he'd always been made to feel bad about—that he longed to go to the surface so much because he was half-Ittallan. But that wasn't true at all. Some people simply enjoyed it. It didn't make them any less—he was still a *naja*. A king. And he had still resurrected the first Ark.

That would never have been accomplished by hiding in Sereth.

The Valendrin cleared his throat with an irritated cough.

'Oh, I do apologise. So many things to keep track of, you know,' Sapora said. The blood mage might have been old and respected, but Sapora was a king. He enjoyed having people wait on *him*, for once.

The Valendrin hissed low. 'Well perhaps you should delegate more, instead of *burdening* yourself with countless irrelevant tasks.'

That time, Sapora couldn't ignore the blatant rudeness. 'When I wish for your counsel, I shall ask for it. As for now, you are ignoring the one task I have assigned you—breaking Malashash's seal.'

The Valendrin sniffed and turned his attention back to the window.

There was no sign of the two Cerastes and the sack they carried any more, and the crowds had resumed as if nothing had passed.

Sapora glanced over his shoulder as the Goldstones were ushered away by the palace stewards. He was alone with the blood mage for a moment. With a sigh, he loosened the button at his cuff and pulled his left sleeve down, revealing his wrist. The thin black line on his skin poked out from under his glove, which Sapora pulled off with his free hand. 'Additionally, I would like you to explain this. I first noticed it on the flight back to the palace after our trip to Povmar.'

Credit to the Valendrin, he didn't offer another snide remark or thinly veiled microaggression. He narrowed his eyes and took Sapora's hand in his own claws, peering down at the skin.

Sapora shivered at his touch; the Valendrin's flesh was as cold as a corpse.

'Hmm. Blood magic often leaves its mark,' the Valendrin muttered, gently touching Sapora's vein with a clawed finger, 'I have not seen this before. It must have something to do with your link to Veynothi, but I cannot say what.'

That didn't inspire confidence. 'Will it get worse?'

'It may grow if you release more Arks. Blood Magic is powerful, and there is always a price. Otherwise there would be thousands of blood mages.'

That went without saying. But he already had the Sevastos under his control. He'd thought that would have mitigated any penance to pay for Veynothi—or any of the other Arks considering they were so intrinsically linked.

A ripple of laughter flowed through him for a split second—the dragon's amusement. Sapora clamped down on the thread that connected them and silenced the god.

This was no laughing matter.

'Are you quite all right, King Sapora?' the Valendrin asked, still clutching his hand.

'Perfectly fine,' Sapora said through gritted teeth. He pulled his hand from the Valendrin and covered it with his glove. 'Malashash is the next Ark. I know his location. You will accompany me to his tomb and assist with the second resurrection.'

'Is that wise? After what you just showed me...shouldn't you consider resting? Perhaps a brief stay in Sereth would—'

'My King! Lord Valendrin!'

Sapora whirled around to see the two Cerastes from the street, escorted by a Varkain of the palace guard in gold and red livery. They hauled their bundle with them, which was definitely the size and shape of an adult body. Someone who had died at Aciel's influence, if the Valendrin's cryptic words were anything to go by. 'You didn't touch the body, did you?' Sapora asked, fumbling with the button on his sleeve.

'No, my liege. We wore gloves at all times and only touched their clothes,' one Cerastes replied—she was taller than her partner, with silver-blonde hair that she wore loose and long, and she looked down her nose at him.

It was a look Sapora was more than familiar with, yet

now he had the jade crown, she couldn't voice her thoughts. Then again, these were his brother's soldiers, and she probably resented having to report to him while Tacio was out of the palace.

'Where are we to take it?' asked the second Cerastes.

'My room would be suitable. There is a large table, and I have my books and tools there,' the Valendrin said.

Sapora shuddered to think what tools they might be, but he couldn't very well send the Cerastes away now. 'I will accompany you.' At the Valendrin's frown, Sapora added, 'I am most interested in observing you work. If it wouldn't be a distraction?'

He knew the blood mage could not state the king was a distraction, even if it were the truth, and he savoured the fleeting panic and indignation that flittered over the Valendrin's face.

'Of course not. Please. This way.'

~

HAVING DISMISSED the Cerastes the moment they delivered the body, Sapora relaxed a little. Only the Valendrin knew of his mark. His weakness. He wanted to keep it that way for as long as possible, however futile it may be.

Sapora hadn't actually been into the rooms he'd assigned his blood mage, and his immediate thought was never to return. The main room was generously sized, with a large window facing the palace gardens—trailing ivy draped over the window and adjoining walls. A large fireplace commanded the room's far wall, atop which various daggers, knives, and small bladed tools were piled up. Two tall, thin glass vials sat in metal rings, and an indiscernible brown substance coated the bottom of both.

In the room's centre, a large stone and wood table sat,

taking up the majority of the space. Despite the flagstone floor and vaulted ceiling, the room was hot and stuffy, as if a bonfire burned low every evening without ventilation.

The scent of blood, ash and sulphur choked the air, and Sapora immediately opened the window to let in a breeze. He coughed, despite himself, and the blood mage let out a chuckle.

'I forget you are unused to the scent of home.'

'The tunnels of Timin Rah smell nothing like this!' Sapora leaned into the open window and sucked in a deep breath.

'To me they do. This is the smell of my work. Of *true* Varkain power.'

Sapora let out a low hiss. It was unbecoming of royalty, but the stench of the room was too thick to ignore. It made his stomach turn.

'Now. Let me see what has happened to the unfortunate people of this city.'

Sapora watched as the Valendrin slowly undid the ropes and carefully peeled back the sack, revealing a portly man of middle years. He was stiff as a board, his skin a sickly shade of blue-green, his bristly beard stuck out at odd angles. An Ittallan, of course, but beyond that, Sapora couldn't discern very much. There was no scent to him any more, other than death. 'I wouldn't touch him if I were you.'

'He is dead. There is no threat.'

'What if there's some lingering curse? People who touched others who were...*infected* often went mad themselves.'

'I don't know about a curse, but lingering effects are worrying.' The Valendrin stepped away from the large table and approached the fireplace, one finger on his chin as he surveyed his array of tools. 'This, I think.' He plucked a slender blade with a small but vicious hook on the end, one of the two glass vials, and returned to the dead Ittallan.

'What are you doing?' Sapora asked. He knew it was a stupid, obvious question, but morbid curiosity was getting the better of him. Already, he leaned away from the window and towards the table, instead of leaving the blood mage to his work. 'You mustn't harm yourself. I need you for Malashash and the other Arks.'

The Valendrin didn't look at him, more concerned with finding some particular spot on the Ittallan's bare arm. 'I am aware, my king. I've no wish to shorten my life either. Death for me would not be the release it is for others.'

Without explaining himself further, he set to work—puncturing the dead skin and collecting the thick, dark blood that oozed slowly from the wound. It had congealed, making the Valendrin's manipulation of it rather messy.

Sapora looked away at the last moment, unwilling to add that visual to his memories, and instead focussed on the gardens. When he had been a child, he'd played among the flowers and vines, enjoying the sun on his skin.

There had been no Varkain in the palace, then.

'What manner of Ark is Malashash?' Sapora asked, after the Valendrin had been working for several minutes.

'You know he is the great defender. What more do you need to know?'

Sapora remained quiet. If Malashash was anything like Veynothi, he didn't think he would be able to control *both* Arks, let alone all four. 'Many thralls were slain to free Veynothi.'

'She feeds off others. Your power becomes hers. Many died to create her, so it is only natural many had to be sacrificed for her resurrection.' The Valendrin approached the fireplace with a vial full of blood and stooped to light it.

'Malashash will need something else to break the seal?' Sapora asked, daring to hope.

'It is possible. The Arks are all different. It would make sense.'

If it was true, it was a relief. The route to Malashash's tomb was not easy. Even *he* struggled to get there, and he'd made the journey into the bowels of the earth three times. But he *could* take the Valendrin without too much difficulty. And from the blood mage's refusal to work on the seal, Sapora was convinced he knew more than he was letting on.

He thought of everything he knew about Malashash. Though both he and Veynothi had been created from the same magic, they were different people with different powers. Veynothi had said so herself.

If Veynothi demanded blood sacrifice, what would a great defender demand?

The room warmed up as the fireplace roared into life, crackling loudly as it chewed through the gathered firewood. It spat an ember out, which singed the rug laid out before it. Sapora only noticed then that there were several large holes burned through. Another expense.

The Valendrin paid the angry fire no mind. He held the vial above the flames and stirred it gently as the contents within began to bubble and smoke.

Sapora coughed as the acrid stench filled the room once again, and he faced the window. 'What *are* you doing?'

'I'm allowing the blood to speak. And it always has much to say of death.'

Sapora swallowed. He didn't like where this was going, nor did he like the question he'd have to ask, but he'd jumped into this with both feet, and it was too late to back out now. 'What does it speak of...?'

The Valendrin held the vial up to the sunlight filtering in through the window. He dipped one finger into the top of the vial, and the substance coated his claw. Slowly, he brought it to his lipless mouth and flicked out his tongue.

Sapora held his breath, watching for any sign of distress. He didn't know how Arillian magic worked in general, much less Aciel's compulsion, and he didn't like that lack of knowledge. Ignorance was terrifying.

The Valendrin convulsed. He dropped the glass vial, which shattered on the stone floor.

Sapora drew one of his scimitars and held the handle tightly. 'Valendrin?'

Sapora's blood mage hunched forward, elbows twitching. Then, so slowly Sapora could hear every one of his ancient bones creaking, the Valendrin turned to face him. His eyes were lifeless and white, rolled back in their sockets. His mouth hung open, jaws half-extended and saliva dripping from black gums onto the floor.

'Valendrin! Speak!' He forced confidence into his words, one eye on the corpse in case it, too, changed—but the Ittallan remained motionless.

'*Sapora. Filthy maggot. You attacked Jato. Tried to murder her! Biting her with your disgusting venom.*' The Valendrin spoke with a voice that was not his own. '*You stole my ereven sphere. Burned my airship. Slaughtered my Arillians.*' The old Varkain jerked uncontrollably, his head twisting at unnatural angles as if he fought whomever possessed him to speak. '*You are a disease upon Linaria. A rot that festers deep in the bowels of the world. You, and the shapeshifters. The filthy mages. And the humans who infest the world like locusts. I will kill every...Last. One. Of. You.*'

The Valendrin gasped for breath, his eyes returning to normal. He stood, panting, in stunned silence for a few seconds.

Then he collapsed to the floor.

12

Isa had barely enough time to let out a squeak of shock when the large man covered Amarah's head with a burlap sack. She vaguely remembered the man from the previous night's discussions by his distinctive glass eye—Rimir. Captain Hanzel's First Mate.

In her surprise, Amarah dropped her scythe, hands leaping to her neck and the tightening noose.

'Let her go!' Isa cried, running across the wide deck to Amarah, all thoughts of her own safety forgotten. She'd only managed to take three steps when the floor disappeared under her as she tripped over a thick coil of rope. Isa flung out her hands to catch her fall, but the rope twisted and snagged around her left ankle. It yanked hard, smashing her into *RaKhanna's* deck.

She split her lip against her teeth and tasted blood. Before she could moan in pain, she was violently whipped back, wood and rope burning her bare arms as she scrambled to hold onto something. She rolled onto her back and saw her attacker, a broad woman with loose, lanky hair, pulling her back towards her. Captain Hanzel.

In one, huge heave, Hanzel pulled Isa closer, spittle

frothing on her lips. Despite her age, the woman had bear-like strength, pulling Isa across the deck like a ragdoll. 'I'll give ya one of my ships, ya ingrate! Nice cabin all to yourself while I get that king's gold! Both you *and* Amarah!' Her eyes were wide, almost sparkling with glee. 'Ya just come along like a good little girl and there'll be no problems!'

Isa hissed. She wasn't going to put up with this. And Hanzel had another thing coming if she thought she was some meek princess who'd do as she was told, just because the sky pirate was bigger than her.

Light engulfed her body as she called upon her *meraki*, shifting her limbs in the blink of an eye into her true form—a wildcat. Isa's transformed state gave her flexibility and manoeuvrability, and she slipped her back leg from the noose of Hanzel's rope. With a roar-like cry, she leapt for the woman, claws fully extended, and slashed at her face and the arm she brought up to deflect the blow.

Her claws slammed into the leather plate armour on Hanzel's arm, and she was knocked back by the sky pirate's brute strength. Landing in the centre of the deck, all hackles raised, she glanced at Amarah.

Her ally was on her knees, hands at her throat where the sack tightened with every passing moment.

Isa leapt to Amarah's aid, only to be grabbed by another pair of hands mid-air and yanked back down to the deck.

Amarah's aggressor, Rimir, clutched the sack with one hand, and threw a short blade to the third pirate who held Isa.

Isa watched the blade sail through the air, and her throat tightened in fear. With another hiss, she kicked and clawed, biting down on the man's hands, trying to get him to drop her before he had a chance to stab the blade into her side.

It worked, and with her fangs drawing blood, the sky pirate dropped her with a yelp. 'She *is* a wildcat, that one,' he laughed, inspecting his bloodied hands. 'Come on kitten, let's get those claws sorted out before you do some damage.'

Isa lashed her tail at the insult. Her form was great for climbing and running, exploring high places and getting her quickly out and away from danger when she needed to. But fighting when outnumbered? She had far less of a chance. She was not a tiger like Palom, and she wasn't a *naja* like her brothers.

She kept her attention on Hanzel and the man in front of her, all the while hearing Amarah's struggle with Rimir behind her. She needed to do *something*, or they were both dead.

As fast as she was, she couldn't flee the battle to get help from Kylos or her other followers and return to *RaKhanna* before Amarah could get away. And from the look in Hanzel's eyes, she wanted Amarah dead. Isa did *not* want that on her conscience.

Not again.

Decision made, Isa crouched low and shifted back, light engulfing her as her body changed once again. Changing back and forth so quickly was never a good thing—it drained a lot of energy—but she couldn't see any way out of their situation that didn't revolve around abandoning Amarah.

Before the light had faded, she darted forward. Isa charged the man with the knife, crouched at the last minute, and kicked at his legs with a sweeping blow.

Her foot connected and she felt the jarring crack as his kneecap dislocated.

He dropped like a stone, and she grabbed the knife before it hit the deck.

She heard the whistle of rope and dodged to the side with all her Ittallan speed, as Hanzel's attack came from behind, snatching thin air instead of her. These pirates were amateurs and opportunists, it seemed. They definitely weren't used to taking on anyone who could *actually* fight back.

She lunged to the side, elbowing Hanzel in the temple and dragging the blade across her throat. As Hanzel fell, Isa kicked out *hard*—her foot connecting with Hanzel's gut.

She didn't know if she'd killed her. Didn't care. Hanzel was no longer a threat—but there was more work to be done.

Pulling one of her own knives from her boot, and now a blade in both hands, Isa tackled Rimir with a battle-cry even her father would be proud of. He grabbed both of her wrists and kept the blade tips away from him, but had to release Amarah to defend himself.

Unrelenting, Isa brought her right knee up and caught his chin in one, swift movement.

By the time Amarah managed to escape his grip and get back on her feet, she stood beside Isa, scythe in hand.

'Big mistake, Rimir,' Amarah spat, blood dripping from her nose. Her breaths came in ragged gasps. 'You *don't* attack me like that, you fucking coward.' She levelled her scythe at him.

Rimir had sunk to one knee, one hand steadying himself against the deck. His eyes were unfocussed.

Seeing the sky pirate so weak awakened something within Isa. She'd tasted battle lust before, had come close to it again when she'd fought Tacio—desperate to stay and slay him instead of fleeing, when all her instincts had told her to run.

The dark sensation crept along her skin like fire, the heat lighting up every muscle in her body. Coupled with the fact that the pirates had tried to take advantage of her and Amarah, it was something Isa could not let go.

Amarah moved first, slashing forward with her scythe.

Rimir had enough awareness to lift his hand to block it, but the blade sliced into his skin, sending a crescent splatter of blood to the deck. Amarah pressed forward, slamming the butt of the blade against his chest.

Already unbalanced, the force of the blow sent Rimir tumbling over the side of the ship.

With her nose full of the scent of blood, Isa raced after him, leaping over the edge of *RaKhanna* and following Rimir to the ground. With knives still clutched in both hands, she landed on Rimir's back and drove her weapons deep into his shoulder blades.

'How dare you!' she screamed, almost hysterical. Both knives were buried, so she pulled another one out, and stabbed again, then again, then again, seeing more and more red with each plunge. 'How dare you!'

Isa screamed over and over until there were no words in her throat, only a roar that gave voice to her rage.

'PRINCESS ISA!'

Amarah's scream cut through to her, and Isa sat back, panting. Blood covered her hands, arms, chest. She could taste it on her lips, too.

'Are you coming or do you wanna slaughter everyone in Estoria?'

Isa staggered to her feet and pulled both knives from Rimir's back. Their handles and her skin were slick with gore.

Her hands trembled, her breathing uneven.

Was this it, now? Everyone who recognised her would attempt to kill her?

Was that what life was going to be like, now she'd turned against Sapora?

'They were after *me*, Isa. You were just in the way,' Amarah said, giving her a hand back onto the deck and ignoring the blood dripping between her fingers. 'Your brother put out a five thousand crown reward this morning on my head. That's what I was tryin' to tell you. That I'm getting out of Estoria, *now*.' Amarah glanced over the side of the ship, then turned away.

Isa tried to swallow the sudden lump in her throat. 'After…you?' she echoed weakly.

'You want some water?' Amarah asked, and Isa thought she saw genuine concern on her face.

Amarah did not look like a woman who'd just been strangled by a supposed associate. 'Sure,' Isa said, unable to think of anything else. She looked back to the deck, but there was no sign of Captain Hanzel or the other crewmate. Had Amarah pushed them off, too?

She didn't want to know. Didn't want to be overcome by that battle-frenzy again. She trembled.

Amarah walked into the captain's cabin scythe-first, and returned a minute later with a large leather pitcher, a dark washcloth, and a long-sleeved tunic that appeared to be padded with leather armour. 'Might wanna change, too. Unless you want all that blood stinking up the place. I'm a bit taller than you, but shouldn't be a bad fit.'

'My things are back at camp. Near Traego's lodge.'

'Ain't got time. I told you. I'm leaving now.'

'Wait. Wait, Amarah! You're really going?'

'After what we just dealt with? All the other pirates'll be worse than Hanzel. I ain't sticking around for that,' Amarah snorted.

'But…but their ships? I'm getting them in a couple of days! They gave their word!'

Amarah cackled. 'Dunno about you, but I wouldn't trust anyone's word here. Trust what they do, not what they *say* they'll do. Hanzel was meant to give you one. Don't think that promise'll come true, now. Even if she survived, you butchered her First Mate. She ain't gonna forgive that.'

Panic flared in Isa's chest. 'What about my throne? I need to get the Ittallan of Val Sharis to join my campaign and stand with me against the Varkain.' Isa shrugged out of her tattered, bloodied clothes, letting them sink to the floor. The Estorian sun was warm on her bare skin, and she wondered if she'd ever be able to enjoy it again, or if she'd have to wear armour for the rest of her days. Isa took the water from Amarah, unstoppered it, and drank deeply. She poured a little over her arms and chest, frantically rinsing herself and using the washcloth to get herself as clean as she could, unsure what to do if Amarah left.

Trying to ignore her memories of blood lust, she didn't know what to do if the sky pirates went back on their word and didn't give her their ships.

Amarah was the only one she could talk to. If the other sky pirates had lied, then *RaKhanna* would be her *only* ship —two ships, actually, remembering Amarah's warship. And from Amarah's words, she wasn't sticking around any longer.

Where would that leave her? And all the Ittallan she'd brought here?

Stranded.

Amarah considered her words for a long moment. 'Come with me, then. I've got my own scores to settle, but I'll fly to Val Sharis to do that. Might be you can do your thing at the same time.'

'What about Kylos? Odi? Palom? All the other followers who are here on *my* word?' Panic grew as Isa pulled on the fresh clothes.

'No time,' Amarah repeated. 'I'm getting outta here. Come with me if you wanna get away from the lies. Stay if you wanna try your luck with the rest of the Ittallan you brought. Your call.'

Isa took another few swigs of water while her heart slowed down to a regular beat. She'd never been on the receiving end of an assassination attempt, and even if it *had* been aimed at Amarah rather than herself, she knew it was only a matter of time before people tried to take her down. Her life was in danger.

As she drank, she remembered herself and Sapora at the ball. The slaughter of the old council, and many Goldstones who'd been present.

"Spring cleaning," she'd called it. She'd almost said that proudly, when Morgen had been beside himself over Eryn and Anahrik's deaths.

She'd *laughed.* What a cold-hearted person she'd been then.

'All right, Isa?' Amarah asked, taking the pitcher back and re-corking the top. 'You coming with me or not? Ain't time to say any goodbyes if you are. If those three were after us, most of Estoria will be on their way here, now. My ship's a prime target.'

'What about sending a message to Odi and the others? I can't disappear without a word!'

'Truth is, they're probably safer here without you. Pirates ain't gonna care for a bunch of Ittallan with no bounty. Your lot all fight back!' Amarah cackled. 'You and me, though? We're worth more than our weight in gold.'

That made sense, but it didn't sit right with her. Isa wanted to get out of this place, but didn't want to give up on what she'd already achieved. She thought quickly. 'If you're *sure* they're safe here—'

'Safe as anywhere else.'

'—then I'll send Ittallan to Estoria. Instead of having all my people at risk on several airships, in full view of everything, I'll tell my followers to come here. *This* will be my base. Outside of Sapora's jurisdiction.'

'Sounds good.' Amarah didn't sound like she was listening as she rummaged around in the cabin.

Isa couldn't believe how quickly everything had changed. Perhaps a sudden disappearance *would* be best? What else was she to do? Run back to the others and end up stranded in Estoria with all the pirates after her?

She couldn't put the Ittallan through that. 'Let's get out of here.'

Amarah kicked her propellers into life and opened her sails as *RaKhanna* lifted off the ground.

Isa wanted to curl up and hide, but forced herself to walk to the edge of the ship and look over the side railing. The trees below blew under the strength of the ship, kicking up sand and dust and swirling it around the Estorian jungle—and over the bloodied bodies of Captain Hanzel and her two crewmates.

Kylos. Aetos. Odi. Palom. Solvi. Chyro.

She considered all of them allies and friends, and owed her life to them.

Now, she was abandoning her people, just when she'd argued that she needed her followers behind her more than ever.

Foolish princess, playing at power.

That's what Tacio had said. Perhaps there was more to what he'd said than just her half-brother being *mean*. Of the three of them, Tacio had spent the most time with Vasil and their Cerastes, had the most respect and confidence of the Varkain. He'd been born in Sereth, raised there. He was a Varkain through and through, understood all their culture and nuances of social situations.

She and Sapora were just playing, always fighting uphill battles where the targets shifted a bit more every day. How would she ever be expected to catch up?

Especially with Sapora placing such a huge bounty on Amarah.

She wondered how long it would be until she had a

bounty of her own. How long before Sapora would give in to Tacio's demands and suggestions. She knew Sapora would want her back at the palace. That went without saying—she was effectively on the run—but how long would it be before it was made official?

RaKhanna rose slowly and turned away from Traego's lodge, and in the clearing beyond, all the Ittallan tents in their makeshift campsite. Trees and buildings shrank in size as Amarah piloted the ship higher and higher, until Isa could hardly make out the details, even with her excellent vision.

And then, in a blur, Amarah flew them out to sea.

~

THEY'D FLOWN in silence for the better part of an hour, when Isa wandered into the captain's cabin. She'd spent the flight so far on deck, warily watching Estoria fade into the distance, expecting a fleet of pirate airships to chase them down at any moment.

But Amarah's confidence had been well-placed, and they saw nothing other than gulls.

Having managed the Imperial Fleet of Taban Yul for three years, Isa still marvelled at the fact a ship as large as *RaKhanna* could be flown by one person. *Khanna* was more acceptable, the ship was half the size. But *RaKhanna* was more formidable. She'd have expected a crew on board, but Amarah seemed more than capable of flying solo, even missing an eye as she was.

'Where are we going?' Isa asked, standing beside the sky pirate whom she now strongly considered an ally—perhaps even a friend. And she hadn't demanded gold every two seconds either, unlike Traego and the other pirate captains.

'Someplace out the way. Someplace safe,' Amarah replied, keeping her gaze straight ahead.

Isa wasn't one for stupid questions, but she couldn't think of anywhere in Linaria where they might be safe. Up until an hour ago, she'd firmly believed they were out of reach in Estoria.

She looked at the sun, at the ocean before them, and gathered they were travelling north-east. In the far distance, just barely touching the horizon, Isa saw land. 'Back to the wetlands?'

'Look at that. You ain't just a pretty face,' Amarah said.

Isa felt her cheeks redden. 'I *can* navigate, you know. I'm more at home on a ship than in the palace. Why does everyone assume because I'm a princess I'm also a naive idiot?'

Amarah adjusted her sails with a shrug.

After the assassination attempt, Isa had been a little shaken up. But Amarah's stalwart confidence and inability to give up or give in to fear kept her going. Isa's confidence grew just watching her.

'Antar will meet us there later. He'll grab some resources and fly my warship. No-one knows he's going, or where. No chance of anyone getting wind of this. Not even Traego.'

Isa heard the slightest waver in Amarah's voice at Traego's name, but didn't comment further. The two obviously shared history, but Isa presumed that even among closely allied thieves, distrust and suspicion ran too deeply for true friendship to ever develop.

She hoped Kylos and Odi would forgive her, and would see the sense in leaving them to lie low in Estoria. She hadn't even had the chance to spend any time with them to rest after their escape. They'd had a brief discussion about their next steps, shared some ideas on approaching the Archigos, but nothing concrete. Every Ittallan that came to

Estoria had risked their life for her. Many had been Sapora's prisoners ever since the attack on the palace. Isa owed the Ittallan so much, and wondered whether they would ever be able to forgive her for leaving them behind.

'The others are safe in Estoria,' Amarah said, as though reading her thoughts. 'Palom, Solvi. Everyone. It's a great place to hide until someone wants to pay for your head. Don't worry. They can all handle themselves if it comes to it. Sky pirates ain't used to much other than Goldstones there. Probably why they were so hurt by the Arillian attack. Not even royalty has any say in Estoria. Too wild.'

Isa scratched her nose. She had wanted to find out more about the Arillian attack. Now that she was alone with Amarah, she saw no reason not to broach the subject. '*Was* it Kohl?'

Amarah snorted, her attention firmly on the sea ahead.

'Amarah?'

'I dunno. Kohl *can* fight. Just like any Arillian. He don't seem to *want* to, though. Unlike *you*.' She looked pointedly at her.

Isa shrugged. 'I defend myself when I have to. Same as anyone else.'

Amarah wrinkled her nose, then looked back to the ocean. 'Wouldn't be how I'd describe that, tell ya the truth, princess.' She rolled her shoulders. 'And Kohl? Maybe. Could've been, but I don't think he has it in him. He's dead inside after everything with Aciel and Jato.'

Isa was grateful Amarah hadn't asked more about her blood lust. 'Why would he have attacked? He did seem more peaceful than other Arillians,' Isa mused aloud. 'Is he being influenced by Jato, too?'

Amarah shook her head. 'It...it ain't something I'm proud of. You know what the pirates are like when it comes to gold...'

Isa narrowed her eyes.

'Your brother has a bounty out for all Arillians—alive or dead. Thing is, Arillians are easier to deal with dead, so...'

'You were killing them?' Isa inferred. Her heart sank at the viciousness of it all. It didn't surprise her that they had fought back, if that was the case. Even Kohl, mild-mannered as he was, would have a breaking point. Everyone did.

Amarah didn't deny it. 'Well there ain't no Arillians left in Estoria now. So, whatever ones were dead are being claimed for. The rest must have flown away. Maybe Kohl was part of it, maybe he weren't. I don't think so, though. Too much of a pacifist.'

Isa wasn't sure. But Amarah had spent far more time in Kohl's company than she had, and the sky pirate had no reason to lie. If anything, Amarah was all about brutal honesty. 'The score you wish to settle. That's...with Jato, isn't it?'

Amarah grunted her assent.

If she was honest with herself, Isa would be happy to let Amarah get the killing blow. Fighting an Arillian—especially one as powerful as Jato—would be a huge risk. Yet, taking advantage of what Amarah wanted to do might help her save the situation. She'd been forced to begin her campaign alone, and didn't want to end up a voiceless passenger on Amarah's ship. She needed to get Amarah to fly them where *she* wanted. Towns where the Archigo lived would be the best start.

Isa paced the deck as she thought.

If she played everything right, and had Amarah work *for* her, then she'd find the silver lining in fleeing Estoria. She'd ensure the Arillian's death was attributed to her. That would get the Ittallan on her side. If it could be made clear that Amarah was acting on behalf of Princess Isa, and the rest of

Val Sharis knew it, *she'd* be the one who saved their country from the Arillian threat.

It would be just as Traego had said. The Ittallan would hail her for putting an end to that danger. It would also put Sapora on the back foot—indebting him to her for ridding Val Sharis of the threat.

And, surely, the tables would finally begin to turn in her favour.

13

Music flowed through the cool evening air, easing the day's stress and soothing fatigue. The ache Morgen felt in his bones faded as the notes of the flutes intertwined with drums, and strings lifted the whole piece to a level of calm and relaxation that Morgen compared to a hot bath.

Once Kalos Topeko had offered his invitation, he'd left, leaving Morgen and Mahlu to tidy up alongside Kalos Ettas and the other Kalosai who'd been working that day. Mahlu had seemed far colder to him than she had been while they'd been working. He wondered if she was unwilling to speak her mind in front of Kalos Ettas, but he didn't get a chance to ask—the moment she had finished, Kalos Ettas dismissed her, and Morgen needed to hurry back to Topeko's and clean up before the ceremony.

Mahlu left so quickly that Morgen didn't even have the chance to wish her well.

He returned to Topeko's home in a flood of apprehension. Mahlu had been trying to tell him something—possibly warn him—and he'd been too excited to be allowed to see the ceremony, to be accepted by the Samolen in one of their most important rituals, that he'd completely ignored it.

He hoped he wouldn't regret it, and that she'd forgive him.

The Kalos waited for him, resplendent in his ceremonial robes. Far more elaborate than those he wore to teach, or day-to-day, they trailed several feet behind him. His headdress was similar to that of the Arch-Kalos, though less elaborate, with only a handful of trailing silks in red, blue, green, and yellow. He held another headdress, a smaller one with silks all in gold—although they were far shorter than the ones he wore. 'Morgen. I had this made for you for tonight.'

'Oh, wow...thank you so much! But...you didn't know if I was coming until an hour ago?' Morgen wanted to be grateful, but he was suspicious of the gift.

Topeko inclined his head. 'I know. But I had hoped you'd want to attend. I know it's been a...difficult time for you here.'

Morgen didn't know what to say. Topeko had been so kind, so patient with him—through all his tantrums and failures. And he still wanted to help. Still wanted Morgen to be part of their culture while he was a student. The back of his throat ran dry and he grew uncomfortably hot. 'Kalos Topeko...I can't thank you enough.' He shuffled forward and gently took the headdress from the scholar.

'They represent the dragon-fire we covet. We recognise its power. Gold is the purest colour—the heart of the flame.' Topeko pointed to his own headdress, where other coloured silks fluttered. 'Red and yellow follow. And then a rainbow of colours—blue, green, purple.'

Morgen gently caressed the silks, listening intently to Topeko lest there was another test coming up. Perhaps words to recite. He'd learned to never take anything said to him at face value.

'Go and bathe. Dress in the robes that have been left for you. I'll meet you outside when you're done, and we'll go to the ceremony together.'

~

MORGEN COULD COUNT on one hand the number of times he'd roamed the streets of Berel at night. Usually, he was so exhausted by the day's training or the exercises Topeko put him through that he simply didn't have the energy to go out exploring after dark. Tonight was something completely different.

The ceremonial robes were heavier than what he was used to, and were weighted, as if he actually wore a full body of armour. Equally, the headdress itched, but he enjoyed the tickle of silk on his cheek. Perhaps now he could be forgiven for his lapse of judgement with the dragon.

He hoped.

Then, he could get back to his studies and enhance his understanding of *Ra*. Possibly even look into *He*, if becoming a Kalosuk was unlikely in the near future. He needed to do *something* to help Linaria recover. Even if there was a way to resurrect Moroda, it wouldn't be enough. Sapora was a threat that needed to be put away. Especially if he had a Sevastos.

The Kalos and the Kalosai walked in companionable silence, with only the stars and the three moons providing light. Two of the moons were full and bright, the third a silver crescent. Morgen had spent much of his youth stargazing, and it always interested him how the stars were different in Corhaven, Ranski, and Val Sharis.

He stared at them now, tracing familiar shapes in his mind's eye.

'I know you've been reaching farther than you can see,

Morgen,' Topeko said, after several minutes had passed. 'I normally have students for at least a year before they attend such a ceremony as this. But there is something...something dogged about the way you study and train. I know you're not Samolen, nor do our rules and culture come naturally to you. I hope I'm making the right judgement.'

Morgen swallowed. This was his opportunity to excel. 'I appreciate your kind words, truly. I guess I *am* always trying to see beyond tomorrow.'

Topeko smiled as Morgen recited one of the scholar's sayings. Morgen had learned the best way to pacify Topeko was to use his own words against him. Whenever he was caught reading the wrong thing or practicing in a way other than had been agreed, Morgen was able to accept the scholar's admonishments and avoid any real punishments.

'There's nothing wrong with trying to see beyond tomorrow. In fact it's a wise thing to try. But in doing so, you cannot lose sight of today. Of what you have before you now.'

Morgen gave Topeko a thin-lipped smile and nodded curtly. Being lectured always reminded him of when he'd been a small child, helpless in his curiosity and sense of adventure, and somehow always winding up getting into trouble. 'I know. I do appreciate what I have,' Morgen answered, a little harsher than he intended.

If Topeko heard his tone, he didn't respond to it. 'That's fine, then. And tonight, you'll have an opportunity to prove that.'

As the scholar led them through the dusty streets into the Old Town, Morgen was grateful for the thick robes. As a desert country, Berel suffered from cripplingly cool evenings, and Morgen found the temperature deeply uncomfortable—his time in the snow-covered town of Povmar hardly compared. But he slogged through it tonight for the chance to prove to Topeko's peers that he was worthy.

He'd never seen the ritual carried out and hadn't realised it was at night, and a child-like delight gripped him. Mahlu's warning seemed ill-placed.

Instead of crossing one of the many bridges which connected Berel New Town with Berel Old Town, Topeko led them down a path to the left—a road Morgen had never even noticed before. He idly wondered if it was a magic path that only appeared during the ritual ceremony, before dismissing the idea as ludicrous.

He'd simply never paid any attention to it before.

The dusty path dropped steeply down towards the lake which surrounded Berel Old Town. Morgen felt the energy and power radiating from the water. It covered his skin, made him feel light on his feet. 'Rhea's breath,' he murmured. The dragon goddess. Linaria's creator.

The fountain from which all magic sprang.

Morgen shivered, though whether it was the cool of the evening air or standing so close to what was essentially raw magic, he couldn't tell. He dropped behind Topeko and lingered half a dozen steps from the lake's edge, staring into it. The water, if it could be called that, didn't resemble any body of water he'd ever seen before. It shone pale blue, almost white, with wisps of mist trailing along the surface. It sat, still, unmoving, and yet Morgen felt in his bones the incredible force within the water. It pulsed as if it breathed. As if it was alive. And it pulled on him as if trying to drag him into its depths.

'Morgen?'

He glanced up to see Topeko halfway along the path, looking back at him. Concern laced his brow, and Morgen suddenly felt ashamed.

Could he help being so captivated by the life blood of

Linaria? He had read books on dragons, from Rhea herself to the ancient Sevastos, and those who lived and flew freely today.

Morgen wondered whether Rhea had simply been a particularly old and powerful Sevastos whose crystal had melted into this pool of energy. She would have had to be enormous for such a vast lake to have been created from her crystal, but it would explain why she was considered the goddess of the world. In fact, some scholars didn't discount that theory.

Standing here, now, in the presence of Rhea's breath, Morgen was inclined to agree.

It felt as though he was in the presence of the most powerful dragon in Linaria. The most powerful dragon that had ever lived, or would ever live.

He licked his lips, his throat dry.

Morgen took a step towards the water, when suddenly Topeko's arms were around his shoulders.

'You don't want to step into there, Morgen,' Topeko said, his usually light, calm voice tinged with concern.

'I'm sorry, I didn't mean to.'

'It's all right. You've been here so long now, I'd forgotten this is the first time you've come so close to the lake. Mesmerising, isn't it?' Topeko quick-marched them back to the path, not letting go of Morgen's shoulders until they were a safe distance from the edge of the lake.

'Like nothing I've ever seen. Like nothing...I've ever felt.' Morgen's voice came out in a throaty whisper, his gaze still locked on the font of pure magic.

Topeko smiled. 'You can see why we call it Rhea's breath? See why all of our power derives from her? And why we *must* respect it?'

'Doesn't it ever run out?' Morgen asked suddenly, thinking of all the bottled Samolen magic he'd encountered while in the Imperial Guard. Not to mention trinkets like the ereven spheres and however many countless others the Samolen created or sold. 'If you've been tapping into it for centuries? Using it to create your cheek jewels? And other ornaments?'

Topeko shook his head as the path narrowed. They were heading towards a large tunnel apparently carved out of the ground itself.

Now he was only steps away, Morgen wasn't sure how he felt being so close to what the Samolen believed to be the presence of the Goddess of Linaria. Or what was left of her, anyway.

Only when they were within the mouth of the tunnel did Morgen relax.

'No. As far as we can tell, the lake has never changed. It's the same mass, the same shape, the same depth. Our use of magic has not affected the lake at all. Rhea is ever-giving.' Topeko smiled in the darkness.

'Depth? You've swum in it?'

'Not personally. And no-one has for a long time. But there were a few brave scholars in the early days who walked into it.' Topko glanced back and grimaced.

The hairs on the back of Morgen's neck stood up. Suddenly the silks were irritating rather than soothing. 'Do I want to ask what happened to them?'

'Better you don't,' Topeko said, 'it wasn't nice, from the accounts. I can point you in the direction of the books if you really want to know...'

'Uh, I'm good,' Morgen said quickly, holding up his hands. 'Where are we going? Is it much further?' As a rule, Morgen wore sandals in Berel. It was too hot for boots. But in the chill of the evening, his feet were getting sore and cold.

They rounded a corner, the walls of the cave pressing

into their sides. It was smooth, as if worn away by a compassionate, artistic hand rather than struck with axes and shovels.

'The lake goes underground. Deep underground. Like any other lake,' Topeko said, 'we travel to an underground version of it. It's been diluted with regular water—when we don't use magic, it's what supplies Berel. It's safer to manipulate the lake there for this ceremony. It's not much further.'

Morgen took a deep breath and followed him through the winding tunnels. Beside them, the cave walls were damp, but he didn't want to risk touching it with his bare hands in case the moisture was pure lake water and burned him or he had some otherwise unpleasant experience.

Just in case.

After Morgen's knees began to cramp, Topeko finally dropped down a small gap in the floor and held his hand out, expectantly. Morgen followed his cue, and after clambering down a ladder, found himself in a vast cavern lit by burning braziers. A handful of Kalos stood in a loose semicircle, talking to one another in hushed voices.

Beyond, the lake swelled, but its glow was fainter down here, and Morgen understood the difference at once. The pull was far weaker, but he could still sense the great power flowing within the water.

'Ah, welcome Kalos Topeko. Welcome Kalosai Morgen,' one of the scholars greeted.

Morgen tore his gaze from the lake to the man who'd spoken, and instantly froze.

Arch-Kalos Dhabra. A man with all four of the Samolen cheek jewels, which shimmered in the low light. Jewelled bracelets coiled up his wrinkled arms, and he stared at Morgen with his mis-matched eyes; one blue, one brown.

He wore a more elaborate robe than those at the university, and wore a headdress of trailing silks that fell over his eyes, briefly masking his hawk-like gaze.

'Arch-Kalos Dhabra.' Topeko dropped to his knees in reverence.

It took Morgen more than a few seconds to regain control of his senses and also sink to the ground.

Now, Mahlu's fear made sense.

What an idiot he'd been. Too keen to regain a foothold in the standing among the Kalos to listen to the clearest warning he'd ever received.

His breathing quickened, his chest tight. He was here to observe, though. The ceremony wasn't about him. Dhabra's attention would be focussed elsewhere.

Morgen threw up excuse after excuse, any thought that would keep him safe. He focussed on a small pebble by his foot, not daring to raise his gaze unless specifically asked to.

'Rise Morgen.' Topeko gently placed a hand on his shoulder. 'Are you well?'

'O—of course,' he stammered, hurrying to stand. 'The honour is mine, Arch-Kalos' he added, with another bow.

Dhabra smiled and tilted his head to the side as he studied Morgen.

Morgen wanted to drop his gaze, but the Arch-Kalos commanded his attention.

Dhabra's blue eye seemed to stare right through him, just as it had done in Topeko's home.

Sheer, freezing terror snaked through Morgen's chest. Could he see the memory of Mahlu's warning? Could he see his own fears and disgust? Could he see that Morgen sought resurrection magic? Or to sever Sapora's connection with the Sevastos and do what he could to save Linaria—even if it meant more violence?

Rooted to the spot, Morgen couldn't move. His mind

raced, tearing through memories and suggestions of the future with lightning-speed.

After several long seconds, the Arch-Kalos appeared to complete his assessment, and stood back, rejoining the group of scholars, allowing Topeko to lead the ceremony.

'Witnesses. Friends. I thank you for your time tonight,' Topeko said, his soft, smooth voice carrying clearly in the cave, and echoing off the water's surface. 'We are gathered to carry out the ritual of our forefathers and join this Kalosai into our fold as a true Samolen. Arch-Kalos Dhabra and I, Kalos Topeko, stand for him. Do you all accept his contribution?'

There were assurances from the crowd, and a ripple of excitement pulsed through their air.

It was only then that Morgen actually looked for the Kalosai who would be the centre of the ritual. He glanced down the line of Samolen gathered, and spotted a young lad who couldn't have been more than fifteen or so. He had the olive skin and dark hair of any Samolen, and Morgen assumed him to be another of Topeko's students from the university.

His robes were yellow and white, his eyes bright green, and he held himself confidently.

He didn't fear the Arch-Kalos as Morgen did.

'Kalosai Cyllin. Have you chosen the path you wish to take?' Topeko asked, his voice rich and well-practiced with ritualistic rites.

'I have chosen,' Cyllin said.

Morgen lingered on the edge of the gathered Kalos, as far away from Dhabra as he could get. He wasn't more than three or four steps from the lake, and had a clear view of events. Suddenly, the unfamiliar words and intonation made him afraid, though he was certain it was simply the presence of the Arch-Kalos.

Topeko continued, 'Then speak and approach the lake, for if Rhea blesses you, you will obtain that which you desire.'

Morgen took a breath as the student spoke, his voice thin and reedy. 'I have chosen the path of the Kaloset, to bring strength to our people, and foster peace. I ask for Rhea's blessing.'

Again, assurances from the gathered scholars. Morgen scrutinised them, trying to remember if any of those present had stood for or against him when he'd been brought to Topeko for judgement. He recognised Kalos Ettas, and wondered if he'd invited Mahlu, too, and she'd declined, or if she had simply been overlooked. Morgen himself was the only Kalosai present—save Cyllin himself.

He wondered how Cyllin's studies would change as a Kaloset. Was he already able to play an instrument, or would one be given to him?

'Kneel before Rhea,' Topeko spoke, as Cyllin reached the edge of the water.

It lapped gently at the shore, confirming the movement that Morgen had sworn he'd felt earlier. Was there something...*alive* in there? His heart beat harder.

Topeko's golden voice continued to instruct Cyllin. 'Touch your hand to the water, and speak your request to Rhea herself.'

Cyllin did as he was bidden, and slowly, hesitantly, he brought his fingertip to the surface.

The moment Cyllin touched the lake, Morgen thought his head would explode.

His breath caught, the cave spun, and that same pull he'd felt from the lake earlier returned tenfold. His vision blurred, narrowed to focus only on the lake's surface. Everything around him shook, and he collapsed to his knees. The hard crunch of stone under his legs was the only indicator that he remained conscious, but he had no control of his body.

A piercing roar tore through his head, so loud he thought it forced blood from his ears and nose.

Even in his terror, he knew it was the snarl of a dragon.

Steam burst from the lake's surface like a geyser. Water plumed twenty feet straight up, slamming into the roof of the cave. Blue flames rose along the water, crackling and spitting.

With another ear-splitting roar, a golden dragon rose from the water. It spread its wings, uncoiled its tail, and filled the cavern. Every scale glittered as water cascaded down its body, bursting into fire the moment they returned to the lake.

The dragon's eyes had no pupils—they stared around the room, white and colourless—gleaming fangs protruding from red gums.

Morgen trembled, digging his fingers into the cave floor to hold himself back. It was as if the dragon tried to pull him in, sucking his soul straight from his body, while his knees remained rooted to the cave floor.

He couldn't breathe. Couldn't see. Just felt a stabbing sensation in his chest and an icy cold grip that covered all his skin as the flames swirled from the water to the cave floor. It crawled along the walls, covering him.

Morgen was certain his hair burned. Smoke filled his nose.

His lungs screamed out for air, but his throat and nose had seized shut. He couldn't cough. Couldn't breathe.

He was drowning. Floating. Being dragged away from himself.

Darkness surrounded him, filled him completely.

'The Goddess has blessed you.'

Arch-Kalos Dhabra's voice echoed somewhere above

him. He heard gentle applause as though a small audience had been mildly entertained by a theatre troupe and were being polite.

Morgen coughed.

Dhabra continued to speak, but Morgen couldn't make out the words. He focussed on his chest, forcing his lungs to work.

He swallowed and opened his eyes. Dizzy, the world swam back into view.

Nothing had changed. The surface of the lake remained still, there were no fires, no dragon's bellow. The Kalos remained in their semi-circle, Cyllin standing before them —now with a green jewel embedded in his cheek. Blood trickled down his face.

Morgen himself was still on his feet. He glanced down at his hands, expecting to see them caked in the dirt and dust of the cave floor, but they were just as clean as when he'd arrived.

Had everything been a hallucination?

The Kalos all spoke among themselves. More rites. More voices.

A wave of nausea boiled up, and Morgen struggled to keep upright.

'Take my hand,' Topeko's voice was right above him.

Morgen glanced up to see the tall scholar towering over him, one hand extended and the brightest smile on his face.

Had he stumbled?

The other Kalos were surrounding the new Kaloset, their attention too focussed on Cyllin to pay him any mind.

'What happened?' Morgen grabbed Topeko's outstretched hand, and warmth flooded him. 'I fell?'

'The ceremony can be a little overwhelming the first time you witness it. We receive a blessing from Rhea. There is much magic in the air.'

'I saw...I think...' Morgen struggled to remember.

'What did you see, Kalosai?'

Morgen gaped, wordless. There was no fire, no smoke. 'Didn't the lake...? Didn't the dragon...?'

'I fear you were perhaps not ready for the amount of magic here. Rest a few days. We can manage without you while you recuperate.'

Morgen nodded absently. Topeko's warmth helped him re-energise, but he sweated profusely, the golden silks sticking to his forehead. Slowly, he relaxed, easing into a smile. He joined the other Kalos in their applause of the new Kaloset.

He *had* been working a lot recently. Proving to himself and the other Samolen that he wasn't a threat. Perhaps a rest *would* do him some good.

Topeko joined the semi-circle and Morgen followed. He'd have time to consider what he saw over the next few days—once he'd had a good, long sleep.

He caught up with Topeko and the others, his breathing back under control. But when he saw Arch-Kalos Dhabra's cold eyes staring right through him, Morgen's smile vanished.

14

Palom shoved trees and bushes out of his path as he forced his way through the jungle, Chyro and Karvou right behind him. He cared nothing for the thorny vines lashing at him, nor the uneven ground that threatened to throw him off balance. All that mattered was his niece.

Solvi's scent was strong, and where he brushed past the bark of the trees, he found it warm from her skin.

He had time.

Thank the dragons above, he had time.

Despite the thick bushes, Chyro kept up with him easily enough—it seemed the young Ittallan had not skimped on his training in the Imperial Guard. At least Palom knew he could be relied on to a reasonable extent. Karvou, with his youthful energy, also kept pace.

Even though he'd had terrible problems with his *Valta Forinja*, Palom almost wished he had that sword with him now. It had led him to *Leillu* when he'd found the unhatched egg. Perhaps it would be able to lead him to the dragon now —and hopefully Solvi.

He cursed under his breath, hacking at a fallen tree trunk that blocked their path with a longsword.

He was too bulky to crawl under it, so he had to cut it to shreds to make a path for them.

'I am going to transform,' Palom said, after a few seconds of cutting at the strong bark and getting nowhere.

'Stop, Palom,' Chyro called.

Palom whirled around to see Chyro staring off to the side, where the trees grew thicker still. He couldn't see what interested Chyro so much. 'What?'

'Water. Running water. I heard a splash.'

'Water splashes all of time. It means nothing,' Palom replied, irritated.

Chryo shook his head. 'No, I heard footsteps through it. She's there. I'm sure.'

Palom had been about to argue, when the younger man darted off, heading towards the sound of the water. Karvou didn't hesitate and charged after him. Palom didn't want to split up, and trusted that Chyro's senses were more acute than his, now he was in his mid-forties, and followed.

Immediately, Palom found himself losing him.

Had *he* been slowing *Chyro* down all this time? The Ittallan had been a Captain of the Imperial Guard, after all. Though Palom had assumed he'd been promoted due to how many people they'd lost against Aciel, not because he'd *actually* thought Chyro was particularly capable.

Palom swallowed his pride and resolved to be kinder to the younger Ittallan if he turned out to be correct about Solvi and *Leillu*.

He'd never forgive himself if anything happened to either of them.

Blood pounded in his ears as he ran, following the sound of Chyro's feet kicking up sand and dirt as he raced towards the water. Palom daren't breathe out of sync in case he lost him. Thankfully, Karvou stayed in sight, and Palom managed to keep on their tracks.

Just as Chyro began to disappear from view, masked by jungle trees and foliage, Palom saw him halt on a small overhang. Palom closed the distance in a few long strides and came to a stop beside the Ittallan, Karvou on his other side, and peered down.

As Chyro had said, there was running water—a large river—coursing through the jungle on its journey to the sea. Though it was extremely wide, there wasn't anything unusual about the water itself.

Unfortunately, the river was the most normal part of the scene below—Palom had *not* expected a leviathan of a creature to be sitting in the middle of it, staring up at them with glistening black eyes.

The sea creature—for it could be nothing else—looked part-fish, part-squid, part-eel. Its dull green flesh seemed to absorb sunlight rather than reflect it, and for several seconds, Palom could only see a writhing mass of wet scales, as he tried to piece together what he could see and smell with what he knew of the world.

'Chyro...Karvou...' Palom muttered, but his companions were equally stunned by the staggering creature.

Karvou whimpered softly. 'This is...'

The creature's bulk was mostly round, until he realised that it was more of a giant eel with a great, elongated body that had looped around itself. Fins spread out along the length of its back, and its squat, round face bore four black eyes.

Leillu flew above it, a streak of blue against the green jungle canopy, roaring in frustration and occasionally letting out a burst of flame, which the creature ignored.

Palom watched as it uncoiled itself, revealing long, large,

clawed limbs—six in all—with webbing between its toes, and wicked talons at the end of each. He'd never seen a creature like it, and despite being a tiger of immeasurable strength, he wanted to do nothing more than to flee this monster.

'Solvi!' Chyro screamed.

Palom followed Chyro's gaze, and saw Solvi unconscious, half in, half out of the water. She'd wrapped her arms around a rock on the river bank, but she wasn't moving. Wet hair covered most of her face, barely obscuring a graze on her forehead. A few paces away, the creature lumbered towards her with a low growl.

'What is this creature...?' Palom snarled, torn between the desires to flee, fight it, and save his niece. It looked ready to finish Solvi off.

'Never seen it before,' Chyro said. 'Maybe Traego knows?'

'Then go get him.'

Chyro froze. 'I'm not leaving you alone to fight that thing! I want to save Solvi, too!'

A low, rumbling growl emanated from the monster and Palom bared his teeth as he readied his *meraki*.

'I may need help. Traego can help. Go.'

Chyro frowned, evidently unhappy by being sent away after finding Solvi and *Leillu*.

'I'll go. I'll run!' Karvou said, breathless.

'You're sure?' Chyro asked.

Palom didn't hear the end of their conversation. He was consumed by his desire to save Solvi, and refused to waste anymore time. In one, swift leap, he threw himself off the cliff face and towards the creature.

Light engulfed him as he fell, and he was not a man when he plunged into the monster, but a tiger with claws and fangs drawn and ready to fight.

His front legs grabbed onto the creature's scales, breaking his fall while he attacked, but despite their sharpness, his claws slid right off the scales as if repelled.

The monster uncoiled itself a little more, its attention now on Palom completely. It let out a low hiss and the water around it bubbled and frothed as it rippled its body in readiness.

Palom snarled as he landed in the water. It swallowed him almost to his chest, but he didn't care. He was an experienced fighter on both land and water, and all he needed to do was keep the monster distracted and away from Solvi—while keeping himself alive in the process—until Traego or one of the other sky pirates that Karvou found was able to come to his aid.

A short way beyond the monster, a mass of brown fur and muscle splashed into the river as Chyro entered the fray, also transformed and ready to fight. He got to his feet, bursting from the water's surface with a bellow that shook Palom.

He needed to get to Solvi and get out, before the situation worsened. Palom snarled again, forcing out all distractions as he tensed, watching the monster for any lapse in concentration so he could dart in and grab Solvi—when his legs were pulled out from under him.

He swallowed water as he went under, his back legs yanked by the creature's whip-like tail. The barbs at the end of its fins bit into his skin and drew blood where they pierced flesh, and Palom let out a snarl of pain.

He writhed away from the creature's tail and came up for air further downstream than he'd have liked to be. His side itched from where the tail had struck him, but he ignored the pain and refocussed his attention.

Above, *Leillu* continued to circle and roar, but the fire

breath she unleashed on the creature did nothing to warrant its attention.

Chyro let out a roar and charged towards the monster in a lumbering gait. The bear's jaws were wide and his fangs were bared, but he was repelled just as easily as the tiger had been.

Palom could spare Chryo no thought in the middle of the battle. He stalked through the water, taking several cautious steps towards the monster. If his claws and Chyro's fangs did no damage, they were at a distinct disadvantage. But all creatures of the sea needed to breathe, and this one spent most of its time above the water from what he'd seen so far.

Perhaps if he used his strength to wrestle the thing and hold its head under water, he could drown it? An ironic death for whatever abomination of nature this thing was, but Solvi's life was more important.

Palom sprang forward with renewed vigour. Keeping himself and Solvi alive was the main focus, but this thing, whatever it was, was a threat to Estoria. To the people who lived there, to the trade and supply of food and materials.

No-one had warned him of such a creature that could threaten them, and Palom wondered where it came from.

He smashed into the monster's side, claws scrabbling for hold, as he tried to pull it over with him with his momentum. The creature groaned and rolled over, and Palom's nose and eyes filled with water as they crashed back into the river together.

The creature writhed, fins flapping and tail slapping at him. It dwarfed Palom, its bulk enormous and slippery. Another barb caught him, puncturing his thigh, and Palom roared in pain. He let go and swam away, leaving a trail of blood in the water as the creature righted itself again.

It snarled at Palom with an otherworldly noise, fins flickering in clear frustration at being attacked.

Palom winced when he came up for air again and put his legs on the river bed. His thigh bled badly, and he could already feel the strength fading from that leg. There'd be no jumping—or even running—for a while now. Not without excruciating pain.

Leillu spat another plume of fire, and the creature—irritated—whipped its tail up to swat at the dragon. Palom drew in a breath of fear, but relaxed when he saw *Leillu* flap her wings and practically leap out of reach.

Chyro charged again, roaring his fury in another attack, and Palom spared a glance at Solvi. She was motionless, her hair and clothes wet with the churning water from their battle, but still in the same place. He swallowed his fear and looked back to the monster, who swivelled around after knocking Chyro back into the river, as though sizing him up.

The creature's skin shimmered in the sunlight, its fins continuing to flicker as it eyed Palom.

He growled again and widened his stance. His leg throbbed and he didn't trust himself to leap or charge, so he held his ground and lowered his head defensively, fangs bared.

As though sensing weakness, the monster let out a low rumble and arched itself towards Palom, approaching with slow caution. Its head alone was almost ten feet wide.

If he wasn't careful, the thing could probably swallow him in a single gulp.

Palom glanced to the water every now and then. He didn't want to be caught off guard by the creature's barbed tail, but could see nothing in the water that posed a threat. Palom turned to the side, tail lashing, hoping to possibly intimidate the creature, causing it to back off.

He saw the monster's intent to strike and dived out of the

way a fraction of a second before it lunged, its mouth agape. Palom saw down the creature's jaws for an instant—needle-like teeth ran all down its throat in waves of circular slices.

What *was* this thing?

He came up for air again and spun round as the creature moved, getting faster and faster with each lunge.

The tiger narrowly avoided two strikes, three, four, before fatigue caught up to him, and the monster managed to knock him back with one of its forelimbs.

Grunting, Palom came up for air. Chyro's roar filled his head over the rushing water.

The thought of fleeing washed over him again, but he couldn't leave Solvi or *Leillu*. Tiring fast, Palom pulled himself from the water and onto the bank. Water fell from his fur, drenching the soil, and he slipped in the mud as he backed away. The trickle of red he left with every step was a concern, but one he couldn't address now.

The creature continued its approach, Solvi forgotten. Even Chyro's aggressive attacks were ignored—it wanted to finish Palom. That much was clear.

He roared again. If he died, at least he'd have protected her.

The monster reached the edge of the water and lumbered onto the ground, pulling itself forward in slow, deliberate heaves. For its size, it was quick in the water. On land, it looked like a newborn stumbling around on unsteady legs.

Palom held his ground. The land sloped upwards towards the treeline. Here, he had a slight advantage. Given the bulk of the creature, Palom wasn't taller than it, but at least he was more comfortable on land than the thing seemed to be.

He saw Chyro raise himself onto his back legs and slash forward with his front claws. Against his better instincts,

Palom launched forward, slamming into the creature with his chest and shoulders.

It let out a cry, as it tottered where it stood, Chyro's claws finally gouging into it, before the monster rolled back into the river with an almighty splash. It sent a wave careening along the water, and washed over the river bank. Palom froze when he saw it cascade over Solvi.

When the water level dropped back to normal, Solvi was gone.

Chyro hadn't noticed, he was too focussed on the fight and keeping himself alive.

Palom let him carry on and stared into the water, looking downstream for any sign of his niece.

He could only see murky, churned up water, and the occasional fish that hadn't been fast enough to get out of the way. Then, the barbed tail of the creature shot out of the murk directly towards him.

Palom leapt to the side, skidding where he landed on the mud. His thigh pulsed in pain, and his lower body collapsed into the sludge.

Where was Solvi?

He had no time to reconsider another course of action.

He leapt back into the water, narrowly avoiding the monster's body as it dived towards him, and came up for air a second later. Frantically he looked for Solvi, for any sign of her. Her hair was dark, and wouldn't be seen easily through the silty water. He couldn't smell, either—blood and mud covered his nose and face, and he didn't have the time to clean himself.

The monster was on top of him a second later, covering Palom with his bulk and forcing him to the bottom of the river. Palom hadn't had the time to draw in a breath, so sudden was the ferocity of the attack, and he scrabbled against the monster's side, slashing and biting as much as he could.

His weaponry scraped right off the creature's scales, and panic rose when he felt his back press against the soft bed of the river. Biting down, Palom desperately tried to get any kind of hold on the creature's armoured scales.

In the darkness, he saw movement and turned his head as the barbed tail shot towards him, slashing him across the cheek and spilling more red into the water.

The tail lashed around, then charged forward in another attack.

Palom turned and opened his mouth to grab onto its fleshy fin with his fangs, and bit down hard.

He immediately felt the tail twist and pull, trying to free itself from his jaws.

Palom tightened his grip until he felt the skin split in his mouth, and acrid, oily blood spewed from the wound.

The pressure above him lifted as the monster retreated, and Palom kicked off the bottom of the river.

He broke the water's surface and gasped. Exhaustion threatened, and it was all he could do to tread water and keep his head above the surface. The monster had retreated a short way, thrashing around and churning up the water and river bed even more.

Chyro took the opportunity to lunge forward, forcing the creature further away from Palom.

His enemy distracted for the moment, Palom turned to look along the river bank, in case Solvi had managed to make it to shore, but it was just as empty as it had been. She was nowhere to be seen.

Water rushing, creatures snarling, and his own pulse deafened him to all else.

He couldn't see her. He *couldn't* see her!

Growling, he swam to the bank—running would be

easier when he didn't have to think about keeping his head out of water, despite the pain—and pulled himself onto the muddy grass. Sparing just a second to shake the mud and silt from his drenched fur, Palom took off down river, adrenaline fuelling his strides as he pushed through the pain of his multiple wounds.

Movement ahead caught his eye as *Leillu* flew above him, her wings speeding her along to match his pace.

He was grateful that he wasn't alone.

Somewhere behind, the monster bellowed, no doubt having knocked Chyro aside again, and the following splash told Palom it was also trailing him.

Ignoring it for now, and trying to capitalise on the short lead he'd built up, Palom ran on, avoiding tree stumps, rocks, and muddy patches where he could, one eye on the water to his right all the while.

Solvi had to be here. She *had* to.

The current wasn't particularly strong. She couldn't have been swept too far downriver.

Whatever fish were in the water had been scared off by the creature, so Palom hoped any movement would be his niece. He'd never forgive himself otherwise.

Another splash, this time uncomfortably close.

He saw the monster break the surface in his peripheral vision and powered on.

His chest burned with every breath, and it felt like his limbs were slowly beginning to stiffen up. He wouldn't be able to run for much longer.

Still he raced onwards, tapping into every inch of his *meraki*, willing his body to give him more strength. He was the great tiger. The saviour of Val Sharis, of Linaria. Forger of the *Valta Forinja*.

He would *not* let this sea creature beat him.

He would *not* lose Solvi.

When the water broke ahead of him, his first thought was the creature had also put on a burst of speed and overtaken him.

But the small form and dark hair told him otherwise.

Leillu had seen too—a flash of blue in the sky as she dived towards her.

Palom skidded to a stop and leapt into the water. He couldn't let the monster reach her first.

Even if it killed him.

The slap of the water sent chills through him—it completely soaked through his fur and now reached his skin.

The monster had no such trouble with the environment, barrelling into Palom before he'd even swum a length.

Its attack knocked the wind from him, and Palom went limp in its claws.

Through sheer luck, the monster pushed him into the riverbank, causing more river water to spill out. It gave Palom an opening to breathe, and he sucked in a lungful of air.

There was no way he could kill this creature. Perhaps damage it, if he was lucky, but there was no way he could defeat it. Blearily, he scanned the water for Chyro, but there was no sign of the bear, and he couldn't hear or smell anything other than the rushing water and the creature that had him pinned.

Again, he wished he had his *Valta Forinja*, despite the weapon's curse. It would have made short work of the monster, reinforced hide or no.

The creature pushed into him again, shoving him deeper into the muddy sludge of the riverbank, as it raked its clawed fins down his body. Palom turned away, so most of the damage was done to his side instead of opening his chest and belly, but each vicious attack sapped more strength from him as the water turned into a dark, bloody mess.

He needed to stay alive longer.

Needed to keep the monster's attention on him.

Perhaps *Leillu* could keep Solvi out of the water until Chyro caught up, or the others arrived.

Another attack, this one smashed his head against the bank.

He let out a roar of anguish as the darkness of the water flooded his vision. The huge form of the creature blocked out all else, its stinking, oily, body surrounding him. It let out a guttural noise—not quite a growl—perhaps an ancient language that Palom could not comprehend.

Unable to hold himself up any more, his head lolled forward. Only by the monster's claws pinning him in place did he not slip under water again and drown.

His blood pumped in his ears, punctuated by splashing water and the snarl of the monster.

Everything else was gone.

Chyro. Solvi. *Leillu*...

He couldn't keep his eyes open.

Suddenly, the pressure on his chest and sides released as the monster let go.

Palom slipped underwater, all his strength having left him. Briefly, he wondered why the monster had released him.

But he had no energy for any other distinct thoughts.

When he felt claws dig into his side and pull him up for air, Palom had no comprehension of what was happening. He felt himself being pulled back up onto the river bank, through the sludgy mud and onto clean grass and jungle foliage.

He took several deep breaths, allowing his vision to come back into focus.

It took several long, painful seconds.

A bear towered over him, its dark brown eyes full of concern.

Palom swallowed and coughed, ejecting water and silt from his mouth and throat.

Was it Chyro? It had to be.

Satisfied that Palom wasn't about to die, the bear took off, racing down the bank towards a small copse of trees.

Palom watched him go, confused. Everything seemed to be moving in slow motion. And...was that a flash of blue in the trees?

He coughed again as his *meraki* flickered, and he shifted back, his tiger form leaving him now he no longer had the energy to sustain it.

The pain intensified a thousand-fold as he rolled over onto his hands and knees. His clothes were ripped and bloody, his skin caked in mud. Opening his mouth, more silty water fell onto the ground and he coughed violently. He hadn't realised quite how much water he'd taken in.

He looked to the river, and saw the monster retreating; Traego's *Otella* firing at it and driving the creature away.

With shaky hands, Palom crawled along the soggy grass until he found strength in his reserves to get himself up onto his feet, using a nearby tree as a crutch. Once steady enough on his feet, he hobbled forward towards the clearing where *Leillu*, Chyro, and Solvi were.

'Please...let her be alive. Please.' He spoke to himself aloud, as if his own words gave himself—and Solvi—strength. 'Rhea, Goddess, if you have mercy...You will let her live.'

He stumbled into the clearing, sending twigs and loose leaves flying as he toppled to his knees.

Solvi lay on her side, breathing shallowly. Chyro knelt by

her chest, transformed back, one of her wrists clutched between his hands.

Leillu bounded over to Palom, knocked into him once, then raced back to Solvi.

'What was that thing?' Chyro asked through gritted teeth, his gaze locked on Solvi.

Unable to speak, Palom winced. He pulled himself over to his niece and pressed his forehead against hers. She was so very cold.

Beside him, Chyro trembled. 'She's going to be okay, isn't she?'

Palom looked her up and down. He couldn't see any lacerations in her clothes, nor blood. Surely she would be okay. Surely.

She was breathing. She had a pulse. She was just so cold.

Otella landed on the opposite bank, fewer trees providing a space for the massive warship. Its propellers caused trees to sway and scattered debris to the ground around them. Palom barely gave it any attention.

'Palom! Chyro!' Traego called. 'You okay?'

Karvou ran ahead, more animated than Palom had ever seen him. He led Traego and his troupe across the river, half-swimming, half-wading through the water, with no regard for his own safety.

At their approach, Palom stepped back and sat on a tree stump, his gaze still on Solvi.

Malot—the Samolen in Traego's crew, he remembered—knelt beside Chyro and rested her hands against Solvi's cheeks. 'She's cold.'

Traego shrugged out of his overcoat and placed it over her. Chyro immediately did the same, although his was somewhat waterlogged, and Traego's troupe removed loose articles of clothing to add to her, bundling her up in whatever they could spare.

They were hardened fighters, all of them. Perhaps other than Judd, a pilot from Corhaven who looked like he'd never been in a conflict in his life. He looked at the others gathered. It appeared Traego had pulled in his entire crew. Then again, the tall Estorian, Antar, was missing. But now wasn't the time to worry where a random member of a sky pirate's crew was. There were enough of them to help Solvi.

He watched as Malot's hands moved along Solvi's body. She would feel her skin, pause for a moment, then move on. 'Take off her boots. Wrap her in the dry clothes. She's taken in a lot of water. This will be hard. I am no healer.'

Palom's heart froze. If only Lathri were here.

Anger and worry rose in him like a double-headed serpent and he rounded on Traego. 'Why did you not warn us? Some great monster like that roaming in jungle!'

Traego was unfazed by the Ittallan's roar. 'I only ever saw it once and it left in a hurry! Makes for a good campfire tale, nothin' more than that.'

'*Good campfire tale*?' Palom echoed, incredulous. 'Tell me *all* of what lives here. All enemies. All dragons. All animals. If our lives are in danger, I *must* know!'

Traego moved forward at a request from Malot that Palom hadn't heard, and together with Chyro, lifted her from the ground.

'I will help.' Palom stood up.

'No. You're too weak. You're bleeding. Badly. Get that wound stemmed. Chyro and Traego can manage,' Malot said, and gave him a look so severe, his panicked rage left him. He instead focussed on his thigh, which still oozed blood. Despite her words, she made no effort to aid him, and she made her way back across the river with Traego and Chyro to *Otella*.

Judd and one of the two cousins on Traego's crew—

Farlan, he thought—helped Palom tie off the wound to keep it from bleeding, and he was sure to grunt his thanks.

Before following them to Traego's airship, he took a moment to look back across the water. There was no sign of the monster. Not even a whiff of oily blood.

Leillu sat up on her haunches and tilted her head to the side, letting out a chirp that seemed enquiring.

Dragons above, what creatures lived in the pirate-infested islands of Estoria?

15

It was late afternoon by the time Isa and Amarah reached the wetlands, and the princess firmly believed it was a cursed place. Or at least a bad omen.

Although she'd never been one to believe in superstitions, the last time she'd been here had only been the day after she'd fled the palace of Taban Yul to escape her brothers. Now, she'd escaped from Estoria after hardly spending any time there.

Perhaps she was looking at it the wrong way. Perhaps the wetlands were her sanctuary, rather than a cursed omen she endured when she'd been forced to flee.

She leaned her arms on the side rail of *RaKhanna* and rested her chin on them. Her hair whipped around, freed of their braids, and she enjoyed having it loose for once. This was her chance to be her true self—not what she'd *had* to be to survive.

Only a short distance away, the marshlands loomed, grey and forever shrouded in thin mist. But at least it was away from the prying eyes of those who would do her or Amarah harm. The northern edge of the wetlands signified Val

Sharis's border with Sereth—the only part of the border that wasn't the Feor Mountains. Heading south and west would be her best bet. Keep away from the Varkain for as long as she could. Any one of them could betray her location to Tacio. Or worse, Sapora.

She could hardly believe the mess she'd managed to get herself into. She didn't even have her essentials with her—just the knives and family stone already on her person, and the borrowed clothes of a sky pirate.

There was no Lathri to offer guidance. No Odi with a kind word. No Kylos to speak sense. No Palom or Solvi for support. No-one. After they'd all worked so hard to get everyone together, she'd fled at the first sign of trouble.

How in Rhea's name would she persuade the other Ittallan to follow her over Sapora without a full retinue?

Amarah kept the ship a clear five hundred feet or so above sea level. They were close enough to the water that she could see the fins of whales and dolphins break the surf, and she whiled away the hours watching them swim and play.

It wasn't long before they were back in Val Sharis—*RaKahanna* was certainly fast. Amarah expertly navigated her new ship over a small inlet, shielded by low cliffs, and landed *RaKhanna* beside one. She folded in the ship's navy sails and wings, making *RaKhanna* rather compact and well-hidden. With the deep mahogany hull, the ship blended in well with the muddy cliffs. No-one would be able to see it unless they knew exactly where to look—or came close.

Isa rubbed her wrists. 'How long are we to be here?'

'Until Antar gets here. Then we'll figure out our next move,' Amarah said, walking out of the cabin and stretching her arms above her head with a yawn.

It was one of the only times Isa had seen the woman without a scythe in hand. 'I wonder if I did the right thing.'

'Too late now. Unless you wanna swim back to Estoria.' Amarah cackled and rolled her shoulders. She brought out a small dark blue ball about the size of her fist, and threw it casually at the deck. The moment it touched the wood, it exploded, sending shimmering light across the whole ship —including Isa. 'I think spending some time away will be a good thing.'

'*Thief Shroud?*'

Amarah grinned. 'You sure you never been a sky pirate before?'

'I pay attention and learn quickly.' At least they were completely hidden now. That lessened some of her fears. 'Do you have a map on board?' Isa knew her country well, but it was always good to get your bearings and see where the nearest towns were. If they were to plan their next moves, Isa needed to get the lay of the land.

'Yeah, inside.' Amarah jerked her thumb over her shoulder.

Isa took her lead, walking past the sky pirate and into the captain's cabin. The room was smaller than she'd thought, and completely sealed off. Amarah's scythe leaned against the only empty section of wall, gleaming in the late afternoon sun. *RaKhanna's* wheel and controls appeared well-worn, but functional, with varnish missing from some of the wooden panels. Shelves filled the walls—other than the vast glass screen that stretched around the cabin—and a large map of Linaria rested on the widest shelf directly behind the wheel.

Isa leaned over the illustration, eyes narrowing over the Val Sharis wetlands. She traced a finger over where she assumed they were hiding. Esta Cona was due south, the closest settlement by far, though it was barely more than a large village. Nari Vela and Ora Ori were two even smaller towns further south. Across the Feor Mountains far to the west, on the opposite coast, lay Gur Bano. North of that fishing village were the towns of Tannon Sona—nestled at the southernmost tip of the Feor Mountains and home to the largest quarry in Val Sharis—and Antir Yul, Taban Yul's smaller, sister city.

Plenty of possibilities.

Thousands of people that she could rally to her cause and have fight for her. *With* her.

Jato was near Taban Yul, on the eastern side of the city, nestled in the plains between it and the mountains. It would be a great step to take her out straight away and begin her campaign with something impactful, but Taban Yul was too far away, and the journey too treacherous to take her on, first. She needed to visit some of the other towns on her way to the capital and recruit people. Using the trade winds would be the most effective route between the towns.

And it seemed silly to travel farther afield when Esta Cona was on her doorstep.

Isa was certain the Archigo of Esta Cona was Kessir, who had attended Summercourt and been snuffed by Sapora and his Varkain, much like most of the others. She could surely take advantage of that tricky relationship, couldn't she?

Tannon Sona or Gur Bano would be good, next. Both were influential towns and supplied the capital; Tannon Sona with marble and stone, Gur Bano with seafood and rich minerals. Even better, both towns were looked after by Archigo Gralla—the wealthiest of all the Val Sharis Archigo, and one whom Isa had actually had conversations with in the past.

First, she'd speak with Archigo Kessir in Esta Cona.

That would put her in a stronger position when she spoke with Archigo Gralla.

Once she had both Archigo and their warriors on her

side, they could make their move against Jato. Amarah would get her revenge, and Isa would be seen as a saviour of Val Sharis.

She could see all the pieces falling into place as she thought it through. It was her best plan. And of course, any Ittallan who got behind her who weren't front-line fighters would travel to Estoria and bolster her numbers there until she'd made Val Sharis safe again.

It made sense.

'That's a big grin. You figuring something out, princess?' Amarah asked.

Isa jumped up to see Amarah leaning against the door-frame of the cabin. She blinked, recovering from her surprise. That was the second time Armarah had managed to sneak up on her. 'Yes. I think I know my next steps.'

'Oh, really? What's that, then?'

'Esta Cona, first. Find the Archigo and speak with them about my plight. They're so close to Estoria, they could join Kylos and the others before we even reach the next town! That'll be Gur Bano or Tannon Sona, depending on the winds. It's been a long time since I've travelled this way, and can't recall how they shift with the seasons. I will need your help with that.'

'We?' Amarah raised an eyebrow.

'Yes. How else am I to fly to the towns of Val Sharis without you and *RaKhanna*? Actually, the warship Antar is coming on will be useful too. Two ships isn't much of a fleet, but two are better than none.'

'Wait, wait, wait, Isa. I said I was leaving Estoria on my own business. Technically you're a stowaway. I have revenge to carry out, and a debt to repay—I've waited too long for both,' Amarah said, her eyebrow still raised.

'You said you were going to help with my campaign.'

'Sure. Once I've done my thing.'

'Think about it, Amarah. Jato is by the capital, and we're stuck in the wetlands. Why not help me for now? Esta Cona is only a league or two south,' Isa pointed at the map, 'minutes away on *RaKhanna*. Besides, I only need an hour at most in town to speak with the Archigo.'

'Givin' orders? At this rate I should be charging ya passage on my ship!' Amarah folded her arms. 'I got people I owe, debts to repay. They come before your campaign. Anyway, keeping you on the move keeps the Varkain stretched thin, which works for me. That's good enough, ain't it?'

'Amarah. We worked well together before, back at the palace when we broke out.'

'When I broke you out.' Amarah snorted.

'I saved you from Captain Hanzel and Rimir back in Estoria. Doesn't that mean you owe me, too? And as I'm right here—'

'Actually that makes us square. I saved you from the palace. You saved me from those cut-throats.' Amarah grinned, as if she'd won a battle.

Isa sighed. She needed to put her foot down if she had any chance of being a good queen. 'Ah, but I gave you your warship. The one Antar is flying? You owe me, to use your own code of honour. They're your ships. Run them as you wish. But *I* get final say on where we travel.' She didn't back down.

Amarah studied her with her one eye. 'You ain't running with me then, you're hiring me. That it?'

'Exactly. Besides, you pledged your ships to me in Estoria. Plans've changed somewhat, I'll admit, but we're both in this situation together. And as you're in my debt, I'm sure you'll think of a more *reasonable* charge for the hire of your ships and services. Especially considering you'll get to take down Jato at the end of it— something you wanted to do anyway.'

'Reasonable charge?' Amarah snorted.

Isa smiled as sweetly as she could.

'Fine. Answer me one thing.'

Isa's stomach dropped in sudden anxiety. 'What?'

'This blood lust of yours. Do I gotta be worried you're gonna go fucking crazy on me? Kill me in my sleep?'

Isa flinched. She turned her head away. 'I'm well-versed in combat.'

'Yeah, so am I, but I don't *butcher* my enemies. I leave 'em when they're down and get away while the going's good. You need a whole wardrobe of clothes every time you fight the amount of gore you get covered in. I saw it with Tacio and thought it was panic. What you did to Rimir today made it clear.'

'It's not every time.' Heat flushed her cheeks. 'It...my father was a warrior. A conqueror. I must have some of that in me.'

'You have it controlled?'

Isa didn't, but she couldn't admit that to Amarah. 'I'm fine until there's blood. Weakness. Some combination, I don't know the exact details.'

The answer seemed to placate Amarah, because she didn't push, but she studied Isa in silence.

'What're you going to do after?' Isa asked, suddenly.

'What?'

'After everything's over. Once I'm queen. What will you do?'

Amarah cackled. 'Don't trick me, Isa. Piracy is outlawed, ain't it?'

'Exceptions have been made before. They can be made again.'

'Damn well hope so.'

'You could be Fleet Master,' Isa ventured.

'I don't think so. I'm not good with takin' orders. I do what I want. The freedom to sail Linaria, that's always been my dream. I'll carry on doing it as long as I can.'

Isa smiled. 'Sounds lovely.'

'I need to help Moroda, too. It's been my goal ever since we fought Aciel. I owe that woman my life. I ain't gonna sit around and do nothing while she's trapped there. Not in my nature.'

Isa saw the large crystal pillar in her mind's eye. Aciel, the damned Arillian, and Moroda, the peacemaker. The woman had wanted to stop the fighting, and had indeed ended one battle. But the floodgates had opened for other would-be conquerors, other powers to rise—including Sapora, and by consequence, the Arks.

Who would have ever imagined such creatures would live again. With Veynothi free, it wouldn't be long before Malashash would be living and breathing again, too.

Isa knew little of the Arks—her histories hadn't covered them in any great depth considering they were thought of as ancient relics—but she knew Malashash had been the great defender of Sereth. He was not an attacking weapon in the way Veynothi and Karekis had been.

Those two had been formidable, Karekis most of all. As the first Ark, he held the most power, did the most damage, and was responsible for wiping the most villages off the map. Isa hated the fact that one of her Ittallan, an old woman called Yfaila, had sold Karekis's location to Tacio. It wouldn't be long before *three* Arks walked again. Solvi had pleaded with her not to punish the old woman, and Isa had acquiesced. She didn't know how long she'd stay that way.

Veynothi was the most feared of all the Arks. She could suck the life out of you, a fact confirmed by Amarah when she'd discovered the Ark's tomb with Traego and Kohl.

Isa shuddered to think what that place must have been like, how they must have felt in Veynothi's presence. Running from or fighting a regular Varkain was challenging enough, let alone one bolstered by ancient blood magic to become an almost unrecognisable creature of terror and death.

Amarah folded her arms. 'It'll probably be dark by the time Antar gets here. We'll spend the night here, leave early tomorrow morning.'

'Sounds good.'

Amarah pulled a small vial of red liquid from her pocket and held it up to the light. It shimmered, and when she unstoppered the cork with her thumb, a small flame burst from the bottle's opening with a crackle.

Isa was impressed. Portable fire.

'Food?'

~

AS AMARAH SUGGESTED, Antar managed to see their *Shroud* even once the sun had set, and carefully manoeuvred the warship to land beside *RaKhanna*. After the propellers stopped, he clambered down the ladder and up onto *RaKhanna*. Another person trailed him; Carav, who looked incredibly sheepish, and constantly glanced over her shoulder.

'Hope you weren't waiting too long cap'n,' Antar greeted, grabbing Amarah's fist in his own and bumping their fore-arms together.

'I ain't grey yet! Well done. No-one ask where you were going?'

'Traego watched me all morning,' Carav said. 'I gave him the slip when he went to check on our steel suppliers.'

'Steel?' Isa asked.

'Guess he wants Palom to set up shop. Having some weapons on hand wouldn't be a bad idea, especially considering Isa's followers are gonna need 'em. Trust Traego to jump on the chance to profit from production,' Amarah said, hands on her hips. 'Anyway, if Sapora or his Varkain come snooping around Estoria, you can bet your life there'll be killings. Best if everyone has a couple blades up their sleeves to defend themselves.'

Isa swallowed. Amarah was so blasé about attacking and killing Varkain. It was hard to remember sometimes that she was half one.

'Let's have a sit down. Need to tell you both about what's happening.' Amarah gestured to the captain's cabin. It was a squeeze for the four of them, but they were all at home on ships, and each found their own spot from which to listen.

Amarah leaned against the wheel, Antar against the far wall, and Carav lingered in the doorway. Isa rested against the glass screen, looking out to the sea every so often in case of anything approaching.

'Hell of a switch up there, Amarah. Thought *you'd* follow Traeg to the ends of Linaria,' Antar said, once they were all settled.

'Don't make me laugh. He's a good ally, but even *that* has a time limit if the papers are anything to go by,' Amarah said. She glanced at Carav. 'King Snake put a bounty on me. Thought it was time to get outta Estoria.'

Antar nodded, knowingly. He folded his arms and turned fully towards Amarah. 'So, you going after Jato? How you planning on taking her down?'

Amarah gestured to Isa and said, 'We both are. I have a score to settle. Princess Isa has a country to run. Both need Jato to be gone. Our princess here has gone to the trouble of hiring me and my ships. I'm captain, but she'll call the shots on where we go. For now.'

Antar looked at Isa, as if noticing her for the first time. She could have sworn he winked. 'Sounds good. I need a hot drink for this. Your ship's stocked?' He raised his chin towards Amarah, who nodded.

Isa watched in amazement as Amarah pulled out the small vial from her satchel for the second time, set it on the table at the back of the cabin, and flames whooshed into life from nothing.

'The Samolen have all sorts of useful tricks.' Amarah grinned at their stunned expressions.

With a pan of water on the boil and Antar pulling mugs of spiced chocolate from Amarah's storage, they all gathered around to discuss their route through Val Sharis, the towns they'd stop at, and how they might go about reaching Taban Yul to kill Aciel's second-in-command.

'This is as stealth a mission as we're gonna get,' Amarah said. 'Two ships, one a warship, we can't take Jato in a full on assault. We need to isolate her from the Arillians she has following her, and get her alone. *I'll* take her on. That ain't up for discussion. Her attacks will reduce my ships to splinters in seconds if we get stupid. Look at what happened to *Khanna*, and I weren't even flying her!'

The group collectively winced. Even Isa, who had loved flying her whole life, keenly felt Amarah's loss when she spoke of her first airship, the one which *RaKhanna* had been named for.

'From what I remember of Taban Yul, Jato's got the whole city surrounded with her storms,' Antar said, 'approaching that'll be hard work.'

'She's focussing on Aciel. On the crystal pillar,' Isa said, drawing everyone's attention. 'If she's distracted, that gives us an advantage.'

'Aciel? Thought Moroda took care of him with that Sevastos?' Amarah asked.

Isa sighed, exasperated. 'So did we. There's this...sickness in the city. Sapora and I thought it was Aciel's influence. Somehow the people in Taban Yul are being affected by him. Hurting themselves. Some even killing themselves.' She shuddered, remembering how she'd felt when she'd touched the woman under Aciel's compulsion. It was not something she'd ever forget.

Amarah bit her lip but didn't say anything.

'I thought we only had *one* Arillian to worry about! Now there's two?' Carav groaned.

'Aciel is still contained. Unless you're walking around in the streets of Taban Yul and get too close to the crystal, you're not going to be bothered by Aciel's compulsion. Jato's focussed on the crystal, not on anyone who might be attacking her.'

Amarah said, 'Well, it's always easier to fight someone who's pissed off, and trust me, Jato is *plenty* pissed off right now. The main reason? She can't fly, on account of me.'

'What?' Isa gasped. The others echoed her incredulity.

'In Oren, we fought. But I hacked at her wings good and proper with my scythe. Damn near chopped one of them off. Unless they can regrow, she's crippled.' Amarah took a long sip of her hot drink.

'So...so how is she in the air, then?' Isa asked.

Amarah shrugged. 'Arillians can keep anything in the air if they want to. It's their domain. She ain't alone, either. Probably got a team of 'em on rotation to keep her airborne. If we can scatter them, fly *RaKhanna* over her, not too high, I can jump. Land right on top of her and finish the job.' She smacked the bottom of her scythe on the floor in her trademark motion. 'When we take her on, Antar's gonna be on my warship. That means I'm trusting *you* to pilot *RaKhanna*, Isa.'

The princess nodded. The two women had developed a

good amount of respect for each other—at least as far as their abilities to fly airships were concerned. It was a far cry from her brother, who only filled her in on details when she pressed for them and usually *after* the event.

She suddenly remembered, vividly, the royal visit to the palace earlier that year during Summercourt. Her own father, the former warrior-king and conqueror of the Ittallan, had utterly ignored her. She meant less than nothing to him because she wasn't a snake.

The idea of taking back her home from the Varkain filled her with a sense of longing, fuelled by rage. This was her mission, her purpose.

She would do whatever it took to win.

Isa said, 'This inlet is safe enough for now. But our ultimate goal is Taban Yul, so we're going to keep on the move. Rallying my people is just as important as slaying Jato. We'll follow the trade winds from Esta Cona west across the Feor Mountains to Tannon Sona. By then, my numbers will be boosted, and we'll be on the right side of the mountains to challenge Jato and save Taban Yul. There are plenty of unmarked villages and hamlets we'll see along the way. Most Ittallan from the capital don't bother themselves with Ittallan there—they don't have enough money for their notice.'

'Know the feeling.' Amarah snorted.

'I'm going to use that to my advantage. And wealth aside, there *are* plenty of Ittallan who are scared enough of Sapora, Tacio, and their Cerastes to report us out of fear of punishment if they don't. We must be careful, especially about drawing attention. You *are* pirates after all.'

She didn't want any mistakes throwing her campaign in jeopardy.

Amarah stepped forward and pointed to the map. 'Esta Cona. That's where we're going in the morning.'

'What about the Imperial Guard posts in town? We ignore 'em?' Carav asked.

'Fine by me,' Isa said. 'We also put out the word that Amarah is after Jato—on my orders. By the time we get to Taban Yul, everyone will know who Amarah is and what she's doing for me. The people are scared of Jato that they might ignore Sapora's bounty on Amarah if she's working to save them from the Arillians.'

'I like your style, Isa. Normally I get people tellin' me I *can't* do what I want.' Amarah took a long swig from her drink and grinned.

'I'm not going to stop anyone enacting their revenge. Especially if it helps me.' Isa grinned back.

'What about all the Ittallan you're planning on recruiting? Two ships is a lotta room, but doubt it'll be enough for all of 'em to jump on board?' Antar asked.

Isa said, 'Estoria is where my followers are going to gather for the time being. Out of Sapora's jurisdiction. The wildness that made me leave should be what keeps them safe. And they can hold their own against the sky pirates. I'm staying here, on the front lines, leading the charge. I'll have the Archigo who join me to send their troops to Estoria. But if we encounter anyone who'll help us here, I'm not going to say no. Extra fighters will be needed—this isn't going to be plain sailing. It goes without saying, but once I'm queen, you'll all be well rewarded for your services. Perhaps even knighthoods?'

Amarah shook her head. 'Thanks, but I'd rather just take your coin. Me, a Goldstone? Hah.'

Isa couldn't believe it. Surely Amarah could see the benefit that came with being part of the nobility? It was what *she* was fighting for, in the end. 'Well, consider what reward you think would be fitting. I'm no Goddess, but I'll have power as queen. If I can give it, I will.'

'Looks like it really is the end of the world if we've got Goldstones wanting to knight sky pirates.' Antar laughed, but it wasn't callous, like those Isa had put up with through her youth. It was bright and genuine, full of joy and good humour.

Isa almost believed she'd already won.

16

It took three hours for the Valendrin to stir back to life after succumbing to Aciel's powers of compulsion, and the warning he'd been forced to speak.

Sapora spent the first few minutes recovering from shock, and the rest of the time debating exactly what to say when the Valendrin awoke.

If this had taken place in Sereth, in full view of other Varkain—Cerastes or otherwise—the Valendrin would have his titles stripped, his money stolen, and would probably end up in the pits fighting thralls for the rest of his days.

Weakness simply was not permitted in their culture.

Even succumbing to powerful Arillian magic.

Sapora wondered whether or not the Valendrin would be grateful to him if he kept his mouth shut. He doubted it. The Varkain were a proud race in general, and the Valendrin were often the worst of them all, save other *naja*.

When the blood mage finally stirred, Sapora immediately sprang into action. 'Welcome back to the world of the living, blood mage. Are you quite yourself again?'

The Valendrin coughed violently. Sapora had left him exactly where he'd crumpled to the floor; clearly his old body pained him, for he winced and groaned as he struggled to pull himself to his feet. He took a moment to catch his breath and glanced around, regaining his bearings. 'W—what happened?'

Sapora blinked slowly. He had more patience than most, and he savoured it when he had the upper hand. 'I believe you fell prey to a *dead* Arillian's magic. The Cerastes are standing guard outside to ensure no-one entered and saw you in...that state.'

Trembling, the Valendrin straightened, pushing himself through evident pain. 'I need no such handouts.'

'They are also waiting to escort you back to Sereth.' Sapora watched the other Varkain carefully, masking his satisfaction when a flicker of fear appeared on the blood mage's face.

'To...to Sereth? How? Jato's storm—'

'Has indeed grounded all but the most essential flights and dedicated pilots. *You'll* be travelling back in a wheeled cart. Like livestock.' Sapora couldn't help himself.

'But...but I...I...' he tried to regain some semblance of confidence and anger, 'I was your father's Valendrin!'

Sapora inclined his chin. 'And you *were* mine, too. I cannot have an advisor who is prey to those birds.' He allowed the blood mage to fret and panic. He had made no such arrangements, of course, hadn't even left the room. But the Valendrin didn't know that. It would be expected, which was what made the lie so easy to believe.

Varkain could smell weakness a league away and were unrelenting once they discovered it. Should any of those elite castes realise the Valendrin had fallen prey to Aciel, it was unlikely he'd ever be welcomed back into Sereth.

All Sapora wanted was to leverage that weakness.

'My king!' the Valendrin sank to his knees and lowered his head to the floor. 'Please reconsider. It was a moment of weakness, yes. But you know what I have done. What I am *capable* of doing! No other Valendrin in Sereth has even *half* my experience. We forego our names when we join the order. I have no other life. No family. Nothing at all that I must do, but serve at your command.'

Begging was always pathetic, though it proved that he was desperate. Sapora let out a long, practiced sigh, as if the Valendrin's words truly stirred his cold heart. 'I'm not sure...'

The Valendrin grasped at the foot of Sapora's robes. 'You seek the other Arks, my king? Allow me to assist with their seals. I will grant you this great treasure and prove myself to you. Prove I am stronger than this moment of...of...insanity.' He gestured wildly to the corpse of the Ittallan still prone on the table in the room's centre. 'I believe Malashash needs only a small ritual, something I can manage alone, without dozens of thralls.'

And there it was.

Again, Sapora allowed silence to fill the room. It fuelled the Valendrin's panic, and it made him more certain he'd selected the right method to deal with the unpleasantness of Aciel's compulsion. He hadn't truly thought the Arillian was powerful enough to speak through the dead, but the rituals of blood magic often transcended death. These days, anything was possible.

He wouldn't dwell on the details, only the facts—which were certainties.

It was the same with Isa. She was gone. He didn't know why she'd left and wouldn't dwell on that. The fact of the matter was she *had* left, and he needed to bring her back. Nothing else entered the equation.

Now, it was Malashash. He needed to resurrect the second Ark. That was next.

Through his own meddling, the blood mage had put himself under Sapora's claws.

The king turned his eyes on the Valendrin. 'Get up.'

At once, the blood mage obeyed, hastily brushing down his crumpled, dirty robes.

'I shall save you the indignity of being carted back to Sereth. For now. I'll leave you to your chambers—rest up. Change. Eat. Whatever you need to do to recover quickly.' Sapora glanced outside, where the sun lit the city. 'I will meet you at the South Gate at third moonrise.'

'Tonight, my king?'

Sapora scowled. 'Yes. Tonight. You shall accompany me to the tomb of Malashash and will help me resurrect him. Bring anything you need for the task.'

Undoubtedly the Valendrin was most unhappy about the new order, but he wisely held most of his emotions back. 'How are we to travel there?'

'It isn't far. We will be taking a covered wagon, in fact, but only as far as the Rio Neva forest. From there, we travel on foot to the site. I have been there before. You will be ready at third moonrise, and we will return to the palace with Malashash.' He gave the Valendrin no more time to retort or argue, sweeping across the room to the door. 'The Southern Gate. You will be alone.'

Final warning given, Sapora exited the chamber and pulled the door closed behind him. The hallway outside was empty—there were no guards stationed outside, Cerastes or otherwise, and he very much doubted the Valendrin would leave his room until their appointed meeting time. No Varkain wanted to be in the presence of another while they were recovering from a wound. While Aciel himself had not left any physical marks—not that Sapora could see—it was clear the blood mage had been shaken.

From now on, the Valendrin would always wonder whether any of the palace Varkain knew about his secret. And that kept him under Sapora's claws. Even if the blood mage never outwardly said he was grateful, Sapora knew it would be a deed that would never be forgotten.

Satisfied he now had a powerful ally loyal to him, Sapora made his way through the palace to his own rooms to prepare.

~

THE DARK, oppressive tunnel hadn't changed since Sapora had last visited.

He'd put off revisiting Malashash for too long, he knew, and he couldn't wait any more. Especially not now he had the Valendrin in tow. There was no excuse to delay the trip.

The palace would soon become a bolt hole instead of a home—Jato's storm grew every day. His Sevastos's hatred was stronger than ever. Sapora needed a guard he could depend upon without question, and he was certain Malashash would be exactly that.

He loved Sereth, in his own way. But the tunnels there were livable: wide, clean, and lit with sconces. The tunnels he had to traverse to reach Malashash, for he'd discovered no other entrances to the tomb in spite of months of research, were old, narrow, and in many places full of stagnant water. He'd even had to dig through part of them with his own hands.

It had seemed his previous traverse to the Ark had left some of the smaller tunnels weak, and parts of their ceilings had collapsed in several locations. As such, the rains had managed to get in, freezing parts of the route and leaving others as little more than deep pits of water.

At least it had flushed out the spiders.

Feeling their webs close around him or the tickle of their feet was more an irritation than a reason to be afraid, but now that they were gone, it truly was just himself and

Malashash alone deep underground, connected only by their blood magic.

The Valendrin would be that conduit once again. His presence and knowledge had enabled him to bring back Veynothi. He had promised to do the same for Malashash.

Since Veynothi had departed Taban Yul, Sapora had revisited the books and tomes he'd been studying for any hint as to the personalities of the Arks. Of course, he'd found nothing. Neither the Valendrin nor the scholars who had deigned to note down the Varkain's greatest weapons during the height of the war had mentioned how self-absorbed Veynothi was, or how critical of authority.

He'd known it had been a futile search, but he'd never been one to be caught unawares, and Veynothi's arrogant petulance had unsteadied him. As king, he expected all of his subjects and servants to obey him. Veynothi's disregard for his authority had been jarring—all the more so as he'd experienced it after his father's deflections.

Every battle he fought had been an uphill one. Did no-one actually support him? He'd followed all their ridiculous laws and traditions, won his jade crown through blood and sweat, proved himself over twice as much as Tacio would have had to, and *still* they chided him.

Still they laughed behind his back.

Just what *was* he supposed to do?

Be a good little snake, live a quiet life in Sereth, and have children who could fawn over Tacio and Vasil?

He'd die before giving in to that.

He had been a prince. Now, he was a king.

Even if he had to prove himself to the entire world by doing the impossible, by bringing back every one of the immortal Arks and saving the stupid people of Linaria from Aciel when he rose again, under it all, Sapora was was terrified that it wouldn't be enough.

He had no doubt that the Arillian *would* awaken and free himself from the Sevastos's crystal prison. The Valendrin's encounter had brought that into stark reality.

Isa had known, too, although she'd been preoccupied with other things while she'd been at the palace.

He cared not for Moroda. The silly girl had been bound to get herself killed. At least in her actions, she had bought him the time he'd needed to move into Taban Yul with many of his Varkain, and start putting in place the changes he'd envisioned since leaving Sereth on his errantry.

Because of Moroda's sacrifice, he'd had the chance to study—and release—the first of the four Arks, and he was well on his way to the second.

If Aciel ever did free himself—and Moroda, too—from the crystal, he ought to thank her for her efforts. Nothing that she'd done it for had come to pass. Sacrifice was very rarely as noble as they thought. But *he'd* been able to benefit. That was a good enough reason for what she'd put herself through.

He heaved himself through a narrow section of the tunnel, crawling on his belly. It was undignified for royalty, but the ends absolutely justified the means. It was a mantra he kept repeating every time he degraded himself. Somewhere behind him, the Valendrin struggled down the tunnel, but he didn't slow or wait for him.

Sapora rounded a corner and was suddenly plunged into the blackness of freezing water. Immediately, he squeezed his eyes shut and forced his nostrils closed. He'd only just made his way out of one icy pool, and now found himself in another.

When his feet touched the soft, silt-filled earth, he kicked straight upwards. His head broke the surface of the water and he inhaled, trying not to gasp and take in the dirty, stagnant air. His lungs ached for a breath of fresh, clean air, but he knew the surface was at least an hour's trek all the way back through dishevelled and broken tunnels.

Not to mention he'd sworn to himself that he wasn't going to return to the surface unless he had Malashash in tow—and he was proving himself stronger than the Valendrin.

He smiled, despite the environment. When Veynothi returned with his sister, he was sure she'd pay him the respect he deserved on seeing her comrade awake and by his side. And for Isa, of course, picked up by one Ark and brought back to another—he was certain she'd see sense and stay in the palace as part of the plans they'd drawn up together in their youth.

He'd forgive whatever had caused her to turn, and keep her in the palace until he was sure she wouldn't flee again. Even after everything she'd done, he did not want to see her on the outside when he finally unleashed his Arks upon Linaria—for he was sure he would have to, and soon.

If Aciel returned and attempted to control him, Sapora needed his full arsenal to keep himself, Tacio, Isa, and his Varkain safe. He was sure two Arks and a Sevastos would be more than a match for Aciel, though he had not halted his search for the remaining two Arks: Brahm and Karekis.

Should all four be brought back...

Sapora swam to the other side of the water-filled pit and licked his fangs at the thought of every single Ark roaming Linaria again. Surely then, even Vasil would have to concede that Sapora was the greater king.

He took several minutes to catch his breath while he waited for the Valendrin to catch up. The cold sapped his strength like a slow poison, and he needed to warm up as the water dripped off him and back into the darkness.

He flicked out his tongue and tasted the air, tested where he was and where he needed to go. Before, when he'd first discovered the tunnel, he'd just guessed where to go, and by some instinct or blind luck, had discovered Malashash's tomb.

Now, he could sense where he'd been, even weeks before. His own scent was faint, but unmistakable, and he used to retrace his exact steps. 'Are you still with me, Valendrin?' Sapora called into the dark, when he heard the splash of water behind him.

'I am, my king.' The trek had been hard going, yet the Valendrin had not uttered a single word of complaint. He was sticking doggedly to his claim of being useful.

'Good. It isn't far, now.' Sapora wondered how Malashash would react. Whether he even remembered him visiting the tomb before.

When he'd freed Veynothi, something inside him trembled, like an autumn leaf that threatened to fall from its tree. The dark markings on the back of his hands were physical evidence of that change.

His thoughts pushed him on, crawling through the tunnels, pulling himself over rocks and around corners where he encountered them, every step bringing him closer to Malashash.

Underfoot, the damp, dank soil suddenly gave way to stone, and adrenaline surged through Sapora. This was the entrance to the tomb. The resting place of the great Varkain defender, Malashash.

Eager, Sapora increased his pace, shuffling forward on his hands and knees where the tunnel forced him low, and then onto his belly. Any other Varkain of good standing—such as Tacio—wouldn't wish to lower themselves to crawling through mud and dirt, like the maggot slur often used against them, but Sapora had always been able to see the bigger picture. He didn't care what he had to do, as long as it resulted in what he wanted. He'd gladly wallow in mud all day if it meant he obtained the powers he desired and could achieve his planned results.

Sapora pulled himself forward, one elbow, then the other, alternating as he squeezed himself through narrower and tighter tunnels, the stone rough against his skin. The Valendrin grunted behind him, but followed. His fear of being ripped apart in Sereth kept him in check.

Sapora smirked. Could Tacio claim to have a Valendrin on his side?

He doubted it.

His rivalry with his brother hadn't really existed growing up. They'd been raised separately—Sapora in the palace of Taban Yul, Tacio in the tunnels of Sereth. Only when Sapora had been of an age to transform had they suddenly been thrust in with each other, and Sapora's eyes had been opened.

He'd known he was a prince since he was young enough to understand the words. He'd been told he would one day rule as king after his father.

Isa, however, a girl born only a few months after him, had been his closest friend as a child. He understood her to be his sister, and they'd played together—wrestling and chasing one another through the palace and across its vast gardens. They'd ignored the glares and snide words of the Goldstones about "mongrels" and "bastards". They'd ignored the fact they looked different—Sapora's grey against Isa's olive skin. As long as they were together, *nothing* in Linaria could stop them.

When Sapora grew old enough to tap into his *meraki* to transform into a cobra—a true *naja*, the form of Varkain royalty—he was told he would be taken to Sereth to see his father.

Knowing that Isa was a little younger, Sapora understood she would follow when she could harness her own *meraki*, and then their fun games and lessons would continue in Sereth while they grew and took on more responsibility about their lineage.

But Isa never followed.

Sapora could never be sure of the exact amount of time he'd been in Sereth—it had been extremely disorienting suddenly living underground in almost perpetual darkness—but he'd visited the surface on numerous occasions and seen the seasons change above ground as he knew them to.

An entire year passed without Isa.

Sapora worried something had happened, that she'd been hurt or perhaps her travelling party had been ambushed. Sky pirates were known to pick off lone vessels, and his own journey to Sereth had been more than a little bumpy.

But none of the Cerastes nor the Imperial Guard in Feoras Sol—the gateway town to Val Sharis—had news of his sister.

When Vasil stated he was to visit the palace of Taban Yul with his youngest son, Tacio, who had been born in Sereth to a Varkain woman, Sapora begged to accompany him. Vasil hadn't liked the idea of it—Sapora certainly remembered his father's irritated disapproval—but eventually Vasil had given in and travelled to the Val Sharis capital with both of his sons.

Sapora had immediately escaped from the Cerastes set to guarding him and combed the palace for any trace of Isa. He'd tapped into his Varkain abilities, sensing and remembering where he'd used to play, where his old rooms had been.

And while Isa's scent was strong, he hadn't been able to find her.

Infuriated, Sapora had returned to Sereth with his father without seeing Isa.

But he'd travelled back to the palace on his own a few months later, without a word to anyone. It was during that trip—unannounced, unexpected, and alone—that he'd finally caught a glimpse of Isa. His strong, funny, cunning sister. The girl he'd played with, hunted with, fought and learned and grown with, had been reduced to tears by a trio of Ittallan Goldstones who were mocking her as a kitten. They'd laughed at her, taunting her about her dirty blood and wild, feral ways.

Sapora's fury had almost ended their lives then and there, had it not been for the Imperial Guard stationed nearby. One of the Goldstones had been scarred for life—losing his left arm at the elbow where Sapora had struck him with his scimitar.

Since then, he'd learned the truth of himself and Isa. Of their mixed heritage and *meraki*, which dictated who they were to become, where they were permitted to live and travel, and how they would forever be treated by others.

He'd vowed to protect her from any who believed her to be lesser than she truly was: royalty. He didn't care what form she took, that she preferred the wide open spaces of Val Sharis to being cooped up indoors like most Varkain, who longed for their tunnels.

Sapora had tried to visit Isa whenever he could—at least twice a year—while he studied in Sereth. He learned language, dance, and drama. He learned to track, to fight, to kill.

He vowed to surpass his father as king as soon as he was ready, to take back the limiting rules and let the Varkain freely roam Val Sharis—or anywhere in Linaria, if they so chose—as they did in Sereth. He vowed to make all Linarians respect the Varkain and see they were as much a part of the world as anyone else—not a people to be ridiculed or feared.

With the Arks at his disposal, he would finally be able to achieve that dream.

Isa would come back, when she understood. She'd always been passionate and headstrong. She never took no for an answer, and was fearless in the face of danger and oppression once he'd helped her see who she was and what she could be. He'd helped her overcome her bullies, taught her how to use her *meraki* to gain advantages over any who might threaten her.

Sapora hated the thought that she was using his lessons against him.

They were a team. They'd *always* been a team.

Whatever had happened while he'd been busy finding his feet as king, or lost in a book about ancient wars and Arks, he could reverse. Whatever Tacio had said, threatened or done, he could overrule.

Everyone else followed him out of fear. Even the damned Valendrin.

Without Isa, Sapora was truly alone.

Without Isa, he had no true allies, no support, no friendship on which to fall back.

Without Isa, he had no purpose in kindness and helping the Ittallan.

Without Isa, he might as well move his Arks forward to slay them all and let the Varkain take over in a conquest so utterly absolute that Vasil's would be scratched from all records, and only his name would remain in the history books.

Sapora blinked rapidly. He didn't dare let any tears fall. Not so close to the Ark, and not with the Valendrin watching.

He pulled himself out the edge of the tunnel and into the wide stone tomb. Dirt scattered around him, darkening the floor and adding another layer of grime to the place.

The blood mage appeared only a few seconds later, his thin, scraggly hair stuck to his damp face, his fingers shaking with exertion.

Sapora gave him a few moments to familiarise himself with the tomb. This time, he did not have the same airship of thralls that he could slay. But Malashash was not Veynothi, and the breaking of his seal would be different to hers—at least, if the Valendrin was correct in his judgement.

From the rudimentary understanding of the Arks he'd gleaned from Veynothi, they were all distinct from one another, even if they had been bound under the same terms.

If only he'd known, Sapora would have tried harder to release Malashash first, before trekking halfway across the world to Corhaven for Veynothi.

Perhaps, if he'd have done that instead, Isa would still be with him in the palace.

Sapora scowled, trying to push the thought from his mind. He was here for Malashash. All else could wait.

'My king, this...this is truly the tomb of Malashash...' The Valendrin could not keep the reverence from his voice.

'Indeed. And we have work to do.' Sapora took a step forward once his eyes had adjusted to the absolute darkness of the tomb. It felt somehow more encompassing than the darkness of the tunnels and the icy water that filled half of them.

With his second step, the ring of torches surrounding Malashash's tomb burst into blue flame.

'*Naja...*' the Ark's whispered voice was expected this time, and the noise echoed for several seconds.

Sapora smiled. Malashash seemed to be ready for his second lease of life. He'd been more of an observer with Veynothi. He wasn't going to make the same mistake a second time. 'Malashash! Ark. Great Defender. I am Sapora, King of the Varkain and Ittallan. I am here to release you from your binding and free you to once again walk upon Linaria under my command.'

The flames flickered, their crackling reverberating across the vast, stone chamber.

The Valendrin appeared transfixed by their light. He then blinked, coming back to himself. 'My king, here are the words I found for the ritual. Speak these with the blood offerings. I have brought my own to break the seal.' He procured a narrow black book, squashed and damp from the journey into the depths of Linaria, but the writing was still legible. He held it before Sapora, using the blue flames to illuminate the words. He raised his other hand, palm facing Malashash, and began to speak in the Varkain's old tongue.

Sapora slipped one scimitar from his sleeve and took it in his left hand. He gripped it tightly and took in a steadying breath. He knew what to expect, and he was ready. He read the page before speaking, to ensure he didn't mess up a single word. 'By my blood, I weaken myself to give you strength.' The blade kissed his hand and drew a line of red. He hissed in pain, but continued on, 'By my blood, I take my power and pass it to you.'

Red droplets oozed down his skin and onto the oval dish at Malashash's stone feet.

'By my blood, I dance with death to give you life.'

The blue flames flashed white for an instant.

He licked his lips and read the next few lines of the book, trying to ignore the Valendrin's chanting.

The Valendrin flicked his wrist, sending sparks of coloured light bouncing around the tomb. He then withdrew a small glass vial and handed it over.

Sapora stared at the vial. The Valendrin's blood was discoloured, thick, and looked nothing like the blood of a living person. But he was a Valendrin. And this was a ceremony. Swallowing once, Sapora spoke, 'By this blood, I feed you our magic. Undoing that which has been done to you.' Sapora flicked the cork out with his thumb and poured the contents of the vial into the dish, on top of his own offering.

Another flash of white-blue light.

Without waiting, he reached into his inside pocket and pulled out the third and final vial. Tacio's blood. 'By this blood, taken from a pure *naja*, I release you from stone.'

The ground shook. Pressure built around them until it seemed as if the very air would split.

With a thundering crack, the stone encasing Malashash shattered and the plinth on which he stood split in two.

The dish of blood disappeared, absorbed into the Ark's flesh as Malashash the immortal returned from stone into his true skin.

The Ark stood for a moment, enormous and otherworldly, before his gold eyes focussed on the two Varkain standing before him.

Sapora didn't hesitate. He bowed and spoke, 'Malashash. Great Defender. I am King Sapora. I welcome you to Linaria, for it has been five thousand years since you last lived.'

'*Naja*. My armour. My shield. Where is it?' Malashash's voice was rough and low, befitting a throat that hadn't worked in several hundred generations.

But his words sent chills down Sapora's spine.

Veynothi's blades had been attached to her—or at least had been in her tomb alongside her. He guessed that grave robbers were loathe to travel into the mountains and risk being slaughtered by the griffin guardians.

Had robbers already been in Malashash's tomb and taken his rightful armour? Or had no-one thought to bury them with Malashash?

'They are not here, Ark,' Sapora said, standing up to look him in the eye.

Even naked and without his armour or weapons, Malashash was a force to be reckoned with. His muscles rippled in the flamelight, and he was all sinew and strength. Sapora didn't fancy his chances in a battle against him, and was grateful that the Ark was on his side.

'Great Ark, I am sure a new set could be fashioned for you?' The Valendrin sank to his knees, arms held over his head in reverence. 'Forgive our lack of knowledge.'

The Ark remained silent as he looked around the empty stone tomb. The fires continued to burn, but lower, and they faded with the magic that had sealed him. They shifted from blue to orange-red, casting a warm glow into the tomb.

Sapora crouched slightly, readying himself for the rush of energy he'd felt on releasing Veynothi. His link to the Sevastos was inextricably linked to the Arks, and when he'd freed her, it felt as though the dragon god itself had reached into his chest and clamped down on his heart with all its fangs.

Even braced, when it hit, Sapora wasn't ready. The sudden wave of energy caused him to buckle, and he gasped with a sudden intake of breath.

Malashash immediately whirled around to look at him, stepping forward, arms raised as if to ward off any attacker. 'King *Naja*?'

Sapora forced his eyes open. He refused to show weakness. 'A small curse from breaking your seal. It is nothing.'

Malashash narrowed his eyes. 'The Sevastos...?'

'Lives. It is in my control, under my command. As is Veynothi.'

If the Ark's stoic expression could show emotion, it came close to it now. 'Veynothi is revived also?'

'You are the second,' Sapora said, wheezing slightly as the rush began to subside. 'When I have the locations of Brahm and...Prince Karekis, they will follow.' He remembered at the last moment to use Karekis's title—he did not want Malashash to respond with as much venom as Veynothi had.

The blood mage, still on his knees, gave a small nod of approval.

When Sapora shook off the last of the pain, Malashash straightened. 'Are we at war once again with the Ittallan? Have they risen up to take Sereth?' Anger tinged the Ark's voice as he balled his clawed hands into fists.

'We are at war, yes, but not with the Ittallan. The Arillians are our greatest threat. Along with the dragons. Linaria is under siege. I wish to protect the Varkain and the Ittallan of Val Sharis. I rule them both and live in the palace of Taban Yul.'

Malashash grew quiet and thoughtful as he mulled over Sapora's words. He took so long that Sapora wasn't sure he'd understood everything, and tried to think of another way of conveying the information so the several thousand year-old creature could comprehend it.

He turned to the Valendrin when the Ark spoke suddenly, preventing Sapora from the need to re-word anything. 'I need armour and weapons. I feel the soil around me has been pulled away and picked apart. My iron is gone. Shattered. Stolen.'

The Valendrin jumped in to defend them. 'There are smiths in Taban Yul. We can re-forge whatever you need. Unfortunately, an Ittallan village was built directly above here. Feoras Sol. They've mined the iron ore in the ground here for centuries.'

Sapora allowed the Valendrin to speak, mostly grateful that this Ark seemed ready to assist him. It was a far cry from Veynothi's petulance.

'Then the forging must be done. At once. I cannot defend without armour,' Malashash said.

Sapora exhaled slowly as the last dregs of the energy rush left him, and his vision snapped back into place, somehow better than it had been before he'd awoken the Ark.

Finally, a servant who acted on orders without threats.

The dark veins on his hand thickened and grew, spreading up his wrist and along his forearm. Sapora pulled his sleeve down to cover it. He could look into that some other time, when he was alone.

Shakily, he got to his feet.

Surely the Valendrin would forgive him a tiny waver in strength considering what they had just achieved. Thankfully, the Valendrin seemed transfixed by Malashash and barely gave him a glance.

When he was sure his voice wouldn't waver, Sapora said, 'You will not have to wait long, Malashash. Once we are back on the surface, you'll find I can move things along quickly. But we have much to discuss. I must explain what has happened to Linaria since you were turned to stone by my Sevastos.'

17

Surprisingly, spending the night on the deck of *RaKhanna* with Amarah, Carav, and Antar, was less uncomfortable than Isa thought it would be. She was a princess, true enough, but she'd also spent her fair share of evenings away from the palace, sleeping in barns or on rooftops under the stars. Anything to get away from the vile looks and comments she received from Goldstones, the council, and the palace staff.

She was no stranger to roughing it.

Besides, she was back in her own country with allies who could be relied on, safe in the knowledge she was taking a step forward. It might not have been in the correct direction, or even the direction she'd *thought* she'd be going in, but she was doing *something*.

Isa could tell Amarah and Antar were hardened fighters with years of experience under their belts. Carav less so, for she was barely seventeen or eighteen, but she was a quick learner and had keen powers of observation. And she seemed absolutely besotted with Amarah—following her around like a lost kitten. Antar, too, was fiercely independent. He wore a belt of knives across his chest, and seemed to have one for any task he was confronted with; a broad blade for cutting food, a broader one for cutting people—he'd winked at her—as well as two long, slim ones that worked as various tools on the ship.

He seemed grateful to have a ship of his own, yet Isa couldn't help but wonder what was to stop him going off and doing his own thing. She didn't know how Amarah could prevent him from stealing the warship, or going back to Traego, for that matter.

She missed her own ships. They were still aboard *Otella*, out of reach for now.

Until she was able to safely return to Estoria, or gain new followers with their own resources, she was stranded with Amarah.

It seemed the sky pirate was going to keep her word, for the moment the sun peeked above the horizon, she was up and about, checking over her ship. 'Ready to go, Isa?'

'I've been ready all my life.'

Amarah cackled. 'I'll take that as a "yes," then. Antar and Carav will be coming with on *RaKhanna*, but we'll all keep our distance from you in town while we do a bit of recon. Safer for us.'

That gave Isa cause for concern. If the sky pirates would be keeping their distance, then she'd effectively be alone in Esta Cona. True, they'd be there in the shadows gathering their own intelligence, but they wouldn't be standing with her.

It wasn't a pleasant thought.

She'd always assumed she'd have a retinue with her—Aetos and Kylos at the very least, Odi also. Odi, in fact, would have been a great asset with the discussions, being the son of the Gal Etra Archigo, and no doubt well-respected.

Alone, Isa would simply have to hope that those within

the town would be on her side, and not treat her like all the other Goldstones had—as a mongrel unworthy of their time.

She wanted to ask Amarah to come with her. Surely Antar and Carav would be perfectly okay to take a look around the town by themselves. It was a selfish thought, she knew. She only wanted Amarah with her so she didn't have to face the unknown alone. The sky pirate had an enormous bounty on her head, and asking her to make such a public appearance would be the quickest way to bring her brothers' wrath upon them.

Besides, asking for that help would be showing weakness and vulnerability. If she was to be a queen, she needed to face everything alone.

Call it practice.

'Is there anything I can do to help prepare?' Isa asked, glancing around the deck of *RaKhanna*.

Amarah rubbed her eye. 'Nah, I have things sorted. We'll leave again at midday, that should give you enough time to get all your talks out the way. Once we're done with our business, we'll wait on the ship and keep an eye on things with a scope. There's a strong wind just before dusk. If we catch that, we'll make good time to the Feor Mountains.'

Isa sighed in relief.

Seeing her reaction, Amarah grinned. 'Thought I was gonna dump ya in the middle of town and leave? Don't be silly. I wanna help ya. Just don't wanna get my head chopped off while doing it!'

It was a reasonable reaction. Isa put her hand across her heart and bowed. 'I swear that you will be well-rewarded for your assistance. I'll never forget this, Amarah.'

Amarah made her way back to the cabin where she started *RaKhanna's* engines.

Isa knew she was playing with fire. This wasn't how

queens were supposed to rise. But the world was no longer the same place it had been when she was a child. Everything had changed, and she had to change with it. Otherwise, she might as well have never left her locked room in the palace.

The deck vibrated underfoot as the propellers sprang into life, and *RaKhanna* gently lifted off the muddy ground. The sails unfurled slowly, gracefully, catching the wind and gently rocking the ship. Isa instinctively widened her stance to counterbalance.

Once they ascended beyond the cliff and into the early morning sunlight, Isa turned her face to the warmth of the sun. It wasn't anywhere near as hot as it had been yesterday —in fact there were several thick clouds already gathering overhead—and Isa wondered whether that would be in her favour or not. Today was the first true step of her campaign.

She *had* to convince the Archigo to join with her and stand against Sapora.

Isa's heart fluttered in her chest, adrenaline coursing through her body at the thought of the challenge she faced. Her knees twitched, as if eager to run—though whether it was towards the challenge or away from it, she wasn't sure. Her body remained tense, no matter how she tried to calm herself. She settled for pacing up and down the length of the ship's deck.

Carav, the young thief, milled around the captain's cabin, watching Amarah as she set to work. Isa could always tell where Carav was because of the myriad necklaces she wore at all times. The metal jingled when she moved and she sounded like a bell chime. It was charming in a vaguely irritating way, and Isa had no idea how she'd become a sky pirate if stealth was such an alien concept to her.

Antar, on the other hand, left Amarah to her job and kept watch near the prow of *RaKhanna*, scope in hand, and with that air of calm, quiet confidence he always seemed to exude.

Isa leaned over the rail and watched the wetlands shrink as the ship gained altitude, listening to the conversation in the cabin with half an ear.

'Aren't you worried about Traego catching you? You have his *Thief's Ink*, don't you?' Carav asked.

Amarah replied, 'He can chase if he wants. But *RaKhanna* is faster than *Otella*. He wouldn't stand a chance.'

A sudden pang of fear shot through Isa's gut. She'd been foolish to assume they'd left all their troubles behind in Estoria. And she hadn't realised that Traego had a method of tracking down Amarah. *Thief's Ink* seemed to be the reason, and that was a concept she didn't know anything about.

Amarah didn't seem bothered in the slightest, so Isa figured she didn't need to be worried, either. Then again, it could simply be Amarah's bravado coming into play and not wanting to worry Carav.

Isa turned her gaze away from the receding land and to the sky behind them, suddenly afraid *Otella* would be on their tracks. As far as she could see, there was nothing in the sky aside from clouds and seabirds.

Her earlier confidence had vanished, and it was with a sense of trepidation that she looked ahead, to Esta Cona.

~

TRUE TO HER WORD, Amarah dropped Isa off in the middle of Esta Cona, in what must have amounted to the town square. She simply lowered the rope ladder and allowed Isa to scramble down and leap the last few feet to drop into the centre of town.

Dread settled squarely over Isa. She had been in the

middle of drafting letters to the Archigo and town guard in Estoria, but she couldn't remember a single word of what she and Odi had written. They'd also worked on a special letter for any Varkain who might have been living in the town or passing through—she didn't want them to report back to Sapora.

She stood alone on a marble statue of a carriage, about to attempt to convince the Archigo who she was, and that she deserved to be Queen of Val Sharis. She had no retinue. No council or advisors. She was just a random Ittallan dropped off in the centre of town by an unregistered airship belonging to a sky pirate.

Amarah hadn't even docked in the hangar.

She knew the sky pirates would land the ship nearby as they trawled through Esta Cona to gather their own intelligence—no doubt about Jato and Amarah's bounty—but Isa still faced this first hurdle alone.

As was to be expected, her abrupt arrival drew plenty of attention.

That was fine. She was used to people staring.

The gathered crowd spoke among themselves, some of the younger Ittallan pointing and gesturing. Clearly no-one had expected their princess to drop out of the sky unannounced, and it appeared to be taking several of them some time to realise just *who* she was.

'Ittallan of Esta Cona! I bid you good morning!' Isa's voice shook. She was unused to delivering speeches and had never felt entirely comfortable talking in front of a large audience. This would have been Odi's job, or Kylos's. Anyone else would usually speak for royalty, especially in public.

Then again, by speaking for herself—even if it was out of necessity—she was setting herself apart from other Ittallan or Varkain royals.

Evidently there were plenty of things she needed to learn.

Even though she'd spent most of the previous night negotiating with a group of unruly sky pirates, somehow talking to her own people was far more intimidating.

'I am Isa, Princess of Val Sharis,' she purposely missed off Sereth, 'and I come to you during Linaria's strife. Please, where is Archigo Kessir? I wish to speak with him, offer my aid, and explain a proposition I have to offer you all.'

That caused additional chatter—more excited this time.

Isa reached into her pocket, relaxing when she felt the familiar weight of her onyx stone. Her family crest was etched into it, and it was an ornament she carried with her at all times.

It was also the only item from her personal effects she still had—everything else had been left in her tent in Estoria. And it was the only proof she had of her name for those who'd never visited Taban Yul or seen her before.

She held it high, drawing gasps and looks of wonder from the crowd.

It didn't take long before a couple of youths raced off away from the square and down one of the main streets. Isa assumed they would be fetching the Imperial Guard. While she waited, she looked around as more and more people gathered. She didn't know what to do. Stay where she was? Standing upon a statue so everyone could see her? Go down and walk among them? Talk to them?

At this point, Kylos would chip in with a reassuring word or advise her on what to do.

She looked around, trying to get her bearings. Esta Cona was opposite to Taban Yul in every conceivable way. It had narrow streets that were half-paved, half churned up clay. None of the buildings had been designed for beauty—function came first out here. The stone would have been mined from the quarry at Tannon Sona, and no-one had bothered to colour it. In Taban Yul, it was common to stroll through various districts and see stunning yellow townhouses with flowering vines trailing down their walls, or poppy-red houses of law and writing, or the hexagonal blue towers that marked the entrance to Traders' Alley. Here, aside from the town being smaller, all the buildings were grey-white and bland, with unadorned fascias and flat rooftops. No plants or flowers grew near, there were no water fountains or music. It was simply a functional town with zero personality.

Even the Ittallan who watched her seemed bland—there were no patterns or colours in their dress, and their simple fabrics were hardwearing.

Bland was the wrong word. Perhaps they were simply poor.

She swallowed thickly. Even as resented as she had been, Isa was still a princess. She lived in a world of palaces, money, and finery. It was worlds apart from the majority of her people. Not all Ittallan were Goldstones, and not all lived in the capital.

She needed to remember that to ensure she did not come across in the same way as Sapora.

'I come alone. There is no Imperial Guard with me, nor Cerestes.' Isa wasn't sure why she added that, but wanted to ensure the Ittallan here knew she wasn't spying for her brother, nor here to push more Ittallan out of their homes or jobs—which would be valid concerns.

She scanned the growing crowd and spotted the familiar blonde hair of Carav. The young sky pirate nodded once, before disappearing into the throng.

'All right, all right, keep moving, unless you want to be fined for loitering!'

Isa whipped around at the sound of a gruff voice barking

across the gathered crowd. A short Ittallan in red and gold livery marched into the square, his puffy face red, black hair stuck to his sweaty forehead. He didn't wear a helm, so Isa couldn't tell if he was a captain or not, and he clapped loudly as if shooing away a scavenging dog. Only a few steps behind him, a tall Ittallan followed, his short purple robes also styled for function over fashion. Kessir was unmistakable with his long dark hair and narrow, hunter's eyes. He'd always been nervous, and seemed to view everyone with deep suspicion.

When Kessir's gaze fell upon Isa, his mouth pulled down into a grimace, his moustache lifting as his lip curled.

So much for making a good first impression.

The soldier of the Imperial Guard shooed away most of the onlookers while Kessir hung back and waited, arms clasped behind his back, watching events unfold. His pale skin was blotchy, as if he'd been caught out in the sun for too long, and his skin peeled a little around his hairline.

Isa had never particularly liked Kessir, but she had little choice.

Before everyone had dispersed, she strode forward, forcing confidence into every step. 'Archigo Kessir. It is an honour to meet you in your hometown. I trust your journey back from Summercourt was comfortable?' Although it was customary for anyone to bow to her, seeing as *she* was royalty and therefore of the highest possible rank, she wanted to show the Archigo respect to get back onto the right foot, and gave him a gentle, polite bow.

Kessir's scowl deepend, and he glanced her up and down as if evaluating her for sale. 'I do believe this is the first time in...well, ever, that you have graced Esta Cona with your presence, my dear Princess Isa. I must say I am most surprised. Are you quite well? There are...rumours that have trickled down to us from the palace...'

His voice was oily, and Isa fought the urge to flinch. 'Rumours have always entertained the townsfolk. I'm sure an esteemed Archigo such as yourself would never listen to such gossip?' She raised an eyebrow and held his gaze, testing him.

Kessir coughed awkwardly and stepped back. 'Of course not. I am above such nonsense. Yet, the Ittallan of Esta Cona seldom receive actual news. Gossip and rumour is often all they hear.' He gestured down the street whence he'd come. 'I'm afraid I had no knowledge of your visit, else I'd have been better prepared. Usually Koraki sends a messenger or steward from the palace and—'

'It's fine,' Isa interrupted. 'If we might speak somewhere in private?'

Kessir and the soldier from his guard shared a brief look, then the Archigo tilted his head in a half-bow. 'Of course, Princess Isa. It would be my honour if you would join me for some tea.'

Pleasantries over, Isa forced the pace back down the street. Kessir wasn't old—he was barely in his fifties—but he was slow and methodical in everything he did. Which included walking, apparently. She took the time during their slow journey to take stock of the town. Many of the buildings sat in various states of disrepair, some with significant chunks of stonework missing or walls half-crumbled.

Esta Cona had been too far out of the way to have been impacted by Aciel's original conquest. She wondered whether Archigo Kessir was simply a poor manager of the towns' funds. He did manage a large swathe of southern Val Sharis, after all. It was entirely possible that he'd squandered the money frivolously instead of in upkeep and maintenance.

On appearances, he didn't seem to have spent the money on himself. She decided there and then to keep a closer eye on Kessir from now on—and even more so when she became queen.

Kessir led them down a crooked set of stairs wedged between two buildings, and onto a narrow walkway on the edge of the river delta. It gave them a stunning view of the Central Ocean, though Estoria was too far beyond the horizon to see.

Small restaurants and cafes nestled against one another, with tables set outside so patrons could enjoy the view. Isa noticed a small Imperial Guard post where a group of blue-armoured Cerastes spoke to one another. They were too far away for her to hear, or even lip read, but she hurried forward when one glanced at her.

Eventually, the Archigo led them to a tea shop on the edge of the parade. The soldier that had followed them stood guard several feet away, giving the princess and the Archigo their privacy. Kessir sat at one of the tables outside—which quickly emptied of other Ittallan—and Isa joined him, feeling altogether out of place.

So far from the main square, she wondered if Amarah and the others even had sight of her anymore.

She ignored her discomfort and focussed on the Archigo.

'What do I owe the honour, Princess Isa?' Kessir asked. He didn't smile. Didn't even pretend to enjoy her presence.

Isa had barely taken a breath to reply when a young serving girl approached their table and placed a large teapot before them. She didn't so much as glance up, simply set the table with cups and condiments, and hurried back into the shop as quickly as she'd arrived.

Kessir ignored her, and Isa tried to recall what she'd been about to say. There was no well-written letter she could simply pass to him. 'Archigo. I shall be blunt as time is short. As you are aware, I am Princess Isa, the daughter of King

Vasil, who conquered Val Sharis more than two decades ago.' She tried to recall how the letter had opened, and Odi's advice on reminding the Archigo of her right to rule. 'My rightful place is on the throne, ruling Val Sharis as your queen. My brother has won the Jade Crown which permits him to rule in Sereth. I wish to ensure this happens. He and the Varkain return to their tunnels, and I rule the land of my birth.'

Kessir lifted his cup to his lips but didn't drink. His eyes watered slightly in the rising steam.

'To that end, I need followers. Resources. Gold.'

She left it there. Ask for too much more and she'd seem desperate. This way, it was a confident request. A demand.

Kessir allowed the silence to hang a little while, before he sipped his tea. 'This is a great ask, Princess. Not just for resources and people. What you ask is treason.'

In her peripheral vision, Isa saw the soldier's hand tighten on the hilt of his sword.

'I ask for you to follow your true and rightful queen. Are you happy with a Varkain upon the throne?'

Kessir's sneer answered for him. 'But are you not yourself part-Varkain, princess?'

'My blood matters only in as much as my right to rule. My *meraki* shows I am an Ittallan, the same as you. The same as those who live in Val Sharis. Besides, your reaction makes your thoughts clear on Sapora in the palace.'

Kessir snorted and looked away. Whomever had been down the promenade, enjoying a morning stroll, had been chased away by the soldier. Two more of his colleagues had appeared since Isa and Kessir had sat down.

The hairs on the back of her neck stood up at being outnumbered, and it took all her effort not to squirm in her seat. She knew she should take the offered drink. Just a small sip would show she was amicable and friendly. But as tense as she was, she couldn't so much as lift the cup to her mouth.

Her gut screamed at her to get out, that she was being surrounded, but she didn't want to mess up her only opportunity with the Archigo. She wouldn't get another chance to sit down with him.

Kessir leaned back in his chair and shouted, 'Zia! Molan! Out here, please.'

Isa fought her flinch. She turned in her seat to see the same serving girl appear, followed by a boy barely ten years old. They obediently approached the table and stood, quiet, awaiting orders. Both were scrawny and underfed, with a gauntness to their faces that Isa found severe.

Something about their behaviour made her skin crawl. When Kessir said nothing further, she asked, 'And who are these two?'

'Zia and Molan. Siblings. They washed up on the coast about a moon before Summercourt,' Kessir said, as if that explained everything.

Isa wasn't sure if he was playing some sort of joke on her. Washed up? What did that mean? Was that some sort of term she was supposed to know? 'Is that right?'

Kessir smiled thinly. 'Indeed. What do you two think of the Varkain? You may speak freely.'

The siblings shared a look, then Zia spoke, 'We escaped Sereth...'

Isa bit her thumbnail. 'You what?'

Zia continued, her voice shaking, 'They took us from our village. Our dad owns the tavern. After the battle in Taban Yul, and Aciel attacked the palace, everything was chaos. Varkain came and raided the town. Rounded us up along with some others.'

Isa's heart went out to them. Kidnapping people and bringing them back to Sereth as thralls was a tradition

Sapora had promised to outlaw as soon as he came to power. While he might have been too late to stop these two being taken, she had little faith he'd actually done anything to prevent it since becoming king.

She wondered whether it was another of his promises that held no water, or if Tacio or some other high-ranking Varkain were continuing with the abductions behind his back.

'I'm sorry you've been through that,' Isa said, though she knew her words weren't anywhere near enough. 'Do you know who I am?'

They nodded.

'I'm going to be queen, soon. That means I'll be in charge of the Imperial Guard in Val Sharis. I'll make sure your family has plenty of gold to rebuild their inn, and your village. I'm going to stop the Varkain taking people from their families. They're going to pay for what they've done.'

Isa looked the youths over. Zia was barely fourteen. What kind of king allowed the Varkain to take his own people and subject them to a life of tortured slavery?

Her blood boiled.

'You're dismissed,' Kessir said, his point made. Both of them scampered off as quickly as they'd arrived.

Isa struggled to keep a lid on her temper. 'Why did you show me that?'

'You saw how they were? Cowering before us?'

She pursed her lips, not trusting herself to speak.

'That's *fear*. All Ittallan fear the Varkain. It's innate. I am the same, though I'm above such animalistic emotions. I *respect* the power of the Varkain. And I *respect* the power of King Sapora, his Sevastos, and the Ark he has.'

Isa shot to her feet, but it was too late. The three soldiers of the Imperial Guard pounced, their weapons drawn and levelled at her before she could do anything.

Kessir finished the rest of his cup of tea and gently dabbed at his lips with a patterned kerchief. 'Captain. If you wouldn't mind sending a message to King Sapora. Inform him that we have caught this treasonous woman, and are keeping her locked up until he is ready to have her collected.'

Isa's breath caught, and several things happened at once.

The rage which had been bubbling within Isa dissipated, giving way to terror.

Scalding tea rushed across her skin as the teapot to her right exploded.

The scent of blood filled her nose as a thin blade pushed through the throat of the soldier nearest her.

Someone grabbed her wrist from behind and yanked her backwards.

'Get down!' Antar yelled. A flick of his wrist and a second blade whizzed through the air to embed itself in the right arm of another guard, causing him to scream in pain and drop his sword.

It was all the distraction Isa needed. She bolted, following the pull of the arm around her wrist—Carav's, now she'd taken a moment to look—and charged along the promenade, away from the shouts of chaos and confusion.

'Got yourself into a right pickle, didn'tcha?' Carav said, racing ahead. 'Amarah saw things were going south *way* before you sat down for tea!'

Isa heard Carav's snide tone but could look past it considering she'd helped get her out of that mess. Antar loped after them, his feet slapping against the paved street as he caught up.

Too close for comfort, the angry shouts and booted feet of the Imperial Guard followed.

Ahead, *RaKhanna* floated down, a rope dangling low.

Isa shifted in a surge of light, her *meraki* changing her

form and giving her a spring in her step. Crouching mid-stride, she leapt into the air, claws drawn, and grasped onto the rope. She didn't wait, trusting that her comrades knew exactly what they were doing, and crawled up as quickly as she was able.

It wobbled underneath as Carav, and then Antar, grabbed on, and *RaKhanna* lifted them all high into the air, away from the baying soldiers.

18

Kohl had been desperate to wait in Gur Bano until morning and take the airship across the Sea of Nami, as he'd originally planned. He needed to keep himself and Fogu out of sight—there was no telling how the townspeople might react to two Arillians in their midst. The bounty for Arillians that King Sapora had levied was valid throughout Linaria. Even if it was only the Estorian pirates who were likely to act on it, it meant that being recognised was more dangerous than ever before. Coupled with the Varkain in town, and it was only a matter of time before they were discovered.

He'd reluctantly taken Fogu's advice, and the two of them had crept away from Gur Bano when the Ittallan and Varkain's conversation had escalated into an altercation. They'd been diligent in ensuring they'd not been followed, and even if they had, Varkain couldn't fly.

The point of travelling to Berel in the first place was to warn the scholars, and hopefully *they* could take steps to safeguard Linaria from the path of destruction it was careening down. If flying directly there put himself at risk, then that was a sacrifice he was willing to make.

He had told Fogu several times to return to Oren, in fact, but the General was too loyal to abandon him now. Kohl was grateful for the company, and had said as much. But he did not wish to risk Fogu's life any more than he already had.

Flying across the Sea of Nami brought with it its own risks. Not only was it a vast ocean many leagues across, but it was full of traffic. The busiest shipping routes in Linaria crossed the Sea of Nami between Corhaven and Val Sharis—not just merchant vessels, but cargo ships; luxury cruisers transporting the world's wealthiest from one continent to another; and dozens upon dozens of unmarked ships belonging to individuals. Some, Kohl feared, were sky pirates. Dragons, too, ruled the skies here —though they were packs of smaller, younger beasts that kept away from any movement that was not their own kind.

The last time Kohl had crossed the ocean, he'd encountered Aciel and Jato on their warship.

That was an experience he never wanted to repeat. Fogu had probably been on the ship as well, not that he'd been able to spot the General at the time.

Kohl shuddered. They'd almost lost Moroda that day. Jato had been close to killing her—probably would have, too, if she hadn't enjoyed *toying* with them for so long first.

The memories made the flight across the sea harder than he'd anticipated, but there was nowhere for them to stop and rest en route. He'd had to rely on Fogu's strength to keep him aloft.

Just like in their escape from Estoria.

Strong trade winds that sped the airships along their routes battered the two Arillians, blowing them off course more than it helped their flight. Kohl's arms numbed after a time, and he glided more than flew, held up by Fogu's seemingly inexhaustible powers.

By the time the vast, orange-red desert appeared on the horizon, Kohl was ready to give up.

In truth, he'd still not fully recovered from his time in Estoria. The drowning pits had taken a lot out of him, as had the sky pirates who'd caught him. He doubted his fingers would ever be straight again. More than that, though, the deaths of his people—frightened and alone in a foreign land—was what ate at his strength most.

Since being plucked from the jaws of death, they'd constantly been on the move, always looking over their shoulders in case of trouble. They'd fought a dragon, crossed the entire width of Val Sharis, and now the Sea of Nami, too. It was too much too soon.

He sighed. He was an Arillian Lord. One of only three. He had the Frost-touch and the ability to commune with the Ice Golems. And yet he was as vulnerable as a newborn.

'My lord?' Fogu ventured once the pair touched down on the nearest patch of land—a tall cliff overlooking the sea to the east, and a small forest to the west. The jagged coastline of Ranski sprawled out to the north and south, giving way to desert. A river flowed through the forest, dividing it, and creating an oasis of green in an otherwise barren landscape. Flowers sprouted among the greenery, splashing a pattern of pinks, yellows, and reds out into the desert.

Ranski had few mountains, in fact its only range was on the far western shore, and under the clear desert sky, Kohl could see Berel on the lake as plainly as he could see the boats and airships on the Sea of Nami.

Phoenixes and dragons were commonplace here, and he had no desire to encounter any of those, either. 'Just need to catch my breath, Fogu,' Kohl replied, after realising he hadn't said anything. He crouched down on the dusty ground, his cloak flapping around in the strong winds so high up. He grasped his hat with his right hand, the fingers on his left stiff and splinted. The makeshift bandage was already fraying, having fared poorly in the sea air during their travel. 'I apologise if I worried you.'

Fogu crouched beside him, arms loosely draped over his knees. 'I've said it so many times now, there's no need to say it again. You know my thoughts.'

'Leave the Linarians to their fate, and go home?' Kohl managed a dry smile. 'We will, just as soon as I've spoken to the scholars here.'

'And if they don't listen?'

'We'll have tried.' Kohl straightened up, glad to give his wings a rest after such a long time in the air. At least here, so far from Taban Yul, he could no longer feel Jato's hateful rage.

One dark thought remained at the back of his mind—what had been said in Gur Bano about there being a sickness in Taban Yul. One so bad it had spooked the Varkain. With Jato so fixated on attacking Taban Yul...could there be a possibility Aciel's influence was somehow affecting those within the Val Sharis capital?

He knew less about the Sevastos magic and its limitations. He'd known there was a good chance that the Sevastos had only sealed Aciel and Moroda away, and they were still alive. He hadn't realised that Aciel's influence could seep *out* of that prison.

Very few people understood Arillian magic, and compulsion itself was rare. If Aciel was able to exert his will on those in the city, it might very well appear as a sickness to observers.

He balled his fists, a dozen thoughts racing around his mind. There were too many powers being disturbed. Linaria was on the brink of destruction, he was certain.

Perhaps it would be for the best if the dragons burned

everything to ash and allowed Linaria to restart from scratch.

'We should keep moving, my lord. Else shelter within those trees,' Fogu said.

Berel was just as hot and arid as Kohl remembered it. The swift desert winds brought dust and grit, which clung to his hair and feathers. He brushed his hand through his hair and shook his head, trying to clear it. 'Probably a good idea.' He flexed the fingers on his good hand, sending out a shower of snowflakes that covered them both. The cooling effect was immediate, and refreshed, Kohl stood up. 'The sooner we get to Berel the better. I'm sure we can find somewhere to rest once we're there.'

Fogu spread his wings and crouched slightly. 'I'll follow your lead, my lord. As always.'

THE SAVING grace of their arduous journey was that if Linaria was at war, the entire country of Ranski was obligated by law to remain neutral. It meant that despite King Sapora's bounties, they were as safe in the mage city of Berel as they would be on their own lands to the far north.

Every city had its bad eggs, but the Samolen were bound by something stronger than personal preferences that could be bribed—it was written into the very magic they wielded.

Despite their decrees, Samolen young and old stared at the two Arillians as they walked along the dusty streets of Berel New Town. Most quickly averted their gaze when Kohl or Fogu looked back, hurrying forward with their own tasks, sand kicked up by sandaled feet.

They moved around in pairs or groups, carrying wood, tools, chunks of stone, most of them aiding someone else.

Some pushed carts of materials along, or stepped out of the Arillians' way when they saw them approach.

'They're rebuilding,' Fogu said, surprised.

Kohl didn't answer. He knew he was staring too, but not at the Samolen. Scorch marks covered half the taller buildings, particularly those near the bridge across the lake into Berel Old Town. Many houses had lost their roof canopies, or were using a patchwork of multicoloured fabrics hastily stitched together.

Coupled with the wide-eyed gazes of the Samolen—and other peoples in the desert capital —and it was clear something terrible had happened here. Quite recently in fact. Even the stench of burning wood and melted stone lingered in the air like mist.

Had they been too late?

He chanced glances into the open doors of the buildings they passed, most of which were houses. Many were occupied, their residents going about their business. There were few—if any—casualties that he could see.

Unease settled in Kohl's stomach the longer they walked, retracing the steps he'd taken with Moroda, Amarah and the others on his first visit to the capital of Ranski, what felt like a lifetime ago. Although both Arillians kept their cloaks on to cover their wings, it was clear the Samolen knew them for what they were the moment they set foot in the city.

'Is it much farther?' Fogu asked, his voice an octave higher. He was doing a poor job of hiding his nerves.

'Fogu, this is the safest place in Linaria right now. Even at home, the Ice Golems can turn on us if they've a mind to! The Samolen are a peaceful people. You know that.'

Fogu let out a snort that didn't seem like approval, keeping his wary gaze scanning ahead and behind, lest they were suddenly set upon. 'And yet it appears they've been under attack.'

'Just because you're peaceful doesn't mean you can't be harmed.' Kohl knew that more than most. In fact, it had been his pacifism that had *led* to more harm—and deaths—than if he'd just fought back whenever he'd been pushed into a corner.

'Well, that's hardly safe, then.'

Kohl couldn't disagree, but it seemed that whatever danger had befallen the city had since passed.

Thankfully, the major roads in Berel were wide and well kept. They passed under stone archways, coloured jewels and flames burning bright, just as Kohl remembered. 'Topeko's home shouldn't be far...'

'Good. I'd hate to think we've flown across half of Linaria just to be turned away.'

'Peace, Fogu. Topeko is a good man. In fact, he was the first person in front of whom I removed my cloak.' Kohl had spent every moment in Berel scouring Topeko's library, looking for books on Arillian magic, compulsion, for anything that might have given him a hint as to Jato's behaviour. And if there was anything he could do to help her.

It had been futile in the end. Jato truly loved Aciel, and followed his campaign because of that, rather than being forced into it like all of the others.

The truth had been worse than his fear.

'There is...something here, my lord,' Fogu said when they reached a part of the street with a clear view of the lake. 'I do not know exactly what, but...'

Kohl stood beside him and closed his eyes to better focus. 'What do you mean?'

'I'm not certain. Some sort of power. It reminds me of the Ice Golems.'

Kohl opened his eyes and pointed to Berel Old Town, which housed the University and the five Sevastos stones that powered the country. 'Berel is a place of power. The dragon magic here is said to be the source of all life.'

Fogu scoffed. 'I can feel that, too. That's the life magic of this place. In every stone, in every breath of wind. What I'm referring to is *more* than that. Dormant. Waiting. Like our Ice Golems.'

Kohl frowned. He'd been here before—admittedly he'd been rather distracted at the time—and he was certain he'd remember feeling a dormant power as strong as the Ice Golems.

Then, he sensed it. A pulse of life. A distant burst as though some vast creature slept, and its breath ghosted through the city for just an instant. Then it was gone.

'I mislike this place, my lord,' Fogu said, his voice low.

Kohl drew his cloak more tightly around himself, despite the heat. 'Come, Fogu. We won't be here for long.' He led them away, deeper into the residential area of the New Town, away from the sights and feelings of the lake magic that pulsed like a heartbeat.

There were fewer Samolen here, too. Most appeared to be in the busier, more touristy sections of the city, which suited the Arillians just fine. Lines of washing hung against walls or in between buildings, and the sound of waterfalls tinkling between fountains brought a calming, natural sound that went far to assuage their nerves.

They crossed another street and Kohl smiled. 'Here we are, friend.' Topeko's home commanded one corner of a small square—a crossroads leading into different parts of the city. It was broad, with a sloping roof of purple fabric and red curtains for doors. It had been built out of the same, sandy stone as the other homes in the area, and a lantern burned brightly above the door, even though the sun was high.

A pair of Samolen with white jewels embedded in their

cheeks exited the house and faltered when they spotted them. One recovered more quickly than his comrade, and bowed low. 'Greetings, Arillians.'

Kohl inclined his head. 'We're here to speak with Topeko. I hope we're not intruding?'

The Samolen's gaze flicked between them both. He crossed one arm over his chest and bowed again, almost apologetic. 'Kalos Topeko is not within. I hope you bring no trouble to our sacred city.' It was not a question, but a statement, and almost rude.

'No trouble at all, friend,' Kohl replied, imitating the bow. 'I *do* have urgent news for Topeko. Do you know where he is? Or when he might return?'

'Kalos Topeko will be teaching at the University. If you are visitors to Berel, why don't we take you on a tour of—'

'That won't be necessary.' Fogu stepped forward, fluttering his wings under his cloak as the Samolen knew exactly what they were. 'We'll wait. Unless that isn't permitted?'

Neither of the two Samolen were in any rush to challenge Fogu's more intimidating stance. The second one straightened up. 'That...that's quite alright. The Kalos will speak to you when he is able, I am sure. But you may have a long wait.'

'Thank you.' Fogu's dismissal couldn't be any clearer, and both Samolen hurried past them, whispering to themselves as they left.

Kohl rounded on his companion. 'Was that *really* necessary?'

'What's the issue? Just getting rid of them. We don't need an audience for one message to one scholar, do we? Anyway, it couldn't be more obvious that they don't want us here.'

Kohl folded his arms. 'I know, but...you didn't need to frighten them. They were only young.'

Fogu pursed his lips and frowned. 'Let's wait inside. I don't want every Samolen in the city staring at us.'

'Fogu! Wait!' Kohl darted after him, one hand outstretched.

Before he reached Fogu, the curtain burst open and a man marched out. Though he wore the robes of the Samolen, he did not share their cheek jewels nor their darker, tanned skin. He was well-built, though not especially tall, with ruffled brown hair, light brown eyes, and dark stubble covering his chin. 'What's all this noise out here?' he snapped, rubbing his bloodshot eyes with one hand.

Even though he'd physically changed since Kohl had last seen him, it was utterly undeniable. '*Morgen*!?' he gasped.

Morgen blinked in the bright sunlight, forehead furrowed in a deep frown. He took a step back and narrowed his eyes, blinking several more times. With eyes as red as they were, and dark circles under them, he looked ill. 'Kohl? It can't be! What in Rhea's name are *you* doing here?'

Kohl chuckled.

A myriad of emotions crossed Morgen's face in the seconds that followed. Shock dominated for the most part, shifting into incredulity and wonder, then darkening to a simmer. He must have remembered something unpleasant.

Kohl's laughter drained. He hadn't seen Morgen since the battle of Taban Yul against Aciel and his forces. Prior to that, he'd abandoned Morgen, Moroda, and Eryn to fight Jato and her Elite Arillians alone, in the wilds of Val Sharis.

Eryn had died in that battle. So had Anahrik, when he and Palom had come to their rescue.

He knew Palom blamed him for their deaths—rightfully so. Morgen harboured similar thoughts, too, it seemed.

Kohl decided to remain neutral. Bringing up the past would only cause pain. 'It's been a long time, Morgen. I hadn't thought you would be here, either. I've come to see Topeko.'

'Kalos Topeko isn't here,' Morgen said coolly. He turned to look at Fogu. 'You and your...friend will have to return another time.'

It was a far cry from the warm welcome Kohl had expected. He spoke before Fogu could step in and make matters worse with his abrupt approach. 'May we wait here for him? It's urgent.'

Morgen hesitated. 'I don't think it would be a good idea.'

'Why not? It's clear some trouble has befallen the city. The news we bring may help prevent more. Dragons are linked, and this place worships them. I think it would be in Topeko's best interests to listen to what we have to say.' It wasn't strictly speaking a lie. Kohl was simply done with being pushed around or pushed away.

He'd apparently said the right thing, however, as Morgen's face of impassivity cracked when he heard the word "dragon."

'What happened here?' Fogu asked.

For once, Kohl didn't wish to reprimand him for being too pushy.

Morgen opened his mouth, then thought better of it. He scratched his forehead and dragged both hands through this hair.

It was in that action that Kohl noticed just how drained the young man looked. His eyes had lost their spark, and he seemed almost resigned. It was something more than tiredness. 'Are you well, Morgen? Can I assist in some way?'

Morgen shrugged. 'If I'm honest, Kohl? You've done enough. I've lost people because of you. I lost *Eryn*.' Morgen's voice broke on the last word.

'For that I am truly sorry. I can never hope for your forgiveness. What I did was inexcusable. But I did it to save my daughter, rather than any malicious intent towards you. I hope, if nothing else, you can understand that.'

The look Morgen gave him was so dark that Kohl took a step back. Morgen had always been cheerful, keen to help and always with a kind word. This Morgen was not the same man he'd travelled with before.

Kohl wasn't sure what he'd been through, but he didn't like it. 'Please, Morgen. This is about Linaria. Not any strife between you and I, or anyone else.'

'You want me to ignore death? *Murder*? You *do* know what Berel stands for, don't you?' Morgen said, though his voice no longer shook.

'We know. This is why we're risking our lives to come here and speak with Topeko,' Kohl said, standing his ground. 'There is nothing you can say that I have not already said to myself, Morgen. No harsh words or criticism or accusation. Save yourself the sadness and rage. It will do you no good to hold onto it and let it fester.'

'You sound like the Kalos,' Morgen said, almost sarcastically. 'Come in then, seeing as you won't leave. You're lucky I'm not permitted to hold a sword, Kohl.'

Morgen pushed back the curtain and walked inside.

Fogu grasped Kohl's arm, holding him back from following. 'Are you sure this is wise, my lord? This man harbours hatred with as much passion as Jato!'

Kohl ignored the mention of his daughter. 'Everyone harbours hatred, Fogu. You must accept that. And as I said to Morgen, this is about more than you or I, or any individual.'

'He *threatened* your life!'

'Arillians!'

Fogu whipped around at the word in time to see a young, blonde woman halfway down the street. She didn't appear to be Samolen either—with pale skin and no cheek jewel. She clutched a wicker basket of food under her elbow and stared at them like a rabbit cornered by a fox.

'Peace, child. We are here to speak with Topeko and Morgen,' Kohl said, hoping that by naming those at the building she would see them as friends. He smiled and opened his arms wide in what he thought was a non-threatening gesture.

Overhead, a phoenix cried, casting a glittering golden-red light upon them as it flew past.

Without another word, the woman spun on her heel and fled down the street, robes billowing out behind her, until she disappeared from view.

19

Palom sat in semi-darkness, the large room illuminated only by a trio of tall, wax candles in the corner.

He didn't want the light. It hurt his eyes too much. Since returning to Traego's lodge in Falice, he'd been told to lie down in the dark and wait to regain his strength.

Malot was Traego's Kalosuk. Although she was a Samolen and had access to their magic, her specialties didn't lie with healing, and she was unfamiliar with Ittallan biology, so treated him like he was some weakling from Corhaven, confined to bed rest for the most part.

Still, she had been kind to him, and had brought him a plate of hot food, for which he was immeasurably grateful.

'Try to eat slowly,' Malot said, leaning forward to grab one of the candles and move it closer.

'No light. Please,' Palom said, his voice rough. He felt sure he'd be coughing up water for the rest of his days. 'It hurts my eyes.'

She left the candle with the others and walked back to him. Her red cheek jewel glinted in the low light, and she smiled thinly. 'Light and warmth will help you recover.'

Palom shovelled a forkful of pan-fried fish and sea vegetables into his mouth. 'Food will help more.'

She huffed and tilted her head, assessing him with narrowed eyes. The silver rings and jewelled studs adorning her ears, nose, and braided hair glinted in the flickering candlelight, making her seem otherworldly. 'You're the worst patient I've had!'

Palom swallowed his mouthful and immediately took another. 'You deal with pirates. And you are not healer.'

'I'm not. But when they have knife wounds or missing limbs, *someone* has to help.'

Palom rested his fork on the edge of his plate, already feeling better. 'Solvi. How is she?'

'The girl?' Malot raised an eyebrow. 'She's fine. She does as she's told more than you. Eat. Rest. *Try* to sleep. There's a bell by your pillow. Ring if you need something.'

Palom grunted his affirmation and took another bite, watching as she let herself out. When the door clicked shut, he put the plate on his bedside table and got to his feet.

She'd bandaged his side and his thigh well in white linen. No fresh blood seeped out when he moved, which had to be a good sign. Unfortunately, the feel of clothes against his skin made him itch, and even the thin blanket on his bed was irritating. Malot was quite certain he'd not been poisoned, but he itched constantly, as though someone draped a tiny feather along his skin, but he couldn't see it to pull it out. He assumed it was his body healing itself, but it was uncomfortable.

He rubbed the back of his neck. He hadn't even seen *Leillu*. Everyone had been focussed on ensuring Solvi was okay—which he completely agreed with—but no-one had thought to tell him what was going on or keep him updated. He didn't even know how long he'd been out—had it been a few hours or a few days?

Palom stood by the window and peered out. Night had fallen, and he knew he'd been in and out of sleep since being brought back, half-remembered memories slipping away as quickly as they appeared. Waking up in an unfamiliar bed with your whole body in pain was unnerving to say the least.

Memories of the battle trickled back bit by bit. The river. The monster. Solvi being washed away. *Leillu* and the bear. Traego's rescue.

That monster was unlike anything he'd seen before, and he'd almost lost his niece to it.

He needed answers. Needed to help.

He couldn't stand being useless.

Palom tapped the bell, accidentally knocking it off the bedside table. Its high-pitched shrill rang over and over again with the sudden movement.

Malot came through the door with a scowl. 'I just told you to rest!'

'I want Traego. Bring him to me. I must speak with him.'

She rolled her eyes. 'You could try being a *little* more polite!'

Palom frowned. 'Please?'

She sighed. 'Traeg and the others are having a meeting right now about what happened. I don't think he'll be done for a while.'

That was understandable. Yet, there was nothing to stop *him* from barging out of the room and marching along the halls and rooms until he found Traego, meeting or no meeting.

He had promised Lathri before she'd died that he would try to be less forceful, to be kinder, gentler. To listen more.

Palom stroked his cheek where the monster's claws had sliced through his flesh. It was swollen and quite tender. He hoped it would heal quickly, though he had to expect a scar from it. Just another one for his collection.

His leg was by far the worst. He couldn't walk without limping.

'Take me to him, then. I was there. Fighting monster. I want to know what he will do about this.'

Malot scrutinised him for a long moment. 'Well, even in your state, I don't think I could stop you if you wanted to force it. Come on.' She held out her arm.

Though he couldn't stand the feel of a shirt, Palom grabbed his large overcoat and slid his arms through the sleeves—loose enough that he didn't feel restricted or irritated by the material.

He winced and he felt around his sides, grimacing when a trickle of blood began to seep through where he'd pressed against his skin.

'I'll get that rebandaged after the meeting. Try not to twist too much. You sure you can manage sitting still?'

Palom grunted in acknowledgement and took her hand. He was certain he'd crush her if he held too tightly, so he used her presence as a guide rather than an aid to his limp.

His vision no longer swam when he moved, and with every step, Palom grew more and more steady, until Malot simply led him down the narrow corridors of Traego's lodge. Torches lit the way, which made him dizzy, but he ignored the rising nausea.

Voices drifted along, muffled by walls, but there was no sign of Solvi. He had to trust that she was fine. The sky pirates here seemed blunt, and would no doubt state it outright if she was badly injured—or worse.

Malot's touch was warm, like Lathri's had been. Palom assumed it was the Samolen magic flowing through them, some connection to all life within Linaria. She and Lathri weren't exactly the same, but they were similar enough that Palom recognised it as the pull of magic.

If Lathri were here, he'd be fighting fit by now.

His stomach tightened in sudden guilt and grief, and he swayed on his feet.

'Heard ya were asking after me?'

Palom looked up. Malot had walked them through an open door to a communal area. Wooden tables and chairs were scattered haphazardly through the room. Pipesmoke hung near the ceiling, drifting out of the open windows and into the night, and the strong scents of spiced coffee and strong vanilla rum assaulted his nose.

Traego, Judd, Farlan, Ernold, Oris, and Karvou all looked at him, enquiring. Traego was the only one on his feet, the bottle of dark rum held in one hand; the others sat on chairs or the edge of tables. Ernold held a pipe between his teeth, but the others nursed large mugs of coffee.

'Palom!' Karvou leapt to his feet, knocking his chair over in his haste to reach Palom.

'Karvou? You should be with Odi and others, not in pirate's den!'

The lad shook his head. 'I wanted to wait for you!'

Palom didn't have the energy to argue with the young man, nor did he want to tell him off for simply being concerned. He looked at Traego and asked, 'Is Solvi okay?'

'That all ya wanted? Course she's fine. Resting up in bed, just like ya.' Traego stared pointedly through the door Malot and Palom and just walked through.

Leillu popped her head out from under one of the tables near the window. At the sound of Palom's voice, she immediately jumped up to meet him, scampering across the room, shoving tables and chairs out of her way with her bulk.

Palom grinned and ran a hand along *Leillu's* snout and horns, before deciding where to sit. Selecting a chair near the window, he limped forward, letting go of Malot's arm. 'Thank you.'

The sky pirates broke into conversation as Palom made his way to a seat.

'You sure you should be up?' Judd asked, getting to his feet and stumbling over to give him a hand. Karvou helped, grabbing Palom's other side.

'I am fine. I can stand. I can walk. I can fight.'

Judd held out a chair for him. 'I guess you're not one for lying down and doing nothing, are you?'

'Is not my way.'

He sat down heavily, trying to keep his upper body as straight as possible. He didn't want to reopen his wounds any more than he had, nor did he want to further distract from the meeting.

Karvou stared at him, eyebrows furrowed.

'I am fine, Karvou. Do not look at me like this.'

Leillu settled down at Palom's feet and grumbled low, like a cat purring, her tail looping around the table.

He smiled, grateful that *Leillu* hadn't been injured during the battle against the monster. He still didn't know what to do with the dragon, especially now she was growing so much. As a hatchling, *Leillu* had been defenceless. Now, she could fly and breathe fire. Surely she would be capable of surviving alone? If that's what she decided to do?

Malot gave him an approving nod, before exiting the room through a door on the far side. Cool night air poured into the room as she left the lodge.

'Right, quiet people,' Traego said, thumping the bottom of his rum bottle onto the nearest table. 'We got shit ta sort out. News spreads like fire in this place, so I'm sure it won't be long before everyone in Estoria knows what happened. We saw that monster off before. I ain't worried about what lurks in the Estorian jungles. What I *do* wanna find out, is what ya all know about Antar and Amarah. Pair o' em fucked off today without so much as a peep.'

'And Carav!' Oris piped up. 'Ain't like my sister to leave without a word!'

'I'm out here, risking my ship and my crew to save this lot,' Traego gestured to Palom and Karvou, 'while they're high-tailing it outta town. Fucking typical. Accidents happen all the time in Estoria, but this is hogshit.'

Palom frowned. Amarah had said something about leaving, hadn't she?

He tried to remember the conversation, whether she'd said anything that would explain her disappearance. He'd been too busy splitting wood for Traego and earning some decent coin to pay much attention to what the thief had to say. And things had taken a turn for the worst with the monster's appearance.

It was no wonder he couldn't remember what she'd said.

Wait. Hadn't Amarah been looking for Princess Isa, too? 'Is anyone else missing?'

'Rest o' my crew is all here, as ya can see,' Traego answered.

'No. I mean Princess Isa. The Ittallan here? Anyone gone?'

Traego shrugged. 'Ain't my concern. I don't even have a headcount. Isa's responsible for her own people. They're just borrowing some o' my land to camp out for a bit. I ain't babysittin' 'em.'

Palom's frown deepened. Traego didn't care what Isa or the Ittallan did—including whether they got themselves hurt or in trouble—as long as he was paid.

'Traeg, I know ya like to keep afloat with the news,' Farlan said, reaching into his pocket and pulling out a crumpled sheet of yellow paper. It looked more like a wet rag than anything else, and he chucked it across the room. 'I reckon this might explain Amarah. Picked it up after the river.'

Traego caught the paper and unfurled it carefully, eyes darting back and forth as he read.

Palom leaned forward, straining to see what had been written, but was too far away to make anything out.

'Yeah, guess it does explain it. Damn.' Traego threw the sheet back into the room, where it fluttered to the floor.

Judd scooped it up and smoothed it out on the table in front of himself, Karvou, and Palom. 'Dragons above, that's a *lot* of money! Sapora must want her badly!'

'A bounty?' Karvou gasped.

'Karvou. I told you. Go with Odi. Stay in the campsite,' Palom ordered.

'I'm not going anywhere until I know you *and* Solvi are both healed!'

Palom sighed. Karvou was too stubborn.

'It's obvious why Amarah's got that big a bounty on her head. Kidnapping royalty, tut tut tut. Antar, though? Nobody seen him nowhere?' Traego folded his arms.

Palom thought back, trying to mentally retrace his steps.

Malot burst back in. 'Traego! We have a problem. Two Varkain outside, and they *don't* look happy.'

Everyone was on their feet in a heartbeat, shoving their chairs back and reaching for concealed weapons. Even Palom stood up, though he didn't feel as stable as he'd thought.

'Coming here?' Traego asked.

Malot nodded. 'In blue armour, too. Not seen anything like it. They're going through the Goldstone villas, asking for Antar. I've told Kylos to get her Ittallan out of sight, but they'll be here any second now!'

'Great. Pair o' snakes is all we need.' Traego unsheathed his curved sword. 'Just one problem after another!'

Palom had to agree. From sea monsters lurking in the jungle, recovering from injuries, missing people, and now Varkain, he was beginning to think coming to Estoria with his princess had been a poor decision. It was too late to change things, now. He just had to deal with it as best he could.

Sensing danger, *Leillu* stood up, opening her wings and letting out a hiss that made everyone turn and stare.

'Is okay, *Leillu*.' Palom rested a hand on the dragon's head. 'You must wait out of sight.' He didn't know if she understood or could simply infer his preferences, but when he pushed her back towards the table, she curled up underneath, though continued to peer out.

A knock at the door made everyone jump. 'We're closed,' Traego barked through the door.

'Open up. We're here on the orders of King Sapora.'

Traego clicked his tongue in irritation. 'So much for telling 'em to get lost, eh?' he whispered to the others. 'Right, weapons low. Let's not give 'em no reason to poison us. We outnumber 'em, if it comes to it.' He nodded to Malot, who opened the door slowly.

One Varkain marched in, shoving past Malot and sending her flying to the ground. The second remained in the doorway, while his companion strolled forward, glancing around the room with a narrowed, predatory gaze. 'Well, well, well. This must be the base of the infamous Captain Traego and his crew. Correct?'

Traego didn't so much as flinch. 'Hardly a secret. What business does the king have with a humble ship merchant like me?'

'Merchant? Don't make me laugh. Even *I* know you by reputation, *pirate*.' The Varkain's voice held no mirth.

Palom fought to keep from snarling. He'd slaughtered Varkain simply for being in his forest. He'd not hesitate to do the same again. Although these two were of a different caste to most Varkain—Cerastes, if he remembered correctly, and they reminded him more of Sapora than anything else—they weren't welcome here. Especially not with Solvi injured.

Karvou grabbed his forearm, and Palom relaxed somewhat.

He watched them move; sinuous, slow, and direct. These were the equivalent to hunter Ittallan, and weren't to be messed with. Any snake was dangerous. But those of a fighting caste needed to be given a wider berth.

'I have paperwork to prove otherwise,' Traego said, continuing his charade of being a merchant ship captain. 'But ya didn't answer my question. Not that the king has any authority on Estoria, far as I know. What does—'

'*We're* asking the questions, thief,' the Varkain snarled. 'We have it on good authority you've a crew member here. An airship pilot. Antar? We would be *most* interested in speaking with him.' Again, he turned his gaze to everyone in the room, as if waiting for some sign that would give Antar away.

'He's a pilot, true enough. But he ain't here at the moment. What's he done that Sapora's so interested in him?'

'*King Sapora* to you, pirate. And it is none of your concern.'

'It *is* my concern. That's my best pilot ya're talking about. Oh, sorry Judd,' Traego glanced at him and shrugged apologetically.

The Varkain seemed to consider his words. Then said, 'You may be aware that sky pirates kidnapped Princess Isa. Stole her from the palace in the middle of the night, not two days ago. While all attempts to follow the thieves have proved futile, there was an unlicensed ship left in the royal hangar. *Narbiot*. It is registered to a family here in Estoria. The only living member of said family we've been able to track down is your pilot, Antar. As you can imagine, we're *quite* keen to speak with him.'

Palom snarled low. Isa and her followers were just beyond the trees—a camp of rebels against the king. Even outnumbered, two Cerastes could do a lot of damage to a group of Ittallan, especially if they were unaware and could not mount a proper defence.

The other Varkain—who had remained in the doorway—glared at him, letting out a low hiss in response.

Palom looked away. He whispered, 'Karvou. Get out of way. Now.'

The second Varkain spoke, 'Wait. I *know* this Ittallan.'

Palom tensed. He knew they could smell blood. His weakness. 'If you know me, then you know to stay out of my way.'

The Cerastes left his post by the door and plucked a short sword from his hip. 'Isn't this the *tiger*? The one Mateli was supposed to kill?'

The other Varkain turned away from Traego and followed his comrade, like two animals on the prowl, following the same blood scent. 'I think you're right. Not in the best condition are you...Palom?'

'Look here, I'll not have—' Traego's anger died on his lips.

Palom hurled himself to the side in time to avoid the first Cerastes' attack. He collided with a table, at just the perfect height to crash into his injured thigh. Palom dropped to the floor in agony, by some fluke dodging the second Varkain's strike.

He had no sword with him—all his belongings, including the rest of his clothes—were in the room he'd been resting in.

Credit to him, Judd leapt forward to his aid, sword in

hand, but the nearest Varkain deflected him with hardly a look.

The two Cerastes had Palom caught between them. Chairs and tables impeded his movement, and he couldn't keep both in his sights at the same time. He let out another warning snarl, ready to tap into his *meraki*.

'Two birds with one stone, isn't that the expression?' said the Varkain who'd recognised him. 'Tracking down the princess to this destitute land and returning with not just the pirates responsible, but the great tiger as well. King Sapora has been waiting to cross paths with you again. Our rewards will be great.'

Palom ignored the jibe. As far as he was concerned, *all* Varkain were the enemy, whether they followed Sapora or not.

Ernold and Farlan circled the Cerastes, with Traego and Judd evening the odds.

'You best leave now, before blood is spilled,' Traego warned.

Four sky pirates and a tiger Ittallan against two Varkain. Although they were Cerastes, the odds were no longer in the snakes' favour.

Palom grimaced at the idea of the two snakes killing everyone and scouring Traego's lodge, coming upon a sleeping Solvi—unguarded and defenceless. Creeping through the Ittallan camp, killing anyone who was unwary. He couldn't stand the thought of it.

Much like in the Rio Neva forest, when he'd been set upon by a trio of Varkain, he needed to put a stop to them. Back then, he'd been under the influence of his cursed *Valta Forinja*. *Emonos*. Now, he was in full control of his actions, and he needed to put down these two Varkain before it led to even more trouble.

They couldn't get back to Sapora with knowledge of Princess Isa's rebels.

With a roar, Palom tapped into his *meraki* and leapt upwards. At eighteen feet nose to tail tip, Palom's tiger form was formidable. It also left him—and everyone else—without much space to manoeuvre in the lodge's common room.

His claws scraped against the Cerastes' armour, leaving deep gouges but not cutting through to their flesh. Traego and the others darted in, slashing with swords and stabbing with blades, now it had turned into an outright brawl.

There was to be no mercy. These snakes could *not* leave. They'd return with reinforcements, and everything would be ruined.

Accidents happened all the time in Estoria—the pirates said so themselves.

This was going to be a *messy* accident.

Palom's fangs crunched through their spear shafts, rendering their weapons useless. Blood filled the air as one Cerastes lunged for Judd—the weakest of the pirates, and clearly with the least battle experience.

Palom followed Judd's attacker, snapping and clawing at the armoured snake.

Leillu launched herself from under the table and let out a furious snarl, coupled with a column of fire. It whooshed past Palom to incinerate the Cerastes leaping for his back.

The snake screamed, tearing off pieces of his armour and throwing them to the floor. The flames caught the tables and loose paperwork, and Judd raced forward to put them out.

Everything turned into chaos. Nose filled with blood and smoke, Palom attacked over and over, half-blind and spurred on by fury and pain. He drove the snakes into the pirates' blades, or bit down whenever he managed to grab hold of one. Shouting filled his ears, disorientating him, and dizziness threatened to overwhelm him.

His wounds reopened, and left the wooden floor slick with blood. He staggered, losing his footing.

The Varkain hissed, the sky pirates screamed, and fire roared in his ears.

A blinding flash of light somewhere from the back of the room dazzled him even more. He squinted to see—this was the light of *meraki*. But...?

He blinked. Karvou?

He had been too young, hadn't he? Or had he misjudged the youth's age?

The Cerastes, too, hissed at the brightness, glaring at whatever new threat had suddenly appeared to challenge them.

When the light faded, Palom lifted his head to get a better look.

A white wolf stood almost as tall as he did, front paws splayed wide, claws black and sharp. Orange eyes glared out between white fur, and Karvou in his true form lifted his lip to reveal a row of ivory fangs. *Now*, things were in their favour.

An Ittallan's first transformation was often unexpected and sudden, and Palom assumed Karvou's surge of emotion had triggered his. The timing of coming into his *meraki* could not have been better, even as loathe as he was to throw him into the middle of a battle against two Cerastes.

Wolf and tiger leapt back into the fray, tearing at limbs and drawing blood with every bite or swipe of the claw.

There was nothing the snakes could do. Outnumbered and overwhelmed, they became prey.

By the time it was all over, exhaustion threatened Palom. He shifted back and immediately sank to his knees, panting heavily. His arms were covered in the blood of the Cerastes, and from his own wounds which had reopened in the strain of transforming and fighting.

Ernold screamed somewhere to his left, clutching his bloody hand where a finger appeared to have been chopped off.

Aside from a few nicks and scratches, the others seemed uninjured. Not so much as a broken bone, though the same could not be said of the room—embers smouldered, several tables had cracked, and most of the chairs would be good for kindling and little else.

Traego wiped his forehead with an angry huff. He stomped forward, kicking debris out of his way, and crushed the nearest Varkain's skull under his steel-toed boot. 'Coming ta *my* home and threatening *my* people? Just for this *damned princess*?'

Malot crept out from behind the door, hurrying to Ernold's side and clutching onto his hand, stemming the flow of blood.

Traego glared at the gore smeared on the bottom of his boot. He spat, and looked back at Palom with fury. 'I tell ya. This princess o' yours is a *lot* more trouble than she's worth.'

20

Adrenaline coiled in the pit of Isa's stomach as Amarah flew them away from Esta Cona. Thankfully, it wasn't far at all to return to the inlet and the warship, which they could use to enhance their firepower, before catching the trade wind to carry them to the Feor Mountains and Tannon Sona beyond.

Isa didn't think her heart rate would ever get back to normal.

Even when she'd taken on Mateli single-handedly, she hadn't been so afraid as she'd been outside that damned teahouse with Archigo Kessir.

Amarah said, 'Plan's simple. Antar gets on the warship and covers our flight across the Feor Mountains. After what happened in town, best we get out of the area double-quick.'

Isa nodded, unable to say much.

'It's one step closer to Jato too.'

Isa was still shaken after Kessir. The Archigo were in place to look after their distinct territories; she'd assumed they would back her, regardless. Lathri had managed to convince so many Ittallan to rally behind her, and it had seemed easy.

She'd struggled at the first hurdle.

No, not struggled. She'd landed face first in the mud and had to be rescued by sky pirates.

Again.

If it hadn't been for Amarah and the others keeping an eye out for her, she'd be in yet another prison, waiting for her brother to send his Varkain to bring her back to the palace.

Perhaps Sapora would have even come himself.

She hated being vulnerable, but knew she should learn from the experience—once she'd calmed down—and be more aware of her surroundings. It didn't matter how many times she escaped the jaws of death, so long as she escaped.

And she wasn't hurt. That had to count for something.

'I think it might be best if you jump onto the warship, too,' Amarah said, when the inlet came back into view. 'Sapora's got a bounty on me, for a start. Everyone in town saw you getting on *RaKhanna*, so swapping ships'll throw off the scent a bit. And you're better defended on the warship with Antar.'

Isa didn't need the additional explanation, but she appreciated that Amarah took the time. It made sense, even though she felt more comfortable with Amarah than Antar. Amarah she knew—in a way. Antar was just another sky pirate. 'What's to stop Antar flying me back to Sapora?'

She didn't mean to sound so paranoid, but after her encounter with Kessir, she didn't want to take any chances. Being overly cautious was exactly how she was going to survive the weeks to come.

'A sky pirate's ship is their everything,' Amarah said, almost wistful. 'Antar has one now, thanks to me. He ain't gonna jeopardise that. Plus I reckon he's a bit scared of you.' She gave Isa a wry smile.

Isa didn't say anything to that. 'The sooner we get to

Tannon Sona, the sooner I can get onto an Ittallan airship and you won't need to shelter me.'

Amarah shrugged, pulling on a lever to fan out her side sails and slow *RaKhanna*. 'You're better company than most of the people who end up travelling on my ship.'

Considering the sort of company Amarah probably kept, Isa didn't think much of her compliment. 'I can't believe I didn't see Kessir's trap. I'm such an idiot.'

'You ain't an idiot. You're hopeful. It's a good thing.'

Isa wasn't so sure.

Before she could say anything, Amarah added, 'Otherwise you'd be too much like Sapora. That'd be much worse.'

'All clear behind. We got a good head start on 'em,' Antar said, strolling back to the captain's cabin from his perch as a lookout. He patted the wall of the cabin. 'Good ship, this.'

'Wasn't sure whether or not to bring both ships. Thought it'd be easier to have everyone on one in case we needed a quick getaway. Looks like I was right,' Amarah said.

'We're lucky it's such a small place. Not a single ship above a class three in their hangar,' Carav said, apparently quite pleased with herself as she caught up with the others, necklaces jingling.

That reminded Isa. What *had* their reconnaissance been? She had no idea what sort of intelligence a tiny town like Esta Cona could offer the sky pirates. Then again, they'd probably raided the town to thieve what they could before taking on Jato.

She hadn't noticed any of them carrying more baggage than normal, but she couldn't be sure. And it wasn't too hard to believe the sky pirates concealed anything they took—it wouldn't do to wander around the streets in the open with massive bags of looted goods in full view.

Isa had to turn a blind eye to it.

She couldn't demand they ferry her around one minute, and reprimand them for how they funded themselves the next.

Antar triple-checked his knives before making his way to the edge of *RaKhanna's* deck. He shouldered his small bag of belongings. 'Ready to go, princess? Air's turbulent by the mountains. Gonna be a bit of a rough ride.'

Isa checked her own blades. She hadn't even thought to grab them when she'd been with Kessir. She needed to be *much* sharper from now on.

Amarah and the others wouldn't always be around to save her skin.

She said, 'I've been flying ships since I was old enough to look over the wheel. The Feor Mountains don't worry me.'.

Antar chuckled as he clambered down the ladder and off the edge of *RaKhanna*.

Isa said, 'Thank you Amarah. See you in Tannon Sona?'

'That's right. Safe flight. Treat my ship well, Antar, you hear?' Amarah called as the Estorian pilot scrambled up the warship.

Isa dwelled on everything as she followed Antar across to the warship, half in a daze.

Ferried from person to person, ship to ship, she felt like cargo. But it was the best way to keep her out of sight and safe. Kessir had always been unpleasant. She shouldn't have been surprised at his treatment of her. But Archigo Gralla would be more amenable. And having the richest Archigo backing her would be the perfect boon.

She strolled to the side of the warship's deck and peered overboard as Antar got himself settled by the wheel. Unsurprisingly, *RaKhanna* was up and in the air before Antar had the warship started.

Antar was a capable pilot, though, and it wasn't long before the warship slowly rose from the ground to join its sister in the air. Isa ran a hand along the guard rail of the far larger ship. Amarah had asked her to commision the ship, and Isa hadn't spared any expense. A class one dreadnought, painted in unassuming colours and capable of matching any of the Imperial warships. Large enough to house a small class four, and with cabins for up to twelve crew, it was formidable. It had cost her thirty-five double-crowns; a considerable amount, to be sure, but nothing more than pocket change for a princess. Not to mention, the cost was only slightly above that of a standard warship in the Imperial Fleet.

Sapora's five-thousand crown bounty on Amarah, though? That equated to thirty-six warships, give or take. A veritable armada.

And it brought into stark realisation how much he hated Amarah. He was ready to set up someone in Linaria for life—and not just them, but their children, grandchildren, and all their descendents for generations, just to get his claws in one sky pirate.

Her brother had fallen down a dark path, and she no longer believed there was any way for him to return from it. She'd tried to talk to him. Asked. Pleaded. But he was too stubborn. He'd dug his heels in and committed himself to his decisions, regardless of the consequences.

She'd realised the same path wasn't as she had thought it would be, and doubled back to find an alternative. It was why she was against Sapora—the one person who'd always stood with her.

The thoughts of her old life swirled in her mind as the warship carried her across the wetlands. Ahead, the Feor Mountains rose in the distance, dark clouds storming at their peaks, and below them sprawled rolling steppes shifting into the marshlands. She'd always loved Val Sharis, considered it the most beautiful place in all of Linaria.

Taban Yul, of course, was the crowning jewel of her land. But even the remote wilds held a rugged beauty that was unsurpassed anywhere else.

She'd visited Corhaven before, and Ranski once, when she had been about fifteen years old. She had clear enough memories of those countries, and while they had their own beauty, they were nothing in comparison to Val Sharis.

Tannon Sona, their destination, was a rich town. Most of the marble that adorned Goldstone manors came from the quarry nearest Tannon Sona. Many business-minded Goldstones had moved there and made their fortunes.

Other than marble and excellent quality building stone, the quarries of Tannon Sona also occasionally threw up raw gemstones. Uncut, many of them would sell for a minimum of two or three hundred crowns.

And of course, the palace at Taban Yul was the largest purchaser of most of their most precious stones. Taban Yul had its rich areas, like any city, and the wealthiest Linarians of all lived there—Ittallan or not.

If anyone would be on the side of trade remaining stable —particularly to the capital—it would be the residents of Tannon Sona. Getting them to stand behind her, a disruptor, would be extremely difficult, and she'd have to rely on her relationship with the Archigo—if a handful of conversations could be called a relationship. Isa was nervous after what had happened with Kessir.

Not to mention every grey cloud on the horizon made her think of Jato and her Arillians. They did *not* want to be caught unawares by those birds. Not before she was ready.

While she had no doubt the warship would have the firepower to fight back, Isa didn't want to start a battle when she was anything less than ready.

On their starboard side, barely five or six ship-lengths

ahead, *RaKhanna* flew at a gentle speed, staying within easy reach.

Isa paced up and down the vast length of the warship deck. Moving helped her think, and standing still staring into the distance didn't ease her nerves. She'd had years of practice of remaining calm under pressure, especially with the Varkain's coils tightening around her a little more every day. Why now was she falling to pieces?

She wondered if, when they crossed the Feor Mountains, she'd see Taban Yul and the palace, all lit up in marble and gold. Sapora would have returned there by now, she was certain. Even a slow ship could reach Corhaven and back within a handful of days, and her brother had been so keen to investigate Veynothi that he'd flown there on his Sevastos.

She had no idea how quickly such a dragon could fly—or for how long—but she'd bet any money that it was faster than most airships. What was he doing now, she wondered. Was he livid? Searching the palace for her? Was he writing a new writ to have a bounty on *her* head, too? Was he basking in the glory and adoration of his fans after returning to the palace with a living Ark?

Princess Isa bit her lip and turned away.

It wouldn't do to think like that.

She'd made her choices and had to live with them.

Worrying or thinking about her brothers, her city, wouldn't help her in her quest right now. She had clear goals that she had to achieve were she to have even the smallest chance of taking her crown from Sapora. Of ruling Val Sharis as its one true queen.

'You all right there, Isa? Gonna wear out the deck all that pacing,' Antar called from the wheel, breaking her thoughts. The large cabin was enclosed, but Antar had all the windows open.

She glanced up, annoyed that her nerves were plain to see. 'I like to keep moving. Helps me think.'

'What you think of that storm ahead?'

She looked into the distance. Storms weren't unusual around the mountains, particularly at high altitudes. 'This ship shouldn't have a problem. Nor should *RaKhanna*, from what I've seen of its capabilities.'

She looked at the grey storm clouds that had been on the horizon since they'd taken flight. They had grown a little, but nothing too worrying. They were still several leagues away—it was just as likely the storm would blow itself out by the time they reached it. A ripple of lightning lit up the clouds in the distance with a bright flash.

'Ah shit,' Antar swore, adjusting the sails and turning the wheel to change their direction, heading south-west.

'Arillians?' Isa voiced her thoughts.

'Ain't nothing else I'd avoid in the sky,' Antar replied. 'Just our luck. Leaving one set of teeth only to fly straight into another.'

Isa scowled. Did Rhea hate her? Was she not allowed to have one day where things went well? 'Watch out!'

A streak of lightning careened through the air, blasting the warship squarely in the side.

Antar swore again, yanking on levers to curl in his sails and drop the ship's altitude. But the warship was built for fighting, not manoeuvrability. *RaKhanna* managed to swerve out of the way, but Amarah had her hands full avoiding more bolts of lightning.

'They're trying to split us up!' Isa cried, at once understanding the Arillians' tactics.

Antar spat and fumbled around with the controls.

Isa had hardly a moment to brace when the ship lurched underfoot as he fired three cannons in quick succession into the swirling thunderclouds. Their smoke trails streamed across the darkening sky, but Isa heard no screams of pain. She didn't think it would be possible to hit as small a target as a moving Arillian with standard fire.

RaKhanna had drifted further away from them in their attempt to avoid impact. 'Can you catch up?'

'Trying!' Antar replied, still fumbling with the controls. 'This thing's a beast to move!'

More lightning. More thunder. The roiling clouds were right above them, now, and with every moment, *RaKhanna* grew further away.

This was bad.

'They'll kill anything in the sky, and that includes ships.'

Isa knew that. She seethed, trying to think of a way out. At least *RaKhanna* was safe, but it meant the Arillians were focussed entirely on them, now.

'We can't run,' Isa said, 'this ship is too slow!'

'Fighting 'em is suicide,' Antar replied, voice louder.

The wind had picked up, and Isa's hair blew around her face. She ran her fingers through it, braiding it quickly and tying it back with twine. 'We're going to be sitting ducks in the air!'

'I know! I know!' Antar pushed the ship's nose down into a dive. 'Fuck it. I don't want this ship to be blasted apart. We gotta surrender.'

Isa couldn't believe it. 'Thought you pirates were fighters!'

Antar laughed. 'We pick our battles carefully. Knowing when to run is better than knowing when to fight. At least this way the ship don't get destroyed. Might be we can talk to 'em on the ground.'

Isa watched the storm grow larger. 'They're trying to *kill* us! What makes you think we can talk to them?'

'Princess, let me know if you got a better idea!' Antar

snapped. '*You're* the one going around talking to all these powerful people. *You* try an' talk to them!'

She didn't have a better idea. But she was allowed to be unhappy about that.

A sudden bolt of lightning shot through the air some leagues above them, and the resultant crash of thunder shook the warship, dropping Isa to her knees.

Her inadvertent scream was drowned out by the rumble, and she struggled to take in a breath. It felt as though the thunder had rippled through her chest.

'Hold on!' Antar roared as the ship groaned and shook, forced into a steeper dive.

Tears streamed from the corners of Isa's eyes as she struggled to recover. She hadn't realised the Arillian's thunder—a by-product of their electrical attacks—could be so powerful. When Aciel had attacked Taban Yul, she'd remained safe, deep inside the castle.

She hadn't been out on one of the warships in the thick of battle, and had no idea of their true devastation until now.

Isa wished Palom had forged one of his *Valta Forinja* for her. The weapons were able to attack with a Sevastos energy used in their core—great for attacking long distance.

Her blades were best for close quarters, as were Antar's, though he had a good arm on him when it came to throwing the knives.

The Arillians would surely be able to pick them off one by one at their leisure, without ever getting close enough to be injured themselves.

Isa swore under her breath as the warship touched down, sinking a little into the muddy ground. The wetlands were more a swamp so close to the sea, and the air was thick with salt, silt, and the scent of mud.

Before Isa disembarked, she checked the ground below.

Would the quagmire suck them up? She didn't fancy wading around in silt-heavy, murky water, nor did she want the soggy ground to catch her footsteps.

But they didn't have any choice.

She slid down the hull of the warship until she reached the cold water below.

Shivering, Isa sank until her feet touched the bottom, and the water came up to her knees. Another splash behind her told her that Antar had followed her lead, and she heard the whoosh of metal as he drew one of his knives in readiness for the Arillian attack.

Isa wracked her brains as she tried to think of a way out of their situation. She hadn't expected to be set upon by Arillians. Wasn't supposed to encounter any until she had several thousand Ittallan fighting with her.

Would she die here, in the waters just outside Esta Cona, with no-one any the wiser of their stand or intentions?

She grimaced. She could pick out individual Arillians against the black storm clouds as they flew closer. At least eight of them.

And...A tiny class five airship some distance behind them?

Isa squinted. It was an airship from the palace, there was no doubt. The gold and red colouring was enough of a give-away, and the style was distinctly Ittallan.

Yet, it was behind the Arillians, whose attention was only focused on herself and her comrade.

Who could possibly be on one of the smallest, personal travelling airships? And why would they be following the Arillians instead of trying to get away from Val Sharis as quickly as possible?

Isa had little time to ponder the motivations of the lone airship traveller, when another, better aimed bolt of lightning scorched the land to her right.

The power carried through the water and stung her. Antar grunted as he felt the brunt of the attack, and the two of them hurried to get out of the water and onto the sodden land. Even though it would be soaked by the water, Isa felt safer from their attacks, more able to leap and roll out of the way in an attempt to evade.

Before they made it onto the land, Antar had thrown one of his short blades straight up.

The suden ferocity and speed of his attack made all the difference. The tip of the blade plunged into one of the Arillian's wings, dropping it from the sky just as the group reached them.

The Arillian screamed as she fell, landing on the muddy ground with a wet squelch that was punctuated by the unmistakable crack of bones shattering from the heavy impact.

Isa raced over to her, mud caking her boots and legs from the water, and slid to a halt when she reached the downed Arillian.

'Get out of...our...skies,' the Arillian heaved as Isa reached her.

'We've landed now,' Isa said, panting slightly.

'No. You're *here*. You're poisoning Linaria. Stealing it from *us*...' Her breaths were ragged now, and blood trickled from the corner of her lips. 'You...are...vermin...Aciel tried. Jato continued...'

Isa scowled at the insult, ignoring the Arillian's blood and her own pounding heart at the scent of it. '*I* am the queen of Val Sharis. *You* are the vermin in my lands.'

The Arillian's lips turned upwards and she laughed, loud and mirthful.

Isa narrowed her eyes. 'I was prepared to be merciful, but not now. You have no remorse.' She tightened her hold on her dagger and rushed forward, plunging the blade into the Arillian's chest and silencing their broken laughter.

The sudden heat from the Arillian's blood made Isa shudder, but she held onto her weapon fast, twisting the handle as she pulled it back out. She wanted to make damned sure that every Arillian she attacked died. There would be no chance of one surviving, like Aciel seemed to have managed.

She had no idea how his power worked, but obviously Jato thought there was a way to revive him, otherwise she wouldn't have spent so long in Val Sharis launching attacks on the capital.

There were another seven Arillians in the air above them, and now they'd seen one of their comrades killed, they'd be ready.

Anger flared within her. Anger at the mistreatment she'd experienced all her life, at the snide looks and filthy comments. At Kessir's trap, and the constant stream of Arillians that plagued her people and lands. 'Come on then! Come and fight me!' Isa screamed. 'You're too cowardly! Fighting me from those heights! Come down to my level and let's see what fight you *really* have in you!'

The powerful fighting spirit came over her again, as it had before when she'd slaughtered Rimir in Estoria. Her muscles tensed, her breathing quickened, and her world shrank to herself and her opponents. Isa's emotions surged. 'Come and avenge her then!'

Isa felt herself cry out, scream or speak, she couldn't tell. She was disconnected somehow, as if she wasn't really there. As if she was floating above herself and the scene, watching it all unfold in slow motion.

The Arillians cried out and swooped down towards her. At least, the stupid ones did. Three of them remained up high, sending down their lightning bolts and waves of wind , while others attacked in a blind rage.

Isa crouched then leapt up to meet the fastest of them, her bloodied blade clutched tightly.

With one, violent motion, she swung the knife up, directly in front of her. It slashed across the arm of the first Arillian that met her, and she grabbed onto him with her other hand.

Bringing her legs up, she stomped on the Arillian's back and leapt up to the next one, half-transforming herself and tapping into her *meraki*, allowing her wildcat reactions to take hold. Isa leapt from Arillian to Arillian as they dived towards her, slashing with the one blade over and over until a particularly strong gust of wind sent it flying into the muddy ground below.

Still, she felt as though she were watching everything unfold in slow motion. She hardly breathed or broke motion as she grabbed another blade from her right boot and continued her deadly, bloody, jumping dance.

Higher and higher she leapt, as if she had wings of her own to keep attacking. Keep the blood pouring.

By the time she touched the ground again, she ached from exertion. She panted, her chest heaving, as around her dead Arillians and bloodied feathers littered the water and sodden ground. She couldn't see or think straight, her hearing swallowed by a loud buzz.

Somewhere to her right, Isa was dimly aware of Antar, but she couldn't spare the energy to even turn to face him, much less speak.

Above, the three Arillians who had held back and attacked from a distance flew away, disappearing into the receding thunderclouds.

'They'll be back with reinforcements soon. We've got to move,' Antar said.

Isa heard, but didn't comprehend. She was too numb. Too spent.

The rage of blood lust left her slowly, leaving her an exhausted, trembling mess.

'Princess Isa? You...you wanna explain what...in Rhea's name that was?' He gestured feebly to the bodies in the mud.

Isa tried to nod. The motion destroyed what was left of her balance, and she toppled over face-first into the muddy water.

Antar raced forward to pull her from the water, looping one of her arms over his shoulders. 'Isa, whatever the fuck that was, you saved the ship.'

Isa swallowed, taking in deep breaths and unable to form a coherent thought or sentence.

The world slowly slipped back into view, not in quite the right colours or brightness, but she could feel her muscles trembling. She could tell they would ache like nothing else within a few minutes.

But she allowed Antar to lead her back to the warship.

She didn't care about the muck or the deaths. Didn't care that more Arillians would be coming back—maybe even Jato herself.

She was no better than Sapora, mindlessly killing. Thoughts of the winter ball floated, unbidden, to her mind's eye.

They'd been doing that a lot recently.

Isa snorted as snot and spit dribbled from her nose and throat, and she let go of Antar to wipe her face.

'We gotta catch up with Amarah and get across the Mountains before the wind changes. To Tannon Sona?' Antar asked. It should have been a statement, but he'd definitely turned to Isa for confirmation as he started up the engines and opened up the sails.

Was he afraid of her?

She flopped onto a flat wooden seat at the back of the cabin and managed a grunt of what she hoped was affirmation. Dimly, she wished she'd had the good sense to bring a cushion with her. The sudden absurdity of the thought rid her of the last of her blood lust, and she broke out into a fit of laughter.

'Princess...Isa?' Antar asked, glancing at her with a raised eyebrow. He made his way to the ship's wheel, leaving muddy footprints in his wake.

'Amarah won't like that...' Isa said. She then laughed at herself for her silliness. After everything that had happened, she worried that Amarah would be upset by a little mud on the deck of her warship?

She must be getting delirious. 'Is there any water?'

'Sure.' Antar tossed her a leather skin.

The water was lukewarm, but tasted heavenly after the intensity of battle and the taste of blood in the air. She wiped her mouth with the back of her hand.

Antar peered at her. 'You...all right? Anything about you I should know about...?'

'I'm fine,' Isa said, once she'd managed to clear the giggles from her system. 'Exhausted. No energy...' She tried to explain, but failed when she struggled to think of the words she needed.

'Rest,' Antar said. 'We only got a small window of opportunity now the last of those Arillians have been fended off.'

Isa waved him away, though the motion made her dizzy again. 'Let's get to the town...as quickly as possible.' She struggled to keep from panting.

Quite what would happen if Aciel freed himself—as Sapora seemed convinced he would—Isa had no idea. Fighting regular Arillians was hard enough, let alone someone with the power of compulsion at his fingertips.

She shuddered and got to her feet, hobbling back to the deck for some fresh air. She collapsed down, her back against the side rails.

'Guess you can't rest just yet, princess,' Antar said as he kicked the warship into life.

The ship's sails billowed out, and Isa pushed herself to standing, leaning on the side rail so she wouldn't topple over. 'What now...The Arillians fled?'

'They did. But someone *else* is here.'

Shivering a little, Isa peered ahead. 'That class five airship from before. I thought it fled with the Arillians...'

'Guess it ain't with them. Maybe it was waiting for the air to clear? I ain't hanging about.'

The warship tilted slightly underfoot as Antar pulled away. The waiting ship was from Taban Yul, that much was for certain. But she had no idea who it was, or why they were simply hanging there, watching them. Her skin crawled, and she shuddered again. 'Quickly Antar. Fast as you can.'

'This ship ain't built for speed!' Antar called back.

'I commissioned it. I know what it can do!' Isa knew they weren't going to win any races, but something about the small airship just watching them gave her chills.

'Heading west. See where the Feor Mountains thin? There's a low valley there. Quickest way to Tannon Sona and the west of Val Sharis, with the wind behind us.'

Isa had to trust that Antar was as good a pilot as he claimed to be. She tried to ignore the fact that many class fives were messenger ships—built for speed.

She had a bad feeling and took several breaths, hating how much her body shook. The warship was powerful and well-built, but in comparison to even the most basic class five airship, they didn't have a chance of getting away.

Antar tried, though. He forced the throttles on at full speed, pulling out every sail to fly as lean as possible.

The class five gained on them, and with it, Isa's gut feeling of dread. 'It isn't working!'

'What d'ya wanna do? Give up and surrender? After all we've been through to get this far?'

'What else is there?'

'Shoot 'em down!'

Isa bit her lip. She'd already caused too much death today. 'Let's face them. We aren't afraid! They won't have much weaponry, will they? Class fives never do.'

Antar didn't respond, but he did slow the ship down to a more comfortable cruising speed.

Would this be the next stupid decision she'd make? Or was it the first good one?

She bit her thumb, watching the small ship draw nearer and nearer. Too exhausted to pace, Isa had no choice but to allow the full weight of dread to wash over her.

'Halt in the name of King Sapora!' a voice yelled from the deck of the ship.

Isa let out a long sigh. At least her brother hadn't sent out strength. She could talk down a messenger, she was sure. Or between herself and Antar, wound them enough to give up the pursuit.

The warship groaned as Antar obeyed the request, fanning out the side sails and hovering in place.

Isa darted into the cabin as quickly as she could—every step weak and shaky. 'Be ready to fend off a couple of messengers.'

'That's the first bit of good news I've heard in weeks.' Antar plucked one of his larger knives from his belt and held it up to the light.

Her own weapons were still caked in the blood and

feathers of the Arillians she'd killed. Not to mention she had hardly any energy left.

'I'll send 'em running. Don't worry!' Antar grinned, all confidence.

'Princess Isa, I presume?'

Ice filled her stomach at the words. The voice instilled terror.

Both she and Antar stepped out of the cabin—Antar sprinting, Isa hobbling—to see the class five ship hovering above the deck of the warship.

Atop the ship, three Varkain stood, looking down at them. Two were in Imperial armour, but the third wore red silks, the handles of six swords jutting out from her back.

Fear stronger than anything she'd experienced before flooded Isa when she looked at that Varkain. Her knees turned to jelly, threatening to drop her to the deck.

One of the armoured Varkain said, 'Princess Isa, you are to come with us. You are now—'

The woman in silks held up her hand, silencing the Varkain. 'Isa. It appears I've come at a bad time for you. Your fighting prowess against those birds was quite entertaining. But my business is more urgent than whatever mortal problem troubles you with them.' She flicked out her forked tongue and tasted the air for a moment. 'Yes. I was correct. You are to tell me where the thieves Amarah and Traego are. They have been in your company recently, I see. I wish to speak with them.'

Though her voice was cordial, she was the embodiment of primal, sinister terror. Isa feared her right down to her bones.

The armoured Varkain gasped. 'V—Veynothi? We are here for the princess, that is all King Sapora ordered!'

Veynothi stepped off the edge of the ship and dropped onto the warship's deck, her robes billowing. '*Sometimes priorities change*. You can tell that to your mongrel king. I have no need of you now. You are dismissed.' She waved her hand, her gaze still locked on Isa.

Isa couldn't move. Could hardly breathe.

The Ark flicked out her tongue again, and her smile deepened, revealing several fangs. 'Once I am done with Amarah and Traeego, I shall have *so much* fun with you, dear, sweet Isa.'

Energy like nothing Isa had ever felt crackled in the air. The pressure increased and her chest tightened every time she took a breath. Part of it was fear giving way to panic. Part of it was the strength of the Ark herself.

Veynothi radiated power. She was a creature that looked like any other Varkain, but Isa knew her to be far, far worse. Something ancient and evil.

Isa swallowed. She wasn't altogether sure whether she would survive this encounter. Her only hope was that the Ark had more interest in tracking down Amarah or Traego than in killing her.

Veynothi flicked out her tongue again, and her sweet smile shifted into a scowl. 'You are a mongrel too, I see. I should have guessed. Whatever happened to true royalty?'

From Isa's previous experience with other Varkain, whenever they asked a question, they rarely wanted an actual answer. She decided to hold her tongue.

In her peripheral vision, Antar clutched a large dagger in each hand, but he was frozen in place—too afraid to move. She hoped he kept still. He was more likely to keep himself alive that way.

She'd barely recovered from her blood lust and wanted to get away as quickly as possible. If she lived to see the light of another dawn, she'd pray to Rhea every day in thanks for her mercy.

'I understand being in the presence of sheer greatness

must be a shock to you,' Veynothi said, bringing Isa back to the present with sudden, unrelenting force. 'I shall ask a second time. The thieves you travel with. Traego. Amarah. You will tell me where they are, now.'

Isa swallowed again. 'They...aren't on this ship.'

Veynothi narrowed her eyes. 'That is *not* what I asked you.'

Isa took a step back, only to be knocked to the deck by a blast of something invisible.

'Do not make me ask again. I could always slaughter you and bring your corpse to the Valendrin. He'll read your blood and get the truth from you that way. It really doesn't matter to me, although I'd rather not be inconvenienced for longer than I have been. I've had a long, *long* wait. You understand.' The sweet smile was back, although Isa saw the threat underneath it.

Before Isa had a chance to respond, Veynothi looked away from her—the Ark's attention drawn by a loud crash on their port side. She flicked out her tongue. 'I thought she was close.'

'Wait!' Antar shouted.

Isa whipped around to see *RaKhanna* a short way ahead of them, wings unfurled and propellers whirring at full speed as Amarah raced away.

Veynothi's smile broadened, and she ignored Isa, turning back to the tiny class five that had brought her here, and the two Varkain messengers huddled atop it. 'To that ship.' She turned away and walked to the side rail, ready to leap back onto her transportation.

Isa saw the Ark had six long, slightly curved blades attached to her back, their tips crossed over one another. She dreaded to think how she fought in battle with those, if her mere presence sent her sprawling to the floor.

The Ark did not give into distraction, that was for sure.

The moment Veynothi realised Amarah was on *RaKhanna*, she lost all interest in Isa.

Within moments, she was back on the class five and away.

The energy that had filled the air disappeared, and Isa took a deep breath.

'What now? That Varkain's gonna destroy Amarah and her ship!' Antar said, watching as Veynothi flew away. Amarah had minutes. 'We can make a break for the mountains while that snake is distracted. Get you to Tannon Sona?'

'We can't leave her!' Dread washed over Isa even as she said it. How could they stand up to an *Ark*?

'Course we can!' Antar replied, racing back into the cabin. He unfurled the remaining sails and cranked up the throttle to full.

'Antar, get the canons ready to fire,' Isa said. 'We have to back up Amarah.'

'Are you outta your mind, princess? You just saw what that...that...*thing* was!'

'She *needs* help. We have more weaponry. Can't we blast Veynothi out of the sky?' Isa honestly didn't know if it was possible.

Amarah would be outmatched.

And so were they.

But she couldn't run. Not after everything she'd done. She could always bargain to go back to the palace in exchange for Amarah's safety, if it came to it. Isa suppressed a shudder. It *wouldn't* come to it.

'I checked the canons back in Estoria. We're loaded and ready to go.' Antar turned the wheel to head towards *RaKhanna*. 'Coulda done with some of Malot's *dragon-breath* on this. But blasting one class five should be easy for this warship.' Frustration clipped his words.

'Prepare yourself. This'll get ugly.' Isa concentrated on her breathing, willing her blood lust to return and give her the strength and confidence to fight.

She slipped her daggers out, wiping them on her sleeves to clear them of the leftover Arillian blood.

'I don't know how this'll play out,' Isa said. The truth was always better than a lie. She only knew a little of the Arks, from what Sapora had told her and from what she'd discovered when snooping through his books. 'Veynothi won't be like any other Varkain you've encountered.'

The Arks were weapons.

They'd wiped out entire cities before, single-handedly.

What chance did a handful of sky pirates and a princess on the run have?

21

With the state of Linaria as it was, not much could surprise Morgen any more. Yet he'd been lost for words at Kohl's sudden reappearance. The Arillian was so utterly out of place that Morgen's brain simply needed a while to catch up.

Naturally, a familiar face was always welcome among a sea of disapproving Kalos. Then he'd remembered.

Eryn. Anahrik. Moroda.

Deep, burning rage swelled in his gut and threatened to overwhelm him. He wanted to lash out, to strike down the Arillian there and then for what he'd done. He desperately wished he had a sword—any sword, not even his *Valta Forinja*. Had Kohl not been such a coward, Linaria would be a very different place today.

The tipped balance of power might have revolved around the dragons, but Kohl was the lynchpin. The point from which everything had diverged. Aciel. Jato. Compulsion. Battles. Life. Death.

Everything.

It all stemmed from Kohl's inaction.

Morgen was still recovering from his experience at the ritual by the lake the previous night, and the frightening look the Arch-Kalos had given him. He still didn't know what it meant, or what the Arch-Kalos had seen in him, much less understand the vision of the dragon and flames. Dealing with Kohl's sudden arrival had put all those thoughts on hold.

The Kalosin healers had eased his headaches and stopped his muscles trembling for the most part, but beyond that, he needed quiet rest.

Two Arillians turning up on his doorstep was *not* quiet rest.

If anything, the stress would cause his thumping headache to return tenfold.

He'd been sitting at the large table eating fruit when he'd heard the commotion outside, and now his appetite had left him. Retaking his seat on the table's bench, he filled three slender glasses from the pitcher of water, pushed two towards the Arillians and drank from the third, mentally bracing himself to deal with Kohl.

Berel was allegedly the safest place in Linaria. A place that revolved around education and peace. Yet war and bloodshed seemed to follow him wherever he went. Even here, in this desert. Even when he tried so hard to stay away from it.

If it wasn't the dragons, it was the damned Arillians.

Morgen closed his eyes and wished that he could turn back time. That he *had* accompanied Amarah when she'd flown through the mountains on her way to Povmar and asked him to join her. It had been a ridiculous request from the sky pirate, one he wouldn't have been able to explain to his comrades—especially as he'd have been abandoning his post in the guard for a second time, ignoring the fact he'd done exactly that a few days later anyway—but he wondered where in the world he'd be right now, had he joined her.

Certainly not stuck here, under the watchful eyes of the Kalos, with a man he'd promised to kill and no feasible way of doing so without signing his own exile.

He had no doubt that Amarah was alive and well, wherever she was. They'd developed a sort of respect for each other—strange, considering they'd been on opposite sides of the law.

Now he had to deal with these two Arillians. It felt like a test of his patience from Rhea herself.

Smoothing down his robes, Morgen wiped his brow. Whatever had happened in the tunnel, whatever vision he'd had or magic he'd experienced, had left a mark on his psyche. It wouldn't be long before the evening music would start and his aches would ease. But he wondered whether they had any music that could ease the constant turmoil and doubts in his mind.

'You're gonna have a long wait. Topeko teaches all day,' Morgen said, when neither Arillian stepped forward to take his offered drink.

'Morgen. You look ill,' Kohl said, his voice flat.

'Desert heat. Takes a lifetime to get used to it.' Morgen wiped his forehead again, feeling foolish and shaky. He had lost weight recently, and even in the forgiving robes, Kohl would be able to see that. It was only natural when you swapped the training circle and physical exercise for books. His muscles had shrunk, his physical strength withering away. Although he'd worked to rebuild the university, it hadn't been much more than pushing and lifting. As exhausting as it was, it was nothing like the drills his captains used to make him do from dawn until dusk.

There was no way he could deny the physical change. They'd just seen the Kalosin leave, and he knew he was sweating profusely. When Kohl didn't answer, Morgen added, 'This...isn't the best time.'

'What happened here? Thought this country was supposed to be at peace,' the other Arillian said, looking down his nose at Topeko's home. 'Looks like a warzone.'

Morgen massaged his temple. 'It *is* at peace.' He didn't really want to say anything that would help Kohl, nor did he want to incriminate himself. If these two didn't know what he'd done, it was two fewer people to admonish him. He settled for most of the truth. 'Dragons attacked. No-one knows why. We've been clearing up the damage since and trying to get back to normal. Restoring the damaged sections of the University mostly.'

The two Arillians shared a glance.

Kohl said, 'We were too late, then. It appears even Berel isn't safe.' He paused, appearing to consider something. 'Morgen, do you still have the *Valta Forinja* that Palom gave you?'

Morgen stiffened. 'No.'

Kohl frowned and turned to his comrade. 'Would the dragon have lied? It had no reason to. Unless it was those in the university that caused it?'

'My lord, I can't claim to understand humans or dragons. Who knows what it meant.'

'Wait,' Morgen said, half-rising from his seat. 'What dragon? Who lied?'

'We shouldn't, my lord.'

Kohl waved the other Arillian away. 'On our way here, we passed by the Feor Mountains and an elder dragon attacked us. That in itself is becoming more commonplace, as I'm sure you're aware. But when we questioned it, the dragon spoke. It said the *Valta Forinja* were the cause of their rage. It also said that power rightfully theirs had been stolen. Misused.'

Morgen's throat tightened. He didn't know where his *Valta Forinja* was, but he'd bet a considerable sum that it was now locked up somewhere in the university with all the other ancient relics and weapons of the past.

If the dragons had attacked the city because *he'd* been there with his *Valta Forinja*...a new wave of guilt washed over him, and he sank back down on the bench.

Then again, how was he meant to to know? Even Palom hadn't known, and he'd *forged* them.

'This is what happens when you play with powers you don't understand, or have any right to control.'

'Kalos Topeko!' Morgen was back on his feet a moment later.

The Kalos loomed large in the doorway, his chest rising and falling quickly. He must have run most of the way through town to get home so quickly.

Before Morgen could even be confused how he knew to hurry back, a small, blonde woman poked her head around the edge of the Kalos's robes. 'Mahlu?' Morgen took a step towards the pair of them.

She flashed him a smile, which died on her lips when she looked back to the Arillians. 'I was coming to see you and offer my well-wishes. But then I saw those two and thought it'd be best to fetch the Kalos. Just in case...'

Morgen didn't need her to finish that sentence. It wasn't in case the Arillians hurt him. It was in case *he* hurt the Arillians, and wound up in even more trouble than before.

It would be like the dragon attack all over again.

His mood darkened.

'Kalosai Morgen.' Topeko inclined his head. 'Kohl, I had not expected to see you again so soon...or at all, if I am to be perfectly honest. Welcome back to my home. Your unannounced visit is most surprising. I take it that not all is well?'

Morgen didn't know how Topeko could remain so

neutral in the face of the traitorous Arillian. He *knew* what Kohl had done, and the consequences his actions had wrought.

Then again, Topeko *was* a Kalos. He didn't just follow the rules. He *breathed* the Samolen culture of peace and neutrality.

'I am deeply honoured and humbled at your welcome, Topeko.' Kohl removed his weather-beaten hat and bowed low. 'This is my good friend, Fogu. We won't be in your way very long, I assure you.'

'Any friend of Amarah or Morgen is a friend here,' Topeko said.

Morgen gritted his teeth. As far as he was concerned, Kohl was *not* a friend.

'I see Kalosai Morgen has already offered you refreshments. Very good. Morgen, would you be so kind as to pour more for Kalosai Mahlu and myself?' Topeko swept into the room, drawing the fabric curtains across the windows and lighting the torches with a wave of his hands.

Morgen shivered as the energy of the room shifted, a little warmth dissipating. He did as he was bid, fetching a fresh jug of cool water from the pantry room to the side.

'I'll help you carry more glasses.' Moments later, Mahlu was beside him. In the relative quiet of the pantry, she pulled him up straight by his shoulders. 'I didn't realise how bad things were. Morgen, you look *terrible*! What happened at the ceremony? He was there, wasn't he? The Arch-Kalos?'

'He was. And...I don't know. I *feel* terrible, like I have a fever.' He shook his head, then immediately regretted it, dizziness and nausea rising up like a double-headed snake. 'I need to rest, that's all. Be fine in a few days.'

'And now *them*.' She glared over her shoulder, where the Arillians dabbled in small talk with Kalos Topeko. 'I know that Arillian. The tall one. Fogu. I'll never forget those eyes.'

'You do?'

'He and his Arillians tore through Iryl on the hunt for recruits during Aciel's war. He sliced through every building, tree, and wall like it was made of soft butter.' Mahlu shuddered.

Morgen reached over and rested a hand on her cheek. 'Kalos Topeko won't let anything happen. Not here. And they're just passing through. I'll make sure of that, no matter how late it is when they finish.' It was an empty promise. As things stood, he wasn't sure he could stay awake another hour.

'I hope.'

They returned to the large table and set down the drinks.

Morgen didn't know what was worse—the Arch-Kalos or what the Arillians had done to Linaria.

Topeko said, 'It isn't surprising. There have been various powers in Linaria's history. Some far greater than others. The dragons have always kept things in balance. But now, there are too many all at once, all vying for dominance,'

'You understand the warning clearly enough. I doubt the other lords of the land will. King Sapora certainly won't, considering he's amassing more of these powers than anyone else. I know not what these Arks are, but I know they are most terrible.' Kohl said, voice tight.

'The Arks...' Topeko trailed off. 'I can hardly believe it.'

'What are they?' Mahlu asked, sipping at her water, eyes darting between everyone gathered like a mouse cornered by a cat.

Topeko said, 'The Samolen, much like Arillians, have always remained apart from Linaria's strife. Above such matters.'

'Perhaps that'll be the end of us all,' Morgen said, sullen. 'Maybe we *should* act.'

'Kalosai Morgen. You're recovering from your recent ordeals. Why don't you get your head down? The heat can be—'

'Apologies Kalos Topeko. I'm fine.' Morgen knew better than to suggest any sort of action around Topeko. The Kalos always wanted to sit and watch and wait. Ultimately doing nothing other than perhaps logging events for it to one day become a new history book that future Kalosai would be forced to study.

But Linaria was *his* home, too. Things had changed. Sapora and Palom and whoever else had awoken these powers, perhaps irrevocably changing things? Morgen didn't want to sit and wait for a dragon to burn them, or worse. 'I am curious. Hasn't the university held the original *Valta Forinja* since they were first created? If that's what's setting the dragons off, if they're really so bad, why haven't the dragons been aggressive towards us before?'

Topeko gave him a long look.

Morgen wondered if Topeko could see into his soul, see all his thoughts and memories, like the Arch-Kalos seemed able to do.

'There are many books which document the history of—'

'Topeko. We do not have time to study Linaria's history, I'm afraid,' Kohl said, his voice gentle but firm. 'If there's anything you know that might help us survive the dragon-fire to come, divert their rage, *anything*—I would be most grateful to hear it.'

Topeko sighed, almost irritated.

'Amarah has a *Valta Forinja*, too. Would she be in danger?' Kohl said.

Morgen's eyebrows shot up. He'd almost forgotten Topeko's relationship with the sky pirate.

'If the dragons' wrath is fuelled by their usage as you

say…then, yes. She would be.' Topeko sighed again, more heavily this time. 'These are weapons of war. Violence. Death. They have no place in Linaria!'

'Unfortunately, Topeko, they *are* here. Dealing with them is what we *must* do,' Kohl said.

Topeko took a long drink, emptying his glass. He refilled it, eyes narrowing as he considered his next words.

'I've wielded a *Valta Forinja*. Ignorantly.' Morgen tried. 'Why are they so awful? What do they have to do with the Arks and the dragons?'

'The *Valta Forinja* are forbidden. But the Arks are far worse.'

Kohl shifted where he stood, apparently uncomfortable. 'I do not doubt Sapora will free the first one soon. The land shifts below us. I doubt it'll ever go back to the way it used to be. Not when the Arks walk again.'

Morgen didn't like where this discussion was going. He'd always been the most comfortable with a sword in one hand, a shield in another. He understood those things. They made sense. But all this?

'According to our teachings, the Varkain are the oldest creatures in Linaria,' Topeko began, 'I am aware the Arillians have their own lore, much of which conflicts with what we teach here. So take this with a pinch of salt if your views are not the same.'

Both Arillians nodded.

Morgen was enraptured by Topeko's words. He could have sworn the Varkain were an off-shoot of the Ittallan race. At least, that's what Palom and Anahrik had told him.

He wondered just how much mis-information had trickled down over the centuries.

Topeko continued, 'And I'm sure you're aware of the Varkain-Ittallan war some few thousand years ago? Linaria was a very different place then. Corhaven was largely uncultivated, home to dozens, hundreds, of nomadic tribes and settlements that moved with them. There were no cities, no fleets of airships, no Imperial Guard. Val Sharis—as it was then—was the richest land in the world. Fertile soil. Gold. Ore. The Ittallan, a much younger race, had risen out of the tunnels of Sereth, crossed the Feor Mountains, and settled in the steppes. They built villages, then towns that would eventually converge and grow to become Taban Yul.'

Morgen leaned forward, almost willing Topeko on.

'Despite the Varkain's preference for life underground, they did not wish to cede any resources to the upstart Ittallan, and so fought them tooth and claw over every scrap of land. Their own blood magic was more powerful, back then. A dark magic not dissimilar to *He*. Many Valendrin claimed that title—blood mage—advising their royal *naja* and giving them the edge in many of the conflicts. However, with the plethora of *meraki* the Ittallan enjoyed, the Varkain were still losing. After all, a tiger is greater than a snake, is it not?'

After seeing Sapora's true form in the ballroom in Taban Yul, and the speed and ferocity with which his fangs dealt death, Morgen wasn't sure he agreed. Then again, if the majority of the Varkain were not of Sapora's caste, then it wouldn't be too far-fetched to assume an army of Ittallan hunters could easily overwhelm the snakes unused to fighting above ground.

'While the Ittallan have their hunters, who excel in combat, the Varkain have what is known as the Old Guard. Shaped by blood magic, they're larger, faster, more aggressive than other Varkain. They would devastate any battalion they came into contact with. However, they had been so twisted that they verged on madness, and would be just as likely to kill their own as they were to kill the Ittallan they'd been set to attack.'

Morgen grimaced at the thought. Going blood-crazed in

the heat of battle wasn't unheard of. But he was certain the idea of that behaviour in a creature like Sapora would give him a fresh wave of nightmares.

'The Valendrin therefore created something to control the Old Guard. Something that would win the war for them.'

'The Arks?' Kohl whispered.

Topeko exhaled through his nose. 'The Arks. Weapons of war so powerful that the Valendrin were only ever able to make four of them. They exhausted every facet of their magic to create the Arks, who would then lead the Old Guard and keep them under control.'

'Veynothi was more than an ancient Varkain. She had... she had powers that...' Kohl pulled his mouth tight, as if in disgust.

'You know of Veynothi?' Topeko gasped.

Kohl shuddered. 'I dare not speak of her.'

Morgen had never seen Kohl look so afraid. Dragons above, what was being unleashed in Linaria? Why was he stuck in Berel?

'I don't know what any of this has to do with dragons and *Valta Forinja*,' Mahlu said.

'You must be slacking in your studies. Shall I inform Kalos Ettas that you require additional reading?' Topeko asked with a wry smile.

'I presume the Arks ruined the Ittallan armies and won the war?' Fogu folded his arms.

Topeko said, 'You'd think so, wouldn't you? But no. They didn't. The war waged against the Ittallan by the Arks was terror incarnate. Entire towns were destroyed, and the death count tolled in the hundreds of thousands. Val Sharis is forever scarred. Before they won the war, the Arks vanished.'

'What?' The tremors were coming back again, and

Morgen clenched his hand around his glass of water to keep them at bay. 'And the *Valta Forinja*?'

'Faced with the Arks, the Ittallan smiths turned to the only power great enough to rival them, pleading for aid.'

Morgen could think of only one thing. 'A Sevastos?'

Topeko nodded. 'And so the *Valta Forinja* were forged. The most powerful weapons in Linaria, fuelled by dragon-ore.'

'It was these weapons that made the Arks disappear?' Kohl asked.

Topeko shrugged. 'It's one of Linaria's greatest mysteries, and I daresay, a Varkain secret. Evidently, the dragons were sick of the war and the destruction it wrought. One lent the Ittallan their strength to end the conflict. It isn't out of the question that another made a bargain to get rid of the Arks.'

Morgen frowned. Most of it made sense, but the ending was shrouded in confusion. 'Is one of the Sevastos stones at the university from one? Who aided the Ittallan to forge the first *Valta Forinja*?'

'Indeed. The other four are those who have aided the Samolen in some way or other. Your books explain this,' Topeko said. 'Having travelled into Sereth after the siege of Taban Yul to offer my congratulations on Sapora's coronation, I mentioned as such. He banished me from Sereth for simply asking about a Sevastos. I think that answers that question.'

'But if a Sevastos helped forge the original *Valta Forinja*, why do they hate them now? Isn't that going back on their word?' Morgen asked.

Topeko laughed. 'The bargain would have been the use of their powers for *one* thing. Like Moroda to seal only Aciel and end *one* battle.. This is why the original *Valta Forinja* are locked in the university, never to be used again, and why the dragons have no anger over this. It is when we wield their magic otherwise in accordance with their agreed terms that there is a problem. Again, this is why we use *Ra* freely, and are forbidden from *He*. One is permitted, the other is not.'

Morgen ran a hand through his hair. He wasn't strong enough to cope with this. It wasn't just a bad story, it was reality.

He knew Sapora had a Sevastos under his control. He didn't know how—considering they seemed to want death as payment for their aid. And even after Topeko's lecture, he was still none-the-wiser.

Perhaps if he actually learned *He*, that destructive, forbidden magic, he would be able to do what none other had. What none had even attempted. Sometimes rules had to be broken to bring about change.

Use that to sever the connection between Sapora and his dragon, and free the god. A Sevastos under the claw of a Varkain was never going to be good for Linaria.

He stared at Kohl and Fogu, who spoke to one another in low voices. Mahlu nursed her cup of water as if it gave her life, hunched down on the bench.

She'd lost so much to Fogu and the Arillians.

Many people had lost things to the various powers fighting for control. The Arillians. The Arks. The *Valta Forinja*. The dragons.

The damned dragons.

Tremors racked his body and he shuddered in place.

'Morgen?' Topeko was beside him, hands on his shoulders, steadying him through the attack.

What was happening to him? What had the Arch-Kalos done?

He hadn't worked up the courage to revisit his memory of that ceremony, and the golden dragon who'd appeared, much less ask Topeko about what it all meant. 'I'm...I'm fine.'

'I think you should lie down for a while. I will deal with our guests, and see them out when we are done.'

Despite Topeko's calm tone, Morgen knew it was a voice that permitted no argument. He wasn't sure he *could* argue, anyway. As he shakily got to his feet, he glanced over to Mahlu. She stared up at him, eyes wide, though he couldn't tell if it was in fright. His own vision was spotty.

With a huff, he picked up his half-empty glass of water and ignored his desire to lead a one-man attack on the palace in Taban Yul and oust Sapora before he destroyed any more lives.

He wouldn't be doing that today. Not any day soon, if things continued this way. Recovering from the intense Samolen magic was his first step. Getting away to learn *He* would be his second.

As Topeko ushered him out of the room, away from the man he wanted to kill, Morgen felt more alone and isolated than he ever had before. At least in Povmar, he had his comrades to talk to and joke with. They all shared a similar humour and despised the cold and the circumstances that had led to their posting in such a distant place.

Here, there was no-one who saw eye to eye with him, save Mahlu.

With a huff, Morgen slumped down on his bed and looked up at the red fabric canopy above. More nightmares would await him when he closed his eyes. Varkain, mostly. But now dragons, Arillians, and Arks.

He needed to change something. Needed to *do* something, before it was too late.

He needed to take his fate into his own hands, starting now.

22

Dark veins snaked up the length of Sapora's right arm. He'd only noticed once he'd emerged from the tunnels and stepped into the dawn sunlight trickling into the cave's entrance. Thankfully, he'd been so caked in dirt that neither of his companions had noticed, but he'd quickly slipped his jacket back on to cover himself, despite the welcome cool air.

He'd need to thoroughly inspect himself as soon as possible to ascertain the extent of the change. For now, the marks had grown all the way from his wrist to—potentially—his shoulder. There wouldn't be much he could do to hide it if the marks kept growing.

Other Varkain would perceive any difference as weakness. He'd experienced it all his life. He did *not* wish to give them any additional ammunition.

Turning on his heel, Sapora surveyed the Valendrin and the Ark. Malashash towered over the Valendrin, overtaking Palom in stature. His grey skin seemed to shimmer in the darkness, and his black hair, slick like oil, reached just past his muscled shoulders. His golden eyes set him apart from other Varkain, and they glowed when the light touched them.

The Valendrin, on the other hand, was ancient, shrivelled, and fawning. Practically lost in the folds of his robes, he had to keep pulling them up and around him so they didn't slip off his bones. A withered creature that looked almost in pain by being alive, it was so deep into its blood magic.

Both dusted themselves off, concerned with the same prideful reputation Sapora associated only with the vain.

He detested both of them. But both were essential to his rule.

The thread to his Sevastos shuddered now he was back above ground, and he clamped down even harder on it.

Quickly, he covered his hands with the fresh pair of gloves he'd tucked into his inside pocket. He smiled as they covered his skin, hiding the marks on his flesh and, for all intents and purposes, acting as armour from those who might look for an opportunity to attack his pride.

Being invisible had been his speciality since boyhood. His means to survive in a cruel world that detested him and ensured he never forgot it. He embraced it, now.

'Is the coach still waiting for us?' the Valendrin asked with a cough.

"Coach" was a great exaggeration for the covered wagon they'd used to travel to this part of the Rio Neva forest. Admittedly, it had cushioned benches inside to make the rickety journey marginally more bearable.

Sapora peered out into the dawn sunlight, and spied the white-grey linen of the wagon's roof nestled between the trees. 'Indeed. Are you quite finished? We must return to the palace quickly. That trip took us all night—who knows what has happened in my absence.'

That got the two Varkain moving, and they hurried across the uneven cave floor to the entrance.

Once in the sunlight, Malashash ground to a halt, swaying slightly. 'It has been...so long.'

Sapora didn't have time for the Ark to get accustomed with sunlight, but knew the creature was practically a god, so he held his tongue. He behaved very differently from Veynothi—far more agreeable—and he had no desire to put that in jeopardy.

The Valendrin did not wait, instead scurrying through the trees and straight into the relative safety of the wagon like a rat finding shelter.

Sapora didn't bother to hide his sneer. To think how far the Valendrin had fallen. One minor mistake, and it was as if his entire world crumbled around him.

'Are you ready to travel, Ark?' Sapora asked.

'I am. How long is the journey to Sereth? I know not this part of the land.'

Two things struck Sapora. Firstly, that Malashash believed they were returning to Sereth. Secondly, how much Linaria's geography must have changed in the five thousand years that had passed since the Ark last walked. 'This is a forest in Val Sharis. The eastern edge rests against the Feor Mountains, and Sereth lays beyond that. We return to the palace in Taban Yul, however.'

'Palace?'

'You *do* know what a palace is?'

Malashash chuckled, though it sounded more like boulders grating against one another. 'I do, my king. But there is no palace in Val Sharis that I know of. Why do we travel there?'

Frustrated, Sapora stepped away from the cave, urging Malashash to hurry to the wagon. 'It is where I reside for now. Where I rule. Taban Yul is the capital city. A glorious beacon of gold and marble.' He hoped by bragging about the wealth of the city, he'd get the Ark to come along.

Malashash remained on the edge of the trees, deep in thought. 'My armour...'

'Yes. We'll get more of it forged for you. I have not forgotten. But I cannot start that until we return. Unless you wish to walk the whole way, why don't you join us in the wagon.' Sapora fought hard to keep his frustration in check.

He'd always been laid back, smooth-spoken, calm. Managing the Sevastos, Veynothi, and now Malashash was taking its toll.

Malashash decided to do as he was bid, and after only another minute of hesitation, he entered the wagon and took his seat beside the Valendrin.

Sapora quickly followed, after tapping the wooden side to get the driver—a young Ittallan with a mop of brown hair—to move out. At least the Ittallan had been ready to go, despite waiting all night.

'Here. Until you have fresh armour.' Sapora lifted the lid of a chest nestled in the corner, revealing red robes of the same cut and style Veynothi had adopted.

Thankfully, the Ark took them without question, looping the fabric around his body until he looked like an ancient statue made living. Malashash's sheer size made it a squeeze, and the wagon rocked uncomfortably as he dressed.

Though Sapora could easily sense the strength of the Ark, it was a raw power that pulsed when he breathed, not the vicious magic of Veynothi, full of malice, designed only to dominate. He'd never considered what it would be like when the Arks walked again. He'd just looked at it as a goal he'd needed to achieve. The details hadn't concerned him.

He supposed it shouldn't surprise him. The Sevastos detested him more than any other, and with two of four

Arks now resurrected, that thread trembled in warning. The magic that bound them ensured the thread would not shatter, but Sapora knew it would if it could.

The Valendrin busied himself by staring out the window as they passed by the ancient trees, though it was clear from his gaze that he wasn't focussed on anything in particular.

Malashash, on the other hand, stared at the roof of the wagon as though fixated on a spot only he could see.

Sapora frowned, following the Ark's gaze, but no matter how much he squinted, he couldn't see anything other than wooden panels and smudged linen. 'What is it, Malashash?'

'Arillians. There are many in these skies.'

Sapora exhaled slowly through his nose. Surely the Ark couldn't see *through* the fabric canopy? He tilted his head in case there was a seam that opened somewhere, but there was nothing.

'They congregate over the mountains. And to the west.'

'Taban Yul,' Sapora said.

'This is where your palace is?'

Sapora nodded.

'Why do you not flee to Sereth?'

Sapora didn't deign to answer. He'd been questioned too often by too many people about everything he did or didn't do. The Ark was his servant. Not his equal.

After a while, Sapora said, 'You are welcome to rid our skies of them. They are keeping their distance for now.' He wasn't sure how—or even if—he was going to broach the subject of Aciel's compulsion sweeping through the city like a plague.

One step at a time.

'Have they attacked Sereth?'

'Not yet.'

'Then there is nothing for me to do.'

Sapora stared at Malashash, his enthusiasm draining

away. Perhaps he wouldn't be so different from Veynothi after all.

HAVING RETURNED to the palace with an Ark in tow once before, Sapora should have been more confident with Malashash.

Sapora had spent most of the journey back in silence, considering his speeches and first orders. Working out the way to best put this to his advantage, and when he could get away to his rooms to inspect the marks growing along his body.

Everything went out the window as they entered the plains leading to Taban Yul. Once the Rio Neva trees were behind them, they all had a clear view of the morning sky, and the swirling thundercloud of Arillians storming overhead.

He didn't need to be an Ark to feel the immense power emanating from the skies.

It was the main reason he'd opted to travel by wagon. Though slower than airship, the skies weren't the friendliest place at the moment. Many ships had been blasted to the ground by the Arillian's electrical attacks, and Jato's storm grew more every day—like she was some great creature drawing breath, readying itself to charge.

His skin crawled at the idea. He knew he was running out of time.

Koraki, the head steward of the palace, had even sent out a few messengers to treat with the Arillian, but none had returned, and the plains were littered with the charred remains of broken airships. Although the Goldstones had not been bothered by the lack of trade given their own private funds, many of Taban Yul's lower classes had struggled. Not only were their districts closer to the Sevastos stone outside—and thusly Aciel's influence—but they had taken to protesting near the palace.

Sapora had ignored them, as he did with all things he considered unworthy of his attention. The Imperial Guard were able to keep the streets clear, for the most part. "Rebel rats," Tacio had called them. Always looking for something to complain about.

Once he had the Arks in place, he would deal with Jato. The citizens would have to be patient.

Pulling on his thread to the Sevastos, Sapora urged it to patrol the skyline. Usually the presence of such an enormous creature was enough to get Jato and her Arillians to back off. It roared in reply, a fiery blaze of anger that careened through his mind like a hurricane.

It wanted to refuse, but was not permitted to do so.

Every command was the same. Every tiny effort, a chore that took all of his strength to enforce.

Even Vasil had reacted with disbelief and arrogance instead of praise and adoration at the news of Veynothi's return.

Sapora gripped the thread harder, aware he clenched his jaw. The Sevastos *would* attack the Arillians threatening Taban Yul if they drew closer to the capital.

A bellow echoed in the distance, and the wagon juddered to a stop.

'Was that...a dragon?' Malashash asked, immediately getting to his feet and shoving his top-half out of the window for a better look.

'It is King Sapora's Sevastos,' the Valendrin replied.

Sapora slowly unclenched his jaw, willing the tension away.

'I see.' Malashash remained where he was.

Sapora wondered if Malashash detested the dragon as

much as Veynothi did. It *was* the reason the four of them had been sealed in the first place. Five thousand years was a long time to hold a grudge, but they had more reason than most.

Even he was unsure of the specifics of their sealing, which explained why it had taken a Valendrin's aid before he'd managed to resurrect them.

There was too much he didn't know.

As the wagon trundled along down the well-worn road towards the capital, Sapora closed his eyes and focussed on his breathing. He needed to ease back into the calm indifference that had served him so well before.

He wondered where Isa was. Whether she'd taken her morning tea and breakfast on the roof as she loved to do, or if she was somewhere buried in the holds of a sky pirate's ship, starved and flayed like a common criminal, or transported like cargo. He didn't know if she'd left of her own volition, or whether she'd been coerced into it, regardless of what Tacio claimed.

Knowing Amarah, it could be either.

'The Arillians draw closer.'

Malashash's words snapped Sapora from his thoughts and brought him back to the present. Had something drawn their attention? 'What? Is there an airship?'

'Airship?'

Malashash's tendency to repeat back words irked Sapora more than he cared to admit. 'A ship that flies. What else is in the sky?'

'Only the Arillians. Brace. They attack.'

Sapora didn't need telling twice—he gripped onto the wall with one hand, grasping onto his scimitar with the other.

The wagon rocked as a bolt of lightning struck the ground beside it. The wood cracked, and one of the large wheels snapped off. Chunks of the wheel flew into the air, thrown by the force of impact. Sapora shifted his feet, moved his weight to balance, and braced as the wagon toppled onto its side.

Poorly-made, the wood and glass windows shattered when they hit the ground, splinters flying in all directions.

Somewhere behind him, the Valendrin yelped, no doubt having braced with both his hands and felt the full brunt of glass shards exploding around them. Sapora had no time to check on him. Slashing with his scimitar, he leapt up through the torn fabric canopy and out into the dazzling sunshine.

The road had been well-made with stone and brick, but the surrounding grass burned.

He doubted the Arillians knew *he* travelled in that wagon. Just his luck they were bored of hunting airships and had turned their sights to the ground. Overhead, a handful of Arillians swirled around, feathers fluttering down.

'King Sapora! Stay clear!' Malashash roared.

Sapora smirked. He could handle a few wayward Arillians.

The sudden creak behind him made him realise the Ark was not discussing the Arillians. He whirled around, taking a large step to his right as the wagon split in two.

Malashash appeared to have punched his way through the cart, the wood splitting either side of him as he emerged from the wreckage, one arm protecting the Valendrin as he heaved him up.

The Ittallan who'd been driving the cart—a young man who reeked of fear—threw off the chunks of wood that had landed on him, scrambled to his feet, and sprinted down the road towards Taban Yul.

Since the Arillian storm, almost all airship flights had been cancelled, and very few people travelled to and from the city on foot. It just wasn't worth the risk. It meant that the few major roads surrounding Taban Yul were empty save the Imperial Guardposts.

Sapora hadn't noticed on their way out, under cover of darkness. But now the sun had risen, they were clear targets.

And so was the Ittallan driver.

'Wait!' Sapora cried, darting after him. His Varkain reactions were unmatched, and he put on a burst of speed, catching up with the Ittallan within a single breath. He grabbed him around the waist, tackling him to the dusty road. 'Get back with us!'

Panicked, the Ittallan thrashed around, whimpering in fear. 'Arillians! Arillians!'

'Calm down and get up!' Sapora snapped, but it was no use. The Ittallan had given into panic.

The air hissed as electricity built up. Sapora's hair lifted, almost weightless. Every instinct screamed at him to get clear.

Sapora released the Ittallan and rolled back.

His ears popped.

Lightning struck.

Sapora remembered at the last moment to squeeze his eyes shut, but the blinding whiteness seared into him, regardless. He turned away, ducking down into the wreckage of the wagon, all thoughts of fighting forgotten as he protected his vision.

The scent of burning flesh was one he'd never forget, and he didn't need to open his eyes again to know the Arillian attack had hit its mark. It was pungent and permeated the air.

Dragons above, he'd tried to help him. But the Ittallan had been too stupid to do anything but flee.

'My king! Are you all right?' Malashash bellowed from somewhere above him.

Still with one eye shut, Sapora pushed himself to his knees, then back onto his feet. 'I'm fine. Can't say the same for our Ittallan friend.'

Malashash scoffed. 'The Ittallan are no friends of mine!'

'It doesn't matter. Get down before—'

Everything around him tightened, superheated in advance of the next lightning strike. He didn't need to look to sense the attack. Sapora dived away from the wagon a moment before it exploded with electrical energy. Debris blasted up, filling the air above him in every direction.

Dammit, where was that Sevastos?

With a snarl, Sapora yanked down hard on the thread connecting him to the dragon, roaring his fury into the order to attack the Arillians.

Above him, two dozen feathered wings flapped in glee; every crackle from every pair of hands at a separate pitch. Twenty-three Arillians.

He risked a glance skywards, confirming what he heard. And in the centre of the ball of feathers—Jato.

She stood out like a sore thumb, her wings jagged, shorter than the others, and barely moving.

Against his better judgement, Sapora took a few seconds to study her. She was certainly less haughty than he remembered on the warship. If anything she looked...

'Malashash. The Arillian in the middle. She's...injured?'

The Ark cast his gaze above and replied immediately. 'Indeed, my king. A weak one.'

Perhaps that was why she'd not attacked the city yet. She wasn't at full strength. Her display of storm clouds was an intimidation tactic, nothing more. Her Arillians were fighting *for* her.

'You may only defend Sereth. But you are sworn to defend your king, are you not?' Sapora said, taking advantage of the lull.

'I am.' Malashash agreed, not taking his eyes from Jato.

'Then defend me. Kill those Arillians.'

The distant bellow of his Sevastos sounded again, far closer this time. At least it was obeying. Surely between the dragon and the Ark, he'd push Jato away?

'My armour. Without it I cannot defend you.'

Sapora hissed. 'I'm sure you can do a good enough job for now. I'm trapped here, in essentially a field. I must get back to the palace. You will help.'

'And me as well,' the Valendrin added, hobbling out of what was left of the wagon to stand beside Sapora. 'If we're to have any chance of resurrecting Brahm and Prince Karekis, I *must* aid the king.'

Sapora rolled his eyes, but if anything could be said to persuade Malashash to do his job, then he wasn't going to argue. The Valendrin's words always carried weight.

The air crackled again.

A high-pitched whine that turned to a hiss.

Another warning.

Sapora shoved the Valendrin to one side and dived in the opposite direction, as a thinner, faster bolt of lightning careened down to blast into the ground. It scorched the stone road, cracking the great slabs and leaving smoke trailing from the damage.

Veynothi was obsessed with herself and her Ark companions.

Malashash was obsessed with his armour.

If the other two were anything alike, then Sapora wasn't sure he'd have the patience to manage all four of them, alongside a dragon that hated being a puppet.

At least with his keen senses, he'd be able to dodge any Arillian attacks while he made a break for the city. The Valendrin would be less lucky, but as he needed him, he'd do his best to keep the blood mage out of harm's way.

Without waiting for Malashash to agree or argue, Sapora grabbed the Valendrin's hand—suppressing the urge to shudder—and took off at a sprint. It wasn't the same burst of speed he put on for sudden attacks or dodges, and it conserved energy.

More lightning strikes, most wildly off-target.

Malashash roared in defiance, the air pulsing with his own brand of magic.

Arillians screamed.

And in the distance, his Sevastos flew along the Feor Mountains, lighting up the sky with its fire.

23

Pain tightened its fist around Palom's side, shocking him from restless sleep into unpleasant wakefulness. His bandages were covered with dried blood. At least it wasn't fresh. Shifting his position, he braced himself for pain, only to be relieved he could turn his upper body without passing out from dizziness.

The blanket was already in a crumpled heap on the floor —Estoria was far too warm for his liking—and he gingerly swung his legs off the low bed, making his way to the cabinet where Malot had left a handful of supplies.

His flesh was tender where he'd been gouged by the monster, but he was definitely healing.

The fight with the Varkain had sapped what remained of his strength, but at least Karvou, Traego, and the other pirates had made it through in one piece.

Karvou. He could hardly believe the young lad had experienced his first taste of *meraki* in the heat of combat. It could happen any time, but being thrown head-first into a battle against the fighting caste of snakes was *not* something he'd have chosen. At least Karvou's father would be proud.

He'd need to ask Kylos or Odi about having a letter sent

back to Tum Metsa to tell Parin the good news. It would definitely be the talk of the town.

Leillu took up most of the floor space in his room. She watched Palom with unblinking eyes, a small puff of smoke rising from her nostrils.

Palom dressed quickly in a loose shirt and pants, gently securing them with a belt, and made his way outside, *Leillu* following him like an ever-present shadow. He passed through a long hallway to the lodge's main room, where the scent of Varkain blood and burnt wood permeated, and hesitated. *Leillu* hissed.

Malot looked up the moment he walked in. She held a damp rag that smelled strongly of alcohol, and paused in the middle of wiping down the tables and floor. 'Good morning Palom. You're looking less like a man who was almost eaten by a monster!' She laughed but quickly stopped when he didn't say anything. Malot cleared her throat. 'Solvi is awake. Said she was going to have a wander down the beach for some fresh air.'

'Where are Varkain?' Palom asked, noticing the two corpses were suspiciously absent.

'Ernold and Farlan have dealt with them.'

Palom wasn't sure exactly what that entailed, but as they were pirates, he didn't care to question it further. If it wasn't a problem to them, he didn't need to worry about it. And he was grateful that Malot had told him about his niece without him having to ask.

He cast his gaze around the room, impressed at how quickly Malot and the others had managed to put it back to rights. There was no sign of Traego, and Antar was still absent. Oris was in the middle of washing the windows along the far wall, and didn't bother looking up. The scent of blood would fade in time.

'Are you feeling better?' Malot asked.

Palom shrugged nonchalantly. 'Is Princess Isa around?'

'Haven't seen her. Kylos visited earlier—asking after you, actually—but most of the Ittallan have kept to their camp or the main part of town. I don't think they want to mix with the likes of us.'

If Palom didn't know any better, he'd say there was a touch of sadness in her voice. He wasn't sure why Kylos would be asking after him, but decided to head over to their camp once he'd seen his niece. He needed to talk to her about Karvou, anyway, and Isa's absence was beginning to worry him.

If Amarah had left in a hurry, had she taken the princess with her?

He cursed himself for not paying more attention to the sky pirate. He'd been too focussed on his wood-chopping task and setting a good example to Karvou.

'Traego?' Palom asked.

'Out with Judd. They're scouting for signs of the monster in case it wanders back into Falice.'

That seemed sensible. At least Traego wanted to keep his land safe, which meant the Ittallan would be kept safe. 'Come on *Leillu*. Fresh air will do us good, too.' Palom nodded to Malot again and skirted around the tables she cleaned.

It couldn't have been too far past dawn, yet the heat Palom stepped into almost sent him to his knees. The air was thick with humid warmth that clung to his skin, and before he'd reached the path to the surrounding jungle, sweat dripped down his forehead.

Leillu, however, chirped happily, and took to the air as if she was perfectly at ease. She disappeared within a few wingbeats, lost in the rich, blue sky.

He took several deep breaths as he walked, inhaling through his nose. A myriad of scents reached him. Varkain and blood. Sky pirates. Several Ittallan. Solvi's scent was faint. Isa's was fainter still.

As much as he was bound to aid his princess, Solvi took priority.

He checked the wind, then followed the well-worn path through the tangle of Estorian jungle until it slipped downhill. Careful not to lose his footing or trip on a trailing vine or bush of thorns, he was grateful when he saw the wide white beach splayed out ahead. Dozens of people milled along the sand, some working with nets and boats, some relaxing.

It didn't take him long to spot his niece among those gathered; sitting on the warm sand, legs in the surf, face turned up to the sun.

Palom hurried along, sending debris flying as he picked up his pace until he almost sprinted towards her.

'*Pali.* You make too much noise. How are you a hunter?'

'I am not trying to sneak up on you,' Palom replied, happy at her good humour. His feet sank in the sand and he kicked out with every step to loosen his footing. 'I was so worried.'

Solvi giggled, her laugh high and light. 'I am okay, *pali.* You worry too much.'

'This is dangerous place. Pirates everywhere. And that... that...monster almost killed you.'

Her joy faded in a flash. 'I know. What *was* it, *pali*? I've never seen it before.'

Palom stared out at the waves, thinking. Small fishing vessels bobbed up and down. He heard the sailors shouting to one another, barking orders and replies as they worked. The monster was of the water. Most likely it came from the sea. 'This is strange time in Linaria. Gods and monsters. Everything is...changing. But I am sure that monster was *emonos*.'

Solvi wrapped her arms around her legs and looked away. 'I know. Thank you for coming to save me.'

Palom snorted. 'I am not leaving you to fight that alone.'

'Chyro helped, too.'

'Chyro is fond of you, I think.'

She giggled again. 'He is a good friend. He would have helped anyone in trouble. Even now, he is in the camp, talking with Kylos and Odi about how he can contribute more.'

The beach grew busy with the morning crowd. Estorians who worked here. Goldstones on holiday. Ruffians and pickpockets looking for an easy opportunity. Even a few Ittallan who had drifted down from Isa's camp for a morning stroll.

One man—tall and lanky, with pockmarked skin and a number of bruises on his arms—caught Palom's attention. He squatted on the beach, digging into the sand furiously like a dog.

'What is he doing?' Solvi stood up and dusted the sand off her skirt.

Palom narrowed his eyes. 'Looks like something is stuck in ground?' He couldn't quite make it out. Something thin and narrow. A stick? A handle? It was black and caked in damp sand.

The man shifted, digging in his heels deeper. He grabbed the end of the tall, black stick with one hand while burrowing around with his other. His hair stuck to his forehead, but he continued to dig away at whatever buried treasure he was in the midst of unearthing.

A few curious individuals congregated nearby, some shouting words of encouragement or suggestions on how better to shovel sand.

Despite himself, Palom made his way across the beach. His curiosity was too great to ignore.

Soft steps behind him meant Solvi, too, wanted to investigate.

The pirate grunted, grabbing hold of the stick with both hands and heaving up. His feet slipped in the uneven surface, his sweaty palms losing grip on whatever it was that he clutched.

Palom was less than five feet away when the silver winding around the black stick shimmered brightly.

His heart leapt into his throat as he felt the unmistakable, red-hot power of the *Valta Forinja*.

Tremors snaked up his arms and legs, rooting him in place.

The pirate gave another grunt, his feet unbalanced in the shifting sand, and hauled out the enormous, glowing scythe in one, smooth movement. Blue light flashed as the blade caught the sun, sending arcs of magic careening in all directions.

Palom wasn't sure he was still breathing.

'*Pali*!' Solvi's mouth hung open.

He didn't need her reaction. He *felt* the weapon's power in his bones. It wasn't just any *Valta Forinja*, randomly washed up on an Estorian beach. It was *his Valta Forinja*. The scythe he'd made for Amarah.

He knew she no longer had it. That was obvious. But he'd never actually asked her what she'd done with it. After ridding himself of his own dual-bladed greatsword, he had no interest in any of the cursed weapons he'd forged.

In fact, he'd almost put them completely out of his mind.

Seeing the scythe now, in all its glory, brought everything rushing back.

He couldn't allow this random sky pirate access to the most powerful weapon in Linaria. Especially considering it belonged to Amarah—and himself.

'You!' Palom bellowed.

The entire crowd jumped, faces turning towards him with a mixture of surprise and annoyance.

Palom strode towards the sky pirate, who clutched the scythe in both hands as if it were a necklace of precious gems. 'Drop that. Now.'

'What? It's mine! I found it!' He pulled the scythe close to his chest and turned away from Palom, sand falling off his arms.

'You did. But *I* made it. Drop it and back away. It is *emonos*!'

The sky pirate made no move to follow Palom's instructions. He licked his lips and shuffled away from the approaching Ittallan. 'You want it? Show me your gold, then! I want fifty crowns!'

Palom fought to keep from snarling. 'It is priceless artefact and it belongs to me. Leave it!'

The sky pirate's eyes widened. 'Priceless, eh? How's about two hundred crowns, then? No. Five hundred!'

'How about five thousand? I get a cut for suggesting the best price,' a random voice from the crowd called out.

'No! Ten thousand! I'll take ten per cent!'

More voices joined in the fray, offering ever-more ludicrous suggestions and how they were entitled to a share.

The original sky pirate grinned, his grip on the blade tightening. 'See? Unless you're a Goldstone, you ain't getting this!'

Palom had no patience left. He tapped into his *meraki*, light inching down his skin, and roared.

'Oh shit, that guy's an Ittallan!'

'Get outta his way!'

'RUN!'

The crowd scattered, racing off in all directions—including the man with the scythe. Apparently he thought it was a rare and priceless treasure, not an actual weapon.

Palom crouched, ready to race after him—even in his state, he'd be able to catch up to a grounded sky pirate.

But he didn't have to—Solvi darted past. She hadn't bothered with her *meraki*, had simply lunged forward, closing the gap between them in a few quick strides. Smashing into the man's side, she knocked him flat to the ground. The scythe went flying, and she bounded after it, leaving him with a new bruise on his upper back.

Solvi didn't touch the scythe, simply stood over it, hands on her hips as though daring the sky pirate to try and take it back from her.

'How dare you!' The man groaned as he got back to his feet. 'That ain't how it works in Estoria!'

'I heard you can take what you want. I took it from you. It's mine now. Wanna try taking it back?' Solvi raised her chin and stared at him levelly. With her wild hair and athletic body, it was clear she was in far better physical condition than the pirate.

He came to the same conclusion, shouted another obscenity about the Ittallan, spat at her feet, and joined the rest of the fleeing crowd.

Palom snorted and hobbled over to Solvi. He was glad she'd stood up for herself, and glad she'd had the foresight not to touch the weapon. With a shudder, he released his *meraki* and crouched to pick up the scythe from the beach.

It was warm to the touch, and thrummed with power.

'Amarah's?' Solvi asked.

'Yes. I will keep this safe.' He didn't want to give into the weapon's power again. But neither was he going to let anyone else fall into its curse. 'Let's take this back to the camp.' His muscles ached, and he knew he shouldn't have transformed while so weak.

Sitting down in the shade with a mug of dark ale was all he wanted to do for the rest of the day. Perhaps with a large bowl of fish stew when his stomach was ready to face food again.

The whir of an airship's engine caught his attention, and he glanced up to see a tiny class five hurtling overhead—a streak of dark copper and grey sails.

'Isn't that one of Princess Isa's ships?' Solvi asked, also staring up.

Palom wasn't the best at recognising different ships, but if his niece said it was, then he had no reason to disbelieve her. 'Princess Isa was just out flying?'

Solvi didn't reply, she just narrowed her eyes.

Then Palom spotted the long overcoat flapping in the wind. Traego.

Wait. What was Traego doing in one of Princess Isa's *personal* ships?

'Shall we speak to him?' Solvi asked, still staring overhead as the ship blasted away towards Traego's base.

'Maybe get Kylos and Odi, too,' Palom said, 'I have many questions for our sky pirate captain.'

~

IT TURNED out that Palom had grossly underestimated Solvi's speed. By the time he'd recovered his breath and strength enough to make his way back up the beach and along the twisting paths through the jungle to Traego's lodge, Solvi was already waiting outside with Kylos, Odi, and Chyro.

'I almost came to look for you, *pali*,' Solvi said with a grin..

'I am not *that* old,' Palom replied.

Solvi giggled.

'I don't see how any of this is a laughing matter,' Kylos said, ever to the point. She stood with her arms folded across her chest, her toe tapping with impatience. 'Our Princess has disappeared and yeh off attacking sky pirates. And what's that?' She gestured to the scythe he carried.

'Is nothing. I saw Princess Isa's ship fly overhead. Thought we should speak with Traego.'

Kylos glared at the scythe, but didn't comment on it. Isa's health was their priority. 'What's that pirate doing flying around in her ship?'

'Technically the ship was on *Otella*. And we are staying here by *his* leave...' Odi said, mediating.

'That doesn't give him the right to use our princess's ship whenever he wants!' Kylos snapped. 'Amarah's gone, too. And Aetos saw Antar flying off in her warship yesterday afternoon.'

Palom frowned. Amarah might have a bounty on her head, but why had Princess Isa left the Ittallan in the dark? They were her allies and confidants.

'This is why we need to speak with Traego. He must know more than he's letting on,' Odi said. He looked at Palom, his gaze flicking down to the scythe. 'It that...?'

'I said *is nothing*.' Palom didn't want to be brought into the conversation about *Valta Forinja* again. Not when there were so many other things at stake. 'Let's go.'

The five of them pushed open the main door and strolled inside. Before Palom had taken a single step, Traego's shouts reverberated through the entire lodge.

If he'd been annoyed the night before, today he was *pissed*.

'—half my fortune! I swear ta Rhea!'

'Someone's upset,' Chyro whispered.

'Do you need some assistance, Captain Traego?' Odi asked, as the group of Ittallan made their way into the communal area.

Palom could still smell the Varkain blood, and wrinkled

his nose. If two high-ranking Cerastes didn't return to the palace, it would only attract more attention. He wasn't sure if he'd done the right thing or not.

'Oh, great, now we have half o' the damned campsite sauntering in. Does a closed door not mean anythin' to ya? Damned Ittallan.' Traego growled. His entire crew—save Antar and Carav—were gathered around the tables. Most looked like a close relative had just died.

'If ya don't mind, I'm kinda in the middle o' somethin' here. So if ya wouldn't mind heading back to ya camp and—'

'How about *yeh* stop treating us like your tenants and see how we can actually help each other. We aren't peasants dumped on yeh land until our lord can pay yeh. This is a battle that'll affect the whole world, so yeh ought to take a more active role in that!' Kylos's eyes burned with her passion. She was utterly unafraid of the pirates, which made sense considering she'd spend a significant chunk of time in the palace dungeons being tortured by Tacio.

'Have ya not noticed? Estoria is under attack by some random monster—its torn up half o' the island and a good chunk o' my money with it. Whole place is gonna crumble any day now!'

That was worrying. Perhaps Traego and Judd had noticed the devastation only after their scouting flight earlier that morning. If the monster had destroyed parts of the island, Traego wouldn't be the only sky pirate affected.

'Where's Princess Isa?' Kylos pressed. 'Yeh were in her ship this morning.'

Traego shrugged. 'I ain't her babysitter! How am I supposed ta know? Anyway, she's a big girl. She can go off if she wants. Likewise while ya on my land, I can help myself to that ship if it ain't bein used.'

'Wait. If the monster has been destroying parts of Estoria, won't it have killed more people? What if Isa's hurt? Or worse?' Chyro asked.

'Who knows. Welcome to go take a wander if ya want. Mostly it's a smokin' crater slowly fillin' with seawater.'

Palom snarled. 'She *should* be your responsibility too! If all you want her for is gold, then having her dead will not help you!'

'Palom has a point,' Malot said. She sat beside Traego and pinched the bridge of her nose.

Traego raised his arms in a huff. 'I swear, everythin's gone ta shit ever since we helped out that princess 'o yours!'

Oris huffed. 'I think it was ever since we went to Veynothi—'

'Oris, one more word outta ya and I'm hurling ya in that fuckin' crater!' Traego snapped.

'I do not understand what is problem. You said you fought monster before. Why only now is it issue?' Palom asked.

'Because only now he's being financially impacted?' Kylos huffed.

Traego shrugged. 'What can I say? I'm a man o' business.' He gave each of them a long, hard look, then relented. 'Fine, fine. Sit down an' keep quiet unless ya got somethin' ta contribute.'

The Ittallan shuffled into the room, some taking a seat at one of the tables, others leaning against the wall. Palom kept by the wall, one eye on the window in case *Leillu* flew by or there were any other threats that decided to intensify all their issues. With things the way they were, he half-expected the monster to turn up again for round two.

'Right. We ain't got all our resources now. Gonna hafta brave the Val Sharis skies to visit some of our other stashes. Anyone seen Ipot about? Or Hanzel?' Traego asked. The pirates mumbled to themselves—a non-committal answer

—and Traego continued, 'We need ta know what in Linaria we are playing with here. We might've chased the monster away a couple o' times, but that didn't stop it razing the jungle. And no-one actually knows what it is? Even us born and bred Estorians?'

Again, more affirmations and mutterings from those seated.

'No-one got a decent explanation? I know there's half a dozen stories but I need *real* ones. Stuff I can work with. Any bounties from south Val Sharis for something like this?'

'Just dragons, Traeg,' Farlan called.

'And that was no dragon,' Traego replied.

'Sea dragons aren't around no more. Even if they was, they don't look like that.'

'I think we can rule out dragons. Didn't have no wings. Didn't breathe no fire. What other options have we got? Come on, come on, I'll give half a crown ta anyone who tells me what that thing actually is. A full crown to anyone that tells me how ta kill it!'

'I think I know,' Chyro said, his voice clear above the ramblings of the crowd as they descended into conversation.

'Hold that,' Traego said, raising his hand for quiet. 'Ya reckon ya know what that thing was?'

'Yes sir,' Chyro said, his old Imperial Guard training slipping through.

'Go on then. Tell me!'

Palom focussed on the young Ittallan, listening intently.

'I think...I think it's Brahm's monster.' Chyro licked his lips.

'Brahm's monster?' Traego repeated, one eyebrow raised.

'That's right.'

Traego rolled his tongue around in his mouth as if unsure whether to reprimand him or laugh at him. 'Don't suppose ya could tell us who the fuck Brahm is and why he's got a monster like that roaming around Estoria?'

Chyro scratched the back of his neck as though self-conscious. 'I...I wasn't sure until I fought it. But we learned about it in training. At the palace in Taban Yul.' He cleared his throat, all eyes in the room on him, the calling birds outside the only sound above his breathing. 'Brahm is one of the four Arks of Sereth. The last one. The weakest. He had a monster to help with...with what he did.'

Traego pursed his lips, his unspoken question prompting Chyro to continue.

'You know...What they did to the Ittallan in Val Sharis? To our homes?'

'In civil war?' Palom asked.

Chyro nodded enthusiastically. 'Yes, exactly. Brahm remained in Sereth, guarding the waterways. This was before airships of course. Everyone travelled long-distance by boat. Back when this land was part of Sereth.'

The crowd muttered again.

'One of the biggest battles during that war took place here. Well. Near here. It's what split the land. The islands drifted away and became Estoria.'

'And ya're saying that monster Palom and ya fought did that?'

'They think it was part of it.'

'And what happened to Brahm?'

Chyro looked to Palom, then back at Traego. 'Well, all the Arks disappeared, didn't they? So no-one knows.'

'And he kept this monster as what? A pet?'

Chyro shrugged. 'Maybe. We don't have all the records. It was five thousand years ago.'

'Well if it's some kind of pet, then Brahm himself must be near,' Malot said.

The crowd broke into excited talk about the amount of

gold they could get from Sapora if they brought him news of another Ark.

'It's *perfect*, Traeg! Sapora'll give us even more gold now and it won't matter that the monster wiped away our stash!' Ernold said, rising from his seat and pumping the air with a fist.

'Exactly. We got the ships to get there, too. Safer flying, right?' Farlan added.

'Wait, wait. Calm down you lot!' Traego snorted. 'First—did ya forget the part where I said the Arks were *causing* us problems? Let's *not* make that worse. Second—if Brahm's been here all the time, how come we've only just seen his monster, huh? More likely the thing has been wandering Linaria looking for Brahm and wound up here!'

Solvi let out a whimper.

Palom's shoulders dropped and he let out a breath. 'Are you okay?' He squeezed Solvi's shoulder.

'Yes. I don't like all the talk of the Arks,' she admitted.

'No-one likes talk of Arks.'

Palom shifted his weight where he sat and winced at the shooting pain through his side. 'I am fine,' he added quickly, seeing Solvi turn to look at him.

'What're we gonna do about it, then?' Traego asked, putting his question out to the room. 'I drove it off before with *Otella*. Twice. But who knows when it'll be back. It can walk on land, so what's ta stop it raiding us one night and destroying all the rest o' our gold and ships? I say we take out a patrol. As many ships as we can. Follow the water upriver until we find it. Flush it out. Drive it ta the ocean, far away from us.'

There were cheers, which was to be expected. This was the sky pirates' home, and no-one wanted a monster like that turning up on their doorstep. If Palom's encounter with it had almost killed him, then tourists or unwary Estorians wouldn't stand a chance.

He knew Traego and the other sky pirate captains were driven by money. Tourists brought in a lot of gold, and no-one would want to travel to Estoria if word spread that a monster haunted the waterways. But he didn't want to help. This was not his battle.

Not to mention the creature was a force to be reckoned with. If Chyro hadn't been there, he would have died, and probably so would Solvi. There was no point in getting involved with the sky pirates' bounty.

But Chyro's words worried him.

Brahm's monster.

Four Arks.

What if Sapora managed to free all of them? He was already well on his way with the first.

All of Linaria would fall under his rule, then. Nothing could stand against those sorts of powers.

He shook his head at the thought. A Sevastos and the Arks. What game was Sapora playing? Who did he think could possibly threaten him with such an arsenal at his control?

'Captain Traego. You're fighting a losing battle.' Odi stood, smoothing down his robes as he straightened up. 'Drive it off again. A hundred times. A thousand. It'll still come back.'

'What ya gettin' at, old man?' Traego asked.

Odi took the insult well. 'There is no way to defeat the Arks. They are immortal. This creature was created by the same blood magic. It, too, will be unbeatable. The best thing would be to flee.'

'I ain't no coward!'

'But you know which battles to fight, and which to flee. This monster is one you should be running from.'

Traego huffed but didn't argue.

'And we are without our princess,' Odi carried on, before anyone else could speak. 'As Kylos suggested, we need to join forces. Truly join forces. I do not know how far you trust the other captains. But perhaps we ought to use the offered ships to find her. Escape this dangerous land and move on, before we're all destroyed.'

Malot lifted her shoulders in a half-shrug. 'Linaria is massive. How would we even know where to search for her?'

'If Princess Isa is with Amarah, can you not track her? Like you did before?' Palom added.

Traego folded his arms, eyes darting left and right as he thought. 'I *could*...'

'Traego. Perhaps we should leave. You always said the skies are safest, right?' Malot said.

'Maybe. But that was before we had dragons and Arillians ragin' about,' Traego replied. 'Then again, everything feels too damned convenient. Antar and Amarah disappearing at the same time as Isa? I get *she* had a bounty on her, but...We had a bit o' an argument. I didn't think much of it...'

'Better to ask them in person, wouldn't you say so?' Odi asked.

'Well. I need ta figure out what's going on with my crew. Antar ain't someone I wanna let run off, knowing all my secret stashes,' Traego said. 'If we leave, Estoria'll be prey for that monster, though.'

Odi turned to look at Palom, and down at the scythe he held. The blade glowed blue in the low light.

Palom tightened his grip. The way Odi stared made him uncomfortable.

'No. I think it will lose interest in Estoria altogether.'

24

Amarah and Carav kept a close eye on the storm clouds ahead. They grew darker and more violent with every passing moment. Where there had been the occasional flash of lightning, it now burst every few seconds. Even from this distance, they felt the rumble of thunder as it made *RaKhanna*'s holds tremble.

Amarah hadn't expected to encounter any Arillians this far east. But if Jato herself was focussed on Taban Yul, her other followers would need to be doing something to keep themselves entertained.

Damned trouble makers.

She didn't know how many there were, and despite the defences installed on *RaKhanna*, anything in the air was at a disadvantage when it came to Arillians.

She'd worked hard to avoid the Arillian's attacks, even though it meant the two ships had been split up. By the time she'd managed to bring *RaKhanna* around, they'd seen her warship land, and the Arillians had fallen prey to Isa's claws. Amarah would never have thought the princess was so capable in battle, but her strength certainly helped. It reminded her of the conversation she'd tried to have about the princess's blood lust.

But she couldn't worry about that now—the main issue was the class five hovering above her warship. Something about it just didn't feel right.

'Shall we try and get closer to the mountains?' Carav furrowed her brows. 'We need to be on the western side, anyway, and the wind will die down before dusk.'

'I ain't leavin' Isa and Antar,' Amarah replied. 'Besides, Jato and the bulk of her forces are there. I don't wanna fly headfirst into an Arillian storm. Even if they don't see us, I ain't losing *another* ship to those birds. Won't be long before more of 'em come to investigate what happened to their friends.'

'I'll keep an eye on them,' Carav said. She clutched the scope in both hands, but she wasn't as good a navigator as Judd or Antar.

Fighting Arillians in a storm. Never a good idea.

She'd come close enough to losing *Khanna* over the Sea of Nami when she'd first encountered Jato, and her Arillians hadn't even been attacking anyone. From the strength of the storm, these ones seemed so riled up it would be like ploughing straight through a wasp's nest.

They needed to cross the mountains further south and avoid any wayward lightning.

She stomped the bottom of her scythe on the deck. 'Pass me that scope. Wanna see what the hold up is.' Amarah rarely had problems flying, but with only one eye, she struggled more with depth perception than she realised she would.

Carav shuffled over and put the brass lens in her hand.

Amarah brought it up to her eye and gasped. It was a small vessel, good for three or four people at most. No cabin, just an open deck and a double mast, vibrantly painted in the red and gold livery of the Imperial Guard.

Definitely a speedy ship from Taban Yul.

She licked her lips and twisted the lens to try and pick out the details of the ship. A woman stood near the prow, and it looked like two others—Varkain—were with her, who flew the ship.

She'd *definitely* seen the woman before. 'Looks like they're all Varkain there.' Amarah kept the lens focussed on the robed woman at the front, trying to recall where she'd seen her before, when realisation dawned. 'Oh fuck.'

'What's wrong?' Carav asked, taking the scope from Amarah for a better look herself.

'Oh fuck. Oh fuck. Shit.' Amarah darted across the deck, shoving crates and barrels out of the way as she grabbed the wheel. 'This is *bad*.'

'What!?' Carav asked, following her into the cabin.

'That's *Veynothi* on that ship! I'd put any money on that. Would never forget her. She's got all her swords and she's *alive*.' Though Amarah had only seen her in stone in her tomb, there was no way she'd ever forget those hateful, golden eyes. 'Damned snake brought her back.' She turned *RaKhanna* away from the storm. 'Can't believe it! Can't fucking believe it!'

'You aren't abandoning Isa are you? Or Antar? You just said you wouldn't!'

'Do you have the *slightest* idea what Veynothi *is*? What she can *do*?'.

'A Varkain?' Carav shrugged. 'I ain't scared of 'em. Are you?'

'This ain't the same. Veynothi is an *Ark*.'

'What's that mean?'

Amarah paused. She didn't know exactly. But her memories of Veynothi's tomb and what she'd done to Kohl while still in stone was enough for her blood to run cold. 'Means we're in trouble if we fight her is all.'

'We can't run!'

'We *are* running!' *RaKhanna* had already pulled away from the warship. She daren't look to see if Veynothi had given chase. She didn't want to be seen as a coward. But equally she didn't want to run into a battle she couldn't win.

'Amarah!'

She scratched the old scar on her cheek as she thought, trying to figure out what to do. 'Carav, you don't get it. We might all die. You understand that? You realise what that *means*? This ain't some scrap. Veynothi is out to *kill*.'

Even as she said it, Amarah felt her mouth dry up. She wasn't warning Carav so much as she was warning herself.

They hadn't even reached Tannon Sona and already their plans were falling apart.

Carav continued to protest, her voice getting higher and higher. 'You're a sky pirate, Amarah! A famous pilot with a reputation older than me! Since when do *you* run from snakes? From someone you promised to help?'

Amarah shook her head. She had her scythe, for what good it would do. She was angry at herself for getting rid of the *Valta Forinja*. At least that thing had range.

Veynothi's ability to render Kohl unconscious in a few seconds rose in her memories.

She was dead. They both were.

There was no two ways about it.

RaKhanna climbed high as they fled. Emotions, thoughts, memories rattled around in her mind. Fast as *RaKhanna* was, she didn't think they'd be able to outrun a class five.

'Amarah! Please?'

'You wanna die, do ya?'

Carav bit her lip. 'I never wanted to stay with Traego,

forever in his debt like Farlan, Ernold, and my brother! He'd never let me be a pilot, even though I watched Judd all the time. I know what to do! I just wanted to be free to fly wherever, like you! You do what you want, when you want. You don't run from fights!'

Amarah didn't know what to say. Carav idolised her more than she'd realised.

Carav said, 'It's just a snake, right? We can take on a snake! And think how rich you'll be knowing you saved the princess?'

Typical the young thief would revert to a reward for the risk.

Fuck it. If she was going to die, she'd go with a bang. And she'd bring Veynothi down with her.

'All right, all right. Quiet.' She kept *RaKhanna* flying ahead. The more distance she put between herself and her warship, the less likely Isa would be dragged into it. 'We can't get away from Veynothi. We'd never outrun that class five.'

'We attack, then? *RaKhanna* has *dragon's breath* stocked, right?'

Carav had a point. Amarah considered her options. Perhaps they'd be lucky and damage the ship. But if not...if Veynothi boarded...

'Amarah?'

'If she gets on board, we're done for...but, maybe...' It was a ridiculous idea. But she didn't have anything else. 'You ever do a tilt and lift with Traego?'

Carav nodded rapidly.

'Good. 'Cause you'll be at the controls.' It was the only chance they had at getting rid of her. And that was hoping Veynothi didn't kill them both, first.

Just her luck she was caught in the middle of Arillians and the Ark.

Could be worse, she supposed. Sapora's damned Sevastos could be here too.

But, if Veynothi was working for Sapora, and *he* wanted her alive, per the bounty...Perhaps that would keep her safe.

Perhaps.

She didn't want to bet on it.

Amarah peered overboard at the wetlands below.

A sudden blast of energy knocked her down and she smashed her nose against the wheel.

Instinctively, Amarah threw out her hand to brace herself, but the strength of the impact didn't stop her nose from cracking. Blood spurted everywhere—it dripped down her face and against the wheel where she had caught it.

Amarah coughed and spluttered, gasping for air against the intense burning in her skull. Bright spots danced across her vision, and she was dimly aware of Carav grabbing onto the wheel and holding *RaKhanna* steady.

'What the fuck was that...' Amarah coughed again, pulling herself up to standing. Nausea rose, and she dry heaved. She pulled on two levers to lock her sails into place in readiness for the last resort manoeuvre.

'No idea, didn't see anything!' Carav yelled from the wheel.

'My scythe...' Amarah muttered, blinking rapidly to clear her vision of the swirling stars which filled it.

'Here.'

Blindly, she groped for Carav and felt the cool steel in her hand. Although disoriented, she felt safer with a weapon in hand. 'All right, what's going on?' Her vision tilted, and she became aware that most of her chest was covered in blood. 'Ugh. Grab me a rag to tie this back.' Her voice was thick with pain. She grabbed hold of the wheel as Carav raced off.

The young woman returned a few moments later and shoved a large square of dark linen into her hand.

Amarah stumbled again as *RaKhanna* suddenly shook under turbulence, then tied the cloth tight around her nose and face. It would have to do.

'I can't see anything in the sky 'cept that other ship.'

Amarah grimaced. 'Brace yourself!'

Her warning preceded Veynothi's next attack, which shook *RaKhanna* as though they were in the middle of a raging storm. 'Dropping altitude!' Amarah yelled, pushing the levers to force the nose of *RaKhanna* down.

She glared through the glass screen at the class five—far too close for comfort. 'Leave *RaKhanna* outta this!'

RaKhanna swung away and Amarah relaxed slightly when she saw the distance between herself and Veynothi opening up. 'Canons ready?'

'Ready!' Carav grinned. 'Wonder what the snake will think of Malot's *dragon's breath*?'

Amarah narrowed her eyes. The ship had definitely made a beeline for them. 'Incoming! Fire!'

Carav held onto the side rail.

Amarah dived, flicking the lever that released one of the *dragons's breath* cannons.

Nimble as *RaKhanna* was, the ship dropped from the sky at Amarah's touch, and Veynothi's next blast of energy soared just above her head. It ripped into her top sails, curling them in on themselves and shaking the ship.

Amarah heard Veynothi cackle, and the sound sent chills up her spine. For all her ship's manoeuvrability, it was no match for raw speed. There would be no getting away.

The *dragon's breath* bellowed as it flew into the air, flames rippling across its body and leaving a plume of dark smoke in its wake. Wings burst from its back and flapped, speeding it straight towards the class five.

Although the messenger ship was fast, it did not enjoy much mobility, and the flames blasted into it with a crack that sounded like thunder.

Amarah could hardly believe it. She thought the battle would be a slog of attacks and well-timed dodges. She hadn't expected Malot's magic to actually connect. 'How's that for aim!'

'Great shot!' Carav punched the air, necklaces jingling.

Amarah allowed herself the ghost of a smile. Perhaps it wouldn't be so impossible.

Her positive thinking disappeared immediately after surfacing when the class five flew out of the smoke. Admittedly, it stuttered somewhat, and was losing control—the flames licked along the masts and wheel. Wood split under the intense heat. The ship wouldn't be in the air long.

Amarah turned the wheel hard to starboard. If they could just stay out of reach—

'You!' Veynothi hissed.

The class five was upon them, and close enough that Amarah had her first look at the newly reawakened Ark.

With her nose a bloody mess and stars occasionally dotting her vision, Amarah struggled to concentrate. The rag made it difficult to breathe—which she had to do through her mouth. This was the worst possible way to start a fight..

Canonfire from her warship joined in the fray as Isa and Antar came within range, smashing into Veynothi's ship and tearing through its mast.

Other than Veynothi herself, the ship had no weaponry to speak of—it was a messenger ship, built to cross vast distances as quickly as possible.

Amarah would thank Rhea, if she could.

'Let's blow it out of the sky!' Carav roared, and Amarah felt herself getting caught up in the emotions of it all.

Adrenaline fuelled her along, and Amarah attacked again, loosing a second wave of *dragon's breath*. 'Damned snake!' She'd keep fighting until the end.

RaKhanna had been well stocked, with plenty of *dragon's breath loaded.* Her warship, though ungainly, boasted even greater firepower even if it didn't have any of Malot's magic.

'Is that the best you can do, Veynothi?' Amarah yelled. She'd always been good at taunting her opponents. An angry enemy was easier to beat. 'For your reputation, I'd have thought you'd be able to take me down more easily!'

Amarah ignored the fact that the last time she'd goaded a powerful opponent—who could also fly—she'd lost *Khanna*. But she'd been alone then, and in a blind fury.

Now, she was in her own space, in her advantage. On an airship.

The small ship shot forward suddenly, charging straight towards *RaKhanna*, sails and wood aflame. An enormous hole had been torn in its hull, and it was losing altitude fast.

She could see Veynothi, one hand held loosely onto the ship's rails. She looked bored.

Amarah pulled back on the throttle, but the other ship was too fast. The class five groaned as the main propellor coughed and died. With a final shudder that tore the sails, it spun wildly, throwing the three occupants into the air.

RaKhanna spun as though on elastic, and Veynothi's ship shot past, narrowly avoiding impact.

Amarah turned and watched it, grinning.

'It appears I've finally caught up with you, thief.'

Veynothi's cool voice was right beside Amarah, and she flinched, jumping back from the Ark who had suddenly appeared on *RaKhanna*. She'd seen her lurch into the air. She hadn't seen her dart down.

Carav came to Amarah's side at once, a length of spiked rope wrapped around her hand.

'Get into the cabin, Carav, keep hold of the wheel,' Amarah whispered. She didn't care too much if Veynothi heard her, but she wanted to keep her attention on the Ark, and refused to let the snake out of her sight. If Carav was out of the way, she was safer. Besides, she needed the other woman in place for this to work.

Carav hesitated for a moment before racing off, leaving Amarah and Veynothi alone on the deck of *RaKhanna.*

Amarah widened her stance, the rag around her nose dripping wet with blood. Every second she kept this snake from Isa was another second the princess had to escape.

'This is *my* ship, Ark,' Amarah said. 'You ain't welcome on it.'

Veynothi's cool smile broadened. 'You were not welcome in my tomb, graverobber. And as you are aware, I am an Ark. I go where I wish.'

Amarah felt the slightest brush of Veynothi's power. It was like the Ark tested the air, seeing where she could push.

The sky pirate knew she couldn't give Veynothi any ground. She remembered, vividly remembered, the fear and panic she'd felt in Veynothi's tomb. Now the creature was awake and walking around, it increased tenfold.

Veynothi didn't look like any Varkain Amarah had ever seen. Although she had the same grey skin, her scales seemed much more defined than on Sapora. Her long, black hair was wild, and her gold eyes seemed to see right through her.

The six swords appeared to be fixed to her back by some invisible force, for Amarah could see no sheath or holder for her weapons.

Everything about this creature was...*wrong*.

Amarah suppressed a shudder. Memories of Varkain attacks in her youth flooded her mind, unbidden.

'You no longer have your *Valta Forinja,* I see?'

Amarah narrowed her eyes and kept her mouth shut.

Veynothi laughed, cold and mirthless. 'Lucky for me.'

Amarah furrowed her brows, but had no time to retort.

Without preamble, the Ark darted forward. She drew one of her swords in a single, swift movement, and slashed down.

Amarah dived to the right, every instinct keeping her out of reach of the drawn blade.

With each step, Veynothi sucked in more energy from the air. She laughed again and struck out with a second sword.

Amarah grimaced.

Every dodge pulled strength and speed from her.

The damned Ark was just having fun before finishing her off. Like every other snake.

Amarah leapt up to her feet, her back to the side rail. 'You Varkain are all the same, whether you're an Ark or a king or the damned maggots on the street!'

Veynothi hissed. 'Despicable last words. I shouldn't have expected any more from a graverobber.'

Amarah tightened her grip on her scythe. Veynothi was certainly one to hold a grudge. 'That why you're after me? Cause I was in that disgusting tomb of yours? You got your sword back. Why don't you fuck off and go grovel to Sapora. I ain't got nothing else of yours! Don't want nothing to do with you!'

Veynothi's eyes flashed. 'You would make an *excellent* thrall. Such fierceness! The Old Guard would enjoy hacking you apart piece by piece.'

'Yeah. Not happening. They tried that before and I cut 'em down to size.' It wasn't strictly speaking the truth, as she'd been left for dead and Traego had saved her life, but Veynothi didn't need to know that. Her youth had been shaped by the amount of battles she'd survived—even when she was saved by someone else. Besides, bravado and implied confidence worked wonders in a fight. At least this explained why Veynothi had ignored Isa and come straight for her.

In fact, she was probably used to people bowing before her, or running away.

Amarah wasn't going to let the snake see her scared. With a grunt of fury, Amarah hurtled towards Veynothi and swung her scythe wide.

The Ark scowled, then dodged, darting to the side almost too fast to see.

Amarah hacked down again and again, taking a step forward, and then another, closing the distance between herself and Veynothi, forcing the Ark against the opposite rails of *RaKhanna*'s deck. The scythe's greater range gave her a tiny advantage.

If she could force Veynothi off her ship, she'd call that a win.

Although Veynothi evaded her attacks, Amarah was cautious of any counter attack by the Ark. She knew of her abilities, knew that she could suck all the energy—all the life—from her in a few heartbeats if she chose.

'You infuriate me, thief.' Veynothi's hiss echoed across the ship, and Amarah frowned.

She attacked again, quickening her pace, not letting the Ark have even a moment's relent.

'This is child's play.'

Amarah danced on the balls of her feet, following the sound of Veynothi's voice, and slashing her scythe in a wide circle.

Veynothi was little more than a dark blur shifting along the deck of her ship like water.

A sudden cry told Amarah that Veynothi had switched targets.

RaKhanna shuddered, then dropped, as Carav lost control of the wheel.

Amarah pushed forward, ignoring the blinding blood on her face and jabbed the blade of her scythe into the captain's cabin. Her aim was true, and the edge of her scythe scored along the top of Veynothi's shoulder.

The Ark hissed and raced past. Amarah only felt the briefest breeze before she was gone.

'You okay Carav?' She leaned forward and pulled her up.

The young woman was visibly shaken. 'I'm fine. She caught me off guard.'

Though her skin was cold, Amarah relaxed. Veynothi hadn't been able to suck the life from her, and she was still on her feet. 'Keep eyes on her. Snake's a damned sight faster than me. Stay ready, on my mark.'

Amarah exited the cabin and closed the door. At least Carav would have some warning the next time Veynothi tried to strike her.

The Ark cackled as she raced around the deck of *RaKhanna*, sending off her own bursts of energy at infrequent intervals.

Amarah raised her scythe to block another sword strike as Veynothi darted out from behind one of the main masts. Every contact felt like a sledgehammer, and forced Amarah back several steps. But she wasn't bleeding. There was no killing blow. 'Out...of practice, Veynothi? All...them years... locked up slow... you down?'

Veynothi's next attack struck like a horse at full gallop. The force of it sapped Amarah's strength, and it took everything she had not to lose her grip on the scythe.

Coupled with the pain in her nose and her poor vision, Amarah realised with sudden terrifying clarity that Veynothi was truly toying with her.

She wondered whether Isa and Antar loomed nearby,

watching but unable to help, or if they'd made a run for it. She hoped they were safe.

Grimacing, she clutched the scythe with both hands. She couldn't afford to let herself be distracted.

Veynothi's cackling grew louder, and seemed to come from all directions.

Amarah backed up to the side of *RaKhanna*, scythe held across her chest as she waited for the Ark to attack her again. Her breathing was laboured, and blood dripped down her chin now the rag around her face was sodden with it.

'You've lost your bite, thief. And I was having *such* fun, too.' Veynothi's drawling voice held the slightest hint of amusement.

It sickened Amarah. 'You're no different than Sapora.'

'Sapora? That mongrel.' Veynothi spat. She walked slowly towards Amarah, almost lazily, her arms hanging loose by her side. Her swords clinked together with each step, each of them locked into place on her back. 'He may be of royal blood, but he is no king. Prince Karekis is the only true ruler of the Varkain.'

Amarah took a breath. Veynothi would easily be able to dodge if she attacked again. She decided to bide her time. Just needed to stay alive. A few more seconds. 'He's no king of mine, either. Isa's better than he is.'

Veynothi smiled. 'Isa? Yes. I'll deal with her once I am finished with you and Traego. Filthy mongrel. I will admit that she is a little more fun than he is.'

Amarah narrowed her eye and took in another breath. Veynothi had to be twenty paces from her. 'I don't care what you're doing. You ain't welcome here. On *RaKhanna*. In Linaria. None of it! You need to go back into stone!'

Veynothi's step faltered for half a heartbeat.

'Now!' Amarah screamed, her lungs and throat burning.

She grabbed onto the rail behind her with one hand, and swung her scythe wildly with the other.

Veynothi smirked and crouched, ready to avoid the blade's edge.

RaKhanna listed under foot, then swung out, groaning with the effort of moving so quickly, in an unnatural direction.

Amarah dug her heels in as the deck tilted vertically.

Veynothi, unsteady and in mid-dodge, slipped. Her eyes went wide.

Then she dropped off *RaKhanna* and into the wetlands below.

25

Kohl's heart weighed heavy as he and Fogu flew north. Berel was about the furthest civilised place from Oren, and they had a long journey back to their floating islands. They decided to make it easier by taking an airship to Iryl, a rich town in Corhaven near the east coast. Topeko had a hand in ensuring they both managed to get seats on the next fast ship, enabling them to leave Ranski as soon as their conversations were over. There were regular ships between Iryl and Berel—many of the richer university students apparently came from the town—and from there they only needed to fly themselves over the narrowest part of the Sea Of Nami to Val Sharis. It brought them dangerously close to Taban Yul, but by keeping to the coast, they could cling to the edge all the way north through the lands of Everwinter until they reached their homeland once again.

He and Fogu hadn't spoken much during their travels and hadn't said a word during their airship flight to Iryl. They'd listened to the people on their night flight, though. Many were well-off Goldstones from Corhaven who'd visited relatives studying in Berel, or had spent time there touring the university and ancient city for fun.

Funny how half the world burned yet Goldstones couldn't possibly postpone their trips.

Kohl had enjoyed listening to their conversations, but Fogu had been less than impressed. He'd kept to himself, arms folded, and stared out the window. Whenever Kohl had tried to attract his attention, Fogu had ignored him.

He knew the General was distracted, so Kohl let him be. There was no point in forcing interaction and drawing attention to themselves.

Fogu hadn't wanted to be part of any journeying at all, and had only accompanied him all the way to Berel out of loyalty. Kohl could understand it. He wanted to be home with his own people, especially considering many were still suffering after being under Aciel's compulsion for so long.

He cast his mind back to Estoria, and wondered whether Amarah thought he was dead or not. After all, they'd gone their separate ways before he'd been attacked by the pirates. After the devastation Fogu had wrought to the island, it was unlikely many pirates would have their full fleets for some time.

At least it meant he'd saved more Arillians from their drowning pits.

And he'd warned the scholars of Ranski, even if it had come too late for the first assault, they now knew more attacks might follow and they could prepare. Whatever happened within Linaria now, he'd done what he could.

Everything was worse than he'd imagined; from dragons to the Varkain, and all the long-dormant powers of Linaria reawakening.

The two of them flew along the west coast of Val Sharis, heading further and further north. The wind grew colder, the clouds overhead more likely to spill snow than rain, and the land below shifted from lush green to white.

He'd risked his own life, and that of Fogu's, by travelling to Berel to warn the scholars. His welcome had been cool, his warnings dismissed. Topeko had been amicable, but it was clear he wanted the Arillians gone just as soon as it was polite to move them on.

Everything he'd tried had been thrown back at him. And he couldn't get Morgen's face out of his mind. The man had fallen into some dark, isolated place. True, he was surrounded by the scholars and students of the university, but it was clear the man was lonely and isolated.

That never boded well.

But as Fogu said, it wasn't his problem.

And one man in the depths of despair was far less of a threat than his daughter on Val Sharis's eastern edge, or the Varkain King and his Arks.

He'd tried. By the Ice Golems, he'd tried.

'My lord. If...I may?'

Kohl hovered in place and glanced behind him. It was the first time Fogu had deigned to speak since they left Berel.

Against the sheer rocky cliffs of Val Sharis's coastline, the sea below was turbulent. Foam and spray slapped against the rocks and sent pebbles crashing into the waves below. They daren't fly too high lest they caught the attention of dragons, passing ships, or one of Jato's Arillians, so they hugged the cliffs like the seabirds that nested in the cracks.

'Yes, Fogu? We're nearly there, now.'

'I know, my lord. I just...All of this strife. It all comes from us.'

Kohl kept quiet.

'And the current issues? What if we talked to Jato? I'm sure she'd—'

'Fogu.' Kohl flapped his wings to keep them moving. He didn't want to talk about Jato. She was off doing her own thing.

'I know we are above conflict in Linaria, but surely things are different when *we've* been part of it? Caused it? Doesn't it then become *our* responsibility?' Fogu flew faster, catching up to Kohl and looking him in the eye. 'When that airship docked in that town. Iryl. I...I remembered. The things Aciel and Jato made me do. The senseless slaughter, the—'

'Fogu!' Kohl shouted. 'I've said it before. I don't know how many more times I must repeat myself. *It wasn't your fault*!'

Fogu shook his head. 'Be that as it may, many people are dead or worse because of me. Because of us.'

'Only the Ice Golems may judge us.'

'And if they judge us to be unworthy? What will you do about it?'

Kohl wasn't sure. As far as he was concerned, he and Jato had cut ties. He'd ignored the fact she was a very large problem in Linaria, with her handful of followers currently laying waste to Val Sharis, wreaking more havoc and sparking more war.

If it didn't happen on their floating islands, it didn't concern him.

It was a dismissive mantra he'd always tried to follow to keep his people safe and at peace. Aciel had been one outlier. A single Arillian with the power of compulsion. Now he'd been sealed away, they could return to their lives. The way things had been.

'Please, my lord.'

Except they couldn't. Jato wouldn't. Nor would those who followed her.

Kohl looked at Fogu, saw the warrior's pleading gaze.

Neither would Fogu.

Kohl sighed.

The Ice Golems had exiled him in favour of Aciel, yet even in his exile, he still had to be a leader. Still had to make the hard decisions, and do the things others couldn't do. His trip to Berel to warn the scholars had been his guilt eating at him, forcing him to do something about Jato without getting his hands dirty.

But now? With the fate of the entire world at stake? Ancient powers unearthed from all corners of Linaria?

Kohl was at a loss.

He continued on, flying slowly as the weight of everything grew heavier. Seagulls screeched at their passing, but he paid them no mind. 'I'm done running. I've tried to help Linaria, but the world seems determined to hate us, regardless. I cannot blame them for that. We have brought war to their shores, slaughtered thousands, and remain aloof, as if we are somehow above them. Better than.'

'We are...'

'*Are* we? Look at the Samolen. They preach peace, yet the dragons—their own sacred gods—attacked them. Their magic is stolen from those beasts. *From dragon-flame begun. From dragon-flame undone*. You must be very foolish to not see those words coming true.' Kohl didn't want to believe it, but he couldn't ignore what he'd seen and heard.

And he knew he had the power to stop them. The dragons. The destruction. The death.

All of it.

If there was no other way. He and the other two Arillians Lords needed to come together, first. Yet, sitting idle would be accepting the end of the world, wouldn't it?

He sighed again, his broken fingers throbbing in the cold, sea breeze. 'I must decide what is best. For us. Our people. For Linaria. The sooner we reach Oren and I can speak with the other two Lords, the sooner I can decide.'

'I have no doubt you will make the right call.' Fogu continued onwards, using the cliff as shelter from the bitter northern winds.

'I appreciate your faith.' It was more than Kohl felt about himself. He'd assumed Jato was having another of her childish tantrums. Flexing her wings. Showing her strength.

But her fixation on Taban Yul made him wonder...the Sevastos had sealed Aciel, but hadn't killed him. It had become apparent that Aciel's will was just as strong as ever, seeping through Taban Yul and influencing those with the misfortune to come into contact with it.

He'd always assumed Aciel had been fully sealed, never to leave a mark on Linaria again.

Alive, but locked away.

If he could influence people...

The repercussions of that changed everything. And it turned it from a problem Linaria had to deal with to one he had to squarely face. If Aciel freed himself, somehow...It was up to him to finish the task, just as he should have done before.

If he hadn't been so cowardly.

He'd not forgotten his promise to seek a way to resurrect Moroda. If it meant releasing Aciel, too, then he would be able to take care of him at the same time.

Kohl pushed his thoughts from his mind. One thing at a time.

First, they needed to get past the Ice Golems.

~

THE FLIGHT UP to Oren was far easier for Fogu and himself than it had been with Amarah and *Khanna*. For one, both he and Fogu could fly under their own power, and were used to the Arillian forces that protected their floating islands from outsiders.

There was no ship to be destroyed this time.

His stomach, however, still lurched in nervous apprehension.

He'd not kept in contact with any of the Arillians since leaving, despite the numerous storms he could have looked into. In fact, it had taken seeing Fogu alone on a beach in Estoria, and his guilt and shame, for him to realise he was letting his people down. They deserved more from him, and he was determined to give it to them.

'Ready for this, my friend?' Kohl asked as they ascended.

'I have been so ready to come home, my lord.'

Kohl's heart ached for home even more now he could see the floating islands in the distance.

When the twin mountains loomed before them, the only true landmark in the barren, frozen landscape, Fogu made a choked noise, and Kohl remembered his General hadn't been home since before Aciel's war. He couldn't fathom the range of emotions his companion felt, but knew they wouldn't be far from his own.

There was no Jato there, now. None of her followers waited to lay into him for being a terrible leader, a terrible father. They were out causing despair throughout Val Sharis.

The silver lining meant Oren would be peaceful, if nothing else.

Of course, there would still be those who were recovering from Aciel's compulsion, and he wondered whether they would ever fully recover. He hoped so. Fogu, too, had been under Aciel's compulsion, and yet seemed well enough. Aside from staring off into the distance when he thought he wasn't looking, Fogu was just as Kohl remembered. He was certainly as strong as he had always been, and just as vocal.

That was another mystery. Why some came through compulsion with few effects, like Fogu, and others lost their minds. Perhaps it was due to Fogu's strength being that much greater than the average Arillian—it was part of why he'd become a General.

But first, they had to cross the threshold, and present themselves to the Golems.

He'd passed them once before, with Amarah, but that was no indication he would receive their blessing a second time. Jato hadn't been on the warpath, then, either.

That alone might change their minds.

'We should go one at a time.' Fogu hovered, staring down at the great army of sentinels spread out for leagues below, turning the white snow into a blur of mottled blue. 'I don't want to be the reason you aren't permitted back.'

'Nonsense, Fogu. You're my General. You're my *friend*. If you aren't permitted home, then I don't wish to return either.' Kohl patted Fogu on the back in what he hoped to be a reassuring gesture. He spoke with more confidence than he felt.

Fogu closed his eyes, nodded in thanks, and the two of them flew low to the ground, skimming across the snow as they approached the gatekeepers to their world.

Ever silent, the rows of giant sentinels looked much the same as when he'd left Oren with Amarah. In their hundreds of thousands, the chunks of living ice were as still and silent as always. Each of their four legs were buried in snow, making it appear as if they sprouted from the ground, like monstrous trees of ice.

Both Arillians landed, the perfect, unblemished snow crunching underfoot.

Towering above them, the sentinels appeared more godlike than the dragons so many Linarians worshipped.

Far, far overhead, Oren floated. Mist had risen in the frigid conditions, and Kohl could barely make out the dark smudge above them—the base of the island.

Bringing his hands up, Kohl let loose a burst of freezing air. It passed over the closest Golem, then shifted through their ranks, leaping from one to the next until each and every one grew aware of their presence and request to enter.

A few moments later, Kohl winced as their words materialised in his mind. Their ancient voices grated—feelings and expressions more than any kind of spoken language.

Returning.

Home.

No.

Danger.

Something rippled. A deep stirring within the ranks of Ice Golems as if they readied themselves to move.

Kohl stood his ground, ignoring the terror clutching at his chest. He sent more icy wind over the Golems, trying to reassure them of his intentions. Most people didn't survive the Golems long enough to attempt a negotiation, but Kohl spoke their same tongue. He had a fraction longer than most. 'I am no danger. I only wish to unite the Arillians. Bring my people together. Keep them safe.'

He held his breath, unsure whether his message was clear enough for the ancient sentinels.

'My lord. Above!'

Kohl leapt back and looked up in time to see a blur of movement. Something—*someone*—had fallen from the island.

Before Kohl could say anything, Fogu leapt into the air, hands held in front of him. The wind he conjured swirled up faster than gravity pulled the person down, and Fogu slowed their approach to land gently in the snow in front of them.

Kohl's heart hammered in his chest—it was an Arillian.

A dead Arillian.

'What is this?' Kohl breathed, his voice trembling. Memories of the Estorian drowning pits fluttered in his mind.

Much death.

Kohl realised then that the Golems were *warning* him of death, not refusing him entry because they thought he brought it. 'What has happened? I must put a stop to this!' Rage swelled within him as he spoke. All the injustice and hatred towards his people. The lives lost.

Danger.

Welcome home.

Kohl looked at Fogu, but knew the General couldn't hear the Golems' voices. 'We're permitted.'

'And...and them?' Fogu crouched low over the body and ran a hand down dead Arillian's cheek. 'He was one of Aciel's army. Young. Strong.'

Cold rage crept through every fibre of Kohl's being. Aciel. Aciel had caused all of this. Even sealed, he *still* inflicted death and sadness on his people. Kohl didn't know if Jato could free Aciel, or was simply drawn to his crystal prison like a moth to flame.

Either way, he'd had enough.

'We've been away too long. The Golems will watch them.' He leapt into the air, feeling stronger than he could remember—funny how powerful an emotion rage could be. 'Let's go home.'

FREEZING wind accompanied them when they landed on the rocks of Oren. It hadn't been long since he'd last been here, but that had been a difficult visit fraught with turmoil. Bringing an outsider to their home was rare enough—worse still that Amarah had been a sky pirate of unscrupulous morals.

It had been Amarah's own fault that Jato had exploded and destroyed *Khanna*.

He gritted his teeth. Another broken promise. He'd not given Amarah a new ship either, hadn't helped her at all.

Fogu landed beside him and sank to his knees, palms flat on the barren ground. 'It has been so long...'

Kohl gave him space while he looked around. Most of the rocky buildings rose in the distance and silhouettes of Arillians flew overhead. There weren't a lot of them. No-one seemed to be anywhere near, strange considering someone must have thrown the dead Arillian off the edge of the island.

Something didn't feel right.

The Ice Golems had warned him of the death.

Kohl wondered if he should have taken Fogu's advice and travelled straight home after escaping Estoria. It wasn't as if Morgen or Topeko had even been pleased to see him, nor grateful for his warning. 'We should go to the flame. That's where the others will be.'

'What is happening here?' Fogu asked, standing up, dust stuck to his palms.

'Aciel's influence lingers.' Kohl scowled. Life on Oren was by no means easy. They didn't enjoy the fertile land of most of Linaria, and only the hardiest plants and animals lived at such altitudes. But it felt worse than before, as though life was strained, somehow.

Nor could he shake the Ice Golems' warning. 'Come, Fogu.'

The two of them flew quickly, spurred on by a gut feeling that something was terribly, terribly wrong. It erased any joy at returning home, at finally being able to show who he was —no more hiding and avoiding others.

Over the generations, Arillians had carved towers and buildings into the sheer rock face and ice, but Kohl felt only sadness at seeing his birthplace. A few of his people flew into their homes, through large, glassless windows carved into the top of the structures.

Were they hiding?

A peal of thunder echoed through the sky, carrying further in the crisp, cool air. Kohl increased his speed, hurrying over Oren's landscape, following the thin air currents until the heart flame glistened ahead.

Even from a distance, there were already dozens upon dozens of Arillians gathered around the fire, staring into it, transfixed. Images flickered in between the orange and yellow flames; mountains; vibrant, green plains; a city of gold and marble; black thunderstorms looming above.

'Jato.' Kohl's cloak flapped around him as he tore through the air, panic seizing him.

At the fire's base, shards of the same living ice of the Golems sprouted—smooth, grey-black—their magic made real through Frost-touch. His fingers tingled.

At their approach, several of the Arillians glanced up, immediately standing and pointing, many shouting to their friends and family. 'Lord Kohl has returned!'

'Can it be?'

'I thought he fled!'

'General Fogu accompanies him!'

'I don't believe it!'

One woman, taller than the others, and swaddled in layers of goat hide to keep the cold off her old bones fluttered her white-blonde wings. She wore her long, blonde hair loose, although bones and varnished pebbles had been threaded through it, making a musical clink when she turned her head, or when the wind caught it.

Tymē.

Kohl landed in front of her and lowered his head, taking her hands in his in respectful greeting. 'You have picked a fine time for a visit,' she said, her voice cold. 'Or was it the pain of our people you felt which finally drew you back?'

'I am pleased to see you too, Tymē. The Golems warned me...'

Tymē closed her eyes and sighed in resignation. 'General Fogu. I thought you, too, had perished. We are fortunate you both live.'

'Tymē.' Fogu bowed his head. 'The world has greatly changed.'

'I imagine it has. Jato's storm grows more every day.'

'Send for Lords Varielle and Dronour. We must speak immediately,' Kohl said.

One of the younger Arillians, pale-faced with a shock of blonde hair, bowed and took to the skies, grabbing two more companions to help deliver the message.

'Any more casualties in Val Sharis?' Kohl almost didn't want to know.

'See for yourself.' Tymē stood aside, leaving both Kohl and Fogu with a clear view of the fire. Up close, he saw every detail of Jato's storm. It spread along the Feor Mountains and into the plains on Taban Yul's eastern side. No airships braved the skies, no people wandered along the road to the great city. A small covered wagon trundled along, having been somewhere in the Rio Neva forest, no doubt.

'She is *your* responsibility, Lord Kohl,' Tymē said. She tightened her furs around her shoulders. 'Whatever transpired between you and Jato, it is no longer personal. I cannot bear to see her bring more destruction to our people.

There are few of us left, after Aciel...She would be better suited at home with us.'

Kohl hated to see Tymē so fragile. She was more than eighty years older than he was, and had always been as strong as the ice itself. A pillar of security within Oren.

He stepped closer to her and placed both hands on her shoulders. She was the closest thing to a mother he'd ever had, and it killed him to see the pain in her eyes. 'I am here to put an end to this. If the Golems must get involved, I shall invoke them. Trust me.'

'If you cannot...if you will not...control her. *We* shall have to. Nothing could be worse than the path we're all falling down.'

Kohl spread his wings. 'It *won't* come to that. She's upset over Aciel. That's understandable. It may take her decades to get over that loss, and—'

'By the Golems!'

The three of them spun around in time to see the black thundercloud flash white. It lit up the sky as if it were the middle of the day, turning the colours of the flames to pale gold.

Kohl's breath caught as lightning struck the ground beside the wagon, almost in slow motion. The strike hadn't been accurate, but it carried enough strength that it incinerated the wooden wheel and sent the eagon tumbling onto its side.

Tymē said something, but Kohl didn't hear. Her words faded into a blur, like he was underwater and couldn't properly listen. Someone else spoke, Fogu, probably, and the entire crowd erupted into a cacophony of noise.

The driver of the wagon raced away, making a break for it. An Ittallan, Kohl assumed. It was futile, of course. You couldn't outrun an Arillian, no matter how fast you were.

But the figure that stepped out of the wagon next gave Kohl pause.

A Varkain dressed in black and silver, one scimitar held in his left hand. Light on his feet, with a lean, athletic build. Who struck faster than anything he'd ever seen.

Sapora.

Jato and her Arillians had just attacked King Sapora.

26

Nightmares plagued Morgen while he slept, and quite often while he was awake. He'd been confined to resting at Topeko's house for the foreseeable future, which carried pros and cons. It meant he didn't have to help rebuild the university for the time being, which was always a bonus, but he saw little and less of Topeko and the other Samolen.

Kohl's visit had thrown him.

Topeko's revelations had left him reeling.

If his *Valta Forinja* was locked up in the University, it was going to be a beacon for the dragons launching a second attack on Berel. Could he even trust the Kalos to keep him safe?

It was only a matter of time before they struck again. Morgen knew it would definitely be his fault if they did. The dragons wouldn't stop until the *Valta Forinja* were destroyed.

Evidently the Samolen ideals of sitting down and waiting out the war wasn't going to help. Not when they were being directly targeted.

If Topeko had his way, Morgen would be stuck under his roof until all the world burned away in dragon-fire. Topeko and the other Kalos were happy to be reduced to ash as long as they didn't fight back.

Morgen couldn't stomach it. Too many people would die.

Staying here any longer was out of the question.

He needed to get his sword and get out. It was the only way he'd be able to protect the people of Berel. The Samolen might not agree with him leaving with his *Valta Forinja*, but it was better than sitting around, peacefully waiting to burn.

And he didn't want to be incinerated by anything else, for that matter. A dragon, Sapora's Sevastos, the Arks —anything.

Morgen wondered if breaking Sapora's hold on his Sevastos would make things better. Linaria's balance of power had been skewed. If he *unskewed* that part, would the world right itself? The *Valta Forinja* might be strong enough to make a difference. If he was going to leave with it anyway, he might as well put it to good use, and cut his nightmares out, too.

Getting away from Arch-Kalos Dhabra would be for the best, at any rate. Topeko *knew* Dhabra was bad news—that was why he'd sent Andel away early. As far as Morgen was concerned, all the Kalos who knew about Dhabra were wilfully complicit in whatever darkness he brought to the Samolen and those students who studied at the universities throughout Ranski.

The man frightened Morgen more than any battle ever had. More than the dragons. He terrified Mahlu, too, and he couldn't abide that.

Morgen shuffled out of his room, hoping the nightmares wouldn't follow him.

He needed to retrieve his sword, whatever the price.

Although it was late morning, the harsh desert sun

already beat down on the city in relentless, crushing waves. His daytime robes were thin and lightweight, and he pulled the shawl over his head to keep as cool as he could.

Thankfully, most Samolen were too busy with their own tasks of the day to pay him much mind, and he blended in relatively well. His skin had darkened during the time he'd spent in Berel, and his robes were from Topeko's own home, so no-one gave him a second look. He was just another Samolen out running errands.

It was better than the stares he usually received.

Morgen wet his chapped lips with his tongue and made his way down the dusty streets towards the university. He kept his head down for the most part, concentrating on his feet and where he walked. Dust covered his sandals, and he kicked out every so often to clear them. That was one thing he wouldn't miss about Ranksi—the damned desert.

He exited the residential district and passed by shops and bakeries as the New Town grew more dense. He didn't particularly want to travel through the more crowded areas, but it was the quickest way to the bridge connecting New and Old Towns, so Morgen was prepared to cope with more people.

It wasn't as if he'd be around too much longer, anyway.

He missed Andel and felt terribly guilty about leaving without having a chance to say farewell, but his own sanity, and the safety of Linaria, were more important.

The bustle of the market swirled around him like a hurricane—noise and movement muddying together. People barged against him, some hurrying him along as they walked in the same direction, others pushing him back as they tried to get past. The scent of spices, fruit, and perfume were thick in the air. Coupled with the overbearing sun, Morgen's head throbbed painfully in the cacophony. Even covered, everything buffeted his senses. It was far more intense than he'd realised it would be outside.

He shook his head to clear it, only for dizziness to swamp him.

Staggering, he instinctively reached out with one hand, missed the wall of the building he walked beside, flailed, and toppled into a rickety market stall. Hands grasping, he grabbed onto the nearest solid thing within reach—which happened to be a large casket of red melons. The casket, the stall holder, and himself tumbled over, the fruit went flying, and several burst open when they smashed into the ground—smearing crimson pulp across the street.

The rich, over-ripe, sickly sweet smell washed over Morgen as he landed face-first in the dust, and his breathing turned into a fit of hacking coughs.

'You damned fool!' the stallholder yelled, hurrying over to collect the few unbroken melons and return them to their casket. 'You just cost me three half-florins!'

Naturally, Morgen had to send the most expensive fruit flying, and not the hard-shelled nuts that could be trampled on by a horse and remain undamaged and perfectly edible.

The man's hands grabbed Morgen by his shoulders and heaved him to his feet. 'Well, lad? You have it? Or will you work it off?'

People stopped in the street, some laughed or pointed at the scene.

The man loomed closer, his shadow blocking out the sun, until he was so close Morgen could smell his breath. Shuddering, Morgen pulled back. He steadied himself, grabbing onto the table behind him—thankfully not sending any other fruit flying. 'Kalos Topeko...'

The stallholder's demeanour shifted. He released Morgen's robes so abruptly that he almost toppled over again. 'Oh, you're one of *his* Kalosai?'

Morgen nodded, too focussed on breathing to speak. Another wave of tremors worked their way up his body, and he fought with everything he had to keep a lid on them.

What was happening to him?

What had the Arch-Kalos *done*?

'I'm on my way to the university,' Morgen stammered. He shuffled further back, pushing his way through the crowd of shoppers and vendors. 'I'll let Kalos Topeko know. Three half-florins. Plus another for the trouble.'

Morgen didn't wait for acknowledgement, nor did he apologise. He simply turned and hurried away, his eyes streaming from dizziness.

He ran blindly, without any idea of where he was going, until a cramp in his calf forced him to skid to a halt. By the time he'd caught his breath back, he glanced up to gather his bearings. Panting heavily, he wiped his forehead again.

Then he realised where he was. 'The path under the lake?' He'd managed to stumble off the main street and onto the slight downhill slope. The gaping mouth of the cave that led under the lake waited below, some fifty or so paces away.

A low wall divided the pathway down—probably explaining why he'd never really noticed it before despite the countless times he'd walked down the main street each day—which also hid him from the view of the baying crowd. Most laughed, but there were a few angry cries here and there.

For a peaceful nation, the Samolen had strong views on honour and how one must conduct themselves.

Morgen didn't care anymore. It had nothing to do with him.

He just needed to catch his breath and—

Light filled his vision. Golden fire raced across his mind.

'Rhea...?' Morgen gasped and dropped to his knees. His muscles spasmed.

He leaned forward, braced himself against the wall, and breathed deeply until the blinding light faded.

Dragons above, *was* he getting ill? Kohl had said so immediately.

It had to be the magic he'd been exposed to during the ritual. Topeko had wanted him to be ready, like Andel, but he hadn't been. Either that, or it was the dark workings of the Arch-Kalos. Perhaps both.

He pushed himself to standing on unsteady legs, until he was certain there would be no more dragon-filled visions.

'Are you okay, Morgen?' It was Mahlu.

He whirled around to see her poking her head over the wall and looking down at him, her forehead creased. 'Um.'

'What happened in the market? Shouldn't you still be at Topeko's? Resting?' She made her way around the edge of the wall and came down to him. She carried a small basket of purple and pink desert flowers, and placed them on the ground—her immediate attention on him.

Morgen waved her away, but remained leaning against the wall for support. 'Not used to the heat. And Kohl's visit...' Morgen trailed off.

Mahlu's expression deepened into a scowl. 'I hate them. Those Arillians.'

Morgen remembered everything he'd lost because of Aciel, Kohl, and Jato. Even this—his time in Berel and his studies with Topeko were being cut short because Arillians were causing trouble. 'Me too.'

She rested a hand on his back. 'Let me help you back to Topeko's. Honestly, I don't know why you think you're well when you obviously—'

'I'm not going back.'

'What do you mean?' Mahlu leaned forward to stare at him. 'You hit your head or something?'

Morgen snorted. 'Arch-Kalos Dhabra definitely did something to my head. *And* the dragon.'

Mahlu shuddered at the mention of the Arch-Kalos. 'The dragon? But that was weeks ago?'

It was the vision of the golden dragon under the lake that Morgen couldn't shake. Every lick of its flames burned like real fire. Ever since then, he'd been dealing with tremors and fatigue, while Topeko treated him like a sick puppy.

None of the other Samolen at the ceremony seemed affected by the dragon—or even aware of it.

He needed to figure out the truth, whatever it took.

'Have you ever been to the lake?' Morgen asked, straightening up and heading down the path, dragging Mahlu along with him.

'No? Why? Should I have?'

'Well, I guess if you only go when you're invited, people like you and me won't ever have the chance to see...'

'See what?' Mahlu pulled away, her eyes getting wide.

He let her go, but continued down the sloping path towards the entrance of the cave. 'I don't know what's going on. What sort of magic is really here. But let me show you what I saw.'

Mahlu loitered where he'd let her go. She held her shoulder with one arm, eyes darting back up to the main street. 'You just said we aren't allowed unless invited.'

'It's not locked. It's not guarded.' Morgen peered into the cave's mouth. The tunnel beyond looked just as he remembered—smooth and slick with water. 'There aren't any ceremonies there. Not in the middle of the day. No-one will be there. No-one will know. Mahlu, I swear to Rhea, it feels like I'm going insane here. Let me show you the place, and you tell me what you see. If you don't see what I did, then I'll go back to Topeko's and sleep until whatever fever I have passes.'

'Morgen...'

'And if you *do* see the same as me, and I'm not delirious...' Morgen trailed off. Even he wasn't sure what it would mean. If he was honest with himself, considering returning to the lake hadn't even occurred to him until that moment.

Now he'd managed to end up by the cave, it seemed silly not to have a look.

Just to prove to himself that he wasn't crazy.

'I'm going. Come with me if you want, Mahlu. But if you don't come, do me a favour? Don't tell Topeko...Dragons above I'm in enough trouble with him as it is.' Going against his better judgement, Morgen turned away from her and headed into the cave's mouth.

Entering it in the middle of the day killed some of the mystery and excitement he'd harboured before. If anything, dread was the most purveying emotion. Water—or what appeared to be water—trickled down the smooth cave walls, creating shallow rivulets. Droplets echoed around him, swallowing his footsteps as he progressed deeper.

This time, Topeko wasn't here to guide him.

Nor protect him.

Morgen steeled himself, wishing he had his sword—not that it would be of much use to a dragon of that size. Even the young drake that had attacked Niversai would have overpowered him.

Thinking back to that night of course made him think of Kohl saving them.

Again, he focussed on his steps. One foot in front of another.

The tunnel curved slightly. Grew darker.

More water dripped.

Shuffling along, step by step, Morgen made his way through the winding tunnel, following the same route he'd taken before. He stumbled once, but caught himself against the wall. His skin tingled where the water touched it, but he knew he was in too deep to back out now.

His pulse pounded in his ears, echoing off the damp tunnel walls.

'Morgen, wait!' Mahlu hissed.

Her footsteps were dulled by the tunnel, but Morgen didn't need to turn around to know she was there. She'd either keep her distance or stay close. It was up to her.

He was more interested in the giant jaws of death he was potentially leading them towards. 'Keep up. It's not far.'

For almost a minute, the two of them moved through the tunnel, wary not to touch anything. Morgen's calf burned with every step, but he continued on regardless. When the ground dropped away under him, he almost overstepped and fell.

Remembering what he'd done with Topeko, he gently fumbled on the floor for a small rope ladder, then clambered down. He dropped off the bottom, landing in the wide cavern underground—and the vast lake that seemed to take up every inch of available space.

Mahlu landed on the ground softly beside him, and gasped.

Even seeing the lake a second time did nothing to diminish the awe-inspiring sight.

There were no flames and no sign of the dragon—just the ever-expanding water pulsing gently, pale blue light reflecting on the cave's roof.

Mahlu pointed. 'Morgen!'

He followed her finger and spotted a man crouched down by the water's edge. From his colourful robes and trailing headdress, Morgen knew it was Dhabra even before he turned around. 'You!'

'Hmph. Dragon-killer. You have come for your final judgement?' Arch-Kalos Dhabra straightened up, unhurried. He clutched a slim blade in one hand, barely longer than his palm, and it dripped with lakewater. His gaze drifted across the pair of them, and he sneered. 'Neither of you will ever become true Kalosai, let alone anything greater. You *are* aware of that, aren't you?' He jabbed the tip of the knife in their direction, punctuating his words with steel. 'Bad blood. It's always bad blood. And *this* one is a killer.' Dhabra pointed the blade at Morgen, light shimmering along its edge.

'*You're* the one with bad blood!' Mahlu screamed, an explosion of anger that made Morgen jump. 'My mother lost *everything*! But you took our money anyway! Took it, took her hope, and ruined us both!'

Dhabra laughed. 'Goldstones are always the same. You cannot throw money at anything you wish and bend it to your will. Rhea's breath doesn't work like that. It chooses *only* the worthy. Neither of you are. Never will be. Topeko enjoys seeing the scum struggle. Thinks he's doing a good job helping the *unfortunate*. But he has contributed to the university and produced some fantastic Kalosin. So I let him play his games every so often.'

Disgust grew in Morgen's belly. He was *not* unfortunate. And he was *not* part of some game.

Dhabra continued, 'Look at you. So full of anger. Rage. Like a fire about to burst and destroy it all. You want to learn *He*, don't you? Topeko thinks he can keep you contained, but *I've* seen the secrets of your soul—seen the true depths of who you are, cretin. Don't you ever wonder why Topeko keeps you in the dark? Swaddled like a babe? Not because you aren't ready. Not because you're stupid. But because of your violence. That darkness grows every second of every day. Look at you, you're trembling with the effort of keeping it at bay.'

'Shut up! Shut *up*!'

'Hmph.' Dhabra smiled as if he'd won some sort of battle. He ignored Morgen and turned his attention to Mahlu. 'And *you*. You may come from a family of gold, but you hide your wretchedness behind your coin. As if it could save you. Kalos Ettas has no doubt you'll flounder and fail, and when you drown, no-one will be left to mourn your worthless corpse.'

'You're just like those Arillians!' Mahlu shook like a leaf. 'Like Aciel demanding Linaria be cleansed! Like Fogu slicing my hometown to ribbons! How *dare* you cast judgement when you're just as bad as the worst of us!' Tears streamed down her cheeks.

Morgen wanted to hold her steady, to comfort her, let her know she wasn't alone. But his fear and hatred of the Arch-Kalos rose like a fountain, and he wasn't sure he could stop it.

'You will *not* rain destruction upon this land. You and your bloodthirsty behaviour are *forbidden*!' Dhabra's voice boomed in the cavern, and several chunks of the ceiling fell into the lake below. He raised the knife. 'I've cut out the stones of so many failures. Spilled their blood in the name of Rhea. Cast them out lest they taint us further. If I must spill more, let Rhea herself judge me for keeping this world cleansed.' Wet with lakewater, Dhabra's blade glowed silver-white.

With sudden dread, Morgen realised the Arch-Kalos meant to attack them both. *Kill* them.

It confused him. Would the Arch-Kalos break the ancient Samolen promise of peace? Had he truly broken it before, so many times? But how could Dhabra hope to harm them with what amounted to a sharpened butter knife.

Arch-Kalos Dhabra's cheek stones glowed. Every colour burned bright as he tapped into *Ra*, and the air grew hot around them. 'I will free you from the troubles of life. Free you of failure, worry, and pain. Of your darkness and despair.' His voice shifted, deepened, as though a thousand tongues spoke with him. 'I judge you both *unworthy*.'

Pain splintered through Morgen's head, as if a metal bolt had been shoved deep into his brain. It laced through him, ear to ear, and he sank to his knees, choking out a cry of anguish.

A memory of Topeko's words fluttered before him. '*The Arch-Kalos isn't like you or me. Or any of the other Kalos. Learn what I'm trying to teach you, and you'll be able to not only defend against powers like that of the Arch-Kalos, but I think you'll learn how to protect those you wish to save.*'

Indignation, terror, and the desire to survive gave Morgen strength when fear should have left him crippled. The pain that had paralyzed him faded. 'You *interrogated* my mind! What gives *you* that right?' His throat burned with the words, but he forced his body to obey.

He'd survived worse.

Mahlu's hatred fuelled his own.

He got to his feet, body shaking with the effort, and called upon *Ra*.

'Boy, you do not understand the chasm between you and I. You are a worm upon the ground, and I am as great as the dragon whose magic I wield!' Dhabra raised both hands, and a blast of energy hurtled across the cavern.

Every hair stood up on end as the energy swelled.

Morgen threw his hands forward, conjuring a rectangular shield before himself and Mahlu.

Dhabra's magic slammed into the shield, crackled at the brief resistance, then crashed through it in a burst of light.

For an instant, Morgen was free. Then Dhabra's magic clamped around him like a vice, knocking Mahlu flying and slamming Morgen to the ground. Slowly, it dragged him across the cavern floor to Dhabra's feet.

'I commend your reflexes. I suppose they would be fast for one like you.' Dhabra looked down at him, tightening the magic around Morgen, binding his arms to his sides and sucking the strength from his legs.

The Arch-Kalos crouched down, knife in hand. He twirled it, as if he took pleasure in what he was about to do. 'But all those who are unworthy are judged sooner or later. By Rhea's word, you will be cleansed from Linaria, never to taint our home with your blood-thirsty nature.'

Morgen squirmed in place, wriggling from side to side as he tried to push free of the magic. Damn it. Dhabra was going to kill him, then Mahlu, and there was nothing he could do about it.

He spat at the Arch-Kalos' feet. One last act of defiance.

'Defiant to the end.'

Morgen scowled. His heart pounded in his ears, but he refused to give Dhabra any satisfaction. There was no Topeko anymore. He was alone.

Dhabra lifted Morgen's chin with the flat of the knife. 'I hope you are ready to meet the Goddess.'

Morgen glared, even though he knew Dhabra could probably see through his brave front to the fear pumping his heart. He'd been cut before by a sword, many times. The idea of being hurt by a blade coated in lakeswater was what gave him more fear than anything else.

He gritted his teeth and kept his mouth shut, braced for the searing heat of the blade slicing his skin.

A sudden shriek broke his concentration. Morgen couldn't turn to see—but a moment later, Dhabra was bowled over as Mahlu lunged into him, her nails scrabbling at his face. 'Dhabra!'

Caught off-guard with Mahlu's surprise attack, the Arch-Kalos let go of his magic for just an instant—it was enough for Morgen to react. He leapt after Mahlu and Dhabra, the two of them wrestling the Arch-Kalos to the ground. Morgen went straight for the weapon, grasping at Dhabra's wrist, digging his thumb in hard. He grinned when Dhabra dropped the blade with a yelp of pain and pushed through Dhabra's magic defence.

Morgen's training kicked in—every movement instinctive. Catching the knife before it clattered to the ground, he grasped the hilt, raised it up, and plunged it into Dhabra's throat.

Bright light spewed out.

Blood spurted, the ground shook, and Morgen's vision went white.

27

Isa's heart thundered in her chest, but she waited, on a knife edge, sweat dripping down the back of her neck.

Suddenly, without warning, *RaKhanna* listed to the extreme—tipping more and more sideways until it was vertical, the port side faced the ground, and someone fell off. Down into the wetlands.

Isa clambered up the mast to get a better look. *RaKhanna* quickly righted itself, then shot forward towards the Feor Mountains, carried by the last of the strong trade winds. 'Quick! After them!'

Antar sprang into action, thrusting the warship forward in *RaKhanna*'s wake.

If that had been Veynothi, Isa did *not* want to be around when she got back onto her vessel. She couldn't even see the tiny class five that had brought her here—she'd lost track in the chaos and confusion—but she doubted Veynothi would be stranded for long.

Even if the Ark took a while to get back on her ship, she wasn't sure Amarah's warship would make it to the mountains, much less beyond, before the Ark caught up.

Perhaps a wiser princess would have fled earlier, but Isa

didn't want to abandon Amarah, not after they'd been through so much together. Amarah had rescued her from the palace, they'd escaped the gold-hungry pirates of Estoria, and had come to an agreement that benefitted them both.

'Keep your eyes peeled for Veynothi,' Isa said.

Antar grunted, too focussed on flying to reply properly.

Isa could hardly believe Sapora had sent Veynothi after her. True, the Ark wanted to hunt Amarah and Traego, but Sapora had unleashed it.

It was like the final hammer blow. If her brother had sent an Ark after her, there would be no reconciliation. There'd be even less chance he'd return to Sereth.

It would come to a fight between them, she knew it.

Isa closed her eyes and the wind rushed through her hair as Antar pushed the warship's speed to its limit.

RaKhanna pulled further and further away, eking out a lead over the larger, heavier warship.

Isa hoped neither of them were hurt badly. They'd been too far away to tell, but the haste with which *RaKhanna* flew told Isa that Amarah didn't fancy a second chance against Veynothi.

She looked beyond *RaKhanna* to the Feor Mountains. She couldn't yet see the valley where they'd pass into the western side of Val Sharis, where Tannon Sona lay beyond.

Something moved near the snow-capped mountains. Isa narrowed her eyes, tried to discern what it was. A large, dark mass, stark against the white-grey backdrop of the snow and storms.

'Antar. Do you see that? On the mountains?' Isa called.

'I see.'

'Any clue as to what it is...?'

'Dragon.'

'You're sure?'

'Seen too many of 'em when I've been flying. Recognise that silhouette anywhere. It's a damned big one, too.'

'Oh, no,' Isa breathed. Don't let it be the Sevastos. *Any* other dragon but that. There were plenty of large dragons in Val Sharis, and the older, bigger ones certainly lived among the peaks of the Feor Mountains. There was more of a chance of it being one of them than of Sapora's Sevastos.

But Rhea had not been on her side lately.

Ahead, *RaKhanna* slowed and hovered in place.

Antar dropped his speed until the warship floated beside *RaKhanna*.

'You all good over there?' Antar called when Amarah hobbled into view. 'Dragons above, what happened to your face?'

Amarah shrugged, scythe in hand. 'Might've broke my nose. Otherwise fine. Isa. Don't tell me that's Sapora's Sevastos.' She pointed a finger towards the mountains.

'It could be,' Isa muttered.

'It *could* be? Or it fucking *is*?'

'Too far away to tell, Amarah.'

The sky pirate smacked the bottom of her scythe on the deck. 'You're the one who lived in the palace with it flying around. What's your gut tell ya? It's another dragon and we go past it? Ain't like we got all day to decide.' Amarah glanced over her shoulder.

Isa chewed the inside of her lip. 'It...probably is.'

'Right, well that's messed up our plans then, ain't it?'

Princess Isa looked back the way they'd come. The wetlands seemed quiet—she couldn't see or hear Veynothi or the airship she'd arrived on. But that wouldn't last long.

'I reckon we cut our losses and head back to the inlet. Anywhere else, even Estoria! Forget going through Val Sharis now there's a damned Ark on the loose and that Sevastos flying about!' Antar said.

Isa sighed. Val Sharis was too dangerous to fly in, but what choice did she have? If she gave up and hid, Sapora would remain on the throne and she would be forced into hiding lest an Ark hunted her down. Or another gold-hungry pirate sold her to Sapora. Whichever came first. 'We *can't* go back.'

'Well we can't fucking go on, can we?' Amarah wiped at her bloody face. 'Maybe we use a *Shroud* and hope it don't see us?'

'Incoming!' Carav yelled.

Isa looked back, but couldn't see Veynothi's airship anywhere. 'Where?'

'From the mountains!'

The dragon roared. Isa gulped. She'd recognise that noise anywhere.

'It's the Sevastos! It's the Sevastos!' Carav yelled.

The two airships—the beginnings of Isa's fleet—broke away from each other, peeling away in opposite directions. There had to be at least two or three leagues between them and the mountains, but Isa knew how quickly the dragon could close that gap.

Did Sapora want her dead *that* badly?

She could do nothing but hold on as Antar flew them away.

'Going for the valley,' Antar said. 'It's not that far and we ain't got much choice.'

Isa grimaced and tightened her grip on the side rail. What else could go wrong? 'Antar! What Amarah just said about a *Shroud*. Can we deploy one?' Isa asked, Amarah's words ringing in her ears.

'We can try?'

'Then *try*! What do I need to do?'

'My pack. I brought a handful with me. Get 'em!'

Isa darted away, lifting the trap door in the centre of the

deck and hurtling down the ladder into the warship's hold. She'd not spent any time down here, to her detriment. Her limbs were stiff and slow—still not recovered from the vicious battle with the Arillians—but she hurried along the interior of the ship, darting from room to room until she spotted Antar's belongings.

Thank goodness the sky pirate had the good sense to bring these with him.

She rooted through his bags; clothes, boots, a compass, twine, more knives than anyone could possibly use in one lifetime, until she found a leather pouch. Inside, dozens of small, glass orbs glittered. Grabbing the pouch, and careful not to let any of the orbs fall out, she raced back onto the deck.

'Good. They're small, so gonna need to use a few. Put one on each side of the main deck. Crack 'em on the floor so they deploy,' Antar said, risking a glance at her, away from the mountains ahead. 'We need to hide the masts as well. Good thing you can climb, princess!'

Isa followed the instruction. She clambered up the three masts and placed an orb at the top of each, their flat bottoms preventing them from rolling around.

'Hurry up, it's gaining!' Antar yelled.

Isa didn't bother turning around. There would be no reasoning with the dragon—it was following orders. *RaKhanna* pulled away, and Isa hoped the ship's speed would be enough to keep them out of danger.

When Isa activated the final orb, the entire ship shimmered for a moment. She clambered back down, one hand massaging her side where a cramp had developed. 'Is that it? Is it done?'

Antar glanced around, hands still on the wheel. 'Think so. I saw the shimmer. Always tough to tell when you're inside the *Shroud*.'

Behind them, the dragon roared again, and unleashed a plume of white-hot fire.

Antar veered off to the left as the fire plunged into the space where the airship had been only a second before.

Isa's relief was palpable.

'We're not out of the woods yet,' Antar said, 'Veynothi could still be around.'

The warship shuddered as the Sevastos gained on them, flapping its wings and covering them in its shadow as it flew over where they had been in its pursuit of *RaKhanna*.

Isa held her breath.

As the last of its tail disappeared, Isa exhaled slowly through her nose. 'Doesn't Amarah have *Shrouds*?'

'Possibly. But *RaKhanna's* faster. She *might* be able to outfly it.'

Isa swallowed. She wasn't sure any airship in the world could outfly a Sevastos. 'I hope so.'

They watched as the Sevastos breathed another plume of fire, and once again the air turned into a dark cloud of smoke.

First Arillians, then an Ark, and now a Sevastos.

If this wasn't Rhea herself telling her to quit, she didn't know what was.

Isa put her thumb nail to her lips as they watched *RaKhanna* evade the enormous beast.

'Don't worry.' Antar poked his head out of the cabin. 'Amarah was able to get rid of Veynothi. She can get rid of a dragon, too!'

Isa's stomach churned. She'd dragged them all into this.They could all have been resting in Estoria now, if it weren't for her. 'Please be okay,' she breathed aloud, gripping the side rails harder than she intended.

'They're almost at the mountains,' Antar said.

Isa could see for herself. She didn't need Antar to spell it out for her. Then again, he was probably just as tense as she was and didn't know what to do.

The dragon seemed to be getting desperate. It sped up and unleashed breath after breath of flame.

Suddenly, when the tip of its fire seemed on top of *RaKhanna*, the airship disappeared.

Isa's breathing steadied. 'Wait. If we can't see *RaKhanna*, and they can't see us, what's to stop us crashing into each other?'

'Sky pirate's instinct.'

Isa took that to mean they were both winging it.

The dragon roared again, pursuing them for another tense minute, before suddenly turning away and flying back towards the mountains, as if someone had pulled it away from them.

Though frustrated at being on a slower ship, Isa felt safe knowing she was hidden from both the Sevastos' and Veynothi's eyes. 'We've made it,' she said, her voice pitching in excitement. 'We've made it! We're safe!'

As the words left her lips, the warship buckled in a sudden burst of energy from behind them. Isa was thrown to her knees by the sudden force and nearly toppled over the side railing. When she pulled herself up, she looked back.

Antar managed to keep the ship in the air, and their *shrouds* held.

Veynothi was angry.

Whether she had attacked them specifically, or had simply burst out a wave of energy in all directions to vent her frustration, Isa couldn't tell.

What she was sure of, however, was that she never wanted to see an Ark again.

ISA HAD NEVER BEEN SO grateful to see a town as when Tannon Sona came into view. It had taken most of the afternoon for the two ships to reach the large town, and only when it was within spitting distance did they remove their *Shrouds*.

Thankfully, there had been no sight or sound of either Veynothi or the Sevastos, and any Arillians they heard were far to the north, accumulating outside Taban Yul.

Guilt laced Isa. She was the princess of Val Sharis. She *should* be in the capital. Even if she could do nothing against Jato's forces, at least she'd be seen there.

She sighed. She had a plan. She had to stick to it.

'You sure you wanna chat to this Archigo? What if he's like the other guy?' Antar asked.

'I know Archigo Gralla. She's the richest of them. And I know her.'

'You do?'

'Well. We've met several times. And spoken. It's more than I had with Kessir.' She really only needed one on her side, because the Archigo listened to themselves more than anyone else. If Gralla backed her, she could convince more to. And the more who were convinced, the more likely the others would fall into place.

'Are you going to keep watch like before?' Isa asked, as Antar brought the ship into the town's docks. Although a far cry from Taban Yul, Tannon Sona was one of the richer towns in Val Sharis, and thus boasted proper docks, well-paved roads, and buildings that weren't in a constant state of disrepair.

Landlocked as it was, there was no no stench of fish or stagnant water, only quarry stone, which carried on the wind. Most buildings had been crafted of white stone, some even embellished with gold or marble, reminiscent of the richer districts of Taban Yul.

'Need to chat with Cap'n Amarah first.' Antar switched off the engines and stretched his arms above his head with a wide yawn.

"Captain Amarah" sounded strange to Isa, but the woman was a captain in her own right—she had a fleet and people working for her. It made sense.

The two of them scrambled off deck and walked along the hangar floor to where *RaKhanna* rested, the whir of the ship's propellers dying down. 'That was fun, weren't it?' Amarah's voice sounded from up on deck.

"Fun" wasn't the word Isa would use, but Amarah sounded in good spirits, so she wasn't about to argue and bring the mood down.

She took the time to glance around. Ships of all sizes and shapes filled the hangar. There were no other class one warships that she could see, but a fair number of threes and fours, one of which seemed to have recently been painted. Mid-size, mid-range ships with limited firepower. Most were probably used to traipse between here and the capital city, with the larger transport vessels for hauling quarry stone or precious gems.

It was mildly concerning that Tannon Sona didn't have any warships.

Carav and Amarah scrambled down the steps carved into *RaKhanna's* hull. Both grinned broadly—at least, she assumed Amarah grinned, the bottom half of her face was obscured by a bloody rag.

'You wanna get that looked at?' Antar asked.

Amarah shrugged. 'Probably.' She didn't seem particularly bothered by it. 'Princess. Where's this Archigo of yours, then?'

'I don't know. I imagine Archigo Gralla will have a residence in town as well as a meeting hall of sorts. Probably best to find the Imperial Guard and—'

'What is with you and constantly waltzing around with the Imperial Guard! You keep forgetting what we are!' Amarah said. Her voice was still light, but Isa caught a whiff of fear from her.

'Sorry. There's no other way. If you want to lay low, or wait on the ships, you can. This won't be anything like Kessir.' Isa hated the limitations of travelling with sky pirates.

'I ain't leaving you alone again.' Amarah stepped forward, wiping grime from her forehead. 'I need to get looked at. No-one knows my ships. You two wait, I'll be back with the princess as soon as possible.'

Isa couldn't believe it. Then again, with the rag covering her face, Amarah wasn't completely recognisable. It was possible that many people had lost their eye from some accident or another. These were dangerous times. 'Are you certain?'

'A broken nose I can deal with. Getting some ice and something to take the edge off the pain would help. Kinda hard to focus on flying when you only got one eye and your vision's full of stars.'

Isa chuckled as the pair walked out of the docks and into the late afternoon sun. The square was bright with white and grey stone, and several well-dressed Ittallan mingled between vendors and buildings, going about their business with hardly a look up. 'I can't believe we got away from that dragon.'

'I can't believe Veynothi *found* me,' Amarah said bitterly. She glanced around, wary.

'Maybe don't mention her name,' Isa whispered. She'd spotted the red and gold livery of the Imperial Guard on patrol, and on the far side of the square, the blue-black armour of half a dozen Cerastes.

'Y'know princess. I smell a trap.'

'Nonsense. I appreciate your caution, but—'

'Ain't nothing cautious about it. You have them damned snakes here!'

'The Cerastes have been posted to every town since Sapora came to power. There's nothing unusual about it. It's a problem for the Imperial Guard to deal with—sharing the workload. Not us.'

'Welcome to Tannon Sona.' A woman of the Imperial Guard greeted them as they walked into the square. 'Princess Isa, I presume?'

Isa recovered from her shock quickly. 'I am. Are you here to escort me to Archigo Gralla?'

'Indeed.' The woman smiled brightly. She turned to Amarah quizzically. 'And you...?'

'This is my pilot. I'd appreciate it if a medic could see her. She had...an altercation during our flight here.' Isa put as much authority into her voice as she could, and maintained eye contact.

If it flustered the guard, she didn't show it. 'Of course. Please, follow me. I'm so sorry to have heard of the...bad time you had at the palace. Archigo Gralla wondered if you might come here, seeking refuge.'

Isa frowned, but said nothing, following the woman as she marched away, leading them deeper into the town.

'Isa...' Amarah hissed.

She dismissed the sky pirate's concern with a wave of her hand. 'Thank you. I shall be glad to meet with the Archigo at once.'

28

Blind fury encompassed Sapora as he ran, like a thief from a shop vendor he'd just stolen from. He was a *king*. He'd *worked* for everything he had. Earned it! Yet he was forced to flee before the Arillians as if he was less than a common rat snake.

Sapora had his pride, if nothing else. But he wasn't so proud that he wouldn't flee when the situation demanded it.

The eastern gate to Taban Yul had been sealed shut ever since the fire in Traders' Alley—caused by Palom, if he recalled correctly. He and the Valendrin had left via the southern gate. But the eastern gate was nearest. And it was where he pushed the Valendrin towards now.

Stumbling along, tripping over his robes, the blood mage slowed him down more than any injury ever could. Not to mention the panic that rolled off him with every step. Sapora turned his lip up, not bothering to look behind him to see if they were being chased. His senses were so attuned he could hear the lightning form before it struck, giving him time to dodge out of the way. Who could claim he wasn't a true Varkain with reflexes like that?

The tell-tale hiss spiked through the air. Sapora shoved

the Valendrin to one side. 'Get down!'

Sapora almost didn't move quickly enough—the electricity scored along the back of his jacket, searing it open. The base of his neck burned—though he wasn't sure if it was from the attack itself or his superheated clothes.

'Get up. Keep running!' Sapora yelled, pushing himself back to his feet.

If he were alone, he could easily get back to the city without being caught out. Having to look after the Valendrin was more than frustrating. It was life-threatening.

He chanced a glance over his shoulder—not to spy upon the Arillians, but to see whether the Ark he'd gone to so much effort to release was actually doing anything to defend them.

His eyes widened when he saw Malashash. The enormous Varkain hissed so deeply that he roared, the sound rolling around the windy plains. Most of the Arillians were split—some continued to fly after himself and the Valendrin, but the majority had turned away—focussing their attention on the giant Varkain who'd made himself a prime target.

Malashash threw his hands up, and the Arilians scattered.

It had to be a blast of energy similar to Veynothi. Perhaps that was a magical attack that linked the two Arks —perhaps all the Arks. Either way, Malashash didn't seem to be in any immediate danger. Any lightning struck seemed to bounce off him as if he were still made of stone.

'My king.' The Valendrin gasped, struggling for breath. 'What are we to do? What if Malashash succumbs?'

'How dare you! Malashash is an *Ark*. Do you truly believe a handful of Arillians will be able to stop him? And I thought you knew more about the Arks than I.' Sapora scowled at the blood mage, infuriated that even now, his decisions were being undermined. 'I *told* you to keep moving. You can rest once we're behind the city gates.'

'But if they take the city—'

Another bolt of lightning.

Sapora brandished his scimitar and waved it at the few Arillians who continued to worry them. 'I will happily cut you to ribbons if you face me like a *true* warrior!'

They laughed. Mocking him.

Another bolt of lightning—this one in jest, rather than to harm them. A few more drifted back to Malashash. There had been twenty-three originally. Now they numbered over thirty. It seemed the entire swarm of birds who were responsible for the enormous thunderstorm were all gathering together.

The Valendrin asked, 'Where is your Sevastos?'

Sapora hissed. He'd like to know that, too. He'd seen it in the distance, flying towards them, fire in its jaws. But in his haste to get away, he'd lost sight of it. It was a shame the invisible thread that connected them did not allow Sapora to know the dragon's location. He tugged on it anyway, hoping his desperation would give the Sevastos some urgency. Had it flown past, to the Feor Mountains? Been distracted by something?

Surely releasing more Arks would tighten his hold on the dragon more than anything else?

Perhaps it was simply bolder now that he'd been bound to Sapora for a while.

'They're turning their attention to us! To Taban Yul!' the blood mage said, his voice trembling. 'It's all over!'

'Keep *running*, Valendrin!' He had no patience for the blood mage's slowness or fear. Not when their enemies had wings.

The two of them raced on, Sapora pushing the Valendrin along, or out of the way of a lightning strike—which, thanks to Malashash's presence—were fewer and fewer. If the Arillians were done preparing and Taban Yul was now under attack, he had to hurry. He'd thought they'd attacked his wagon simply because it was there, not as a precursor to a full-on assault.

Approaching the city from the east brought them into the battlefield of the city's previous siege against Aciel. The Sevastos crystal which sealed him—and Moroda—stood tall and proud several meters from the edge of the city's walls. It remained unguarded, for now. Too many soldiers had ended up injured or worse.

Even at this distance, the power emanating from the dragon stone could not be ignored.

Sapora had spent little time in Ranski and had not studied any form of magic before. Yet even he felt the power was not the burning flames of a dragon, but the cool compulsion of the damned Arillian. He wondered if Aciel could see through the eyes of those he compelled, or if he was simply replaying his final thoughts through his victims—over and over until they could not take living any longer.

The Valendrin, one of the most powerful and experienced in all of Sereth, had fallen prey to it. Sapora suppressed a shudder as they approached the crippled eastern gate—a welcome sight as it loomed overhead. Both he and the Valendrin were exhausted, their breathing heavy. Sapora hated his weakness. Not long before, he'd have been able to make that same run and hardly be out of breath.

His left arm twinged, reminding him of the growing marks.

He ignored it, and tried to remember the name of the guards posted by the eastern gate. Nothing came to mind.

Thankfully, the Valendrin spoke before he could think any more about it. 'Captain Tethkari! It is your king and his Valendrin. Open this gate at once!'

'My Lord Valendrin!' a muffled voice carried through from the other side.

Chains worked and the locks unhinged, swinging the enormous wooden gate open a crack—just enough for the two slender Varkain to slip through.

'Are you all right, my king? You're bleeding!' Captain Tethkari said. He turned to the two soldiers of the Imperial Guard beside him. 'Quick, grab a medic—'

'Not necessary,' Sapora interrupted the captain. He raised his chin. 'It looks like Jato and her Arillians are moving, and the city is about to be under siege.' He spoke quickly, hoping to mask his heavy breathing by relaying the orders in between breaths. 'Have every wall manned, every ballista brought out. Oh, and a third Varkain will follow behind us. Dressed in red. Malashash.'

Recognition flickered in Captain Tethkari's dark green eyes at the name. Shock. Astonishment. Fear. He floundered for a moment, unsure what to say.

Sapora continued, 'Have him escorted to the palace at once. I'll be waiting atop the north tower. Do not dally. Understood?' North tower was the tallest of the palace towers, and would afford him the greatest view of the city and the plains beyond.

'Yes sir. I mean, yes my liege. I'll have my two soldiers accompany you. I'll escort the Ark myself.'

It was a refreshing change to have a competent captain of the guard. 'Good. Have this gate resealed the moment Malashash is inside the city.'

'Yes my liege. At once.'

Sapora grabbed hold of the Valendrin and led him back to the palace.

Sapora marched through the richer districts towards the palace. Here, many of the roads had been paved with gold—or at least had gold detailing along their edges. 'Inside your homes! Trade is cancelled!' It wasn't much of a practiced speech. Sapora had expected to return to his city with another Ark in tow, glorious in his achievements. He hadn't expected to return to a city under siege. Attacking him had no doubt been the inciting incident for Jato. Or perhaps her storm had now reached peak strength. Who knew.

He had to deal with it now.

The two young soldiers with him—one Ittallan, one Varkain—echoed his words and used their spears to herd people out of the way of their king.

'What is happening?' A woman peered out at him. She grasped the heavily jewelled necklace around her throat as if it gave her comfort.

Sapora glared at her bony wrist, at the coloured powders on her face. 'Are you *blind*? We've Arillians on our doorstep! Have you not heard the thunder? Seen the lightning strikes? They're attacking!'

She and other Goldstones darted out of the way, affronted at Sapora's brusque manner.

The Valendrin said nothing, simply followed him like an obedient puppy.

Overhead bird Ittallan flew. Eagles. Ravens. Storks. Many of the Imperial Guard were still Ittallan, and Sapora hoped that his short briefing to Captain Tethkari at the city gate had resulted in word spreading through the rest of his city's military.

He snorted, angry, as he marched through the streets. He'd wanted Veynothi to be back by now. Then Isa would be safe in the palace, and he'd have a warrior Ark to set upon Jato and any Arillians who dared attack the city.

Truthfully, he'd thought Jato a bit of a spoiled brat.

When she and her Arillians had set up camp in the plains between Taban Yul and the Feor Mountains, it had the telltale signs of a childish tantrum. He hadn't *actually* expected her to harm him, or the capital. Destroy a few airships, yes, and throw her weight around somewhat.

But nothing like this.

He wondered what had changed to spark it.

It wasn't as if he even knew what she wanted. Every envoy and messenger ship that had been sent had ended up charred by their storms.

Two members of the Imperial Guard stood at attention at the base of the wide marble staircase which led to the palace's main entrance. Gold-topped pillars depicting famous Ittallan from the past shimmered in the sunlight. A roaring bear on its rear legs. A boar with tusks that could impale a man.

Sapora gave them a cursory glance as he whipped past the two guards. 'Battle stations. Now.'

They fell in line between Sapora, the Valendrin, and the other two soldiers Tethkari had sent to accompany them. 'The city is to be sealed off. No-one in or out, save Veynothi or Isa.'

'What about Prince Tacio, my king?' the Varkain soldier asked.

Sapora grunted. 'Yes, yes, or my brother.'

'Where will you go, my liege? What are your orders?' asked the Valendrin once they reached the top of the stairs.

Sapora paused and turned around, looking down on his city. Parts of it were still damaged from his Sevastos. But it was full of Ittallan and those Varkain who had made the journey from Sereth to start a new life here.

They'd all die to Jato's storm unless he did something to protect them. 'Fighting the Arillians will result in more of you dying. Get the city secured. The people inside. Defend them. I will monitor the situation atop the north tower. Safer than risking another ship in the air, and I'm faster at dodging than any airship, too. Prepare yourself and await further orders. Valendrin, you will wait for Malashash, then join me at the tower. I want to see what she's doing.'

Orders given, Sapora whirled around and strolled through the open palace doors. Enormous slabs of oak, they stretched over ten feet high, intricately decorated with gold, silver, and countless gemstones.

Everything here was vanity and wealth. None of it meant *anything*.

He had brought the Arks back. Given them life. They were his to command. To control.

He didn't care about Jato or why she had decided to storm the city. He refused to let her take anything away from him. Not after everything he'd been through.

Sapora swept along corridors and up flights of stairs.

Everything inside the palace was chaos. Imperial Guard or Cerastes, officer or captain, every capable fighter jumped into action—grabbing shields, weapons, armour.

He hissed. Armour. How were the smiths of the city to forge armour for Malashash while everything was shut down?

Another problem. Malashash had fought well enough against the Arillians outside. He'd have to make do for just a little longer.

Sapora himself never wore armour. Most of his opponents were too slow to hit him. And he hated feeling encumbered by heavy chain links or metal plating. Besides, you didn't want to be wearing metal armour when you were struck by lighting.

He ascended the final, winding staircase of the north tower. It had been a favourite haunt of his sister's, and he knew why. So high up—the tallest tower of the palace by some margin—it offered unparalleled views of the city and beyond. It would give him a birds' eye view of the Arillians' movements, and hopefully would give him the space to think of some sort of plan to get out of this mess.

Opening the hatch, Sapora stepped out onto the flat tower roof. Only fifteen feet or so in diameter, and without any guard rail, he felt more exposed here than ever. A strong breeze could easily blow off the unwary. But for any Arillian to reach him here, they'd need to fly over the city walls. So far, that was one thing they'd avoided.

Where was that Sevastos?

A distant roar, somewhere along the Feor Mountains. There.

It wasn't too far. It would be on the other side of the Arillian thundercloud from the sound of it. Perhaps they could catch the birds in a pincer movement? The dragon would flush them close to the city, and the ballista on the city walls would pierce them. Dragon-fire would mop up any Arillians that his weapons failed to hit.

Assuming the dragon was more controlled this time, and didn't burn down half the wall, either. He called the dragon back again. Whatever it was doing could wait.

Happy he had at least some idea in mind, he now needed to wait for Captain Tethkari, Malashash, and the Valendrin to arrive so he could relay his orders. Until then, he didn't want to lose sight of Jato and what her Arillians were doing.

Sapora lifted himself onto his tiptoes. He'd never been particularly tall, and didn't want to miss a single thing if he could help it. Past the eastern wall, the top of the Sevastos crystal glittered dully. Even from here, the pulsing power was undeniable.

His arm twitched again, and he cautiously lifted the edge of his sleeve to peek at his skin. He expected the same dark veins as before, so he wasn't shocked when he saw them. Shrugging out of his jacket, he rolled his shoulder forward to see the black veins had twisted up the entire length of his left arm, across his shoulder, and most likely down his back.

He'd need a mirror to check how far they had spread.

With hiss, he pulled the jacket back on. It had to be related to resurrecting the Arks, which meant there wouldn't be any point in staring at it until after Jato had been dealt with.

Another peal of thunder tore across the sky—this one far louder than any before. The dark thunderclouds grew larger, reaching almost to the city limits. They flashed white with every ripple of lightning.

The air grew tight and goosebumps rose on Sapora's flesh. More lightning—far more powerful. He felt the hiss of it as power gathered overhead.

Sapora crouched, braced to roll or dart out of the way.

But the strike wasn't meant for him.

In fact, he doubted any of the Arillians were even aware he watched them atop the tower.

Sapora held his breath as light burst from the clouds above, and a bolt of lightning careened through the sky, zig-zagging, pulsing, until it smashed into the Sevastos stone.

The shockwave of impact sent a blast of wind across the city. It ripped trees from their roots, pulled rooftops apart, and dropped everyone standing to the ground. Sapora lay flat, claws grasping at the tower's edge as he turned his face away from the wind. With one eye squinting shut, he stared down at the maze of streets below. Red and gold stood out, the armour of the Imperial Guard. Dozens, hundreds, of townspeople were thrown to the ground. Some pressed themselves against buildings, walls, or cowered under porches, waiting for the shockwave to pass.

Sapora looked back up. Gently getting to his feet, he

returned his attention to the sky and the Arillians above. They flew in circles and loops, their wings flapping wildly as they sent more gusts of wind in all directions. The thunder-clouds grew bigger, their darkness coating the city like a blanket, and turning the dull, overcast day as dark as night.

He glared.

They surrounded him. His city.

Along the dual city walls, the Imperial Guard rolled out several ballista, but it would take them time to get set up. And despite his confidence in his strategy, they still required the Arillians to be within shooting distance for the bolts to hit their marks.

He needed the dragon to corral them. They were all sitting targets, otherwise.

The Sevastos crystal pulsed again, faster this time. Sapora hissed involuntarily. Instinctively afraid of the power that crystal contained.

Realisation suddenly dawned on him.

Were they...were they trying to split the crystal open?

They couldn't. Surely?

Sapora bit down on the fear that threatened to rise within his chest. He had nothing to be afraid of. He had a Valendrin under his command. Two Arks. One of Linaria's strongest dragons.

He was *untouchable.*

He never needed to be afraid as long as he lived.

And yet...

'My king! Malashash has returned!' the Valendrin called from the stairwell below him.

Sapora stepped aside, making room for the Varkain to get onto the tower top. The Ark looked no worse for wear, considering he'd taken on two dozen Arillians alone—and without the armour he kept going on about.

Captain Tethkari, despite being in the presence of an

Ark, was remarkably composed. It was clear how and why he'd become a captain.

The Valendrin was a mess. His robes were in shambles, and his frail body trembled.

'The Imperial Guard are at work following your orders, my king,' Captain Tethkari reported immediately. He cast his own gaze down at the city for a long moment. 'We will keep the people safe. We've been used to running short while the city has been locked down. We'll do whatever it takes to get this siege finished with.'

Sapora wasn't overly pleased with the man's loose tongue. He was a captain, to be given orders and to delegate. But if he was competent, as he appeared to be, Sapora would forgive him speaking his mind when he wasn't asked for his opinion.

Sapora turned to the Ark. 'Malashash. Are you ready to fight for your king?'

'Birds are the same now as five thousand years ago.' Although his words were confident, Malashash spoke with little enthusiasm. He glared across the city's walls, watching the Arillians with wary eyes. 'It is easier to defend Sereth.'

'Yes, but we aren't in Sereth, unfortunately. We'll have to make do.' Sapora didn't mean to snap, but he didn't want the Ark to talk back to him, particularly not in front of Captain Tethkari. He'd only met the young Varkain a couple of times, and hadn't yet got the measure of the man.

He didn't want rumours to fester about his inability to fully control and command the Arks. There'd be mutinies within his own ranks of soldiers at the first hint of weakness otherwise.

More energy flickered through the air and Sapora glowered. 'Brace yourselves. Another bolt.'

The Varkain huddled down, keeping their bodies low, their senses alert.

Another bolt of lightning soared down from the dark clouds above, splitting the sky in two. Electricity crackled and sparked as it followed the path of the previous strike, zig-zagging towards the Sevastos crystal, where it smashed into it.

The blow was more powerful than before, and the resulting shockwave ripped up everything in the city that wasn't nailed down. Debris filled the air, knocked around by the resulting gust of wind.

'My king...the crystal! The crystal!' The blood mage gasped, the first to get back to his feet. He pointed towards the Sevastos crystal, unnecessarily.

Although Sapora's rule had revolved around resurrecting the Arks and dabbling with ancient powers and magic beyond his understanding, he'd never once considered the Sevastos crystal.

The thought that it could break had never even occurred to him.

A crack ran down the length of the crystal, bright white against the dark blue.

'My king. It is...it is him. Again. He lives!' The Valendrin sank to his knees, giving into his sheer terror.

Sapora didn't need him to elaborate. He'd spent time in Aciel's presence before. Aciel was not a man he'd ever forget.

Considering the Valendrin had fallen prey to some remnants of Aciel's compulsion, Sapora glowered at the potential results the cracked crystal would have.

'What does this mean?' Malashash asked, his voice still gruff.

'*It means I can finally kill every one of you filthy maggots!*' Captain Tethkari's eyes had rolled back. A lopsided grin plastered on his face revealed rows of jagged teeth, and he raised his sword—pointing the tip at Sapora's throat.

29

Isa had never particularly enjoyed the aromas that wafted from Taban Yul's smoking rooms. The acrid stench burned her throat more than anything else, and she'd always kept upwind of the districts where they sprung up like a fungus.

She knew many Goldstones frequented those places—enjoying the ceremony of selecting a pipe, mixing the scents to go into it, and wasting hours—if not days—in the pillowed rooms of Taban Yul's most popular smoking lounges, while flutes and harps played dulcet tones.

Archigo Gralla, it appeared, shared their enjoyment of those luxuries.

Isa shouldn't have been surprised. Gralla was wealthy. Those with too much money and not enough time often found *interesting* ways of spending said money.

The smoking rooms of Tannon Sona were larger than any of Taban Yul's finest establishments. Perhaps they used the rooms to mask the scent of stone and dust from the quarries. Perhaps it was simply a cultural thing—those Ittallan of central Val Sharis enjoyed their pipes more than any others. Perhaps there were simply more wealthy people here.

Isa, despite her heritage as a princess, had never considered herself wealthy. Wealth meant you could do whatever you wanted, and people would fall over themselves to help you. While she'd always had access to gold, the snide looks and hateful comments had always made her feel like she'd stolen it.

It meant that when she, Amarah, and the soldier who escorted them arrived outside *Oriol's Den*—Tannon Sona's most prestigious smoking room—to meet with the Archigo, Isa felt even more out of place than when she'd approached Archigo Kessir.

Amarah, on the other hand, relaxed. 'This'll *definitely* dull the pain!'

'I'll have a medic attend, regardless. I'll be waiting outside if Archigo Gralla requires anything else,' the woman said, adjusting her golden helm.

'We're not here to have fun. This is business,' Isa said, once they were out of earshot. 'You have to be on your best form!'

Amarah cackled and took off the bloody rag that had been wrapped around her face, shoving it in her pocket. 'Isa you worry too much. I just need something for the pain. Ain't gonna do anything that'll stop me being able to fight or fly, believe me!'

Isa wasn't so sure, considering how much Amarah's eye had lit up when she'd realised where they were going.

'Besides, I still don't trust no-one here. Them Cerastes looked awful shifty.'

Isa didn't find their presence comforting, either. The Cerastes followed Tacio's orders first and foremost, so their presence did nothing but remind her of him.

'The sooner we speak with Archigo Gralla, the sooner

we can leave,' Isa said. It was all she could do, now they were here.

She took a deep breath, then made her way through the entrance foyer. Heat smacked her in the face, along with the pungent flavours of cinnamon, ginger, and chocolate. There were other fruits and spices, too, and a scent that reminded her of fermented pears.

Immediately it made her dizzy and she swayed on her feet.

Amarah grabbed her arm and held her up. 'Stay with us, princess! You wanna make a good impression, don't you?'

Embarrassed, Isa shook her off. 'I'm fine. Don't fuss.' The smoking lounge was dark and low-ceilinged—heavy drapes covered the windows. Stale smoke lingered in the air like a thick mist, and the myriad cushions seemed to retain heat like an oven. Small oil lamps flickered low, dotted around the walls and on small tables. The pungent smoke did a good job of covering up the sour stink of stale sweat that otherwise permeated the lounge.

Such a place would usually be full of patrons, but only members of the Imperial Guard seemed to be present—all standing at attention against the walls. Six of them.

'Quite a welcome,' Amarah whispered.

Isa ignored her and walked through the plush room, nodding to each member of the guard she passed. A door lay open at the far end, the heavy drapes pushed to one side to allow entrance. 'Archigo Gralla must be in there.'

'Isa. This place is perfect for an ambush. We're outnumbered here.'

'Hush. It'll be fine.' Isa didn't know if it would be, especially after her experience with Kessir, but she had no alternative. Without Gralla's aid, her campaign wouldn't even get off the ground. Gralla had the money, the contacts, and the influence to make a real difference.

The door opened to a small, circular room at the back of the parlour. Archigo Gralla herself sat at a low table, lost in her heavy robes. Her grey hair looked like it had recently come unbound—it was a mass of wispy curls that fell about her narrow shoulders. Her eyes, though red, were bright and alert. Her nose twitched. 'Well, well. If it isn't Princess Isa, come to grace me with her presence.'

'Archigo Gralla. It has been too long.' Isa did her best to incline her head but was uncomfortably forced to stoop under the low ceiling.

'Please, sit. Your...friend is welcome, too.' Gralla's voice was husky, as though she'd lost the core of it some years ago.

'I'll wait outside if it's all the same. Your woman out front said she'd get me a medic,' Amarah replied. She gingerly touched her broken nose to emphasise her point.

'But of course. So much blood will inevitably draw scavengers...'

Isa shared a look with Amarah, hoping she didn't come across as too timid. She'd slipped one of her knives up her right-hand sleeve—it could be in her grasp with just the flick of her wrist, if necessary.

When Amarah left, Isa did as she was bid by the older woman and sat down on one of the plump cushions spread around the table. The oil lamp on the table's centre flickered once.

This was the polar opposite of her meeting with Kessir. She hoped the results would be the polar opposite, too. Ignoring the doubt screaming at her, Isa spoke confidently, 'I trust your travels after Summercourt were safe?'

'Yes. Thankfully, your Arillian gatekeepers didn't affect my ship. I only travel lightly, you see. Makes me less of a target for the most part.'

Isa didn't like her tone. 'They aren't *my* gatekeepers. And I'm dealing with them.'

'Oh, are you?' Gralla lifted her smoking pipe to her lips. It was long and slender, and looked like it had been gilded with gold and emeralds. She took a long drag and leaned back in her cushions. 'How is that when you are here, in my *Oriol's Den*?'

Isa straightened up where Gralla sank down. 'The woman I travel with has agreed to kill Jato in my honour. For I wish to rise as queen of Val Sharis. Getting rid of Jato is my gift to the Ittallan.'

'Hmm. You *are* a princess. If anything were to happen to your brothers...?'

Isa shifted, uncomfortable. This was the truth she had to face. She wasn't going to run from it or flinch. 'If they were to leave Val Sharis and return to Sereth, that would be the easiest path, with the least bloodshed.'

'And if they refuse? The palace of Val Sharis is not a home any would throw away lightly.'

Isa doubled down. 'Then I will do what must be done.'

'Which is...?' Gralla took another drag, and breathed out a ring of smoke as if they had all the time in the world for idle chit chat.

Isa fought the urge to cough. Her eyes watered. 'I am the daughter of the warrior-king Vasil. I excel in combat. If it comes to it...I'll have to kill. I'm good at that.' She remembered the Arillians she'd slaughtered only that morning, and suddenly wondered if she stank of blood. Gralla's cryptic words about blood and scavengers had put her on edge.

Then again, in the depths of the smoking room, it was unlikely. *She'd* be smelling like pipesmoke for weeks.

Gralla considered her. 'There's more to being strong than how effective you are at killing people. Take away Sapora's venom, and what is he? Same for Vasil *the*

Conqueror. Weak.' She laughed dryly. 'Good leaders—good queens—need more than a knife concealed up a sleeve.'

Isa held her tongue for a moment. She'd spent her entire life on the sidelines, observing others, trying to keep one step ahead and out of trouble. The quickest way to show yourself as a fool was to speak or act without thinking. She ignored the barb. 'I plan to be a great queen. One who listens to her subjects instead of terrorising them.'

Gralla laughed. 'I'd hope not terrorising them would be the bare minimum.' She took another long drag, studying Isa all the while.

'And I will listen to the advice of my council. I will not become queen alone. I will become queen because I am the one my people *want*. An Ittallan like them, who does not thirst for domination and blood in the way the Varkain do.' She really wished she had Odi with her. Or at least the letters he'd been crafting for her. He was always so eloquent with his words.

'You think you're a better ruler than Sapora? More fit? What if these people who want you on the throne have only said so because *anyone* is better than Sapora?'

Isa didn't know how to react. 'It's possible...'

Gralla raised an eyebrow. 'And you're fine with that? You don't *only* want loyal followers?'

'Not everyone will see me for who I am. Many see me as a bastard child. I'll show them I am their true queen. Show them that a life in fear of your ruler is not the only choice.'

Gralla blew out more smoke and smiled. 'This kills pain, you know. Smoke a lot of it and you stop feeling much of anything.'

Isa narrowed her eyes and leaned away from the rings that continued to pour from Gralla's lips.

'Not like it'll save your life. But anything that dulls the

ache and lets you keep going has to be worth it, right?' Gralla closed her eyes.

Isa didn't care about the reasons for the smoking lounge. She was sure there were as many excuses as there were people who visited the establishments. 'Not for me, thank you.'

'Hmm. Pity. It might help.'

Something about Gralla's voice set Isa's teeth on edge. She held her breath, listening. Boots outside. It could have been townspeople, or the Imperial Guard, or even Antar or Carav come to check on them.

Isa rose to her feet. 'Amarah was right? A trap!'

'For me as well.' Gralla opened her eyes. 'Treason, that's what they'll say when they arrest me. Because I don't want to live in fear of my ruler, either. But if you're victorious, my people and I are behind you, queen.'

Isa curled her lip and drew the short knife from her sleeve.

Gralla laughed. 'Try that.' She gestured with her chin.

Isa turned to see a sword mounted to the wall above the door. Although it didn't have a scabbard, it looked sharp enough. She reached up and plucked it down. Heavier than she was used to, the sword had been expertly crafted, and was well-balanced.

'Give you a bit more reach.' Gralla winked.

'Isa!' Amarah screamed from outside. Even with her senses dulled by the fog of smoke, Isa heard the sky pirate easily enough. Without waiting for Gralla's permission, she raced back through the smoking lounge.

She'd not been inside for long, yet coming out into fresh air and sunlight dazed her. Blinking rapidly, Isa saw Amarah, her back against the building's wall, half a dozen Cerastes surrounding them.

'I hope you got us some help,' Amarah said, not taking

her gaze off the nearest Varkain. Her scythe was levelled at him, the blade glinting in the sun.

It was no *Valta Forinja*, which would have given them the advantage, and they were outnumbered. Isa was not a fan of their odds. 'Hard to say. Kind of been interrupted.'

'Isa! I knew you were a traitor, but I'd never have figured you were so low class.'

The Cerastes uniformly took a step back, making space in their ranks for Prince Tacio to approach the two women with his usual lazy gait.

'Took me a while to track you down, I'll admit. Thankfully my Cerastes always have their eyes and ears open. Look how far you've fallen.' Tacio folded his arms and halted, out of striking reach of either the sword or scythe. He gave Amarah a cursory glance, but his attention lingered on Isa. 'You three. Sort out the Archigo. Gralla won't put up much of a fight, don't worry.' Tacio ordered, and three of his Cerastes broke away from the group. They hurtled forward, shoving past Isa and Amarah as they raced into the door faster than they could blink.

'Gonna help her?' Amarah questioned.

'Not with these Cerastes. She has her own people in there. They'll protect her.' Isa didn't much like their chances. One on one, she could hold Tacio off. But not with all the other snakes waiting to attack, their blades gleaming.

Tacio grinned broadly. He had them pinned. He was going to take his time and savour the situation. He'd always been a terrible loser, but he was an even worse winner. 'Who needs an Ark when you have me!'

The Cerastes chuckled, their stances casual.

Isa swallowed. 'Are you here to gloat or to fight?'

'Both,' Tacio replied. 'Sapora wants you back alive. I can abide by that. But a princess on the run? These are dangerous times, Isa. Getting hurt is an inevitability.'

Isa darted forward, using the element of surprise while her brother was in the middle of talking. The sword weighed heavy in her hand, but it was sharp, and she lunged forward like a viper strike.

Tacio shifted to his right at the last moment, bringing up his own short sword, the blades sending sparks into the air as they clashed. 'I wasn't finished. I thought you learned manners.' He pressed his sword against hers, shoving her back with ease.

Isa blinked. Her head was still fuzzy from the smoke.

She *really* didn't like her odds.

'Hold back. Wait for an opening,' Amarah whispered.

'An *opening*? Like I'd give you one, thief.' Tacio scowled. 'I can hear your heartbeat. I can smell the fear leaking from your skin. You think I won't hear you whispering to each other? Figure out your desperate plans? What do you take me for?'

'I take you for a maggot, like the others,' Amarah replied, bold as ever.

Tacio snarled. 'Maggot!?'

'Prince Tacio! Isn't she the one with the bounty?' one of the Cerastes said, lowering his spear slightly. 'I saw the posters. Amarah? The sky pirate?'

'Hmm?' Tacio's scowl disappeared, replaced by a quizzical frown. 'Don't tell me I can't kill this one, either? After such an insult, I'd love to see your head severed from your body.'

'Pretty sure she's just for the fighting pits. Why would the king want a sky pirate?' the Cerastes replied.

Amarah snorted her indignation.

Isa calculated their chances. Everything was coming to a head. She should have known better than to think she could outrun the Varkain. They were worse than bloodhounds on a scent. Especially when there were personal reasons thrown in for the hunt.

If Tacio had his way, both of them would be dead already.

It was only by Sapora's requests for herself and Amarah to remain alive.

Behind her, the grunts and shouts of Tacio's Cerastes against Gralla's Imperial Guard grew louder. Tables toppled over, fabric tore, and glass lamps smashed.

'Don't you worry about her, sister,' Tacio said with a sneer. 'I haven't decided yet if I'll execute her for treason or draw out her torture over months. I guess that depends on you.'

She hated being at her brother's mercy. She'd always hated it.

'What has the Archigo ever done to you? You ignored Gralla at Summercourt,' Isa said.

Tacio chuckled. 'We usually ignore things that are beneath us. All the Archigo have been visited by my Cerastes. They are to give up any information on you the moment they have it. Gralla did not. Therefore she is no longer an Archigo, but an Ittallan revolter. A peasant waving a pitchfork.'

'I've only just arrived!'

'Hmph. Treasonous Archigo. She invited you into this stinking den instead of reporting your arrival. It was by chance I'd been searching the quarry only this morning, thinking you might've hidden away in there. Cowering like a trapped rat.'

Isa tightened her grip on the sword's hilt. How badly she wanted to sever *his* neck.

'Will you come willingly? Or shall it be a fight? All my swords against yours.'

Isa bent her knees slightly. 'Keep the Cerastes out of it and I'll kill you where you stand.'

Tacio's easy demeanour vanished. 'Laughable. You're nothing but a mongrel.'

Isa realised then that Tacio hadn't told the Cerastes of her earlier fight with him. Then again, he was a high-ranking Varkain who'd lost in single combat. Yes, she'd fled, but she'd definitely managed to get the better of him before her escape.

In fact...when she looked at him more closely, she saw the powders covering her claw marks on his face.

She smiled. Everything was a show with Tacio. Nothing more than bravado.

She wondered what would happen if she killed him there and then. Would the Cerastes flee? Would they attack her? Or would they throw their spears at her feet and pledge their allegiance?

'Isa, you don't wanna be fighting him,' Amarah said, wary.

'I have no choice. Tacio, you hear me? I challenge you. Fight me. If I win, I continue my campaign. I *am* going to become queen. What'll happen when I throw *you* into my dungeon?'

Around her, the Cerastes laughed again.

'Going for queen, are you? Hah. Here I'd put gold on you scampering off to some distant corner of the world and chasing mice for the rest of your days.'

Tacio's insult hurt, but she let him have his fun. It wasn't as if she hadn't heard it all a thousand times before. And he still hadn't agreed to fight her.

'I am the *true* queen of Val Sharis. Take Sapora and return to Sereth. All your Cerastes. All your Varkain. You miss your tunnels, I'm sure. No-one needs to get hurt, let alone die.'

The Varkain muttered among themselves.

'Hush!' Tacio silenced. 'You're here to do a job. So *do it*!'

Isa's smile deepened. He hadn't met her challenge. The coward.

She leapt to meet the first Cerastes, deflecting his spear with her sword before driving it into him. The sword tip glanced off his armour, but she followed the blade's momentum and danced inside his guard, where she drove her dagger into his throat with her other hand.

The other Cerastes gave her a wide berth after that—none in any rush to tackle her.

'You sacrifice your own Cerastes, Tacio?' Isa kept one eye on her brother while looking out for incoming attacks. 'Are you afraid to challenge me? Afraid you'll lose again?'

'Silence, cat!' Tacio snapped. 'I am your prince! *You* do as *I* tell you!'

Isa laughed. In her peripheral vision, she saw Amarah lunge into a Cerastes, her scythe batting away the spear. She fought defensively, keeping the Varkain at bay and staying out of reach of their attacks.

It was a good technique to keep them safe, but it wouldn't last. Varkain had more patience and stamina than most. She needed to rile Tacio—force him to make a mistake. Something she could take advantage of.

Before she could turn her attention to the next Cerastes, a knife flew through the air. It whistled past her nose and embedded itself in the forearm of a Varkain. He screamed in pain, one hand clasping the blade's hilt.

All eyes turned down the street, where Antar and Carav raced towards them. Antar already had another throwing blade in hand, but he'd lost the element of surprise, and the Varkain easily dodged the next knife.

'Think we need to get outta here!' Amarah said.

Isa wasn't so sure. Running again was not what she

wanted. It might have been the sky pirate's code—to flee any encounter you couldn't win—but she was no coward, and refused to run from her brother. Not to mention Archigo Gralla was as much a victim of this as she was, and far from the first Ittallan—Archigo or not—to fall victim to the Varkain's bullying tactic.

Besides, she *knew* she could take on Tacio—if he was brave enough to face her a second time.

Her main concern were the Cerastes he'd brought with him. There was little stopping them getting involved and overwhelming her allies—they were Varkain fighters, and could quickly turn the tables. She tried again. 'Tacio. Call your Cerastes off. Your problem is with me, so fight me like a true *naja*!' Picking at his pride was about the only thing she could do.

Tacio did not take the bait. 'And dirty my new cloak? I think not. As I said before, you are beneath me. I'll have my Cerastes drag you back to Taban Yul in the cargo hold, and Sapora will deal with you as he sees fit. He is *our* king, after all.'

So much for showing him up as a coward.

Their attention split between Isa, Amarah, and the two new arrivals, the Cerastes group broke up and reformed—as smooth as water—to keep both sets of challengers in view.

Antar didn't hold back. He didn't even slow down to assess the situation. He simply hurtled into the group of Cerastes like a boulder, his hands a blur as they stabbed and sliced with different daggers.

Isa was impressed with his guts. She and Amarah pressed forward with sword and scythe, clashing against the Cerastes weaponry—bouncing off their swords and armour, and occasionally cutting into Varkain flesh.

What had begun as a standoff had turned into chaos. The scent of blood and pipe smoke filled the air as they fought. Screams rang out around her, as the fighting from inside the smoking lounge spilled out onto the streets, and the red and gold livery of the Imperial Guard entered the fray.

Isa dodged left, right, backwards, struck forwards. Any metal that glinted near her was a potential threat, which she avoided at all costs.

Sweat prickled the back of her neck as the heat of the smoking den and the day mingled, and all thoughts were pushed from her mind, save one thing—survive. Her blood lust crept along her arms slowly, in sync with the beating of her heart. But it wasn't enough. The Cerastes were too well-armoured, too strong, and she couldn't tap into that sweetly destructive, yet maddenning, side of herself without blood, a display of weakness, and some surge of emotion.

Isa gritted her teeth. If she didn't do something, they wouldn't last much longer.

Carav dropped to the floor—her necklaces jingling the only sign that something had happened.

Isa darted in between Amarah and an overly tall Cerastes as she crossed the street—which had turned into a battlefield. Skidding to a halt, she sank to her knees.

Blood gushed from the young woman's shoulder—a Varkain bite.

'Dragons above!' Isa swore. 'Amarah! You have that rag still?'

Admittedly, she was surprised her voice carried over the clash of fighting, but only a few seconds later and Amarah hurried into view.

'Shit. Bitten?'

'Looks like it. Just hope it was a shallow bite...' Isa knew it was wishful thinking, but there wasn't much else to be said. She could only act.

Antar backed up to them, still facing his aggressors, a

long knife in each hand. The normally full belt he wore around his chest was empty—most of his weapons lost on the floor, or embedded in an unfortunate Varkain. 'What's the plan, cap'n?'

'My plan was to get the fuck outta here, but I got overruled.' Amarah pressed the rag of dark cloth to Carav's shoulder, while the remaining Cerastes surrounded the small group, spear tips keeping them locked down. Their fight was finished.

They shoved Archigo Gralla into their huddle, along with two of her Imperial soldiers—the other four having fallen to Varkain fangs.

Isa glared at the Cerastes and counted heads. Although they'd managed to down three of them, and injure several others, Tacio's the elite fighters had the upper hand.

They'd lost.

Tacio applauded lazily. 'Good bit of blood sport. Not had any real entertainment since I was last in Sereth! Archigo, as I'm sure you'll expect, your titles and lands will be stripped. We'll appoint a new Archigo once I'm back at the palace. Oh, but before we go...' Tacio nodded to one Cerastes, who entered the building warily.

Isa heard a match light, and braced.

'There. Just to clear the air somewhat, you understand? A terrible blast when one of the lamps caught fire. Mixed with the smoke and cushions...' Tacio mimed an explosion. 'We couldn't save the poor old Archigo Gralla, unfortunately.'

'Bastard,' Gralla said. A thin line of blood trickled down her forehead. 'You fought well, Isa,'

Isa nodded, too focussed on keeping Carav's bleeding staunched. 'You as well.'

Tacio had them all cornered and she didn't know what she could do.

Carav's pulse weakened under Isa's hands. 'No, no, no. Come on, Carav. Stay with us!'

Tacio snorted. 'You do what it takes to win.' As the smoking rooms burned, he waved a hand to his Cerastes. 'Leave the dead for the crows. Get these loaded up on the ship. I've had enough of travelling in Val Sharis for a lifetime.'

'Yes, Prince Tacio.' The Cerastes moved as one, every movement in sync with their neighbours. They forced Isa and the others to their feet—although she refused to leave Carav and hauled the younger woman over her shoulder. She could only hope it hadn't been enough venom to kill her.

Slowly, painfully, they followed Tacio through the streets towards the airship hangar. Behind them, smoke rose gently into the sky.

30

Getting the sky pirates to agree on anything seemed nigh impossible. None of them voted on anything unanimously, and they all liked to fight amongst themselves whenever there was a minor disagreement. Although Traego had agreed to follow Amarah's *Thief's Ink* to locate her—and hopefully Princess Isa too—actually getting in the air and on Amarah's trail was like pulling teeth.

Palom, Solvi, Kylos, and half a dozen other Ittallan had wanted to leap into action. Many had rested since arriving in Estoria and were well recovered from the palace escape. More still had bought or fashioned weapons, shields, armour, and fairly unscrupulous materials from the myriad of shops and sellers in Estoria.

Palom himself was more than ready to go, even if he still ached.

He'd come here to aid their princess. Help her become queen.

Lathri had died for Isa's cause, and he wasn't going to let her death be in vain.

Eventually Aetos had taken a bearing from Traego and

flown ahead, keen to get moving. He was used to scouting ahead, which reminded Palom—rather painfully—of Anahrik. *Leillu*, too, seemed eager to be on the move. She took to the air at every opportunity, often disappearing for hours at a time. It was a mild concern, but she never came back injured or harmed in any way. Perhaps it was simply part of the young dragon growing up and discovering her independence.

Time was of the essence. He didn't know why Princess Isa had left, but if she travelled with Amarah—who had an enormous bounty on her head from King Sapora—it was safe to say they were both probably in danger.

He wished he'd paid more attention to Amarah's plea for him to come with her.

Judd was a capable pilot and had been ordered by Traego to fly one of Isa's small, class five airships. Kylos had argued to go with him as she considered herself Isa's highest ranking member of her following—essentially a general. Solvi and Chyro had wedged themselves on board, too. Kylos also brought a satchel of the princess's belongings, as well as the letters she and Odi had been working on since their arrival. She didn't know what was going on, and stated she was preparing for any and all eventualities.

It left Palom flying with Traego on his *Otella*, alongside the rest of the sky pirate's crew, as well as Karvou, and thirty other Ittallan fighters. He'd wanted Karvou to stay in Estoria and guard their base, but the lad had refused to leave Palom's side. He was a fighter now, anyway, and would be of use if they ran into trouble.

Palom couldn't disagree.

Odi had opted to remain in Estoria with the bulk of Isa's followers. Dangerous as it was, having a base in Estoria made sense, so he agreed to remain and fortify their stronghold as much as possible while they continued to buy and build resources in readiness to move the moment they had to.

Palom was happy to let Odi run the base. He was used to organising people, and as the son of an Archigo, his talents lay in managing people and resources. It meant that Palom could focus on the more important things—Solvi and Princess Isa.

Traego's main priority was visiting his caches of gold, jewels, and other valuables to ensure he could stay well financed throughout his time away from Estoria.

Palom knew it was a reasonable priority for the man. An ancient monster *had* charged through the Estorian islands and destroyed much of his land and accumulated wealth. But none of it mattered if Isa didn't end up on the throne.

Under Sapora's rule, they were all pawns and playthings, waiting to be picked off by an Ark or a dragon as the Varkain saw fit.

Isa would bring balance to Linaria. She cared for the Ittallan in a way the Varkain never could. She was one of them, for a start.

He *believed* in her.

Everything would fall into place and Linaria would return to some form of normality. It had to.

Traego and Malot had also worked for several hours on their stash of bottled Samolen magic—chief among which were *Thief Shrouds*. Many had been destroyed by Brahm's monster, so Malot had worked double-time to replenish what they had, and ensure *Otella* had all the firepower it would need for the flight across countries.

They knew they were travelling deep into Val Sharis, where the skies were most fraught with danger, and Traego couldn't afford to lose his flagship.

At least they were as prepared as they could be, even if it had delayed their departure by several hours. Palom took a deep breath as Traego navigated *Otella* away from Estoria. Aetos, *Leillu*, and Judd were already tiny dots in the distance —their superior flying speed enabling them to eke out a lead over the slower, bulkier warship.

Somehow, the vast ocean below seemed ominous. It reminded him of the massive monster—which had come from the sea. It may have been Brahm's monster, but it lived in the water, guarding waterways and attacking those it deemed a threat.

He didn't like any of it.

Ancient gods and magic deserved to remain in the history books.

Their princess had fled. Considering she'd worked so hard just to reach Estoria, the thought of someone—or something—pushing her to flee worried him.

Palom had armed himself with a new sword. He'd not had the time to forge one of his own, but the smiths on Estoria weren't half-bad. The new sword represented a fresh start, a new goal. It had yet to be tested, but the blade was sharp and the steel was good. Pirates trusted in their weapons—they were their tools of the trade for all intents and purposes. It was to be expected their weapons were of excellent quality.

He'd also brought along Amarah's scythe. Uncomfortable letting a *Valta Forinja* fall into the wrong hands—he couldn't even fathom the devastation one could wrought in the hands of a rash and impulsive sky pirate—he felt obligated to bring it with him. Better with him—its maker—than a random pirate who was more likely to lop his own head off with it.

It meant the return of *emonos*, but there was little he could do about that. At least he'd experienced it before and knew what to expect. Still, he didn't appreciate the weapon's darkness already spreading over him. It made him worry more. Think unreasonable thoughts. But he knew it was the weapon's doing and clamped down on them before they became words or actions he'd regret.

Odi's dark look also rattled around his mind. He knew the weapon was *emonos*, and had suggested the monster might be drawn to it. Palom suppressed a snarl. These days it felt like all of Linaria was imploding in on itself.

'Deploying the *Shrouds*!' Traego called from the captain's cabin.

Palom made his way along the open deck to the ship's prow. A tusked boar-head had been carved out of wood—though yellowed with age—a rather strange figurehead considering the man wasn't an Ittallan, but Palom could not claim to understand the workings of sky pirates. At least it made *Otella* recognisable from a distance. That, along with the faded paintwork and sails. It was clear that Traego had been traipsing around Linaria in this ship for decades.

Karvou leaned over the side railing, the wind ruffling his dark hair.

Light shimmered along every surface of the ship as Traego's thief's magic worked. Palom had been unsure of it at first, but considering it had been responsible for them getting away from Tacio at the palace, he knew it had its uses.

Palom preferred facing opponents in the open. Honourably. That had gone out the window when he'd been under the influence of his *Valta Forinja*. Perhaps it would go out the window again.

'Are you feeling okay, Palom?' Karvou asked, turning around as Palom approached.

'Are you?'

Karvou shrugged. 'I always thought I'd spend my whole life in Tum Metsa. Take over my father's shop, you know? This is an adventure.'

'Adventures are dangerous.'

'That's the *fun* part!'

Palom frowned. Karvou was too green to comprehend the level of danger the world was in. 'What about when Cerastes attacked? You were not afraid?'

Karvou thought about it. 'Sure. A bit? But look at what happened!' He held up a clenched fist as if that explained everything. 'A wolf! Can you believe it? Dad's only a hare.'

Palom *could* believe it. He'd have bet money on Karvou being a hunter. 'And now you are in service to Princess Isa. Will you fight for her? Die for her?'

The young lad nodded, enthusiastic.

Palom didn't press the matter. In the heat of a fight, it wasn't unusual to give in to battle lust and excitement. But regret often followed after—especially when there had been deaths. Whether it was those you'd killed, or allies you'd lost, the thrilling danger of fighting never lasted long.

'You know King Sapora, don't you? Dad said you travelled with him.'

Karvou's question caught Palom off-guard. 'I did travel with him. But I cannot say I know him.'

'He's a bad king. Why didn't you do anything about him before?'

Palom fought the urge to laugh. 'Not all problems are solved by killing. And Sapora had done nothing wrong then.' It wasn't strictly speaking true. Sapora *had* been the instigator of many conflicts aboard *Khanna*, especially towards himself and Anahrik. The Varkain had done whatever he'd wanted. It was no different once they'd realised he was a prince, and it was no different now he was king. Amarah and Sapora had fought most of all; so headstrong they clashed constantly. 'It is in past. No point in thinking what should have been done. Have you been out of Tum Metsa before?'

'Of course,' Karvou replied, 'but never away from the north. Estoria was so hot! I didn't realise days could be so warm!'

Palom let out a dry chuckle. For all his bravado, Karvou was still a kid. Out of his depth. He couldn't bear the thought of anything happening to him and wished he'd stayed behind in Estoria. At least then he'd be out of immediate danger, instead of flying straight towards it.

Otella was not fast. Warships had never been built that way. But the flight was comfortable. So large, Palom hardly felt any turbulence at all. It was a far cry from Amarah's old *Khanna*. 'Karvou, why don't you get some rest. The journey will take time, you should save your strength. I think there will be much fighting to come. You must be ready for it, yes?'

Karvou seemed about to argue, before he shrugged and did as he was told, wandering off.

'The cabins are below. You can use any that are unlocked.'

Palom glanced up to see Malot giving the youth directions. At her words, Karvou happily made his way down into the lower ship.

'He is very fond of you,' the Samolen woman said, once she realised Palom was looking at her.

Palom inclined his head. 'You are fond of Traego.'

'We're crew.' She said it so matter-of-factly, as if it didn't warrant any further explanation.

'Then, what happened with Antar? *He* was crew.'

Malot's face soured. 'I don't know. That's part of what we're going to find out.'

'I thought we were looking for Amarah and Princess Isa?'

'We are. Amarah might know more about Antar. He might even be with her.'

Palom sensed the simmering anger brewing within her

and decided to stop talking about what was evidently a sore subject. 'How does ink work? How does Traego track Amarah?'

Malot walked past him, her hair blowing wildly in the breeze. 'More Samolen magic. Not from me, though. I mostly work on improving *Thief Shrouds* and keeping *Otella* in tip-top condition.'

Palom tilted his head to one side. 'More magic?'

'*Thief's Ink*, they call it. You use enchanted ink to mark someone. Mostly people use it to keep an eye on those who owe them a debt, so they can never really get away from you. Nasty, really. But Traego's always used it to mark his crew. That way, if ever they get split up on a job, or lost somewhere, he can always find them and help them out.'

'Seems like good idea.'

'Amarah and Traego met years ago. They were still kids, really. She's been marked since then.'

Palom blinked in surprise. 'I do not think Amarah would like to be found any time.'

Malot laughed. 'There's a lot of trust that Traego won't randomly show up whenever he needs something off her. But...he did loan her some gold when we were all in Estoria for her new ship. Before everything kicked off. He could always claim he's coming to collect that debt, if she kicks up a fuss about being tracked down.'

That made sense. A sudden dark thought entered his mind. He wasn't sure if it was his, or had been spurred on by the presence of his *Valta Forinja*—which he kept wrapped up in a locked cabin deep in the ship's hold. 'Does it work if the marked one is dead?'

Malot's smile fell from her lips. 'Yes. As long as the mark is still intact, it will always work. It works on inanimate objects, too. In case you ever store something and want to find it. It's how Traego always finds his caches and secret hideouts, even if someone steals something or it gets moved. And even buried underneath the ice and snow of the Ever-winter. If you have a mark, you'll always know exactly where it is.'

Palom grimaced. He hoped they weren't about to discover Amarah and Isa's bodies somewhere in the wilds of Val Sharis.

~

'TANNON SONA. THAT'S THE PLACE.' Oris jabbed a thumb at the map mounted on the back wall of Traego's cabin.

'Ya sure?' Traego asked.

'I'm sure!'

Trageo's entire crew, along with Palom and Karvou, had all piled into the cabin. Their flight had taken them cross-country, through the night, and into the following morning. Palom smelled the quarry dust in the air, along with the distant tang of smoke. He recalled his father considering sending him here to work in the quarry when he'd been much younger. He'd given some excuse about the Feoras Sol mines being too dangerous.

Palom had argued the matter until his father had ceded and had remained in town with his family ever since.

'The ink can't lie. Amarah's definitely stopped there, and that's the town name.'

Palom looked out the window. No-one could ignore the enormous black storm roiling further north—over Taban Yul. Even from several leagues away, he saw the ripple of sheet lightning through the dark clouds. It made every hair stand on edge.

Arillians.

Leillu hissed on deck, her tail lashing and her wings

beating as she stared at them in the distance. She bared her small, sharp teeth, and fire flickered in her throat.

'*Leillu.* Is okay. We are not going to Arillians. They are not coming here,' Palom said, trying to comfort the little dragon.

'I ain't been ta Tannon Sona in a couple o' years.' Traego stroked his chin.

'I was here last summer. Had to move a shipment of pretty rock for some Goldstone,' Farlan said. 'It's full of Goldies. Smoking lounges are good, too.' He chuckled.

'Well, we ain't got any time for none o' that, so let's stick ta the plan. This is Sapora's country now, there's gonna be snakes everywhere.'

Karvou scoffed. 'We took care of them before!'

'That was two snakes on our home ground. This could be different,' Ernold warned. He flexed his mace nervously, running a thumb over and over the points as if it brought him some comfort.

'They got a big enough hangar as far as I recall. Could dock *Otella* there and scout the place out before we do anything ta bring the snakes down on us.' Traego peered out the window. Tannon Sona itself was only a few minutes away, a dark smudge on the lush green land below. 'Dragons above, I dunno whether to fly on, wait, land...'

'Traego! Something's coming!' Oris piped up and leapt out of the cabin, scope already in hand. He raised it to his eye and held his breath. 'Yep! It's that eagle again!'

'Aetos!' Karvou raced out onto the deck.

'He will have news.' Palom turned to Traego. 'You can make good decision, now.'

Traego nodded. 'Better be a fast report. Wanna get moving, or get landing, or get doing whatever we gotta do, before those Arillians come down on us.'

Traego didn't have to wait long.

Aetos landed on deck abruptly, dark feathers floating away as he transformed back. 'She's there!'

'Princess Isa?' Palom gasped.

'Amarah?' Traego yelled at the same time.

Aetos took several deep breaths and grabbed hold of the ship's side rail to steady himself. 'Both. Antar and Carav, too.'

'Is my sister all right?' Oris asked, rushing over to him.

Aetos's eyes were wide. 'They're all surrounded by Cerastes. Prince Tacio, too. Judd and the others have already landed in town for a closer look. It's going to be a bloodbath unless we do something.'

Palom let out a low growl. 'We go to Tannon Sona! We *must* help Princess Isa!'

'And risk my crew if there's a bloodbath?' Traego spat. 'Not happening.'

'You came here to help her, did you not?' Palom argued.

'I came here ta find out what happened ta Amarah, Antar, and Carav. I know that now. Gotta keep my distance and keep the rest o' my crew and ships safe.'

'Judd is there. Will you not help him? What if Cerastes kill him? Or rest of your crew?'

'Judd ain't no fighter.' Traego laughed and held his stomach. 'He's probably dropping ya friends off and will come straight back ta me. Poor guy, your Ittallan are stronger than him. Doubt he had a choice *but* to land if that's what they told him ta do!'

Palom could easily imagine Solvi, Kylos, or Chyro overpowering Traego's pilot. And if that was the case, Judd would be back in the air on Isa's class five any minute now. He snarled again and paced the deck. 'I will *not* stand by while my princess is attacked by Tacio and his Cerastes!'

'Ya welcome ta jump off my ship if ya want.'

Palom glowered.

'What are you *waiting* for?' Aetos snapped, staring at each of the sky pirates. 'I thought you pirates worked for gold and glory! What if you kill Tacio? You'd be hailed as heroes!'

Traego laughed aloud, his whole body shaking. 'Heroes? We'd be strung up for treason! We're already walking a very thin line by helping Isa. Don't wanna slide any further down the snake's throat if I can help it!'

'There is no further to slide down!' Palom roared. 'You helped free Princess Isa from her prison. Her followers are on your land. You are either on her side or you are not. And you *are*!' He wanted to draw his sword to strengthen his point, but he knew that was the *Valta Forinja's* influence. He bit back a snarl and stared Traego in the eyes. 'You are already most of way there. Let us work together to defeat Cerastes and help Isa!'

Traego's easy confidence faltered for a moment. His gaze darted to the rest of his crew; Malot, Ernold, Farlan, Oris.

'I am willing to help the princess,' Malot said, the silver rings in her braids clinking together softly as she approached them. 'I know not if she will be a good queen, but she is better than Sapora, and all the devastation he has brought. He was the one who sent Cerastes into our home.' The red jewel embedded in her cheek flashed brightly.

'Traeg, you know I'm always up for a good scrap!' Farlan grinned. 'Get me a scar for the other side of me face!' All the pirates laughed as he tapped the slash down his left cheek—a war wound from his first encounter with the monster, he'd continually boasted about.

Palom said, 'If Princess Isa loses...If she dies...more than just your ship will be at risk. All Linaria may fall to Sapora and his Arks.' Palom hoped his tone was less confrontational and more persuasive.

'There's no time! Princess Isa needs our help *now*!' Aetos

shouted. He transformed again, his *meraki* covering him in light as his limbs changed. Within a few seconds, an eagle stood where a man had before, and took to the air, wings powering towards the town below.

'You would be helping Amarah, too. Adding to her debt?' Malot suggested.

Traego thought about it for a moment. 'All right, all right. I can see I'm outnumbered here! But any damage to *Otella* and I'm taking it outta ya cuts!' He pointed a finger at each member of his crew before heading back into the cabin and grabbing hold of the wheel.

Relief flooded Palom when Traego steered the ship closer to Tannon Sona and descended. 'Are you ready, *Leillu*? I want you to keep out of way. Keep safe.'

The dragon chirped at him, her bright eyes blinking.

Palom tried to calm himself. Any emotions would be blown out of proportion by the *Valta Forinja*. It was why he'd gone to the trouble of wrapping it up and locking it in his cabin, so no-one could accidentally stumble upon it. Even though he'd last touched it two days ago on the beach in Estoria, its effects still bothered him.

He wondered if that curse was worthwhile. With the *Valta Forinja* in his grasp, he'd make short work of the Cerastes there, no matter how many there were. Tacio, too.

But the physical pain and psychological torment he'd have to ensure again…

Not to mention he'd be doing Lathri a disservice after recognising she'd been correct, and the weapon had been *emonos*.

He wasn't convinced he was strong enough. And there was no Lathri to speak sense into him, this time.

No. He wouldn't turn to darkness for this. If it was his time to die, he'd die willingly—fighting for his princess, and for change in Val Sharis.

Palom spotted Isa's class five ship docked closest to the entrance, but there was no sign of Judd or any of the Ittallan he'd flown. He also recognised *RaKhanna* on the far side, and Amarah's warship. They were definitely in the right place. He took several deep breaths through his nose, trying to figure out what had happened. There were dozens of Varkain—all of whom had come from one airship in particular. It was a larger transport vessel, and it stank of fresh paint.

'Why does that ship smell bad?' He pointed.

Traego strolled over to it, a deep frown on his face. 'I can't smell nothin'.'

'My nose is better than yours.'

Traego stared up at the ship, hands on his hips. 'Hang on a minute...' He dragged a fingernail along the hull. Brown paint peeled away at his touch, revealing bright red underneath. 'Probably from the capital, but they painted over the colours. See? Imperial ship. Probably why they ain't docked in the hangar for the Imperial Guard. Definitely tryin' ta hide 'emselves. Setting up an ambush?'

Palom was impressed. It was a good disguise. Even Traego hadn't realised what it was until he'd investigated it more closely, and his livelihood revolved around seeing through those sorts of disguises. 'Is good you have discovered this ruse. But Princess Isa awaits!'

'Hold up, Palom. Didn't ya hear me? It could be an ambush!'

Fear shot through Palom's gut. 'Then we must move *faster*! They will only be ambushing princess!'

The other Ittallan clambered off *Otella* alongside Traego's crew. Altogether, they were a force to be reckoned with, a collection of hunters eager to defend their rightful queen.

Keen to reach Isa before anything happened to her, Palom led them out of the hangar and into the town. He'd expected it to be a bustle of activity in the middle of the afternoon, but the streets were empty. Dark smoke rose in the distance—something was burning.

'Where is everyone?' Oris said, stepping into the sunlight. 'What's going on?'

'The Cerastes,' Palom said, voice grim. He glanced up and saw the black eagle circling overhead. 'Aetos. Come!' He didn't give them any time to argue, simply raced off into the large square and down a street that seemed to lead towards where the eagle hovered.

Footsteps behind him told Palom at least some of the others followed. Karvou would definitely be on his heels, as would the other Ittallan, and he hoped Traego and the others would be quick to follow—trying to find Judd and Amarah, if nothing else.

Palom skidded to a halt at the edge of one street, the white-grey paving bright in the sunlight. He'd raced past an alleyway, blinked, and almost missed the blue-black armour of Cerastes marching in the opposite direction along a parallel street. He held out a hand to halt Karvou and the others, then pressed a finger to his lips for silence.

Varkain senses were highly attuned—even more so than Ittallan senses. The Cerastes would know they were there before they had a chance to launch their own ambush.

But Palom wanted a closer look before he did anything rash.

He shimmied down the narrow alley, his back flush with a stone townhouse, ivy draping down the walls. The Cerastes had passed, and he carefully poked his head around the corner of the building to peer down the otherwise deserted street. Princess Isa! He whispered, 'They are there.'

Karvou appeared at his side a moment later, followed shortly by a handful of Ittallan, Traego, and the rest of his crew.

'What's the plan?' Malot asked, her voice wavering slightly. 'I can't see Judd or any of the others.'

'They aren't with the Cerastes. That means they're safe?' Karvou asked.

Palom said, 'They are probably doing same as us. Scouting. Looking for opening to move in.'

'Wait!' Traego said, his voice louder than Palom liked. 'The ship in the hangar! The disguised one! Set up for an ambush. It's theirs?'

'It did smell of Varkain.' Palom agreed, and the other Ittallan assented with a low murmur..

'Oris, Karvou. You get back ta the hangar. Quick as ya can. Do what ya can ta sabotage the ship. Make sure it can't get off the ground!' Traego spoke quickly, excited.

'But the Cerastes—'

'Hide in *Otella* once you're done. Or *RaKhanna*, if the Varkain are so good at sensing people. Do what ya can, then get outta there. Got it?'

'Yessir!' Oris grinned, racing back down the alley.

Karvou glanced at Palom once, as if asking for permission, then ran after him.

'What good will that do? You have just put them in danger!' Palom snarled.

'Keep calm, tiger. We snatch what's ours from the snakes an' bail. When they try an' come after us, they won't be able ta get their ship off the ground!'

Palom thought about it.

'Oris knows how ships work. Karvou is another pair of hands, so they'll work quickly. Plus I didn't think ya wanted that lad in the thick of fighting more Cerastes? Not with Prince Tacio there, too?'

Palom had to admit the sky pirate was right.

'Good. Ya ready for an assault on them snakes, then?'

Palom wasn't sure why Traego had suddenly changed his tune from reluctant ally to wanting to get stuck into the thick of things, but he wasn't about to argue. It was only a short walk from where they were to the hangar. And he did not want the Cerastes getting there while Karvou was still on their ship.

He raced into the street, following the path of the Cerastes. Farlan and Ernold followed close behind, keeping up with Palom's loping strides, three more Ittallan behind them. At their speed, it wasn't long before the Varkain came into view.

Palom roared the moment he saw them—the noise echoing off the stone buildings and rooting the Cerastes in their steps. They recovered quickly, raising their spears and turning to face him. 'Let Princess Isa and allies go! Or we kill you where you stand!'

The Cerastes hissed in retaliation.

Palom smelled blood and looked more closely. Princess Isa and several others were surrounded by the armoured Varkain; Isa herself was battered and bloody; the lower half of Amarah's face was covered with drying blood; even Antar wasn't without injury. But Carav—he gasped. Isa carried the woman over one shoulder. The very *unconscious* woman.

'What's this? A vigilante come to defend your Archigo and the princess?' Tacio made his way to the front of the group and glared at Palom. 'Oh goodness, and all this riff raff with you? Looks like I *will* get some deaths after all!'

'Prince Tacio. Isa is your sister! Let her go!' Palom snarled. On the street's opposite side, he saw Kylos creeping close to the snakes. She *had* been waiting, too. That meant Solvi and Chyro were with her.

They could do this!

'Isa is a traitor. Like the former Archigo Gralla, here. Sapora is our king. Anything done or said otherwise is treason.' Tacio drew his short sword. 'The punishment for which is death.'

Palom couldn't take it anymore. 'Sapora is *no* king of mine! Long live Queen Isa!'

'Long live Queen Isa!' Kylos screamed, charging the Cerastes like a runaway train.

Echoes of, 'long live Queen Isa,' bounced around the street as Chyro, Solvi, and the Ittallan that had flown with them took up the cry, their voices swirling around the Cerastes like wind.

Overhead, Aetos screeched—his high-pitched cry shrill in the air.

Although the sky pirates didn't shout the same words, they roared and slammed their weapons together or banged them against the stone buildings. Anything to make more noise and intimidate their opponents.

Palom knew exactly how many of them there were, but the cacophony of noise grew until it sounded like a small army surrounded the Cerastes. The snakes glanced around in all directions, as if expecting to see said army materialise at any moment.

Palom let out another snarl, drew his own sword, and lunged forward. His sword a blur, Palom struck over and over, forcing the snakes apart and away from Princess Isa and the others. Carav was in bad shape, and so was Archigo Gralla. 'We'll clear path for you! Run for hangar!'

'Oh no you don't!' one Cerastes spat, darting in with his spear. The tip of the blade caught Palom square in the chest, but his layers of boiled armour plating deflected the blow's impact, and he turned it away. Bringing up his sword, he severed the spear's wooden shaft, rendering the Cerastes weaponless. 'Run, and I will not kill you.'

Around him, the clash of swords, spears, cudgels, and other weapons rang in his ears. A blinding flash of light preceded the transformations of those Ittallan who tapped into their *meraki*. Solvi and Chyro joined in, and the enormous snow leopard and bear entered the fray with teeth bared and claws drawn. Other Ittallan snarled and roared—Aetos swooped down, talons slashing against any exposed skin—alongside an owl, a lynx, two bulls, and the largest elephant Palom had ever seen. Their roars were deafening, and their sheer strength bowled over many of the Cerastes, shattering their spears and crushing their armour.

The snakes scattered, tried to regroup, their movements creating an opening. 'RUN!' Palom's bellow carried over the clash of battle, and Antar was the first to break away. He carried Carav over one shoulder but was strong enough to get up to a full sprint.

'Amarah!' Palom roared.

The sky pirate pulled her scythe from the back of a downed Cerastes, and she wiped blood from her cheek. 'About time we had some help! Dragons above, *this* is what it's like to fight with the Ittallan!'

Palom didn't have time to address her compliment. 'Get Isa to ships!'

Amarah jabbed the butt of her scythe into the back of a Varkain's knee to save Gralla from an incoming attack, before grabbing Isa's elbow and wheeling her around. 'You heard the man! Come on!'

'Archigo Gralla?' the princess said, panting with exertion.

'I'll help,' Palom said. 'Get away, or this will be for nothing!'

'Stop right there!' Tacio hissed, hurrying to the end of the street and blocking off their escape. 'You're *not* getting past me!'

'Ya outnumbered and outclassed!' Traego said. 'Ya Varkain are cut down or injured. Only have seven left. Get out the way if ya know what's good for ya!'

Although his Cerastes moved over to stand beside him, Tacio blinked, taking stock of the situation. Realisation slowly dawned, and he turned a shade paler when he understood the difference in numbers had now shifted away from his favour. 'You traitorous *wretch*!' Tacio spat at his sister's feet. 'You think this is *over*? This is *one* encounter! Sapora has Veynothi after you, and if you think for one second that—'

'We met her.' Isa's breaths came in gasps, but she'd lost none of her defiance. 'We dealt with her, same as we're dealing with you. This is the new world, brother. *My* new world. I suggest you take Sapora and get back to your tunnels if you want to live.' She brandished her sword at him. Sweat-stained and with bloodied clothes, Isa looked every bit the warrior her father had been.

Tacio seemed to think so, too, because he didn't reply immediately. His gaze darted between Palom and their allies, calculating.

Solvi slunk over to Isa, standing behind her and baring her fangs in a low growl, tail lashing left to right, sweeping away broken spears.

'Isa. You have sealed your fate. Sapora might want you alive, but after *this*? You've just signed your own death warrant.'

'As have you, unless you return to Sereth.'

The standoff didn't last long. One Cerastes with more sense than the others threw down his spear, the blade clattering on the stone streets. The others followed suit, dropping their weapons and backing away, allowing the Ittallan to pass.

Tacio hissed in fury but sheathed his sword. He wasn't foolish enough to press the fight when it was clear he wouldn't be winning it.

Traego and the others pushed forward, sweeping Palom up in their movements. The Ittallan cheered, repeating, 'Long live Queen Isa,' over and over, until Palom could hear nothing but their voices.

They helped their injured along, carrying those too weak to walk, making their way past the furious, incredulous glares of the Varkain, and back to the hangar where their ships waited to take them away.

31

Morgen stared at his blood-coated hands in stunned shock, his mouth half-open, his breaths coming in furious gasps. He'd injured people before. Killed them. Because he'd been ordered to, or it had been the right thing to do.

Arch-Kalos Dhabra had *attacked* him. Attacked Mahlu.

Had been about to kill them both.

Yet, Morgen had killed him in cold blood.

The viscous liquid dripped slowly off his fingers and the squelch of it hitting the ground echoed.

'...Morgen?' Mahlu's voice sounded very far away.

He didn't know what to do. Couldn't comprehend *what* he'd done. Everything had turned white, as if fire burned away his eyes. But now he could see the sticky redness all over his palms, the knife still clutched in one hand—so tightly that his knuckles had turned white.

His tremors had stopped. Replaced by something worse. A numbness he couldn't explain or understand, and a pain deep in his head.

Mahlu placed a hand on his shoulder, but he couldn't tear his eyes away from his bloodied hands.

'Morgen, we should go...' her voice was soft, hesitant. Fearful?

Something had awoken within him when the light from Dhabra's death filled the cavern. No, maybe it had only filled *him*. Something cold and twisted, like a metal splinter deep in his mind. He shuddered. 'I don't...' his mouth worked, but he didn't know what he was saying.

Drip. Drip. Drip.

Blood oozed along the cave floor.

'Leave that.' Mahlu reached over him, gently uncurling his clenched fingers from the hilt of the small blade. Blood completely covered the metal—there was no sign of the water from the lake. No more of Rhea's breath.

At Mahlu's touch, the blade clattered noisily to the ground. Morgen watched it fall, as if it was in slow motion. When he moved his eyes, he saw Dhabra's body. He let out a gasp as if seeing it for the first time. 'Arch...Arch-Kalos?'

Mahlu scurried over to Dhabra and placed her hands over his face—his mouth forever open in a wordless cry of shock and pain. She gently pulled his exquisite headdress away from him, bundling the silks up into one neat parcel.

'What are—'

'Let's go, Morgen.' Mahlu's hands were around his shoulders again, hauling him to his feet. Morgen let her lead, too stunned and too overwhelmed to argue. 'We have to get out of here.' She turned him away from Dhabra, away from the lake, and back to the ladder.

'Wait. The dragon...Mahlu? Did you see...' Sentences half-formed, fluttering away before he could give them voice.

'I didn't see one. Keep walking, there you go. Look, we're at the ladder now. Can you climb?'

He reached out for the nearest rung of the rope ladder, nailed into the rock. His fingers slipped. 'Too much blood.'

'Try again, Morgen. Come on, quickly.'

With her encouragement, Morgen managed to clamber onto the ladder, and up out of the cavern. Every step cleared his mind a little more, his shock fading into infrequent heart palpitations.

'Good. Your breathing is better!' Mahlu encouraged.

The heavy pain lingered in his head. Something had changed within him. Something fundamental.

'We...you have to get your things. From Topeko's. Then we need to leave.'

'My sword,' Morgen muttered. They crept along the tunnel as quickly as they could—Mahlu stopping every so often to wait for him to catch up. Every step was stronger than the one before. 'My *Valta Forinja*. I need it.'

'Morgen, after what we just did, we have to get out of the country! Samolen or not, we'll hang for this! There's no time!'

'I *need* it.' Morgen blinked rapidly, eyes adjusting as they stepped out from the darkness and into the bright sunlight. 'It'll be at the university.'

Mahlu held Dhabra's headdress under one arm and tucked in a loose trail of silk. 'It's the middle of the day. It'll be full!'

'*I have to*!' It was the clearest, strongest thought he'd had for days. 'Then we can get away. Why...why did you take that?' He jerked his chin towards the bundle she carried.

'You wouldn't understand!'

'I need my *Valta Forinja*. Keeping it here makes this place a target for more dragon attacks. I'm saving the city from that. And I'll do more good with it than the Kalos would ever do with it locked up. I'm going to help save Linaria from Sapora. Stop the Arks. Whatever it takes to make a difference. To stop more people dying. Sitting here, practicing peace, none of it will help in the end. We'll all burn while the Samolen never lift a finger!' The warm sunlight seemed to burn away the fog of confusion in his mind, leaving only clear desires—getting his *Valta Forinja* and getting out of the country.

It wouldn't absolve him of murdering the Arch-Kalos, but his intentions were pure.

Mahlu tightened her grip on the headdress. She slumped her shoulders. 'Justice. That's what this is. For everything he did to my family. I'm taking this to my mother.'

'In Iryl?'

She nodded.

'Fine. You have your own things? Grab them. I'll meet you at Topeko's when I'm done at the university. His house is closest to the docks anyway.'

Mahlu almost smiled, then caught herself. 'What about gold? I don't have much...'

'I'll cover the tickets. Go.'

She didn't hesitate—dashing along the dusty street, Dhabra's headdress held tight.

Morgen didn't know what he was doing, didn't know what was going on. He'd made a decision and had just fallen off the edge of a cliff.

There was no going back.

~

MORGEN RINSED his hands in one of the many fountains on the edge of Berel New Town, the flowing water changing from clear to rust red. In the heat, the blood had thickened and dried, and cracked blood fell off his skin in chunks. He was going to the university to steal. It made no difference whether or not he was covered in the blood of the man he'd just murdered. But somehow, it felt wrong to enter that sacred place of learning with crimson up his arms.

With his robes covered in dust and dirt, his hair in disarray, and his overall appearance generally dishevelled, he expected more attention from the people he passed. Thankfully, in the height of the day, most of the Kalos were indoors with their students, and many residents and visitors would be taking shelter from the intense desert heat.

It gave him a small window of opportunity.

He crossed the bridge into the Old Town, not bothering to peer over the side at the vast lake below. He'd already sampled enough of Rhea's breath to last him a lifetime. His head continued to throb, and the longer he spent in the sun, the worse it would get, so he pushed himself to jog.

Morgen had visited the university many times, but he'd never gone to the parts sectioned off for ancient artefacts or confiscated items. He knew there would be one—Topeko had taken Palom and Anahrik there on their very first visit to the city.

He just had to search quickly and methodically.

Five enormous Sevastos stones dominated the university courtyard, set up in a wide circle around the centre. Morgen stared at them as he passed, felt their power much as he'd felt the power below the lake. Had that been a figment of his imagination? A fever dream? Or did a real dragon dwell there? Mahlu didn't seem to think so.

It didn't matter anymore.

It wasn't as if he was going to remain here, studying like a good Kalosai.

Not now.

A few Kalosai sat outside, sharing heavy books or eating lunch. Most gave him little more than a cursory glance.

Morgen stopped before walking inside and turned to a pair of young Kalosai sitting on a low wall, their blue cheek jewels sparkling. 'You two. Where are the artefacts kept?' Morgen was surprised at how flat his own voice sounded.

The students paused their conversation and looked up sharply. 'Um, which ones? I can find a Kalos who could—'

'No. *You* tell me.'

They shared an uneasy glance with one another, which only irritated Morgen. 'Well, the oldest books are in the south wing. The library sprawls—'

'Not those. The *Valta Forinja*. My sword was taken there. *Where* is it?' Morgen raised his voice.

They jumped, stumbling off the walls. 'I don't...that's not...'

'I don't *care* what you think. Take me there!' Morgen hated resorting to intimidation, but he didn't have time to waste and his headache was worsening. After what he'd done to the Arch-Kalos, nothing seemed that bad anymore. He waved his hand in frustration and the gesture blasted both students apart—sending them sprawling.

Morgen frowned in surprise. His headache lessened. He felt the pull of magic as though he'd just lit a torch, but it was somehow colder. Less tangible. A strange version of the *Ra* he'd practiced.

Was it something to do with that light when he'd killed the Arch-Kalos?

'O—okay!' the first student yelped, getting to his feet and hurrying through the entrance, leaving his books on the courtyard floor.

Morgen turned to the other, who cowered by the wall. 'Keep studying. Keep quiet.'

They nodded frantically, and Morgen ran after the first Kalosai. He didn't have time to figure out the new magic he seemed able to wield.

At first Morgen was suspicious. The Kalosai might've run straight to the nearest Kalos, and then everything would be over. But true to his word, the student navigated them down staircases and along quieter and quieter corridors until they arrived at a large, steel door. 'In here.'

'Open it.'

'It's locked.'

'Open it,' Morgen repeated.

'I—I can't! I don't have the key, only the Kalos have access to it, and—'

Morgen huffed, his irritation growing. He raised both hands, the tingling pull of the magic coursing within him as before. He squeezed his palms into a fist, focussing on the door's lock.

Something clicked.

The hinges shattered.

And the door cracked open.

The Kalosai gasped. 'What...How? Are you a Kalosuk? You don't have a jewel, and—'

'Be quiet!' Morgen snapped, waving his left arm angrily. Magic swelled and sent the Kalosai flying into the opposite wall.

So, this was *He*.

Morgen thought he'd be elated, but only grim determination pushed him on as he walked into the room of forbidden artefacts and weapons. Many books, bottles, and boxes lined the walls—stacked up on rows upon rows of shelving. He didn't know what was inside, nor did he care to. The Samolen were incredibly diverse in their magic and what could be achieved. He wondered whether most of the illegal imported stuff was produced right here, under the nose of the Kalos.

Or whether the Arch-Kalos managed the whole thing.

Dhabra must've known how to use *He*. It was the only way he'd have an advantage over the other Kalos. What gave him the right to *cleanse* their ranks, as he'd said. Casting Rhea's judgement.

Morgen's stomach turned. Even though he'd rinsed his hands, he saw Dhabra's blood dripping between his fingers in his mind's eye.

With a vaulted ceiling and few lights, Morgen wondered how anyone found their way back out of such a room. It seemed to extend forever. And there was no sign of his sword, nor the other *Valta Forinja*. Cursing under his breath, he rushed along, glancing this way and that for any sign of his sword.

He didn't know how long he'd spent in the university already. Too long.

Someone was bound to notice the missing Kalosai. He only hoped it would take far longer for the Arch-Kalos' absence to be detected.

With a sudden thought, he flicked his right arm and sent the entire row of metal racking sprawling to the ground. It hit the floor with an almighty crash as dozens—hundreds of items went flying. The next shelf fell in a similar manner. Then the next, each one crashing to the floor like a set of dominos.

Although the room was deep in the bowels of the university, *someone* would have heard that.

Thankfully, the crashed shelves cleared a path to the end of the room, and his eyes lit up. He licked his lips and made his way across, clambering over the metal racking and countless items that now littered the floor.

There, at the room's farthest wall, he spied the glint of a sword. He made his way over to them, grinning broadly as he saw a metal cage that held several ancient weapons. Many had crumbled over the centuries they'd been locked up here, their blades rusted and hilts faded, but their power was unmistakable. Beside the collection of swords, pikes, and daggers—his own short sword. It was the only one without layers of dust caked into it, and it was the only one that called out to him.

It took no effort for Morgen to tap into *He* and rend the locks from the cages.

Morgen grasped the hilt of his sword and relaxed into the power that thrummed within. He held all the power of a Sevastos. With access to *He* in one hand, and his *Valta Forinja* in the other, there was nothing that could touch him.

No battle he could lose. No enemy that could defeat him.

Even the myriad footsteps charging down the stairs outside the chamber gave him no cause for concern. The panicked shouting and screaming of dozens of Samolen meant nothing.

He was finally going to avenge Eryn's death. He'd already avenged Mahlu's family with what he'd done to the Arch-Kalos. He'd ensure she remained safe. Then, he would slay Sapora, releasing the god from his claws, and bring balance back to Linaria.

If the Samolen didn't like it, that was their tough luck. He couldn't sit around and wait. Not when he had all this strength at his fingertips. After years of being squashed down, following orders he didn't believe in, and running from his nightmares—he was going to make a difference.

Save Linaria, before it was too late.

The footsteps outside turned to shouts. Surprise. Anger.

'Stop right there!'

'What have you done?'

'The Arch-Kalos will hear of this!'

Their voices blurred together, became meaningless.

Morgen's head burned as if the metal splinter buried itself deeper, twisting hard. His unsheathed sword sent out a wave of blue light, as if happy to once again be in the hands of its master. Morgen didn't want to hurt them. Not if he didn't have to. 'Step aside, I'm leaving. I've only taken what's mine. I haven't touched anything else.'

'You cannot take *anything* from this room! It is forbidden!' one Kalos roared.

Morgen barely glanced up. The door was so far away, and they were *so* loud. He picked his way across the debris, careful not to accidentally crush anything underfoot. He was being deliberate. Respectful of their artefacts. Couldn't they see all the trouble he was going to for their sake?

'This is mine. It shouldn't have been put here,' Morgen said, too focussed on where he stepped to pay much attention to the Samolen blocking the door. He needed to get out, get back to Topeko's and grab the rest of his things, then leave with Mahlu. Nothing else mattered.

'Stay where you are, or we'll use force!'

Morgen looked up, then. Kalos Ettas blocked the doorway, three others behind him. 'Stand aside.'

Something in his voice must've worried the Kalos, because they didn't immediately reply. They muttered to one another, one shook his head. Ettas stepped back but raised his hand. 'Kalosai Morgen! Your time here has been fraught with rule-breaking and violence. When Topeko hears of this, you'll likely have your mind stripped and be cast out into the desert! Stop this madness now, and I'll—'

Ettas never finished his sentence.

Morgen waved his left hand, a smooth, diagonal strike in mid-air. Magic filled that movement, and a wall of crushing pressure knocked Ettas to the ground as if he'd been punched by a boulder. Morgen glanced at the other Kalos. Blue light flickered from his palm, the physical manifestation of *He*. 'Stand aside,' Morgen repeated.

'The Kalosai uses *He*!' one shrieked.

Morgen stepped over Ettas's body. Blood trickled from

the Kalos' temple. Morgen didn't know if he was dead or if he'd simply knocked the man unconscious.

He found he didn't much care.

'I am no Kalosai. I have renounced your ways. Not that I was ever part of them before.' Morgen shoved past the Kalos and walked down the corridor. The young Kalosai who'd brought him to the room remained where he'd left him, although he was awake and watched Morgen with wary eyes. A large bruise had grown across his cheek where he'd hit the wall.

Morgen said, 'I have no quarrel with you Samolen. Even though I have every right to after how you treated me. What you put me through. Stay where you are, if you know what's good for you. I'm leaving this damned desert.'

MORGEN WASN'T QUITE sure when he'd made it back to Kalos Topeko's house. After what had happened in the university, everything blurred together into one, painful, headache-induced mess. His feet carried him the whole way there, with little conscious input.

His head throbbed, although every use of *He* had lessened it. His fingers seemed to glow pale blue, shimmering as if underwater.

Mahlu was already inside when he arrived. She had a large satchel over one shoulder and had tied her blonde hair back with a leather cord. She had another smaller bag open on the table, with dried meat, fruit, nuts, and wrapped cheese inside. She'd been in the middle of topping up the bag with as much food as she could fit in, and looked up when he entered the room. 'Morgen! Dragons above, I've been so worried. Are you okay?'

'Fine. You got everything you need?'

'Yeah. I found a bag for you, too. It's in your room. What...what did you do?' She looked at his glowing sword/

'Good. I won't be long.' Morgen ignored her question and made his way through Topeko's house to his own room. The door had been left open, and he saw that Mahlu had also gone to the trouble of stripping his bed sheets and stuffing them in the bottom of the large bag.

He travelled light, as a rule. Rummaging through the wooden trunk at the end of his bed, he pulled out a pouch of florins and half-crowns, a razor, hairbrush, and the only other clean clothes he had left. At the very bottom of the trunk was the linen he'd used to carefully wrap his sword in. He took it out, inspected it, then shoved it in the bag.

Along with this *Valta Forinja*, he didn't need anything else.

Once he had his headache under control, he swapped his sandals for his boots, shouldered his bag—far less heavy now he'd offloaded all the books and tomes he'd originally brought back—and made for the door.

He didn't know exactly how he was going to challenge Sapora. Their first step was getting out of Ranski—if he focussed on one thing at a time, everything would be all right. He was sure.

'It has finally come to this.'

Morgen wasn't surprised to see Topeko arrive when he rejoined Mahlu.

The Kalos seemed to have aged ten years since he'd last seen him. Grey streaked through his dark hair, and lines creased his forehead even without frowning. 'I tried so very hard, Morgen. I hope you know that.' He sounded pitiful.

Morgen ignored him and crossed the floor to Mahlu, securing the bag of food and resting a hand on hers, hoping it would reassure her. 'Time to go.'

'Perhaps the Arch-Kalos was right. You *are* beyond saving,' Topeko said.

Morgen scowled. 'I don't need saving. *You* all do.'

'What could we possibly need saving from? There is no strife here.'

'Yourselves. You'll sit here while the world burns. You'll do nothing.' Just speaking about it made rage boil within him. A kettle on the brink of overflowing. 'Arillians. Dragons. Sevastos. Arks. Varkain. All of it. You'll sit and wait for everyone to kill each other.'

'I see nothing wrong with remaining passive.'

Morgen raised his arms in fury. 'Open your eyes! Half the university burned down because of the dragons! I didn't see your sacred god rise up and defend you!'

Topeko tapped his cheek jewel, which flared with purple light. 'We defended ourselves using Rhea's breath. Come, now, Morgen, this is the most basic—'

'I'm *done*. No more, Topeko. I'm leaving.'

'I cannot permit that.' Sadness tinged his voice. 'You have stolen the forbidden weapon, destroyed university property. Exile and death is all that awaits you now.'

Morgen shrugged. 'Death comes for everyone. I'd rather not sit around and do nothing, waiting for it.'

'I know. You'd rather meet it head-on.' Topeko shook his head. 'If that is what you wish, there is nothing I can do to change that. But, Kalosai or not, I cannot let you leave. You understand that?'

'Morgen...' Mahlu whispered.

Morgen squeezed her hand. 'Don't worry, Mahlu. I won't let anything happen to you. I promise.'

'You have brought this Kalosai into your madness. Morgen, how—'

'Kalos Topeko. Thank you for the lessons and lectures. Let us go, and no further harm will come to you or this city.'

Morgen hoped the Kalos would take him up on his offer. Killing the Arch-Kalos had been one thing. Hurting Topeko would be something else.

'No, Morgen. I cannot in good faith let you leave. Not after this. You must face judgement, and I cannot protect you from the Arch-Kalos again.'

Morgen laughed. A small chuckle at first, but it soon burst into a full belly-laugh that shook his entire body head to toe. He grasped his stomach with his free hand, almost doubled over. Tears fell as he laughed, and he squeezed his eyes shut. The tears didn't stop.

His laughter turned to sobbing, then coughing as the shock of everything collapsed around him. His head throbbed, the magic he wielded threatening to explode. Morgen couldn't control it. Couldn't control himself.

He raised his *Valta Forinja* and blue light streaked off the blade, filling the room with an ethereal glow despite it being the middle of the day.

Topeko stepped forward, hands raised. He threw up a shield of pure *Ra*.

Morgen opened one eye and wiped the wetness away. Suddenly, the magic was no longer invisible. He'd always been able to faintly see its outline, but now, with whatever it was awakened within him, he saw the furious purple smoke manipulated by Topeko's master hands. Morgen clenched his fist and slashed the sword down in a vertical strike. Reacting faster than he could blink, the *Valta Forinja* unleashed a blade of blue light. It cut into the floor as it zoomed to Topeko, only to dissipate against the Kalos's shield.

'I'll not hurt you, Morgen,' Topeko said. 'Stop this and face your judgement like a man.'

'There is *no judgement*!' Morgen yelled, sending strike after strike at Topeko—each one bouncing harmlessly off his shield wall and dissipating, although they tore up the floor with a devastating effect. 'Don't you see? Don't you *understand*?'

Topeko walked forward, closing the gap between them, his shield of *Ra* keeping him safe from Morgen's attacks. 'Judgement is for everyone. You. Mahlu. Even me.'

Morgen's strikes grew faster, clumsier. He stepped back, suddenly worried about Topeko's sheer defensive strength. Through blurred vision, he gritted his teeth, tried to focus. 'No more! No more judgement!' He rolled to the side, his training tapping in, forcing him to look for another opening. Raising both hands to bring the sword down in a powerful, two-handed strike, Topeko crossed both palms and wind filled the room, sucking the strength from his arms.

Morgen almost dropped his sword.

Fine. Topeko could defend against the *Valta Forinja*.

He'd simply change his approach. His head flared with pain and Morgen relished it. The pain gave his magic strength. He tapped into it, pulling the pain like a physical thing through the air. *Ra* was the magical energy of the world, channeled into a form he created. *He* was the other side of that coin. Where *Ra* defended, healed, saved; *He* attacked, damaged, and killed.

The exertion took its toll. Morgen sweated, his knees trembled. Out of the corner of his eye, Mahlu watched, abject terror on her face.

This was it. He had to get rid of Topeko so they could be free.

Morgen sent the bolt of *He* at the Kalos. It pierced through his shield, sucked in the magic of it, and impaled Topeko in the stomach.

'You've desecrated the teachings!' Topeko roared.

Morgen shaped and folded the ball of raw energy as it flickered before him.

'Magic is *Ra*! It is life! It is creation! It is re-birth! This... this is *not* magic!'

More *He* formed at Morgen's beckoning. Its blue darker than his *Valta Forinja*. Wilder. Like wind and fire and lightning all rolled into one, swirling mass of energy. Power. He shaped it with his mind, using his hands to form the chaotic swirl into a ball. His headache lessened the more he fed it, rolling his hands around and around one another, the power within thrumming with strength.

'Morgen!' Topeko screamed, his voice cracking.

Morgen threw the ball of energy across the room.

It thundered into Topeko, blasted through him and slammed into the wall—splitting the wood. The Kalos's scream filled the air.

Morgen laughed. 'Magic comes from the dragons. Your sacred gods. Look at how destructive they are. *He* is just as important as *Ra*. Moreso, given how long you've ignored it...'

The edges of Topeko's defensive wall of magic fractured.

'Dragons are *death*. Stands to reason their magic causes it, too.' Morgen watched, unblinking, as smoke rose in great waves from the damage he'd caused to Topeko's home. 'Look at the *Valta Forinja*. If that's not dragon magic, I don't know what is. You hide from the truth. I get it. The truth hurts. But, Topeko, I...I'm *embracing* the truth. Letting it *strengthen* me.'

'Morgen...' Topeko's wall evaporated, and he collapsed to the floor, clutching his bleeding belly. Blood bubbled up, seeping through his robes. 'It's...not possible.'

Morgen held out his arm and Mahlu grabbed their belongings and joined him, tears streaming down her cheeks. He said, 'I told you. There's no more judgement.'

'Then you...the Arch-Kalos...?' Topeko coughed, his breathing laboured. 'Morgen, what have...you...done?'

Morgen picked up his sword and grabbed his bag from

Mahlu, before wrapping one arm around her shoulder. 'I haven't done anything yet. Sapora and the Arillians must pay for what *they've* done. I'm gonna stop them, Topeko. I'm gonna save Linaria. You should be proud of me and everything I'm going to achieve. I bet none of your Kalosai have ever saved the world.'

Morgen and Mahlu walked through the shattered doorway, leaving Topeko in a growing pool of blood.

32

Amarah sat on the stool in front of *RaKhanna's* controls, one finger on the wheel to keep her ship flying straight while her mind wandered.

The Archigo of Tannon Sona had brought her pipe with her—apparently she never left home without it—and thanks to the smoke, Amarah hardly felt the pain of her broken nose anymore, much less the myriad of cuts and scrapes that lined her arms and chest after their encounter with the Cerastes.

She was just glad she'd pulled through it without being bitten.

Gralla had to be the first Goldstone who actually had decent taste.

Amarah's thoughts kept returning to the people she owed. Moroda's debt was the oldest, and Amarah wanted to return to her hunt for a Sevastos. After Kohl and his Arillians had let her down, she couldn't think of any way she could try and save her other than one of the most ancient dragons. She wanted to get her revenge on Jato, too. She also wanted to fly anywhere *but* their current destination.

She wanted a damned lot of things, but Rhea wasn't having any of it, apparently.

If Kohl hadn't let her down in Oren, perhaps some of his old Arillian magic would have worked on Moroda and the Sevastos crystal, and she'd have been free to hunt Jato as she pleased.

If she hadn't answered Princess Isa's desperate cry for help, she wouldn't have been mixed up in the second Ittallan-Varkain war that brewed. It was more than a fight for the throne. It was a generations' long hatred that had flared back into life, and she'd rather *not* be caught in the middle of it.

Fighting alongside sky pirates and thieves was one thing. Fighting alongside tigers, bears, and bulls was quite something else.

Idly, she scratched her cheek. The horizontal scar under her eye itched as night drew in, and the cold with it. Another facet her of her past. Another thing she'd fled from.

Traego had resumed authority when they'd all made it to the hangar, full of victorious joy both at surviving the battle and being reunited with their princess. He'd taken Carav on board *Otella* so Malot could keep an eye on her. She'd been stirring back into consciousness, but recovering from a Varkain bite often took several days. Traego had then told them their next location and said to split up and fly under *Shrouds*, which made sense. Amarah didn't want Veynothi or Sapora's dragon to find her again.

Their destination had worried her and she'd immediately refused.

Then Traego had argued the point, and with Tacio and the Cerastes still in the town, she'd had no choice but to agree.

So she flew *RaKhanna* and a small contingent of Isa's

followers to the last place in Linaria she ever wanted to go—or thought she would go: Sereth.

She could hardly believe it.

But where else could they have gone? Nowhere in Val Sharis was safe. The Estorian pirates wanted their heads. Ranski would throw them out for their unwillingness to uphold peace. And Corhaven was just as much in Sapora's pocket as Val Sharis was. Traego had justified it was the one place he'd never think to look.

Isa had argued against it.

Yet there were leagues of disused, abandoned tunnels all over Sereth. Under the volcano, for a start. Princess Isa could rest and recover there.

Amarah snorted. If someone had told her a few days ago that she'd end up flying to Sereth—of her own accord—she'd have assumed they were mad. Despite the sense Traego had spoken, it didn't sit well with her.

Admittedly, Isa's behaviour didn't sit well with her either. She'd had her first glimpse of it when they'd fled Estoria, attacked by Captain Hanzel and her First Mate, Rimir. Isa had flown into a rage that had seemed to blind and deafen her to everything but the battle. She'd turned self-defense into a bloodbath. The same thing had happened with the Arillians over the wetlands.

Thankfully, Isa had been too drained after those encounters to put up much of a fight against Tacio, but her actions were worrying. Perhaps she had more Varkain blood in her than she cared to admit.

At least Amarah had managed to grab an emerald the size of a child's fist while they'd been in Esta Cona—she, Antar, and Carav had been sure to scope out the place and help themselves to anything they happened upon. Amarah knew Traego was bound to catch up with her sooner or later, she'd constantly been touching the *Thief's Ink* on her wrist as if it would tell her whenever Traego tracked her. If she was no longer in his debt, she would be free to do as she wished again—for the first time since before she'd stupidly got herself arrested in Niversai however many months ago.

The emerald weighed heavy in her pocket, along with her thoughts. Amarah leaned back on the stool, stifling a yawn and closing her good eye for just a moment.

Princess Isa had chosen to fly on *RaKhanna*, along with Archigo Gralla, Kylos, Solvi, and most of the Ittallan who'd shown up to fight back at the last minute. It meant all the chatter on deck was either about Isa's campaign or how the Archigo could help. Amarah wasn't interested in any of it.

Mostly, she was frustrated that her own desires and goals had been put on hold yet again.

Once they landed and she'd had time to rest up, she was going to do her own thing. Isa had left Estoria with her because she'd needed a ship. Amarah had allowed it, because she'd needed gold. It had been mutually beneficial.

Now, she was no longer needed.

And while Isa and her followers discussed the political side of taking the throne and her subsequent rule, all Amarah could think about was Veynothi and the Sevastos. None of them stood a chance against powers like that, and it had been by pure luck they'd survived both encounters with all their limbs attached.

Overhead, the third moon rose, pale and yellow in an inky black sky. Stars twinkled, and even so high up, Amarah heard an owl or two in the trees far below. It was peaceful.

A vast country, Sereth's true size was impossible to ascertain—everything was underground, sequestered away in labyrinthine tunnels. Dense forests sprawled over the land above, fed by wide rivers, the resulting landscape rich in wildlife. Aside from a handful of outposts built close to the

Feor Mountains, Sereth was the same as it had been for millenia.

Their specific destination was Mount Kozue, one of the most easterly places in the world, and Sereth's only real landmark above ground. An extinct volcano, the land surrounding it was barren—stripped of the lush green that covered the rest of the country.

But it was the only place for an airship to land. So far from anything resembling civilisation, it was the last place the Varkain would look for them. And there was something ironic about the fact that they'd chosen to hide right under the snakes' noses.

Amarah stifled another yawn and stretched both arms above her, holding them there until her shoulders cracked. It had been a *long* few days.

'*Otella* is already there?' Kylos asked. 'Guess we took a gentle flight.'

'I'm just looking forward to being on solid ground again. Even if it is in Sereth,' Isa said.

'Whassat, Isa? Bored of flying?' Amarah called out. 'Here I was thinking you'd've made a natural sky pirate!'

'Isa is not afraid teh get her hands dirty, or do what must be done,' Kylos said, affronted. 'It doesn't mean she's a common thief who relishes such acts.'

Amarah cackled and pulled in her sails, gently lowering *RaKhanna* to the rocky ground. 'Gonna be a bumpy landing. No soft jungle grass here!' It was mostly true—the bottoms of airships were designed to be flat, for easier ground landings—but no ship had ever been built to comfortably land at the base of a sleeping volcano.

She winced as the hull crunched on rocks, mini shockwaves running up her arms as she held firm on the wheel and controls.

Her passengers immediately sprang to life, grabbing their belongings and shuffling around on deck. Isa led them, walking confidently now she had more of her followers with her, and had been able to sit and rest for a day or so while they flew.

A good sleep would do anyone wonders.

'Thank you, Amarah. I truly appreciate your assistance. That will be all for now,' Isa said as she led the Ittallan off *RaKhanna*.

Amarah snorted. What was she, some Imperial pilot the princess could order about? She followed the others off. She needed to have a candid conversation with Traego at any rate—it was because of *him* she'd had to get away from Estoria in the first place.

It was not a conversation she was looking forward to.

Mostly she was grateful that, for the first time in what felt like weeks, she could slow down and catch her breath before some other monster from Linaria's past rose up to attack her. She couldn't remember the last time she'd just sat and enjoyed herself without being in the middle of another adventure or battle.

Truthfully, she didn't know what she'd say to Traego. She clutched her wrist as she walked the short distance between *RaKhanna* and *Otella*, her fingers wrapping around her *Thief's Ink*.

'Amarah.'

She whirled around at the sound of her name and saw Palom approach. He held a long, thin bundle, wrapped in a patchwork of linens. 'Palom. You made me jump.' She scratched her old scar again. 'You all right?'

'I am okay. You?'

Amarah nodded, suddenly wary. Her gaze was drawn to the bundle he held. 'Whassat?'

Instead of answering, Palom unfolded the top of the

linen to reveal a curved blade that glowed blue in the evening darkness.

Her breath caught. 'That's...my scythe. Where d'you get it?'

'Buried in beach on Estoria. Some pirate found it. I took it back.'

It made sense. She'd thrown it away when that damned monster had attacked. Her *Valta Forinja* had enhanced her fears and paranoia to the point she'd been frozen in place by a panic attack, unable to do anything but cry and hyperventilate until Traego had kicked the weapon out of her grasp.

She'd not even gone back to look for it.

Amarah tore her gaze away from the weapon and back to Palom, unsure. 'I dunno if I want it.'

'It is *emonos*.'

'Meaning?'

Palom covered the blade's edge and secured the linen with twine, hiding the *Valta Forinja* from view. 'It means...is not good.'

'That's an understatement. Damned strong, though.' She didn't have to think hard to remember back to the battle outside Taban Yul against Aciel and his Arillians. The *Valta Forinja* had been the reason they'd survived. And every other battle she'd been thrown into, come to think of it.

But after everything it had done to her? She suppressed a shiver. 'What you gonna do with it?'

'I do not know. I wanted to see if you wanted it. But, now...'

'What happened to your sword?'

Palom shrugged. 'Buried in snow. North Val Sharis.'

That didn't surprise her. 'It affected you, too?'

He nodded, the muscles in his arm tense.

Amarah couldn't comprehend what was going through his mind. Palom had forged the mythical weapons. Their formidability couldn't be questioned, but it was a damned steep cost to pay to wield them. 'I'll stick with my normal scythe, thanks. Do what you want with that. It's yours, anyway. I just borrowed it.' She hoped that didn't come across as ungrateful. The *Valta Forinja* had kept her out of danger on more than one occasion. And if she'd had any other weapon when she'd challenged Jato, she'd be dead.

But she couldn't afford to lose her senses. 'I need to talk to Traeg. Figure out what's going on.'

'Why did you leave? Take Princess Isa with you? You said you were running, but I did not ask the reasons.'

Amarah adjusted her eye patch and walked past him, eager to get on board *Otella*. 'Had to get away for a bit. Isa chose to come with me. Unfortunately, Sapora put a huge bounty on me, and—'

'I saw poster.'

'Then you know why I had to leave. Even Traego wanted some of the bounty.'

Palom put a hand on her shoulder, halting her. 'Traego was confused why you left.'

That didn't make sense. 'Carav said Traego was considering selling me to Sapora!'

Palom frowned. 'No? He has been worried for you. Antar as well.'

Amarah blinked. That didn't make sense. 'I thought...' She shook her head. It didn't matter. 'Anyway, I need to make sure Traego don't come after me again. I'm done runnin' from everyone. I got my own stuff to do.'

'You are leaving?'

'I got debts to pay. Got revenge to chase.'

Palom stared at her for a while, one massive hand still resting on her shoulder. 'You never fight for other people. Do you?'

'Where's that come from?' Amarah laughed, the cackle

resounding in the clear night sky. She didn't need to explain herself to the Ittallan. 'I do what I want, Palom. Always have. No need to be surprised!'

'Hmm.' Palom released her with a frown.

Amarah left him alone and clambered up the steps carved in *Otella's* side.

Farlan blocked the way to the deck. He stood by the side rail at the top of the ladder, arms folded, his nose screwed up. 'Oh, it's *you*.'

'You can sound a bit happier, y'know.' Amarah kept her feet on the steps and grasped the side rail with both hands. 'Gonna move so I can get on board?'

Farlan scratched his chin, considering. 'Traeg! Got your traitor wants ta come up. Shall I let her?'

Amarah scowled. Traitor? 'Hey, I had shit I needed to sort out! Traeg understands. I ain't no traitor!'

'Yeah, let her up.' Traego's reply was faint, as if he was on the far end of the ship.

'Looks like you got lucky this time.' Farlan leaned back, giving Amarah just enough room to squeeze up onto the deck.

She was sure to shove past him, digging her elbow into his gut to show just how little she appreciated his tone. Amarah stomped across the deck, her mood completely soured by Farlan's attitude. 'Traeg?'

'Over here.'

A small flame flickered near *Otella's* prow, around which Amarah could just pick out the silhouettes of Traego, Antar, Isa, Kylos, and Malot.

'Private meeting? Hope I ain't interrupting.' Amarah thumped the bottom of her scythe on the deck.

'Nah I was gonna send for ya if ya hadn't turned up soon.' Traego waved at the only empty stool around the fire. 'Sit. Think we gotta have some words, me an' ya.'

'Yeah, I reckon we do.' Amarah sat. She didn't like being an outsider. She and Traego had always been close, and yet had often butted heads. This was the first time she could remember feeling as if they were on opposite sides. 'How's Carav doing?'

'She'll be fine. Just needs rest. I've cleaned up her wounds, got rid of any lingering venom. That's all I can do for now,' Malot replied. In the light of the fire, her red cheek jewel looked almost like a smear of blood on her face. Her jewelled ears and the silver bangles laced through her dark hair glowed softly.

Amarah didn't like the sudden reminder of her birthplace.

'O' course, she wouldn't have *been* hurt if ya hadn't taken her when ya left Estoria.'

Amarah folded her arms at the accusation in Traego's voice. Everyone was against her tonight, it seemed. 'Well, maybe *you* shouldn't have said you wanted in on Sapora's bounty. I know you did the Veynothi job for king snake. Only a small step for you to sell me to him for even more crowns.'

Traego scowled. 'Amarah, I don't have a clue what ya on about.'

She shifted in her seat, trying to get more comfortable. 'You know exactly what I'm on about. Sapora's bounty. Three thousand crowns? Ringing any bells?'

'I didn't have a fucking clue where ya'd raced off ta 'til the first night when Ernold handed me a piece o' paper with ya name scrawled on it!'

Amarah pursed her lips. Traego was brutally honest most of the time. 'Well good thing I left when I did. The first thing you do after finding out about the bounty is track me down!'

'Because o' this lot.' Traego jerked his thumb at Isa and

Kylos. 'Damned Ittallan were on the verge o' rioting. That great big monster came back and tore up half the island. Estoria was a damned death trap.'

Amarah narrowed her eye. Had Carav lied about Traego's knowledge of the bounty? To get her to leave? 'So... you *ain't* gonna drop me off at Taban Yul?'

Traego erupted into laughter. 'Amarah ya more use ta me on my side than the gold Sapora can give me. I don't sell out my crew. Not unless they give me cause ta. I thought ya knew that.' His voice quickly grew serious. 'I ain't Cyd and I ain't Ipot, or any of them other half-baked captains. Come on, Amarah. How long we known each other?'

Amarah chewed her lip. Her life had revolved around trusting no-one but herself. Using others when it was convenient. Paying back debts so she could never owe anyone. All she wanted was to be free. To sail Linaria's skies as she wished.

She hated the way Traego looked at her. It was the way *she'd* looked at the Kalos in Berel when they'd accused her of doing something she hadn't. As a child, she couldn't fight back. Nothing could compare to the anger, hatred, and fear she'd felt at the injustice of her upbringing.

Dismissing the others gathered around the fire, she said, 'Traeg, I panicked. I—'

'Fuck sake, Amarah. I thought ya were better than that.'

'Can we save your squabbling for another time? We need to work out what we're doing,' Kylos interjected.

Amarah wanted to get away again. She pulled out the emerald from her pocket and passed it to Traego. Her voice had grown soft. 'Here. This should cover what you gave me for *RaKhanna*, right?'

Traego studied it longer than Amarah thought he would. Did he doubt its authenticity?

She quickly added, 'Traeg, you know it's worth plenty! More than—'

'It's at least double.' Traego admitted, taking it from her and staring at the gem. 'Ya didn't need ta...'

'Means *RaKhanna's* fully mine, right? Fly where I want?'

Traego nodded.

'As long as it helps *my* campaign. I hired you, remember?' Isa said, speaking for the first time since Amarah had arrived. 'You agreed.'

'Terms've changed. You wanted a ship to get around in. The other sky pirates in Estoria might've let you down, but you got *Otella* now,' Amarah said.

'Wait,' Traego said. 'I don't remember being privy ta any discussions ya had!'

'You were there when Isa addressed all the captains. You said you'd help. I did her a personal favour. Now *Otella* is here and you got your followers back, my part in our agreement is over.' Amarah looked at the princess.

'Why are you so keen to leave? Thought you were on our side,' Kylos asked.

'I wanna do my own thing.'

'And how much of "yeh own thing" do yeh think yeh'll be able to do while Sapora remains in power? With his Sevastos and his Arks, and that *insane* bounty on yeh head?' Kylos sneered. 'We *all* know about that, now.'

Amarah shrugged and stood up. 'Don't matter. I'm free.'

'What about Jato?' Isa asked, her voice quiet but clear.

'I'll get to her when I get to her.' She just wanted to get away. Shame and embarrassment were emotions she'd never learned to manage particularly well. She couldn't believe she'd fled from Traego, believed he wanted the bounty on her life. Believed Carav, that besotted idiot.

'Amarah. Ya need ta be honest with us,' Traego said. He hadn't pocketed the emerald. 'Antar said ya gave him ya ship.

Fuck me, if that's all my crew needs ta turn on me, I'm a shit captain.'

'I didn't turn on you! Just flew under a different colour for a bit is all.' Antar leaned back in his chair and returned his attention to wiping his blades down with a cloth.

'It's still my warship,' Amarah said quickly. 'Antar's borrowing it for a bit.'

'A bit? Ya were plannin' on coming back, then, were ya? Both of ya?'

'Once everything died down.'

Traego's face didn't budge. 'What ya so keen ta run off ta and get sorted, then? If it ain't Jato?'

Amarah looked at the faces staring at her. Traego—an ally she'd believed the worst of. Isa—the princess she'd offered to help. Antar—whom she'd promised her own ship and freedom. There were too many of them. She sat back down and sighed. 'You know me and Kohl went off to his homeland. Tried to find some Arillian magic he'd said would help Moroda?'

They nodded, the crackling fire the only sound bar the distant conversation of Ittallan on the ground.

'Needless to say things went to shit and now I'm back where I started. But it was a Sevastos that put Moroda there. It's a Sevastos that Sapora has under his claws. Catching my drift?'

'You're gonna look for your own Sevastos? That even possible?' Antar raised an eyebrow.

'Moroda found one. Why can't I? And when I do, I'll ask it to help. Besides, we ain't gonna have much luck against Sapora without one. Fight fire with fire, ain't that what you're always saying, Traeg?' Amarah hoped by focussing on the practical next steps, she could detract from her misjudgement of him and the others.

'You want to leave me, now that I've had my first victory,

have my ships together?' Isa asked, incredulous. 'Archigo Gralla is on my side. It won't be easy, but she'll have more people join me—here, if they're fighting fit, in Estoria if they want to get away from Sapora's Varkain. Staying with us is the best thing you can do.'

Amarah disagreed. 'You can't use *Thief Shrouds* forever. Malot's good but you'd need her working night and day for the rest of her life if you wanna sneak around Val Sharis without that dragon spotting us. Come on Isa, you know what it was like!'

The princess grew quiet, pensive.

'This is helping you out in a roundabout way, ain't it? If I get something that'll give us an edge against Sapora?'

'Getting rid of Jato *was* going to be the edge.' Isa stood up and flicked her hair.

'Until we clear the skies, we ain't got no chance of getting *near* her. I know you go battle crazy when you fight, but I'm just flesh and blood.' Amarah had meant it as a joke, but Isa seemed to hunker down within herself. Amarah tried to backpedal. 'Hey, you're good in a scrap. Nothing wrong with that.'

'*Good in a scrap*? Understatement of the century.' Antar laughed, plucking up another knife and running his thumb along its edge.

'Veynothi is a problem, too,' Isa said, her cheeks flushed. 'She's hunting us down. Me under Sapora's orders. You and Traego for what you stole from her.'

Amarah shuddered, remembering the Ark's golden eyes. They'd pierced her soul. 'How we gonna deal with her? Ain't as if we can just...put her back in stone? I'd rather *not* have that damned snake following me everywhere I go.'

'It was the Sevastos that did it,' Isa said. 'Sapora's Sevastos, I mean. It's what binds them together.'

'Ya what?' Traego turned to her.

Isa pinched the bridge of her nose, remembering. 'I didn't know. Not until the Valendrin told me. He explained the Sevastos had been asked to kill the Arks. But...you know, they're immortal? It couldn't kill them. It just...it turned them to stone.'

'That's why the Arks disappeared?' Kylos asked.

'That's what the Valendrin said. I don't know why he'd lie. He was talking to Sapora, Tacio, and myself.'

'Wait, weren't that thousands of years ago? What's it still doing around now? Why ain't there a crystal like in Berel? All the other Sevastos stones are there, after they helped people,' Amarah said.

'Because it *didn't* fulfil its promise. The Arks still live. Even in stone, they weren't dead.'

'Huh.' That explained why Sapora had a god flying around doing his bidding. It still didn't help with the fact that both enormous powers had made Linaria more dangerous than ever.

'Hang on a minute. The Sevastos follows Sapora because o' its unfinished job with the Arks? Am I understandin' that right?' Traego asked.

'That's correct.' Isa confirmed, running a hand through her hair.

'Then all we gotta do ta break Sapora's hold on it, is kill the Arks? It'll die. Just leave the massive crystal, like Amarah said are in Berel?'

'I suppose? But killing the Arks...We fought Veynothi! There's no way you can beat her!' Amarah scoffed.

'Does it matter?' Traego was getting excited now. He was always the most animated when he had a plan forming. 'Ya missin' the point! Kill the Arks, ya kill his hold on the Sevastos! Don't ya get it?'

It was so ludicrous that Amarah clapped slowly.

Traego rolled his eyes. 'Now ya just being petty.'

'No, I ain't.' Amarah didn't know how to make him understand. 'That Sevastos is the most powerful thing in the world. Aside from these Arks, right? And Sapora's got it on a pretty tight leash.'

They raised their eyebrows.

'What do you think it's gonna do when that leash snaps? It's gonna go fucking ballistic. I would, if I'd been chained up Rhea knows how many years and forced to do things I didn't wanna. From dragon-flame, remember...'

'From dragon-flame begun, from dragon-flame undone,' Malot whispered.

Traego gestured wildly with one hand. 'Oh, so instead of freeing the Sevastos, we'll let King Snake keep his little pet then, is that it? Dragons above, I thought ya hated Sapora.'

'I *do* hate the snake,' Amarah snapped, growing more frustrated. 'I'm just sayin' you gotta be prepared for the Sevastos to go on a proper rampage when it ain't under control anymore. A last hurrah before it dies. What if it burns half the world on its own?'

'You don't know it'll do that,' Antar said, though he didn't sound confident. He glanced nervously at Malot.

Amarah said, 'No, but I got a feelin' it will. It's not gonna turn around and thank us. We're the same as Sapora to it. *We're* the ones killin' Linaria. *We're* the ones who'll burn.' She hated where she'd grown up, hated the education forced down her throat—one she'd not managed to understand, let alone learn. But Topeko's words had been a nagging worry in the back of her mind ever since they'd defeated Aciel. Malot's repetition just emphasised the warning they held.

'How's this. You lot figure out how to hold your own against the Arks. *I'm* gonna find another Sevastos.'

'And how long will it take yeh teh find a Sevastos?' Kylos asked.

'Who knows. Moroda managed it. I'm sure if I talk with Topeko, he'll be able to help. Especially as I'm not trying to kill anything. Then, I'll kill Jato. That'll be your signal princess,' Amarah said.

They broke into chatter, and Amarah grinned, her earlier shame passing.

She didn't need anything else. She had her ship. She had her freedom.

Whether Isa permitted it or not, she couldn't stop her flying away—although it would be nice to have the princess on her side. They'd been through a lot together.

Amarah leaned back in her stool, stretching her legs out and pointing her toes towards the fire to chase away the night chill.

Soon, she would have her revenge.

33

As night coated the land in darkness, Palom wandered through the grounded airships and small campfires where the Ittallan were settling down for the evening. Sereth was lush and wild, untouched since people first walked in Linaria. But the land they'd chosen to rest in, under the shadow of the volcano, was the complete opposite. Black, grey, and red rocks covered the ground, ranging in size from enormous boulders to pebbles so small they were basically sand.

Palom didn't like how it felt underfoot. Unnatural. No soil. No grass. No trees. Just the barren landscape and the enormous volcano which dominated. Admittedly, if they were to move into the lush areas of Sereth, they'd be closer to the Varkain themselves. Hundreds of thousands—millions, even—of the snakes lived in their underground cities. Many lived entirely below the surface, going their whole lives without ever seeing the sun.

He couldn't imagine a life like that. Then again, he couldn't imagine being a snake. The thought of it went against his nature so much that it evoked nausea.

Traego's plan to hide here had been a good one, even if it

hadn't sat well with any of the Ittallan. The Varkain were their oldest enemies. In fact, there were no races in the world who were on good terms with them.

Princess Isa had spent time with her followers, briefly, before being summoned by Traego to a meeting on his ship. Kylos had gone with her. Now Isa was back, Kylos had refused to let the princess out of her sight in fear she'd be whisked off again and leave them stranded. He found it comforting that Isa had people who were determined to keep her safe.

Farlan had let him on board to return the wrapped *Valta Forinja*. He was almost glad that Amarah hadn't wanted it back. If she'd taken it willingly, she would have been *emonos* too. He didn't know what that would mean for their party, but he would have to keep a closer eye on her.

Traego and the others spoke long into the night, and Palom was happy to leave them to it. *Leillu* stuck close to the group, keeping within the bounds of the volcano, even though he was certain there would be good hunting for her in the lush forests to the north and west. Even the dragon seemed withdrawn in this desolate place. 'I do not like it here, either, *Leillu*.'

She chirped low at him, opening one eye.

He sat by the bottom of *Otella's* ladder, his dragon nestled up against his side, her heat radiating like fire.

Solvi had been to see him, as had Karvou, and half a dozen other Ittallan. Despite being away from their princess for so long, and currently hiding on enemy ground, the Ittallan were in surprisingly high spirits. Even those who had been wounded by Tacio's Cerastes were doing well. They'd not lost anyone, had their princess back, and were safe.

He held an apple in one hand and polished it against his leather jerkin. They were all traitors to the crown. Any one of them could be beheaded for what they'd done. He leaned back, his head touching the wooden hull of the warship that seemed to rise up above him impossibly high. Far beyond the top of the warship, three moons hung low and yellow.

It reminded him of Sol, and he wondered what was happening back home.

Taking a bite of the apple, Palom wrinkled his nose. Too soft and tart. It wasn't the right sort of apple—the kind that grew in the Rio Neva forest where he'd grown up. His father, Manilo, was the Archigo of Feoras Sol now. Palom wanted to tell the princess that she had the support of Sol, forever and always. But Sol could offer little by way of resources—people or supplies. His people were simple folk, mostly keeping to themselves and following the old ways more than the commerce-driven cities of Val Sharis. Mining the Feor Mountains for iron ore was the only way the village had survived so many generations.

Yet, having their support in spirit had to count for *something*, didn't it?

He wasn't sure what more he could do to help.

He'd planned on setting up shop in Estoria and forging weapons to aid her cause. But like all their plans so far, that, too, was out the window.

Every so often, a chunk of conversation drifted down to him. No-one seemed to be angry, which was always a good sign. He carried his sword with him, and was ready to leap up at the first hint of trouble. Kylos could look after herself. As could the princess for that matter. But he didn't like the idea of them facing off against the sky pirates alone, if anything went wrong.

And he didn't trust Traego at all.

None of the sky pirate captains had made good on their promises. To them, their word was no oath they swore by. It was used only for trickery designed to line their pockets with gold.

Never any honour.

Footsteps above. Boots crunched. Belts clinked.

Palom got to his feet and backed away from the ladder, chucking the half-eaten apple away. *Leillu* stretched her wings and yawned wide. 'We are not going anywhere,' he said to her, though his attention was on the people scrambling down the steps.

'Palom! Is everything well?' Princess Isa asked once she had disembarked.

'Everything is fine. Aside from being here.' Palom shrugged. 'And you?'

Kylos leapt off *Otella*, landing softly on the hard rocks. 'About as well as yeh can expect from a sky pirate.' She dusted off her palms and glanced at the princess with bright brown-orange eyes. 'Traego wants teh scout the area. I offered teh go, but he wants teh fly.' Kylos's scowl made it obvious what she thought of that.

'He *would* be faster. And *Otella* has firepower where Aetos does not. Besides, your brother has done so much for me. He deserves to rest!' Isa said.

'I thought point of coming here was safety. Surely there is nothing to scout?' Palom frowned.

'That's what I said. But yeh can never be too careful, I s'pose,' Kylos replied.

'You have worked much. You rest. *I* will go with Traego and keep eye on him.'

'An eye on him? You don't think he's up to something, do you?' Isa asked, her shoulders dropping.

'I do not know. Is why I will go and keep eye on him.'

'If you wouldn't mind? I've been away from the Ittallan here so long. I need to see them properly and rest. Kylos, Chyro and the others can set up a perimeter here, just in case anything wanders close. Apparently there aren't any Varkain settlements anywhere near, and even if they were, they'd be underground.' Isa peered through the gap between the parked ships to where several fires blazed brightly, the silhouettes of her Ittallan settling in for another rough night.

Palom said, 'I will watch him. Rest, princess. You have earned this.' He grabbed hold of the nearest step of the ladder, carved right into the wooden hull of *Otella*. 'I will be back soon and report. Do not worry.'

Leillu leapt into the air behind him, the wind from her wings a mini gale.

Farlan remained at the top. 'Oi, Traeg ain't called for you, so—'

'I am seeing Captain Traego.' Palom barged past Farlan. Although the sky pirate was a big man—strong and well-built—Palom was a tiger. There was no way he was stopping Palom from getting on board.

'Oi! Stop, you!'

'Captain Traego?' Palom boomed, ignoring Farlan's protests. 'You are going to scout, yes? I will come with you.'

The captain poked his head out of the cabin, a scowl on his face. 'What? Even my crew ain't coming! They been ordered ta rest up and tend ta the injured!'

'I am not your crew. I am not resting.' Palom crossed the deck quickly. 'You are not ordering me about. Princess Isa said it would be good idea if I come along.'

'Princess Isa ain't got no authority on my ship! I don't need ya help ta see if we got an angry Varkain on our tail!' Traego argued, already kicking his engines into life. The rest of his crew—Malot, Antar, Judd, Ernold—made their way off the ship. Farlan glared for a while before deciding to give up the fight, and also scampered down the steps.

'An Ittallan's senses are not to be ignored. I will not speak about your running of ship. I will just keep watch and listen.' Palom squared himself.

Leillu landed beside him, flexing her wings and lashing her tail.

'*Leillu* is also coming with.'

Traego peered out of the cabin again, the scowl on his face deepening. 'Oh great, now I got a fire hazard, too? Look, Palom. I appreciate ya generosity, but it ain't needed. So take ya dragon and get off my ship!'

'Is not happening, Traego. You take your route. I will watch by front of ship. *Leillu* will not cause fire, do not worry.'

Traego opened his mouth to argue again, then huffed. 'Fuck sake, Palom. Ya got some nerve, I tell ya.'

Palom smiled. Even though he was known as "the great tiger," a fact that he'd hated, it had its benefits. 'Good. I am sure our scouting mission will be fast.'

Traego muttered to himself as he navigated *Otella* off the barren rock and into the cool night air.

Palom didn't for one minute believe that Traego was scouting for Princess Isa's sake. Everything a sky pirate did *had* to benefit themselves in some way. At least while he was on *Otella*, he could keep an eye out for any threats while Traego did whatever it was he was doing.

Peering over the side rail into the dark landscape, their makeshift campsite seemed an enormous beacon. Dozens of campfires burned brightly, the contrast even greater against the barren scenery. There were no towns or settlements above ground in Sereth, although there were plenty of tunnels. Most were disused according to Chyro—why would you live so close to a volcano in case one day it awoke—so the chances of any Varkain spotting them was low.

But Palom didn't like it. It seemed too great a risk. 'Their fires are bright.'

Traego didn't reply.

Palom smirked. He wondered how often Traego's command was ever questioned—or overruled. He busied himself with staying alert, patrolling around the edge of *Otella's* deck, working his way across from one side to the other, then back again, ensuring he had a clear view of their surroundings as they flew. Although his vision was better than most, he did not have a scope, and so couldn't see every tiny detail. 'We are flying south, no?'

'Place called Eshkol. Tiny little outpost. Well, I guess it's bigger underground.'

'In Sereth?'

'Uh-huh. We occasionally get Varkain in Estoria. Eshkol is usually where they're from. There's a small beach there. I'm heading to a cove by the water. Ya can guard the ship while we're there.'

'You are meant to be scouting for Princess Isa.' Palom spoke through gritted teeth, annoyed that his assumption about Traego's actions had been proven true.

'Ya scouting for her. I can get on with my business.'

'What business?'

'None o' yours.'

Palom snorted. It was true, he didn't particularly care what business Traego had, as long as it didn't affect Princess Isa or the rest of the Ittallan. 'See this, *Leillu*? I did good work for Traego, yes? Honest work. This is how he treats me.'

Leillu tilted her head to the side, then flapped her wings. She let out a noise—more squeak than roar.

'Exactly right *Leillu*. Is much rudeness.'

Palom grinned when he heard Traego huff. For such a carefree and easy-going sky pirate, Traego certainly had his limits of what he would tolerate. 'Why did you not reprimand Amarah and Antar?'

'What?'

'You know. Tell off? For leaving.'

'I ain't that kinda captain.'

Palom snorted. 'All sky pirates are same. Driven by gold. Jewels. Whatever brings you money.'

'And all ya Ittallan are crazed animals slobbering all over the place.'

Anger flared. 'This is not true.'

'Exactly.'

Palom conceded the point. Perhaps it meant not all Varkain were the same, but that was a harder pill to swallow —even with evidence.

He was glad Traego hadn't decided to take his crew and flee. It seemed that they really were without a home while Estoria was under attack by Brahm's monster. He balled his hands into fists. Odi's words had been ominous. He'd not paid them much attention at the time, but now he had space to think, he wondered whether travelling to the seaside was actually a mistake.

Amarah's *Valta Forinja* was still on board, albeit wrapped up in the ship's hold. Would that monster somehow track them down and attack again?

He shuddered to think about it.

'Maybe same is not true of Arillians,' Palom muttered.

'Maybe. Them and dragons are what we never go near.'

'*Dimok vrakataj* is what we call them in old tongue.'

'*Dimok vrakataj*?' Traego repeated.

'It means,' Palom paused, thinking about it, 'bringer of storms.'

'Storm-bringer is a good description of them damned birds. Still ain't got a clue what happened ta Kohl. But he certainly left with a bang. Now I got half the pirates in Estoria wantin' my blood an' blamin' me 'cause I brought him ta the island.'

'Do they not already want your blood?'

Traego chuckled. 'Well, more'n they normally do.'

Palom tried not to think about Kohl. He'd promised to kill him if ever he saw him again. Everywhere the Arillian went, he brought misery and death. 'I hope Amarah kills Jato soon.'

'Well she's on her way towards that goal.'

Palom raised an eyebrow. A long strip of grey-yellow appeared below them as the shoreline of Sereth's south coast came into view. 'She is?'

Traego let out a short bark of laughter. 'If ya hadn't been in such a hurry ta come with me, ya'd've seen her go.'

'Go?' Palom felt stupid for repeating, but shock had slowed his reactions. 'I didn't know...'

'She'll be back. Always is.'

A blast of energy slammed into *Otella*, tearing the main sail in half and dropping the ship several feet in altitude. *Otella* groaned low, several planks of wooden hull peeling away.

Palom drew his greatsword the moment he felt the shift in the air—almost before he'd consciously realised it. The blade glinted in the yellow moonlight, but he couldn't see anything that had caused the attack. 'Face my blade like warrior!'

Laughter echoed around them. Another burst of energy.

'I'm gettin' *Otella* out the sky! Dragons above! Knew I shoulda used a *Shroud*! Thought it'd be *safe*!' Traego fumbled with the controls, pulling on levers and nose-diving the ship towards the beach below.

Palom let out a snarl.

Leillu hissed and leapt into the air, uncomfortable with the unsteady ship under her claws. She roared as she beat her wings, getting away from *Otella*.

Another blast of invisible energy knocked her from the sky.

'*Leillu*!' Palom screamed, racing to the edge of the deck. He watched as she fell, limp, to the sandy beach below.

Without thought of his own safety, Palom leapt over the edge, diving after her.

The drop had to be fifty feet, or thereabouts. But panic had taken over, and Palom could think of nothing but the safety of his dragon companion.

She landed with a yelp on the beach, crumpling into a heap.

Palom landed beside her a few seconds later. He dropped his sword in the sand and dived towards the dragon, covering her with his body lest there were more invisible strikes he had to contend with. '*Leillu*?' he gasped, one hand on the dragon's cheek. He ignored the pain in his shins.

She trembled under his touch, her body rising and falling with shallow, panicked breaths.

'*Asfali*. You are okay. Stay down. I will fight for you.' The prayer was out of his mouth before he realised what he said.

Leillu chirped, her voice weak.

A short way ahead, *Otella* landed, crunching into the sand with an almighty groan, and sending shockwaves along the beach. Palom braced, one hand on the ground, one on *Leillu* to shelter her from the debris splintering off the ship's hull and the heaps of sand it threw up.

'Non-Varkain are not permitted in this place.' A cold voice cut through the pain and fear like a blade. 'You shall perish for this transgression.'

Deep, primal fear grabbed Palom by the throat and refused to let go. He struggled to breathe.

Leillu whimpered.

He glanced down at the dragon. No blood. Thank Rhea.

'How dare you!' Palom growled, getting to his feet. Terror clutched at his chest. 'I am afraid of no Varkain!'

She slithered into view, striding along the beach as if she owned it. 'I am more than any Varkain you know.' She was tall, with dark hair that fell to the back of her knees. Her skin was typical grey, slightly darker than Sapora, which made her golden eyes seem to glow. Her body was wreathed in thick, red silks of traditional Varkain royalty. The same invisible power that had attacked the ship emanated from her with every step. And poking just over her shoulders were the hilts of swords. Four of them. No—six.

What kind of Varkain fought with so many weapons?

What Varkain could hit him with invisible energy?

Palom straightened, then took a step forward to pick up his own sword from the sand.

Then he realised. '*Emonos*! You...you are Ark?'

A cool smile seemed to split her face in half, rows of ivory fangs poking out from her lips.

It was answer enough for him.

He didn't know where she'd come from or how she'd found them—she was far too close for comfort. It had been less than an hours' flight from the volcano to Eshkol. There would be nothing stopping her from tracking down Isa and destroying the Ittallan gathered there.

He lifted his sword, the tip pointed directly at her. 'I am not afraid of you.'

The Ark cackled. 'Then you must be *very* stupid.' She flicked out her tongue and her eyes shimmered. 'A hunter? No wonder you are so bold. I shall have *fun* with you.' She held her left arm to the side. One of the swords leapt off her back and flew into her waiting hand. 'Let us dance, hunter.'

Palom leapt forward, sword grasped in both hands. He charged over the sand, closing the gap between them in seconds, focussed only on keeping the Ark's attention on himself—not *Leillu*, Traego, or Isa further beyond. He roared as he swung, the blade arcing towards her with all the strength he could muster.

Her blade lifted to meet his, the metal screaming as they kissed—sparks leaping along the length of both weapons.

The vibration shook his fingers, wrists, and arms, but Palom held on, weathering the blow.

He forced her back one step, their blades still pressing against one another, sparks jumping in all directions.

'You are strong,' she said, her voice like silk.

Palom pulled back and swung again, a swift uppercut aimed for her hip.

She stepped away, spinning and grabbing another sword in the same, smooth movement, and blocked his attack. 'You are fast, too. But not enough of either. Not against *me*.'

Palom moved with her, pushing her back with blows.

She blocked every one and hissed at him. 'I am an Ark! You are beneath me, Ittallan!'

'I am Palom. Tiger of Feoras Sol. I have killed Varkain. Arillians. I will defend Linaria against your kind!'

The Ark laughed. 'Interesting, but not good enough, *tiger*.' Then she was on the offensive, darting forward, slipping inside his guard and forcing him to defend against her blades.

His arms stung where her swords sliced into his flesh, but he endured.

'I am Veynothi. I forget how many Ittallan I have killed. Buildings razed. Families slaughtered. You are simply the next mark on my ever-growing tally. Isa will follow, soon enough.'

Veynothi must have seen his shock, because she laughed again, pushed him back with another invisible blow, then raised her two swords in readiness. 'Yes. The mongrel princess will fall to me, soon enough. Once I have—'

Her whole body jerked, eyes wide. Her mouth hung open, limp.

The tip of a long, curved sword appeared through her belly, skewering her.

Palom froze, unsure what had happened.

'No-one hurts Isa. Not while she owes me.' Traego leaned over Veynothi's shoulder, his mouth close to her ear. 'Ya should've told that ta King Sapora.' He twisted the blade and wrenched it out of her body.

Palom braced himself for an explosion of blood and gore —Traego's sword had a serrated edge—but nothing happened.

Veynothi straightened, the sly grin returning. There was no sign of pain on her features. 'Traego. Thief. I've been looking for you.'

The sky pirate gasped. 'Oh, shit.'

She whipped around faster than any of them could blink. She knocked Traego's sword from his hand in one, quick, snap of his wrist.

Traego screamed.

Palom lunged forward.

But Veynothi was faster. With another slash, she drew an arc of crimson on the sand and smacked Traego to his knees. 'You were right, thief. I *was* locked in stone.' She placed one bare foot over his chest, pinning him face-down into the sand. 'But I'm out, now. And I can get you.'

34

Watching *Otella* sail away, shortly followed by *RaKhanna*, Isa wondered if she was doing the right thing. She'd waited so long to build her fleet, and the moment everyone was back together, two of her strongest ships had left.

Traego would be back. Palom would make sure of that.

Amarah, on the other hand? Who knew when she'd return—if she'd even be successful.

Isa had never travelled to Sereth before. Almost all of it was underground, and Vasil didn't permit non-Varkain in his country aside from the thralls who were collected or recruited—their terms for it, she preferred "kidnapped." She'd never had much interest in visiting a place that hated her so vehemently, so she'd always mentally scrubbed the country from her mind.

For her, the world ended at the Feor Mountains, at the Val Sharis-Sereth border.

Now, with Amarah and her sky pirate allies, she had effectively travelled off the map into the deep unknown.

Goosebumps rose along her arms just thinking about it.

This was what she wanted. To keep a step ahead of her enemies, whoever they might be.

Sapora would never consider looking for her in Sereth because it was already his by right. There was no conflict here. And no-one ever willingly went to Sereth. It meant there wouldn't be any surprises, unlike in Estoria.

Here she was, princess of the Varkain and Ittallan, hiding in her father's country, waiting for sky pirates and rebellious Ittallan to join her in her quest for revenge, and take back the land she believed was hers to rule.

She wondered what Vasil, what *Sapora*, would think if they saw her now.

How far she'd come. Or fallen, if Tacio's words were anything to go by.

Isa sat on the prow of one of her twin ships, legs dangling over the edge. She'd made sure they were offloaded before Traego flew away in *Otella*. She wasn't about to make the same mistake twice and accidentally ground herself. Kylos had insisted she stay put and have something to eat, and had gone away to rustle up a meal for her.

For the first time in a long time, Isa was alone. Although night had settled in, she could see well enough. Her first impression of Sereth was of a wasteland.

She supposed that would be obvious, given their location: Mount Kozue was a volcano. Long-since dormant, the history of its eruptions had left clear marks on Sereth; a barren landscape covered in black-red soil and rocks, with only a handful of sparse trees to break up the monotony.

If a land could look anything like death, it did here.

She knew the Varkain lived in their subterranean world, and was sure it would be more inviting, but above ground appeared utterly desolate. A far cry from the lush greenery that covered the rest of the country.

It was no wonder that Sapora had always been keen to get away. If given the choice of a marble palace bathed in sunlight or a city of tunnels plunged in constant darkness, she knew which option she'd choose.

Was she truly a princess of the Varkain, too? If that's how she felt about their country?

Linaria would be better off if she ruled the Ittallan of Val Sharis, and Sapora could be king of the snakes in Sereth, if that's what he wanted. Or Tacio. She didn't care, really, as long as she had her palace back and her people behind her.

She'd rather there was no more bloodshed between them, but after her encounter in Tannon Sona, she'd come to the realisation that it was wishful thinking.

The joint rule over the two races instigated by their father's bloody conquering of Val Sharis had never really taken root. How could you wipe away thousands of years of war and hatred? The truce between the Ittallan and Varkain had been difficult to uphold, with skirmishes carried out on both sides, despite it being forbidden by law. At least Vasil had left Val Sharis to rule themselves with a council of Ittallan.

Sapora's ideals of uniting the Ittallan and Varkain properly had seemed noble at the time—and needed, considering their own mixed blood—but the reality of it hadn't been simple. The Ittallan and the Varkain simply had too much animosity between them.

Her fighting instincts and blood lust came from her father, of that she had no doubt.

But she was no snake. Never had been. One trait didn't define her.

Perhaps it was for their best—and the good of all Linaria—for the Varkain to return to Sereth and the Ittallan to reign supreme in Val Sharis, and especially in Taban Yul. Those Varkain who'd pushed existing residents out would be sent back unless they bought their way in like any other Ittallan wishing to live in the capital.

It would be a true end to the war between her two people.

She'd reinstate a council of Ittallan, maybe even put Odi on it, if he accepted the job. His network would be invaluable, and she wanted people she could trust by her side. Lathri would have been her first choice of council advisor, but everything had gone wrong, and she no longer had the leader of the rebellion with her.

She still felt guilty for that. Lathri had given her life to get Isa out of the palace. Isa would not let her death be in vain.

She shivered.

'Cold? I can grab yeh a blanket if yeh want one.'

Isa gritted her teeth to keep them from chattering. It *had* suddenly become cold. A cool wind blew from the north. It seemed to cut into every patch of bare skin. 'Thanks. I'll wait it out a little longer,' she said, acknowledging Kylos's offer and taking the food from her. It was cold meat—spiced duck, from the smell of it—with shredded fruits and vegetables wrapped in crisp flatbread. She gratefully took a bite, the taste immediately transporting her back to Estoria.

The majority of her followers were still on that tropical island, holding down the forte. Those who were with her now were fighters, ready to leap into action at a moment's notice. She grinned without realising it, excitement racing through her from head to toe. This was the beginning of her own army.

Those who believed in her.

'Thank you, Kylos,' Isa said, remembering her manners after the third bite.

'Yeh welcome. I was honestly afraid we'd never see yeh again.'

Isa couldn't remember the last time anyone had shown her genuine concern, or cared where she was—without an ulterior motive. 'I apologise for worrying you.'

'Yeh did a good job. Archigo Gralla is on board. That's a massive step forward. Everyone in the *country* knows Gralla!'

'It is a step forward. A shame she's stuck here with us and not in Estoria with her people. She's not a warrior. She'd be better off there. That would be incredible for their motivation.' Isa didn't care about the petulance in her voice.

'Well, nothing's really gone teh plan, has it?' Kylos chewed on her own dinner. 'But we adapt. That's what we've always done teh survive. This is still progress. We'll be able teh get her teh the others soon enough.'

Isa had to commend the woman's positivity. She was blunt. Sometimes more so than even Amarah, but Kylos was never malicious. She simply wanted what was best for her family and the rest of the Ittallan. Her tune had changed after Isa had rescued her from the palace dungeons—the air of skepticism Kylos had always carried towards her vanishing overnight, and she'd been a constant shadow ever since. Even after Lathri's passing, she'd endured, always acting in the best interests of her people, and managing the Ittallan in Isa's absence.

'Give it a few days and Tannon Sona will calm down again. Can ferry Archigo Gralla back, have her take steps teh move her people to Estoria. The Imperial Guard of the town will follow her orders. Most of 'em follow individual Archigo, anyway. Any who're on Sapora or Tacio's side would probably have already gone with 'em.'

'Just think, by the time we get back to Estoria, there'll be an army waiting for us.' Isa imagined gathering her troops and sailing for Val Sharis with an army at her side.

'Exactly. Then we'll get rid of that dirty snake!'

Kylos's words stung. She was against Sapora, true, but he was still her brother. He'd fought oppression all his life, too.

'How is Carav doing?' Isa asked, changing the subject.

Kylos took another two large bites, finishing the rest of her food. 'She's good, considering. Those sky pirates are hard teh keep down. Malot is looking after her for the most part. Our fighters definitely got off lighter. A night or two teh recover their strength is all they'll need.'

That was reassuring. She knew the Ittallan were tough. They'd been oppressed for so long, constantly fighting against the Varkain for their right to live on their own lands. This *would* be the end of it. Not only being named queen, but ending the war between Ittallan and Varkain—for good.

Isa changed into the fresh clothes Kylos had brought for her, but she kept Gralla's sword attached to her hip. Although she was more used to fighting in close quarters with knives, she wasn't a bad hand with a sword. She would never be able to wield something bigger, like Palom's greatsword, but the short blade at her hip was more than comfortable. She also liked the idea of fighting with a weapon gifted to her by the Archigo. If nothing else, it was a visual representation that the Archigo stood with her. A queen *of* the people, instead of a king *above* them.

It was strange. Lathri had claimed the people wanted her as queen. Isa had struggled to believe it, but Lathri's goals had aligned with her own desires for respect—and in some way, to instil justice against those who'd always put her down. It hadn't been exclusively the Varkain. There were plenty of Ittallan Goldstones who had looked down at her.

Many on the council, too.

Even the palace staff had begrudgingly followed orders or obeyed commands whenever they came from her. She'd lost track of the number of times Koraki would conveniently forget a request or deliberately misconstrue it. Not to mention the huffing and eye rolls she'd endured whenever she'd entered a room.

Sapora had been the only thing to keep the staff in line.

And it was only out of fear.

The more time she'd spent away from the palace, the more she'd realised that place was a bubble. Most people in Val Sharis feared or despised the Varkain, and having one on the throne had sown the seeds of rebellion.

People saw her as one of them. An Ittallan. Not a mongrel or a half-breed who didn't fit in either world, but someone worthy of following. Of fighting with, and dying for.

The battle against Tacio and his Cerastes in Tannon Sona had proven that to Isa in a way that she could hardly believe. It boosted her confidence, gave her strength.

When she patrolled the makeshift campsite, the Ittallan revered her. They clutched her hands in theirs, wished her well, offered to share their food—some even bowed. It was the complete opposite of what she'd been used to in the palace. And even though she'd left them in Estoria when fear and paranoia had taken hold, they didn't begrudge her for it.

She wondered if their positive mood would last when it came to marching on the palace and standing their ground against Sapora, Tacio, and their snakes. After all, she was about to lead them into another civil war. There would be deaths on both sides.

Would she be forgiven for that, too, she wondered.

'Yeh awful quiet, princess. If yeh don't mind me sayin' so,' Kylos said.

'I have...many things on my mind.'

Kylos nodded knowingly. 'Anythin' I can help yeh with, just say the word!'

In truth, Isa didn't know *what* would help. She thought

best when she moved, not when she sat down and talked about things. She'd always been like it, even as a child. Always moving. Always thinking—it was the only way she could figure anything out. 'I might patrol again.'

'Chyro and Aetos are on duty,' Kylos said. 'Yeh can sit and save energy.'

Isa scowled. 'I'm fine to—'

'Please. We nearly lost yeh once already. Let 'em do what they followed yeh for.'

She didn't like it, even though Kylos made sense.

'I'll get yeh a blanket. It's late. Try and get some sleep if yeh can. I imagine once that Traego comes back, we'll have a better idea of our surroundings and figure out where yeh can go next.'

'All right, Kylos. Thank you.' Isa wasn't at all grateful, but she was used to putting on manners for other people. She didn't want to be pushed and pulled around, told what to do, when to sleep, when to work. But she was exhausted, physically and mentally. With a full belly, laying down to get some rest wasn't a bad idea.

She sat down, her back resting against the mast on her ship, as she watched Kylos make her way towards one of the nearest fires to get her a blanket.

Isa smiled at how much things had changed, and closed her eyes.

~

SLEEP DIDN'T COME EASILY. While most of the Ittallan eventually drifted off, their fires burning low in the cool night air, sleep eluded the princess. She had too many things on her mind, too many problems to work out.

Traego hadn't said when he would be back. How long did it take to scout the area, anyway? She assumed it came down to how far out he went. At this rate, he wouldn't be back until dawn. Isa tried to push the worry away. Palom was with him. She didn't need to concern herself with the sky pirate if he had the great tiger as an escort.

Amarah had left on her mission to find a Sevastos.

There'd been so many misunderstandings between herself and Amarah that Isa was amazed she still did anything in aid of her campaign.

Biting insects and flies buzzed around the low flames, their high-pitched wings making Isa flinch every time one came too near—further distracting her from sleep. It was a small price to pay to be safe.

Another insect hissed.

She flinched involuntarily and rolled onto her other side. Her tiny class five was brilliant at travelling quickly. But it made an awful bed. Even with a blanket on the floor and another over her, it was awkward and squashed. More used to sleeping in a barn than on a bed, Isa had thought roughing it would be easy. But a class five was nothing like the comparative luxury of Amarah's *RaKhanna* or Traego's *Otella*.

Another buzz. Another hiss.

Wait.

Isa sat up, fully alert. She held her breath, ears straining to hear over the snoring and muttering of dozens of sleeping Ittallan.

'What is it princess?' Solvi slunk towards her, a shadow in the dark. 'Is something wrong?'

Isa shouldn't have been surprised the young Ittallan was also awake. 'I'm not sure. Thought I heard something.'

Solvi deftly leapt onto the deck of the tiny airship and turned her face to the wind. Eyes closed, she listened.

Isa closed her eyes, too, listening intently. It had almost sounded like...

'A Varkain?' Solvi whispered. 'I thought no-one lived near the volcano?'

'So did I,' Isa whispered back. 'I'm going to investigate.'

'Princess, you mustn't! Let me wake Kylos or Chyro!'

'And start a panic? Don't be silly. Sounds like there's only one.' Isa scrambled off the edge of the ship, dropping a few feet to the ground. The rocks and pebbles slipped underfoot, rolling away. 'Keep back, Solvi. No need for you to get involved.'

Isa stalked through the darkness, keeping away from the low fires to stay hidden. A Varkain might have superior hearing and speed, but her night vision was unmatched. One hand on the scabbard of her sword, Isa prowled along as stealthily as she could. The Varkain didn't hiss again, but she knew the rough direction it had come from.

She hoped it was a young one. A child, perhaps, who had decided to explore some of the disused tunnels. It was the sort of thing she and Sapora had done as children—escaping the watchful eyes of the guard in whose care they'd been placed, while they explored hidden or sealed off areas of the palace or city. She'd discovered the old stairwell to the back of the dungeons that way.

If that was the case, all they'd need would be a stern telling off. Perhaps a show of her blade to prove she wasn't joking, and that would be the end of it.

Light snoring filled the air around her, muddling her hearing. She paused frequently, ears straining. More than once, Isa wondered if she'd misheard, or the Varkain who'd hissed had simply run off.

If that was the case, she had to act fast. She couldn't risk being spotted by even a single Varkain—they wouldn't be long coming back with reinforcements, or worse, a Cerastes—and they'd be in even more trouble.

Pebbles shifted under her every step, and she threatened

to slip. Isa swore under her breath with every stumble.

'Even a kitten like you can lose their footing here,' a voice whispered somewhere to her left.

Isa whirled around to face the voice. She'd recognise it anywhere. 'Tacio. I should have known it was you slithering around in the dark.'

He laughed, mirthless, then went quiet.

Isa fought to keep dread from rising and followed the sound of his laughter as it echoed away. She didn't care that she was walking into a very obvious trap. Didn't care to know how he'd managed to track her down after they'd tried so hard to hide themselves.

She was going to put a stop to him once and for all.

She'd already beaten him twice. There was no more time for games.

The thought of him so close to her Ittallan made her toes curl. How *dare* he try to take everything from her. Was she permitted nothing in life unless she took it for herself? Fought for it, tooth and claw?

Isa almost snarled as she ran towards him. He could have been alone, he could have had an entire battalion of Cerastes waiting with him.

None of it mattered.

Racing along in the dark, she tried to avoid patches of ground that moved under her feet—a twisted ankle now would be the worst thing that could happen to her—while gaining on her half-brother. She saw him ahead, keeping as still as a statue.

She grasped the hilt of her sword, ready to draw it as she closed in on him, and put on a final burst of speed.

The ground gave way—rocks and stones crumbling into a massive hole that suddenly appeared beneath her feet. Isa yelped in surprise as solid ground disintegrated into nothing, and she plummeted into the widening hole.

35

There was no denying it.

Aciel's power washed through the city like a hurricane the moment lightning had cracked the crystal. Sapora had known the Arillian lived, even if he didn't understand *how*.

Now, the floodgates had opened.

His time had run out.

Captain Tethkari's body twitched. He took a step towards Sapora. Raised his sword.

Sapora dodged to the right, a moment before the other Varkain struck, his movement bringing him to the edge of the tower's top. Malashash, thankfully, appeared unaffected by Aciel's compulsion. The Valendrin, however, sank to his knees, clutched his head, and murmured as if overcome by pain, fear, or both. Sapora ignored him, his attention on Tethkari as the captain spun on his heel, bringing his sword around for another strike.

'Captain! Cease this! Sapora is your *king*!' Malashash roared, diving in between the two. Tethkari's sword slammed into the Ark's arm and it rebounded with a deafening crack.

'He is not himself. Arillian magic has done this!' Sapora

hissed. He jumped back, away from Tethkari and the Ark. Malashash could deal with Tethkari. That was his job.

Sapora turned his attention back to the city wall and the crystal beyond. Light burst from the crack, spilling out like water. Arillians filled the air, lightning snapping in all directions along with gale force winds. More of them flew away, circling high and diving back down, sending more wind over to the city.

Lightning streaked over the walls and into the nearest buildings, crashing into them, sending sparks flying in all directions.

His soldiers on the city walls leapt into action, firing bolts from their ballista and scattering the Arillians even further. Beyond the plains, the Feor Mountains loomed, dark and misty. A dragon appeared—his Sevastos.

'About time,' Sapora muttered under his breath. He had no idea where the dragon had been, or what it had been doing, but that was in the past. It was here now, thank Rhea, and it could help them turn the tide of this siege before it was too late.

Several bolts flew through the air, missing their targets, only to be blasted off by more lightning struck in retaliation. The ballista had been set up at regular intervals, prepared since the first Arillian storm appeared on the city's horizon, but only now called into action.

The Arillians had never been close enough to launch a full scale attack—nor for him to launch one on them—and had been kept at bay by the Sevastos patrolling Taban Yul's skies, aside from when it had decided to go off on a long flight.

Sapora wasn't sure if they'd waited for the dragon to be out of range before they attacked the city, or it was just coincidence.

The Arillians had downed almost all ships flying into or

out of the city, forcing supplies to be brought to Val Sharis by ship and carted over the land in wagons. It sowed more seeds of discontent within the city, which was why he'd been so desperate to resurrect the Arks. Once he had those, he'd be unstoppable. He could put an end to the Arillians on his doorstep, weed out any rebels within his city, and find Isa.

He hadn't expected Jato to make the first move, and he detested being on the back foot.

Malashash and Tethkari clashed behind him. The captain attempted—and failed—to get past the Ark to attack Sapora. He hissed, his eyes empty. Aciel wanted *him* dead, then. The Arillian's warning through the Valendrin had been more than a threat—his control over the captain was proof of that.

Sapora wondered how much power Aciel had while sealed. If that seal could be broken by Jato's lightning, he hoped the Sevastos dragons were not weaker than he'd originally thought. But the crystal remained whole, and even now, the light that had poured out began to slow.

He needed to stop it. Sapora raised his scimitar to the sky. Weak sunlight filtered through the clouds and glinted off the flat of the blade like a beacon. 'If you want to kill the king, Jato, I am right here!' He didn't know how well his voice would carry, or if the Arillians would even take notice of him.

'King Sapora?' the Valendrin moaned. He remained on his knees, cowering.

'Aciel's compulsion might be awakened, but Jato is the one causing *this*. Their leader,' Sapora said, his gaze still locked on the flock of Arillians outside the city walls. He gestured to the damaged ballista, the injured soldiers on the walls, and the scent of electrical burning. '*I'll* take her out.'

'My king!' Malashash's warning almost came too late.

Captain Tethkari ducked past the Ark and hurled himself at Sapora.

Fast as Sapora was, Tethkari was faster. With a roar any Ittallan would be proud of, the captain careened into Sapora's midriff, arms wrapping around his back in a tight grip. The momentum of Tethkari's movement pushed him off-balance, teetering on the edge of the tower.

Sapora opened his arms wide, trying to balance, to slow himself.

'*Only death awaits you, maggot.*'

Sapora drove his scimitar into the back of Tethkari's neck—the only part of him he could reach. It crunched through bone. Blood gushed from the wound, Tethkari shuddered and went limp.

They both fell off the tower's edge.

Something cold raced through Sapora's belly at the sudden realisation there was nothing underfoot.

'My king!'

Hands as rough as stone clutched the front of Sapora's silk robe—the fabric immediately tearing. Malashash pulled harder and grabbed Sapora under the shoulder with his other arm.

The violent yank hurt, but the Ark caught Sapora mid-air, and pulled him back onto the tower.

Sapora winced, staggering once he was back on his feet.

'Are you well, my king?' Malashash asked.

Sapora ran a hand through his hair. His heart pounded painfully. It was the most fear he'd experienced in his life.

He'd been a hair's breadth away. It had thrown him so much that he didn't even think to reprimand Malashash for letting his guard down in the first place.

And Tethkari has been so promising. Strong, fast, obedient. Aciel had taken him away in an instant. Forced him to kill his own captain.

'Your shirt,' the Valendrin said, shakily getting to his feet. He pointed at the ripped fabric.

Sapora waved him away, only to notice his jacket sleeve had peeled away at the seams where Malashash had grabbed it. The fabric split apart, and his sleeve ripped away, taken by a gust of wind barely a moment later.

The robe Sapora wore underneath his jacket was short-sleeved and lightweight, better for speed and manoeuvrability. With his bare arm now revealed, he, Malashash, and the Valendrin saw the myriad of black lines criss crossing the length of his skin like the roots of a vast tree, from fingertip to beyond his shoulder. They pulsed with his heartbeat.

'M—my king!' both his servants gasped in unison.

Sapora scowled. There was no *time* for this. Aciel was on the brink of release, Jato and her Arillians were launching a full scale attack on the city, and his Sevasos was as defiant as ever.

There was no Veynothi. No Tacio. No Isa.

'It is nothing,' Sapora said. There was no point in hiding it any longer, so he opted to ignore it.

'But—' Malashash began.

'I said it is *nothing*.' Sapora curled his lip as he turned his back to them, attention returning to the battle rampaging along the city's walls, more upset about Tethkari's death than he cared to admit.

Many of the decorative, golden status that topped the walls had been damaged or outright destroyed. White marble had blackened, and several members of the Imperial Guard limped away, injured by the Arillians' strikes. 'We may not live to see this day out. If we do survive, worry about it then.' Sapora clenched his fist, his vision blurred.

There would be plenty of time for investigations and discussions about his skin changes *after* the Arillians had been dealt with. He needed to focus on the here and now.

Another slip up like with Tethkari, and everything would be for nothing.

And if Aciel's compulsion had broken free...could affect his own soldiers...

'Malashash! I need you in the city. Get into the streets. Ensure my soldiers are not under Aciel's command, like Tethkari. Keep the people inside and safe!'

'At once, my king.' Malashash bowed, raced ahead, and leapt off the tower's edge.

Sapora blinked as the Ark darted past him, a light breeze the only thing he felt, for Malashash moved so quickly. The grey and red robed mass of the defender disappeared into the streets of Taban Yul. Sapora was impressed. He knew the Arks were immortal, but surely they felt *pain*? A drop from that height would have killed him. Malashash had willingly made the jump.

Sapora couldn't stand to think that Aciel could control another member of the guard. Forcing them to slaughter their own people was underhanded, even for his taste.

The only silver lining in this entire farce was that Aciel appeared to only be able to fully control one person at a time. It made sense, considering he was sealed. He didn't know how much longer that would remain true.

More lightning charged along the city walls, scorching the streets with every flash. Buildings burned. People screamed. Rooftops caught alight.

Sapora glared at the destruction below.

'What are your orders, King Sapora?' the Valendrin asked, hobbling to Sapora's side and clutching his robes like a Goldstone woman might clutch her skirts at a ball. Thankfully, he'd stopped whimpering like a kicked puppy.

Evacuating the city was not an option. It was too large, there was too little time, and he couldn't trust any of his captains to not suddenly turn on the people. Aciel was like a ghost, invisible save when he possessed others—forcing them to speak or act against their will.

And if Sapora was forced to kill all his own warriors...

No. He wouldn't let that happen. This was *his* city. He was charged with keeping it safe.

If he couldn't defend it from one Arillian, then he might as well give the jade crown to Tacio.

Containing Aciel was about the only thing he *could* do. The crystal had done a reasonably good job of that thus far, save a little of Aciel's strength seeping out. But the crystal wouldn't hold for long if Jato and her followers had anything to do with it.

It left only one course of action.

'I will kill Jato. Scatter the remaining Arillians with the Sevastos. Left to it, they might split the crystal and there'll be no turning back if that happens.' Sapora had always assumed Aciel would free himself at some point. He knew a Sevastos was nothing more than a beast, one that could be tamed, broken, and killed. Their magic, though formidable, was not infallible.

It was only going to be a matter of time, and it was why he'd wanted to amass all the power in Linaria to stop the damned Arillian when he rose again.

He had *not* expected Aciel's compulsion to slow things down and affect his city before he was ready.

Sapora exhaled slowly. How in all of Linaria was he meant to kill Jato while she flew hundreds of feet in the air?

'Why not have the Sevastos burn them all?'

Sapora folded his arms, ignoring the Valendrin's stares at his bare skin. 'It *must* be me. The people of the city will never respect me, otherwise. Not truly.' But the Valendrin's words gave him an idea of just how to get Jato's attention.

Aciel spoke through his people.

He would speak through someone else, too.

Sapora clamped down hard on the thread connecting himself with the Sevastos. The dragon wouldn't be immune to their lightning, but it was so old and powerful that it could endure their assault long enough for his message.

'Fly to them. Hover. Speak my words.'

A snarl was his answer, but the dragon obeyed. Resplendent in vivid red scales, the enormous beast growled low, wings spread wide as it soared over the plains towards Taban Yul. The Sevastos was indeed a creature of incredible strength and beauty. Perhaps the oldest of any dragon living, as it had served his ancestors five thousand years ago, and it was all the stronger for its age. It would serve its purpose well enough.

Although it was at least a league from the city walls, the Sevastos's presence spread awe and fear through the people.

Beside him, the Valendrin trembled.

'You have nothing to fear. It is a beast. We are above them,' Sapora said.

'Yes, King Sapora. Of course. It...it's just—'

'Hush. They will hear me speak.'

With a deafening bellow, the Sevastos crossed the plains effortlessly, its enormous wings taking up the entire sky. Several Arillians let loose bolts of lightning to deter it as it grew closer to them, but their attacks bounced off its hardened scales like raindrops.

When their attacks proved ineffective, more of them flew away, gusts of wind thrown in all directions, only to wheel back a moment later. They whirled around in a wide arc, circling around the centre of their group—Jato.

Sapora narrowed his eyes as the Sevastos drew nearer.

He took a breath and spoke. The dragon opened its mouth, the king's words booming from its throat so loud that not just the Arillians heard, but the entirety of Taban Yul.

'Jato. You and your Arillians have caused nothing but destruction since you arrived in my land. This will cease immediately, else I shall rend you from existence. So speaks Sapora, King of Val Sharis and Sereth.'

It seemed to Sapora that Taban Yul went quiet at the words. Fires still raged, buildings still crumbled. But the people halted in their terror, looking up and around for the enormous dragon who spoke with the king's voice, and the enemy at their gates who now had to answer his challenge.

Even the Valendrin held his breath.

Sapora concentrated on the Sevastos, who explained that Jato laughed at his words. From the dragon's tone, it, too, shared in the Arillians' amusement. He wasn't sure whether Jato would give in to his bait and accept his challenge or simply lay waste to the city.

From his brief encounter with her on her warship, he recalled she had something of a temper.

'Laugh all you like. But you refuse to fight me? You are nothing but a weakling. A coward, held up by those in your service too stupid to see the truth.'

Their hilarity ceased at once.

Sapora braced himself. His left arm throbbed now the marks were exposed to the cool air. *'I challenge you, Jato. But do not get your hopes up for victory. I have never been bested in combat. This is how I won the jade crown. Became king. And it is how I will save Taban Yul from you and your despicable people.'*

'Is that wise? Her allies could intervene and—'

'Her followers will lose faith the moment my fangs sink into her. Those under Aciel's compulsion were the same at the end of the last battle. This one will be no different.' Sapora drew his other scimitar, inspecting it out of habit. He didn't need to. The edge was as sharp as always.

'And your arm?'

Sapora scowled at him. 'My arm is *your* area of expertise,

blood mage. Unless it is going to fall off, I do not have time to concern myself with it. Taban Yul burns,' he gestured over the city, 'I am trying to put a halt to this siege in the swiftest way possible. You doubt my skills?'

'Never, my king.' The Valendrin prostrated himself.

Sapora had never been keen on fawning behaviour, but it was better than being second-guessed at every step. 'Good.'

'Where will you do battle? Here, she would have the advantage.'

Sapora hadn't wanted to walk through the palace with his arm exposed, let alone in the city streets. Far too many people would see the marks. Tongues would wag. Fear and confusion would grow like a festering wound.

Then again, Tethkari had managed to get the better of him on the tower roof, and he was only another Varkain. Admittedly a highly trained one, but he had still come close to perishing. Even if Jato's wings had been clipped, she could still use lightning. At such close range, dodging would be impossible.

Sapora licked his lips as he thought, considering his admittedly few possibilities for what would give him the greatest advantage.

The Sevastos spoke in his mind only two words: *she accepts.*

Taban Yul had often been referred to as the city of gold, despite only a handful of streets having any gold on them. Rumours, gossip, and fantastical stories were always more widespread than an often mundane truth, especially when it came to the Ittallan flaunting their wealth.

Sapora had thought the city earned its nickname

because of the Goldstones who lived there. They brought their wealth with them, constructed ever taller, larger, and more opulent houses, employing people and helping the city grow. The richer districts congregated near the palace. They enjoyed vast gardens, exotic artefacts, statues, and fountains carved from marble, silver, or gold.

When Sapora's Sevastos had awoken after being transported from Sereth, it had laid waste to the fleet of ships attacking the palace. Its fires had burned indiscriminately, damaging parts of Taban Yul.

Yet, the Goldstones had not been affected. Their districts were far enough away from the site of destruction, and they continued living as if nothing had changed.

When Aciel's will began to creep through the city, infecting people and killing the most unfortunate, it had been largely confined to the eastern districts, where the poor congregated.

Again, the Goldstones had not been affected.

But when Sapora strolled through the city, the Valendrin at his side, he saw the terror plain on their faces for the first time. Goldstones were *not* immune to Arillian lightning. They were as likely to be killed as a homeless peasant.

They shrieked their indignation; their fear, their anger that he had not protected them. Their homes burned, or were irrevocably damaged. They demanded recompense.

In fact, they were so concerned with their own monetary value and losses, that they didn't notice—or comment—on the black marks snaking along his arms.

But among the crowds of people pushing and shoving to get away, or get close to the king, Sapora saw Varkain. His own people, watching from alleys and low doorways. Huddled together for comfort and safety.

Their eyes flicked down to his bare skin, and their expressions shifted from wonder to disgust.

They recoiled.

Sapora added their disgusted reactions to his own, personal armour. He wore it day and night, a mental block that kept the opinions of the stupid or the unworthy from affecting him. More fuel for his internal fire that burned cold.

His entire life revolved around doubters telling him what he could and couldn't do, then throwing their thoughts back in their face as he overcame more of his perceived weaknesses.

Slaughtering Jato in full view of his Sevastos, the Valendrin, an Ark, and a city of his people was the next milestone.

Malashash met them at one of the larger squares in the middle of Taban Yul. A row of the Imperial Guard lined up along the edges of the square—four on each, sixteen in total—their spears held aloft.

Sapora half-expected any one of their eyes to roll back and turn white, but there was nothing aside from steely determination on their faces. They barred entrance to the square at each of the roads intersecting it, not that there were many people trying to get a good viewing spot, considering sections of the city burned.

Perhaps Aciel was not as strong as Sapora had first assumed, and needed time to possess another person. He hoped that would be the case, for he was confident Jato would be long dead by then. And he didn't want one of his soldiers to turn on him in the middle of the fight.

'The two districts closest to the eastern gate have been cleared. We're working our way west, using taverns and halls to house the citizens. Don't want them out in the open,' Malashash said.

'Good.' Sapora could only acknowledge their efforts. His eyes were cast skywards, where the Sevastos and close to one hundred Arillians filled the air. Thunder rippled around them, but no bolts of lightning were thrown. No hiss preceding a sneak attack.

Jato stood out among the others. One wing was considerably shorter than the other, though both were in bad shape. Jagged and rough, the feathers looked like they'd been sawn clean off. She wore the same armour he remembered from the warship—more ceremonial than functional—and her short, blonde hair was wild, like her eyes.

'Are you certain?' the Valendrin whispered.

Sapora ignored him, strolling out into the centre of the square. Daily markets were held here, vendors wheeling in their carts to flaunt their goods from all over Val Sharis and beyond each morning. The market had dwindled over the past few weeks as supplies struggled to make it past the Arillians, then the council had agreed to turn it into a weekly market instead of daily. Everything had been cleared away, save a few empty barrels bundled in one corner of the square.

It meant the paved street was wide and mercifully empty, surrounded on all four sides by tall buildings—counting houses, merchants guilds, a house of laws, and the mint itself, where all Linarian coins were produced.

Behind the tall, white buildings, thick, black smoke rose from parts of Taban Yul that were still aflame. It was a stark contrast of colour and brightness.

Across the square, Jato and a handful of her Arillians landed, loose feathers carried away on the wind they brought with them.

'The maggot calls himself *king*.' Jato's voice carried over the noise.

Sapora wasn't surprised that her first words to him were an insult. He smirked. 'You can't even fly. You can hardly call *yourself* an Arillian.'

Jato pulled herself up to her full height, shoving the handful of Arillians with her out of the way. She strolled across the square, sending out a flurry of cool wind with every step.

Sapora braced against it. Arillians were all about intimidation, and Jato was grounded. She'd be zero threat. As long as her followers kept out of it, of course. He bent his knees slightly, readying himself. There were no more dramatic announcements, no controlling the crowd.

He was here to kill Jato, nothing more needed to be said.

The Sevastos hovered, plunging the square into shadow, its wingbeats creating more wind above the two combatants.

Jato held her palms up and spread her wings wide, revealing the extent of the damage to them. She was missing patches of feathers, two large sections of her left wing had been cut up, and some chunks were completely gone.

Sapora knew she needed her wings to fly. She didn't need them to attack.

Blue light flickered at her palms, bright and dazzling. Sparks of electricity jumped between her fingers as she created a ball of lightning. 'I'll enjoy cutting you down piece by piece!' Jato threw the ball of electricity towards his face.

Sapora dived to the ground, her attack whizzing overhead as he rolled towards her. He came up and immediately darted to the right as she fired another attack at him, faster than the first. The electricity scored along his bare arm, burning his skin where it struck.

He groaned in pain but didn't have time to do anything other than dodge her next attack. She sent balls and bolts of lightning faster than he could blink—he'd never known an Arillian to attack so quickly. Her furious onslaught meant Spora couldn't get within striking distance.

His side ached and his skin burned where her attacks caught him, and he panted, every breath painful. The

Varkain used stealth to attack—ambushing their targets and striking too quickly for them to get away. The element of surprise was everything. And when he didn't have it, his outright speed usually gave him the upper hand.

He was not designed for long, drawn out battles. It was why the gauntlet to win the jade crown was so taxing.

Jato laughed again. 'Maggot getting tired? Too bad. I'm having *far* too much fun to stop, now. And once you're nothing more than a smoking pile in the dirt, I'll shatter the dragon crystal sealing my Aciel and bring him back!' Her laughter stretched towards the heavens.

Sapora lunged, his scimitar slashing at her chest.

She brought her arm up to block his strike, her vambrace connecting with his blade.

Sapora slammed his other scimitar into her body, the blade digging into her unprotected torso. When it sliced through her clothes, he pressed harder—into her flesh.

Jato yelped and kicked out with her heavy boot, the toe digging into his thigh and dropping him to his knees.

He let go of the blade in her torso and tightened his hold on the one she'd deflected. Cutting down quickly, his blade caught her leg, but skittered off her greaves. Sapora rolled away and stood up, panting. He'd lost one scimitar but had drawn blood.

It was a start.

Jato grimaced as she pulled the blade out of her—the edge biting in, but not deep, given the small amount of blood on the weapon. 'By the Golems. I don't know how long it's been since someone was able to cause me physical pain.' Her voice was low, almost reverent.

Sapora snorted. 'Hold still and I'll deal you pain like you'd never thought possible.'

She laughed, but it wasn't a high cackle. 'Try it, maggot. You're already dead, you know.' She waved her hand, and a fierce gust of wind knocked Sapora back several paces.

He grimaced.

'Those marks on your flesh. They'll kill you,' Jato said, walking towards him casually. Another blast of wind—so ferocious it was like a solid wall.

Sapora narrowed his eyes. Of all people to see his skin, he hadn't expected the Arillian to understand what they meant. 'You're lying.'

Jato's lip twitched. 'Why would I lie? You're only a maggot. I'm going to kill you. Consider it a mercy. You deserve the slow death those marks will give you, but you have chosen to face me here, and die today. I have permitted you that privilege.'

Something cold rippled through him. He clenched and unclenched his fist, wishing he could dart forward and pick up the scimitar she'd discarded.

She fired a short burst of lightning at him—a continuous stream that scorched the paving stones black and sent debris flying.

People around him cheered or cried out—a mixture of Ittallan and Varkain citizens, and the Imperial Guard who tried to keep them out of harm's way. Clearly the city being half on fire did not deter people from watching him fight Jato despite them trying to flee only a few minutes previously.

He hoped Malashash was able to keep everyone under control, especially if Aciel's compulsion took over another of his soldiers.

Sapora's thought wandered to the marks on his arm, what they had to do with the Arks, and how Jato—of all people—knew what they meant.

He took a deep breath. Losing focus was the quickest

way to come off worse in a fight, and Jato would be fighting to the death.

He fought in front of an *Ark*. The thought of letting Malashash see how weak he was spurred him on. 'I care little for the opinions of birds. *Your* blood will stain these streets. Not mine!' Sapora lunged instead of dodging her next attack, nipping inside her guard and bringing up his scimitar across her chin in a violent uppercut.

Jato leapt back, flapping her wings uselessly to get away, but the crimson slash across her face was bright against her pale skin.

His blade had cut off the tip of her nose. Now she'd moved away, Sapora bent over to pick up his other scimitar. A weapon in each hand again, he breathed a sigh of relief. He was back in control.

Jato clutched her face with one hand, blood pouring from her chin, nose, and forehead. 'H—how dare you!' The ball of lightning she hurled at him was bigger and faster than any before. Sparks flared out in every direction, lighting up the square and bouncing off the armour of the Imperial Guard.

Sapora couldn't get out of the way in time, and the electrical energy careened into him, stinging every nerve ending. Gritting his teeth, Sapora weathered the pain, but it left his vision spotty, his fingers twitching. He tasted blood.

'Look at what you've done to me, maggot!' Jato practically snarled, spittle flying from her lips. She battered him into the ground with more wind, lightning crackling all the while. Blood poured off her face as she stalked towards him, every step another blast of frigid wind that kept him pinned in place.

Sapora groaned, his face pressed into the ground. Loose paving slabs and pebbles swirled around in her raging storm, flung against him, tearing skin and clothes indiscriminately. He turned his head, watching her approach through one eye.

'Once Aciel is free, he—'

Sapora grabbed hold of her ankle, holding it in a vice-like grip. 'That'll *never* happen, Jato.' Pushing her down, he pulled himself up and kicked her in the chin. Her head snapped backwards, and he held one scimitar across her exposed throat. He pressed the edge into her skin and crouched down beside her, taking a moment to catch his breath now he had his prey under control.

She glared at him with bloodshot eyes, wings fluttering uselessly.

Wind and lightning burst around them—a tempest of fury and pain. But Sapora was too close for it to be effective. The wind ruffled his hair and jacket but couldn't harm him. He leaned forward, savouring the pleasure of his mastery. The battle was his. 'I should have killed you on that airship. Unfortunately, I was somewhat out of practice, back then.'

Sapora opened his jaws wide, his fangs extending. His voice shifted into a low grumble. 'I won't repeat that mistake.' He bit down, fangs piercing her flesh and drawing blood.

It had been a long time since he'd killed anything with his own venom—the preferred Varkain way to end a battle. There was a dizzying pleasure in it. Something that couldn't be explained, seeing a life slowly sicken and wither away at his own touch.

Jato gasped.

Sapora backed off, blood dripping from his scimitar and mouth.

She clutched her throat, but already her breathing had slowed, her tongue thickening and eyes bulging as the venom crept through her body.

Sapora took a shuddering breath. Overhead, the

Sevastos bellowed, unleashing a plume of white-hot fire at the remaining Arillians, their screams of anguish shifting into screams of pain.

Something loud filled his head. A roaring as if he stood under a rushing waterfall, and it was nothing to do with the dragon or the flapping wings. The noise grew in intensity, almost burning loud in his head. He blinked slowly, turning around with a scowl.

The Valendrin raced across the square, Malashash in tow. Behind them, more of his own Varkain ran, Ittallan, too. Soldiers. Citizens. They waved, frantic, their mouths open, leaping over broken slabs of paving and avoiding the damage caused by Jato's lightning.

Sapora blinked again.

Were they...were they *cheering*?

'You are victorious!' the blood mage cheered, his face more animated than Sapora had ever seen.

'A battle of a true warrior. I am greatly honoured to serve you.' Malashash bowed low, his red silk robes the same colour as the blood pooling on the paved street.

Sapora didn't know what to do, how to react. He'd been confident in his victory, but there had been several moments where even his own assurances had wavered.

'My king, a Varkain entered the palace while you were atop the tower. We ordered him to wait, considering the situation,' Malashash said, suddenly remembering. 'Once this has been cleared, I shall bring you to him.'

People wanting to see the king wasn't new. Sapora shrugged, somehow lost amidst all the praise and cheering. 'Did he have a name?'

'Roke. Said he returned with word of a Captain of the Imperial Guard named Morgen.'

The Ark's words brought the world into sudden, bright, clarity. Sapora wiped his blades clean on his torn robes, then sheathed them. They'd need to be thoroughly cleaned and treated as soon as possible. Malashash needed his armour forging, too.

More work to do.

He looked up. Despite parts of Taban Yul being on fire and the crystal sealing Aciel cracked, the city cheered him. Jato lay dying and her Arillians were driven off, re-opening the skies for trade and travel.

The Ittallan citizens looked at him through tears of joy as they screamed and hugged one another in celebration. They didn't see him as a disgusting Varkain or a mongrel, unworthy of the palace. They saw him as Malashash did—as their true king and the saviour of their city.

Sapora raised his chin as the Imperial Guard celebrated along with the people, before trying half-heartedly to clear the streets and make way for King Sapora as he returned to the palace victorious.

36

Several things happened when Veynothi dropped Traego to the ground. Paralysing shock took hold, numbing Palom's body and halting his reactions. Palom had seen—and partaken in—plenty of battles in his life, especially against Varkain. But he'd never seen anything happen quite as fast as the Ark taking down Traego. Especially considering Traego had already plunged his sword *through* her belly, and she was unaffected. There wasn't so much as a drop of blood in the sand. Once the shock passed, he realised he'd failed Princess Isa.

He'd promised her that he'd return with Traego. Veynothi had now made him break that promise.

He stood, lost, as the Ark focussed on the sky pirate.

What could he do? Taking Veynothi on...he'd killed Varkain before, but she wasn't anything like those.

Fleeing wasn't an option either—he had no idea how to fly an airship with Traego down.

If by some miracle he survived his encounter with Veynothi, he'd have no way of finding his way back to Isa and the others. Nor would they know where he was, unless Aetos, or any of the other Ittallan who could fly happened along this way when they inevitably came searching for them.

Thankfully, the Ark was more interested in Traego than in himself. There was a chance he could slip away, unnoticed, and Veynothi would leave once she tired of torturing Traego. But it wouldn't be long before she found the Ittallan camp and decimated it.

Challenging her would be suicidal. Their brief fight had thrown that into stark reality.

Leillu was out of action, whimpering with every breath, curled up in a heap on the sand.

Dragons above, what was he *supposed* to do? There was nothing that didn't result in his own demise, or in the deaths of the Ittallan he'd sworn to protect.

Traego groaned, his voice muffled by the sand currently pressing into his face, Veynothi's foot keeping him down as she relished in his suffering.

Damn it. He could do nothing *but* face her—he couldn't wait for the Ark to grow bored of Traego and turn her attention to him. Far better he stood up and met his fate head on. Against his better judgement, Palom raised his sword. 'Veynothi! Leave him!'

Veyothi didn't respond, just pressed her foot harder down on Traego's chest, the claws at the end of her toes digging into his collarbone.

Palom roared and charged forward, crossing the distance between them in a few strides, kicking up sand with every step. He swung his sword down in one ferocious strike, only to have his blade cleave through thin air.

The Ark appeared to his left, having moved faster than he could see. 'So, *you* want my attention first. That's interesting. Most Ittallan run from me when they have the chance.'

'Leave this place.' Palom slashed at her, refusing to rise to her insult. 'You have made point with Traego. You can go.'

She dodged his attack easily, stepping out of range of his strike. 'You don't give me orders.' She smiled and flicked out her tongue. 'Wait. That scent...' Veynothi lowered her own sword and turned to face Palom fully, her pupils constricting into slits. 'I didn't think I was mistaken in my tracking. But why is Amarah's scent on *you*? You're an Ittallan!'

'I said to leave this place!'

She scowled at him, lips turning up and revealing her fangs. 'Hmph. This place is the home of the Varkain. Sacred to us. It is *you* who is not welcome here.' Veynothi turned away, sending off an invisible wave of power.

Palom grimaced as it smacked into him—then she sucked it back in, taking his strength in the same movement. His grip faltered and he dropped his weapon. 'N—no!'

Veynothi breathed in deeply. 'Ah, *much* better.' She flexed her fingers. 'Now I feel *awake*!' She rolled her shoulders and ran her fingers through her waist-length hair. 'Ittallan. You will tell me where Amarah is, and I will let you live. Think carefully on your next words.' The Ark watched him, her gaze as sharp as her fangs.

It was clear her threats weren't empty. Palom took a step back, painfully aware both *Leillu* and Traego were unprotected. They only lived by her mercy. He'd never forgive himself if he did anything that brought them harm.

Unfortunately, he didn't have an answer. Amarah had left. She very likely was no longer in Sereth. And he had no idea where she'd gone. He doubted Veynothi would be happy with that information—not that he would tell the Ark even if he knew where Amarah was.

Traego groaned, his face pressed into the sand, but he was alive.

'Veynothi. You are *emonos*. I will not help you.'

She pursed her lips. 'Most unfortunate. I tracked her this far. I'll continue to track her even after this beach runs red with your blood.' She grasped two of her swords, power radiating from her as she squared up to face him, stronger now she'd sucked in some of Palom's own strength.

Although Palom stood almost three feet taller than Veynothi, the power she exuded made him feel as weak as a lamb. He pushed through the fear and faced her, concerned only with stalling her as long as he could in the hopes he could think of a way out of this mess.

Veynothi was the fiercest of the Arks, the most violent. She was responsible for more Ittallan deaths than any other. He'd learned of the Arks as a boy—his father had taken the history of Val Sharis extremely seriously, ensuring both his sons understood where they had come from, and the threats the Ittallan had faced over the generations.

It was clear that Veynothi was every bit as terrible as her reputation suggested—a mythical nightmare made flesh.

She stepped carefully to the side, taking her time, toying with him.

Palom circled her, drawing closer to Traego and *Otella*—small chunks of the hull scattered along the beach from its earlier crash-landing.

And an idea dawned on him.

A terrible, suicidal, *wonderful* idea.

'What is wrong...?' Veynothi asked, no doubt sensing the change in Palom's heart rate.

He lowered his gaze, a deep growl forming in his chest. Calculating the distance to *Otella*, Veynothi, Traego, and the sea, Palom tensed, ready to spring. With a snarl, he surged forward, sword held in front of him.

Veynothi stepped back, lazily avoiding the blow.

Palom feinted to the left, then hurled his sword at her. He'd done the same thing to a group of Arillians who'd attacked him before, and he was betting on the Ark sharing an identical moment of confusion. It would give him a tiny window.

The Ark hesitated for an instant and leapt away, bringing her close to the shore where the cool sea lapped against the Sereth shoreline.

In that moment, Palom spun on his heel, the momentum of his sword throw whipping him around quickly. He dug his boots into the sand and kicked away, throwing himself against *Otella's* side. Grabbing hold of the steps carved into the ship, he heaved himself up, half-leaping, half-pulling, until he scrambled onto the deck.

Palom daren't look behind him, but he hoped Veynothi was too caught off-guard to react with her usual speed. He raced along the deck, skidding at the last moment to the hatch which led into the ship's hold.

An angry hiss behind him signified his time was up.

The Ark was on his heels.

He wrenched the hatch open and leapt into the narrow opening—foregoing the ladder and jumping down the seven foot drop into *Otella's* hold. Without waiting, Palom ran down the corridor, his feet following a familiar path to his own room. It was locked, as he'd left it, and he fumbled in his pocket for the key.

'It will do you no good to hide from me.' Veynothi's voice carried down the corridor.

Although *Otella* was a former warship, and thus of great size, the corridors were narrow and the ceilings were low, and Palom felt as if he were trapped in the bowels of Sereth with her.

He found the single brass key and pulled it from his pocket, but before he had the chance to slip it into the keyhole, another of Veynothi's invisible attacks slammed into him. The key fell from his hand and bounced down the corridor with a clink.

'No lock can hold me.' The Ark laughed again. She walked down the corridor, one sword in each hand, their tips scraping along the walls on either side as she approached. Her grin broadened, fangs splitting her face in two.

Palom flinched at the high-pitched shriek of metal on wood made, and dropped to the floor, searching for the key. His pulse pounded in his ears, his vision spotty in the fear that gripped him so closely in her presence. He couldn't so much as form a retort.

'This is over, now. You fought well, tiger. But not well enough.' Veynothi raised her right arm, the sword held high.

Palom snarled, instinct taking over.

She could suck all the energy from him if she wanted. Render him too weak to fight back, as she had done to Traego and *Leillu*. But she was as cold, sadistic, and merciless as all Varkain were, and wanted to see her opponent suffer instead of fighting honourably. Dying to her would be *emonos*. Unclean.

He had no sword to defend himself with, and yet she advanced on him without mercy, two swords against zero defence, a twisted smile on her face as she relished every moment of her utter domination.

She struck, sweeping down with one sword and across with another, the two weapons forcing him further from the door.

Palom braced himself, shoved his shoulder into her strike, and collided with both swords. His boiled leather jerkin had been toughened over the years, but her swords cut straight through it, slicing into the meat of his shoulder and thigh. Grimacing through the pain, Palom kept pushing, forcing her off-balance and shoving her away as he stepped back to the locked door.

There was no sign of the key—he could have stepped on it for all he knew—and he daren't risk turning his back to the Ark. Blood trickled down his shoulder, and his thigh throbbed painfully, but adrenaline coursed through him, giving him the strength to force himself through the injury.

Veynothi clearly hadn't expected her attack to be met, much less forced away, and she dropped one sword, steadying herself against the wall. 'You arrogant tiger!'

Palom snatched up the dropped blade. A jolt ran through his arm the moment he touched it, his entire arm spasming. He almost let go again, but instead turned and hacked the steel into the door's lock. One strike. Two. Three. Veynothi recovered herself by the fourth strike, but the lock snapped, wood splintered, and the door to his cabin opened with a loud creak.

'Don't touch my sword with your filthy hands, Ittallan!' Veynothi roared, drawing more energy from him as her rage grew.

Door broken down, Palom flung the sword back at Veynothi as her attack reached him, and the strength went from his legs. His fingers burned from where he'd touched the hilt, and he fell into the room.

Gasping for breath, he crawled across the floor, steeling himself for even more unpleasantness as the wrapped *Valta Forinja* lay on the empty bunk. Waiting.

He had no idea if it would make any difference against Veynothi, but it was more powerful than any regular weapon. And if he was to survive long enough to protect his friends and loved ones from an Ark, he *had* to use its strength. Whatever the cost.

It was a sacrifice he was willing to make.

'That scent...' Veynothi whispered, now in the doorway. She blocked his way out.

He'd committed.

Palom forced himself to stand, his legs trembling with effort and the pain in his thigh. With a snarl, he picked up the scythe and tore off the linen covering the blade. This way, he held only the cloth and not the handle itself. Even so, the scythe's power thrummed through him and goosebumps raised on his arms and legs at the feel of it. Palom tightened his grip and pointed the curved blade directly at Veynothi.

'That is...' Her voice trailed off.

'You know what this is?' Palom asked. The tables had turned. 'This is *emonos*. Like you.'

'How do you have Amarah's weapon?'

'It is *my* weapon. I forged it. And others, too.' Blue light crackled around the edge of the blade as if it, too, snarled at the Ark.

'You forged the *Valta Forinja?*' She leapt forward, mouth agape and fangs bared, bringing up two swords in both hands.

Palom slashed the scythe diagonally across the room—an arc of blue energy shot out, slicing into the wall, doorframe, and Veynothi herself.

She screamed and dropped like a stone to the cabin's floor, a line of dark blood oozing from her grey flesh where the *Valta Forinja's* power had cut into her.

That was unexpected. He'd hoped the power of the scythe would be enough to get her to back off or wear her out. He hadn't thought it would actually *harm* the immortal creature. Palom smiled. Not for the thrill of victory suddenly becoming an option. Not even because the Ark had been hurt. But because he had the power to make her leave, and keep *Leillu*, Traego, and Isa safe.

She staggered to her feet, eyes glittering with fury, blood dripping from her collarbone and the side of her neck. 'Stolen magic.' Veynothi spat and backed away, through the damaged door frame and into the corridor. She still radiated power, but it swirled around her body like a shield. She didn't lunge at him or try to draw more energy away.

Palom hadn't realised she would know of his weapon. Then again, the Arks were ancient. She probably knew of the original *Valta Forinja*—the first ever created in Linaria. 'If you know what this is, then you know you are defeated, Veynothi.' He staggered out of the cabin after her, the light from the scythe turning the inside of *Otella* a vibrant turquoise blue. It flashed of its own accord, like a cornered animal snapping wildly.

She hissed again. 'You use stolen magic to fight me? Coward. Cast it aside and stand tall to meet your fate like a true tiger!'

Palom didn't give in. It wasn't just his own life at stake. There were too many others whose fate would be decided by his actions tonight. Letting them down wasn't something he could do. It was the only reason he wielded the *Valta Forinja* again. 'Leave the ship. Leave Traego and *Leillu*. Then leave this place.'

Veynothi stood underneath the open hatch to the deck, a shaft of moonlight bathing her from above. In its eerie light, she almost looked like she was made of stone. She glared at him, then at the scythe, her invisible power whirling around her body.

Palom held the handle as tight as he dared. He didn't want to touch the weapon itself, didn't want to give in to the paranoia, fear, and hatred that the cursed scythe would elicit. He held his ground against the Ark, meeting her glare for glare, until with sudden speed, she leapt vertically—through the hatch and onto *Otella's* deck.

He hurried after her as quickly as he could, but he couldn't bear his full weight on the thigh that had been cut. There was no guarantee she hadn't leapt up to slaughter

Traego where he lay, and Palom wasn't as fast as the Ark even without being injured. He scrambled after her, the bulky scythe slowing his progress.

The weapon's shaft thwacked onto the side of the ship as he clambered up the ladder, but Palom daren't let go of it, not even for a second. Veynothi was too fast, too strong. Even having her out of his sight increased his heart rate to a sickening speed.

Palom pulled himself through the hatch with a grunt, and rolled onto the deck, *Valta Forinja* clutched tight. Where had Veynothi gone? He gazed over the ship's deck and the open captain's cabin. No sign of the Ark. Waves crashed against the beach, the only sound that reached him.

Crossing the deck, he peered over the side. *Leillu* and Traego were exactly where he'd left them, thank Rhea. It took him several worrying seconds before he spotted her. Veynothi stood in the water, the waves lapping gently at her bare feet, illuminated by moonlight. She still held a sword in one hand, but her stance was defensive rather than aggressive.

'Veynothi. You leave. Now.' High up on the deck of the warship, he had a clear view along the length of the beach and the sea beyond. He leaned on the side railing, grateful it could keep him on his feet. Sweat trickled down his forehead despite the cold night air.

The *Valta Forinja* flickered, sending out waves of blue light that danced over one another as they faded away into darkness. If a weapon could be alive, the *Valta Forinja* came close. Despite forging four of them, he didn't understand their workings. They fought with the power of a Sevastos, and slowly corrupted their wielders. But they seemed alive in some way; coercing him to go certain places, or act in certain ways.

Right now it seemed active. Awake. And eager to fight Veynothi.

Something moved in Palom's peripheral vision—far out to sea. Bubbles burst up from the depths, foaming on the surface of the dark water.

Veynothi heard it too, turning away from the beach to face the water beyond.

Taking a deep breath, Palom straightened, narrowing his eyes as he tried to make out the details on the waves. A barbed fin protruded from the water, sending spray high.

He'd recognise that fin anywhere. 'No. Rhea do not let this be so. Please...'

The monster from Estoria broke the water's surface with a bellow that shook the beach. Something fell off the desk in the captain's cabin and rolled across the deck, but Palom ignored it. He could hardly believe that creature was here. In the flesh. Alongside Veynothi.

He fought to keep his breathing even.

'All these years alone must have been terrible for you.' Veynothi stretched out one arm and gently stroked the monster's scales with the back of one finger, cooing to it as if it were a kitten.

It rumbled in reply, a deep vibration that Palom felt in his bones. It opened its mouth, circular rows of fangs gleaming, and spoke in a guttural, grating language that sent shivers up his spine. He didn't understand anything until it spoke the Ark's name, 'Veynothi.'

She replied in kind, slipping into the ancient Varkain dialect.

Palom took his chance to get off the ship while she was distracted, clambering down gingerly. This trip to Estoria was meant to be a chance for him to lie low and rest, and he'd immediately found himself caught up in another excursion that had ended in blood.

Traego hadn't moved, but he breathed. *Leillu* was much the same.

Palom held his breath, not willing to go to their aid while the Ark was still in sight. If Veynothi was on the edge of leaving, he didn't want to do anything that would change her mind.

'Tiger. I was correct. You have met Brahm's pet before, I see. He's been tracking you little rats all over the seas. Tracking that filthy magic you stole.' Veynothi's voice caught Palom's attention. 'You scarred him. Traego, too. And when he saw that thief, Amarah, with my sword, he immediately came to my side. Or what he thought was my side. You disgusting vermin.'

Palom raised the scythe, an arc of blue shining bright. 'You wish to continue our battle?' Given them no time to argue, he hurled another blast of energy at the pair.

It crashed into the beach, carving out a small crater and sending up an enormous splash. Seawater immediately poured into the deep hole, and the monster roared in defiance with another ear-splitting cry.

Veynothi's eyes flashed in anger and she scowled. But she didn't retaliate. 'Not today, tiger. I would prefer to have my prince with me when you and I meet again.'

Palom faltered. 'Your...prince? But, Sapora is king, and—'

She laughed, cutting him off abruptly. 'That mongrel? Don't be so stupid. Prince Karekis is the only royalty I follow. I imagine the mongrel king has resurrected Malashash by now. Our unit is halfway restored. When we're all back, we'll wipe you from the face of Linaria.' She snapped her fingers to illustrate her point.

Palom said nothing. In truth, the pain from his thigh had intensified during his climb down *Otella*, and it took every ounce of strength to keep his leg from trembling. Show any weakness in front of a Varkain, and they'd be upon you before you could blink.

Thankfully, Veynothi seemed to have taken advantage of the monster's appearance, lingering with it and speaking to it in their ancient tongue. 'I will be back for you, Palom the Great Tiger of Val Sharis. And your thieving friends. We'll all be back for you.' She sheathed her swords and wiped her still bleeding neck with one hand. '*You* will suffer the most for what you have done to me tonight.'

'I await your fight.' Palom let out a snarl, and Veynothi turned away from him.

The Ark clambered onto the monster's back, her clawed hands easily finding purchase on the creature's scales. She manoeuvred herself deftly between its fins and protruding spines until she nestled down just behind its head and clutched it tightly.

With another low rumble, the monster turned away, pulling itself along the sand and back into the beckoning sea.

Palom watched, tense. He half-considered launching more attacks with his *Valta Forinja* to properly see them off, but held back. He didn't want to use the weapon any more than he had to—even the little he had used it tonight might well have been too much.

Nightmares would plague him again.

Once the monster and the Ark had disappeared, swallowed up by the sea, Palom hobbled over to Traego. 'She is gone, Traego. You are safe.'

The sky pirate groaned.

Leaving him there for the moment—he'd spent an age lying down, another minute wouldn't hurt—Palom crossed the beach to his dragon. '*Leillu*. You are okay now? *Leillu*?' He crouched down and scooped her up in his arms, awkwardly balancing the dragon's shape and weight with the *Valta Forinja*.

Leillu chirped, tried to flutter her wings, but didn't have the strength for it. Her eyes opened once, focussed on him, then closed, her breathing slowing to a normal rate.

Palom checked her carefully, but couldn't discern any broken bones, and she wasn't bleeding or wounded. 'You will rest. Come on. Let us see Traego.' He heaved her up over one shoulder and limped back to *Otella's* side. 'Traego. Get up. We must go.'

Another groan from the sky pirate.

Palom carefully shoved his boot under Traego and turned him over.

Traego yelped in pain and sat up, clutching his left arm. A piece of broken bone protruded from his wrist, blood congealing around the wound. His jacket had been torn open and a long gash along his chest also dripped blood, but it didn't appear life-threatening. His face was paler than normal, his eyes dull and bloodshot. His hair was full of sand, which fell all over him as he moved.

'You will not get better sitting on beach. Can you fly ship?'

'With a fuckin' broken wrist?' Traego coughed. 'The fuck was that?'

It was obvious what Traego asked about. '*That* was Veynothi. An Ark.'

Traego trembled, his face paling even more. 'Gimme a hand up?'

Palom adjusted *Leillu*, rested the scythe against his body, and hauled Traego to his feet with a grunt. 'She is gone now. We should leave, too.'

'Wait. Need ta get my stash.' Traego took a step forward and almost stumbled over again. He gritted his teeth and continued on. 'There's a cave along the beach. Just up here a short ways.'

Palom frowned. 'We should get back to Princess Isa.'

'I know that!' Traego snapped, glancing over his shoulder. 'But I ain't comin' all the way out here just ta get beat up and go back empty handed.' He clutched his head and swayed.

Palom said, 'You and *Leillu* wait on ship. I will go to cove. You are in no position to go off on your own.'

Traego halted.

'Just tell me what I am looking for and I will find this for you.'

The sky pirate coughed again, several long hacks, then spat a gob of something red into the sand and wiped his mouth. After a moment of debate, he slumped his shoulders. 'Fine. At least I know what ta tell Isa when we get back.'

'What is that?'

'We know how ta kill an Ark.'

37

Isa's world shrank from a barren landscape to a cramped, underground tunnel lit by a narrow shaft of moonlight that trickled down the gaping hole she'd fallen through.

Bruises littered her body where she'd been flung against the rocky ground, and a large gash across her cheek stung badly—probably not helped by the dirt that had managed to get into it.

She landed on her feet in a huge dust cloud, but had scraped her arms and legs as she'd tried to grab hold of anything to slow her fall. Loose rocks and chunks of soil fell around her—some from the ground above still disintegrating, some from the walls of the shaft she'd fallen down.

Isa covered her mouth with her sleeve and coughed several times, blinking rapidly to adjust to the sudden murkiness of the underground. Surrounded by the same black-red rock as above, the tunnel seemed an even darker and more foreboding place. The shaft ended four feet above her head. Not an insurmountable distance to jump. Isa crouched and leapt straight up, her fingers scrabbling against the rock, which immediately broke away into dust.

She jumped again and again, each time struggling for purchase, but the walls of the shaft were too weak to hold her weight. Now matter how hard she tried to grip, it all crumbled away under her fingers. She cursed, coughing again at the dust cloud thrown up by her constant jumping and the rocky soil disintegrating.

'Damn you, Tacio.'

It had been a trap, of course.

In single combat, she was better than he was. While he was undoubtedly a skilled fighter, her blood lust gave her the edge. Now she was in his world of tunnels and darkness, she wasn't sure she'd have the advantage any more. He'd purposely led her somewhere he had the upper hand.

Traego had deliberately taken them to Mount Kozue because it was an uninhabited area of Sereth—all the tunnels underfoot were disused. It also meant that she was alone underground, the tunnels unkempt and messy—some even collapsed in places.

She suppressed a shiver. It wasn't terribly far back to the Ittallan camp—she just needed to get her bearings, find another way out, and get back to them.

Catching her breath, Isa headed along the tunnel. There was no point in trying to clamber up the way she'd fallen in.

It was difficult to keep her sense of direction in the dark—with no moon or stars to guide her, she relied on her own instincts and best guess. She could quite easily be walking in the completely opposite direction and end up in some other part of Sereth where Varkain lived.

Her cheek continued to sting, fouling her mood. Thankfully she'd kept hold of her sword, so she wasn't completely defenceless, but she wasn't sure what good it would do if she had to use it in such a confined space.

Although her footsteps had always been light, in the quiet of the tunnel, they seemed like a horse thundering along. The noise put her on edge, and she clutched her sword with both hands as if it gave her greater strength.

Even her breathing seemed louder than normal.

She supposed all noises were confined to the tunnel, and sounds she was used to dissipating simply bounced back to her ears. Isa didn't like it. It wasn't unlike being drunk, when your senses were warped and nothing made sense.

She'd been walking less than a minute when the tunnel split into three pathways. Each of them led in roughly the same direction, but they were too dark to see properly down. What if they curved and led back to the inhabited areas of Sereth? There was no way she'd survive stumbling into a group of Varkain. They'd overwhelm her, and the game would be up.

Isa scowled, looking down each tunnel individually, as if the best route would somehow reveal itself if she stared at it long enough.

Water trickled from somewhere along one tunnel. Droplets dripped every few seconds.

Not that one. Varkain were more likely to live near fresh water.

She eyed the other two. Both tunnels disappeared into darkness. Both appeared identical.

A hiss echoed some way behind her.

She flinched. Tacio.

Isa picked the tunnel on the right and darted down it, hoping he was too far behind to have seen her move. She didn't want to hide and wait, holding her breath and hoping he'd pass. He could hear her heartbeat for one thing—admittedly he needed to be close enough to see her for that—and she didn't trust herself to hold her nerve. So she sprinted away, following the tunnel as it wound further to the right before levelling out.

More tunnels split off the one she raced down—gaping

holes on either side that could lead to her freedom, or straight into a nest of Varkain.

She sprinted, taking the first left, the sixth right, the second left, until she had no idea where she'd come from or where she'd been. Panting, she leaned against the wall to catch her breath. If she didn't know where she was, Tacio couldn't know either.

The wall was slippery with water, and she wiped her palm on her sleeve, still clutching the sword in her other hand. Sheathing it at her hip would be sensible—running with a chunk of metal held aloft took far more effort—but she didn't want to put it away in case she stumbled into danger and couldn't react quickly enough.

At least Solvi hadn't come with her—the young Ittallan would be trapped in the tunnels, otherwise, and she'd already been put in far too much danger. In Taban Yul, Solvi had come into contact with Aciel's compulsion and spent several days recovering with Lathri. In Estoria, Brahm's monster had almost killed her. Despite the constant risks, she'd stuck with her through it all.

Isa wiped her forehead and looked back the way she'd come. Piles of rocky soil lined the wall where part of it had collapsed on itself, merging two tunnels into one. The damned place was like a rabbit's warren.

No light penetrated so deep, and there weren't any sconces to show the way, as Sapora had once told her would be in Sereth. She was trapped in a labyrinth of disused tunnels in the dark, and somewhere, Tacio hunted her.

She hated the thought of it. He would be in his element—not only was he in the country of his birth, he had the advantage of growing up in Sereth. He knew the tunnels like she knew the city of Taban Yul. He might have even played in these ones, or explored them.

If it had been a rooftop chase, the odds would be reversed.

'Damned snake,' Isa swore again. She needed to get back to the surface. Walking along the tunnel, she turned down new paths as they appeared only if they led up. She tried to keep moving. Every time she stopped was another opportunity for Tacio to gain on her.

It wasn't long before a cramp developed in her calf, and her walking turned to hobbling. Sweat trickled down the back of her neck, tickling her skin and irritating her. She wished she'd braided her hair back—it made traversing the narrow paths far easier, but she'd taken to wearing it loose since leaving Estoria.

She dreaded to think how many hairs and footsteps she'd left, and how easy it would be for Tacio to track her. Dread settled in the pit of her stomach and refused to move.

All she could do was ignore it and keep going.

With no sense of time, Isa pushed on, through the aches and bleeding, hoping to find another break in the tunnel above where she could clamber out, or even better, a tunnel that led directly to the surface. Behind her, soft hissing reverberated every now and then—although it was so faint and sound carried in such a bizarre way down here, that Isa wasn't sure her mind hadn't made it up to keep her on her toes.

Eventually the ground sloped upwards. She grinned, picking up her pace, resting her left hand against the wall for support as she hurried along. Faint light trickled down, but she was too far away to tell if it opened to the surface or if there was another gap in the tunnel's roof.

The wall beside her disappeared.

Isa withdrew her hand before she stumbled—and a snake's head almost two feet wide shot out of the gap in the wall. Fangs bared, it struck at her with lightning speed.

Isa's feet slipped on the slope and she ducked as the Varkain's fangs collided with the wall above her head. Debris fell above her, coating her in dirt and soil. Her hand shot out instinctively and brushed against the snake's enormous body, pushing at it.

She grunted in pain as she toppled to the ground and rolled away.

The transformed Varkain—a Cerastes, if the horns above its eyes and keeled scales were anything to go by—wheeled around to follow her back down the slope.

In the darkness, she could only make out the glint of its eyes and fangs when it opened its mouth—but she felt its forked tongue flicking out. The tip touched her bare arm, and she recoiled, slashing with her sword in the same movement.

It backed off with another hiss, and Isa turned to run down the slope. She made it back into the main tunnel and whirled around, sword at the ready.

The Cerastes weaved after her. Despite its massive size, the Varkain was at home in the smooth, tight spaces of the Sereth underground, and it was on her in a heartbeat. It struck again, but Isa had space to dodge. She darted to the left, going by the sound of its movement rather than seeing it react, and brought up her sword to keep it at bay. 'Tacio doesn't give up easily, does he?' Isa's breathing was heavy, her vision blurred by dirt in her eye—which stung as much as the gash on her cheek.

It didn't reply—they couldn't speak when transformed—but it coiled its body into the larger tunnel and arched its neck, looking for another opening to strike.

She steeled herself. There could be dozens down here with her—not to mention Tacio himself. Her heart fluttered, and the Cerastes loomed closer. Killing a Varkain was one thing. Surviving an encounter with a transformed Varkain in the tunnels of Sereth was something else.

If she turned her back on it, she was dead.

Yet facing this one left her wide open to any others that tracked her down.

She took a step towards the snake, thrusting the sword in half-hearted jabs to get it to back off. If she needed her blood lust to kick in at any point, now was the time. But it wasn't something she had any control over. Sometimes when she fought, nothing happened. Other times, it reared its ugly head the moment the first drop of blood spilled.

The Cerastes hissed again, writhing its body as it shifted in the tunnel and stared at her with wide, unblinking eyes.

Isa gulped. Like when she'd challenged Mateli, she couldn't give it the chance to make the first move. She *had* to act.

She snarled, channelling her inner-warrior, and darted forward, aiming for the Cerastes' massive body. The tip of the sword skittered off its scales, and her momentum carried her on—tripping over one of the snake's enormous coils.

It flinched at her touch, slithering away in the blink of an eye. With an angry hiss, it curled up several feet away from her and struck again, once in the spot Isa had just been, and again when she dodged it.

Isa brought up her sword at the last moment, and the Varkain's mouth slammed into the flat of the blade, bouncing off.

The force of the strike pushed Isa back. Sharp pain laced through her wrist on impact, but she'd blocked its blow and avoided being bitten. Gritting her teeth, she tried to keep her eye on the snake, but in the pitch-dark of the tunnel, she couldn't see details. It moved, she could tell that much, and she could hear its scales sliding against the loose soil—

An idea struck her.

She widened her stance, making herself a more appealing target, and held the sword high in her right hand. Isa squeezed the hilt, waiting for the sound of moving scales as the Varkain lunged again.

The moment she heard it, Isa whacked the sword on the tunnel wall as hard as she could. Rocks and soil collapsed as the metal bit in, tumbling down as part of the tunnel collapsed.

She darted back as the effect snowballed—more and more rocks fell, soil flung from the now gaping hole in the wall, and covered the Cerastes mid-strike.

Isa didn't wait to see if the Cerastes was down for good or not. She turned away from it and sprinted down the wide tunnel as fast as she could, pushing through the cramp in her leg and letting fear fuel her onwards. She timed her breathing with every fourth step, keeping herself in rhythm as she ran, all the while feeling for another incline.

Anything to get her away from the main tunnel and back to the surface.

Heart pounding, she flung herself down another opening and skidded to a halt. Tapping into her own *meraki* and racing through the tunnels in her true form would help with visibility. Her night vision was excellent, but as a wild-cat, she needed almost no light to navigate. Avoiding any more Varkain would also be easier. But transforming would mean she'd have to leave her sword behind—not a risk she wanted to take when she might run straight into a Varkain's waiting jaws.

She could manage.

She hoped.

Holding the sword tight to her chest, Isa slipped down to the ground, resting her back against the tunnel wall. Careful not to put too much pressure against it lest it collapsed, she tried to take control of her breathing and fear.

Sweat had stuck loose hair to her face, and she pushed it out of the way, wiping more dirt and grime along her forehead.

She hadn't even challenged Sapora for the throne yet, and here she was fighting Tacio and his Cerastes for her life.

Damn it all.

She'd learned at a young age that nothing in life was easy. If you wanted something, you had to fight for it. Even living, apparently.

Tacio was here to settle a score. She'd hurt him—physically as well as his pride. She wasn't sure which he hated more. He'd always been a proud peacock, and Isa had wished Sapora hadn't brought him to the palace. Their plans had been ruined anyway, but she and Sapora could have had a chance to salvage them had Tacio not got himself involved.

Her heartbeat slowed, but she was mentally shattered. Everything over the past few weeks had taken its toll on her. She almost laughed. Tacio didn't have to lift a finger—she'd probably wander around down here until she died of exhaustion.

Isa's bottom lip quivered. Everyone had worked so hard to stop her. They'd taken her birthright. Her childhood. Her freedom. Whether she sat there—meek—and accepted it, or fought back, it all went wrong. People had died on account of her. People who believed in her and what she stood for.

Or was it just as Gralla had said—they only followed her because she was an alternative to Sapora.

She stared at her hands—what little she could see of her palms in the dark. There was as much blood on her hands as on Sapora's. He owned it. Seemed almost proud of it. *She* tried to hide it. She'd not forgotten the way Amarah had looked at her after she'd slaughtered Rimir back in Estoria.

Even Antar's confident attitude had faded after she'd killed those Arillians to defend their ship.

Isa snorted. She was just as bad as Sapora. Worse. Because she pretended to be someone—something—so much better than she truly was: the bastard daughter of a bloodthirsty Varkain conqueror.

Solvi was waiting for her, though. On the surface. Palom, too. And Kylos. Aetos. Odi. Chyro. So many Ittallan had given up their lives, had committed treason, to back her cause. She laughed. Would it all be for nothing if she met her end lost somewhere in a Varkain's tunnel?

No. She couldn't. She wouldn't!

So caught up in glaring at her hands and the metaphorical blood dripping off it, Isa almost missed the subtle shift in the shadows to her right. A hint of movement, sensed rather than seen. She blinked, and the Varkain surged towards her.

Isa flattened herself to the wall—the only thing she could do.

The new Varkain missed its strike and coiled around her, trying to trap her against the wall. This snake was larger than the Cerastes by some margin, but the bands of grey stippling along its body and its deep golden-red eyes were unforgettable. A *naja*.

'Tacio!' Isa rolled away from him.

Though the enormous snake couldn't talk, he seemed to smile, twisting his body expertly in the tunnel to keep Isa in front of him. Every breath came out as a hiss so low it was a growl, growing with intensity as he slithered closer.

Isa broke away.

Clambering over the few coils that had surrounded her, she sprinted.

The *naja* followed, its throaty growl seeming to penetrate her mind even when she built up a lead over him. His snarling hiss echoed in the dark, the sound filling every gap, every space, and Isa couldn't get away from it.

Darting to the side, down a narrow tunnel that she'd not seen until the last minute, Isa felt the whoosh of air on the back of her legs as Tacio struck. Immediately rolling to the ground, she passed through the gap and out of range.

But it wasn't another tunnel. It was a gap between two large boulders wedged in the wall of the main tunnel that led to a tiny cave. There was nowhere to go save back the way she'd come.

However, the opening was too small for Tacio—or any other Cerastes he had with him—to fit through. Staying in the cramped space gave her some room to breathe. Her chest rose and fell quickly. She was out of stamina, and out of courage.

Isa crouched down, one arm wrapped around her knees, the other grasping the hilt of her sword, blade tip pointed at the entrance in case Tacio tried to come through. The space was high enough for her to stand, and wide enough to take three or four steps, but that was all.

There was no light. No breeze. No escape.

Outside, Tacio's snarling hiss grew louder as he realised where she'd gone, and couldn't reach her.

If he wanted to fight, he'd have to come in and challenge her with a blade in hand.

Isa could take her time to recover, but she knew the Varkain could slip into stasis at any point. They could practically wait out an ice age if they had a mind to.

It took them a few seconds to return to normal, however.

If Tacio wanted to wait, then she could sneak away while he was slipping in between stasis and true wakefulness.

Isa ran her free hand through her hair, leaving streaks of dirt and blood in it. Her fingers trembled, but she couldn't do much about it. She had no idea how long she'd been down here. An hour. Five? Or had it only been minutes, the panicked fear warping all sense of time even more than the darkness itself?

She bit down on the urge to whimper.

'Sapora has the first Ark, you know.' Tacio whispered through the crack in the tunnel.

She froze at his sudden voice.

'And really, he has *you* to thank for that.'

Isa refused to rise to his bait. She saw the hint of movement on the other side, the glint of metal in the dark as he paced outside her hiding space.

'All those followers of yours. The ones we captured after the attack on the palace. Oh yes, I know all about that. Those traitorous moles in the Imperial Guard.' He chuckled.

She wasn't sure if he was bluffing or if he really knew about her betrayal. Surely there was no way Tacio could have discovered her message to Morgen.

Could he?

Tacio continued, 'Veynothi. All the Arks. They were created with blood magic. And they needed blood to break their seals. Do you remember what the Valendrin said, dear sister? Before you ran off to tell your little gang of rats?'

Isa turned her head away and crawled to the edge of the space she'd found herself in. She gently picked at the wall with one finger, sending loose soil to the ground. She wondered if digging her way out was a possibility. Whether Tacio would notice...

She worked at the wall as quickly as she dared, and only when Tacio spoke.

He was good at bragging and had always loved the sound of his own voice.

She ignored his words. They were meaningless barbs designed to elicit a reaction. The kind of teasing she'd endured for years. Her eyes stung, but she couldn't do anything.

When she didn't reply, Tacio spoke again. 'Where do you suppose he found enough people to kill? Get enough blood to resurrect Veynothi? *Your* followers. Those who kept their silence. Who vowed to protect you. They all died, in the end. Every one of them. They may have been willing to die for you, but they brought back the first Ark. All those deaths on *your* head.'

Isa stopped working, tears trickling down her face and stinging the graze on her cheek. Her fingers slipped from the wall and she braced herself on the ground, palms flat in the dirt.

Tacio laughed softly and tapped the tip of his sword against the floor of the tunnel, the sound echoing, like the ticking of a clock. 'Even if you get what you want, kitten princess. Even if you become the queen you are so desperate to be...The palace will always smell of blood.'

38

Oren had always been home to Kohl. He'd been born there, as had his father before him, and his grandfather before him, all the way back to when the islands had been at ground level, before the Ice Golems had seen fit to raise the Arillians above the rest of Linaria.

Yet, he always worried he'd be an outsider.

Ever since his conflict with Aciel, something in his heart had never been quite as it used to be.

Sure, he had Fogu back on his side, but losing Jato had hit him hard. Harder than he would have liked it to. Harder than he'd thought it would.

He'd known when she'd revealed she was interested in being with Aciel that he'd have a hard battle on his hands. How silly he'd been back then to have not realised it was a losing battle.

Now, he watched his daughter and her followers—almost one hundred strong—attack King Sapora and the city of Taban Yul.

'My lord?' Fogu spoke, but Kohl couldn't tear his eyes from the scene playing out before him like a vision from a nightmare. The fire at the heart of Oren was fuelled by the same magic that gave the Ice Golems life, that gave the Arillian Lords their Frost-touch, and it gave them the ability to see into any storm—Arillian-made or otherwise—across Linaria. Jato's thunderstorm was enormous, stretching from the ridge of the Feor Mountains, across the plains, right up to the doorstep of Taban Yul.

More Arillians had been arriving each day, Tymē had explained, after hunting down any dragons they could find and slaughtering them.

Now her forces were at full strength. There was no sign of Sapora's Sevastos.

And they'd attacked.

He watched it play out. The wagon had only been the beginning. Now, Jato and her Arillians loosed their lightning on the city, destroying buildings and damaging the walls around Taban Yul. The Imperial Guard retaliated, sending off their own ballista bolts into the flurry of Arillians. Most of them were too nimble, but two—three—plummeted from the sky, their wings skewered by the vicious metal.

He trembled as he watched. Several more Arillians arrived until he was certain the entire population of Oren surrounded the fire, watching everything unfold alongside him.

His breathing had grown short. 'Jato, what are you doing...?'

Lightning flashed, and the plume of electricity crashed into the Sevastos crystal just outside the city's eastern gate.

Kohl *felt* the force of the blast, even though Oren was hundreds of leagues away. There was something fierce in that blow. Emotional anguish. Torment. Jato had put everything into that blast.

Under the weight of Jato's combined attacks, the crystal cracked, spewing out white light in all directions.

The Arillians gathered by the fire burst into shocked conversation. Heads shook. Hangs wrung. Wings flapped. 'It...she *cannot*!' Kohl didn't know what to say. He couldn't believe his own eyes.

'She *has*, my lord. She's damaged the Sevastos stone!' Fogu said, leaning closer to the flames as if it would give him a more detailed vision. 'By the Ice Golems, I'd never have thought it possible she could break the seal. A Sevastos is, is...'

Kohl tried to regain his composure. He'd tracked down dragons for Aciel for a long while. Killed dozens. He knew what a Sevastos was capable of. Jato's power astonished him. 'The crystal is only damaged. But I've no idea how long it'll hold given that onslaught.'

'Sapora will retaliate,' Fogu said, echoing the statements of the other Arillians. 'She may be in danger.'

Kohl raised his shoulders. 'Against a Varkain? Sapora has no chance. Jato will wipe out the city with that storm.' He couldn't fathom how many people lived in Taban Yul—how many would die to his daughter's rage and unyielding desire for retribution. Aciel lived. It wouldn't be long before he was free to walk again, putting Linaria back in the terrible position it had been in to begin with.

His people would be at risk. After losing so many lives, it was unfair that they'd be put through the same torture as before under Aciel's compulsion.

He couldn't let that happen. Not again.

Kohl tore his gaze away from the flames and stared at the sky, hoping the two Lords would not take long to arrive. The distance between each of the floating islands was minimal, and an Arillian Lord could make the trek in less than an hour. No doubt they would have been keeping an eye on things in Linaria with their own village fires, and would wish to speak with him. Jato was of Oren. As Oren's Lord, she was *his* responsibility—blood relation notwithstanding.

He clutched his broken fingers and returned his attention to the battlefield Taban Yul had become. Jato's Arillians had whipped themselves into a frenzy, flying high and wheeling low, sending off stray bolts of lightning every chance they had.

'She can't control them,' Tymē said. 'Look at them. As wild as feral goats. They'll destroy each other once they're done with the city. Mark my words, this will not end well for any of us.'

Kohl frowned. He hoped they had more sense than that, but daren't say anything to object to Tymē's observation. The unfortunate truth was that she was right.

With the city taken and Aciel able to be freed, what was to stop Jato and her followers doing as they pleased? A storm of that size could move across the length of Val Sharis, unimpeded, killing any dragon—any person—they chose.

He needed to get her back. Even if she refused to speak with him, he could get her home, take away her armour, keep her from her followers, and restrain her if he had to. If that didn't work, the Ice Golems would be her final judgement.

'Any sign of the other Lords?' Kohl asked Tymē.

'Not yet. They'll come to the heart fire anyway,' she replied, still watching events unfold through the ten-foot high flames. She pursed her lips as she watched. There was no humour in her gaze.

Kohl couldn't remember the last time he'd seen Dronour or Varielle, Lords of Sirvat and Matsu, respectively. In fact, it had been decades since he'd even visited the other Arillian islands. A deeply tribal people, Arillians liked to keep to themselves and their own customs. It wasn't unheard of for individuals to flit between the three Lords' domains—Aciel had been born on Sirvat—but for the most part, they ruled themselves and kept on their own islands.

The three Arillian leaders hadn't ever come together during Kohl's lifetime. Perhaps if he'd called a meeting before Aciel had exiled him, things would have worked out differently. That was the wonderful thing about hindsight.

Kohl wouldn't make the same mistake again. It was why he'd summoned them the moment he arrived on Oren. There'd be no more hesitating from now on.

A collective gasp rippled through the Arillians gathered and Kohl looked into the flames. Sapora's Sevastos had appeared, gliding in from high in the Feor Mountains. Although they heard no sound through their magical storms, Kohl knew the enormous dragon bellowed its challenge as it approached Jato's group.

He sucked in a breath, hoping Jato wouldn't be stupid enough to attack the dragon. It was clear why the majority of Linarians worshipped them as gods. Its wingspan alone would be enough to put fear into the hearts of any who saw it, Arillian or not.

Then, something happened that Kohl could not understand. The Sevatos hovered a short way from the centre of the group. A few of Jato's Arillians hurled lightning at it, but the dragon didn't fight back. There were no flames of fury nor swipes of its claws.

'Is it speaking?' Fogu suggested.

'Possibly.' There was no other reason for its behaviour. Kohl knew he was in the right place—in Oren, with his people—but he so desperately wanted to be in Taban Yul.

Fogu put a hand on his shoulder. 'Lord Varielle arrives.'

Kohl glanced up in time to see the Lord swoop overhead.

Varielle was a youthful Arillian, perhaps eighty years old, and the youngest of the Lords by over two decades. Her grey-black hair grew a short way past her shoulders, the colour matching her wings. Individual blue feathers poked out in odd patterns, giving her wings an unusual sheen, particularly when the sun hit her. She carried a gold and white spear, more for ceremony than combat, and travelled with two Generals, whose names Kohl did not know, to his shame.

Another reminder of how much time he'd spent away from his people.

'Lord Varielle.' Kohl took to the wing to greet her in mid-air, a short distance above the fire.

'Lord Kohl.' She inclined her head, but her gaze was drawn to the scenes playing out in the fire rather than to him.

Fogu leapt into the air and hovered next to Kohl. He inclined his head to all three of the new arrivals and gestured wide with both arms. 'Welcome to Oren, Lord Varielle. I am General Fogu. I apologise for the lack of formality but—'

'We're in the middle of a crisis.' Varielle cut him off. 'No need to sugarcoat it, Fogu. I know why you called me. Lord Dronour is here also, I presume?'

'On his way,' Kohl answered, before Fogu could speak for him again. 'I thought it time we convened. Before the situation worsened.'

Varielle narrowed her pale blue eyes. 'What is your explanation for her?' She pointed at the fire below them, where Jato and a few of her Arillians flew over the city walls. 'Aciel had only just been dealt with and now General Jato is on the rampage? Are you *trying* to plunge us into another war, Kohl? By the Golems, any Arillian who passes through Oren seems to be cursed with a rather destructive nature!'

Kohl ignored the insult when she dropped his title. 'My good Lord Varielle, if anything, I am trying to ensure we are prepared for the next war. It's inevitable. Regardless of Jato's actions, Aciel is alive. So long as he lives, he is a threat to all Arillians, not to mention the rest of Linaria.'

She snorted. 'Eight hundred and seventy-three people. That's how many Aciel took with him on his campaign. Do you know how many returned?'

Kohl met her eyes but said nothing.

'Forty-nine. Of which half are unfit to fly, much less rejoin the village and get on with work. Matsu doesn't *have* enough people to lose this many.'

'Which is why you, Lord Dronour, and I will ensure such things never happen again.' Kohl had to be firm with Varielle. With all the Arillians.

'Lord Kohl!' Tymē cried out.

Kohl dived down and landed heavily beside her. She didn't need to say anything. She simply stared at the flames with her mouth half open. Fogu landed a moment later, followed by Varielle and her two Generals.

Although the fire showed the landscape below an Arillian storm, it could not show anything that was not in direct view of their thunderclouds. It meant Kohl had to strain his eyes just to get a glimpse of why Tymē had called him down in the middle of his discussion with another Arillian Lord.

He didn't particularly want to see the citizens of Taban Yul slaughtered, or see their terror as they fled before another of the famed, devastating Arillian storms.

But that wasn't what he saw.

On the far edge of the storm, deep within the city itself, Jato and Sapora fought one another. They moved quickly, throwing out attacks and dodging others.

He saw his daughter's shredded wings, her wild eyes.

And her blood as it spilled onto the white streets.

Lord Dronour arrived at some point during the evening. Fogu had poked his head through the open window—a gaping hole in the building—to notify him.

Kohl hadn't really listened.

Outside was chaos. Arillians wailed, cried, shouted in various states of distress. Despite their rocky relationship, General Jato had been well-loved by the Arillians of Oren. She was confident, proud, skilled in battle—traits of any would-be Arillian Lord. It had been expected that, on Kohl's passing, she would become the new Lord of Oren and obtain the Frost-touch to convene with the Ice Golems on their behalf.

Her relationship with the low-class Aciel had been unusual but not despised.

Only Kohl had objected to it.

To see her death after her heartbreak, battles with her father, and her own self-inflicted exile was more than his people could take. They mourned loudly. They wailed their grief. White flowers plucked from the steepest inclines along Oren were scattered on the ground around the village fire in symbolism of her death.

Kohl had effectively locked himself inside one of the larger buildings in Oren. Used for communal gatherings when the weather was too poor to meet outside, he sat on one of the stone seats and stared out the window, his mind and body numb.

He would never forget the sight of his own people at the Estorian drowning pits. And he'd never forget seeing Jato bleed out, Varkain venom running through her, on the streets of Taban Yul.

Something died within him both times. Some part of him that he'd never be able to get back.

He knew it was beyond rude to invite the other two Arillian Lords to Oren, then keep them waiting immediately after their arrival. But after everything he'd been through, everything he'd faced, he needed time to process his thoughts so he didn't come across as a gibbering mess.

Eventually, once the sun had set, he knew he had to face reality. There would be time for grieving later.

Lord Varielle, with her youthful energy, and Lord Dronour—almost three hundred years old—came the moment he gave Fogu the word. They shared their condolences, said the expected words of sorrow, then it was straight to business.

Much of it passed as a blur for Kohl. There were certain details of their conversation he'd never be able to recall. But the gist of it was the same. The two Lords had wanted to deal with things for years, but Kohl had always vyed for peace and put a halt to their plans.

There was no point, anymore. He'd been pushed beyond his limit.

Arillians had been banished to the distant north after they'd lost the Great War. Banished to a land where the ground was hard, few plants or animals could survive, and where his people coped on the fringes of society.

They would continue to be beaten for something their ancestors had done unless something changed.

'We must end this. I see no other way.' Kohl's voice had been without emotion. 'We did this. It was our fault. But when will our punishment end? When every Arillian is dead, like my daughter? No. Enough have lost daughters, families. We must put a stop to this. We can't wait until the rest of Linaria finishes us off. We've suffered enough. Aciel tried to fight back, and went about it the wrong way. Now, it is up to us to unite the Airllians behind a single goal.'

All three Lords were in agreement. All three would speak with the Ice Golems to set their decision in motion.

There would be no more Arillian deaths in Linaria from

this day forward. There would be consequences for those who had slain their people. And their law would be enforced.

Linarians would repent for what they had done to the Arillian people. It was beyond time they were judged.

'My lord?' Fogu broke his thoughts. 'Are you ready for the gathering now? I can tell the others you're still resting…?'

'No. Now is fine. Thank you, General. I'll be there in a minute.'

How long had it been since he'd convened his people?

Fogu, at least, was still respected. Most Arillians were happy to listen to him, to follow him. Their enthusiastic response to his arrival had put his General at ease—he'd been so ashamed of taking part in Aciel's campaign that he'd thought he'd never be worthy to go home again.

Kohl had been correct that he'd be welcomed home. That, at least, had been something good in the tangle of pain and loss.

Through the window, he could still see what remained of Jato's tower. It had felt like another lifetime when he'd returned here with Amarah. Somewhere out on the ice was what was left of *Khanna*. Little more than splinters, now. Probably frozen over, never to be rediscovered.

He pushed away the looming guilt. Amarah was clearly doing fine on her own—probably had another airship by now, knowing her. The sky pirate was nothing if not independent and competent. He needn't worry about her. Needn't feel guilty about what had happened to her.

He'd done everything in his power to stop the fight and had saved her life.

Perhaps not her eye, but certainly her life.

Knowing he couldn't put it off any longer, Kohl fluttered his wings and put his hat on as if it were a piece of armour that could protect him from his terrible grief.

With a small heave, he pushed off the smooth floor and slipped gracefully through the large entranceway on his wings, following Fogu.

The Arillians of Oren, his people, waited by the fire, alongside Lords Varielle and Dronour with their Generals. His own General stood near the front, having no doubt just addressed them. As Kohl flew near, he saw Tymē sitting on a large, flat boulder, one young child curled up on her lap, playing with the braids in her blonde hair. Despite the late hour, his people needed strong leadership, and most were present for his requested gathering.

Kohl couldn't bring himself to smile. 'My people. We have lost another Arillian today. Another daughter. General Jato.' His voice cracked on her name and he paused, taking several breaths. 'It has been long, far too long, since I lived up to my title as your Lord. Since I stopped trying to escape my responsibilities and problems. I ask your forgiveness, and understand that I will not fail you again.'

The crowd broke out into whispers. Oren was the most densely populated of the three Arillian settlements. Even after those who'd suffered at Aciel's hand were missing, there were still over ten thousand gathered. Their whispers suddenly grew into shouts.

Kohl raised his hand for quiet. 'I am welcome here, as I was before Aciel's ascension. The Golems have permitted General Fogu and I back home.'

His words, spoken low and calmly, cut through the crowd.

'I want peace. I have *always* wanted peace. But Linaria—more than just Oren—is unable to enjoy this through no fault of our own.'

The last few whispers in the crowd fell silent at his words.

Lord Varielle stepped up. 'Matsu has suffered greatly.

We've lost people. Friends. Loved ones. Those of you who visited my village these last few months have seen the devastation of my land.'

'Sirvat, too, has not escaped unscathed. We may never recover,' Lord Dronour added, his reedy voice thin.

Kohl continued, 'Those of you who travelled with Aciel on his campaign will have seen the state of Linaria. Will know the unrest between the peoples of this world. Borders between countries, races...even families are battlegrounds.' Kohl took a moment to catch his breath, and let his words hang. 'There is no one person responsible for this strife. No one group we can remove to scourge Linaria of this brewing war. With the dragons attacking Linarians, a king holding a Sevastos hostage, and Aciel's seal broken, there are too many elements, too many variables. The battles commencing now are some of the worst I have ever seen. Arillians are hunted down and slaughtered for gold. If they do not stop—and soon—I fear Linaria will be lost to us all.'

Fogu looked gravely on as if to emphasise Kohl's words, but he said nothing.

'We must defend ourselves before it's too late, and Linaria is destroyed.'

Kohl sensed the wavering nerves. Arillians glanced at one another, worried. Some held each other's hands, or held their children close.

'And what would you have us do, Kohl? To prevent this terrible fate?' It was Tymē. It was always Tymē. Her eyes held a grim steeliness that made Kohl think she already knew what he was going to ask of them.

'We will end this. We cannot sit up here and hide. Not when so much of the pain in Linaria has been caused by Arillian hands. I will *not* stand by and have Arillians be responsible for the destruction of our world. We came close to it in the Great War, and now Aciel has tried it again. Is *still* trying. We three Lords *will* end what he started. We will no longer cower in fear. We have the Frost-touch for a reason, and we mean to use it to the fullest of our abilities. There will be no more suffering.'

Lord Varielle raised her chin. 'We will convene with the Ice Golems, for they are the only ones who may judge our actions and pass sentence. We hope to end this chapter of death in Linaria, before our world is lost.'

Kohl, Varielle, and Dronour took to the air, their Generals following a moment later.

Kohl flew with grim determination. He'd never have thought it would come to this. Never thought Jato would be lost to him because of the Varkain.

Every time he closed his eyes, he saw her—skin stained crimson, unable to breathe.

Fogu caught up, flying alongside him while the other Lords and Generals stayed in formation a short distance behind. 'Whatever they say, I am with you until the end, my lord.'

Kohl looked at him. 'Thank you, my friend.'

They reached the edge of the floating island and dived down towards the tundra of ice and snow that spread out far below. The Everwinter stretched as far as northern Val Sharis—the influence of the Ice Golems and the Frost-touch that gave them life.

Before the dragons had risen, the Everwinter covered Linaria in its entirety. It was the beginning of everything, before any creatures walked on the land. The Varkain burrowed underneath, coveting heat and hibernating through the harshest winters. The Arillians flew above, gods of the world—untouchable.

Life had been in perfect balance.

Varielle, Dronour, and he wished to restore that balance.

It was the only way to end the constant cycle of destruction and save Linaria from dragon-fire.

Rows upon rows of Ice Golems stood in the snow. Silent sentinels, ever-watchful, guarding the last bastion of Arillian land from any who might wish to bring them harm. Carved from the ice and made living, they were ancient, immortal entities whose sole purpose was to guard the Arillians and provide judgement on their actions.

Kohl wondered how they would feel about casting judgement on the rest of Linaria.

For the second time in as many days, Kohl landed at their feet. Conversations between Arillians up in the relative isolation of Oren's meeting house was one thing. Actually asking the Golems was something else.

This time, he wouldn't speak alone. He, Varielle, and Dronour would all impart their request at the same time. A request in unity carried more weight. And as long as the request was for the good of Arillians as a whole, it was likely to be carried out.

Should the Ice Golems disagree, it would be a very different scenario.

Many Arillians had tried to worm their way out of some debt or ask for unwarranted assistance with a minor gripe. Most survived with little more than their pride hurt.

Kohl's face still bore the scars of the last time he'd offended the Ice Golems. He'd been lucky to get away. If they deemed him a threat, there would be nothing he could do.

Headless, the Ice Golems had no facial features, no emotional reactions to anything. They were a construct made living—each one an identical copy of the one before; hulking masses of ice, four-legged, four-armed monstrosities whose sheer bulk usually deterred any would-be assailants of the floating islands. They seemed to grow out of the ground—snow piled up about their legs and atop their shoulders. An everlasting feature of the landscape. Unchanging and eternal.

Kohl removed his hat and clutched it to his chest. To his left, Varielle held out her spear. To his right, Dronour clasped his hands behind his back. With a shuddering breath, Kohl closed his eyes. The three Arillian Lords called upon their Frost-touch, and reached out to the great sentinels with a gust of freezing air—their request written into the ice.

As one, the Ice Golems stirred as the magic of the Lords awakened them.

Kohl braced himself for their reply, which came immediately—a powerful emotion and distinct words in his mind.

A war to end all strife.

Return to the beginning.

Before the dragons drew breath.

Where no creature could harm Arillians.

Save Linaria before it turns to ash.

Kohl tensed. He knew the other two Lords heard the same answer, but he daren't turn his attention from the Ice Golems to see their reactions.

Unbidden, the memory of Jato's death flashed in his mind. It was swiftly followed by the Arillians in Estoria—bound by sky pirates, drowned in sea water. His memory of the Ark Veynothi, and the power she'd wielded while locked in stone. His own experience of capture by the sky pirates, and subsequent rescue by Fogu. His conversation with the elder dragon, and its hatred of the *Valta Forinja*. His time in Berel with the scholars. Their dedication to peace. The dragon-fire that had damaged so much of their city. And the hidden power he and Fogu had sensed while they were there. A sleeping force. Waiting.

Return Linaria to frozen tundra.

Together.

Kohl bit down on the urge to flinch as the Ice Golems spoke in unison, the power of their voices an explosion in his mind. The ground trembled beneath his feet, and Kohl's eyes snapped open.

He and the others took to the air as ice cracked underfoot and chunks of snow hurtled to the ground, fallen from the Golems' shoulders.

He'd spoken with the Golems many times. Had seen them bring Oren to the ground once. He'd only ever seen them move when they'd hurt him. Panic flared in his chest and he beat his wings, putting more distance between himself and the army below.

His throat tightened and his eyes burned from the memories he'd been forced to relive, unsure whether it was his own mind tormenting him, or if the Golems had somehow been able to manipulate his thoughts to see what he had experienced for themselves.

'They agree.' Lord Dronour said, his voice an octave higher. 'Three hundred years and now the Ice Golems awaken. Truly awaken. This is a momentous occasion! I am honoured to share it with you, Lords.' His large brown wings flapped slowly, keeping him aloft.

Kohl inclined his head in acknowledgement, but couldn't pull his eyes away from the Golems as they took their first steps, leaving small craters in the snow—marking where they had stood for millennia. Wind flared up above the army as they moved, a gust on the scale of a hurricane that swirled around their numbers.

His hands twitched with sudden cold, and Kohl realised the Ice Golems were calling upon the Lords' Frost-touch. Enormous chunks of ice formed along the base of Oren, slowly creeping up the sides as the Golems summoned it into being.

Varielle raised her spear, a beam of white light shooting

from the tip to the floating island. Ice burst into being where the light touched the land. Dronour, too, raised his hands. Massive chunks of ice crawled along the edge of the islands, spreading over every inch of it like a vast, shield.

Kohl and Fogu flew higher, until they were in line with the village—in time to see ice forming along the buildings and land, peaking into spikes at the top like a castle tower.

'It is a fortress, my lord. A floating fortress of Everwinter ice!'

The ice that had grown was the same blue-grey the Golems themselves were made of, the same as the base of the fire in the heart of their village. Imbued with the Arillians' most ancient magic, power emanated from the fortress as the ice grew higher and thicker. An impenetrable barrier coating every inch of the floating islands. Ice covered the white petals scattered for Jato, forever freezing them in place.

There were three main settlements within the Arillian's lands—Oren, Sirvat, and Matsu. But there were also countless other islands, some large enough for dwellings, others little more than floating debris. The Golems' ice formed along each and every one.

It was awe-inspiring. And though it was not enough to completely force the grief of Jato's death from Kohl's mind, it gave him a new purpose. A new focus.

He flew ahead of the islands, Fogu at his side, the other Lords behind him. They moved south, away from the two mountains that marked Oren, away from the barren landscape to which they'd been banished since the end of the Great War.

The army of Ice Golems marched below, the floating fortress of ice moved above, and Kohl—along with the Arillian Lords and their Generals—led them towards retribution.

39

Amarah flew east from Sereth in *RaKhanna*. It meant most of her journey took her across the Great Western Ocean—a foreboding expanse of water highly susceptible to summer storms—but it meant she didn't have to risk crossing Val Sharis or the Sea of Nami, where there were far worse dangers than strong winds.

She'd never flown this way around Linaria before. All her previous flights had required stops along the way—towns or villages that she could steal from to finance her next trip, usually. Flying alone was peaceful. The quiet ocean below almost lulled her into a false sense of security—that half the world *wasn't* on fire, and everything would be okay.

For the first time in as long as she could remember, she was flying on her own terms. She didn't owe Traego, didn't have to worry about him chasing her.

Moroda's debt was the oldest, and she needed to address that sooner rather than later. She'd relied on Kohl for his Arillian magic which was meant to help free Moroda from the Sevastos crystal. He'd also promised to get her a new ship after Jato had destroyed *Khanna*. And he'd promised to help her track down a Sevastos.

Amarah snorted. This was why she *didn't* rely on other people.

Ranski stretched out ahead of her—a hardy land of desert heat and dusty roads. Having sworn never to return when she'd left at fourteen, she'd already broken that vow by travelling back there once before. Now, she was back for a second time.

Ranski's western coast was home to a low mountain range—the only one in the country. It didn't have a name, but it spread from the southern tip along the jagged western shore until it reached the Corhaven border.

Phoenixes often nested in those mountains—as did the few dragons who called Ranski their home. There weren't as many of the fire-breathing beasts here as in Val Sharis, but Amarah peered down more often than not, in case a flash of red or green scales preceded another attack.

A high-pitched screech caught her attention, and Amarah glanced to her starboard side in time to see a phoenix with vivid orange-gold scales flying alongside *RaKhanna*. It held its talons close to its body, and Amarah scowled. 'Don't even *think* about getting any closer to my ship!'

The phoenix let out a high keening call and flapped its wings to keep pace before gliding again. It looked over at her every so often with its jewel-black eyes. It was larger than an eagle, but with narrower wings, a broader tail, and scales instead of feathers. Opening its golden beak, it let out another cry, then angled its wings upwards and veered away—diving into the depths of the mountains below.

If Topeko had been aboard *RaKhanna*, he'd have heralded it as a sign from Rhea.

After all, phoenixes were creatures that followed Rhea's

children, who were born of fire and lived and died in an endless cycle of rebirth. He'd have said it was something to do with one age of Linaria ending, and another beginning.

Amarah had never had the time for such nonsense, and wasn't superstitious in the slightest.

But she viewed the phoenix's arrival with a healthy degree of suspicion. They followed dragons—everyone knew that. If it led one of those creatures to her ship, Rhea herself wouldn't be able to save the beast from her wrath. Potential trouble was all the phoenix's appearance meant to her.

Amarah rubbed her eyebrows. If Moroda had figured out how to find a Sevastos, surely she, a famed treasure hunter who made her living finding hidden things, would be able to do the same.

And she'd do it without Kohl the dragon slayer.

Ranski opened up underneath her ship, a wide mass of yellows, golds, and browns. The Zona River flowed from north to south, splitting Ranski down the middle with a streak of blue. Berel lay on the river's other side, perched atop the lake of Rhea's breath—the university and Old Town dominating the middle of the lake. Greenery dotted the land close to Berel, adding much needed colour to a landscape of browns and yellows.

She'd flown through the entire night, and dawn had only just begun to light Linaria. It meant Amarah didn't have any sunburn or blisters on her shoulders, and remained cool and comfortable while she flew towards the heart of the desert. The long flight also meant her energy was spent, and she was looking forward to the rejuvenating magic the Samolen played each morning.

As a child, she'd promised herself she'd leave Berel and never return. Not unless she was dragged back kicking and screaming. Topeko had been the only good thing in her youth. The only person who'd shown her kindness and patience. Her parents had essentially given her up to the university in the hopes she would learn something useful. The Kalos had been horrific to her. And the Arch-Kalos had been the worst of all—the man who'd given her the final push to run away at fourteen years old. She glared at the city, mixed emotions fighting for dominance. There was no need to go to the university. No chance she'd encounter any of the Kalos and relive those memories.

Amarah brought *RaKhanna* around Berel's south side, towards the small hangar she always used to dock her ship. There were larger docks that catered to tourists and visitors, but the small hangar was closer to Topeko's home and was far quieter.

As she dropped in altitude, she frowned. She couldn't hear the morning music that usually played. The streets were silent, almost empty—there was hardly anyone outside. Amarah leaned forward, listening hard. Usually at this altitude their music carried high and clear.

And there was nothing.

Had something happened? Perhaps some new rule had been introduced?

Amarah dismissed the thought as soon as it appeared. The music every dawn and dusk was an integral part of Samolen culture. It wouldn't just...stop.

Several buildings lay blackened, their fabric rooftops burned or replaced with a patchwork of material. Even the university across the lake in the Old Town had walls that had been badly damaged.

With an innate sense that something wasn't right, Amarah brought in *RaKhanna* to land—the larger ship taking up far more space than *Khanna* ever had. There were a few class fives in the hangar already, and none of them looked like they had flown recently.

Amarah picked up her scythe and strolled along the deck. No Samolen to greet her.

She pursed her lips and clambered down from *RaKhanna*, the feeling of *wrongness* growing with every step. It had been over twenty years since she'd lived here. Aside from her brief visit with Moroda and the others—which had only lasted two days while essential repairs had been carried out on her ship—she'd not been anywhere near the country.

Was she misremembering?

Tightening her grip on the scythe, Amarah made her way down the stone hangar steps and onto the sandy ground. Heat drenched her and she took a breath. Definitely back in Ranski.

Although the docks were small, there was usually at least one or two Samolen in attendance—waiting to escort visitors to the university or give directions to wherever they were staying in town. She frowned, keeping a close lookout for any obvious threats, as she made her way along the streets of Berel New Town.

It hadn't changed much since her last visit, aside from the fact the streets were deserted. No robed Samolen milled about, no children laughed as they played and chased each other. There didn't even seem to be any birds singing.

'What in Rhea's name...?'

Breath held, Amarah hurried down familiar pathways, crossing into residential districts and looping around the back of a large section of houses. It had always been the quickest way to Topeko's, and even as a child she'd been fascinated by airships and so had often snuck away from her classes to watch the different types arriving and leaving.

When she spotted the purple fabric roof of Topeko's house, relief flooded her. She kept low for the moment, hiding behind a low wall that ringed the houses opposite. She didn't know what she was afraid of, exactly—the

Samolen weren't known for their aggression—but something had shifted in the city, and until she knew exactly what it was, she would take every precaution. Curtains had been drawn across the windows of Topeko's house. Odd, in the morning—Topeko had always been an early riser—but not unusual. It fuelled her suspicion.

Amarah glanced around, listening for anything dangerous.

Footsteps approached from her left. A pair of them. No, three.

She ducked down again, barely peeking around the corner of the stone wall for fear of being spotted.

Three Samolen. Two were healers—Kalosin—the third man stood about a head taller than the other two. She could tell he was a Kalos by the purple cheek jewel he wore and the fact his robes were a little more elaborate, with more silver weaved into the sleeves. A large bruise covered his temple. And he marched the two Kalosin along, his robes sweeping up with every step.

Narrowing her eye, she watched the three walk straight into Topeko's house.

Something was *wrong*. Terribly, terribly wrong.

No-one barged into the house of another. The Samolen were too formal and followed their rules of politeness too well.

She darted across the road to the entrance. Samolen protocol dictated she put her scythe away, but if Topeko was in trouble, she might need it. So Amarah kept her hold on it as she pushed through the curtain door—more heavy, purple fabric—and into the relative gloom of the entranceway. 'Topeko!'

Three Samolen looked up—the same ones who'd just walked in.

Amarah blinked, taking a moment to absorb the scene in

front of her. The usually pristine walls and floors had been shredded, chunks of wood gouged from the table and shelves. Books littered the floor, pages in disarray and scattered around the room. Topeko's enormous table—that she'd eaten at as a child—had been split in two; bowls and glasses on the floor, some of which had shattered. Both benches were in several pieces, splinters poking out from where they'd been snapped. But aside from the chaos and confusion of the mess, the worst thing by far was the dried and cracked bloodstain in the centre of the room. 'Where's Topeko?'

'Put that weapon down!' the Kalos said, straightening up and raising one palm.

She tossed her scythe to the floor and raced forward. 'Topeko? Topeko!'

The Kalos caught her as she tried to barge past him, both hands on her shoulders.

'Where's Topeko? What happened?'

'Calm yourself, child,' one of the Kalosin said gently. Her white stone flashed. 'You are Amarah, are you not? Kalos Topeko spoke of you often. Are you hurt? Shall I look at your eye?'

'I won't be calm until someone tells me what the fuck happened! Where's Topeko? Is he all right? Is this his blood?'

'Screaming and shouting isn't going to help the situation,' the Kalos said.

Amarah shook herself like a dog, trying to wriggle out of his hold, but he had her in a firm grip, and she couldn't get away. 'I *am* calm! I'm fine! Tell me what happened? Topeko's like a...a...an uncle to me.' She'd been about to say "dad," but that was a step too far, even if she did care deeply about the old scholar.

'There was an altercation,' the first Kalosin said. She

spoke calmly, as if discussing what she'd eaten for breakfast. 'One of the students desecrated the teachings. Turned violent.'

That couldn't be right. All the Samolen taught was peace, and how their magic could keep said peace going until the end of time. They were bound *by law*. 'That can't be right! Someone from outside must've broke in! Is Topeko okay?'

'He is in a bad way. He's resting at the moment, which is why we need you to be quiet. Can you do that, Amarah? It would help the Kalos if you controlled your emotions.' She gave her a smile, which only made Amarah angrier. Then, with a tiny wave of the Kalosin's hand, the rage bubbling up dissipated and heat filled the room.

Amarah stopped struggling.

The Kalos released her and stepped back. 'Better?'

Her gaze darted between the three Samolen, who'd evidently been in the middle of cleaning up the room. 'Can I see him? When did this happen? I'll track the bastard down, mark my words! You might not wanna fight back, but I will!'

Although the Kalosin flinched at her curse, they didn't reprimand her. 'I would prefer you didn't see Kalos Topeko. He needs absolute rest and quiet. We've summoned Andel to help comfort him during this time, but he may be some days arriving.'

'Andel's gone?'

'Visiting the other universities. How long has it been since you were here last, Amarah?' she asked again, her voice sickly sweet.

It grated. 'Too long. I'm gonna go see him. I won't disturb him. Trust me, I don't want Topeko any worse off than he is already.'

The Kalosin looked to the Kalos as if for permission.

He frowned at Amarah, then sighed. 'I'll come with you. This is...a very sensitive matter.'

Amarah shrugged. 'Can't stop ya.' She left the healers to their work and walked to the large hallway. How could the Samolen have let this happen? For someone to have hurt Topeko—put him in a bad way—they had to be professionals. Other than books, what did Topeko have that was of any value? It wasn't as if he kept a pot of gold hidden under his bed. Perhaps whoever had carried out the attack had scared everyone off, and that was why the streets were empty.

The Kalos followed her a few steps behind. 'This *really* isn't the best time, Amarah.'

'I don't give a fuck. I'm here now.' Having an escort didn't bother her. She could always ignore him. 'What in Rhea's name happened?'

'Too many things. Too much darkness.'

A typically Samolen answer—vague, overly mysterious, and not at all helpful. She snorted. She'd get a better answer from Topeko—the only Kalos who had ever been straight with her. 'Who are you, anyway? First on the scene?'

He cleared his throat, indignant. 'I am Kalos Ettas, a fellow teacher at the university.'

'Why are *you* here, then? Breaking the teachings is a bad thing, ain't it? Is Arch-Kalos off terrorising some other non-Samolen?' Amarah remembered the Arch-Kalos and his vicious insults at her inability to do magic. Something about her being broken and having tainted blood.

Ettas halted, his cheeks reddening. 'You really are as uncouth as they say.'

'Who's *they*?'

'It matters not. Lower your voice, please. He's in here.'

They stopped outside a closed door near the rear of the house. Despite herself, Amarah trembled as Ettas gently knocked, then pushed the door open. 'Kalos Topeko? You have a visitor. I know you aren't to be disturbed at the moment, but she was quite insistent.'

Amarah hovered in the doorway, waiting for Ettas to push the door open wide enough so she could get a good look at the room before she stepped inside.

But when she saw Topeko, all her survival instincts went out the window. He lay under several blankets, one arm dangling off the edge of the bed. Topeko, like most of the Samolen, had skin darkened under the desert sun, but it was pale and blotchy. His breathing came out in a rasp, his eyes firmly closed.

'Topeko!' Amarah rushed into the room, grasping his hand in her own. 'Dragons above, what have you got yourself into?' She perched on the end of the bed and stared down at him. His chest had been bound in bandages, but she could still see and smell the blood leaking from his wounds. Deep lacerations across his chest and arms added grim red lines across his skin. 'What happened? What was he savaged by? *Axes*?' Amarah was incredulous.

Ettas closed the door gently behind him as he entered the room. 'One of his new students. You know how Topeko likes to train up less than—'

She glared at him.

The Kalos cleared his throat. 'That is to say, he likes to work with...*challenging* individuals. For whom success would be difficult but hard-earned.'

She looked back at Topeko. His pulse was weak. 'And? He helped *me*.'

'Yes, well, we know all about you. *This* one was a man of the Imperial Guard. So accustomed to violence, he's been nothing but trouble since the moment he arrived.'

'Someone from the Imperial Guard? What they wanna do studying magic here? The Guard is stretched thin in

Corhaven and Val Sharis. Didn't think any of 'em would be able to leave.'

Ettas shrugged. 'It matters not the reason, as long as they are willing to cast aside their rage and follow the teachings. Kalos Topeko tried. Kalosai Andel was a good influence, too.'

Amarah frowned at the thought. She knew what they taught. She knew there were people who willingly travelled to the university to gain an education in a particular field of magic. It didn't make sense that someone with the training and background of a soldier would throw that away to practice peace.

Ettas said, 'The dragons have been highly-strung of late. A few even drew their breath over the university. Nothing has gone well since he arrived.'

That explained the burned buildings she'd seen on her flight in. Amarah didn't say anything, her focus on her old tutor.

'This young Kalosai, this man of the sword, brought his weapon to the dragon and attacked it. The dragon's blood still stains the street where they fought.' Ettas scowled at his own words, his nose wrinkling.

'Impressive. Most dragons would just melt any sword someone swung at it.'

Ettas shook his head. 'This was no ordinary sword. It was a *Valta Forinja*.'

Amarah's jaw dropped. It *couldn't* be. 'What you say?'

The Kalos rolled his eyes. 'The originals were forged thousands of years—'

'I *know* what the damned thing is! Was it a short sword? Was it *Morgen*?' There was no way it could be him. She'd last seen Morgen on the outskirts of Povmar, a remote village in the furthest reaches of Corhaven. It was nowhere near Ranksi.

'You *know* him?' Ettas gasped.

Amarah looked back at Topeko. His eyelids fluttered, his breathing hitched for a moment, then settled down. She recalled the sight of blood, the destroyed furniture. Morgen had always been keen to uphold the law and follow orders. Even orders he didn't agree with. He'd been quick to leap into action and defend others—perhaps a little too quick, if she was honest. He'd been kind-hearted and helpful. Dedicated. He'd killed only when he had to, and fled when he didn't. She pursed her lips. 'Nah. I don't think I do know him.'

'Hmm.' Ettas folded his arms and dropped his voice to a whisper. 'To answer your earlier question, the Arch-Kalos himself did not escape Morgen's wrath. I am the most senior Kalos at the university right now. One of my own students was also caught up in this mess. So I felt it my duty to be with Kalot Topeko and the Kalosin.'

Amarah stood up. 'What?'

Ettas dropped his gaze to the floor, head bowing low. 'Morgen left...quite some trail of destruction. Kalosai Mahlu disappeared at the same time. Either she left with him or we have another body yet to discover.'

What was going on with Morgen? It couldn't be the same soft-hearted soldier who'd arrested her back in Niversai, who'd gone to find a medic for her, and had let her roam free once he'd caught up with her in Burian forest. The same man who'd taught Moroda and Eryn how to defend themselves, had leapt to their aid when assaulted by Jato's Arillians. Who'd *grieved* at their deaths.

'Where's the Arch-Kalos?' Amarah asked.

'His body is at the university.'

'How in Rhea's name did *Morgen* overpower him? That can't be right. You've got it wrong. Morgen ain't like that, and even if he was, he ain't *that* strong.'

Ettas rubbed his forehead, a nervous twitch most Goldstones had. 'Morgen appears to have used *He*. I do not know how. None of us would have taught it to him. I fear the Arch-Kalos was right—his blood is bad. Tainted. It was only a matter of time before he snapped. All the signs were there—'

Ettas continued to ramble on, words spilling out like a torrent.

'Whatever Morgen did—if it *was* him—I don't believe he killed the Arch-Kalos. He's the most powerful Samolen in Linaria for Rhea's sake!'

'Don't you think *we* thought the same thing?' Ettas snapped.

Topeko groaned and coughed weakly.

Amarah sat back down and grasped his hand. 'It's all right, Topeko. Sorry, your Kalos is getting a bit wound up. You'll be okay, won't you?' She stared at Ettas as she spoke.

He shrugged.

'Where'd the Arch-Kalos die? I wanna see this for myself.'

~

AMARAH LEFT Topeko in the hands of the Kalosin. Admittedly, if she stayed, she'd work herself up into just as much of a state as Ettas had.

She'd come back to Berel looking for a huge plate of the only decent food in Linaria, a catch-up with Topeko, and information on how to find a Sevastos in order to do some good.

The last thing she'd expected was to walk into a bloodbath, discover her old ally had murdered the Arch-Kalos, and had tried to do the same to Topeko. The Arch-Kalos she didn't care for. Topeko was another matter entirely.

He was as close to family as it got. Even her sky pirate allies were capable of stabbing each other in the back. Topeko was above that—he was the epitome of total honesty.

She couldn't believe Morgen had caused all that destruction. Had almost killed Topeko. She refused to believe it. The man had stayed in Niversai with Topeko after Aciel's battle. He'd gone back to rebuild the city and *help* people. Somewhere along the line, he'd been posted out to Povmar and had guarded the little village in the snow, protecting the villagers from griffins.

That's when she'd last seen him.

Other than the fact he'd grown a beard, he was exactly as she remembered.

Since then, Veynothi had been released, an enormous sea monster had attacked Estoria, and she'd gained a new ship.

When she thought of it that way, a lot had changed in a short amount of time. But had Morgen's personality really shifted *that* much? Had what he'd been through really driven him to hurt and kill innocent people?

Amarah followed the path under the lake, as Ettas had directed her before she left Topeko's home. She knew all about the ceremonies down here—the rituals in which Kalosai obtained their proper cheek jewel, and were indoctrinated fully into their magical society.

It had repulsed her as a child and it repulsed her now. The physical manifestation of everything she'd never be. Of all her failings.

Ettas had permitted her to carry her scythe in case Morgen had left any traps they'd not found, which she held tightly as she navigated the winding tunnel. Under the lake had been one place she'd never been permitted to see, so she'd decided it wasn't worth her time.

It was always easier to run away from something you didn't like.

One of the two Kalosin escorted her to the tunnel opening, and waited for her outside—partly because they didn't want to visit the site of the Arch-Kalos' death, and partly because Amarah told her to wait.

Amarah wanted to be alone while she investigated.

She'd been so concerned about Isa becoming queen and outrunning the bounty on her head that she'd hardly spared a thought for what happened in the rest of Linaria. Dragons had been worrying Val Sharis. Ranski had always been so far away that she'd never even considered the idea of anything going wrong there, nor it affecting her.

Water dripped from the tunnel's ceiling, the drops echoing.

Something rumbled deep in the earth, like a beast sleeping. Amarah held her breath, waited for it to pass, then continued. A hole appeared in the ground ahead of her, and she slid down the ladder, dropping into a vast cavern. She landed with a thud, her knees twinging on impact.

With a wince, Amarah made her way towards the lake. She'd only taken a few steps when she noticed the blood stains on the dusty ground by the water's edge. 'Dhabra.'

She walked over to it, wary of anyone else down here, then crouched low for a better look.

Was it truly the blood of the Arch-Kalos? It had smeared, no doubt from when the other Samolen had heaved his body away. Deep lines had been gouged in the sand close by. Clear signs of a struggle. There were too many footprints to discern any more information—but something *had* happened down here not too long ago.

Amarah wondered if the Arch-Kalos had died instantly or been left to bleed out.

She hoped it had been a slow, painful death.

Amarah approached the lake water. 'Rhea's breath. Really.' Samolen cheek jewels were forged from it. A lake of power that fuelled the country and the Samolen magic, wherever they were in Linaria. Something she'd never been able to achieve.

The surface of the water rippled.

She raised her scythe, just in case. As far as she knew, nothing lived in the lake. No fish. No plants. Nothing that could move. 'Who's there?' Perhaps *this* was the true cause of Dhabra's death, not Morgen.

Water splashed, and Amarah stepped back—she didn't want it touching her.

Grasping the handle of her scythe in both hands, Amarah shouted out to the water, 'Did you kill Dhabra?'

'*I did not kill the Arch-Kalos.*' A female voice drifted through the cave, reverberating off the walls and ceiling. '*But I watched the one who did.*'

Amarah swallowed. Too many thoughts cascaded through her mind at once.

'*I thought he would kill the girl in his rage. But he was satisfied with his first taste of blood.*'

'Who are you?' Amarah spun around, but she couldn't see who spoke. The only movement was the rippling lake water. 'Where are you?'

In response, flames surged across the water. Bright gold, they covered every inch of the lake and crawled up the walls of the cavern.

Amarah gasped. She'd never heard of fire across the lake before. Never heard of a voice down here, either. She had buried her head in the sand and ignored many of her problems, weaknesses, and the things she didn't understand—but surely she'd have heard a *rumour* of this before now?

She didn't know what kind of magic this was. After everything with Veynothi and the sea monster, anything was possible. Amarah decided to stick to logic for now. 'Was it Morgen?'

The flames flickered and grew brighter. '*And Mahlu. Together, they slaughtered the Arch-Kalos.*'

'Why?'

'*Linaria is on the brink of destruction. Our fires will destroy everything. Morgen wishes to stop this. Violently. The Arch-Kalos opposed him.*'

Amarah blinked. '*Our* fires? You mean...you're a...you're a dragon?' Was this day going to throw any more surprises at her?

The fire crackled and spat, shifting to blue. It reminded Amarah of the fires in Veynothi's tomb, and she leapt back. A dragon burst from the water, sending up a shower of spray around itself. Every scale looked like it had been carved out of the purest gold, and even with its wings folded tight against its body, the enormous beast filled the cavern, its tail curling around its body.

Amarah crossed the scythe over her chest—not that it would offer any protection if the dragon decided to breathe fire. She'd be incinerated in a heartbeat. The dragon was so large that a single fang rivalled the length of her scythe. She wondered how quickly she could run back to the ladder.

As if reading her mind, the dragon spoke, '*I have no desire to kill you.*'

'Yeah, not buying that.' Amarah backed away slowly.

'*You came to see this place and now you flee?*'

'I was trying to find out what happened to Dhabra. See if I could figure anything out. If I'd known there was a bloody dragon down here...'

The dragon pulled back her lips, exposing dagger-like fangs. It could have been her version of laughter. Amarah wasn't sure, nor did she care to stay and find out. Every fibre of her being screamed at her to run before the dragon decided she wanted an Amarah-shaped snack.

'*Morgen has access to all our magic, now. The half that the Samolen use, and the half that they shun. Life and death. The Arch-Kalos passed it to him.*'

Anger flared within her. After his escapades down here, Morgen had nearly killed Topeko, and not for any reason that she could discern. 'Why didn't you stop him? You're a dragon! You could have burned everything!'

'*It is not my place to meddle in your affairs.*'

Something clicked for Amarah. Her knees went weak. 'Wait. You...Are you Rhea?'

The dragon laughed again. 'The Kalos called me that, once.'

'But you aren't the creator of Linara? You're just another dragon? Like any of the others?'

'*Your eyes are not so easily deceived.*'

'A Sevastos, then? Why are you in the lake?'

The dragon closed her eyes for a moment. '*I am old. Sleep lasts decades. I leave the skies to my younger brethren. The Samolen syphon a little of my magic and I can sleep as long as I wish.*'

Amarah scratched her head, unconcerned with the hows or whys. 'I want your help. Undo the work of a Sevastos who sealed my...friend. Can you do that?'

Smoke poured from the dragon's nose. '*It is within my power. But why would I undo what another has given their life for?*'

'I thought you dragons like to bargain with us?'

Again, the dragon seemed to laugh.

It had grown warm in the cavern, with the flames crackling away, and Amarah felt as if she was trapped in the middle of a clay oven.

She tried again. 'My friend is in there. Sealed away in

crystal. She tried to stop a war. Tried to stop Aciel. If it weren't for her, none of us would be here. The damned Arillians would've taken over everything.' She thought back to her time in Taban Yul before freeing Isa. Aciel's power had hung in the air, even then. Affecting people of the city. 'It was for nothing if Aciel's still able to hurt people. Or kill 'em. I owe Moroda, and I wanna stop this.'

'Do you understand what you ask? I smell you are of Samolen blood, but I have never seen you in this cave before. The Kalos have never prayed for you to take my power.'

Amarah shrugged. 'I wasn't ever worth it, I guess.'

The dragon studied her. Water dripped from her scales, bursting into flame the moment they touched the lake below. *'You ask me to give you my power. What do you offer in return?'*

Amarah flinched. 'I dunno? I ain't got nothing to give. Only my ship, but that's my freedom. I can get you gold? Jewels? What's your payment?'

Lowering her head to look Amarah in the eye, the dragon let out another rumble, power pulsing from her body as waves of heat when she moved. *'I agree to help you, because I think this will stop the death raining upon Linaria. But you must give your life to take this gift.'*

'What?'

'You ask me to sacrifice. The lake's power will dry up if I leave. The Samolen will no longer be able to create jewels of power. Their city will slowly perish and return to desert. I have lived within these waters for thousands of years. It is no wonder they worship me as a Goddess, even if they are misplaced.'

Amarah stammered. 'But...I would...'

'You will perish, as I will. As they will.'

Amarah couldn't speak. She'd wanted to help Moroda since the Goldstone stopped the fighting. Pay her back for all she'd done. She'd finally encountered a dragon capable of doing it—and could hardly believe it had been the one responsible for the Samolen's magic. The *one* thing she'd never been able to tap into. The innate energy the Kalos had sworn every person had access to.

Amarah had been denied it her whole life.

And now the source of the power, perhaps the oldest dragon living, had agreed to help her.

She'd get everything she wanted—repaying debts and the last laugh at those Kalos who'd always called her worthless and broken. Who'd forced her to run away.

Amarah had flown many ships in her lifetime. She wondered how it would be to soar atop the wings of a golden dragon.

Had Morgen known about the Sevastos? Or had he fallen so far down a dark path that he couldn't tell what was right anymore? Amarah couldn't wrap her head around the change.

She scratched her nose.

RaKhanna. Topeko. Palom. Traego. Isa. Revenge on Jato. Revenge on Morgen.

She had so many things to live for, so many things she wanted to do. And yet without the dragon's help, she couldn't free Moroda.

Giving up everything she still had to do, still wanted to do.

She blinked, realising the dragon waited.

Amarah held her scythe close. Out of the corner of her eye, she saw Dhabra's blood, dry and dark on the ground. Some wrongs had already been righted without her being anywhere near.

She chewed the inside of her lip, considering.

'No deal, dragon.' Amarah backed away and grabbed hold of the ladder. 'But if you care about Linaria, about it not being destroyed, maybe you should stop being like the

Samolen. Stop preaching peace, or that you're above the rest of us. If you wanna do something to help, *do* it. We aren't all willing to die for you. We'll figure it out ourselves if we have to.'

Bowing its head, the dragon slunk back into the water without another word, the flames dying with it, disappearing as quickly as they had arrived, and leaving the cavern full of steam.

Amarah climbed up the ladder, her breaths short as she came down from the shock of insulting an apex predator, a goddess, and living to tell the tale. She could already imagine the look on Topeko's face when he recovered. She looked forward to him telling her off for being so reckless.

Amarah smirked.

She'd find another way to help Moroda.

And she'd do it on her own terms.

40

Debris piled up at Isa's feet as she continued to dig into the cave wall that trapped her. Tears blurred her vision, but it didn't matter in the pitch dark. Despite her tolerance for insults, Tacio's words had cut deeply. For once, it wasn't the fact she was a cat. It was the fact her actions had allowed others to suffer and die for a cause they vehemently opposed.

It was worse because he was right: those deaths *were* on her head. People had died for her, but their deaths had brought Veynothi back to life. If those people hadn't been following her, they'd never have been captured and used for such a hideous purpose.

And when she took her throne—because she was damned if she was going to fail after everything she'd been through—that thought would stay with her until the day she died. The palace itself would be forever tainted.

Soil caked her fingernails, but she'd made decent progress as she dug through the cave wall. It would spill out into another tunnel, then she'd be on the run again. At least she'd had time to recover some of her energy while kneeling on the floor, even if shoveling soil with her bare hands took a great deal of effort.

Tacio had stopped taunting her for a while. He would have heard her crying, she was certain. But it was evident from his vicious attacks—and his Cerastes—that he wanted to do more than upset her. There was no more returning her to the palace. This was life and death.

She'd always hated his smug face and arrogance. A preening peacock who delighted in belittling others and tormenting those he perceived as beneath him. That was pretty much everyone, other than their father.

She'd brought him down a peg or two when she'd escaped from the palace. But instead of simmering down, he'd practically boiled over—resolute in his goal to teach Isa her place for hurting him.

Isa flinched when a worm fell out of the soil and crawled along the back of her hand. Shaking her finger, she flicked it away, then felt a gentle breeze from the other side of the hole she'd dug. Biting down on her scream for joy, she grabbed the sword, using its edge to widen the gap—she didn't want the whole thing to collapse on her head as she was crawling through it.

She paused for a moment, listening intently for any signs of movement from Tacio. She hadn't heard him walk away, but he'd been silent for quite some time now. It was possible he'd put himself into stasis, waiting for her to grow too hungry or thirsty to stay hidden any longer, ready to pounce when she inevitably made a break for it.

If that was the case, and he heard her scramble out the back of the cave, she'd have a good minute or two head start on him. She planned to use every second of it.

His earlier taunts might have upset her. But they'd also stoked her own fires of anger. Tacio and Sapora would pay for what they had done to her people. They weren't lambs to be slaughtered, or thralls to be used and thrown away as the Varkain saw fit.

The Ittallan were worth far more than that—and she was determined to prove it.

Isa slid the sword along the ground, pushing it all the way out of the cave and into the adjacent tunnel. Again, she waited, listening. Only once certain that no Varkain lay in wait outside, Isa tapped into her *meraki*. Light engulfed her, brightening the cavern for a brief moment. In her true form, Isa was small enough to dart through the hole she'd made, and she slipped through, ears flat and tail held low. Her paws carried her silently along.

On the other side, she breathed deeply. Fresh air flowed through here. Isa swivelled her ears, listening as she tried to work out the best move. Tacio wasn't far away, even if he hadn't realised that she'd escaped yet.

She padded along the tunnel towards the clear air, nose twitching. The tunnel curved around and upwards and she stopped, looking up. Her eyes were far better in her true form, and she saw a hint of moonlight at the far end of the slope. Freedom!

Darting back to her sword, she transformed back, scooped it up, then pelted along the tunnel towards the cool night air. Her joy grew with every stride that brought her closer to freedom from the underground, and closer to her people.

She didn't care if the Varkain heard her footsteps or breathing—she was so close to getting out of the tunnels that it didn't matter. She'd fight them again if she had to—but on open ground, where she had the advantage, and their transformed states were more a hindrance than a threat.

In a confined space—like a tunnel in the dark—the Varkain reigned supreme. But on open ground, she'd *always* be better. At worst, she could flee—and she was faster than them in a sprint than trapped in a tunnel.

Cool air stung her bloodied cheeks as she powered up the final incline. Part of the ceiling had collapsed here, enabling her to see the moonlight that signalled her escape. If the tunnels here were lived in and had been maintained, she might very well have died down there—starved to death if she didn't go out to meet Tacio and his Cerastes' fangs.

'The cowardly cat runs away!'

Isa laughed at the insult hurled at her from several feet behind. It sounded like a Cerastes—Tacio's voice grated more. None of it mattered. They could say what they wanted —she was *free*. She'd rolled around in the dirt like a filthy animal. She looked nothing like the regal queen she purported to be. But she'd done what had been necessary.

Her laughter carried, and she sprinted on, fuelled by her own elation. The sky was no longer ink black, but navy, and bright along the horizon. Dawn was not far off. Dragons above, she'd been underground a long time. Solvi would be looking for her. Kylos and Aetos, too, if Solvi had woken them up.

She only hoped her tunnel wanderings hadn't taken her too far from the camp.

Thankfully, the volcano acted as an unmissable landmark, and she headed towards it. As long as she kept it ahead of her, and the sea to her right, there was no way she wouldn't find the others.

'You're continuing on this farcical campaign of yours, then?' Tacio called.

Isa slowed and turned around, while continuing to back off. He stood where she'd appeared from the tunnel, two Cerastes with him.

He tilted his head. 'Even though they'll call you the blood queen for all the death you've brought to the Ittallan?'

Isa scowled and shouted back, 'It's better than the kitten princess!'

The Cerastes chuckled, but Tacio wasn't moved. He had to be thirty feet away now, the distance growing every second.

Isa raised her arms in a shrug. 'This is it Tacio! You've thrown your best at me and I've beaten you! I've won! Go back underground and stay there before you embarrass yourself even more!'

'My *best*? Don't make me laugh!' Tacio crouched, then darted forward. Putting all the speed of a strike into his movement, he dashed towards her, covering the distance between them in three quick lunges.

Isa had expected it. Nothing was really out of range of a Varkain if they wanted the kill badly enough. She held her sword out, defending herself against his inevitable strike.

Tacio's blade bounced off hers, and he held it high, panting from his sudden exertion.

'Do you really want to do this, Tacio? After what happened last time?'

'Last time, I had you trapped until your friends turned up.'

Isa smirked and raised an eyebrow, her jubilation of the clear air above her giving her more confidence. 'Only because of your Cerastes. I'm talking about you and me. One on one. Who came out of *that* worse off? I see the powders you use to cover your skin. Hiding that shame.'

'That was different. You had an airship waiting to fly you to safety. Look around you, Isa. There's nothing here. I'll keep my Cerastes out of it. They'll be here to witness the true victor.'

Isa chanced a look at them. They hadn't moved from the tunnel's gaping mouth.

'You see?' Tacio said, 'you need so many people to keep

you up, keep you safe. Whatever happens, all their deaths cannot be erased. How could you in good faith become queen, knowing there are so many bodies behind you?'

Isa's jubilation shifted into rage. 'I don't know if you've noticed, but being king *isn't* about being the best. Sapora needs me. You. The Valendrin. The Arks. He does none of it himself. At least I have people who *choose* to follow me instead of following out of fear of death! I'm not perfect and have never said I was. You preen like you're a damned peacock!'

Tacio laughed, once. 'I don't roll around in the muck like a pig. Disgracing myself with the company I keep. We are the children of Vasil the conqueror! We *are* above the riff raff.'

'I'm acting like it. You're the spoiled child who hates not getting his own way.' Isa lunged with the sword, bringing it up in a swift strike. She didn't care to talk to him. Their world views were too different, too extreme from one another. From the moment they'd met, they'd been at odds. The years had done nothing to change that.

Tacio darted to the side, but her blade caught the edge of his sleeve, slicing through it at the wrist.

'I'm going to be Queen of the Ittallan. I will atone for my mistakes. That is not your concern. Stay in Sereth, Tacio. I'll try and convince Sapora to join you. You can rule the Varkain there.'

For a moment, it looked as if Tacio considered her words. He didn't snap back a barbed retort, nor did he scoff at her suggestion. His gaze fell on her weapon, then at his own blade—more a long dagger than a sword. He curled his lip, one fang poking out. 'You travel with thieves and pirates, scum from the bottom of my boot, and pretend you have a right to the throne? Hah. You won't see the truth of the horrors you've already brought to the Ittallan, fine. That's on you. I thought I could get you to give up this silly quest to be queen. You're not a child anymore, Isa. These are real lives you're playing with.'

Isa kept a careful watch, waiting for the slightest hint Tacio was about to strike.

'I have yet to play my own trump card. You're *filth*. You aren't fit to live, let alone rule!' Tacio charged at her, blade low, aiming for her legs.

Isa leapt high, soaring clear over him and landing several paces away. 'What trump card?'

Tacio circled her, every step slow and deliberate. 'Sapora isn't the only one who knows where the Arks are.'

Isa gasped. 'Yfaila. I'd forgotten about her.'

Tacio's grin broadened, his eyes glinting in the low light of pre-dawn. 'Ah yes. Thanks to one of *your* Ittallan, I know where Prince Karekis is. Did you know only a pure Varkain of royal blood can break his seal? Not Sapora. Certainly not you. Only *I* can.'

Isa couldn't believe it. 'Not only are you against me, you're against Sapora, too?'

'I was born to be king. I rule the Cerastes. I have the strongest blood. Veynothi will respect me when I have Prince Karekis at my side. Don't worry, Isa. We'll all return to Sereth once the fighting's done. The Val Sharis Council will report to me, and pay Sereth homage, just as they did with Vasil. Put things back where they ought to be, before anything gets more out of hand.'

She couldn't believe it. The entire time she'd thought Sapora would be her greatest adversary for the throne, while Tacio had acted like a true snake and been putting other plans into motion. Tacio was always going to be a thorn in her side. For all his whining about going back to Sereth, he was inconveniencing himself just to teach *her* a lesson.

Before she could respond, Tacio was on her again, slashing so quickly she almost tripped over her own feet trying to stay out of his reach. The rocks and loose pebbles underfoot didn't help, and she turned her back to him in order to leap away.

The tip of his blade caught one shoulder blade, and she winced. Finally with some distance between herself and him, she caught her breath. The wound stung, but she'd survived worse. She was still covered in the cuts and grazes she'd picked up in the tunnels, and her arms throbbed.

An eagle screeched high above. Isa glanced up, but couldn't spot it in the dark sky. She cursed a moment later, because Tacio struck again, taking advantage of her momentary distraction. For all his bravado and arrogance, he was a skilled fighter, and his blade caught her a few more times—drawing blood every time it did.

She snarled and struck back, heaving the sword around in a powerful strike that clipped his ankle and knocked him off-balance. If he wasn't bluffing about Prince Karekis, that would be the biggest problem added to everything she needed to overcome. Veynothi was already too much—she'd survived *her* through pure luck. Luck ran out, eventually.

With a surge of strength, Isa forced herself to go on the offensive. The sword seemed to grow heavier with every swing, but she pushed through the fatigue and ache in her muscles, attacking Tacio with deadly precision.

She feinted to the right, then slammed the sword into his torso—catching his hip and drawing blood for the first time.

Her heart raced, each slash more furious than the last, driving Tacio away.

He met her onslaught with equal fury, parrying the attacks of the heavier weapon and keeping her blade away from him.

They wore a rut among the shifting stones and rocks on the ground with their constant dancing around one another, and Isa had to focus more on where she stepped than on attacking Tacio. Her skin prickled with sweat.

Somewhere to the east, a wolf howled.

Tacio paused for a moment, and Isa leapt back, widening the gap between herself and him. Already, she could feel her blood lust creeping through her, waiting to be unleashed. She didn't want it to. Tacio's words about the palace smelling of blood would stay with her forever. She didn't want to go mad in the heat of battle—that was *not* how a queen was supposed to act.

It might have worked for Vasil, a warrior-king and conqueror, but not her.

Even Archigo Gralla had said there was more to power than killing your enemies effectively.

She wasn't Vasil. Or Sapora. Or Tacio. She was *more* than they were. People loved her. Would fight for her—live and die for her. And she would do the same for them. *That* was the difference. The Varkain saw people as a means to an end—a stepping stone on their own rise to accumulating more power and prestige.

Isa saw them as people who would rise *with* her.

A voice for the voiceless.

Tacio pointed the tip of his blade to an indiscernible spot on the landscape behind Isa's shoulder. 'You see? Your followers, racing to your aid. Coming to save the lost kitten.'

Isa glanced past him to the tunnel she'd escaped from. The same two Cerastes remained in place, watching. Tacio didn't have any reinforcements, then. She'd heard Aetos cry, and the wolf howl was the young Karvou—Palom had taken him under his wing. Three against three were better odds. If Solvi, Chyro, or any of the others had come, too, then the

Varkain would have no chance. It would be like Tannon Sona all over again.

Tacio seemed to come to the same conclusions, because he lowered his blade.

Isa kept hold of her sword. She wasn't so naive as to put away her fang while she was within Tacio's striking range. She focussed on her ragged breathing, trying to stay in control of her blood lust. Now there was a little space between herself and Tacio, it wasn't affecting her as intensely. The more time passed with her in control, the less likely it was to take over.

Tacio attacked suddenly—putting on a burst of speed that put him within arm's reach of Isa in less than a heartbeat. His blade caught her across the forearm as she brought up her sword to deflect his strike, but the force of it knocked her to the ground.

Isa braced herself with both hands, dropping her sword in the same movement. The rocks dug into her palms—one particularly sharp one even cut the edge of her thumb. She flinched and rolled away, narrowly avoiding Tacio's second strike, which plunged into the ground where her throat had been a second earlier.

Coughing, she pushed herself up onto her hands and knees, ready to dodge again.

A bellow from behind distracted her, along with heavy steps charging along. Isa straightened to see an enormous bear hurtling towards them. 'Chyro.'

Beyond, Karvou loped forward, the white fur of the wolf stark against the dark backdrop. Solvi followed, as did Kylos. Overhead, Aetos circled, screeching all the while.

The fight was over.

Isa smiled, her hair a mess and her clothes ruined, but she was victorious. Tacio hadn't been able to put her out of action, and now her reinforcements were seconds away.

Judging by the look of utter contempt on Tacio's face, he knew it, too. He darted towards her and slashed across her face with his own claws. She spun away, her sword now out of reach. In her peripheral vision, the two Cerastes ran towards them. With Aetos and the others charging in, she needed to stop this before it became a bloodbath.

Isa dropped to the ground and rolled away from him. She scooped up a pile of rocky soil and flung it at his face as he dived after her.

Tacio grunted and squeezed his eyes shut, fingers scrabbling at his face.

Isa reached down, grabbed the long dagger he'd dropped, and drew it across the back of his knee. When he staggered, she kicked him down, blade pressed against the thin skin of his throat.

Tacio coughed and spluttered, one eye shut, the other watering. 'How *dare* you use such underhanded tactics!'

Isa gulped down air and grinned. She tasted blood between her lips. 'You do what it takes to win.'

He hissed.

A flash of light burst from Isa's left, and she glanced across in time to see the red fox shift back into Kylos. 'I'll ask later what in Rhea's name happened tonight, princess. I'm just glad yeh in one piece.' She appraised her. 'Well, just about in one piece.'

'I appreciate your concern, Kylos,' Isa said, the edge of the blade pressed against Tacio. She could practically hear his pulse. The desire to open his throat from ear to ear was almost too great. It wouldn't take much effort at all. Like drawing a nail across a file.

'What yeh waitin' for, princess? Kill him!' Kylos said. 'If yeh don't wanna kill yeh own flesh and blood, I understand. Give me the blade an' I'll gladly spill his blood.'

Isa didn't know if it would be better to kill him herself, let Kylos get her revenge, or just let the snake go.

None of them appealed to her.

Chyro, Solvi, and Karvou transformed back and formed a semicircle around Isa and Tacio. The Cerastes halted a few steps from their downed leader. All eyes were locked on her.

Tacio glared at her with one eye, his entire body tense.

Isa knew he wouldn't beg. He was far too proud for that.

'Isa! Remember what this snake did teh me! *Teh Lathri*!' Kylos said through gritted teeth. 'Cut him an' let him bleed out. He don't deserve a quick death.'

Isa's fingers trembled.

'If yeh can't kill *this* snake, what yeh gonna be like when yeh fight Sapora?'

Tacio's earlier words circled her mind. All those deaths on her head. Her followers' blood taken to raise Veynothi.

Isa, the Blood Queen.

She couldn't take him prisoner. She had no use for prisoners. All she wanted was for Tacio and Sapora to stay in Sereth, and leave Val Sharis to her. Surely everyone in Linaria saw that as well-balanced?

But that was the foolish dream of a child where things were simpler, and people did what you wanted. The reality was vastly different. Tacio had his own goals, as did Sapora. None of them aligned with hers anymore.

There was more to being queen than killing people. There was more to power than death.

Kylos spoke again, but Isa tuned her out. Her focus shrank to the blade in her hand, and Tacio's throat.

She was better than the Varkain.

Isa dropped her sword and stepped away from Tacio. 'Get out of my sight, snake. This is your final warning. Your Cerastes witnessed your defeat.'

The Ittallan broke into furious shouting around her, but Isa ignored them.

Tacio scrambled to his feet and backed up to his two Cerastes. One eye remained shut, dirt poking under his eyelashes. He gaped at her, wordless. His clothes were in tatters, his jewellery missing, his flesh marred by her sword. Blood trickled from a dozen wounds.

He shook his head, a smirk tugging on the corner of his lips, but didn't say anything. The three Varkain retreated, disappearing back down the tunnel, their footsteps fading away.

'Princess Isa. Far be it for me teh question yeh motives, but...' Kylos trailed off.

'You *should* have killed him.' Solvi said, her voice quiet. 'He was the king's brother. A real threat to us.'

Isa didn't reply. Tacio's warning that he'd release Prince Karekis, the first Ark, was her most immediate concern. She didn't want her people to hate her, nor did she want her ascension to the throne to be paved in blood. She'd be no better than Sapora or the Arks he raised.

Nothing would change if you simply killed those who disagreed with you. Memories of the ball flooded her mind, when Sapora had killed most of the council. He'd killed many who'd looked at him the wrong way, or muttered insults under their breath.

She'd realised that everything had changed from that moment onwards. When she hadn't been sure she'd wanted to walk down that path any longer.

The incredulous gawking of her followers bore into her. She wouldn't apologise for her decision—she was done apologising. 'Maybe I should have killed him. But that would have brought me down to his level. I'm no Varkain. And I'm no blood queen. I'm better than they are.' Isa stared after Tacio for a long while, until she realised the early morning sun warmed her skin.

Chyro said, 'Back to the camp, Princess Isa?' He offered an arm to her.

'Thank you for coming. All of you. Let's go. It has been... a long night.'

Although she felt the uncertain stares of her followers, Isa walked across the barren wasteland with her head held high.

~

IT WAS morning by the time Isa returned to the Ittallan camp, nestled against the base of the volcano. *Otella* had returned, docked awkwardly, like an ungainly frog squatting on the flat ground. Isa had never been so pleased to see an airship before.

She'd have run the last few feet, but after a night of terror in the tunnels, coupled with fighting for her life against Tacio, she didn't have the energy. Even her sword on her hip felt too heavy. Chyro, Solvi, and Karvou had offered to carry things for her, but she'd refused. Kylos had been unusually silent the entire walk back to their camp.

It was to be expected. Isa wasn't sure she'd made the right call—whether her people's perception of her was more important than the death of another Varkain.

Killing Tacio might have solved one problem and avenged Lathri's death.

But it would also have brought Sapora down upon her with all his wrath. They weren't able to survive a direct onslaught from the Sevastos, let alone more Arks. Until they were in a stronger position, wishing down greater threats upon them was something Isa *had* to avoid.

She'd give Kylos some time. Isa was certain she'd come around.

'Princess Isa!' Palom called, making his way towards them from the base of *Otella*.

Isa narrowed her eyes. Palom was limping. 'Trouble in Sereth?'

Palom snorted once. 'The Ark. Veynothi.'

Isa halted mid-step, and Solvi almost walked into her, she'd stopped so abruptly. 'Veynothi?'

'She is gone. Traego was hurt, but is fine. Broken wrist. Shaken up.' He gestured to the airship, but Isa couldn't discern any movement on the deck. Palom continued, '*Leillu*, too, was hurt. These Arks are...*emonos*.'

Isa knew that. 'Take me to Traego.'

Palom took a moment to acknowledge the Ittallan with her, before leading the princess over to *Otella* and scrambling up the steps.

Isa couldn't believe it. They'd last seen Veynothi in the wetlands. Had she been able to track them down? She shivered at the thought of it. Too many fangs all around her, all desperate for her throat.

Traego sat upright in his cabin, a heavy blanket wrapped around his shoulders, a thick bandage around his wrist. His entire crew—Malot, Judd, Antar, Farlan, Ernold, and Oris—fussed around him, bringing a waterskin, a bottle of rum, and some figs. Even Carav, who hobbled around with her arm in a sling, had appeared from her bed to help the captain.

Leillu curled up by Traego's feet, shoving herself in the small gap between the ship's controls and where Traego sat, a blanket across her wings. The dragon opened her eyes as Isa and Palom approached, and let out a low whine.

Palom smiled. 'I am back, *Leillu*. Sleep.'

'Ah, princess. Glad ta see ya well,' Traego croaked. 'That Ark o' Sapora's...she's unforgettable, ain't she?'

'You should not joke about Ark.' Palom waved a hand dismissively. 'You see princess? He is fine.'

It didn't appear anything could destroy Traego's cheerful nature. Isa said, 'I'm lucky you did go on patrol. Otherwise she could have come upon the camp and killed everyone.'

Traego nodded, his face pale. He grabbed the offered rum from Judd with his good hand and took a deep swig.

'How did you escape her?' Isa asked.

Palom stiffened. 'It...we were lucky.'

'So were we,' Isa said, thinking back to her own encounter with the Ark. It had been Amarah's quick thinking that had kept them safe. 'But how can she be gone? Sereth is her home, she'd be able to follow you, surely?'

Palom exhaled through his nose. 'I am not proud.'

'You have to do what it takes,' Isa said, as gently as she could considering what she'd done that morning. She doubted Palom would be happy to discover she'd let Lathri's torturer live. That was a truth she was going to keep quiet about for as long as possible.

'I used this. It...it hurt her. She bled.' Palom walked to the cabin and pulled out a package bundled in linen that Isa hadn't noticed before. '*Valta Forinja*. The scythe I forged for Amarah.'

Isa blinked.

'That's right, princess. This'll kill the Ark,' Traego added. 'I drove my sword right through her an' she didn't even flinch. That thing, though?'

'Would it truly kill her? I thought...I thought the Arks were immortal...' Isa's gaze was glued to the glowing blue blade.

Palom shrugged. 'It hurt her. She fled with Estorian

monster. Maybe to rest. Maybe to regroup. She was afraid of *Valta Forinja*. But, we should not stay here long, I think.'

This changed everything. She'd always learned that the Arks were unstoppable, immortal killers. The Varkain's ultimate weapon—capable of wiping entire cities off the face of Linaria.

If they had a weakness...

'May I?' Isa held out her hand.

After a brief moment of hesitation, Palom handed the scythe to her.

The moment she touched it, Isa felt the energy within. It pulsed like a heartbeat. Blue light cascaded from the tip of the blade.

Leillu raised her head and snarled, smoke pouring from her nostrils.

'Is *emonos*, princess. Cursed. There is reason I don't use my *Valta Forinja*. Why Amarah abandoned hers.'

'That scythe damn near killed Amarah in the middle o' a fight,' Traego said. 'Had ta kick it away. She couldn't move. Speak. Nothin'. Definitely a dangerous thing ta hold.'

Isa gasped. The possibilities that had opened now she had this weapon at her fingertips...

Not even Sapora, not even his Arks, could stand up to it.

'Princess...?' Palom's voice broke her from her reverie.

Isa hurriedly covered the blade in linen. 'This is a good thing to have in my arsenal.'

Palom and Traego exchanged looks.

'Be careful, princess. The originals are locked away for good reason,' Malot said, the Samolen's jewel shining bright red in the morning sun. 'Do not fall into the depths of despair with it.'

'Believe me, Malot, that's the *last* thing I want.' With the *Valta Forinja* in her control, she could defeat any opponent. And if she could keep control of her blood lust when she had Tacio on his knees, her blade at his throat, she could withstand any curse the weapon attempted to bestow upon her.

Isa carefully handed the scythe back to Palom, and walked across *Otella's* deck. Peering over the side, she saw her Ittallan below. Thirty fighters, the only ones who'd left Estoria to come to her aid. Odi managed her main base on the tropical island. But this was her fighting force.

'My followers!' Isa opened her arms wide, the sun bathing them in warm, golden light. 'We have come close to defeat at the hands of Sapora, Tacio, and Veynothi. Some wish to follow me because I am an alternative to snakes ruling Val Sharis. I will prove to you that I am a queen worthy of your support. Sapora has unleashed the Arks upon Linaria, declaring himself an enemy of the Ittallan. I vow to fight them. I will *not* flee. I will *not* abandon you.'

They stared up at her. Some frowned. Some smiled. Kylos leaned against a tent pole, arms folded.

'I will ensure the Ittallan rise above the disasters we've endured at Sapora's command. To prove my intent, I vow to hunt down and kill the Arks. I will kill Jato, who terrorises our beautiful capital city. More Ittallan will join our cause, our base in Estoria. Archigo Gralla has already begun this process, and more Archigo will follow her lead. Our numbers will swell.'

Shouts rang out from the Ittallan. They stamped their feet in unison and cheered her name.

A thrill of excitement rippled down Isa's spine. It pushed away her fatigue and pain, the aches across her body. She was *more* than the bastard child of a Varkain conqueror, driven to blood lust in the heat of battle.

She spoke for the oppressed, the unloved, the forgotten. Whether they saw it now, or came to her side in time, she would be there for them.

Isa drew the sword at her hip and held it high. Sunlight caught it and made Tacio's blood glitter.

She raised her voice to a shout. 'Together, we will march on Taban Yul. We will drive Sapora from the palace. And you will have an Ittallan on the throne—your true queen!'

End

NOTE FROM THE AUTHOR

Thank you for reading *Isa*!

If you enjoyed *Isa*, please consider leaving a review on Amazon and Goodreads.

Book reviews are crucial for indie authors like me, and even a couple of lines can make a huge difference. They're also the best way readers can discover new books!

Can't wait to get back into the World of Linaria?

Subscribe to my mailing list and you'll be the first to hear news, announcements, and special offers.

Plus, you'll also get to enjoy freebies, including a high-res digital map of Linaria and a free spin-off novella—*Rise of a Sky Pirate*—just for signing up!

www.llmcneil.com